THE GIRLS

THE GIRLS
Henry de Montherlant

A Tetralogy of Novels

THE GIRLS

PITY FOR WOMEN

THE HIPPOGRIFF

THE LEPERS

Translated from the French by Terence Kilmartin
Introduction by Peter Quennell

Carroll & Graf Publishers, Inc.
New York

CONTENTS

INTRODUCTION

Byron often talked of the letters he received from women. They had begun to arrive in 1812, when he took the London world by storm; and they continued to pursue him during the years of Italian exile until he left Genoa bound for Greece and death. Some were from old acquaintances, like Lady Caroline Lamb, whom he remembered far too clearly; others from admirers he had met once or twice, and was anxious not to meet again; but many of his correspondents were total strangers, and wrote simply because they reverenced his genius and believed that he alone, in an unfriendly world, could give them the appreciation that they felt they needed. Though Byron did not always reply, he seldom threw away their scribblings. He was an inveterate hoarder of every kind of written record; and even the wildest and most ridiculous effusion passed at once into his personal archives.

Those archives can still be examined. Here, among others, are the letters of a mad peeress, an unhappy Swiss governess, an ill-starred actress, a disconsolate housemaid, a famous *demi-mondaine*, and an impressionable day-dreaming girl who addressed Byron as 'My dear Papa'. Some letters are hastily scrawled; some blotted and blistered with tears; some written in a flowing copperplate hand on expensive gilt-edged paper. But all are romantic and enthusiastic; and all do their best to establish an emotional link between the writer and the poet. Every correspondent endeavours to stake out her claim to the great man's sympathy and interest.

Nearly thirty years ago, when I first read through these letters and edited a sheaf for publication*, I was immediately reminded of Henry de Montherlant's sequence, *Les jeunes filles, Pitié pour les femmes, Le Démon du bien* and *Les Lépreuses*, of which the last volume had recently appeared. Montherlant, too, describes a celebrated writer beset by wild, enthusiastic

---

*To Lord Byron by George Paston & Peter Quennell, Murray, 1939.

women, each of whom has managed to convince herself that only she can understand her hero. Costals' correspondents, however, though just as unfortunate, are less numerous and varied than those of Byron, his chief epistolary persecutors being Thérèse Pantevin, a crack-brained country girl who confuses her passion for Costals with her love of God, and Andrée Hacquebaut, a provincial bluestocking, who aspires one day to become his mistress. Both are rebuffed; of many of their letters the recipient notes: *'Cette lettre est restée sans résponse'* Often he does not open the envelope; and, when Andrée eventually visits Paris and makes a forlorn and desperate attempt to force her way into his intimacy, he stages a particularly atrocious scene in which, with another young woman acting as hidden eye-witness, she has her pride demolished and her pretensions humbled. Costals exhibits certain Byronic features; his fund of patience is strictly limited; and, if he is driven too far, his cynical good humour is apt to turn to downright cruelty.

The character of Costals has frequently puzzled critics; and some readers have not unnaturally assumed that it is based upon a self-portrait. This Montherlant has always denied. *'Le caractère de Costals'*, he remarks at the head of *Les jeunes filles*, *'est, en partie du moins, un caractère de "libertin" ou de "mauvais sujet" (comme on disait autrefois). Il a donc fallu lui donner des particularités convenables à ce caractère. S'il est sûr que l'auteur a mis de soi dans ce personnage, il reste qu'il y a en celui-ci nombre de traits qui sont du domaine purement objectif....'* The *Avertissement* to *Pitié pour les femmes* includes an equally emphatic declaration: *'L'auteur rappelle ici ... qu'il a peint en Costals un personnage que, de propos délibéré, il a voulu inquiétant, voire par moments odieux. Et que les propos et les actes de ce personnage ne sauraient être, sans injustice, prêtés à celui qui l'a conçu.'*

Yet Montherlant admits that there is something of himself in Costals; and his reader will observe that many of Costals' opinions on life are also to be found, more or less accurately reproduced, among his published notebook jottings. To judge from his *Carnets*, Montherlant bears as much, and as little, resemblance to Costals as Byron bore to Childe Harold; each fictitious character is a literary *persona*, which incorporates some of the traits of the artist who produced it, but does not pretend to be a full-length likeness. Costals is the moving spirit who controls the story, the exponent of a system of ideas, a voice that denounces and derides, a principle against which the other characters react. Although Montherlant tells us a good deal about his habits, tastes and antecedents, he remains a somewhat enigmatic figure – a personification of the writer's beliefs and prejudices rather than an individual human being.

But then, *Les jeunes filles* has little in common with the average modern novel; for Montherlant rejects the conventions of story-telling that most novelists have inherited from their nineteenth-century predecessors. '*Si ce roman*,' he writes in his second volume, '*sacrifiait aux règles du genre, telles qu'elles sont établies en France, la scène à la cuisine, entre Costals et Solange, y eût été placée à la fin.... Mais la vie, qui ne sait pas vivre, prétend sottement se dérober aux convenances du roman français.*' *Les jeunes filles* is not a 'well-constructed' book in the accepted meaning of the phrase, but follows its own rules of construction and possesses its own interior harmony. It includes a mass of exceedingly diverse material – letters, notes, comments, asides, together with long passages of straightforward narrative – and is written, as the story develops, from several different points of view. One is that of the narrator, who sometimes blends into his imaginary novelist; another is the redoubtable Costals speaking in his proper person. Yet the subsidiary characters are also allowed a hearing; and there comes a moment when the ridiculous Madame Dandillot – a commonplace middle-class matron, described as resembling a policeman's horse – suddenly dominates the scene and exhibits all her hidden virtues. Her intrinsic absurdity and vulgarity are redeemed by the unselfish strength of her maternal love; and, as she looks down on her sleeping daughter, she becomes a great and good woman. Although this is an aspect of his prospective mother-in-law that has escaped Costals, and seems to be strangely at odds with the narrator's previous attitude, it inspires him to produce a particularly moving passage on the theme of love and sleep:

'*Brusquement elle se tut, comme une petite boîte à musique qui s'enraye.... Elle dit: "Tu dors?" Pas de réponse. Elle alluma. Solange dormait, un peu de salive au coin de la bouche.... Comme la nuit est grande sur le monde, et comme la terre est silencieuse quand on regarde dormir ce qu'on aime! Celui qu'obsède la disparate enclose dans chaque objet, et qui veut y voir une des clefs de la nature, ne méditera-t-il pas sur la tendresse humaine, qui est à la fois le comble de l'inquiétude et le comble du repos?*'

Costals, as it happens, is also a devoted parent; he has an illegitimate son, child of a discarded mistress, for whom he feels a deep, but undemanding, love. Brunet monopolizes his strongest affections; otherwise he distrusts and despises love, more especially romantic love, since he sees it as the arch-foe of his personal integrity and independence; and Costals cherishes the belief that he is, above all else, a free man. '*C'est une de mes grandes forces,*' writes Montherlant in his *Carnets*, '*d'échapper à l'amour en connaissant, mêlées, la sensualité et la tendresse.*' Similarly, Costals has done his best to exclude love – at least, as it is understood by the average woman – both from his life and from his work. '*Je connais bien l'amour;*' he tells Andrée Hacquebaut. '*C'est un sentiment pour lequel je n'ai pas d'estime. D'ailleurs il n'existe pas dans la nature; il est une invention des femmes. . . . Dans chacun des livres que j'ai publiés vous trouverez, sous une forme ou l'autre, cette affirmation: "Ce qui m'importe par-dessus tout, c'est d'aimer". Mais il ne s'agit jamais de l'amour. Il s'agit d'un composé d'affection et de désir, qui n'est pas l'amour.*'

It is the conflict between these two different theories of love that provides the basic drama of *Les jeunes filles*. According to Costals, love, 'the invention of women', is always enervating and demoralizing: moreover, romantic love may lead to marriage; and marriage is the fatal 'hippogriff'; whereas the emotion that blends desire and tenderness suffuses the heart with peace and the mind with energy. In an interview, the author has claimed that *Les jeunes filles* has a definitely 'salubrious' message. Nor will he agree that it constitutes an attack on Woman: '*J'y suis souvent dur pour les femmes.*

Mais, dans toute mon œuvre, ne suis-je pas aussi dur pour les hommes? ... Ce que j'attaque, ce n'est pas la femme, c'est l'idolatrie de la femme, c'est la conception "cour d'amour" de la femme, c'est la situation privilégiée de la femme. Dans Les jeunes filles, au lieu de cultiver les imperfections de la femme avec une complaisance béate, j'ai voulu la traiter d'égale à égal....'

This, however, though it may be true of Montherlant – his plays present the opposite sex in a much softer and more advantageous light – is not entirely true of Costals, whose attitude towards women is certainly harsh, and who makes very little attempt to treat his female associates upon an equal footing. The personage Montherlant describes is at once a rake and a misogynist; and, as a 'libertin', he belongs to the same family as Richardson's Lovelace, Choderlos de Laclos' Valmont or, indeed, as Casanova. Like Costals, Lovelace is a 'marriage-hater'; and he believes that, by conquering Clarissa Harlowe, he is merely reconciling 'herself to herself' and illustrating the 'triumph of nature' over an outworn social code. He, too, is 'noted for his vivacity and courage', and possesses, we are told, 'sound health and ... a soul and body fitted for and pleased with each other.' Though highly educated, he represents natural man as opposed to sentimental, artificial woman.

Valmont, on the other hand, resembles Costals only in his more Machiavellian aspects; but Montherlant's description of how the novelist humiliates Andrée while Solange lurks behind a curtain, and of the meaner details of his treatment of Solange, might well have been imagined by Laclos. As for Casanova, he had more generous feelings than Costals, but often voices much the same opinions. Thus Costals remarks that, if he had a daughter, *'Je la désirerai sûrement un jour'*; and Casanova admits that he could never understand *'comment un père pouvait tendrement aimer sa charmante fille sans avoir du moins un fois couché avec elle.'* But, in Casanova's life, women were the centre of existence; and Costals announces that, *'à la rigueur, je puis répéter à cent ou cent cinquante femmes les mêmes paroles, en étant sincère à chaque coup, parce que la femme reste dans le superficiel de ma vie.'* Casanova was occasionally cruel because he loved too violently and indiscriminately; Costals is cruel because the desire he experiences is apt to conceal a fundamental distaste.

Here he has many distinguished predecessors; a strain of fierce misogyny runs through European thought and writing. Shakespeare himself was not immune from it; and just as Costals is moved to protest against the weakness and untidiness of the flaccid female organism, Berowne in *Love's Labour's Lost* compares it to an ill-functioning piece of household clockwork:

> What I! I love! I sue! I seek a wife!
> A woman that is like a German clock,
> Still a-repairing, ever out of frame,
> And never going aright . . .

– an image that Shakespeare apparently derived from a popular sixteenth-century proverb.

Another poetic misogynist was the author of *Les Fleurs du mal*. He, too, attacked '*l'idolâtrie de la femme*', declared that it had always astonished him that women were allowed to enter churches – '*Quelle conversation peuvent-elles avoir avec Dieu?*' – and asserted that in a woman's composition physical and spiritual qualities were inextricably bound up together: '*La femme ne sait pas séparer l'âme du corps. Elle est simpliste comme les animaux.*' In short, Woman was the antithesis of the Dandy; by which Baudelaire, of course, meant not a modern Beau Brummell, but the 'well-born soul', the literary aristocrat, perpetually at war with the world in which he finds himself. To sum up, Woman is essentially a vulgar being; and at this point one recollects Costals' remark on the change that overtakes a woman's personality as soon as she begins to hum: '*Solange fredonna la mélopée des Bateliers. . . . Costals pensa qu'il y a, en toute femme, une grue prête à ressortir, et qui ressort quand elle chantonne.*'

In *Les jeunes filles* Montherlant expresses his view of the opposite sex more eloquently, forcibly and unreservedly than in any of his earlier or later novels. But it is already obvious in such books as *Le Songe* and *Les Bestaires*, published in 1922 and 1926 respectively. Each introduces a young man who represents the noblest type of human comradeship; and each draws the portrait of a girl who stands for the opposing principle, and who offers, not steady, unselfish affection, but self-centred and self-destructive love. *Gentillesse* – a word difficult to translate – is one of Montherlant's and Costals' favourite virtues; and, among the characters who appear in *Les jeunes filles*, Brunet, Costals' adolescent son, alone exhibits this redeeming quality. Solange puzzles, distracts and annoys; his association with Brunet is refreshingly uncomplicated and straightforward. '*Je n'aime pas*,' reflects Costals, '*ce qui est une occasion de bêtise pour l'homme, et c'est pourquoi je n'aime pas la femme.... Eternelle supériorité des gosses sur les femmes....*' This superiority, moreover, is not only spiritual and emotional; the hero suggests that it is also physical. In Solange's embrace, he notes that her body is strangely scentless, and that even her hair has a weak and faded aroma. '*Pourquoi Costals évoqua-t-il l'odeur si bonne et si vivace des cheveux de son fils? Il ignorait que c'est un règle, que les cheveux des jeunes garçons sentent plus fort et meilleur que ceux des femmes.*' This comparison temporarily deadens his desire; and soon afterwards, for the first time in his relationship with Solange, he feels a humiliating lack of energy.

During the course of an interview on the subject of *Les jeunes filles*, from which I have already quoted, Montherlant admits that he may, now and then, have been inclined to generalize much too widely and too freely – '*j'y dis trop "les femmes" et "les hommes"*'; and that a certain simplification has at times resulted. With this criticism many of his readers will agree. Costals is an extremely dogmatic personage; and, like most dogmatists, he is apt to assume that he has mastered the whole art of living. Besides being entirely self-sufficient, he is, he repeatedly claims, a thoroughly happy and harmonious character; '*la mélancolie est le petit luxe des âmes pauvres*'. Thanks both to his natural lucidity and to his '*discipline d'égoisme*', he can confront the universe without alarm: '*Les gens disent qu'on est malheureux quand on voit trop tout ce qui est. Moi, je vois tout ce qui est, et je suis très heureux.*' The life he leads is 'perfectly intelligent'; he has neither fears nor misgivings.

Such self-sufficiency, a reader may object, is seldom found in real life; but Montherlant the artist keeps a wary eye on

Costals the dogmatic theorist. His hero is slightly incredible only so long as he remains invincible, '*avec sa jeunesse, sa santé, son impudence, son œuvre, son gracieux fils, son collier de maîtresses très jeunes, et tous les avantages de la puissance . . .*' But, although Costals never quite vails his sword or drops his intellectual panache, *Les jeunes filles* is still the story of his successive misadventures. He falls into the trap that has been laid by Solange; he becomes engaged; he is nearly overtaken and devoured by the appalling Hippogriff. In the last volume, having temporarily escaped from Solange, he seeks a refuge among the Atlas Mountains, and there suspects that he has contracted leprosy – a symbolic disaster that sends him hurrying back towards a European hospital.

I have suggested elsewhere that Montherlant is a remarkably gifted comic novelist; and the story of Costals' brush with Death, and of his long struggle against that legendary monster, Marriage, is told with wonderfully enlivening humour. Few characters in fiction have been more savagely treated than Andrée Hacquebaut and Solange Dandillot; but Montherlant is far too good an artist to pass a summary verdict on his own creations. The ridiculous bluestocking has a kind of farouche dignity that even Costals cannot quite extinguish; and one reader at least has never lost his regard for the unhappy young girl. Although Solange has a limited, commonplace mind, she is patient, affectionate and good-natured and, despite Costals' ferocious diatribes, by no means altogether stupid.

Style is a quality that seldom ranks very high in the contemporary critic's scale of values; but it would be impossible to discuss Montherlant the novelist without considering his achievement as a modern master of the French language. His prose style is uncommonly rich and various – tart, idiomatic, incisive, when he attacks some typical or controversial issue; measured, euphonious, poetic, when he deals with wider and less transitory themes. He has always loved nature, and shown a deep understanding of the life of plants and animals. What could be more vivid than his description, in *Le Démon du bien*, of the four cats whom Costals meets in an Italian restaurant; or, on another plane, his picture, in *Les Lépreuses*, of the desolate landscape of the High Atlas?

'Rose rougeâtre de la terre. Blanc de la neige. Bleu des ombres aux flancs des monts. Sur le versant d'en dessous, des oueds avaient oubliés leur mission dans la vie . . . étaient devenus des pistes, encombrées de galets, qu'on ne distinguait plus que par leurs rubans de lauriers-roses; et puis un ruisseau de glace rouge, comme un ruisseau de gelée à la groseille, ou comme une tranchée pleine de sang frais coagulé. Des troupeaux de moutons, qui avaient la couleur même de la sécheresse, passaient au-dessus de leurs têtes, se déplaçaient avec le rhythme des ombres, et le chien croquait la neige durcie. Des bergers momifiés étaient là depuis cinq mille ans. Des sauterelles, figées elles aussi, sur les buissons neigeux, guettées par la fluxion de poitrine. Et de grands faucons blancs qui glissaient et viraient avec des grâces d'almée.'

Like every genuine style, that of Henry de Montherlant is no mere adventitious decoration, but arises naturally from his subject as he enlarges and develops it. Montherlant's efforts as a controversialist should never blind us to the fact that he is primarily an accomplished artist. *Les jeunes filles* may be read and enjoyed as a deliberately controversial book – an attack on 'the cult of Woman', on the place that Woman has come to occupy in the modern European world; and as such it may have helped to break down many masculine taboos and phobias. But it is also an imaginative work of art, which, having absorbed and digested its subject matter, presents us with something far more valuable and lasting. Circumstances change; social problems vary; one day the unending War of the Sexes may be fought under completely different standards. But, so long as literature continues to play a part in our lives, Montherlant's story of *Les jeunes filles* is a book that will retain its youthful freshness.

PETER QUENNELL

FOREWORD

The author would like to point out that in Costals he has deliberately painted a character whom he intended to be disquieting and even, at times, odious; and that this character's words and actions cannot in fairness be attributed to its creator.

The author made the central character of *La Rose de sable*, Lieutenant Auligny, a man endowed with the highest moral qualities: patriotism, charity, a horror of violence, a passion for justice and an acute sensitivity to injustice (to the point of being made ill by it), an almost excessive sensibility and scrupulousness, a sense of human solidarity, an anxiety, amounting to obsession, to put himself out for others and to avoid injuring them, etc.

This character, as central as that of Costals is here, takes up the major part of a work of nearly six hundred pages, and innumerable details lend it that 'autobiographical' aspect which some have claimed to discern in Costals.

One might well wonder whether the critics and the public, on reading *La Rose de sable*, would attribute to the author the same abundance of virtues as they attributed to him of vices after reading *The Girls*.

H.M.

THE GIRLS

Mademoiselle Thérèse Pantevin   to M. Pierre Costals
La Vallée Maurienne   *Avenue Henri-Martin*
near Avranches   *Paris*
(Manche)

26 September 1926

†
A.M.D.G.

Thank you, Monsieur and dearly beloved, for never answering my letters. They were unworthy of me. Three letters in three years, and not a single reply! But now the time has come for me to tell you my secret.

Ever since I first came across your books, I have loved you. When I saw your photograph in a newspaper, my passion was aroused. For three months, from November the 11th, 1923, to February the 2nd, 1924, I wrote to you every day. But I did not send the letters, I was too ashamed. I sent only one of them. You did not reply. And yet, as I gazed at your photograph, the look in your eyes, your whole expression, revealed to me my happy fate: you did not love me, no, but you had found a place for me in your thoughts.

With my letter of August the 15th, 1924 – the Feast of the Assumption of the Blessed Virgin – I reminded you of my existence. And a few days later, I caught a certain gleam on your face in that same photograph which told me that my letter had struck home.

On April the 11th last, I wrote to you a third time. But so great was my fear of displeasing you by an excess of boldness that the terms in which I wrote must have left you in doubt as to my feelings. I did not dare tell you of my love, and it was killing me. So then I wrote you a great confession in a six-page letter which I began on the last Saturday of the month of the Rosary and finished on the eve of the Immaculate Conception. But I did not send that either.

I think of you, I suffer, I must tell you all: I love you. I wish you no harm whatsoever.

How I have suffered! When you know me you will understand. I am not a self-sufficient sort of woman. Separated from
you I have been nothing, I could do nothing. I have wept, I
have prayed, I have meditated, but this inner life is all the
life I have had. Why should I take anything out of myself
unless it could be dedicated to the man for whom I was made?
For God created man for His glory, and woman for the glory
of man. Oh! what you could not do for me! Make me live,
my friend, for without you I am incapable of living. All I need
is to be loved, and I feel capable of so much love.

I love you and I know that in telling you so I am fulfilling
God's will. My friend, have you never dreamed of what our
love will be in Eternity?

Soon it will be October ... the last flowers are in the fields.
I could not bear to see them die in vain. I picked them, making
the sign of the Cross as I did so. I put four sprigs of them
from us both on the grave of twin kittens that died two years
ago. I am sending you three sprigs, and am keeping three
more which I shall lay at the foot of my little statue of the
Sacred Heart.

This time I beg you to answer me, so that I may give free
rein to my tender feelings and, if your heart responds to mine,
grow accustomed to my happiness.

My friend, our task is to reconstruct the Kingdom of God.
If you desire this Kingdom, and the kingdom of my heart, give
me a sign.

I kiss your pen, and sign myself

> Marie Paradis
>> for 'Thérèse Pantevin' no longer exists.

(Do not put your name on your envelope.)

This letter remained unanswered.

Mademoiselle Andrée Hacquebaut   to Pierre Costals
Saint-Léonard   *Paris*
(Loiret)

3 October 1926

Dear great Costals,

During the summer I was out of doors nearly all the time,

and the house had ceased to be of any importance to me. With
the first cold weather, one fits it out like an ark in which to
sail through the deluge of winter, and it is only now, much
more than in the spring when my mother died, that I realize
what it means to be living in Saint-Léonard (Loiret) with a
stupid, deaf old uncle, when one is poor, unmarried, an orphan
without brothers or sisters, and pushing thirty.

And yet, this melancholy is, as it were, swallowed up by the
anniversary each October brings. It is now four years to the
very day since I first read a book of yours. The power you
have over people! Last night I wept – real tears – on re-reading
Fragility. (Did I tell you I had had an adorable binding made
for it in green morocco? The only beautiful thing in the
desert of ugliness and mediocrity in which I live. A hundred
and fifty francs. Half my month's pocket money. . . .) There
are days when I cannot pick up a newspaper without finding
your name in it, cannot open my mouth without mentioning
you (I pronounce your name more often than a woman pro-
nounces the name of her lover), cannot think without feeling
your thoughts intermingled with mine. You are not so much
a man as an element in which my life is steeped, as though in
air or water. No one else has the 'feel' of you as I have. No,
no one, I won't have it! I'm not jealous of the people you love
– not even the 'fine ladies' – but of those who love you.
Allow me at least the unique position of having loved your
work more than anyone. I know it almost by heart, so much
so that sentences of yours often spring to my lips or my pen,
expressing my thought better than I myself could have done :
you speak, and it is myself I hear. This is no doubt the effect
of your talent, which conquered me from the very first, but
it also has to do with the sort of affinity one notices between
oneself and certain persons from whom one might appear
to be separated by an abyss. Throughout my life, so joyless
and at times so tormented, this mysterious fellow-feeling has
uplifted and sustained me. How I have matured through reading you! You have turned over people's souls as one turns
over the soil, revealing their own riches to them. For four
years, your work has been as it were a mouthpiece for one
who has no literary talent, just as your happiness has been

a requital for one who is unhappy. Being as eager as you to
live life to the full, and yet knowing only self-denial and
yearning in this wretched life of mine – wretched and
absurdly paradoxical since I have acquired a culture which
remains unexploited – fettered as I am by loneliness and lack
of money, I had, so to speak, delegated to you all this fervour,
all this appetite for life. Far from envying you, as so many
others do, I had, if I may say so, something of the feeling of
parents whose own lives have been a failure and who live
to see their children succeed (so you see you are my son, in
spite of your thirty-three years!). Walled in as I was, I was
glad that someone should triumph over all obstacles and
barriers. That was my recompense. If at any time you had
ceased to be yourself, or ceased to be happy, you would have
proved yourself unworthy of my trust, you would have betrayed me – me and many others, for I know there were
many who felt as I did.

I am proud that you write what you write. I am proud
that you live as you live. That a man of your kind should be
a success with the public (which is almost unheard of) recon-
ciles me to the world: it means that all is not lost. I could
not bear it if you were not loved, and it's now three years
since I said to my best friend: 'If you hadn't loved Costals
(as a writer), I wouldn't have given much for our friendship.'
I am always terrified that you may do something that is not
quite 'the thing'. Whenever I read an article of yours in a
newspaper I always get the sort of shiver of apprehension my
mother apparently used to get when I was a toddler and a
neighbour warned her: 'Dédée's playing by the pond.' But
what you write is always what I expected, just as, when I
met you, you were as I had imagined you. O God, let this
miracle never cease! It's a wonderful feeling, you know, to
be able to put such trust in a free man.

When I met you! How can I forget your kindness, your
straightforwardness, your courtesy! You, the inaccessible
Costals! A very big and very famous brother, but a brother
all the same. The ideal comrade, with whom one is on an
equal footing, provided one holds one's head up a little. I
was half afraid you would give me the sort of reception which

a writer with your ... all-conquering reputation might give to a young female admirer come to visit him, and anything at all suggestive of physical desire on either side would have humiliated me. Even today I would give you my life, but I cannot imagine myself giving you a kiss. Although religion no longer has any hold over me, something has remained of my very devout and scrupulous childhood (never reading a book on the sly, and never wanting to). Your reserve was an exquisite discovery for me: 'reserve' equals 'power', in a man as much as in a woman. And moreover, it proved to me that in your eyes I was not like all the others. Everything you did for me – advising me what to read, finding me that job in Paris, which I lost through my own fault – showed me how kind you were, something one could not have guessed from your books. (Kind when you choose, be it said. There are things about you that upset me a little, as you know. Although of course you have special prerogatives.)

In a month's time, I shall be going to Paris for a few days on business connected with my mother's estate. Tell me you will be there then.

Yours with a solemn hand-clasp,

A.H.

Forgive the length of this letter. I can't help myself. But I promise not to write again for a fortnight.

This letter remained unanswered.

2501 – Girl, 28, blonde, pretty, Catholic, 20,000 frs. savings, would marry gent. in good situation.

2529 – Girl, 25, bronzed, slim, very pretty, good legs, no private means, typist provincial town, would marry gent. with steady job. Seeks above all tenderness.

2530 – Aristocratic lady, 40, only daughter, mildly intellectual, living in chateau, 200,000 frs. dowry, would marry distinguished Catholic gent. even without means, pref. nobleman.

2550 – Girl, 21, daughter naval officer, orphan, attractive, light-brown hair, hazel eyes, small, slim, good figure, living Finisterre, no financial prospects.

2554 – Widow, 49, lively, affectionate, sensitive, warm-hearted, rich inner life, distinguished, excellent health, ideal housewife, superior in every way, income 25,000 frs., house-owner, wishes communicate view marriage sincere respectable gentleman similar financial position in order achieve peace and security in mutual trust and affection. Serious. Give exact address.

2563 – Artistic girl, personal qualities, warm-hearted, plucky, independent, living alone, desires marriage nice young man.

2565 – Marchioness, very tall, blue-green eyes, natural blonde hair, good figure, attractive, elegant, distinguished, accustomed fashionable society, good jewellery, would marry good-looking gent. American type.

2574 – Decent, healthy girl, living country with mother, seeks marriage.

2576a – Working girl, brunette, 29, gentle, docile, conscien-tious, 600 frs. per month, slight curable T.B., would marry gent. under 45 really anxious make her happy. Means unim-portant. Would leave provinces.

Extract from *Happy Ever After*,
monthly matrimonial gazette, October 1926.

1899 – Bachelor, thirtyish, fine physique, 5ft 9ins., well edu-cated, every endowment, would marry girl with substantial dowry.

1907 – Clerk, 23, medium height, sportsman, would marry woman who could make him independent.

1910 – Veterinary surgeon, 24, well-to-do, handsome, tall, fine eyes, Ramon Novarro type, seeks, view marriage, senti-mental companion with at least 600,000 frs. dowry.

1929 – Widower, 63, elegant, healthy, Belgian, liberal pro-fession, decorated Order of Leopold, private income 4,000 frs., would marry widow or spinster of good physique, fairly stout, loving, not spendthrift, with minimum income 20,000. Has suffered.

1930 – Schoolmaster, Mayenne, 28, due promotion soon, would marry freethinking colleague with substantial means.

1931 – Young man, 5ft 10ins., very smart, very good dancer, fine athlete, wishes meet blonde girl of independent means view marriage. Motor-car trips.

1940 – Gentleman, university graduate, fiftyish, kind, considerate, disinterested, craving tenderness, seeks view marriage young person pref. under 23, genteel, distinguished, well educated, cultured, tender, devoted, character irreproachable, very pretty, good housekeeper, outwardly simple but really seductive, with minimum dowry 500,000 frs. and expectations if poss.

1945 – Colonial warrant officer, clean bill of health, slim, blond, curly hair, aquiline nose, oval face, sensitive, violinist, Tunisian outpost, would marry girl 17-20 with dowry who loves radiant sun, eternal azure of the land of mirages and infinite sands.

1947 – Mechanic, bachelor, 18, seeks view marriage correspondent who could help him set up in business.

1950 – Captain, 33, horseman, promotion imminent, Officer Legion of Honour, fine physique, brown hair, distinguished, elegant, serious, good-humoured despite having suffered, very straightforward, wishes bring happiness to young person even with a child, tall, pleasant, sentimental and ideal, perfectly educated, Catholic, in order build happy durable home based profound affection and high moral qualities. Situation and means immaterial.

1958 – Young man, 21, good-looking, modest means, seeks sister soul with fortune.

1962 – Viscount, only son, 27, certified noble ancestry dating back sixteenth century, no personal fortune at present but substantial expectations, perfect in every way, would marry person with very large fortune, religion and age immaterial, whose parents could provide occupation for son-in-law.

1967 – Road mender, 29, no private means, Paris suburbs, hopes find young woman for marriage.

Happy Ever After, October 1926.

A man reading a page of matrimonial advertisements can give rein, one after another, to several of the different men that are in him: the laughing man, the lusting man, the thinking man; and inside the 'thinking man' there is also a man who weeps.

The laughing man. Ah, yes! he will laugh himself sick. The high opinion most of these poor creatures have of themselves. The importance they attach to blond hair and Catholicism. The regulation height of the gentlemen. The 'expectations' of the young ladies – and what expectations! An inexhaustible mine of absurdity.

On the second page of the journal, 'the editors are at the disposal of their readers to provide them with any help they may need for the success of their plans, and if need be to write direct to subscribers in any terms which may be desired, at a fee of 2fr. 50 per letter.'

On the back page, a box advertising a 'lady detective and her sleuths, shadows, etc. ...' Perfect! One must think of everything when setting up house. (But might not the lady detective be the editor of the journal herself, a Penelope ready to destroy what she has woven?) A good mark, too, for the advertisement for 'quick loans': we all know how expensive women are.

When the laughing man has had a good laugh and a good sneer, etc. ... to the point of thinking, if he is a bit sour: 'Let's have a nice little war to clean up all this riff-raff' (although it's true, adds this deplorable man, that one of the horrors of war, to which attention is never sufficiently drawn, is that women are spared) – when the laughing man has had a good laugh, he turns the switch and the lusting man appears. The man who cannot read 'Girl, 22' without a quiver of excitement.

Behind each of these advertisements a face, a body, an unknown something which, after all, may well be a heart. Behind these printed pages, a hundred and fifty living women, living at this very moment, each of whom wants a man – and why not me? – each of whom, since she is there, is ready for adventure, legal or illegal (the legal being a thousand times worse than the other), each of whom has reached such a pitch of deprivation that she is ready to offer herself to the first comer. The men, for their part, demand 'large fortunes'. We read this, for instance: 'Gentleman wishes meet young pretty woman with large fortune view marriage.' Full stop. You: young, pretty, with large fortune. Me ... well, me, 'a gentle-man': aren't you satisfied? Most of the women do at least specify 'gentleman with job' – bed and board. The bed first. And what more natural, what more respect-worthy than this demand? 'You don't feel poverty any more when you're under a blanket', as a Marseilles street-walker once rather splendidly observed. (Sometimes you feel a different sort of poverty. But that's another matter.) The lecherous man, scanning these pages, sees them pulsating as the sea pulsates, swarming as the Roman arena swarmed when the beasts were let loose in it. There are too many of them, and he loses heart – like the art-lover confronted with two thousand pieces in a museum. A herd of women enclosed in the arena. Menacing as the beasts of the arena, and yet, like them, half innocent and defenceless: all victims, even the worst. It is simply a matter of shooting an arrow into the heap. Brutes, cads and perverts, swindlers and blackmailers, all the archers are up there choos-ing their prey. Every kind of threat against the race of woman. Extremes of candour and baseness, deceptions, disappoint-ments, all the social dramas, even happiness, simmer in the witches' cauldron of a matrimonial gazette. Absurdity and pathos too, as in everything that has to do with life – and this is life itself, a microcosm of life.

As for the thinking man, *he* sees this matrimonial journal, so ridiculous from one point of view, as an extremely valuable piece of social machinery.

The author remembers coming across the alluring phrase *select company* in an advertising brochure for some spa hotel. And one often hears people say to each other: 'You should go to the So-and-So's. You'll make a lot of social connections there.' Whereupon every well-born person draws himself up and recalls the remark of the old aristocratic lady who, on her death-bed, pestered no doubt by tiresome visitors, left her grand-children with this final word of advice: 'Above all, avoid social connections.'

And yet, after this initial reaction, one is struck by all the misfortunes engendered by the lack of connections. It seems a trite thing to say; but in fact it is less widely realized than one might think. One is struck by the vast number of agreeable things people lack simply because they have not known which door to knock at. And it is surely tragic to think of those doors simply waiting to be opened on to gardens of Eden which remained closed because people passed them by.

The people who wait all their lives for the one person who was made for them – *who always exists* – and who die without having met that person: the men who fail to find an outlet for their abilities and waste their lives in inferior jobs: the girls who remain unmarried when they could have made a man happy as well as themselves: the people who sink ever deeper into penury when there are charitable organizations which might have been expressly created for them; and all this because none of them happened to know of this person, that organization, that vacancy – it is a problem that can haunt one.

And it applies to small things as well as big. There is the book which, at a particular moment, might have raised your spirits, but which you did not know about. There is the place that would have made the perfect setting for your love affair, the treatment that would have cured your illness, the scheme that would have enabled you to gain time. They were all there waiting for you, but no one pointed them out to you because you had too few connections. The promised land is all around you, and you do not know it – like a wasp trying to get out of a room, endlessly beating and buzzing against the window-pane although the window is ajar a few inches away. A man is thrown into the water with his wrists tied, and no one has taught him the knack of freeing himself – yet such a knack exists.

This counterpoint of offers and appeals resembles the flight of birds criss-crossing in the vastness of space until at last some of them meet and they fly off two by two. Montaigne tells us that his father would have liked to see in every town 'a certain place appointed, to which those who needed anything could betake themselves. Such a one desires company for a journey to Paris. Another requires a servant of a certain quality. Yet another a master, etc. . . .' And he cites the example of two 'most excellent persons' who died in penury and who would have been succoured if their sad plight had been known. Truly, the man who first thought of using a gazette to help people find what they seek should have a statue erected in his honour. Anything designed to bring people together deserves encouragement, even when they are brought together for sentimental ends, with all the silliness and triviality that implies.

The old lady who enjoined her family with fierce pride, 'Above all, avoid connections', was condemning anyone who took her at her word to all the miseries of non-fulfilment – of soul as well as body – and an agonizing regret for all that could have been theirs for the asking, but which eluded them. Turning in on oneself is bad for all except strong and exceptional natures, and even then only on condition that it is relative and not continuous. Others pay dearly for it. One cannot shut oneself up in one's room with impunity. One cannot live on oneself alone with impunity. One cannot send one's fellow-creatures 'packing' with impunity. And it is right that this should be so, since turning in on oneself – unless it is dictated by high intellectual or spiritual motives – is more often than not the result of idleness, egotism, impotence, in short that 'fear of living' which has not yet been sufficiently recognized as one of the major evils that afflict humanity.

Thérèse Pantevin   to Pierre Costals
La Vallée Maurienne   *Paris*

6 October 1926

†
A.M.D.G.

My Beloved, once again you have failed to answer me! God has not permitted it; blessed be His Holy Name.

Convinced that your silence means that great things are happening – no doubt you are working – I will respect that silence. Yes, until All Saints Day even. On that date I will send you another *De Profundis*.

31

I kiss your right hand, the one that writes.

Marie Paradis

P.S. Do not put your name on the envelope.

This letter remained unanswered.

Thérèse Pantevin — to Pierre Costals
La Vallée Maurienne — *Paris*

All Saints Day

Quick, let me have something to hold in my hands which has felt your breath on it! If you only knew the people around me! If you only knew what a horrible thing it is to be entirely dependent on a power that does not wish you well. Only you can save me. Give me life, so that I can be sure of having it for all eternity.

This is a supreme adjuration. You are the breath of life to me: do not let me expire.

Marie

I have had my photo taken, and am sending it to you. As you see, I am young but not pretty. And in fact the photo flatters me.

(Do not put your name on the envelope.)

Pierre Costals — to Thérèse Pantevin
Paris — *La Vallée Maurienne*

Mademoiselle,

I never for a moment imagined that one day I should find myself answering one of your extravagant missives. Alas! I was touched by the most recent ones; the damage is done. You say that your life is in my hands. We know all about that. But the possibility that you may really believe it is one that I must face. Ought I, in that case, to ignore these appeals?

32

I cannot be so hard-hearted. Let us see what can be done for you.

There is no chance of the feeling you think you have for me ever arousing the slightest echo on my side. Do not persist in it: it would be like beating your head against a wall; you would wear yourself out. And besides, even if you were to reach me, you would get nothing from me, for I have nothing to give to anyone. Let me tell you this once and for all. Do not imagine that I shall ever weaken.

However, if that path is closed to you, it is not the only one. There is obviously a certain force in you, and it would be a pity to waste it on the first oaf you came across, with whom you might become infatuated for want of anyone better. When allowance is made for the element of sentimental gush in your devotion, which comes of your sex and age, what remains is perhaps not wholly bad; though it would be strange if God were to find it acceptable. I do not know exactly what he is, having not an atom of faith. But in him, or in the idea you have of him, you will certainly be better off than in making a 'home'. Homes! Plague centres, every one of them. If there is anything I can do for you, it is to encourage you in this quest, and to follow your progress with sympathy from afar – although, as I say, I believe neither in the divinity of Jesus Christ nor in the divinity of anyone else. But the rarefied heights of non-belief are familiar to me. They will be my prayer for you, if you wish. For it is all the same thing. Luckily.

Do not write me letters eight pages long every three days, as you will no doubt consider yourself entitled to do after this one. I tell you frankly, I shall leave them unread. My interest in you amounts to my being able to read a letter from you about once every three weeks, not every three days. Do not give in to the urge to write to me until you have put up such a fight as will have done you credit. And do not expect me to answer you. I will only answer you if I feel inclined, which is to say that my replies will be few and far between.

Upon which, I remain, Mademoiselle, yours sincerely,

Costals

Pierre Costals   to Mademoiselle Rachel Guigui
Paris   *Carqueiranne (Var)*

6 November 1926

Dear Guiguite,

Could I ask you to post from Carqueiranne (with apologies
for sending it to you in a sealed envelope) this letter addressed
to a young lady in the Loiret who has been wishing me well
(from the Loiret) for the past four years. Since she has literally
nothing else to do but think about me, you can imagine what
a good time she has. Plain, anything but desirable, but intelligent, cultivated, worthy. She is an orphan (her father was a
country solicitor of no standing), she learnt Latin all by herself, etc. ... in fact altogether most estimable. I have a certain
sympathy for her, being acutely aware of what it must be like
to be a penniless spinster approaching thirty, and of a fairly
superior type, in Saint-Léonard (Loiret) of all places. It's
pathetic to see a woman of this calibre condemned either to
turn into a sour old virgin, or to marry a local shopkeeper,
or to take a lover (which might not be easy, since nature has
not been over-kind to her), and let herself go. I keep up the
illusion of friendship with her, because I know it bolsters her
up. She is coming to Paris in a day or two, and this time I
don't want to see her. A woman who loves you, but whom
you neither love nor desire, is just possible as a correspondent.
But face to face, ouch! I am giving the strictest orders at
home to say I have left for the Midi.

There is another young lady, this time from the Manche,
to whom I've just written after leaving unanswered three or
four letters she has sent me over the past three years. The
other day she sent me her photograph – she's a proper little
peasant, in a black orphan's smock; you couldn't imagine anything more ill-favoured. She's completely mad (in the mystical
mode), and would be nothing without her madness, which is
her only asset. A remark in one of her letters struck a chord
in me, and opened, if not my heart, at least that place deep
inside one where kindness and pity are thought to dwell: 'If
you only knew what a terrible thing it is to be entirely dependent on a power that does not wish you well!' I imagine

34

she means her family. Since it is not easy, with piety, to distinguish the boundary between madness and sublimity, I have
plumped for sublimity and would like her to take advice as
to whether she may not be made for the convent: anything
would be better than that farmyard with all those cow-hands
full of contempt for the little mystic. I'm sure that you, dear
Guiguite, who are imbued with the humane spirit of Israel,
would have approved of my answering her in the end. I know
it was rash of me: good deeds are always rash. But I
don't like refusing people the little bit of happiness they ask
of you when their paths cross yours.

Nothing in particular to say to you, except to thank you
for the pleasure you have given me so faithfully for so many
months. Now that you are at Carqueiranne (I hope you had
a good journey), you will have seen the fishermen's nets held
up on the surface of the water by fragments of cork. My
nights with you are like those fragments of cork holding me
up on the surface of life. Without those nights, and the nights
spent with my other little companions, I believe I would sink
like a stone, what with the stupidity of my family, the vile-
ness of my fellow-writers, and the time my friends make me
waste.

I hope the latest of your protectors is a fine figure of a man
and a nice chap. Come back to me in good form at the end
of the month. I don't think I should mind losing you: it
would amuse me to have a gap to fill. But on the whole I
should be glad if you stayed.

Dear Guiguite, I love the pleasure I have with you, I love
the pleasure I give you; in short, you are eighteen and I like
you. Good-bye, my dear.

Your devoted servant,

C.

Pierre Costals   to Andrée Hacquebaut
Paris   *Saint-Léonard*

*[Letter dated from Carqueiranne and enclosed with the
preceding one.]*

7 November 1926

Dear Mademoiselle,

What a bore! Here I am in this God-forsaken place, where I shall be stuck all the time you are in Paris. If I had been nearer, I would willingly have popped up to Paris to spare you this disappointment. But from here! ...

If you need help of any kind in Paris, a letter of introduction, or anything, let me know at once at Carqueiranne, 'c/o Mlle Rachel Guigui, 14 rue de la Plage.' Mlle Guigui is an elderly Jewess with whom I am lodging for a few days. Incorrigible as I am, I shall no doubt end up by falling into her arms, assuming that one can be inflamed by a person called Guigui, which I find hard to believe.

As I write to you, I can see from my window the irradiations of the zenith multiply themselves in sparkling facets on the shimmering methylene-blue of the sea. Then I think what it must be like to spend eleven months of the year at Saint-Léonard (Loiret).... And the beauty of the sea no longer seems quite so innocent.

Cordially yours,

C.

Well, no! I've just lied to you. I can't see the sea at all at the moment, for the simple reason that I am writing this in a café in Carqueiranne from which it is not visible. Even to tell you this harmless lie would have been painful to me. It is true that, in spite of all appearances to the contrary, it does happen that I do things that are painful to me. Rarely, but sometimes.

Andrée Hacquebaut   to Pierre Costals
Hôtel des Beaux-Arts   *Carqueiranne*
Paris

11 November 1926

Costals, dear Costals, was your letter from Carqueiranne a disappointment to me? Yes and no. Yes, because to come to Paris and miss you is too idiotic. No, because a little letter like that easily makes up for a few moments of your presence. Your niceness! Still the same after all these years! So you would really, if you had not been so far away, have 'popped up' to Paris simply to see me! And your adorable postscript, the *guilt* I can detect in you for having told me an insignificant little lie! How could one not love you, in spite of your moods, your weeks of silence, your harsh words, the teasing, rather disturbing side of you, the cruel mischievousness, when all this is mitigated and absolved by your truly *divine* goodness and delicacy of feeling? I have had nothing but joy through you.

I am alone in my room in this little hotel. The fire is roaring; down below, Paris stirs and bustles in the rain. Your letter is on the table in front of me. It will help me to live through these few days in Paris without you. It will help me, too, to say to you everything I have to say. For this is a very solemn letter.

During the summer at Saint-Léonard I find almost acceptable a pattern of life which in winter makes me shudder with horror. There are, even at Saint-Léonard, nice young men to go boating or bathing with, to while away the time with, and they suffice. With the beginning of the cold weather, with lamps and books, all that comes to an end. The cold · makes me feel the need for the things of the mind. And then I am drawn to Paris. A few hours in Paris – yesterday Beethoven at the Salle Gaveau, this morning the Fragonards at the Galerie Charpentier – and I say to myself: No, it's impossible! I have no vanity about being what I am, but I must recognize it. And what I am makes me refuse to marry a nonentity. I have always had the idea firmly rooted in my mind that a woman's love cannot be an act of condescension, since in the carnal act it is she who is the victim.

A provincial girl without means and without connections, I cannot make a 'good' marriage which would bring me money and position – for example a marriage in Paris, into a cultivated, well-to-do milieu (to find a cultivated husband I should have to live in Paris half the year, independently, and I can't afford that). A 'good' marriage being impossible, I only want a marriage that will allow me to be overtly in love. If I were to remain equally lonely and deprived, and in addition

tied for life to a man who bored me but whom nevertheless I
cared for sufficiently not to want to make him feel it, with
all the disadvantages I have now, minus my freedom, plus
innumerable worries, what would be the point? Only a great
love and the knowledge of performing a really fruitful task
would make the sacrifice of my liberty worth while.

There are two or three young men here who would, I
think, willingly marry me. They are not unattractive: young,
pleasant, perfectly decent and well-bred. One of them at least
I could perhaps succeed in loving if I really put my mind to
it. But in what a limited environment – provincial trades-
people – oblivious to poetry, to everything profound or subtle
or disinterested. A married man can perhaps detach himself
from his environment. But a married woman? She cannot cut
herself off either from her husband or from his circle, or even
risk shocking them. Can you imagine how devastating it is
for a woman to be even the slightest bit superior? That is the
crux of my tragedy. The pleasure of disdaining mediocrities
has to be paid for. And liking mediocrities must be paid for
by the mediocrity of the pleasure one gets from them. Ah!
what a wife I would have been for an artist! For to be an
artist's wife one must love the artist even more than the man,
dedicate oneself to making the former great and the latter
happy. And then, how restful to be alone together, to understand each other's unspoken thoughts.

I have a horror of old maids. I pity the unhappily married.
Illicit love revolts me. So? ... And I shall be thirty in April!
Thirty, the crucial age.... My head spins. I'm terrified of
botching everything. Oh Costals, what am I to do with my
life?

One thing alone sustains me: your existence. You alone
give me the poise a woman needs. If I shut my eyes an instant
and tell myself that *you exist*, I feel assuaged. Yes, one must
thank creatures such as you for existing, simply for existing!
Is fire diminished by needing something to kindle it? I love
you like a torch with which I set myself alight. So what has
happened to me is this: you have made every other man
uninteresting to me, for the rest of my life, and every other
future meaningless. I can no longer envisage any normal

happiness – I mean a commonplace marriage – without my whole being revolting against the insipidity of it, because I shall never have the strength to devote my life to a man I scarcely love at all. Imagine a mortal woman who had loved Jupiter, and could not then love any man, though wanting desperately to be able to love one.

How I should have liked to be able to do something for you, for your work! But I can do nothing, nothing! If I could write, I should write articles about you, or a book. I almost wish that you were poor, sickly, unrecognized. I almost wish that you were wandering in search of your life's work, as I am searching for mine. Your weakness would be my strength. But no, you are entirely self-sufficient, you are embedded, as it were, in your solitude, and what makes others hate you – your self-assurance – is for me a matter for regret. There is no hope of my ever being able to feel this bond between us, this unique bond: a conviction on your part that you can put your trust in me absolutely. But tell me, at least, that you will never need such devotion! For if, one day, you did come to need it, how terrible if I could not respond to your appeal because I was bogged down in some dreary task, undertaken out of despair of ever finding anything better to do!

Once, as I was writing to you, this sentence came to the tip of my pen: 'I love you with all my heart.' I did not dare write it, in case you misunderstood. Now that you know me, now that you realize that I am not and never will be 'in love' with you, I can write it with complete confidence, I can write it without the slightest reticence: I love you with all my heart.

You must not answer; you must forget this letter or keep only an impression of tenderness from it, if possible. Above all, you must not make me atone for it by changing your attitude towards me.

A.H.

P.S. I am having a dark-red dress made for the winter, all velvety and light. And I've bought myself a grey coat, very delicate and chic – oh! so chic – which looks as though it might have come from a smart couturier (it is in fact a copy). I shall also buy a tight-fitting grey feather toque, because it is so kind to the face. .... You see how light-hearted I am in spite of you.

To be elegant, perhaps even pretty. .... And all for what, for whom? For the Saint-Léonardins. ....

Goodnight, Monsieur

Pierre Costals   to Andrée Hacquebaut
Paris   *Saint-Léonard*

26 November 1926

Dear Mademoiselle,

I write in answer to your esteemed letter of the 11th inst. with the regulation fortnight's delay. One week during which I did not even open your envelope (a little quarantine to which I submit all letters from women, after which time there is a chance that they may no longer be contagious). And one week during which I put off replying to you day after day because the thought of it bored me. Forgive me, but I find it difficult to remain completely serious when people tell me they love me.

The fact is that I did not find your letter at all agreeable. Why leave the nice, friendly plane we were on for the vulgarity and tediousness of 'sentiment'? You have now moved on to such exalted heights that I doubt whether I shall be able to follow you. I treated you with complete naturalness, as an intelligent comrade, if you like. Now I shall have to watch my step. Now I shall feel I have obligations towards you: an obligation to show myself worthy of your sublime gift of yourself, an obligation to treat you with infinite consideration (of which this letter is already a sample), an obligation to give you in return something more or less in proportion with what you have done me the honour of offering me. So many obligations! And obligations, alas, have never been my strong suit. I'm afraid you have been both clumsy and rash. You should have kept it all to yourself, so that I could have gone on pretending that I hadn't understood.

To change the subject: you surprised me one day by confessing your ignorance of English literature. I have just inherited the library of an old lady who had, I suppose, a kind

of feeling for me which it should be easy for you to reconstruct by analogy. Would you like me to send you a little
parcel of English literature in translation? I already have the
books in English. And it distresses me to think that a girl like
you might spend her whole life without having been brought
into contact with the genius of England.

Cordially yours, dear Mademoiselle. But keep a tight rein
on yourself, I beg of you.

C.

Andrée Hacquebaut   to Pierre Costals
Saint-Léonard   *Paris*

November 1926

How absurd you are! Imagine thinking that I wanted to lay
hands on you! And immediately you shake with fright, in
your ferocious desire for independence.

What, after all, does it all amount to? As I have told you,
you are like a god to me. And isn't a god more or less a mirror
in which to contemplate oneself and see oneself in a better
light? Does one not create him in one's own image, only
better? That is what you are, my sublimated double, the
strongest, the proudest, the best of me. I have, then, a calm,
cold passion for you. And beside this, my friendship. You are
at once a god and a chum – isn't that delicious?

What obligations does it impose on you? Give me what you
have given me up to now – I ask nothing more. I shall never
weigh more than a feather in your life. How small one would
be prepared to make oneself, in order to remain close to the
man one loves! As long as I can write to you, I shall not be
really unhappy. And what do I care even if you grow tired
of me, since I shall never grow tired of you, and I shall still
have your books? At the worst, even if you no longer gave
me anything more than you give everyone else, it would still
be a noble gift. Hence my attachment to you is calm and
relaxed.

41

I fancy Mme de Beaumont, who loved Chateaubriand more than Chateaubriand loved her, must have written to him as I am writing to you.

How deep-rooted the idea of mutual obligation is! One tells a person again and again : 'Don't worry. For your sake and for mine, I do not and will not love you. I have a passionate friendship for you, because it gives me pleasure, because I want it, because it makes me happy, because it is gratifying to think about another person, to look after him, to make him happy. I ask nothing of you. You owe me nothing. I love you at my own risk.' And the other person imagines that you love him with an irresistible love and are miserable because it is not requited. Nothing of the kind.

You will not, no, you cannot resent this melancholy half-offering of mine, finer in quality than the offerings of other women. Do not withhold your esteem from me. And write to me sometimes, I beg of you. When you maintain an absolute silence for a long time, I begin to fade away, I lapse into a sort of moral and spiritual lethargy. To understand becomes a matter of indifference to me, if I cannot make you share the fruit of my conquest.

I give you my hand.

A.H.

I accept with gratitude your offer of English books, although I would have preferred not to owe you anything for the moment.

Pierre Costals   to Andrée Hacquebaut
Paris   *Saint-Léonard*

30 November 1926

I recognize, dear Mademoiselle, that loving me is no fun. The moment I realize that someone cares for me, I'm disconcerted and annoyed. My next impulse is to put myself on the defensive. I have had a deep attachment for three or four people in my life, and they were always people I could have sworn were not even remotely drawn towards me. I think if they had loved me I should have been inclined to steer clear of them.

To be loved more than one loves oneself is one of the crosses of life. Because it obliges one either to feign a recipro- cal passion which one does not feel, or to cause pain by one's coldness and the rebuffs one administers. In either case there is constraint (and a man like me cannot feel constrained with- out the risk of turning nasty), and in either case pain. As Bossuet so powerfully put it: 'To love someone too much is to do him an irreparable wrong.' It's almost what I once wrote myself: 'To love without being loved is to do more harm than good.' The consequence is to be found in La Rochefoucauld: 'We are more prepared to love those who hate us than those who love us more than we would wish.' And your humble servant concludes: one should never tell people one loves them without asking their forgiveness.

Anyone I love takes away part of my freedom, but in that case it is I who wished it; and there is so much pleasure in loving that one gladly sacrifices something for its sake. Any- one who loves me takes away all my freedom. Anyone who admires me (as a writer) threatens to take it away from me. I even fear those who understand me, which is why I spend so much time covering my tracks – both in my private life and in the persona I express through my books. What would have delighted me, had I loved God, is the thought that God gives nothing in return.

I am equally afraid, needless to say, of being the object of a physical desire which I could not reciprocate. I would prefer to have an utterly passive woman, a block of wood, in my arms than a woman who got more pleasure from contact with me than I from contact with her. I can remember some truly hellish nights. . . . There will surely be demonesses in hell who desire one without one's desiring them. It is inconceivable that a God who is an expert in torture will not have thought of that.

I know so well how painful it is to be loved more than one loves oneself that I have always kept a careful watch on myself when I felt that *I* loved more than I was loved. That has happened to me sometimes, of course, and also to feel that my desire was only tolerated out of complaisance : the person concerned had scruples, or else was frigid. How careful I was then to make my presence felt as little as possible, how gingerly I advanced, how attentively I watched for the first sign of lassitude, in order to go into reverse, to meet less frequently ! ... Needless to say I suffered. But I knew that it was vital for my own sake, that I would lose everything if I tried to impose myself, and that anyhow it was I who was in the wrong for loving too much.

I know all about love : it's a feeling I have little respect for. Besides, it doesn't exist in nature; it's an invention of women. If a price were put on my head I should feel safer in the wilds, like a hunted animal, than with a woman who was in love with me. But there is affection. And there is affection mixed with desire, a splendid thing. In *every one* of the books I have published you will find, in one form or another, this affirmation : 'What matters to me above everything is loving.' But it is never a question of 'love'. It is a compound of affection and desire, which is not the same thing. 'A compound of affection and desire – what's that if it isn't love?' Well, no, it isn't love. 'Explain.' ... I don't feel like it. Women do not understand these things.

And finally, I don't like people needing me, intellectually, 'emotionally', or carnally. The inexplicable pleasure which my presence inspires in certain people diminishes them in my eyes. What do I care about having a place in someone else's universe !

I enclose an article I wrote on the subject many years ago. I would write it differently today. It is overstated and lacking in subtlety. But on the basic point I haven't changed.

One word more. You mention Pauline de Beaumont. I suspect Chateaubriand would not have done what he did for her if she hadn't been dying. He knew it was only for a brief moment.

My compliments to you, dear Mademoiselle.

C.

Fragment of an article by Costals

'The ideal in love is to love without being loved in return.'

...For the repugnance which some men feel for being loved, I can see several reasons, contradictory of course, inconsistency being a characteristic of the male.

Pride. – The desire to *keep the initiative.* In the love that others bear us, there is always something which eludes us, which threatens to catch us off guard, perhaps to overwhelm us, which has designs on us, which seeks to control us. Even in love, even when we are two, we do not want to be two, we want to remain alone.

Humility, or, if this seems too strong a word, absence of conceit. – The humility of a clear-sighted man, who does not think himself especially handsome or especially worthy, and finds it somehow *ridiculous* that his slightest gesture, word, silence, etc., can create happiness or misery. What an unfair power he is given! I have no great opinion of a man who is conceited enough to think aloud : 'She loves me', who does not try at least to minimize the thing by saying : 'She's getting worked up about me.' Whereby, no doubt, he belittles the woman, but only because he has first of all belittled himself.

An attitude that I would compare, for instance, to that of a writer who finds it *ridiculous* to have 'disciples', because he knows what his personality is made of, and what his 'message' adds up to. Any man worthy of the name despises the influence he exercises, in whatever direction, and puts up with having to exercise it as the price he must pay for his urge to express himself. *We* do not want to be dependent. How then can we approve of those who would depend on us? It is an exalted view of human nature that makes one refuse to be a leader.

Dignity. – Embarrassment and shame at the *passive* role a man who is loved has to play. For him, the state of being loved is suitable only to women, animals and children. For a man to allow himself to be embraced, caressed, held hands with, looked at with swimming eyes – ugh! (Even the majority of children, however effeminate they may be in France,

45

thoroughly dislike being kissed. They put up with it out of politeness, and because they have to, grown-ups being more muscular than they are. Their impatience with these slobberings is obvious to everyone except the slobberer, who thinks they are delighted by it.)

The desire to *remain free*, to protect oneself. – A man who is loved is a prisoner. No need to dwell on this, since it is well known.

Thérèse Pantevin   to Pierre Costals
La Vallée Maurienne   *Paris*

3 December 1926

A.M.D.G.

You have answered me! You have written to me to say that you would be willing to read a letter from me every three weeks! I have read this and kissed these words. Do not let me languish. If you could only see how pale I am! Quick, write some more words for me to kiss.

I crushed your letter against my breast, against my medals, until they hurt me, and the more they hurt the more it did me good. Everything that hurts me does me good. I dream of you coming into my room, but if you really came in I would probably begin to cry.

If I could, I would gladly leave the 'plague centre'. But where could I go? I ought to set out, like Abraham, walking straight ahead without knowing where, in the holy freedom of the children of God. For I dare not go to you. I would not know what to say to you, you would not be able to drag a word out of me ... and yet I await a sign from you, in spite of my terrible fear of disappointing you. But I don't spend all my time in the house; I'm often in the fields. I go to the local town three or four times a year. Last week we went to the fair at N— and I enjoyed myself very much. You see I don't deserve to be a nun, if that is what you meant.

However, do not start thinking I'm a flibbertigibbet. Every day I repose in the Eucharist, as I repose body and soul beside you in the silence of each night, and then everything that exists reposes in me. And I pray for my poor father, who does not believe in God, and who treats me so roughly. Do you know what he said just now at supper? 'It would be better to rear pigs than daughters.' He was looking at me when he said it.

Good-bye, my friend. My heart is heavy with all I have to give you. Love me just one jot as much as I love you, and Eternity will take us to its bosom.

Marie Paradis

Pierre Costals
Paris

to Thérèse Pantevin
La Vallée Maurienne

9 December 1926

Mademoiselle,

If you belong to Jesus Christ, you must not belong to him in a muddled way. Granted that God exists, he has given love to human beings only that they may give it back to him and him alone. Must I remind you of St Augustine's words: 'The soul can only reach God by approaching him without human intervention,' or the mystic (Meister Eckhart) who goes so far as to say: 'Do you know why God is God? It is because he is independent of all creatures.' You dishonour God by mixing him up with me. Such sloppiness is nauseating. When I see Jesus Christ mixed up with the human species (mixed, not juxtaposed, for juxtaposition occurs in all of us), I always think of the Princess Palatine's story of the schoolboy who had pictures of saints painted on his bottom so as not to be whipped.

You tell me you don't 'deserve' to take the veil. Say rather 'I am not destined' or 'I have not been chosen'. That is quite possible. But do not speak of deserving. Just as the love of one person for another has no need to be deserved, so the grace God gives a person to consecrate to him is given to that person in preference to an infinity of deserving persons without his having deserved it. I would even go so far as to say that, if

I were God, what I should like in a person would be my grace, just because it is privilege. This said, you are right not to be too self-satisfied. To be too firmly convinced that God approves of an action is often a clear sign that it is not being done for him and through his spirit, just as it is often a sign that a human action is defective to be too sure that it will be applauded.

Perhaps there are forces within you that could be harnessed to God's purposes. I don't know what you may have to lose by it, but I know it's negligible. It must have been one of the Fathers of the Church who invented the expression: he who loses wins. It pains me to think of you becoming involved in the imbecility of the world. You go to town, you go to the fair, and far from being overwhelmed with disgust by what you see there, you take pleasure in it. If you believe, what are you doing in the world? There is nothing innocent in the world once one believes (to enjoy the taste of a glass of water is to slap Christ's face); nothing that can even be justified. However trifling your activity, it is ridiculous; I should like to see your actions die out one by one, as lights go out at midnight in a town. One of my fellow-writers having spoken of the 'virtue of contempt', an ecclesiastic, writing in some review or other, danced a veritable fandango of scorn and derision: 'The virtue of contempt! A fine sort of Christian!' But the Gospel is full of Christ's contempt for the world; and this very morning I read somewhere: 'What a joy to know how contemptible the world is! How weak one is not to despise it as much as it deserves!' Who wrote that? The 'gentle' Fénelon, the 'swan'. (*Medit. V*) But better still – the last word in fact: the dying Jesus prays for his executioners, and refuses to pray for the world. *Non pro mundo rogo.* 'I pray not for the world.' (*St John* XVII, 9). *There's* a thunderbolt that impresses me more than the one that occurred when he expired. He prays for his executioners, because that is an extravagance worthy of his genius, but he refuses to pray for the corrupt and foolish multitude which he cursed in the Gospel. 'I pray not for the world, but for them which thou hast given me.' Wonderful, shattering words – it does me good to hear them! and now, Mademoiselle, be one of those for whom Jesus does not pray.

The sin against the Holy Ghost touches me deeply. Maybe there is at this moment a religious house waiting for you to bury yourself in body and soul, as I bury myself body and soul in my writings; it awaits you as the earth awaits the morning dew. That you are alive, I can believe. But alive with spiritual life? I have no means of knowing what there is in you; perhaps there is nothing. You have no more pressing objective than to find out what your impulses and inclinations amount to. Only a priest can disentangle them. A good confessor is the foundation of the edifice you must build. Go and see Father M— at the monastery of the — at L—. I know Father M—; he has the distinction of having been the greatest sinner in the world – which means that he will understand your sins the better, knowing what sin is. He will induce in you such a state of humility that the confession of those sins will be as enjoyable to you as the flames were to the martyrs. He will never anticipate the grace within you, supposing it to be there, but will follow it humbly and firmly, after testing it with the greatest care. Although today people no longer enter into religion unthinkingly, as they used to do (and as people continue to enter into matrimony), the Church cannot be too careful in making sure of a vocation. You should not be made a nun by men but by God.

You pray for your father? You would do better to pray for yourself. Have you forgotten how insistent the Gospel is on that point? And you would do better to read the Gospel, and understand it, than to go so often to Mass, to Communion, etc. Abuses are often more dangerous than errors, because one is less on one's guard against them. Piety should be devoid of gestures, like sorrow, and, I might almost venture to say, as silent. How eloquent the silence of Moses before God!

Do not cease to remind yourself, whatever I may write to you, that I am not a Christian believer. Faith is darkness – the expression falls frequently from religious pens; and I am all crude brightness. Do not cease to bear in mind that I have no faith, that I do not miss it, that I do not ever expect to have it, that I do not ever wish to have it. 'There is a road which, though it may sometimes appear the right one, leads to hell.' Perhaps I am that road. In imagination and in hope I have damned myself a hundred thousand times. In action – in the total and absolute fulfilment of my desires – I have damned myself another hundred thousand times. And in memories and regrets I have damned myself another hundred thousand times. And that is part of my glory. And I have helped enough women to damnation to help one in the opposite direction. For I am a spirit of grace, and spirits of grace radiate like grace itself, which assumes every form. And I am – essentially – *he-who-assumes-every-form*.

I have written to you in a language that must be partly incomprehensible to you. You may forage what you can from it.

Forgive me, Mademoiselle, for my presumption.

Costals

Andrée Hacquebaut
Saint-Léonard

to Pierre Costals
Paris

24 December 1926

You do not write to me for more than three weeks. Then at last a slender post-card with no more than a dozen words on it brings me your greetings and asks for my news. My news? I cannot go on telling you *ad infinitum* that I'm unhappy. I must, however, find some way out of this state of crisis which is killing me. The day when it is proved to me beyond a shadow of doubt that every outlet is closed to me as far as love is concerned – and that day cannot be far off – I shall persist no longer. It would be horrible to cling on. The only alternative is voluntary renunciation, a pure and dignified life. I belong to the sacrificial generation, the girls whose chances of love were decimated by the war with its toll of young men : we too are widows. As for man-hunting, for adventure, I am not yet ripe for that.

It seems to me that such a renunciation would open up fresh fields for me. 'I'm beaten, it's all over and done with. Therefore, everything that happens to me from now on will be a bonus. Since I no longer seek, it may be that I've already found.' I have often noticed in myself a sudden reversal of this kind when I reach the climax of some experience I've been going through: a burst of furious pride, a sort of emotional desiccation and detachment, a sudden asperity towards fate: 'After all, come what may, I still have myself.'

I still have you, too, of course. In my confusion and despair I have a kind of peace: "He cannot, he will not be my happiness. But he is my truth. He does not want me to love him – I would fail to please him and would destroy myself. Nevertheless, it fills me with a great peace, in spite of my life's failure, when so many women will never find the man who would make their hearts throb, or will love heaven knows whom out of the need to love, it fills me with a great peace to have discovered at least this certainty: that there exists a man who is everything to me, whom I could have loved with my whole being. I no longer need to search or to wait – the exhausting fate of lonely women.' Yes, telling myself this appeases me. The impression of having *achieved*, of having *had*, of escaping at last from that vague and indefinable torment, from the inordinate appetite for love – the renouncing of a precise treasure, and not innumerable and unknown possible treasures – why, in comparison it's almost tantamount to possessing.

Christmas! An abyss of boredom and mediocrity with the people among whom I have to spend it. A day of rain and nostalgia and misery. Why are there days when all those hostile things which at other times lie dormant and innocuous rise up and assail one all at once? It's agonizing to have to undergo this onslaught. And I think of the Christmases of those who love one another, of the adorable Christmas in *Werther*. What a pity I can no longer put my shoes in the fireplace! I would have put two pairs, because there are four things I long for madly: a husband (with love), a gramophone, a book about Cosima Wagner, and a hat decorated with an aigrette, a hat I won't describe to you, because you would make fun of me.

A Happy New Year! I'm very fond of you, you know, Costals. And if happiness could be given like a diamond, it would long ago have passed from my hand into yours. Once more I offer you my undying devotion. But when, oh when will you ever make use of it?

A.H.

This letter remained unanswered.

Saint-Léonard. January. Seven degrees of frost. At night, in spite of the stove, the water freezes in the Hacquebaut house.

What is most immediately striking about Andrée's room is that everything in it, furniture, hangings, objects, is at least twenty years old and looks it: for twenty years nothing has been bought, or next to nothing. The only things of any beauty are some reproductions of famous pictures, chosen with taste, and a very unfeminine taste (a taste in which there is a feeling for grandeur).

The sound of a hooter outside. How often this hooter has made her heart miss a beat! In spite of the cold, she opens the window. The postman's big bicycle-lamp lights up the door of the neighbouring house. Then it moves, comes nearer. As the lamp passes Andrée flings out a wish to it as though it were a shooting star: 'O God, make it stop!' But the lamp moves away into the distance. Out there, too, is the man she calls to, who also goes by without stopping.

Already fairly isolated from humanity, she is isolated even more by the cold. The snow-bound atmosphere muffles sounds. Everything lives in slow motion, everything shrivels up. Express trains no longer run. The mail arrives a day late. But what does it matter, after all? Never a letter from Costals. Luckily she knows that in February she will be going to Paris for a month.

She had always suffered from the feeling of having nobody at the other end of the line, from not knowing what person, what cause to dedicate herself to. As a child she already showed symptoms of the disease that Costals, in a neologism worthy of a medical student, called Andrée's 'letteritis'. In those days she used to write letters to herself, rather like the English poet in the last war, who at each port of call on the way to the Dardanelles, hired an urchin to wave a handkerchief when the steamer sailed (Costals professed to find such a trait utterly *repulsive:* he could not possibly have shaken hands with a man with that sort of sensibility). Later on, she had contributed for some time to the correspondence columns of the women's papers, which are the young girl's substitute for men, as lap-dogs are the grown woman's substitute for babies. This correspondence had ceased when she began writing to Costals.

She scribbled page after page to him, for hours on end, stopping only because of cramp in her hand. As with most women, what she wrote in the form of letters was in fact her diary – huge pages without margins, unnumbered, with words scratched out or written over, and lines added in every direction and even across other lines. Whenever Costals received one of these letters, he would weigh it in his hand with a sigh, assessing the number of pages it must contain: for a man who, like most men, could not read long letters, it was an affliction every time. It was unusual for the envelope not to be held together with bits of stamp paper lest it should burst under the weight. Inside, Costals would often find a photograph of Andrée which he would tear up in a rage and throw into the waste paper basket without even glancing at it. Ah! if she had seen him then it would have been like a dagger in her heart. But also, in an instant, she would have seen the light at last. Unless, incurably, she were to think: 'Only love could account for such a fit of rage. What has he got against me today?' Sometimes she would perfume her letters with such a pungent scent that he was obliged to hang them out on clothes pegs for the night; but even this was not enough, and the drawer of his desk would reek for days on end. If he complained to her, she would complain back: how could friendship be affected by such trifles? She was incapable of realizing (1) that there was no friendship, and (2) if there had been, yes, it would have been affected, because in anything to do with the quality of personal relations, there are no trifles. It was the same with her writing-paper, which was of an 'impossible' format. As Costals kept her letters, he had pointed out to her how awkward they were for his files, overlapping them and destroying their neatness. It was a waste of breath – so much so that he was occasionally provoked into throwing some of her letters away out of sheer exasperation at seeing their edges frayed like lace in his files.

From time to time, Costals would send a reply to these letters – illegible little notes, scribbled as fast as he could manage, in which he put down whatever came into his head – literally anything – and in which he always teased her a little, because it was in his nature to tease. *She* believed that one only teases people one loves. In her more lucid moments, she found these notes touching in their goodwill, which indeed they were.

At the beginning, she had also sent him little presents – baskets of flowers or fruit. At first he had been weak or lazy or charitable enough to accept them: 'She would be very hurt if I refused them.' When she sent him a rather elegant cigarette-holder, he sent it back with a friendly letter. For a year she stopped sending presents, then began again – eau de Cologne, sachets of lavender. He wrote to her: 'Dear Mademoiselle, I shall not return your little presents any more. I shall give them automatically to my mistresses' (which was what he had done). That did it. There were no more little presents.

Andrée's other cure for boredom was reading. Books borrowed, books ordered from a lending library, books even bought (mad extravagance – books costing thirty francs!): she read until her eyes ached. Almost always worth-while books. And almost always something interesting in the reflections she scribbled in the margins.

Letter-writing, reading, what else? She ordered prospectuses from travel agencies, catalogues of rare books, manuscripts, records, catalogues from big stores, and thumbed through them interminably, marking what she would have liked to have, almost without bitterness. She did not resent the fact that millions of fools, thanks to their ill-gotten fortunes, could enjoy the art, the luxury, the things of the mind, which were denied to her. She had tried to 'write', but soon realized that she had no literary talent. Sometimes, at the end of her tether, she would go out and walk aimlessly in the countryside, although she had no feeling for nature, at least the nature round Saint-Léonard. She would only have liked it as a background for living people.

There were times when this life was bearable, when, if she did not feel happy, she was not exactly unhappy. Reading a good book, she would say to herself: 'To think that there are women who work seven hours a day in an office!' At other times she was bored to distraction – so much time on her hands that she did not know what to do with – but nonetheless she resisted manual work, from an acute sense of the value of time. While her mother was alive she had never wanted to help her with the housework, to darn, or sew her dresses. 'Imagine making jam when I could spend the time improving my mind, discovering a great writer I haven't read, learning something, no matter what, if only from reading Larousse!' Only an acute attack of misery would drive her to take up a manual chore. Thus. whenever she felt particularly distressed, she took to darning her stockings. It had become a formula : great unhappiness = darning of stockings – so much so that the crimson 'egg' she used for this purpose gave her a twinge when she came across it in her more serene moments. Since her mother's death, she had had to get down to minor household chores – but never without a feeling of vehement impatience. It was something she simply could not accept.

One day Costals had said to her: 'If I had had the misfortune to have a daughter, I should have been stiff with anxiety until she was married off, all the more so if she had no money. Parents are terribly proud of themselves when they produce a brat, and go round trumpeting it to the world, but when it comes to bringing it up with a little intelligence, nothing doing. Of course I realize how awful it must be for decent people to do what has to be done to get a daughter settled – intrigue, entertain, etc. – because everything connected with marriage is unquestionably the greatest nonsense that can happen in the life of a human being. But they shouldn't have got themselves into the mess in the first place! It's always the same – producing children, and then not knowing what to do with them. So much care and attention and conscientiousness about birth, and so much frivolity, blindness and stupidity about education. And then we come to the parents who haven't enough money to get their daughters married off, and go on waiting, waiting for God knows what, waiting until she

55

becomes crabbed and can't afford to be so choosy. I know some really criminal parents, whose daughter was made for marriage, but who condemned her to celibacy in order to keep her with them. All this is simply to explain to you that there is only one thing for you to do – to take a job in Paris that is not too exacting and that provides you with your bread and butter, and to concentrate, to the exclusion of everything else, on *meeting people*, in other words looking for a husband. Your sole aim, for the time being, should be to make social contacts.'

Mademoiselle had taken offence at these words. She was like those bogus artists who rail against the bourgeoisie but who are more bourgeois than anyone. 'Make social contacts' – so that was the advice he gave to a superior girl like her!

'You who despise society, you who wallow in solitude, you tell me that!'

'I live in solitude because I've won and paid for the right to live in solitude. When I was twenty-five *I* "met people" too. It's because I did things that bored me then that I can now do what I like. It's not a question of whether "meeting people" is fun. It's a question of whether you want to remain a penniless spinster in Saint-Léonard (Loiret). If not, you must make a suitable marriage, and you will only make a suitable marriage if you have an inexhaustible supply of suitable gentlemen parading in front of you, like stallions parading round a paddock. Which you can only do in Paris. Find a job there. If you like, I can help you to find one.'

'I'll be saddled with her the whole time,' Costals had thought to himself. In spite of which, in this unfortunate fit of altruism he not only told her, 'I'll help you to find a job', but went further: 'I'll introduce you to people.' She agreed.

If she had not been in love with him, he might perhaps have taken her on as his secretary, his own having just left him. But imagine taking on as secretary a woman who is in love with you! ... Costals had a friend called M. Armand Pailhès, an excellent man, a splendid paterfamilias, who was secretary-general of a big firm of robbers (a company formed for the reconstruction of the war-devastated North). He offered a job as a typist, and so Andrée landed in Paris.

But when it came to doing a job that encroached on her inner life, Andrée bridled – she could not help it. She could not work for half an hour without heaving sighs which infuriated her boss. She would spend twenty minutes at a time in the lavatory reading Nietzsche. She arrived late and left early. After three or four days, with a volume of Valéry lying in her half-open drawer, she would bury herself in 'pure poetry' as soon as her boss's back was turned. Her habit of suddenly closing the drawer if he looked round gave her away. Apart from this, although she considered that her tact was nothing less than heroic, her notes to Costals, at the rate of one every three days ('Won't you come to the concert of Spanish music on Sunday? . . .' 'I'm going to the exhibition of prints at the Bibliothèque Nationale on Saturday. If by any chance you were free. . . .') exasperated him. He excused himself two or three times, did not reply to the next few letters, and finished by tearing them up without opening them. And it must be admitted that he did nothing about 'introducing her to people'. He too considered himself heroic, for having got her settled in Paris, and his heroism was strictly limited. Take Andrée to parties! He would rather die. In short, both regarded themselves as heroic, which is always a bad sign. When, at the end of the month, enlightened about the girl's behaviour, M. Pailhès found a pretext to give her back her cherished freedom, everyone was happy, Andrée included. To live in Paris but to be imprisoned in that stupid office, to have everything she loved within arm's reach but to be unable to enjoy it, was worse than the provinces, where at least, if she suffered, she suffered without irritation. It was almost with a sigh of relief that she took the train back to Saint-Léonard.

In the waiting-room of the War Pensioners' Review Board, awaiting examination, two hundred average Frenchmen, ex-service men, neither bourgeois nor plebeian, but of that intermediate class which is the backbone of France, with their characteristic French tendency to be buttoned up to the eyebrows, and their pallid and, my God, so unprepossessing Parisian faces.

A restless crowd, with men coming and going, edging in and out, like bulls in a herd when they sense a man approaching; the one-legged men in particular stubbornly refuse to sit down. One man jumps at every name that is called; another asks the way to the lavatory: the thought that his request for a renewal of his pension will be refused has upset his inside. But there are also some quiet little men, old lags, reading their newspapers. How wonderfully brave of that one over there to open the *Action Française* in the middle of the crowd! (If they don't reduce *his* disablement scale, there's no government left.) And the doleful faces of the seriously wounded, escorted by their 'good ladies'. And the bourgeois with the red ribbon of the Legion of Honour, sitting not with the common herd but a little apart, on the only chair in the room, in order to make it clear that his respectability has remained intact throughout this grim ordeal. (Costals, on entering, had put his gloves in his pocket so as not to be the only person there wearing them.)

Costals imagined all these men in uniform, and then he loved them, whereas in their civilian clothes he had a tendency, typically ruling class, to regard them as malingerers. 'That fat one, for instance. . . . Is it possible,' our professional psychologist asks himself, 'to be ill and fat at the same time? And this one here with his shifty look, there's obviously nothing wrong with him, absolutely nothing.' Whereupon the man with the shifty look turns round and shows the professional psychologist an empty coat-sleeve.

A wave of respect, hope, fear, a sudden sharpening of attention, as a doctor passes through. Some of them salute him, to remind him who they are, although he has never seen them in his life. He passes by with his cigarette in the air – not that he is a smoker (he is nothing of the sort), but because smoking being forbidden here, it is a sign of his power. To two or three poor devils who are particularly keen saluters he offers, or rather *tenders* his hand, without stopping or turning his head. As he goes through, the man of power moves the men aside by taking them by the arm with an air of affable superiority, as one touches the backs of sheep when one is trying to make one's way through a flock. At first, when they do not know who is taking their arm from behind, they start indignantly; but as soon as they see who it is, their faces light up: the man of power has *touched* them, unworthy as they are! Ah yes, they are in good hands!

If the doctor stops to speak to one of them, he is suddenly surrounded by three or four, then six, then ten, who crowd around him shamelessly and listen, hoping to pick up a hint which will help them to obtain something, or simply hasten their turn. They are suddenly so humble, so insanely, incorrigibly respectful towards people in authority, so ready to accept anything, that it is painful to see.

A placard warns: 'Doctors are strictly forbidden to accept fees on the premises of the Review Board.' Why, O Administration, do you have to put the idea into our heads that there may be something shady about such fees? We know perfectly well that everything to do with pensions is as pure as the driven snow.

What a superb play of expressions on the face of one of the men when a doctor leaves the room by the outer door! He struggles against his natural shyness, finally overcomes it, and quickly makes for the exit behind the doctor, whom he will buttonhole outside; and he lowers his eyes, feigning indifference, so that the others will not spot his game and follow him in order to accost the doctor at the same time.

Some men leave, but more come in – so much so that (utterly convinced as one is that one will be the last to go in) one tells oneself that there will never be an end to it. Which is indeed a very 'wartime' sentiment.

From time to time an assistant appears at the door of one of the consulting rooms and calls out the names of the men whose turn it is. Those whose civilian lives are on a par with their military ones for wretchedness, the eternal second-raters, answer 'Present!' like keen young recruits. When one of the assistants shouts the names in a stentorian voice, some of the men laugh, and the others, realizing that it was funny, laugh too. A great wave of laughter. They are suddenly right back at the Front.

Some of the men hunch their backs on the way into the

consulting-room to make themselves look iller. Others preen themselves and look ingratiating, thinking that this will make the best impression. The room concerned with the 'respiratory and circulatory systems' is much the most popular, because malingering is easiest there. Through the open door, the surgery appears bathed in a limpid, greenish glow, like an aquarium or an oriental night. One can catch a glimpse of what is happening in the consulting-room. One man tries to read what the doctor is writing about him, and goes on talking, lying into the void, while the doctor stands there casually turning his back on him. Another breathes heavily, oppressively. Another comes out pulling up his trousers, and the price-tag is still to be seen on his underpants, bought only yesterday because he was ashamed of his old ones. His furtive look betrays the fact that he has hoodwinked the doctor, or thinks he has hood-winked him, and he walks with his eyes lowered, like a man going to the Communion rail, to hide the gleam of triumph in his eyes which might give him away. Others come out with collars and ties undone, which accentuates the guard-room aspect of the place (on his way here Costals had made the taxi-driver hurry, thinking that if he were five minutes late he would be court-martialled). Some of the men argue the toss as they come out, with their rapacious, tubercular Parisian faces. But they are peaceable rebels, very French. A swig of white wine and it will all be over – or another doctor has only to cross the room for that awful gleam of humility to appear in their eyes again. They hope to get something out of him, so they cease to be rebels. One only rebels when one has nothing to lose by it.

As the hours go by, exhaustion begins to set in. Even the cripples have given up standing. The herd has become stupefied. When one sees how they have acquiesced, how one has acquiesced oneself, in waiting from half-past eight until ten minutes to twelve, one understands how *it* lasted four and a half years. . . .

A blind man came out of one of the rooms, led by a girl – and for Costals the war atmosphere collapsed there and then like a burst balloon. She had slender, slanting eyes – bluish below her black hair, as in Andalusia, and as disturbing as dark eyes in a real blonde; a tiny forehead (ah, nice and stupid!); curls down her neck – and although he had always proclaimed that he only liked clean-shaven necks, the pleasure of contradicting himself (his privilege, like God's) now made him adore these curls. Her skin was stretched so tight that it might have been marble, and it was matt, though her nose shone a little, as marble statues are polished in places where they have been kissed a great deal. She held her head a little to one side, as though to indicate the point on her neck where she should be kissed. He loved the way she patted and re-arranged her hair: the gesture of the midinette. He liked this community of gestures among women. Her body was well-rounded and yet slender: what is known as *morbidezza*, is it not?

As she passed by, Costals sniffed the odour she left in her wake, his nose quivering like a dog's. The couple went out. Without a moment's hesitation, Costals followed them. He would concoct a pretty lie for the head of the Review Board.

He was about to offer to find them a taxi. But they were hardly in the street before an empty taxi drew up. They hailed it, and it was the distinguished novelist who was left standing on the pavement.

He was delighted. 'Now I shall be able to work in peace,' he said to himself.

On the very day she arrived in Paris Andrée went to a concert. In the past these hours of music had meant so much to her in her loveless life. They were a substitute for all the other ecstasies. It was as though thousands of lovers clasped her in their arms. What a let-down it was, afterwards, from this seventh heaven to the Parisian street! At such moments she felt strongly that she could never marry an ordinary person. This time she was bored at the concert – a mixture of dejection and indifference. This music, which she had once loved so desperately, for want of anything else to love, now seemed to her so insipid by comparison with the proximity of Costals.

Costals spoiled her taste for everything else, demolished every-thing around her, everything she relied on, created a vacuum as though he wanted her to love nothing but himself. It was no longer Beethoven, it was he, his 'music of perdition'. Listen-ing to the Pastoral Symphony, with its imitations of bird calls, she found it puerile. The sounds reached her across a layer of distraction and boredom. Actually, she was not listening, she could not listen. The most trashy music would have accom-panied her daydreams quite as well.

Costals had invited her to dinner the following night. The restaurant was a little twenty-franc bistro. They talked of nothing but literature. Flanked on either side by other diners a few feet away, she did not dare speak of what lay nearest her heart. But in fact she scarcely felt the need to. She was in Paris for a month : there was no hurry. And moreover, now that she was with him she felt a profound sense of unison, as though they were brother and sister. (She kept coming back to the phrase 'brother and sister' – although now she was thinking 'Byron and Augusta', which was to give it an extra twist.) Such peace, such well-being, such security, such aban-don! An impression of the futility of words, and a feeling of being marvellously alone, almost more alone than when she was by herself. . .

She was astonished to find herself unperturbed. It must, she thought, be due to their profound intellectual understanding, stronger than love and superior to it. And also because, ever since Costals' harsh letter, she was trying hard to keep to the plane of virile friendship on which he wanted her to remain, and to hold romance at bay. She had no desire, even, when she was with him, to indulge in those chaste caresses which girls love, except for an occasional longing to kiss his hand. And even this did not seem to her to be an amorous gesture, but rather an overflowing of gratitude, as though she could not find words to express her feelings, or dared not, or could not say them.

As for him, at the other side of the table, his eyes never rested on her, but looked over her head; but she did not notice it. Besides, he never looked at anyone he did not desire; always beyond them.

At one point, however, his eyes fell on the girl's bare fore-
arms – and he could not take them away. Her arms were dirty.
He tried in vain to persuade himself that their greyish tinge
was the natural colour of the skin : the illusion was impossible.
For a long while he kept his eyes glued to her arms, unable to
utter another word. Perhaps, if he had desired her at all, he
might have found her even more desirable (a big 'if'). Since
he did not desire her, the sight froze him.

The atmosphere of cheerful banter created by Costals (and
quickly recaptured) became even more animated towards the
end of the meal. Andrée thought it must be the effect of the
wine, or even of her presence. In fact this gaiety had sprung
up suddenly in Costals the moment he had decided he was
going to cut the evening short and pretend he had to get away
early : it was the gaiety of the horse that sniffs the stable.

She accepted her dismissal with good grace, and went home
on foot. This calm and serenity sustained her at each of their
meetings. After the agonies induced by Costals' long silences,
during which she longed for something shattering to happen to
cure her of her love – silences which might have driven her
to all kinds of folly – when she saw him again everything
became simple and peaceful, everything happened in the same
natural, easy rhythm – so much so that she found herself being
almost cold with him.

On leaving her, Costals had said : 'I'll get in touch with you
in two or three days.' A week having elapsed, she wrote to
him. Costals groaned, but decided that it would be cruel to go
on depriving her of another meeting during this paltry month
in Paris by which she had set so much store. He had two
appointments in the same district, the avenue Marceau, two
days later, one at four o'clock, the other at eight. Between
them he would be free. He arranged to meet her at half past
five in the rue Quentin-Bauchart, on the pavement in front of
number 5. He would be leaving this house at that time, after
visiting some friends.

On the pavement in the rue Quentin-Bauchart at twenty-five past five, Andrée was already accusing Costals of being late. Obviously he had forgotten their appointment; he had come out early and gone away. She was a little surprised at this rendezvous in the street after dark, on a bitterly cold day in early February. 'Would he make such a rendezvous with a woman he really loved, or who meant anything at all to him?' But he emerged, her heart leapt, and off they went side by side down the dark street with its red and white lights.

'I'm not in very good form,' Costals said straight off. 'The other day I saw in a shop a piece of jade which I coveted. A thousand francs. I decided to go back to the shop that evening and buy it. And then I ran into an old lady who used to keep a flower stall where I bought violets for my girl-friends a few years ago. She's a widow; she told me her two children were both ill, her brother treated her badly, and she was destitute. Crash! There I was, utterly disarmed. I was ashamed to buy my piece of jade, and pressed the thousand-franc note into her hand. I haven't got over it yet.'

'What do you mean?'

'I haven't yet got over the irritation I felt at giving her the thousand francs instead of buying the piece of jade.'

'What was to stop you buying the jade as well?'

'Oh! I bought it all right, but it wasn't the same thing. What annoys me is to have given away a thousand francs out of pure charity. It's ruined my week.'

'Nonsense, the satisfaction of ... no, I won't say "of duty done" – that would be too pompous. But after all, don't you feel a certain satisfaction at having given pleasure to an old woman you were sorry for?'

'No. I feel. . . .'

'Go on, say it: you feel regret.'

'Yes, regret. I'm ashamed. And at the same time there's something else that worries me. I feel that a thousand francs. . . . What's a thousand francs? I'm tormented by the desire to give her more.'

'How complicated you are!'

'But you don't know what pity is. It's a feeling that can ruin your life. Luckily I know how to protect myself. I have a very strict egotist's discipline. If I hadn't I wouldn't have written my books. I had to choose. You'll be able to test this egotism one day, God willing. . . .'

'Did he do what he has done for me out of pity?' she wondered. She believed that he was fond of her, but could not make out in what way. Perhaps he would have been just as kind, just as devoted, to a male friend. Yet there were times when she thought to herself that one isn't as helpful and sensitive as that simply out of kindness. Had she not been afraid of annoying him, she would have asked him whether he treated her as he did out of pure comradeship – an exquisite sense of comradeship – or whether there was an element of love in it. In other words – how could she put it? – whether he was attracted to her.

But Costals, having caught sight of a notice-board advertising a flat to let, glanced up at the building and said:

'I've been haunted by the idea of moving ever since I can remember. Would you mind coming with me while I have a look at this place? I've rather fallen for the house.'

A few minutes later the concierge was showing them round the flat. What a strange sensation for Andrée! Almost as though they were a young married couple, or engaged. It made her feel dizzy . . . and it was even more extraordinary when the concierge said to her:

'Everything works very well. Perhaps Madame would care to see . . . the hot water. . . .'

'Madame'. . . . And in the bathroom! Was it really possible that Costals did not realize how provocative it was for a girl – and a girl of whose love for him he was well aware – to be shown round a flat which he thought of making his home? Was it possible that he had no ulterior motive? And she was not too badly dressed to be taken for his wife! Meanwhile he was asking her advice: should that window be walled up, this wall knocked through? She answered mechanically, like a good housewife, but her soul was elsewhere, borne away as though on a gust of wind to a realm so unexpected and improbable that it frightened her.

'Six rooms . . .' she said for the sake of saying something. 'Isn't it rather on the large side?'

'Not at all. Drawing-room, dining-room, my study, my bedroom, a junk-room, and then the other bedroom, the "tomb of
the unknown woman"....'

'Tomb? Are you a Bluebeard?'

'No, "tomb" in another sense – a double sense.* The room
in which women fall. And the room in which their illusions
tumble down.'

Was it really possible that he could be so lacking in tact
if. . . . She felt as though in a dream, in an abyss. On the way
downstairs, she was afraid she might lose her balance.

Outside, the cold gripped her. She shivered. Now he was
walking beside her, and his long overcoat, tight at the waist,
flapped against his legs like a skirt (like a German officer's
great-coat, she thought) to the rhythm of his footsteps which
rang out with a power and majesty which startled her. His
gloved hands were clasped together over his stomach in an
attitude which he maintained almost throughout their entire
meeting – an attitude Andrée found somehow hieratic. It
seemed to her that she was walking beside a Homeric hero.

'What torture all these domestic problems are,' he was saying. 'My family are always on at me: "You must get married,
you need a woman to look after you." That's a moral way of
looking at marriage, don't you think? Marry for social or
family reasons, or to make a girl happy – not at all. It's simply
a question of having someone there to see that you're not
swindled when you buy the upholstery. Fancy getting married
on those terms! One might just as well engage a housekeeper,
whom one can always get rid of if she won't do. Whereas a
wife. . . .'

Costals was obsessed with the idea of the wrongness of
marriage for a writer – a real writer, who takes his art
seriously. He was inexhaustible on the subject. For five minutes,
without drawing breath, he railed against marriage, extrava-
gantly and, it must be said, tastelessly. Truths, half-truths and
sophistries welled from his lips, accompanied by bitter jibes. A
great burst of eloquence. He was like a cup full to the brim

---

*Untranslatable pun on the words *tomber*, to fall, and *tombeau*,
tomb (*Translator's note*).

and continually overflowing, like the basins of Moroccan fountains.

'You see how I trust you,' he said at the end. 'I talk to you as I would to a man.' Regardless of the fact that almost everything he had said had wounded the woman who walked at his side, numb with cold, hurrying to keep up with him along the dark avenues. Had he not raised her to the seventh heaven, only to plunge her back into the abyss? At first she had ventured a few remarks in favour of writers marrying. She was sure these remarks were sound, but she felt so self-conscious that now she did not know what to say, the words refused to 'come out'; she was like a schoolboy being tortured by a sadistic examiner, knowing the answers perfectly well but standing there like an idiot, overcome with nerves, his mind a blank. Nevertheless, incapable of rejecting the idea that the visit to the flat was not unintentional, she began to think that he was only saying all this to provoke her into taking the opposite view, and to hear it from her lips. She allowed herself to indulge in this fantasy, this madness, this senseless daydream. . . . Then she thought it would be cunning to switch from wives to children.

'Yes, but what about children! How can a man like you, Costals, who are a sort of fertility god, have no children? I must confess that it's always surprised me. Your personality is incomplete without them. Even if only from the point of view of your work, think what riches you're depriving yourself of!'

To every word she had said before, the fertility god had been ready with a lightning retort: a vicious thrust of the foil, and each time a hit. Now, for the first time, he did not answer. She thought she had found his Achilles heel. She turned towards him, saw his upturned face and his limpid eyes, in which she seemed to see an expression of sadness, intensely moving in a man as overconfident as he. Ah! how she adored him when she saw him weakened!

'Your son, Costals! His little arms around your neck. . . . Think how he would need you. . . . All the messages you send out into the void, for a crowd of indifferent people, concentrated on a person who was flesh of your flesh, a person you loved. . . . No, you're not a complete man if you haven't experienced that. But I can tell that you regret it. No, don't deny it! You can't hide it from me any more. Women have these intuitions, you know....'

He was like a punch-drunk boxer, who can no longer defend himself, his eyes staring into space, those eyes in which Andrée seemed to read a message of defeat. Sensing her opportunity, she brought the conversation round from children to herself. The darkness gave her courage, and the fact of not looking at him. She looked only at their two shadows, side by side, which loomed up, turned, vanished, reappeared, according to the play of the street lamps. And she thrilled at the thought of all the passers-by who knew nothing about them, suspected nothing. For she still imagined that there was something to 'know'.

'Sometimes I think that, whatever you may say, you need to be loved, you don't dislike being loved, in spite of all your blasphemies against love. But something tells me that you may perhaps relent a little. You gave yourself away, Costals, unwittingly: I saw your look of sadness and longing when I spoke to you about that non-existent son and about the element of sterility in your love life. Something tells me that you hanker after another form of tenderness. I can understand how one might feel ill at ease if one were loved the wrong way. But I, for instance, do I love you the wrong way? Isn't my affection for you a source of sweetness and not an infliction? Don't you understand that it's the most ardent and passionate love that is most capable of renunciation and self-sacrifice? Let me love you, so that I can stop having to hold back for fear of displeasing you, saying "affection" when I mean "love". What do I want? More warmth, more life, more activity. Oh, to be able to do things for you – anything! Not to have to go away again in three weeks' time with so cruelly little to treasure.... Because what suffices me here, once I'm far away.... I should like, for instance – how shall I put it – should like you to call me by my Christian name, or even "my dear". It's been "dear Mademoiselle" for four years! You might be talking to your piano teacher. I should like you to write to me more often – a few lines every fortnight (it isn't much to ask). I should like you to treat me as a little girl, if only a stupid and sulky little girl. I should like to see you in places that are more appropriate, more suited to you – gardens, the country, art galleries. . . . I don't know what I want exactly. . . . But I don't want things as they were, as they are, as you've wished them to be. I don't demand that it should last for ever, only that I should enjoy you more, be closer to you, as long as it does last. And I should still like an answer to the question : has my affection given you some happiness? Have I the right to think that I'm to some extent necessary to you? Have you felt less alone for the assurance I've brought you of being passionately understood and loved, loved in everything that makes you what you are, in the quintessence of your being as in your smallest idiosyncrasies, your irony, your fooling, your unkindnesses even, God forgive me? If you don't give me the terrible answer Satan gave to Eloa, it will be happiness enough for me.'

'What a fantasy world she lives in!' thought Costals. 'Andrée Hacquebaut's affection giving me happiness! She has a mania for denying the obvious, and another typically feminine mania – wanting me to be unhappy so as to be able to console me. The idea of her consoling me for my alleged unhappiness, when it's she and her kind, meaning all those women who give you a love you haven't asked for, who are responsible for spoiling my happiness! No, the whole thing is too farcical. And yet at the same time one can respect and pity it. How can I get out of it without hurting her?' The thought of the harm he could do her by simply telling her, in one short sentence, *how things stood*, paralysed him – like a man playing at boxing with a child and hardly daring to move for fear of hurting it. 'God, how maddening the girl is! What a mess I've got myself into!'

He was still dragging her along with his long strides. In the past twenty minutes they had passed through one gloomy and almost deserted street after another (rue Christophe Colomb, rue Georges-Bizet, rue Magellan, etc.). These streets, with their blocks of expensive flats and private houses, and very few shops, were almost entirely plunged in darkness. The rare passers-by were hunched up against the cold. Cars were parked along the edge of the pavement. Andrée wondered

why Costals did not take her into a tea-shop or a café,
as any other man would have done. But no – walk! walk!
(Costals had in fact thought of going into a café, but in the
restaurant the other day Andrée had got stuck in the revolving
doors so that she could neither get in nor out, and the waiters
had laughed. And she was so dowdy and frumpish – let's face
it, he was a little ashamed of her. So he preferred to let her
catch pneumonia rather than suffer an affront to his vanity
on her account.) Each new street they took seemed to Andrée
even darker than the one before, and, although at first she
braced herself against this glimpse of sky amidst her inner
clouds, she ended up by thinking that the object of this
Wandering Jew act of Costals' was simply to find a suitable
place to kiss her; and if the expedition was becoming rather
prolonged, it was because he could not make up his mind – a
proof that he really loved her. As they turned into the rue
Keppler, a particularly dark and deserted street, she was certain that it was there that her destiny would be fulfilled.
Never would she forget those details: the terrier seated beside
a chauffeur in a parked limousine, staring at her with an
almost human intensity; the lantern on a heap of paving-
stones, as moving as a sanctuary lamp. But they came out of
that insidious street without anything having happened. Then
Costals said:

'I've listened to you with great interest, and I'm extremely
touched by what you say. But I've already given you my
answer. Our friendship was a very excellent thing. But the
heart infects everything. On the plane of friendship, or on the
plane of sensuality, things are healthy, and wounds, if they
develop, are clean-cut. When the heart intervenes, the wound
spreads, everything goes wrong. I've seen it happen so often.'

'What you say is absurd. The heart infects nothing; on the
contrary, it purifies everything. It's really too idiotic! So it's
"the plane of sensuality" that is pure? If I had a great physical
passion for you, you'd forgive me for it. If I were provocative, if I gave you to understand that it was only pleasure I
was after, you might despise me perhaps, but you'd accept it.
But when I offer you love, how embarrassing, how boring! If
only people would leave one in peace with their love! When

I offer you my love as the very basis of my life, the life of a girl still intact and (though I say it who shouldn't) fairly superior, how dull and ridiculous! You don't care for my love. You don't want *everything* from me, you only want a little. And I can't give you only a little. You have treated me as a sister. You have given me a privileged position at your side, as a sultan chooses his favourite concubine or his vizier from the crowd, and now you want me to stay there like a good girl without raising my voice, and content myself with what you give me – with delightful generosity, true, but that isn't enough for me any more. Imagine having the right to nothing more than friendship! Friendships can be beautiful, marvellous even – like yours – sweet, consoling, touching, fraternal, but they are inadequate nonetheless, terribly inadequate. I cannot survive with you through friendship alone, nor indeed will I. There is something buoyant in me that transcends all that – transcends it utterly. So much inner strength that remains untapped. . . . I'm brimming over with the desire to give. I demand everything, and by "everything" I don't mean necessarily that you should abandon the disinterestedness you exploit so cleverly. . . .' ('Ah!' he thought to himself, 'a touch of asperity! Here's a little mouse who's asking to be eaten up. That, too, might have been expected.') 'No. I'm quite sincere when I tell you, as I've told you many times, that you have never penetrated to the source of my inmost feelings, or you've touched it only fleetingly, when you were feeling particularly kind and sweet. What I ask is the right to love you, to cherish you with all my strength and all my heart. Your coldness has always restrained me. I cannot love you if you do not want me to.'

'How can I be so frivolous as to allow you to give me a love I can't respond to? You see, I've used up all my feelings. I gave everything in a first love affair, at sixteen. From seventeen onwards I would have answered you as I do today: "Friendship, yes. Love, ecstasy, the whole shooting match: too late".'

'Too late! Always the same devastating words: too late! Ah! well, my life is finished.'

He felt sorry for her. 'When I was seventeen,' he said

gravely, 'and was beginning to move in society, I immediately began flirting a great deal, and I remember my mother saying to me then: "You mustn't excite young girls when your intentions aren't serious. It isn't fair." I'm beginning to wonder whether I haven't behaved badly towards you.'

'Good heavens, you haven't behaved badly towards me at all, not voluntarily. You're the most upright of men. . . .'

'Me, upright! I lie the whole time.'

He blinked his eyelids. Why had this cry escaped his lips? He felt a violent flush rise to his cheeks, and bowed his head.

'Of course you sometimes lie, like everyone else. All the same you're the most upright, the most noble of men.'

'Nobility again! You're going to make me take a violent dislike to myself one of these days with all this talk of nobility, and it would be a bore for me to dislike myself. I shall have to say to you what I said to an Italian servant who had worked for some prince or other and who, when he came to work for me, used to call me "Your Honour" at every turn. "If Your Honour would care. . . ." "I think Your Honour had better. . . ." Finally I got so irritated that I said to him: "Don't keep talking about my honour. You'll end up by making it real".'

'How impossible you are! Always joking at the most solemn moments. . . . Anyway, whether you like it or not, I repeat: you're an absolutely upright man. But you've been guilty of a certain rashness as far as I'm concerned. You shouldn't have let me get to this point.'

It was on the tip of his tongue to answer: 'Haven't I given you enough proofs of my indifference?' but he could not bring himself to do so. What he said was:

'So friendship isn't possible between a young man and a young woman?'

'Oh yes, the sort of impotence such a friendship represents must be possible in certain cases. With a very young girl for instance. When I was eighteen, I should have asked for nothing better than what I have now: a masculine friendship, especially with you, would have been everything I desired. But being the woman I am, a woman of whose age, loneliness, anguish, desperation and need for love you are not unaware, how could I help falling in love with such a magnificent friend as you? I offered you my love; you rejected it. But when I told you I was coming to Paris, far from making it clear to me that you did not want to see me again, as you ought to have done . . .' ('There's my reward!' thought Costals), 'you invited me to dinner. You encouraged me to think about you, you showed me that I wasn't unattractive to you. . . .' ('That's a good one!') 'You've done everything you possibly could to make me lose my heart to you. Because in refusing yourself, dear sir, you offer yourself. And that is what you will not see. To allow oneself to be loved is tantamount to loving. You are wrong in thinking that one can only offer oneself by promises or caresses. You have offered yourself without either promises or caresses, but just as surely, in your good-natured frivolity. . . . Do you know what your trouble is, Costals? Not being able to be nasty to me.'

'Well, well, how profound we are! So that's it, I'm "too nice"?'

'Yes, you are "too nice". In future, Costals, in your relations with women, don't be "too nice". Out of pity for them. And then you should drum this axiom into your head: "No friendships with unmarried girls." Because each one of them will believe you like her best. And because, unconsciously, you will give each of them the impression that you like her best. Even when you aren't trying to seduce, you behave like a seducer – and then you're genuinely astonished and furious afterwards, when the harm is done. You're so extraordinarily lacking in conceit! Perhaps that's what causes the trouble.'

'But after all, I can't pretend there aren't thousands of men as intelligent as I am, and much better looking. Just look around, and you will surely find one who will give you back as much as you give and more.'

'How exasperating you are! I'd like to give you a good shaking. I'm sick and tired of telling you that a woman only loves once, and that for me you are that once, you are irreplaceable as far as I'm concerned. You refuse to face the reality, which is that my true life is my love for you.'

'I don't know which of the two of us won't face up to reality,' he said gently.

'And besides, what a charming answer: "Why don't you look elsewhere?" to a woman who tells you: "I love you more than my life. Or rather, quite simply, you *are* my life".'

'How lucky you are to find that simple. As far as I'm concerned we're in a stew, a real sentimental stew.'

'You talk about love like a schoolboy. You ought to be ashamed of your childishness about such a subject.'

'A man without childishness is a monster.'

'*You're* a monster because you're too childish.'

Her voice was full of tears. Costals went on in a more affable tone:

'You're the one who's absurd, my poor girl, for giving me the power to make you unhappy. Do you know how I'd like you to be? I'd like to be able to say the most cruel and wounding things to you without your minding in the least.'

Her only reply was a shrug of the shoulders. Then she added:

' "My poor girl." Careful, don't start being "too nice" again.'

'Well, I must say you really are maddening! If I'm brusque with you it won't do. If I'm nice to you it won't do. I'm getting fed up with all this slop. After all, what am I doing here?'

Costals had never taken much part in the emotional brawling which women try to impose on any man who comes near them, not even with the ones he liked. And to have to indulge in it with a woman he was indifferent to. . . .

But it was too much for Andrée. The tears gushed from her eyes.

'There, there, my dear girl! Stop crying. If women only knew how much they lose by their whimperings. A man has to be a saint, when he sees they're hurt, not to want to hurt them more. But I am such a saint. Although . . . women have to be continually enlightened (I mean one always has to be explaining to them), enlightened, pampered, consoled, petted, appeased. I must admit I've no vocation for wet-nursing or for handling cases of porcelain. I like the things of the heart to be treated fairly briskly, without too much fuss, without going on about it as if there weren't other things in life. I

believe that the more one really loves, the less one talks about
it. . . . You silly girl, do you want to kill yourself!' (He had
grasped her by the arm. She was so distraught that in crossing
the street she had allowed a car to brush past her in a quite
terrifying way.) 'Well, you're lucky I didn't push you under
it! It's a sort of reflex I have with women when a car goes by.
Especially with those I like best. However, up to now I've
always resisted the impulse. And in your case, as you see, I
had the reflex to protect you. And yet you complain!'

'No, Costals, I don't complain. I know you're fond of me.
There are moments when I think of you as a kindly father
figure, and of how nice it would have been to be created,
re-created by you from scratch. Have I reproached you? If
so, forget it. I can't imagine what nonsense I must have
talked. . . . I'm not myself today. . . . I don't want you to feel
under any obligation towards me. Even if, one day, by some
miracle of fate, I were to acquire a privileged position with
you, I wouldn't wish for any other bond between us but your
tenderness, never your pity or your charity, as with the
flower-seller . . .'

'What she doesn't want is the one thing I can give her,'
Costals thought to himself. 'And what's this "miracle of fate"
that might give her a privileged position with me? What new
chimera is she riding off on now?'

It was perhaps the third or fourth time they had walked
round the square des Etats-Unis, marked by the dainty feet of
countesses and dotted with statues of Liberators and Bene-
factors and Enthusiasts. The leaves of the spindle-trees glowed
in the nocturnal gloom, as though each manservant daily
polished the foliage opposite the house of his noble master.
The windows with their closed shutters called to mind a row
of strong-boxes in the vaults of a bank. There were a few
humble people about who, in this opulent setting, looked like
prisoners-of-war working for the enemy: black-faced coal-men,
paid to be disfigured; a little butcher's boy bringing the
countesses' meat, slipping down through a tiny tradesmen's
entrance, like a cat through a hole in a door. It was Costals
who noticed these things, because his mind was free. Andrée
noticed nothing. Novelists have always gone into elaborate

detail about the settings in which their lovers meet; but only the novelists notice these details; the lovers see nothing, immersed as they are in their slop.

As they circled the square des Etats-Unis, Andrée noticed only the darkness of its green arbours, its lonely paths, and that almost suspect nook with its benches (just behind the statue of the Enthusiast), and her crazy hopes revived: here she was among these groves at night with this man, and – whether he kissed her or not – he could not have brought her there by chance. And he had called her 'my dear'. Would a man say 'my dear' to a woman he was indifferent to, to a woman with whom he did not feel to some extent intimate? Perhaps he would, after all (when one lives at Saint-Léonard one ends up by not knowing what's done and what isn't). And he had taken her by the arm and said 'Silly girl!' For the first time, he had *touched* her. (At that moment she had raised her eyes to see if she could read the plaque bearing the name of the street, so that for the rest of her life this memory should be linked to a precise spot.) She began to believe that he had held her arm for a long time, squeezing it in a mean-ingful way, and that a man did not say 'Silly girl!' unless he felt a certain tenderness. All her earlier clear-sightedness – 'You give each one the impression that you like her best' – had dimmed, like a sky clouding over. Passionately she wished that he would take her arm, or that she could dare to take his. But they left the square with its dark thickets, and her hopes subsided. Where was he leading her now? Were they going to resume their fearful chase through those streets in which there was nothing but chemists and flower-shops?* Once, indeed, she had complained of the cold, but he had replied with a winning air: 'A nice dry cold.... Very healthy!'

'Anyhow,' he said, 'we must clear up this question of friend-ship between men and women.'

'No, no, let's forget it, there's no point....'

'Well then, here we have an intelligent, shrewd (when she chooses to be), cultivated, self-made girl, a girl who knows my work better than I do myself, and knows it intelligently – in

---

*A symbol, perhaps, of the ruling class (*Author's note*).

short, a girl worthy of the highest praise. She vegetates in Saint-Léonard (Loiret), that is to say in an indescribable back-water. . . .'

'I beg your pardon,' she said with a smile, 'Saint-Léonard (Loiret) has three thousand one hundred and eighty inhabitants. Important textile mills. Birthplace of the great agronomist Leveilley. . . .'

Now she was trying to adopt his tone. She felt rather ridiculous being a woman, and thought he was quite right to be a healthy, cheerful overgrown schoolboy made for bachelor friendships and easy-going love affairs, whose only fault was to be too down-to-earth and not to take himself seriously enough.

'I offer this interesting young woman the sympathy which is her due. She seems very pleased. For years she goes on tell-ing me in a thousand different ways that I have saved her, that I "have given her nothing but joy". . . . You see, I know your letters by heart too,' he interjected, succumbing once more to his natural imprudence. . . . 'One fine day, I realize she's going to fall in love with me, and that I shall be unable to respond adequately to her love, because I'm not a man of love but a man of pleasure. (Yes, there it is, I like pleasure. And pleasure likes me too.) So I take up my finest pen and I write to her and say: "Dear Mademoiselle, I have regretfully perceived that you were about to fall in love with me. Don't deny it: I saw it with my lynx-like eye (am I, or am I not, our 'eminent psychologist'?) And so, from today onwards, nothing doing. I shall write to you no more. I shall return your letters unopened. When you come to Paris, 'Monsieur is away'. I opened the door of enlightenment to you; now I am closing it again. I dragged you away from the birthplace of the great agronomist Leveilley; now I am sending you back there. Good-bye, dear Mademoiselle. The best of luck to you." I ask you to consider a moment, quite calmly, what you would have thought of such a letter. You don't answer? Well, you would have thought this: "He's a swine. What a fine friend-ship he must have had for me, when it can be destroyed at one blow! And what conceit! He thinks every woman wants to fling herself at him. Just like men. You talk to them of friendship: they assume you mean sex. Afterwards they accuse you of thinking of nothing else." You would have suffered then what you are suffering now, and with good reason. Why didn't I write you that letter? Because I didn't want to lose your friendship, because I knew that my friendship was a help to you, and because I should have loathed myself for plunging a dagger into your heart. . . . Well, then, did I behave badly in not breaking with you?'

'Of course not, I know very well how kind you are.'

'You'll have to pay a forfeit every time you mention my kindness.'

'Oh, you're really too mischievous,' she said, half laughing.

It was true, she no longer knew whether he was kind or cruel. Now she was rather inclined to think that it was she who was in the wrong. But she no longer really knew; everything was getting mixed up in her mind. What she would have liked would have been to be back at her hotel; alone with herself, decanting all the happiness and all the pain he had poured into her, to see which, the happiness or the pain, would float above the other. What she would have liked most of all was not to feel cold any more. But at the hotel she would still be cold. She repeated to herself a saying of Costals': 'Cold is a disease of the planet', and more especially a remark of St Thérèse of Lisieux, a remark so ordinary on the surface, but in reality most moving: 'You don't know what it's like to have been cold for seven years.' She was worn out (they had been walking for two hours) and her fatigue was befuddling her brain; her eyelids were aching, and she could feel a headache coming on. She said to herself: 'What a night it's going to be!' But having invoked his presence month after month at Saint-Léonard, she could never be the first to put an end to it. She would collapse, exhausted, on to the pavement rather than give the signal for his 'Good-bye, dear Mademoiselle. I'll get in touch with you one of these days.'

In the avenue Marceau the north wind swept out from each side-street with a bombastic flourish. From the top of the avenue Pierre-Ier the Champs-Elysées could be seen below, a valley of light. She longed for him to decide to go down there. She would be warmed by those lights, those human beings, the noise, the movement, the luxury. They would go into a café and listen to some music: she would show him a shop where there were 'ensembles' for 390 francs – incredible, they might have come from one of the big fashion houses ... but no, that would be impossible, it might look like cadging.... Suddenly, for the first time, it struck her that he had not thought of buying her a few francs' worth of flowers at any of the florists they had passed, even though they had stopped in front of one of them. No, not even one of those bunches of violets which, he had so tactfully informed her, he used to buy 'for his girl-friends'. In fact he had never given her anything at all except books – oh yes, he was generous enough with books ('You see, I'm an intellectual girl ... so naturally! ...'). She fought against the unexpected bitterness it caused her, considering it naïve and vulgar. But Costals turned his back on the Champs-Elysées, the Promised Land, and plunged once more down one of the drearier streets, as though he took pleasure in pacing up and down like a caged beast, as though he enjoyed this spasmodic, nightmarish flight, like some legendary descent into hell. Almost fainting, her thighs aching with fatigue, dabbing at a drip on the end of her nose ('I'm sure my nose is red'), biting her lips from which she thought the cold and the pain must have drained all colour, and, with all this, a pressing need to obey a little call of nature, she heard him hold forth ('hold forth' was the word that came to her mind, she was so weary of him):

'According to your theory, then, the magnificent realm of friendship between man and woman would become forbidden territory. Women would be penned in the "heart and senses" domain, incapable of being raised to a nobler, more rarefied world. And, for fear of disappointing them, a man would have to avoid social contact with any young women not destined for his bed, licit or illicit – in other words, when all is said and done, the vast majority of women. He would have to rush past them with lowered eyes like a seminarist: *"Noli me tangere*, ladies! Because you might think I was in love with you, which I'm very far from being – no offence meant." Or like the young Kabyles. A Kabyle once told me that, in his village, boys who had reached the age of fifteen and were not yet married were packed off by their parents to Algiers, so as not to be an object of temptation to the girls of the village. And whenever they returned to the village for a few days (on the occasion of a funeral, a wedding, or for the feast of A'id) they had to give warning of their comings and goings by shouting "trec, trec, trec", so that the girls could go and hide, such a temptation were boys to them. In future I too shall say "trec, trec, trec", so that the girls can take cover. Or rather I shall have a rattle, like a leper. . . . '

He went on to say something rather cruel: 'Girls are like those stray dogs you can't throw a friendly glance at without their assuming that you're calling them and will welcome them with open arms, and without their wagging their tails and scrabbling at your trouser-legs.'

He embroidered on this. As always when he was talking or writing to someone he was indifferent to, he said more or less anything that came into his head (Andrée had never been aware of this in their relations with each other). Just as matadors regard anything that happens to them in bull-rings outside Spain, successes as well as failures, as non-existent, so Costals, a born writer, really only took trouble with one of his modes of expression – books. Conversation and corre-spondence belonged to the sphere of relaxation and spare time; in those spheres he did not mind what he said; it did not count.

Suddenly he stopped dead.

'Do you understand what I'm saying?'

'Of course.'

'Well, I don't. For some time now it's ceased to have any meaning – pure word-spinning. If you can't see that, what's the use of talking to you? In short,' he concluded, 'since, according to you, it was my duty to break with you, and I've delayed all too long, it's quite simple. . . . I cannot give you what you want from me. Let us, therefore, cease to know one another.'

'No! No!' cried Andrée, springing up from the depths of her torpor, 'you have no right to desert me now. But you're not serious, are you?'

' "Have no right",' Costals thought. 'Ah, well, as I've always said, the trouble with charity is that you have to go on with it.'

As though she had read his thoughts, she went on:

'Loving commits one, doing good commits one. One hasn't the right to love people in the same way as one dispenses charity, anonymously, without entering their lives....'

'Let's stay as we are, then. Only, from now on, don't complain of the situation. You're the one who wants it.'

'I shall never complain of anything again, I give you my solemn word. There's only one thing I want: not to lose you. ... You know what the key to it all is,' she said point-blank. 'The fact that you're a man who has always jilted and never been jilted. One can sense it.'

'It's not true. I've been jilted twice, and in the most cruel way.'

'And ... you were hurt?'

'No, I found it quite natural. What could be more legitimate than to have had enough of someone? I've felt it too often myself not to understand it in others. When I see a woman with whom I've had months of intimacy drop me from her life overnight, no longer want to have anything to do with me, I recognize myself.'

She was silent, as though stunned. But then he said:

'Goodness! I must leave you. I'm dining with some people at eight, and it's now ten to.'

'Shall we see each other again?' she asked, feeling at the end of her tether, incapable of further speech, of uttering anything more than a few banal remarks.

'Of course. I'll get in touch with you.'

'Don't leave it too long.... If I write to you, you probably won't answer. To think that you've never given me your telephone number!'

'I thought you were supposed not to complain any more.'

'Sorry.'

'Even if I did give you my telephone number it wouldn't make any difference, because it's permanently switched off: "the silence of those infinite spaces" reassures me. And do you know who drove me to take this step, which is irritating for friends or business people who want to talk to me, and inconvenient for me since I'm liable to miss things that might be important? Women, and women only. Women in general, with their daily or twice-daily calls, each one lasting a quarter of an hour, and always about nothing. And a particular category of women, who are the most dangerous of all: the women who love me and whom I do not love. Result: I get three express letters from women per day, always about nothing, of course. And there's nothing more exasperating than to be pestered with letters from people one doesn't love when one expects every post to bring a letter from somebody one does. Well, good-bye, dear Mademoiselle, and don't catch cold.'

He had spoken to her in a tone that froze her to such an extent that she wondered whether she might not faint. She gave him her hand mechanically. She had no feeling left.

She walked away. He called after her: 'Hey!'

She stopped. He came up to her. Alternating waves of sincerity and trickery, of gravity and mockery, flashed across his features. And it was true that he felt more lively and restless than she, like a mischievous dog jumping round a sheep and having the greatest fun teasing it.

'Am I a swine?'

'I don't know. Leave me alone.... Leave me alone....'

'Good-bye.'

He went off, and after a few steps lit a cigarette. He felt ten years younger now that she was no longer there. A woman going away and leaving him alone meant ten years' reprieve if he did not love her. One or two years if he did.

Andrée did not sleep a wink. Lying in bed, she turned over on her right side, and her anguish fell to the right, then on her left side, and her anguish fell to the left, like a lump inside her body. She kept wanting to change the position of her legs, which were still aching after the evening's frantic trek. The too-narrow sheet added to her misery: she kept finding herself uncovered, and felt (or believed) she was catching cold. In the morning, she cried from seven o'clock until twenty-five past. How cruel he had been, and at the same time how gentle! At all costs she must know 'where she stood' with him. She sent him an express letter, telling him she had cried from six to eight, and 'beseeching' him to telephone her at noon at the hotel. Having paid for the letter with a two-franc piece, she left the change to the post office clerk, who muttered a few sardonic words about forsaken women.

Costals did not telephone. The express letter had made him furious. The mere sight of Andrée's handwriting exasperated him. 'She means nothing to me. I owe her nothing. I've put myself out for her dozens of times. I take her out to dinner and then on top of that I give up two and a half hours of my life to her – yes, two and a half hours! I rack my brains trying to find a way out of the ridiculous position she has put me in without hurting her feelings. And now she comes back at me with express letters, tearful letters. So I'm expected to see her three hours running every other day! Well, this time, no.' At noon, he sent her a telegram saying he had to leave for Besançon to see a sick uncle, and would write to her on his return.

Andrée sat and waited in her room on the sixth floor of her squalid hotel (she had asked the prices of six hotels before deciding on this one), with its draughty windows, its stinking bedside table, the drawer in which she had found some old bits of soiled cotton-wool. Sitting on the only chair beside a meagre wood fire, her overcoat round her shoulders, she thought she could never have experienced such an agony of distress. Oh, God! if only she knew what was in his mind! She guessed that she must have irritated him by writing, but it would have been impossible for her not to write. Her mind swung back and forth like a pair of maladjusted scales. One moment she thought of them walking, walking like lost souls along those lugubrious avenues in the frightful cold, and his every word seemed like a knife twisted in a wound. The next moment she was at the other extreme, exaggerating and inventing as she went along: 'Those minutes will have been the only happy minutes of my life. Even when he teased me, he was so kind, so tender and serious, perhaps unwittingly. He was unhappy about not having any children, he wanted to confide in me, seemed to be looking for sympathy. How touching he was when he talked about his mother! Has he ever spoken to another woman about his mother?' Just as she imagined that Costals had been confiding in her, when he had merely been thinking aloud, no more and no less than when he prostituted himself to fifty thousand readers, in the same way she genuinely believed that, because she had held his hand for rather a long time when they shook hands on meeting, it was he who had held hers. She could still hear the clatter of 'his German officer's footsteps' on the asphalt; she could still see him listening to her with 'the imperceptible smile of the gods' on his lips. The idea that he had contemplated marrying her – even in a moment of aberration – seemed to her less probable than the day before, and yet: 'I know I'm unworthy of such luck; I realize all that divides us, if only from the social point of view; I'm neither crazy nor romantic. So there must have been something for this eventuality, which I had never, never dreamed of, to have suddenly seemed plausible.' She even reached the point of wanting passionately to walk with him again one evening through those gloomy avenues, to walk and walk until she had to beg for mercy; and what had seemed to her 'frightful' and 'lugubrious' a moment before was what she now pinned all her hopes on.

At half past eleven she went down to the reception to wait for the telephone call, her eyes glued to her wrist-watch. Nothing happened. At one o'clock she returned to her room, incapable of lunching, and went on waiting. She was in Paris for only a month, and yet she was waiting for the time to go by! At two o'clock she received Costals' message, and sensed that he was lying. She went round to the avenue Henri-Martin, and inquired of the concierge:

'Is M. Costals in Paris?'

'Yes, Mademoiselle.'

But upstairs the servant told her:

'M. Costals is in Besançon.'

Next morning she went back to the avenue Henri-Martin. She had no doubt that he was there, but could not bear not to know. She needed a verdict one way or the other, however unpleasant, to rest upon a certainty, or die upon it.

'Is M. Costals back?'

'No, Mademoiselle. We don't know when he'll be back.'

She went away and wandered around, unable to bring herself to leave the neighbourhood, looking everywhere for
Costals, wallowing in the bitter thought that he and she were
both in Paris and the days were flowing by in an emptiness
no different from Saint-Léonard. And soon she would have to
return to Saint-Léonard, return without a ray of hope to a
hell of loneliness and despair. Her peregrinations (no question
about it, she was born to tramp the streets!) were aimed not
so much at meeting Costals as at providing her with a sort of
opiate: sitting idly in her hotel room she might have had a fit
of hysterics. She went into a church, the name of which she
did not know, and spent an hour there, half frozen, repeating
to herself: 'Oh, no, God cannot make one suffer more than a
man can.' She wrote this sentence on a piece of paper she
found in her bag, bought a cheap envelope, slipped it inside it
and took it round to Costals' concierge.

She paced up and down outside the house for an hour, just
as, when she happened to be in Paris and Costals was away,
she used to pass underneath his windows nearly every night
to see if they were lit up. She went pale when she saw a man
whom she took for him. She caught sight of herself in a shop
window, and was horrified by her ugliness: 'My God, what
have you done to me? Who is this stranger?' (she had not
thought of God when she was in the church). She met a
woman selling violets and bought a bunch – 'I shall be more
generous than he' – and going back to Costals' house, laid
them on the floor of the landing against the door of his flat.
Out in the street again she realized, too late, that her gesture
would only do her harm, that the servant would find the
flowers and make fun of her. She thought of going up to take
them back, but it would be the fifth time the concierge had
seen her in two days.... She dared not.

At nightfall, frozen stiff, she made her way to the underground. But oh! the temptation to take a taxi. She would
have done so for a short trip. But her hotel was so far that it
would cost her at least twelve francs. It was typical of her,
this habit of stopping short amid the storms of her emotional

life to tot up money. In the underground, people stared at her: people wear their sadness as they do a garment. She felt full of compassion, all kindness, weakness and abandon; she offered her seat (an unconscious reflex action, for she could see nothing) to an old man who was standing. She changed trains in a state of utter bewilderment, horrified by the labyrinthine passages, the rush for the automatic gates which shut in your face, those automatic gates that corral people like animals, as though they were a herd of pigs being sorted out by machines in an American factory. And she thought she was going to faint when she finally got off, what with her utter exhaustion, the nervous tension, her sleepless night, and no lunch. It seemed to her that only the strength of her heartbeats sustained her. Her eyelids were aching. All her anguish and distress seemed to be concentrated in this pain in her eyeballs. She went into a bar and ordered a coffee, despite her fear of being taken for a whore. There was a crowd of workmen at the counter. She had to stand behind them, stretching her arm between two men to reach her glass. But she felt that, without the coffee, she could not have stood up a moment longer. Suddenly one of the workmen smiled at her, and his smile eased her pain. But it only lasted a moment; outside, the pain welled up again.

Back at the hotel, she noticed that a forty-franc bottle of scent had been stolen from her room. During the last few days this scent had been her only consolation: she had sniffed it when she was feeling particularly tormented. She also learned from the waiter that she was being charged three francs a day more for her room than other guests had to pay for it (because of her smart appearance, of course!). She attracted blow after blow, like a wounded hen being pecked by the whole poultry-yard.

She would cheerfully have spent hundreds of francs in a single day if she had been happy. When she was unhappy, the thought of money spent – or wasted – gnawed at her, and there were moments when she told herself that she must leave Paris simply in order to stop the leakage.

She wept.... Tears of uncertainty – it was too stupid. After all, it would be time enough to shed them when it all came to an end. She began to think that he was putting her to the test, teasing her rather cruelly, in order to dazzle her the more with joy for all the suffering he had inflicted on her. She applied to him the remark made about M. de Chavigny in Musset's *Un Caprice:* 'He is mischievous, but he is not bad.' In the end she drew some consolation from her suffering, telling herself that it was a decisive test, that she now knew better than ever how much she loved this man, and what the quality of her love was, since she could put up with his behaviour in this way. For all her horrible doubts about him, she had never felt a moment's anger or resentment. She loved him just as much, but simply did not understand. She also told herself: 'Anything that happens to me now will be paradise after all this.' In spite of the grinding neuralgia which had not left her for two days and upon which all the pills in the world had failed to make an impression, she settled down to write him a long letter, scribbling, scribbling away across the calm paper. But the ceiling light was too high and too dim, and she had to give up.

Next morning, at a quarter to eight, Costals heard a ring at the door of his flat. His servant did not come down until eight o'clock, and anyhow had a key. Costals went from the bathroom into the hall with the lather still on his cheeks.

'What is it?' he asked through the door.

'It's me.'

'Who's "me"?'

'Andrée.'

'Andrée? Andrée who?'

He knew only too well. But he wanted to punish her. Ringing at his door at a quarter to eight! And that note: 'God cannot make one suffer more than a man can'! And those flowers on his doorstep, as though it were a tombstone! Enough to cover him with ridicule in the eyes of all the tenants! He had thrown them in the dustbin at once, after crushing them in his rage.

'Andrée Hacquebaut.'

'I can't let you in. I got back last night. But I haven't shaved.'

'What difference does that make? Let me in, please.'

'You must say "for the love of God".'

'For the love of God!'

'I'd be delighted to let you in. Only I'm stark naked.'

'You refuse to see me?'

'At this moment, yes.'

'Is that your last word?'

'Please don't insist.'

'All right. I shall take the eight fifty-six train to Saint-Léonard. You'll have nothing more to fear from me.'

'No, no. I'll telephone you at noon.'

'Yes, just like the other day! Good-bye!'

He heard her footsteps receding. After a while he half-opened the door. He wondered whether he might not find her still there, crouching on the stairs. There was no one. But in front of the door were the fresh imprints of her wet shoes, going in every direction, as though a hunted beast had trampled there.

At eleven o'clock he heaved a sigh and telephoned the hotel. He was told that she had paid her bill and left.

At first he was profoundly relieved. Then he felt remorse. She was to have spent a month in Paris, and it was going to be such a treat for her! As a novelist he was too accustomed to putting himself in other people's skins not to realize how much she must have suffered, and he was moved by it. He wrote to her:

Dear Mademoiselle,

Your sudden departure has left me puzzled. I cannot for a moment believe that it was due to my not receiving you at half past seven in the morning. Once, my mother refused to let me into her room. Being a sensitive child, I was upset and wondered in what way I could have incurred her displeasure. When she came home that evening, she called me in, kissed me, treated me exactly as usual, but refused to explain why her door had been closed to me that morning. Years later she confessed to me: she had run out of face-powder, and did not want me to see her without any powder on. And I was fourteen! When she was about to die, she gave orders that I was not to be allowed into her room after she was dead until they had bandaged her chin. . . . Well, I'm her son. You accuse me of not being vain enough : and yet, in certain respects, I'm terribly punctilious. This morning, for example, even if you had been in flames on the landing as a result of some heater exploding or God knows what, I probably wouldn't have gone to your help because I hadn't shaved. The fact that I was naked had nothing to do with it, mind you. No doubt you know how men are made : you must have seen statues. And besides, I was dressed.

Your absurd departure has deprived me of the pleasure of taking you to the Monet exhibition, as I had planned. I was so looking forward to it.

Cordially yours.

How very like him Andrée found this letter ! Kindliness, jokes, and even a touch of impropriety, which she smiled at without being disturbed by it. And again the allusions to his mother, which she found so moving . . . But she did not regret having returned to Saint-Léonard. She had a feeling that, had she stayed in Paris, he would have continued to make her suffer. Whereas this friendly letter mysteriously – yes, really unaccountably – dissolved her pain. Full, as always, of Costals' books, she remembered a saying in one of them : 'Absence brings people closer.' Why did he understand everything so well in his books and pretend not to understand in life ?

One morning, some days after this scene, Costals was in Cannes. The sea could be seen from the villa, still grey after the riotous winter storms. The novelist was reading Malebranche – *La Recherche de Ja Vérité*.

From the next room came the sound of a clear young voice singing to itself. Costals raised his head. When he heard his son singing in the house, he felt as though the house were flying through the air. Sometimes both father and son would sing, each on a different floor. He listened for a while, then could not resist any longer and made his way to the child's room.

As soon as he opened the door the voice stopped. The boy
pretended to be asleep. Costals was familiar with this trick.
As with all boys of his age (he would be fourteen in three
months' time), Philippe's jokes and gags, though they did not
last long, and were buried forever from one day to the next,
were persistent while they did last. Even if he had not heard
him singing, Costals would have known that his son was not
asleep: his face was dry, and he always perspired in his sleep.
'Open your eyes, donkey, or I'll drop my cigarette ash on
your face.'

Costals sat down on the bed...and jumped up again. He
turned back the sheet and found a foil. Philippe had discovered fencing a fortnight before and, still in the first flush
of this discovery, took his foil to bed with him – as Cardinal
de Maillé, newly promoted to the Sacred College, slept with
his red hat, according to Saint-Simon.

Sitting down again, Costals took his son's hands, never quite
clean, with their long, delicate fingers (*Les jeunes garçons aux
mains larges et limpides*, he had written one day when he had
a penchant for alexandrines), and kissed them. The boy had a
tanned face and straight black hair. On the front of his
pyjamas the stains of breakfast chocolate were proudly displayed. He was still pretending to be asleep. One could see
at once that if he had no wings it was because he had wished
it so (but what about the cloven hoof?). Scattered on the floor
around the bed, like gobs of spittle around an Arab, was a
large quantity of small change (Philippe insisted on having his
pocket money in this form so that he could jingle it in his
pocket – 'But why?' – 'To show off, of course!'), a comb
(broken), a mirror (broken), a fountain-pen (broken), a wallet,
an empty scent bottle – all the things which boys' pockets are
eternally stuffed with, and which slip out whenever they lie
down. There was also a padlock, for Philippe did not want his
rabbits to be killed, and every time the cook brought their
food, Master Philippe had to be fetched to open and shut the
hutch himself.

Suddenly Philippe seized his father's head, pulled it down,
and kissed it. Then he squeezed it violently between his arms,
no longer the caressing child but a child who fancies himself

as a wrestling champion. There followed a great deal of horse-play, which he liked best of all, being very sensitive to touch. Whenever Costals warned him that he was going to break something, or that he was ruining the pillow, he replied: 'That's a detail' – it was the catch-phrase of the moment. Finally Philippe pinned down his father's shoulders with his knees (the sheet, by this time, was all over the place), and in that position bent forward and nibbled his nose.

'You've hurt me, you idiot!'

'Cry-baby! Sissy, sissy!' (and he made faces at him).

Eventually the excitement died down. Philippe got back under the sheet and buried himself in *Cri-Cri*.* Costals, stretched out on top of the bed, returned to his Malebranche.

Costals had had this bastard son at the age of twenty-one. The chosen intermediary was a woman who in law was an adulteress so that there could be no question of her having any rights whatever over the child. At the age of six Philippe had been entrusted to the care of an old friend of Costals, Mlle du Peyron de Larchant, a spinster of about fifty, who had all the advantages of maternal love for the brat without any of its grave drawbacks. Although she also loved Costals like a son, she had never been in love with him, and this guaranteed the stability and probity of her affection. Costals had arranged things in this way because it seemed to him disgraceful that anyone but he should have any rights over his son. He was, moreover, convinced of the pernicious influence mothers generally have on children, a view shared by a large number of educationists and moralists, who dare not admit it openly for fear of offending time-honoured conventions, which are always exquisitely chivalrous.

Philippe lived partly in Marseilles, partly in Cannes. Costals spent ten days or so with him every month, being convinced from experience that a highly-strung man cannot love a person with whom he cohabits, or even merely sees every day. The arrangement had worked extremely satisfactorily for fourteen years. Which proves nothing.

Philippe, who was known as Brunet because of his brown

---

*A boys' magazine of the 1920's (*Translator's note*).

skin (he called his father 'La Dine', a nickname for which no explanation, sensible or otherwise, was forthcoming), was still, at the age of nearly fourteen, physically very much a child: undeveloped, and his voice still unbroken. In character also he was very much a child, but at the same time terribly quick-witted and alert: a little backward physically, very advanced mentally. He was not an adolescent, he was a precocious child: not at all the same thing. One day in Paris at the age of ten, finding himself without enough money to go home by underground, he had gone and sung in people's courtyards until he had made enough for his fare. When he was eleven, Costals, who himself had not been born innocent (innocents do not notice such things), had discovered a hole made by Philippe in the door of Mlle du Peyron's bathroom.

He was not a rebellious or ill-natured or even wearisome child – wearisome as children are in their high spirits. Not one of those children whose mien one studies anxiously when they wake up in the morning to see if they are in a good or a bad mood and whether the day will be possible or unbearable. He was a little highly-seasoned, but he was straight. He was not pure, but he was healthy. He zigzagged violently, but without ever leaving the road. Disinterested; warm-hearted; intelligent, in a down-to-earth way (all Costals' efforts to inject him with a more high-flown conception of the universe – a philosophy of the universe – had failed); and with the restfulness one finds in boys who are not interested in sport. Although at first sight he appeared to be a typical French boy of 1927 – in other words a horrible little guttersnipe – he was not a gutter-snipe, for he was never mean or nasty: he never did anything despicable.

The surest way of winning the confidence and friendship of a young boy is not to be his father. Brunet, however, con-fided in his father far more than most boys. He also lied to him less than is usual. Costals did not always understand his son, and he was sometimes annoyed by this, or rather irritated with himself on account of it. Whereas with women he could tell almost without fail what was going to be produced out of the hat, what was going to be their reaction in any given circumstance, with Philippe he was not so sure. Perhaps it

was because women's reactions have something mass-pro-
duced, or – shall we say? – traditional* about them. Perhaps
it was simply because what happened inside their heads did
not seem worth bothering about. He considered them far less
mysterious than men, especially in childhood. There is no
comparison, from this point of view, between boys and girls.
Who was it (Vauvenargues or Chamfort?) who said, cruelly,
that one must choose between loving women and understanding them? Costals loved them, and had never tried to
understand them, had never even wondered whether there was
anything in them to understand.

'La Dine!'

'Shut up! Let me read Malebranche.'

'You make me sick with your branch! I say, I had a lovely
dream last night.'

'What did you dream?'

'I dreamt I was eating noodles with tomato sauce.'

'Is that what you interrupted me for? What a pain in the
neck the child is!'

There was more horse-play. Suddenly, at the height of the
struggle, Brunet, with his face a few inches away from his
father's, stopped and studied it attentively.

'I'm looking at you. I'd forgotten your face. Yesterday at
the station I wondered if I'd recognize you when you got off
the puff-puff. Luckily I remembered your overcoat. It's a
pretty awful one! A fifteen-hundred-franc overcoat! Really,
you have no taste. I shall have to come with you when you
buy your togs.'

'He too forgets faces. . . .' Costals mused. He himself was
liable to forget the faces of his mistresses, his best friends, to
forget everything, in fact. When one of his own traits came
back at him like this from his son, he felt a bit uneasy. 'Nonsense! he's a good kid, and I love him – so we should get by
all right.' (Which was anticipating a bit.)

Meanwhile Brunet was still staring at his father. 'I'm fond of

_____

*'In France, women are too much alike. They have the same way
of being pretty, of entering a room, of writing, of loving, of
quarrelling. No matter how often you change from one to another,
it always seems to be the same one.' – Prince de Ligne

you, you know. You're a good sort,' he said at last, and kissed him. Costals kissed him back, on his eyelids, rather from a sort of sense of the proprieties, of the necessary reciprocities, than from any keen impulse.

'Is that the way you kiss women?' the boy asked. 'Go on, show me how you do it.'

'Shh.... Now, now.'

'Had you ever kissed a woman by the time you were four-teen?'

'Of course.'

'I kissed Francine Finoune. She said to me: "Give me a kiss and I'll take you to the cinema." So I kissed her.'

'Where?'

'There.' (He pointed to a spot on his cheek.)

'And did you like it?'

Philippe eyed his father as though, by the mere suggestion that this kiss might have given pleasure, he had insulted him.

'Oh, come off it.'

'The day you find you like kissing Francine Finoune, you must let me know, because I shall have one or two things to tell you.'

'Catch me telling you that! Anyway, we've quarrelled. She asked me for ten francs. So I gave her a clout.'

'She takes you to the cinema, and yet you refuse her ten francs. Is that fair?'

'Oh, that's a detail.'

Costals searched his pocket for a cigarette ... and found a roll of peppermints. Hardly a week ever passed without Brunet giving his father some such 'surprise', a little present slipped into his pocket – sweets, a packet of cigarettes, or some such thing. Costals gave the child a light. This was the signal for another standing joke – Brunet blowing, rapidly one after the other, several puffs of smoke into Costals' hair. The latter then had to don his son's beret as quickly as possible. When he took it off, his head would be smoking. Vast amusement, each time as fresh as ever. The smouldering skull of the genius!

'Poor La Dine, I'm wasting your time.'

'It's never a waste of time being with you.'

Costals had stretched himself out on the bed again; having

94

abandoned *La Recherche de la Vérité*, he was reading *Cri-Cri* over his son's shoulder. Philippe burst out laughing every other minute. He seemed to be not quite himself unless he had a pretext for laughing, and everything was a pretext. He would throw his head right back, and in the middle of his brown face, at the summit of his whole being, his dazzling white teeth, small and regular as the incisors of a cat, shone like snow on a mountain top. Scarcely for a moment, during the hour they had been together, had he ceased to laugh – radiating sweetness and good humour. One could see at once that he was a child who was rid of his parents. All this was well attuned to Costals' own constant good humour – the natural condition of a man of sense.

A wire-haired fox terrier appeared in the doorway, gave a muffled 'woof' of approval, and disappeared after this benison. The terrier, who answered to the name Hairynose, was the only person in the house who maintained a high moral tone. He often watched with a look of severity as Costals and his son played the fool; it was obvious that he was judging them. The examination would end with a deep sigh. Then this paragon would put his nose to his behind and go back to sleep.

Several times Costals tried to get up, but Brunet held out his arms towards him, stretching them as a cat stretches out its fore-paws, and Costals, who knew this gesture well and found it touching, gave in.

After a time, Brunet crumpled up his *Cri-Cri* and threw it aside violently, as though suddenly horrified at having enjoyed it; then he bent down and laid his head on his father's chest. With him there was always, beneath the playfulness, a desire for physical contact; he was always finding reasons for rubbing against his father, either in their rough-and-tumbles, or by suddenly clasping him in his arms and trying to make him dance the fox-trot, or jumping on his back, or taking his arm in the street. (And then there was his girlish way of giving a start and turning away his head whenever anything painful or cruel was mentioned, such as an operation, or even a thermometer.) Costals, finding himself close to him like this, and touched by his need for affection, felt that the least he could do was to kiss him again. He thought to himself: 'He's charming, he's cuddly, he smells good, the softness of his skin is not of this world. And yet I haven't the same sort of tenderness for him that I have for a woman. Why? It's strange.' The fact was that Costals was capable of feeling strong tenderness only for people he desired. He thought the bridge of Philippe's nose, just below the eyes, was too wide (like a lion cub, perhaps), and this single small feature that he did not like prevented him from responding with complete spontaneity to his son's caresses. And he watched himself, afraid of appearing cold – for he was very fond of his son – and making sure that, in the matter of caresses, he would always have something to spare. He also wondered, as he wondered about women: 'Why does he enjoy embracing me?' And he could not understand.

At this point Old Mother Hubbard (their nickname for the old lady) poked her head round the half-open door like a little tousled field mouse and beamed at the charming spectacle they presented.

Andrée Hacquebaut   to Pierre Costals
Saint-Léonard   *Paris*

15 March 1927

Not a day has passed since my return without the tears springing to my eyes under the impact of a painful memory. But it only lasts a few seconds. The rest of the time I live, I laugh, I talk, I write. Apparently unscathed. What brings my wound home to *me* is the fact that I can no longer sing. Before, I used to sing all the time, even in my worst moments. Now it not only won't 'come' to me, but if I make an effort it won't 'come out'. Oh Costals, what makes men suffer? There is only one suffering: loneliness of heart. I have made a list of my blessings: freedom, health, leisure, my daily bread (dry bread, but still), comparative youth, and so on. And yet, telling myself that other human beings might passionately envy all this does not make me any happier. Even if the list could be extended *ad infinitum*, I would only have to put down the absence of love on the debit side for the whole of the credit column to be reduced to zero. The truth is that I no longer enjoy anything. Only on Saturday did I find a little peace, when I went to Confession in order not to break completely with the practice of religion. With God and yourself together forbidding me to love you, I ought to be convinced!

I had a dream the other night. Its origin is easy to guess. We were walking through Paris in the rain. And I kept forgetting things – once it was a fur – and I would climb back up interminable staircases while you waited for me below at the corner of the street. I would rejoin you, we would set off again, once again I would find I had forgotten something, I would go back, climb the stairs again, search again. . . . And, as usual in dreams, the search involved unbelievable trouble, I had to rummage through a mass of things, there was no end to it, and I was obsessed all the time with the fear that you would have got tired of waiting. But I always found you on the pavement waiting for me, your face contorted with impatience, like an angry little cat. This dream consoled me a little, as a sign that you were not lost to me.

And yet, if I were to judge by your silence. . . .

Oh, no reproach intended, no sulking (I know what sulking costs me). I cannot conceive of there ever being the slightest shadow of reproach between us. Whatever you do, whatever happens, *nothing* will ever weaken my admiration for you, my devotion and gratitude. But my affection is beginning to succumb, from anæmia, because it feels wasted. It cannot go on living off itself for ever. That would be a superhuman task, like having to go on filling the Danaids' bottomless barrel, until one collapses. It might be possible for a girl of twenty. At thirty (minus thirty-nine days!) one no longer has the energy. I can sense that you are deeply involved elsewhere. All my enthusiasm is dead. Permanently wrapped up in you as I am, how could I possibly endure without torment those long deserts in our friendship?

What have I had from you? Such meagre oases! Not an hour of intimacy. Two years ago, you had me to your house several times. Since then, always outside – at concerts, in restaurants, in the street. It's as though you were afraid of something. There remained your letters, rare as they were.

(I would have far preferred you to do nothing for me in the practical sphere but to write to me more often. My correspondence with you is an eternal monologue.) But if even the letters disappear! Remove both physical presence *and* letters from a friendship, and what remains? I know there are men who go for weeks, even months, without seeing or writing to one another, and yet remain firm and devoted friends. But I am not a man. Each empty post leaves me crushed for a whole hour, and upsets my entire day. A word from you, on the other hand, is like a drop of oil on a fire : it kindles a passionate fervour in me. . . .

If I am to keep a small corner in your heart, I must first of all write you shorter letters, mustn't I?

Your
Andrée.

I have decided to laugh as little as possible from now on, because of my wrinkles.

This letter remained unanswered.

Andrée Hacquebaut   to Pierre Costals
Saint-Léonard   *Paris*

31 March 1927

What does this silence mean – this barrier of silence that I have to break through to reach you? I love you as one loves a child who has a heart disease and is doomed to die at twenty. I know I shall lose what little I have of you, that is to say the right to correspond with you, etc. – your presence in my life, the slight interest you have in me. I also know that I shall make no attempt to cling on to you. All I ask is not to be stabbed in the back : it's the only expression I can think of to describe these appalling betrayals through silence, which leave me floundering in ignorance and incomprehension, groping in the void like a blind man with his stick, or a mystic seeking God in the darkness of spiritual desolation. Even the mystics have need of the sacraments, which are a substitute for the real presence. I love everything about you : even your raillery and your harshness give me happiness, and anyway they fortify me against you; whereas your silence paralyses and destroys me. You can deal me blow after blow and I shall be able to withstand them. But do not take a cowardly advantage of the weapons of silence and absence.

If you only knew what it is not to have any contact with you – either in person or through letters – that is not broken up by these weeks of total separation! The lack of *continuity* between us! All these things that come to nothing, that absence makes abortive, when it was essential to strike while the iron was hot. Everything evaporates through absence, like the heat of a room through an open door. How do you expect anything to develop, or even survive, between us in such a disjointed situation? No sooner have I left you than I find the words I ought to have said to you (such a stream of things I ought to tell you to explain this or that, to rectify the idea you have of me . . .), but I cannot say them because we see each other so rarely. So I am reduced to my letters, which irritate you and which have no effect on you, and it is only in my room, alone, that I speak out to you and convince you.

It is not your behaviour I'm complaining of, you understand. It isn't even your indifference to my distress. It isn't *you* at all, it's the uncertainty – that abyss of absolute uncertainty within whose depths anything can lie hidden without one's knowing: accident, illness, changes of heart, ill-founded grievances, misunderstandings. . . .

Write to me anything you like, but write to me. Be it only an empty envelope – like those the Maréchal de Luxembourg asked Rousseau to send him – so that I know you are still alive.

I believe in you in spite of everything, as one must, our preacher used to say, believe in God in spite of everything.

Andrée.

This letter remained unanswered.

Andrée Hacquebaut   to Pierre Costals
Saint-Léonard   *Paris*

23 April 1927
9 p.m.

I am thirty years old today, Costals.

It is Sunday. Sunday, a bad day for me even at the best of times. The weather has been divine, too divine. Alas, I'm beginning to know them, these desolate springtimes, these summers that go by one after the other like empty baskets: not one of them, not one, has fulfilled its promise. How terrible it is, this sensation of sterility in a season when everything aspires towards renewal. Must one always see these intoxicating things through a horrible veil of deprivation? What is the point of being pretty? (For how much longer?)

This afternoon there was the usual hubbub of the *boule*-players. Seven times, from my room, I heard the hotel gramophone play the famous tune from *Louise: Depuis le jour où je me suis donnée* ... From time to time there were cheers and rounds of applause, for there was some kind of reunion party going on. Before dinner there was a thunderstorm. Now everything at the hotel is lit up *al giorno*, the tables on the terrace glistening, rain-soaked. The soft air brings me the sound of dance music, and the sweet orange smell from a languishing acacia branch. I can see two young men in dinner jackets coming out of the hotel, their shirt-fronts shining, too, and their patent leather shoes in the mud. Their carefree happiness pains me.

I am thirty. That's that. The age of waiting is over, the age of realization has begun: I have reached the turning-point. What I need now is a past rather than a future, memories rather than hopes. This is the age at which film stars in America commit suicide, because they have nothing more to expect from life. I still have *everything*.

In my mind's eye I see myself at the bedside of a dead child or a dead husband. Of course it must be terrible to have had and then to have no longer; but not to have had at all is worse. If only I were younger, or older! Younger, I wouldn't yet have had enough of this purely cerebral life and this purely platonic, intellectual, cold friendship: when I first met you, I didn't care about love, I didn't need it, I was sufficient unto myself, my body didn't interest me. Older, I should no longer be in a position to 'make a life' for myself, I should no longer have anything to lose by resigning myself to friendship pure and simple, I could even be quite happy with it. Thirty, for me, is either too early or too late.

Costals, I tell you quite simply and sadly: I am not trying to cling on to you. I have always known that, whatever I did, I would not attract you for ever. I have lived, I am still living, in the constant expectation of your growing weary of me, forgetting me, and the silence in which you have immured yourself during the past two months confirms my fears. Perhaps this is a psychological error: you have stuck so faithfully to your 'good works' on my behalf for four years! But I don't want to rely on the past as a gauge for the future. And besides, I don't even know if it was a question of 'good works' on your part or a genuine inclination. You have never cared to enlighten me on that point.

This being so, why should I go on being discreet and circumspect with you? Why should I go on being adroit? I'm inclined to think I've been only too discreet, and I know very well that no sort of finesse means anything to you. You get tired of things for no reason, simply because they have 'gone on long enough', because they have 'served their purpose', because 'one must have a change'. There's no point in trying to *deserve well* of you; it's simply a matter of trying to make the best of the short period during which one has a place in your life and if possible turn it into something more solid, beautiful, and happy.

Never, never, never will you be able to accuse me of being the female enemy. Never, no matter what you do, will you see me turn against you, or reproach you. I am your *friend*. But I cannot go on being nothing but a friend. I am like a soul in Purgatory, a woman of thirty, highly-strung, unhappy, with none of the outlets men have: brief affairs, travel, work, vanity, ambition. For twenty years I've walked in a straight line between two high banks. So you must be a little indulgent when you hear what I have to say to you.

What I have to say to you is this. Your friendship can do nothing more for my happiness. It is like a pearl found in the desert by a Bedouin dying of thirst. I am no longer at an age when half-measures and half-attachments can suffice; I must have total happiness or total despair. I am hungry for plenitude, and it is a passionate plenitude that I need. I am no longer interested in all those spiritual values which I prized so highly when I was younger; I am no longer interested in you in that sense; I have had enough of being loved fastidiously. This pure friendship is a beautiful thing, but it isn't a tangible thing of which I can be sure as I am sure of what I eat or what I drink; it's a fleshless thing, arid, stifling, intermittent, spasmodic, and in any case flagging, exhausting itself in the long run – all absence, waiting, emptiness – in which I have all the self-denials of love without any of its benefits. A sterile, spent thing, unless it can be infused with new sap. To be loved is to be at once desired, cossetted, possessed and cherished. All the rest is moonshine.

I should like to have my share of you, to take my fill of you, to be able to live on my repletion. Here, then, is what I propose. I do so calmly and coolly: I've thought a great deal about what I am going to write to you. I propose that we exchange this moribund friendship for two months during which you would give yourself to me passionately, during which I would be entirely yours. I am ready to give you my solemn word that once this time had elapsed you would never hear from me again if that was your wish.

These brief weeks of desperate plenitude (desperate for me) might perhaps give you some pleasure. For me they would be everything – everything, that is to say *something*, in this life of mine in which there is *nothing*, something for me to hold on to, the memory of which would remain with me, inviolate, which nothing and nobody could take away from me, a satisfaction of a different kind from the psychological satisfaction you have, it's true, given me up to now. With such a memory, I could snap my fingers at the banal happiness of married women. Having possessed you once, my life will not have been wasted. What dazzling peace for the rest of my days!

You must not think that, even at thirty, I have an inordinate need of physical love. A cerebral need, rather. It is really my conscience that tells me I ought to experience it. To get it over with. To be inoculated. Appeased. Mentally appeased, I mean. Like settling down in a train one was afraid of missing. As far as the senses are concerned, I am still a very little girl. Everything I have to offer you is fresh and new as at the break of day, completely worthy, in its simplicity, of your greatness. I would never forgive you if you forced me to offer it without love.

And please do not bring up that word 'affair' which you sometimes use so crudely. For me, everything that comes within your aura loses its ordinary meaning. Lover, mistress, liaison, affair – these words no longer mean anything: there is simply love. And, within the context of love, every liberty, every audacity, all consumed by its radiance.

Yes, it is I who have written this letter! Only two years ago, I should have died rather than contemplate the step which I am taking towards you. But what do I care about the world's opinion, when I know that what I would give you is radiantly pure and perhaps sublime?

A ndrée

This letter remained unanswered.

The most striking thing about man's – the male's – conception of happiness is that no such conception exists. There is a book of Alain's entitled: *Propos sur le bonheur.* But nowhere in this book is there any mention of happiness. This is highly significant. Most men have no conception of happiness.

Saint-Preux, in *La Nouvelle Héloïse*, cries out: 'O God, my soul was made for suffering: give me one that is made for happiness!' Well, God did not hear his prayer: the soul of the male is not made for happiness. In his eyes, happiness is a negative state – insipid in the literal sense of the word – which one only becomes aware of as a result of a glaring *un*-happiness; happiness is obtainable only by not thinking about it. One day you take a look at yourself and realize that you are not too badly off: so you tell yourself you are happy. And you take as your guiding principle the famous platitude that happiness comes only to those who do not seek it. To look for happiness, to speak of it as of something concrete, is regarded as unmanly. It was a man, Goethe, who spoke of 'the duty of happiness'. And it was also a man, Stendhal, who made that magnificent remark, so far-reaching it embodies a whole philosophy and a whole ethic: 'There is nothing in the world I respect as much as happiness.' But these were superior men, and it is precisely because they transcend the ordinary human categories that they think like this. To the average man, anyone who admits to a respect for happiness is suspect. As for 'the duty of happiness', in spite of Goethe it has always received, together with the notion of 'live and let live', the worst possible press. You may say to a man, even a young man: 'One empty hour, one wasted hour – think of the remorse, as death draws near, for not having devoted it to the pursuit of happiness!' and he will be taken aback. 'Whose happiness do you mean?' he will ask. 'Other people's? The country's?' And if you answer fiercely: 'No! MINE!' he will be shocked. He cannot understand how you can think of your own happiness; he has never thought of his. The male is always telling himself, quite cheerfully: 'Tomorrow you'll start living.' And if he knows what he means by 'living' it is already quite an achievement. Another young man, almost a youth, with everything in his favour, having heard someone use the word 'living', in the sense of making the most of life, asks him: 'But what do you mean by "living"?' For him, to live means to work, to scratch a living. If he were asked what happiness was, he would no doubt reply: 'Doing one's duty, finding a task to fulfil, a discipline, etc.' In other words, what he means by happiness is the method he has chosen, or, more probably, has had imposed on him, of killing time. And even this is not enough; when men kill time in too easy and pleasant a way they grow sick of it. One has often heard of the sort of malaise that comes over a man when he reaches a standstill, a state of quiescent equilibrium in which he no longer feels any desires: it is similar to the sort of malaise one feels in a motor-boat on a dead calm sea when the engine fails. Whence the fact that the consciousness of happiness gives such a powerful sensation of loneliness. This is often misunderstood.

However, it does sometimes happen that a man has a positive conception of happiness. In this case happiness lies in the satisfaction of vanity (with all kinds of individual variations, of course, since each man's idea of his own happiness is absolutely incomprehensible to everyone else). Vanity is man's predominant passion. It is not true that one can make a man do absolutely anything for money. But one can make most men do anything one wants by appealing to their vanity. Most men would go without food and drink for a whole day if by doing so they were to obtain a sop to their vanity at the end of it. A man without vanity is a bit of a freak: he casts a chill, and is given a wide berth. Thus for men it is not so much a question of *being* happy as of making people believe they are. A young doctor in the North African desert, recently married, once remarked ingenuously, without realizing how splendid his remark was: 'I'm extremely happy. But if only I could tell someone about it.' Most men would be only too delighted with the happiness of the sage. Fundamentally, that is what they like: how they all yearn to go into retreat! But people would not believe they were happy, people would think they had given up, or were incompetent, so off they go on the other tack, giving themselves airs, plunging into the shameful and ridiculous bustle we normally find them in, making lots of telephone calls, and soon a day of happiness for them is a day on which they have made plenty of telephone calls, in other words a day on which they have been very important. And in this way happiness-as-the-satisfaction-of-vanity merges with the happiness-which-comes-without-thinking-about-it which we mentioned earlier.

Women, on the other hand, have a positive idea of happiness. For, if man is more restless, woman is more alive. No woman would ask, like the afore-mentioned young man: 'What do you mean by "living"?' She has no need of explanations. To live, for her, is to feel. All women prefer to burn themselves out rather than be extinguished; all women prefer to be devoured rather than ignored. And in their 'feeling', what mobility, what profuseness of reaction! When one sees how a woman, if the

man she loves seems to love her less – even a little less –
suffers as much as if he no longer loved her at all; when one
sees how, later, if she realizes that he still loves her as much
as ever, not only does she feel wonderfully happy, but her joy
is redoubled by the joy of being forgiven for having suspected
him – when one sees this and compares it with the sluggish-
ness of men, one grasps the meaning of the word 'alive'.

In fact, the succession of minor pleasures which, according
to men, is what ultimately constitutes happiness, as a mass of
little stars makes up the Milky Way, seems no more capable
of doing so in women's eyes than, for Christians, a thousand
venial sins are capable of making up one mortal sin. For
women, happiness is a clearly defined state, endowed with its
own individual personality, a tangible reality that is extremely
alive, powerful and sensitive. A woman will tell you she is
happy as she will tell you she is hot or cold. 'What are you
thinking?' – 'That I'm happy.' 'Why do you want to do this
or that?' – 'In order to be happy!' (this in such a vehement
tone, with an 'of course' implied). 'I'm afraid of your doing
this or that.' – 'Do you think I want to ruin my happiness?'
She will give you a description of her happiness, telling you,
for example: 'When I'm happy, I don't talk', or 'When I'm
happy I always feel well.' She will know precisely when it
begins and when it ends. There is a book in the Bibliothèque
Rose entitled *A Fortnight of Happiness*. It is a book by a
woman, and this is obvious from the title alone: no man
would ever have had the notion that happiness can be cut
into slices like a cake. And a woman will enjoy this 'fortnight
of happiness' – meaning any limited period of happiness, any
obviously ephemeral happiness – much more than a man
would. For a woman any happiness, however short-lived, is
better than nothing. If you tell a girl you would love to marry
her but for one reason or another it is inevitable that she will
begin to be unhappy within a year, she is sure to reply: 'Well
then, I shall have had a year of happiness.' A man in her
place would think of the threat to his future, and would weigh
up the risks. The idea of happiness is so strong in women that
they can see nothing else; all risks are blotted out.

The only acceptable future for a woman is a happy

marriage. Thus she is dependent on men, and knows it from an early age. However true it is that male adolescents suffer from their impotence, as boys they live in the present, as young men they think of the future as a substance they will fashion by themselves. Girls, on the other hand, are afraid of the future. A boy knows that his future will be what he wants it to be; a girl knows that her future will be what a man wants it to be. Her dreams of happiness during this period of uncertainty will be all the more ardent if this happiness is threatened in advance.

Similarly, women attach far more importance than men to the conditions of happiness. It was a woman who once wrote that, as room thermometers indicate the correct temperature for *orange-trees*, *silk-worms*, etc., the word *happiness* ought to be opposite the 25 degrees centigrade line. When one returns from long stays in North Africa, Spain or Italy to the leprous Parisian winter, ten degrees below, to the darkness, the dirt, the ugliness, the inconveniences, the nastiness, the strained unhealthy life, what astonishes one is not so much this accumulation of horrors as the fact that most men put up with it: thanks to them, life goes on. But women, in the midst of this hell on earth, daydream of other things, pine away for other things, and sometimes fall into despair. There was once a novel for girls entitled *L'Age où l'on croit aux îles*. Women are always at the age when one believes in islands, in other words the age when one believes in happiness.

This positive idea of happiness that women have, and the demands they make on it, no doubt arise from the state of unsatisfaction which is their lot. Not that all women are martyrs by any means! Nevertheless, when one thinks of the condition of the sexes in society, the word that springs to mind for women is *unhappiness*, and for men *worries*. There is a striking custom in the Moslem marriage ceremony as celebrated in Algiers. A woman advances towards the young couple and pours jasmine water into the cupped hands of the bride. The groom bends down and drinks it. The woman proceeds to do the same with the bridegroom; but just as the bride is about to drink from his hands, he opens them and lets the water escape. What an appalling custom – laying it down as a principle that man should be happy and woman not. There is something about the picture of the little girl bending down to drink the water and being refused it that makes one shudder. True, that is the Moslem world; in Europe the unhappiness of woman is not laid down as a sacred principle in advance. But even in Europe, whereas the happiness of women is dependent on that of men, men are not much concerned about making women happy. It is rare to find a public man risking his career, an industrialist endangering his business, a writer sacrificing his work, to make a woman happy (by marrying her, for instance). In fact, quite apart from any question of sacrifice, one never sees a man marrying a woman who wants to marry him more than he wants to marry her, simply in order to make her happy. Whereas there are millions of women who dream of marriage simply in order to discharge an overflow of loving devotion on a husband and children.

Dreams are born of dissatisfaction: no satisfied person dreams (or, if he is an artist, he dreams only in a calculated way.) Where do people (even men) dream of happiness? In slums, in hospitals, in prisons. Women dream of happiness and think about it, because they have not got it. If a man suffers through a woman, he has everything else to console himself with. But what has she got? A woman can never realize herself completely: she is too dependent on men. She therefore dreams continually of the unattainable. A poetess once wrote a book under the title *Waiting* – a title as feminine as our *Fortnight of Happiness*. Women are always waiting, hopefully up to a certain age, hopelessly thereafter. This dreaming of happiness, so peculiar to women, is incomprehensible to men. They call it naïvety, emotionalism, romanticism, Bovaryism – always with a suggestion of superiority and disdain. There is an even more contemptuous word: soulfulness. If a woman admits to being happy, a man will tell her it's exhibitionism. If she sings all day long, a man will say she is a bit simple-minded – for him, she could not possibly be happy unless she was simple. If a poet writes that he would rather not go to the Italian lakes at all than go there without his beloved, there will always be a critic ready to say: 'Shop-girl's talk.' (If it is 'shop-girl's talk' for a woman to say: 'It would be absolute torture for me to see, for example, a Titian I like when I'm in the company of someone I dislike', so much the better for shop-girls.) The girl who waits for a husband a little too long, and vainly decorates the unknown beloved's altar in her heart, would simply appear comic to that same beloved: he thinks, or pretends to think, that it is simply a drama of the flesh, when in fact it is the soul consumed with the desire to give itself. (Whether this unhappiness is greater than that of many married women is another question.) A young woman who dreams of a happiness she does not possess interests him only to the extent that he can hope to benefit from it: he has no more respect for her longing because of this. As for the old maid and all her regrets, for them he has only jeers, not to say insults: the attitude of men towards spinsters, in France at least, is a disgrace.

The feminine conception of happiness suffers the fate of all feminine conceptions: it does not interest men. Men are not interested in women when their senses are satisfied, and the day she realizes this for the first time is one of the tragedies in a woman's life. Galatea flees into the willows, hoping to be caught; a moment later the man runs from the willows, but this time it's for good – he does not want to be caught. Men are bored or irritated by women as soon as they have ceased to enjoy them, just as the smoke from a cigarette inhaled with pleasure a few moments ago is bothersome when it rises from the cigarette after one has put it down three-quarters finished with no intention of taking it up again. It is because they have nothing to say to each other that couples quarrel; it is a way of passing the time. A man has to make an effort, out of politeness, or good nature, or a sense of duty, to devote some of his time to the woman who has satisfied his desires; when he does so, he always has the feeling that he is doing her a favour. Only rakes are permanently interested in women, because with them curiosity – the soul of desire – is permanently alive: hence the indulgent attitude of women towards them, even the most serious women. 'The happiness of women,' a character in a novel has perceptively remarked, 'the happiness of women comes from men, but the happiness of men comes from themselves. The only thing a woman can do for a man is avoid disturbing his happiness.' The terrible thing is that women – powerless and naïve – long to do for men what men do for them. A woman who is happy and loved (and who loves) asks for nothing more. A man who loves and is loved needs something else as well. Leaving aside the question of money, a man always makes a present to a woman by marrying her, because marriage is a vital necessity for her but not for him. Women marry because marriage is for them the only key to happiness, whereas men marry because Tom, Dick and Harry do; they marry out of habitude, if not hebetude. Naturally they do not admit this, because they are unaware of it. Thoughtlessness makes men marry, just as thoughtlessness makes them go to war. One shudders at the thought of what would become of society if men began to be governed by reason; it would perish, as we see peoples perish before our very eyes because they are too intelligent.

Man and woman confront each other, and society says to them: 'You know nothing about him? You know nothing about her? Well, have a try. Go ahead and make the best of it.' Indeed, were it not for the mating urge, each sex would stay where it was. Not out of shyness, as in Vigny's poem, but simply like two species impervious to each other and with nothing to say to each other. Nature has made them antithetical, incapable of agreeing, or capable of agreeing only on the ruin of something, and we watch this strange spectacle of beings who are driven towards each other although they seem not to be made for each other.

Woman is made for one man; man is made for life, and incidentally for all women. Woman is made to arrive and stay put; man is made to act and move on: she begins loving when he has finished; people talk of women 'teasing' when they ought to talk of men. Man takes and throws away again; woman gives herself, and what has once been given cannot be taken back, or only with difficulty. Woman thinks love can do everything – not only *her* love, but the love man bears her, which she always exaggerates. She will eloquently maintain that love has no limits; man sees the limits not only of woman's love but of his own, whose poverty he is only too well aware of. Not only are they out of step, but supply and demand are badly synchronized between them. Men seldom feel anything for women except desire, which women find tiresome; women seldom feel anything for men except tenderness, which men find tiresome. Women offer more tenderness than men can stand; fortunately there are children to absorb the surplus, as long as they need it. Women say: 'Ah, how foolish men are to sacrifice, for the sake of ideas, or glory, or money, time that should be devoted to love, to true love! It teaches one so many things! Think how many men fail to attain to the highest spheres (intellectual, social, religious, etc.) because they have not allowed love to live and grow in them!' And men reply: 'How can love live and grow in me? It can only die there. These embers cannot be fanned into flame: artifice is worse than useless. Why ask me to be other than what nature made me? Nature made me a man – that is, a member of a loveless species.'

Such is this hybrid couple from whom spring most of the ills of mankind without either of them being to blame, but only nature, which brought them together without matching them, throwing in the best and the worst as in all her other works, wherein nothing is not muddled, confused, impure, two-sided, *pace* the ignorant and the sage, who never see more than one side.

'What!' you will say, ' "the source of most of the ills of mankind" – what an exaggeration!' But just open your newspaper. Dramas of jealousy, dramas of adultery, dramas of divorce, dramas of abortion, crimes of passion. And all those family dramas which would not exist without an initial couple. And all the things one never hears about. It is not the free union that seems to be cursed, it is the couple, whatever form it takes, and perhaps more especially in marriage. At the basis of it a monstrous gamble: the man being forced to take a partner for life when there is no good reason why it should be this one rather than the next, since millions of others are equally worthy of his love. The man driven by nature to repeat the same words of love to a dozen women including the one who is destined for him – false if he hides the truth from her, cruel if he admits it. The man driven by nature to deceive his wife, with all the lies and baseness this entails – culpable if he yields to nature's commands, unhappy if he resists them. The girl who grows to womanhood in the midst of tears, and to motherhood in the midst of sighs. The child, a natural occurrence that makes woman ugly and deformed. The act which is supposed to be supremely natural, but which can only be performed at certain periods, in certain conditions, with certain precautions. The terror of pregnancy, or the terror of disease, hovering like a spectre above every love-bed. The so-called supremely natural act surrounded by a whole pharmacopoeia which sullies it and poisons it and makes it ridiculous. What man, indeed, if he only stops to think for a moment, will not admit to himself, when he approaches a woman, that he is entangling himself in a mesh of misfortunes, or at any rate risks, and that he is tempting Providence? And yet he wants it, women want it, society wants it, and nature, if she were capable of wanting anything, would want it too. For that is what love is – the thread of fire which binds the living to the earth and justifies the Creation. You will ask me, dear reader, what I am driving at. The answer is that I am simply registering my astonishment at the fact that an impulse so basic as that of one sex towards the other should be forced by its very nature to cause so many ills. It seems to me that what nature should condemn is what is done against her, not what she prescribes. But no, she reserves all her severity for those who follow her and without whom she would not exist. Unless everything is nature's, and we are mistaken in seeing her in one place rather than another.

Pierre Costals   to M. Armand Pailhès
Paris   *Toulouse*

                                                       27 April 1927
My dear Pailhès,

A letter from poor Andrée H. She offers herself to me in the most formal terms. If she persists, I shall of course be obliged to refuse her, in no less formal terms.

In so far as I understand the French attitude in these matters, I should guess that her reaction will be as follows: 'A real man does not behave in such a way. Either he's a cad, or he's impotent. It is disgraceful to insult a woman in such a way.'

What do you think? But first of all, here is my defence.

Totally lacking in worldly wisdom, Andrée is incapable of distinguishing the element of civility pure and simple, of complaisance, of good-nature if you like, in my attitude towards her. Where I am concerned, she takes politeness for keen interest, benevolence for predilection, pity for friendship. God forgive me, I suspect that at times she thinks I'm in love with her. If I send a book to a colleague with whom I am on perfectly amicable terms, with the dedication 'affectionate regards', it does not enter his head for a moment that I really have any affection for him. A similar dedication would make Andrée swoon with joy: 'He has declared his love!'

The truth is that I regard her with sympathy, respect, and a certain admiration. That is all, and it's a great deal.

All? No, understanding too. I know that people find Andrée antipathetic. They complain that she thinks herself superior – but supposing she is, in some respects? That she is 'literary' – but in fact, although she is stuffed with reading, she is still perfectly natural, completely devoid of affectation, unlike so many of these female bookworms who adopt, more or less unconsciously, opinions and attitudes which they think will impress. Andrée's writing is also revealing: simplicity itself, flowing like water from a spring. The fact is that, unlike all those others, she has a simple, powerful temperament, she's a *Natur* (and you know that to call anyone *eine Natur* was for Goethe the highest praise). And I even forgive her, up to a point, her lack of dignity. For after all, the girl loves, and love and dignity make bad bed-fellows. She wants to be happy: what could be more natural? I too, when I want to be happy, go at it as hard as I can. In short, she irritates me but I understand her, and defend her when she is attacked, for I could not swear that in her position I wouldn't be irritating too – more discreetly than she, of course, or at least so I hope.

When all this is said, the fact remains that she is ugly, graceless, badly dressed, and utterly unfeminine. As you yourself said to me: 'She looks like a housemaid.' The human face is a curious invention: it must be very nice, or else!

And then, even if she were not obviously unprepossessing, she doesn't attract me, and that in itself is enough to justify my attitude. There are women who have nothing to recommend them, but this nothing arouses my desire. Andrée's nothing gets me down. Drain that cup to the dregs* – no, never!

I am capable of making the gesture of taking this woman. To succeed in something one despises is a noble and difficult thing – because one must conquer oneself as well as others – but it has always been within my power. To succeed in something that disgusts me is something I am also capable of. I should escape with nothing worse than that deadly depression one experiences after having consummated the carnal act with somebody who doesn't appeal to one. But what I cannot do is feign love. In being possessed by me, she would feel my disgust, and it would stab her to the heart. I should have undergone this harrowing ordeal, and to what end? To make her suffer!

Even supposing she doesn't suffer, should one take a woman out of pity? It's 'a good talking point', as my fellow-writers say. Of course it can happen that one takes a woman because one is sorry for her, just as it can happen that one takes a woman because she has made one angry. But there must be a basis of desire, which there is not, and never will be, between me and Andrée. One of my friends, who is very unhappily married, said to me one day à propos of his wife: 'I go on with her out of pity. She's young. She needs it.' I've never forgotten that remark, which seemed to me to be appalling. But you can satisfy a woman out of pity, even though she makes you unhappy, if she is your wife, if she is part of your life, someone you see continually. You cannot satisfy, out of pity alone, a stranger who repels you physically and for whom you feel no affection.

Furthermore, whatever anyone may say, it really is something to make a woman of a well-brought-up young lady, even one of thirty. It creates a bond, involves risks, perhaps responsibilities, perhaps long-term consequences: nothing can

---

*An untranslatable pun here: *Boire cette coupe jusqu'au lit* (bed) instead of *lie* (dregs) (*Translator's note*).

alter the fact that the thing has happened. And so, I consider it the purest folly to incur all this for the sake of somebody to whom I am indifferent. Colette's mother used to say to her: 'Don't do anything foolish unless it's really going to give you pleasure.' And I don't want to feel under any obligations to her.

One final reason, a shabby one if you like, but after all I'm not a saint. By disposition and on principle I have, since adolescence, kept all my love affairs secret, even the most flattering ones. By disposition, being naturally secretive (which goes hand in hand with false confidences). On principle, because a young woman will yield to me all the more easily if she knows that nothing will leak out, and because my reputation as a libertine, since no names can be attached to it, remains on the whole vague enough not to interfere with my enterprises. And inevitably Andrée, who is as incontinent in speech as on paper, would go round advertising the fact that she was my mistress. I have always prided myself on the fact that, with a few rare exceptions, nobody has been able to name my women-friends. And the whole of Paris, faced with an ugly duckling like Andrée, would exclaim: 'Now we know what excites him', and from this one sample imagine the rest!

And lastly, even without all that, there is something else which in itself would be enough to restrain me from becoming her lover: something about the shape of her face and her forehead reminds me of my great-uncle Costals de Pradels, and you will appreciate that I don't want the family mixed up in all this ... Who would have believed it? I too have my scruples....*

Costals

Andrée Hacquebaut   to Pierre Costals
Saint-Léonard   Paris
                                                   30 April 1927

You have left unanswered the most solemn letter a proud

---

*The rest of this letter has no bearing on our subject (*Author's note*).

and pure young woman could write to a man. My other letters did not necessarily call for replies; this one demanded one. If you do not answer the letter I am writing to you now, I shall consider that, for the first time, you have *behaved badly* towards me. It will be the first *real* crack in my esteem for you.

I am thirty; I have no experience of love, and unless you change your attitude, I never shall. Because you have occupied too great a place in my heart. Who else could love you as I do? No one – it wouldn't be possible. Not one of your mistresses loves you as I do. (Indeed, this is one reason why you prefer them to me.) You are the being one meets once in a lifetime, the decisive, the definitive being who leaves his mark for ever, without whom a woman's life is bound to be abortive, truncated, without flower or fruit. You are my master. God knows I haven't the soul of a slave, and yet I submit to you without the slightest effort or the slightest humility, remaining nevertheless on the same plane as you, at once your subject and your equal. I do not believe there could possibly be a more delicious sensation than that, for a woman like me, if you were my master in the full sense of the word. Which is to explain that I could not, even if I wanted to, offer to another man a sort of residuum of myself, when all that is best in me belongs to you: in my view, it would be a defilement. And besides, I am now incapable of taking an interest in another man. Men who are not you bore me. They do not dominate me. It is I who would dominate them. And I cannot belong to a man who does not dominate me in everything; it would be impossible, everything inside me rebels against it. My destiny as a woman is to love in submission and respect; I must feel myself transcended. You see, even if I were offered the most tempting marriages, now.... Like women who have a religious vocation, I've weighed it all up. On one side of the scale, all the material goods of this world, and on the other my vocation, which is to love you. And my vocation wins hands down.

You are both too much and too little in my life. Too much for me to be able to love anyone else. Too little for me to be fulfilled and satisfied. You give me too much for me to be able to break off relations with you without a terrible wrench. You give me too little for it not to be as painfully inadequate as nothing at all. Your friendship is a torture to me, and the rupture of that friendship would be torture too. You are like a knife in my heart. To leave it there is painful; but to pull it out would be to drain my life away. I am torn between my friendship for you, my spiritual need of you, my need to be loved spiritually by you – and my desire for love, my desire to *live*, if only for a few months : my flesh, too, has a legitimate need to be loved. If I do not want to lose you, I must sacrifice my flesh. I must die a virgin, or forget your very name. I must forgo marriage, sexual pleasure, motherhood, a healthy, normal life, and exhaust myself in a hopeless passion for someone who is fond of me, no doubt, but who has no need of me, either as a person to give to or as a person to take from. For you do not want even my self-sacrifice. You want nothing of me.

You once told me that women who looked at you with melting eyes 'sent you up the wall'. Have you ever seen me look at you like that? Do I ever foist myself on you or cling to you? If that were the case, I would understand your resistance : one owes nothing to people who bore one. But it is not the case, and I would take good care that it wasn't : a man's boredom is far too humiliating for a woman. My love is a loving comradeship. I do not desire you, but you are the only man whose desires I could accept without revulsion. I repeat, I can only love someone who is superior to me. I would rather be tortured by self-denial than give myself beneath me. I would prefer marriage, even a mediocre marriage, to a mediocre love affair. What then? Marriage, and your friendship on the side? First of all, no husband would tolerate such a friendship. And then, the mere thought of a man touching me sends me back to you, and I imagine all the heart-rending regrets for what might have been.

I have wanted, and I still want, with all my strength, your well-being and mine. Is it possible that it has all been to no purpose? Hurt me, if honesty demands it of you, but do not let me down. Let us assume that in these two months of intimacy there would be no pleasure for you who are surfeited elsewhere; they might at least be a psychological experiment from which your books could reap some benefit. I should be your guinea-pig, a guinea-pig of a particularly rare and precious species: a thinking guinea-pig, a guinea-pig which could if necessary take notes on what it felt and pass them on to you. In default of pleasure, you would be furthering your work, and as for me, if I knew that I was contributing towards it in however small a way, my happiness would be redoubled. And then, who knows, pleasure may come : your catalogue of women perhaps does not include a thirty-year-old provincial girl, as cultivated in mind as she is intact in body (and much prettier in body than in face). You have so often written that a man's only motive in love is curiosity, how could you not feel curiosity for that sort of object? And after all, me or another. . . .

One of two things. Either you have a genuine affection for me, in which case no harm would be done, for you would know you were making me happy, and your affection would be gratified; and perhaps our relationship, begun in friendship, would end in friendship; love would have been deliciously enclosed between two layers of friendship, like a jewel between two layers of tissue paper. If not, if you are indifferent to me, then what have you to fear? It would cause you no regret to see this experiment detach you completely from me.

I have the impression of beating against a wall. The wall hasn't given yet, but by dint of perseverance. . . . You have no idea what a woman's will-power can be.

Andrée

Pierre Costals
Paris

to Andrée Hacquebaut
Saint-Léonard

2 May 1927

Dear Mademoiselle,
This is to acknowledge your two March letters in which you complain of my silence, and your two April letters in which you offer yourself to me. So you see that I've read you.
You are obsessed with the idea of happiness. So am I. You have no idea how keenly I feel the tragedy of a situation in

which neither body nor soul obtains what it desires. I could write page after page on the subject, even more forcefully than you. If in this matter we are in complete sympathy – *sumpathein*: to suffer with, to suffer from the same suffering as – it is because, from this point of view, *I have been you*. Not only during adolescence, bound hand and foot as I was by my shyness and my ignorance of the world, but even later, when I was already a man, during certain desolate periods of my life. True, they did not last long. Today I have everything I like, and I like everything I have.

And so, I repeat, your suffering is not of the kind I need to imagine in order to be able to sympathize with. I know what it's like; it's intolerable, and your situation is intolerable. You are really very unlucky.

That said, if I understand your last two letters aright, you wish to give yourself to me. Allow me to say, dear Mademoiselle, that this idea does not seem to me a happy one.

1. Physiologically I am somewhat peculiar. I only desire : (a) girls of under twenty-two years of age; (b) passive, bovine girls; (c) long, thin girls with raven hair. So you see that you do not at all fulfil the required conditions, which are an absolute *sine qua non*. Whatever your attractions, upon which I will not expatiate – you know them only too well – I do not feel capable of responding to the desire which you do me the honour of conceiving for me. Nature (the wretch!) would remain deaf to my appeals. And, as they say, you can take a horse to water but you cannot make it drink.

2. (Just for the record.) The act which you have in mind would be an immense disappointment to you, especially after the way you have worked yourself up to it. You have no idea what these apish antics are like. A love-scene overheard through a partition sounds like a session at the dentist's. I don't know whether you have ever heard the things a woman murmurs when she gives herself. No? Well, it's a pity, because you would have become a Carmelite there and then. (But let's be fair; I ought to add '... and what a man says when he's trying to pick up a woman?' Surely not, because you would have shot yourself long since.)

I must also put you on your guard against your belief in the efficacy of desire and will-power. You know my views on the ineptitude of women. One example of this seems to me to be their faith in the power of persistence. No doubt there are men with whom it works. But I belong to the opposite species. And I tell you : no, never!

Come now, be brave! Please believe that I am whole-heartedly with you in your affliction. But anyway, why be so set on me when the world is full of gentlemen with multi-farious assets whom you could make supremely happy? You beat against me like a bird against the window of a lighthouse. You will not break this window. You will break yourself against it, and you will fall to the ground. Good-bye, dear Mademoiselle. I hope I can still count on your friendship, with no ill-feelings. You know I am determined to be forgiven everything.

Sincerely yours,

C.

P.S. – You did not put enough stamps on your last letter. It is the fourth time at least that this has happened, and it's inevitable with the packed envelopes you send me. So I have to pay exorbitant surcharges. You should buy yourself some scales.

Pierre Costals
Paris

to Armand Pailhès
Toulouse

2 May 1927

... Another letter from poor Andrée, offering herself right, left and centre. She loves me so much I'm amazed she hasn't yet murdered me. But let her try! She'll get a hot reception. I'm not so easy to get rid of. And I would leap at the opportunity getting rid of *her*. I don't blame her. I understand her and pity her. She once wrote to me : 'To understand is to love. If I understand you so well, it's because I love you.' Well, I understand her and I don't love her. I'm profoundly indifferent to her; even the thought of making her suffer gives me no pleasure. Which is why I will not give her her two months of love. Or a week of love ('charity week'). Or a night of love. Not even 'an hour with'.*

I wish you had read the letter I wrote her! Not wishing to give the poor girl my reasons, which could all be summed up as follows: 'I will not love you and I will not take you, because I do not love you and I do not want you', I racked my brains to find a way of refusing her without being too wounding.

This is not the first time I've been in such a jam. As a young man I had to get a doctor friend of mine to tell an over-enthusiastic American lady that the Venus of the streets had not left me unscathed – which was pure invention. Three years ago I was pestered by the Baroness Fléchier, a woman of fifty years and more. One evening, around midnight, at the end of a tête-à-tête which until then, by sheer strength of will, I had managed to maintain on an exalted level, she put her scrawny old arms under my nose and said: 'You're the first man I've entertained at such an hour who hasn't kissed my arms.' In this predicament, I naturally had to concoct some excuse. I was ashamed of the one I had used against the lady from Alabama, so I told her that unfortunately I was not attracted by women. Since I keep my love affairs a dead secret, I thought this might get by. She believed me, or at any rate pretended to, and I, in a fit of good humour at the thought of my let-off, went and overdid it by swearing to her that never in my life had I held a woman in my arms! On this basis we remained good friends.

I was loth to give either of these excuses to a 'young' girl, and I wrote to Andrée the most unbelievable nonsense. I told her I only liked tall, thin, twenty-year-olds with raven hair, and that they must also be totally inert. And I told her the act of love was apish. Which it is. But it's also something else.

And to think that it's all so simple! A single spark of desire, and the thing would have happened four years ago. You know my cosmogony? 'In the beginning was Desire.' Yes, and if

---

*The reference is to a well-known book entitled *Une heure avec* ... published in the 1920's – a collection of interviews with famous people (*Translator's note*).

there's no desire, there's no beginning.... Incidentally, I saw a stunning girl at the Doignys' last night. Such a ravishing little creature! I had noticed her and followed her for a moment last February at the Review Board, where she was escorting a blind man (an orphaned cousin, she will tell me). While everyone else was jabbering away and paralysing me with compliments, she said nothing. To say nothing to me is, as you know, the surest way of 'saying' a lot to me. Simplicity always scores a point with me – especially after 'remarkable' persons of the Andrée type. I guessed from the very first that this child was not very intelligent, because she's too pretty. (You know I've never – never – found the two things together in a woman: intelligence and beauty.) Eventually she addressed a few words to me – banality itself, of the choicest kind. Naturally I couldn't help teasing her.

'You say you've read me. What have you read of mine, Mademoiselle?'

She thought....

'Let me see.... Ah, yes. *Rien que la terre.*'

'Sorry. That's by Morand.'

She was quite unruffled:

'I know I've read something of yours. I can't remember either the title or the subject, but I remember liking it.'

Bravo! But her ordeal was not yet over. I threw her a sombre look:

'And ... and ... have you any reservations about my art, Mademoiselle?'

She opened her eyes wide. 'No, you haven't any reservations, have you?' I repeated in an impassioned voice. She shook her head. So all was well.

And how ravishing she is! A little round head, like a bird's, and perfectly made hands, literally translucent at the fingertips, like onyx. The beauty of these extremities, and of her nails, would suggest that she was of noble blood, which unfortunately she isn't.

I contrived to leave with her, and we found ourselves in the avenue de Wagram. Her conversation was as flat as the pavement, and her acidulous voice made a bad impression on me. But I was touched by her little mule's steps as she walked along beside me – I walking like a mountain, and she like a shrub (there's a good pair of similes for you). All the women stared at her – without warmth – and men turned round. And as for me, there was that prompt familiarity which showed that she attracted me. And the old, vulgar vanity of walking beside a pretty girl knowing that one is taken for her lover. 'Yes, but they must realize from the sound of her voice that she's still a virgin.' And that was a bit of a dampener.

I felt slightly awkward not knowing her name. When you desire a woman whose name you don't know, learning her name is a kind of preliminary sketch for the act of possessing her. The name is already a soul. She is called Solange Dandillot. *Sol*: ground, and *ange*: angel – the two extremes, and I'm equally at home with both!

And she's the granddaughter of a public prosecutor! That alone would have been enough to make me want her.

She told me a little about her life, with a characteristically French directness, very refreshing after the eternal self-romanticizing of German virgins. I escorted her home to the avenue de Villiers. Good address; that helped to make me love her. (Oh! . . .) She tells me she has no girl-friends. And there's nothing better for a girl than to have no girl-friends – except to have no parents. I offered to take her to the Piérards' next week, and she accepted. I wrote at once to the Piérards, simply for the pleasure of writing her name.

Why am I telling you all this? Because here is an angel who will not get away from me. Her wings are weighted with lead; all one has to do is to leave her to tire herself out. And this is the answer to the divagations of poor Andrée, who spends her time seeking God knows what God knows where. The Andrée story can be summed up in a single phrase, which would make a good title for a light comedy: *If only she had been pretty*.

(I put 'angel' in the feminine. And indeed, since angels are pure spirits, I don't see why they are invariably represented in male form, unless it is to satisfy the unacknowledged homosexuality of the human species.)

Andrée Hacquebaut   to Pierre Costals
Saint-Léonard   *Paris*

Friday, 4 May

I once showed a letter of yours to one of my friends who is
a graphologist, without telling her who the writer was. 'Beware
of this man', she told me. 'He is of the race of serpents.' And
it's quite true : you are the masculine serpent in all its
hideousness. Another of my friends once swallowed a snake's
egg while drinking from a well. The egg hatched in her diges-
tive system, and it was not till long afterwards, when she was
X-rayed, that they found she had a snake inside her body. In
the same way, I let you into my heart some time ago in all
innocence. And now I see the reptile there.

Treacherous and hard-hearted killer! Oh, no complaints, it's
a nice clean job. No blood, nothing compromising. And a wonderful alibi : 'What, me! After all I've done for her! I who
even now am "in complete sympathy" with her, I who understand her suffering so well, I who have lavished encouragement and condolence and consolation on her!' Your con-
dolences make me want to slap your face – your charitable
advice, your insulting detachment, your disinterestedness,
which is nothing more than impotence or sadism. 'Never!' you
say. And why? Because I'm thirty years old, because I'm not
'passive', etc., etc. The most squalid street-girl has enjoyed
your caresses as she might enjoy those of any other man,
whereas a woman for whom you are everything, a woman for
whom those caresses would have been the summit of human
happiness, not for what she would have received from you
(you're not God's gift to women), but for what she would have
given you. . . . The woman of the gutter or the brothel, whom
you despise, gets that from you, whilst I, whom you love with
your heart, with your kindness. . . . Your kindness! What does
it amount to? The kindness of a man who watches his friend
drown without lifting a finger! But it isn't even a question of
kindness, but of fairness. Fairness means responding to the
love that is offered to you with an equal love.

'I can only love girls of under twenty-two.' Rubbish! In
Fragility, Maurice says to Christine : 'You no longer have the

eyes of a girl, but those of a woman. Now there's something behind them' (p. 211). That is not the sort of thing one tosses off idly. One must have felt it. You can only love 'passive, bovine' women? Do you want them made of wood, or stone, or iron, or reinforced concrete? But anyhow you're lying. Remember what you wrote about the Polish girl: 'I love the (physical) pleasure I give her. Even if that were all, it would be enough' (*Purple*, p. 162). You can only love 'long, thin' persons? That's a good one! Must I remind you of the description of Hélène in *Fragility* or Lydia in *Purple*?* And my 'persistence'? Me, persist! Me, want to intrude on your life, when I spend my own trying to extricate myself from you and you from me; when I have reached the point of longing for you to offend me even more deeply than you have already, so that my wounded pride may assuage the pain of losing you; when, in exchange for something durable, our friendship, I offer you the means of getting rid of me for ever! 'The act which you have in mind would be an immense disappointment to you.' Why? That's a typically masculine idea. Woman excels in enlarging, ennobling everything with her imagination and heart, while man belittles everything with his carping spirit, not to say his natural pettiness. A woman loves more than ever after being physically possessed, especially by the man who initiated her. The opposite is unheard of, if my friends are to be believed. And even if it did turn out to be a disappointment, wouldn't this be infinitely preferable to the slow poison of unfulfilment, which makes it impossible to free yourself from the other person? And even if it did turn out to be distasteful, what a relief to have got it out of one's system at last! No more Costals! Disappointment, I welcome you! Disgust, I welcome you! But of course such a solution would offend your pride. You do not want me, since you cheerfully allow me to disappear from your life, but you want to lose me with all the honours of war. No woman must be allowed to see you as other than a hero. You're afraid of being deglamorized,

---

*A number of quotations from Costals' work, all with the same object of proving his inconsistency, have been omitted here. They occupy two whole pages, back and front, of Andrée's letter (*Author's note*).

poor angel. Well, I can tell you that the true hero is the man who dispenses happiness. And if I were to be disgusted by anything, it would not be 'the act of love' with you, it would be your cowardice in avoiding it. My admiration for you has been shaken, for the first time, by your pathetic excuses. Yes indeed, I have nothing but pity and contempt for your miserable affection, which is too lukewarm to assimilate the flesh, for fear of having to cope with its ferments. There's my fertility God! People envy you, and yet your life is mean and shabby – yes, do you realize that? Oh, all those 'superior' men! Impotent parasites! It would serve them right if the common people, the horny-handed sons of toil, cut off their heads – and other parts as well, since they don't know how to use them to give happiness to those who need happiness more than life itself. Ah! why did you not take me if only to humiliate me? You could cure me of a love that is killing me, and you won't! So one must suffer 'nobly', eh? One must be sublime. Monsieur is very strong on sacrifice – the sacrifice of others, of course. 'In any case we'll remain friends, won't we?' In other words: 'It would be the simplest thing in the world for me to give you the happiness you desire. But I do not wish to. Nevertheless I want you to remain in my life, just enough to gratify me without inconveniencing me or complicating my existence. I don't like your face or your body or your appearance; you can give that vulgar part of yourself to whomsover you like. But please, dear Mademoiselle, keep the more ethereal parts exclusively for me. Not to mention (*for the record*) the right to make you suffer.' Well, I've had enough of heroism. You've cured me of heroism. For life.

I used to have dreams of a man dominating me, sweeping me off my feet. I chose a conquistador, a solitary prince, a man ten times more masculine, more intelligent, more self-sufficient, more wonderful than anyone else, the man who said in reply to the Catholic interviewer who reproached him with having abused the gift of pleasure: 'Well, what of it! I've rejoiced in God's creation.' To him I would have given my mind, my youth, my virgin body, my lips which have never once been kissed. Him I should have been only too happy to obey. For him I was ready to sacrifice everything, my life, even

my honour. I offer him all this, and he will have none of it!
I foresaw everything, accepted everything: *during*, the loss of
my peace of mind; *afterwards*, the wrenching apart, his infidelity, his neglect, my despair, my lost reputation. I foresaw
it all, except that my offering might be rejected. I foresaw
everything that would happen *afterwards*: what I did not
foresee was that there would be no *afterwards*. I wanted your
embrace, and all I got was your 'kindness' and your pity:
either a patronizing and paternal old man, or a capricious,
teasing boy. My psychology was that of simple, humble people,
who believe that desire is inevitable between a man and a
woman who are young and normal and fond of each other.
I hadn't thought of the affectations of the upper classes and the
'intellectual élite.' There, you make me talk like a Communist.

Saturday

'Never!' Your 'never!' You know, even if you knocked that
'never' into my head like a nail, I should still rebound under
the hammer. For if I really believed in that 'never', there would
be nothing for it but to lie down and die: there are things one
could die of, literally, without much effort; one has only to
let oneself go. But I don't believe in it, I can't believe in it.
One day you'll suffer, you'll pay the penalty for never in your
life having forgone a single desire, not even a passing whim,
and for having forced a creature who adores you to forgo a
desire that for her was unique, irreplaceable, vital. And when
that day comes, Costals, there will be no more 'nevers'. No, I
cannot believe that if, one day, I were reduced to crawling at
your feet and begging you to give me, not two months, but
a single week of illusory happiness, you would refuse me. It's
not that in itself it means so very much to me. But to know
that it will happen some time, some day. All I ask of you is
one week, and then it will be finished for ever, if you so wish.
During that week I should be capable of burning up my whole
life and dying, like Lucifer, in the flames. No, no, no, I cannot
believe you will go on refusing me forever. Even if you took
me without either love or desire, like a woman you picked up
in the street....

Sunday

It's First Communion Day. Bright sunshine. A dazzling May morning . . . I wept as I listened to those little girls' voices. A few years more, and, like me. . . . I flung myself on to my knees beside my bed, and said : 'My God, give me the strength to convince him !'

In a little while I shall be taking this letter to the post in the same hand as my missal. You see what you drive me to. I would not have to write such things if I were yours.

This letter crossed the following one.

Pierre Costals   to Andrée Hacquebaut
Paris   *Saint-Léonard*

6 May 1927

Dear Mademoiselle,

My last letter was more cavalier than chivalrous. Almost as soon as it had gone, I was smitten with remorse. Forgive me for it.

Logically, that letter must have given you the impression that I was making fun of your predicament. In fact, not only do I not find it funny, but I feel it personally and respect it. However, I must tell you why, and you must take my word for it; for you will never understand how a man of my sort came to find himself in a similar situation to yours. I will not try and explain it to you. Apart from the fact that it touches all too closely on my private life, I cannot really explain it to myself. I have come to the conclusion that it was an ordeal of the kind that initiates have to undergo, or like the descent into Hades of the gods of antiquity who alternated between a sojourn on earth and a sojourn in the underworld.

Years ago, for several months – say six months – I was 'walled in' like you. I had a solid mass of tenderness all ready, God knows, to be given to more or less anybody as long as they aroused my desire (for I have never seriously loved anyone I did not desire). But I could not make contact. And I felt certain that the world was full of girls who would have been

only too happy to receive the tenderness and the pleasure that
I was only too happy to give them; and they longed for it in
vain, as I longed for it in vain. But still I could not make
contact.

Do you know, Mademoiselle, I brushed against people in the
street simply out of the need for human contact. I really did.
I was younger than I am today; my freedom was unlimited;
I had money to burn, and I've always been ready to pay for
my pleasures – and for the pleasures of those I love. But I
could not make contact. They were afraid of my desire, I
don't know why. I saw people steer clear of me to whom
I only wished to give and from whom I asked nothing in return,
except what they themselves desired. And yet it seemed to me
that my tenderness must be visible on my face, like perspiration, or like mist on a window-pane, blurring it.... I suppose
it cannot be seen in this way. People fled as I approached, like
sheep scuttling down the embankment on either side of a
road as a car approaches. The whole human race was trickling
through my fingers. There was something unforgettable about
the expression of fear in eyes one would have liked to close
with almost paternal kisses. Those girls one would have treated
like goddesses.... I don't know what was wrong with me.
Perhaps I had been guilty of some terrible infringement of the
law, and it showed on my face. Perhaps it was merely the
result of some misunderstanding, some calumny.... All around
me I saw people coming together and going off two by two.
But *I* could still make no contact. And it was spring, then
summer; these things always happen in summer (August is a
terrible month for the unsatisfied): the days are 'too beautiful', nature seems happier than one is oneself – Heaven knows
I went through it. And all the time this one obsession, and a
total inability to work, to tear myself away from this obsession. Loveless days going by one after the other. Another loveless day. Another day of defeat. And yet it *counted*, each day
counted and brought me nearer to the grave – a right that only
happy days should have. I have a horrifying memory of those
days, and a strong desire to help others who long to give but
can find no one to give to. It is a particularly tragic thing for
women, for all sorts of obvious reasons: their youth passes

more quickly, they are more dependent, more susceptible to
other people's opinion of them, etc. I could almost take you
to task for not complaining loudly enough about *your* case, as
though you were not fully aware of your tragedy.

How did I get over it? I don't know. It just 'happened'.
How? Just 'like that'. You will say this is a strange answer
from a man who prides himself on being clear-sighted. But
there it is. Nature, for a time, was against me; then she was
on my side. Like a wind that changes during a game: now
against you, now for you. Since then, I have put more trust
in nature.

Let me conclude with a comparison similar to the one I
made in my last letter. A bird flies into a room by mistake.
It flutters around, seeking a way out. But there is none. Or
rather there is, but the bird cannot see it, because birds cannot
see everything, poor things. Suddenly it sees a thin streak of
light – a half-open door. It swoops, and finds itself in a lumber-
room lit by a paraffin lamp. But there again there is no way
out, and again it beats against the walls. That bird is you, and
the lumber-room with its paraffin lamp is me (you recognize
my well-known modesty).

For, of course, nothing has changed as far as our relationship
is concerned. Me, 'take' you (as you so nicely put it)? No,
never.

Good heavens! For once, this is a long letter.

Believe me, yours sympathetically,

C.

P.S. I forgot to tell you that during the time I was unable to
'make contact' with women, I had four little sleeping companions, each one nicer than the next, whom I was very fond
of. So I was only 'walled in' by a sort of mental blockage.

Costals' Notebook

At the Piérards'! O charming one! I want to lift her up in the
palms of my hands, like a marine Venus in her shell. Exactly
the right size for me: if she were smaller, I would overwhelm

her; if bigger, there would be too much of her. She is much admired, which pleases me as though I were her papa. Dance with her. She dances so demurely that I wonder if she does it to tease me.

She came with the Saulniers. So, neither father nor mother. Divine absence! May it last for ever! If only girls knew how much they would gain by being foundlings.

No profound desire for her body. No sign of the tornado of desire – dry mouth, tottering legs, etc. An urge to say sweet, caressing things – an urge aroused by her, though these words could well have fallen on other ears than hers . . .

How like a little cat as she watches me write my name in a book I had brought her, as if she expected to see a little bird fly out of my pen. (Before setting out, I had solemnly kissed the cover of this book that I was about to give her.) Exactly like a cat perched on your desk watching you write. And again like a cat when we were sitting side by side and I felt her body leaning lightly against mine, like a river against its bank.

My hand on the arm of her chair in a caressing gesture, a gesture of possession almost. Once, but fleetingly, almost imperceptibly, she put her hand on my arm. Yet she is very reserved. Obviously she is pleased that she attracts me, but with an entrancing simplicity and naturalness. Not a grain of coquetry, in spite of her looks. Simply, almost negligently dressed. Is this an affectation? She claims not to like social life, not to like luxury, etc. Making allowances for a bit of affectation, which is conceivable, there must be some truth in this, for, being what she is, if she liked social life one would meet her everywhere.

Apart from what she says about her own character (she speaks from the heart when she speaks about herself – like most young girls), nothing, literally nothing memorable about her conversation. Her intellectual education is nil. But so much the better: schooling is for fools. A girl who has obtained some diploma or other, even if she later forgets all she has learnt, will still retain, it seems to me, like a pretty vase which once contained a nauseous liquid, the bad smell of the half-knowledge she once ingurgitated.

She is twenty-one, it appears. Let's say twenty-two. One wouldn't think it: she looks really young.

She spoke of her father: 'Papa used to be very interested in physical culture. He's a real enthusiast.'

'Is he ... does he have a profession?'

'No, he does nothing. ...' As she said this, she was visibly embarrassed. She's ashamed that her father lives on a private income! When she pronounced the word 'enthusiast' I gave a shudder, as though I had touched a snake.

She talked of one of her cousins. The fact that she had a cousin seemed to me strange, offensive, almost a provocation. O foundlings!

My behaviour was as bad as hers was good – taking her by the arm, propelling her to the buffet with my hands round her waist, trying to show off *urbi et orbi* that she was mine. How course and vulgar and naïvely pleased with myself! Like a cavalry sergeant. One often sees a man with a pleasant and intelligent face suddenly transformed into an idiot, his smile at once inane and conceited, his whole attitude at once awkward and affected. What has happened? He has just met a woman who attracts him. And inside him it is just the same. For the apparition of an attractive woman instantly lowers a man's self-respect, as sharply as a lump of ice lowers the temperature of a drink. Which is why anyone who loves humanity cannot love women. But *I* don't care a damn for humanity, and I love women.

I would have invited her to the cinema, but to have her see a film full of half-naked gigolos – no thanks! And anyhow, it wouldn't suit such an 1890-ish young person. The Opéra-Comique seemed rather to suggest itself. I told her I had a box for Tuesday. 'I'll ask my parents and telephone you.'

The box will be a *baignoire*,* and I shall have booked all the seats in it. Unfortunately we shall have those maddening musicians to reckon with, with their passion for noise. Ah well, if words are forbidden, gestures will have to do instead.

Of course, she may well refuse: because she hasn't the same degree of vitality as I have.

Next day – At one o'clock last night, my heart was still beating

*Big ground-floor box (behind the stalls) (*Translator's note*).

as fast as at eight o'clock in the evening when I left her. And then I was visited by a dream in which this chit of a girl betrayed me, as though I must realize that she was already capable of making me suffer. Oh, I didn't really suffer, but I felt a twinge.

Waiting for her telephone call: anxious all morning, convinced that the telephone would be out of order just at the moment she called, starting up at every bicycle bell in the street.

The telephone! She'll come! When I hear her voice on the telephone, Priapus himself could not outreach me – whereas, even when I was dancing with her, I could echo the words of the prophet: 'Tyre, though thou be sought for, yet shalt thou never be found again.'

I think of the day that voice will get on my nerves when I hear it on the telephone – and I shall leave France in order not to hear it any more.

How disgraceful of her parents to let her go out alone with Pierre Costals! A fine way to behave! Now, if anything happens, whose fault will it be? It's disheartening to see all moral standards crumbling like this in the France of 1927.

Wednesday – Opéra-Comique. *Madame Butterfly.*
After Madame Butterfly,
Ouch!

Yesterday a sergeant, today an undergraduate.

Not a sign of life from the object. Or rather, yes, one: in the second act she moved her chair a little away from mine. Can the object be virtuous? The thought sent a shiver down my spine. I was crestfallen: 'I'll have to start again from scratch. . . .'

Paralysed. By her reserve. By the absurdity of a novelist kissing a girl in a box at the Opéra-Comique. I wanted to be 'ninetyish', but I had gone too far. A telltale remark by the usherette had revealed that I had reserved every seat in the box; how could the object not have guessed? The absurdity of this too carefully planned evening!

Not even the knowledge of my superiority over her from so many points of view could lift me out of my doldrums.

This knowledge became blurred, and I could only see what made me her inferior. She, a pretty twenty-year-old, and I an intellectual, an old thinking-pot of thirty-four.

Our conversation was a veritable swamp of platitude. I watched her hands, as though I hoped to see her twisting them in her anxiety at my failure to declare myself. When I said: 'It's frantically boring', she answered: 'Yes'. This 'yes' cut me to the quick; doubtless I expected her to throw herself into my arms, saying: 'How could anything be boring with you, my beloved?' The situation became so intolerable that I suggested we should leave. She said 'yes' once more without a moment's hesitation, which cut me to the quick once more. (How childish her 'yeses' are! The intonation of a doll when one squeezes its stomach.) We left, eyed by the usherettes with looks that powerfully suggested this thought: 'Well, well! There's a couple who must have been having a good time. But they can't hold out any longer, so off they go to the hotel.'

In short: a cold douche in the *baignoire*.*

The evening has made two things clear at least: that she is not in love with me, and that I am not in love with her.

Perhaps it was simply that, like racing cyclists, neither of us wanted to be the first to start. Perhaps her behaviour was calculated, to keep me in suspense. A rash calculation, then, for what's to prevent me from dropping her here and now? I'm not the man to persist if a woman refuses; there are a hundred more where she came from; they're all interchangeable. I'm glad to find that I don't love her any more than I did, and am therefore still free: I can take what I want from this game.

If today's set-back is not the sort of disaster from which one never recovers, it is the rock-bottom from which one may spring up even higher than before. What a leap it will be, with the impetus gained from the recoil. As a matter of fact I'm going to write to her: thus keeping the undergraduate touch. By means of this letter, I shall be reversing the situation, giving her back the initiative, driving her into a corner. My cards are on the table; now it's up to her.

*A pun here: *baignoire* = 'bath' as well as 'box' (*Translator's note*).

The ethics of honour, or simply the proprieties, were invented to provide an exact counterpart to natural ethics, thus allowing us to win both ways.

If Rosine is ugly and importunate, natural ethics to the fore: 'How could I be such a monster! Me, do such a thing to your venerable father! (or your husband, my best friend!).' But if she is attractive and aloof: 'How could I be such a boor as to remain insensible to your charms? I refuse to be so insulting.'

One finds the two alternatives in every field. If someone insults you: 'What! kill someone for such a trifle? Is that what honour demands?' or else, contrariwise: 'I killed him because I was insulted. My honour....' Etc.

Pierre Costals	to Mademoiselle Solange Dandillot
Paris	*Avenue de Villiers, Paris*

12 May 1927

You must admit, dear Mademoiselle, that last night was not quite the thing, and that indeed we provided a somewhat distressing spectacle. You made me very nervous – froze me in fact. Did you do it on purpose? Or am I simply a donkey?

It will come as no surprise to you, I think, to learn that I have a rather special feeling towards you. If you find it objectionable, let us leave it at that. I shall feel some regret, perhaps a twinge of pain, but I do not want to be importunate, and after all, the world is big enough. If, on the other hand, like an intelligent girl, you would like us to try our luck again, just tell me. Only in that case you must also tell me that you will allow me a certain degree of familiarity with you, and a modicum of those gestures which not only Nature, but Society itself, expected of us last night. Those august moral personages are at present overcome with amazement and wrath at our attitude; it is up to us to appease them. But you must make your intentions clear to me, for I do not feel inclined to offer you a purely platonic friendship, and even less do I feel inclined to be spurned by a woman, something that has never happened to me in my life.*

---

*This is a lie (*Author's note*).

Write to me or telephone me. But I'd prefer a nice letter; letters are more substantial. Not to mention all the advantages of the written word (I know what I mean, even if you don't).

Once more: failing a note or a telephone call from you telling me whether I behaved well or whether I behaved in an awkward and ill-bred manner last night, we shall not see each other again. It depends entirely on you.

Au revoir, my dear Mademoiselle, or adieu. It is possible that I am about to entertain for you a feeling with a touch of profundity about it (but I'm not yet absolutely sure). There is an impulse there that it would be a pity to waste. See if it displeases you or not, without considering my pleasure but thinking only of your own. And give me your answer with the same frankness and trust that I pride myself on having shown here.

Costals

Written by Costals in his diary

Have written her a letter that isn't up to much. How strange it is that when I write to an unknown or scarcely known woman who attracts me, I can avoid flannel only through passion or cynicism. The language of passion being out of the question, this missive is a compromise between twaddle and impertinence. She will enjoy the twaddle, will fail to notice the impertinence, and will telephone me within 24 hours.

(In fact I have no idea. I'm incapable of foreseeing her reactions in any given circumstance. In dealing with her I have the impression that I'm the Quai d'Orsay*: I do everything gropingly and by the grace of God.)

There's something poignant for me in imagining the happiness I might have given to other women with such a letter but have refused them. And this feeling has a great deal of charm.

The fact that I find it charming ought to make me feel that I'm a cad. Am I a cad? Brunet, at any rate, pays me compliments: 'Don't you think it's terrific to have a pater like you?' In fact, he's amazed: 'Why are you so nice?'

---

*The French Foreign Office (*Translator's note*).

The thing is that there are some people I love and some I don't. That sounds too simple. But it's the key to it all.

No, the heart is not affected, nor the flesh, but something is. Whence comes this obscure and passionate desire to please her? If only I could hear a tremor in her voice....

Mademoiselle Dandillot did not write a 'nice letter'. She telephoned. The gist of her reply was: 'I must confess that I didn't really understand your letter. But I like you very much. So why don't we meet again?' They arranged to go to a concert. Costals chose the most expensive in Paris, because when one goes out with a woman it does not matter whether a thing is good or bad, but only that it should cost a great deal of money.

The entry of the female chorus conjured up a vision of lady prisoners at the gates of Saint-Lazare: ancient, deformed, sinister, incredibly frumpish. Then came the musicians, squat little fellows with handkerchiefs tucked into their necks like diners: *Froggy for ever!** The efforts of these poor wretches to look like artists (long hair down their necks, locks falling over their temples) were enough to bring tears to one's eyes. Sitting on metal garden chairs in an unbelievable church-hall décor – squalid 'foliage' and peeling 'pilasters' – they offered a spectacle which seemed so enchanting to some of the audience that they examined it through opera-glasses.†

---

*In English in the original (*Translator's note*).

†Need I point out that this chapter is a sort of leg-pull written by someone who allows himself an occasional flight of fancy, and that only those without a sense of humour could take offence at it? One can caricature what one loves all the more sharply the more one loves it. The things I have written or could have written about Algeria and Spain! Sympathy with music-lovers, gratitude towards musicians: such being my sincere feelings, I can allow myself to cut a few capers. And I seem to remember that in some of my other books I have spoken of music (church music, Russian, Spanish and Arab music, etc.) with a seriousness and enthusiasm which should, if necessary, excuse these pages (*Author's note*).

'If music softens manners', said Costals, 'it doesn't ennoble faces. There are about sixty musicians there, so I realize they can't all be expected to have genius written all over their faces. But why don't they give them masks, as in the theatre of antiquity, or hide them in a pit as at Bayreuth?'

Monsieur was *very* fastidious. However, Solange seemed to approve. But he felt that she was in a mood to approve of everything he said. He cast his eyes over the audience, and the extraordinary ugliness of these men and women, the squalid, grotesque and antiquated décor of the hall, made him look away. Literally repelled, his eyes swivelled up to the ceiling, in the hope of seeing the forms of a nobler humanity painted there. But on the ceiling too there was nothing but fussily decorated gilt plaster, blackened with dirt as though by factory smoke. It was obvious that generations had breathed in this hall. If Costals had not been with Solange, he would have left at once: it was almost more than he could bear.

Soon, the lights were switched on and platform and auditorium were brilliantly illuminated. It was a monstrous idea; both, in fact, should have been plunged in darkness.

As there was some delay in starting, people began to grow impatient and to drum their feet. But after a few seconds it died down. Then there was another little outburst, equally short-lived. Odd little gusts of bad temper in this crowd, odd because so brief. Even an outburst of patriotism would have lasted a few seconds longer.

At last the conductor lowered his baton and all the people on the platform began simultaneously to make a noise.

As the musicians frenziedly wielded their bows it seemed to Costals that he could smell the lady-violinists' armpits, and he was moved by this; it was the best part of the show, he thought.

Solange, sitting sideways, had moved closer to him. He stroked her smooth, clear neck. He noticed that she had brought her face close to his, as thought to enter his aura. Little islands of skin showed here and there through her blouse, like sand-banks in a white salt flat. The features of her face that he found unattractive he saw as emergency exits through which he could escape should the occasion arise, or as ambiguous clauses in a contract: that rather heavy chin would one day allow him to leave her with a light heart. He kissed the nape of her neck; she did not flinch (that little-girl odour of her hair!) And his blood stirred like foliage as his hand traced, through her dress, her suspenders and her long thighs. He was surprised that such a respectable girl allowed her thighs to be stroked in public. He had not realized that already she wanted anything he wanted.

'I think there's something ... how shall I put it? oppressive about that first movement (of the symphony),' said Mlle Dandillot, who was indeed oppressed, but for other reasons. 'Don't you?'

'I don't think anything.... Look here, tell me honestly, do you like music?' he asked after a moment with a suspicious look.

She raised her eyebrows as if to say: 'So so....' Then she said:

'What I don't like is church music.'

'Ah!' he thought, 'how unaffected she is! The delightful thing about her is that she has no interest in anything. So she doesn't try to dazzle you with specialized knowledge. And also that she hasn't an idea in her head, which for a woman, is the surest way of not having wrong ones.'

He put his arm around her. She was leaning right over now, almost lying on him. Pretending to pick something up from the floor, he kissed her body, scenting the rubbery odour of her suspender-belt through her skirt. From time to time he pressed his face against the nape of her neck and kept it there, as though to absorb, slowly, everything this woman had to give. 'No', he told himself delightedly, 'never has anyone behaved as badly as this with a woman in public!' He had always enjoyed being self-contradictory, and it pleased him to think that if he had seen another couple behaving in this way, he would have found it difficult to restrain himself from calling out to them: 'I say, what are hotels for?'

Leaning back a little, he saw behind Solange's back the young woman in the seat next to her; she was sitting well back in her seat, listening with her mouth half-open and her eyes closed. She was not pretty, but Costals desired her: (1) because he found it appropriate that, at the very moment he was caressing one young woman for the first time, he should desire another; (2) because she appeared to be asleep and this inevitably aroused in him the idea of taking advantage of her sleep; and (3) because it struck him that in order to experience such ecstasy from something as insipid as this music, she must be mentally deranged, and since he only liked simple, healthy girls like Solange there was something agreeable about wanting a deranged woman.

Suddenly the young woman flung her head back in a wild gesture, like the caracara bird when it has finished its call, the very picture of sensual delight. It was obvious that one of those sounds had penetrated to the most sensitive point of her being.

So Costals stretched his arm behind Solange's seat and placed his hand on the back of the other seat in such a way that the other woman's shoulder leaned against it. But the gentle pressure he imparted to it produced no reaction from the young woman, who was completely engrossed in her semiquavers. He gave up. And in any case, since these contortions gave him cramp in his arm, the game was not worth the candle. Anyone foolish enough to imagine that all this was just a try-on, a sly and underhanded sacristan's trick, will be disconcerted to know that: (1) Costals really wanted to embark on a serious adventure with the unknown woman, to arrange a meeting with her, and (2) to do so without attracting Solange's attention (for example by passing a note to the unknown woman behind Solange's back) would have been excellent sport, like one of those feats at the circus during which the band stops, and therefore not at all the work of a sacristan but rather of an archangel.

The noise from the platform ceased and there was some applause, accompanied by demonstrations of hatred on the part of a few members of the audience against those who were applauding.

Thereafter the music took a new turn from which it was clear that this was the real classical thing.

'Well, do you like *this*?' Costals asked Solange.

'I don't mind it.'

'You don't.... Splendid! Absolutely splendid!'

'You don't understand,' she said, a bit nettled. 'The cubist music they were playing before this gave me the creeps. But this I don't mind.'

'I can see you don't care two hoots for it,' said Costals, 'and that's as it should be. You're a good child.'

'But I *do* care!' said Solange, with the woman's genius for squandering her advantage.

'No, no,' said Costals, chivalrous as ever, 'You don't care two hoots.' He was interrupted by a chorus of 'Ssh!'

Suddenly the most terrible cries rang out on the platform. It was as though a woman, at the very instant of giving birth, learned that she had not only lost all her money but that her lover had abandoned her. On hearing these yelps, Costals screwed up his face and instinctively tried to block his ears, but the hall exploded in a thunder of cheers. Such profound disagreements bring home to a man that a society is no longer for him. Costals remembered the truly 'immortal' pages in *La Nouvelle Héloïse* on the Frenchman's idea of music. 'They can appreciate no other effects but vocal outbursts; they are sensitive only to noise,' writes Rousseau.

'I don't think women are made for singing,' said Solange. 'Could that be profound?' the writer wondered. 'But what is profundity? A chamber pot is profound, too.'

Raucous voices (young people's?) were shouting 'Encore!' and people were still clapping: public manifestations of admiration in Europe are more or less what one would expect from the savages of Oceania. Three or four times the singers returned to take a bow. And Costals thought: 'Poor fellows!' The conductor, who was an obvious charlatan (for which reason he was admired, especially by the women), left the platform and returned several times, doubtless in order to receive several rations of applause. These re-entries were exactly like those of a clown. And yet the entire audience was in the seventh heaven.

Thereafter, as though to cure everyone's eardrums, the genii of music, or rather the bank clerks, played very softly: it might have been a clyster-pipe band. There were even moments when, literally, not a sound could be heard. These moments were magnificent.

Costals looked round the audience. A third of it was made up of people who spontaneously enjoyed the noise they heard; another third of people who enjoyed it only through an intellectual effort, remembering everything they had heard and read about each piece; the remaining third consisting of people who felt nothing, but absolutely nothing. All of them, however, adopted the most elegant poses in order to receive this manna. Pig-faced men with eye-glasses pretended that the slightest whisper in the hall spoiled their ecstasy. Pig-faced men in spectacles bent down towards their brats (for six-year-old children were to be seen in the audience, evidently brought there as a punishment for some grave misdemeanour) to draw their attention to some sacrosanct passage so that they should know once and for all that that was where they ought to feel moved. A number of women, like Solange's neighbour, considered it unseemly to do otherwise than keep their eyes closed. In unanimous mutual mimicry these people aped one another's earnest expressions, while from the platform the miasma of sound continued inexhaustibly to spread.

'They're depraved,' said Costals, casting a look of reprobation round the hall. 'Apart from the simpletons – for the donkey must have his bran.* At all events, an unhealthy place, and I wouldn't like to take the responsibility of chaperoning you here any longer. Shall we go?'

'Yes.'

Always that 'yes'! Had he said to her: 'Let's stay', or 'Come to my flat', or 'Let's go to Kamchatka', it seemed to him that her answer would have been the same: 'Yes.' And when he repeated it to himself with the same intonation she used, something stirred in his heart, like a bird in its nest.

So they left this temple of collective auto-suggestion. Costals remembered that when he was twelve years old his grandmother had taken him to another temple of the same sort. They were doing *Le Malade imaginaire*. When it came to the scene in which the actors pursue each other into the auditorium, the old lady, who from the beginning had shown signs of impatience, got up and said: 'Come on, let's go. It's *too*

_____
*An untranslatable pun here. The French has *son*, which = 'sound' or 'bran' (*Translator's note*).

142

stupid.' An unforgettable impression it had made, on a child who was already only too inclined to judge for himself. *There* was a family in which received ideas cut no ice.

He could have taken a taxi, but preferred to see her home on foot: they both needed time to recover. He was so confident of obtaining whatever he wanted from her that he thought it advisable to keep something to look forward to: what, after all, would be left once he had taken her? Besides, for him it was a matter of principle that a self-respecting man should let a few opportunities slip. Accustomed to success in everything, he took pride in loading the dice against himself.

Not far from her house he stopped her underneath a street-lamp and stood in front of her, gripping her arms. Assuming no doubt that he was about to kiss her, she took a few steps backwards into the shadow – out of shyness or modesty. He drew her towards him; her arms hung limp, and she did not lift her face. As he bent down to kiss her on the mouth, she suddenly let her head fall so low that Costals' lips brushed the fringe of her hair. Putting a finger under her chin, he lifted her head and kissed her on the forehead; she remained quite still. Feeling a little dampened, he walked on, and she followed him. He had to force himself a bit in order to sound friendly as he asked: 'Do you want to go to the Bois after dinner on Friday?' Calmly, but with an eager expression on her face, she agreed. 'Your nose is shiny,' he told her. 'Powder it.'

As soon as Costals had turned away from her after saying good-bye, Mademoiselle Dandillot, instead of following him with her eyes until he had disappeared, which would have been the recognized thing to do, pressed the button on the outer door and climbed the stairway, the lift being out of order. As soon as she began the ascent, she had a painful intuition that she would be unable to reach the fourth floor, on which she lived, without something happening which she dreaded but could not define. She went up gripping the banister with one hand while the other kept contact with the wall, against which she scraped her hand-bag, tearing the leather on a nail. She reached the door of her flat, like an exhausted swimmer reaching a buoy, opened it, went into her bedroom, and sat down on her bed. 'What's the matter with me?' she said out loud, making a face. A late tram rattled past below; she winced and said, again out loud: 'Oh, those trams!' then winced again on hearing a motor-horn. Then she thought she had left the electric light on, not only in the hall but even in the rooms where she had not been; she went to see. By now her whole body was shot through with the sort of vibration that shakes a steamer when it pitches heavily and the propeller revolves outside the water. She lay down, her hands gripping the edges of the mattress, rolled over first to the right and then to the left, like the carcass of a dog being rolled over by the surf. She got up and removed her dress, so impatiently that she forgot to unfasten it and her head got stuck in it. She snatched a magazine from the table and tore it in two, her face still contorted, then tore the pieces in two. 'Am I going to have a fit of hysterics?' A sudden wave of nausea overcame her, and she felt herself turn pale. She went over to the mirror, overcome with an obscure desire to give herself a fright. Then her stomach heaved violently and sent her flying to the wash-stand, where, clutching the basin with one hand and holding her forehead with the other, she vomited.

When she felt better, she put on her night-dress and lay down on her bed without taking off her shoes. Her love for Costals became confused in her mind with the relief of having vomited. A sentence engraved itself in her head, mysterious and inevitable as an inscription in a phylactery: 'He has given me profound peace.' The whole of her life until these last few days seemed to her like a broad stretch of landscape, even and serene. Then a shell had fallen. And now the countryside was shattered and transformed, but the calm and the light remained the same. She turned over and stretched herself out on her stomach in a familiar, childish position, burying her fore-arms under the bolster to seek the coolness there, as one buries them in the desert sand, which becomes colder and colder the deeper one goes. She said again: 'He has given me profound peace,' and dropped her shoes off by scraping the heels against the side of the bed. Then she went to the book-shelf, took down the novel Costals had given her, got into bed, put out the light, and lay down still holding the book, which she slid under the sheet, a finger between the pages.

Thérèse Pantevin   to Pierre Costals
La Vallée Maurienne   *Paris*

15 May 1927

My Beloved,

I suffer, I am plagued with temptations, I suffer. Yesterday in church, while the priest was reciting the litany of the Blessed Virgin, I interspersed her name with yours. 'Heart most gentle. Heart most mild. Heart most wonderful. Heart without stain.' And I thought to myself that I ought to add: *Miserere mei*, 'Have pity on me.'

Have pity on me, Monsieur. I am a poor girl. Pity is the real miracle, not Our Lord's walking on the water. Pity is all-embracing and sufficient to itself. I think it can even dispense with an object.

Take me in your lap so that I do not die.

Marie

Write to me and tell me you have pity on me.

Andrée Hacquebaut   to Pierre Costals
Saint-Léonard   *Paris*

Tuesday, 19 May 1927

Your last letter crossed with mine. It has softened my rancour without reviving my ardour. You have a way of rubbing salt in wounds which you're ostensibly trying to heal.... You're a past master at distilling the sugar and the acid at one and the same time, at simultaneously licking and biting, like a wild animal. Are you by nature fundamentally good, but corrupted by a perverse intellect? Or fundamentally bad, but with enough decency to feel some remorse? Do you play at being good, or do you play at being bad, or do you just play? Perhaps it's a terrible law of nature that the

145

superior man lends but never gives himself. In fact you've written as much : 'A creator who gives himself surrenders himself.' But *you* take the art of self-withdrawal to the ultimate pitch of refinement. Everything that comes from you is equivocal, double-edged. And the disturbing thing is that the first impression you give is one of simplicity and directness. You pour out poison and medicine in turn, almost simultaneously, but in such a subtle way that one is neither killed by the poison nor cured by the medicine. One remains in an ambiguous state which would be suffering enough in itself even if the elements of suffering were not dominant in it. Before your last letter I sustained myself on the horror I felt for you : for the one before was a masterpiece of pure malice. (Malice, that supreme banality, from a person one has placed above everyone else ! And all that time wasted in fighting against one another, when it could be spent fighting side by side !) That horror had something solid about it, which I found almost restful. Your last letter – apart from the postscript, which must be a joke – shows so much understanding that one no longer knows where one is.... My heart goes out to you in spite of myself, as from a little sister to a big brother – that feeling which used to be so familiar to me. You stab me to the heart, yet it is with you that I am tempted to seek refuge. Then one says to oneself : 'If he understands so well, and yet does not lift a finger to save me, he is all the more criminal.' One feels more resentful towards you, and yet one cannot help having a sort of insane confidence in you. One can neither hate you wholeheartedly nor love you wholeheartedly : one adores you in a fog of anger and reproach, one hates you without being absolutely sure that it isn't love. Is that what you wanted, you who appear so passionate but are in fact so much in control of everything you do? Are you a sort of satanic alchemist concocting the feelings you want people to have for you with the same icy indifference as you measure out the feelings you entertain for others? Or is your attitude spontaneous, natural, guileless, unaware? Whatever it is, I don't know what you're like to those who do not love you, but I do know what you're like to those who do. *Flagellum amantibus* : a scourge to those who love him.

As for me, if you're playing some abominable game with me, which at this moment I'm inclined to believe you are (I mean at the very moment of writing these words, for at other moments I tell myself you're merely a child juxtaposed with a man rich in solemn meditation and weighty experience, Faust and Eliakim inextricably merged, in other words a monster – though if you are such a monster you cannot help yourself and are forgiven) – if you're playing a game with me quite consciously, I can only tell you I'm not strong enough for you, and cry 'Pax'. And in any case I'm not playing any more. You were once an element of vitality, of inner fecundity, of active torment in my life. Now there's nothing. You dry everything up, like the wind. You have mummified the tenderness, so fresh, so deep, so absolute, which I felt for you. Like a sort of white frost, you have blighted feelings which, had they flowered, could have brought forth wonderful fruit. So much so that you have relieved me (in this at least you operated a cure) of the misery and the fear of growing old. I wanted to stay young during the time I loved and was loved, because to my mind a woman of forty in bed.... But now, what does it matter? There are moments now when it seems to me that I can no longer give you anything at all, moments when it seems to me that you have pulled out by the roots everything that blossomed inside me, and that you could fall ill, even die, without my feeling anything. Quite honestly, even that time in Paris I wasn't all that sorry to leave you. I went home drunk, as it were, with a sort of deliverance, and for a week I was almost happy by comparison. As soon as I got home, I removed your photograph from the wall of my room. But it was really only a gesture. I put it back later. Why not? It was doing me neither good nor harm. I can see myself writing you a solemn farewell, and next time I come to Paris, asking you to kiss me like a sister, so that at least I shall have had one kiss from you. It would be the only thing I should ever have asked of you. Because I would have you know *once and for all* that I have never begged anything from you, your company, your friendship, your intimacy, or your love. I offered, and you turned me down; quite a different matter. My pride permitted me to offer. It would not permit me to beg.

Wednesday

As I have said: all I feel towards you now is emptiness, exhaustion – the very thing you wanted. And yet, this emptiness is itself a feeling, is still superfluous in my life. As long as you are still in my life, as long as I have still not cut all the threads that bind me to you, I shall not be available for anyone else. I shall *never* dissociate – my body to another, my heart to you. And if another should give me or allow me love, or its semblance, I shall not keep my friendship for you. (Not much loss.... For to have from a man what I have from you is to have lost him already. Nothing in the present, nothing in the future, nothing to remember.... And anyhow, a woman doesn't go on giving her friendship to a man who has refused it.) You are the only friend I could not keep in a normal life. Costals, the friend of the family, my children's favourite uncle, no, never! The reverse side of my feeling for you is nothingness, just as the reverse side of your sensual excesses is Jansenism. You will represent lost love for me, not friendship. You won't turn the torrent into an irrigation channel, nor the wild pony into a plough-horse. And so desperately, at the moment, do I need that normal life in which you can have no part, so desperately do I need to embrace reality rather than dreams, to hold in my arms a man or a child of my own, so grateful will I be to the nice ordinary chap who allows me to love him, that I shall give myself to him entirely, with my will at least. Even more than this, though I don't much care for children, in my desperation I have reached the point of wanting a child without a husband. Because, since the man refuses to be loved, and one cannot bear him if one does not love him, only the child can take one out of oneself. And so, whatever happened, I should no longer need you. Yes, I should infinitely prefer to have a beloved creature in my arms, *even if he didn't love me at all*, than to have his purest, most exclusive tenderness in his absence.

Friday

I can bear it no longer, I can bear it no longer. A human being has a certain capacity for suffering; beyond that, he

dies or finds release no matter how. Suffering cannot indefinitely remain suffering; it changes into something else. For four
months – ever since Paris – you have kept me living in a house
on fire. Either I had to die of asphyxiation, or jump out of the
window and break my back – which is what I have done.

I don't beg, I shall never beg anything at all from you. But
I tell you again, solemnly, irrevocably: if I have to give up
hope of being yours some day, life will no longer have any
meaning for me. After all, Costals, after all, I must live! Is
there not a single sentence in the hundreds of letters I've
written to you that might touch your heart even now? I want
to go on hoping, persuading myself that your attitude is the
result of scruples. When you come to realize, in six months'
or a year's time, that you're ruining my life, perhaps.... Perhaps between now and then you'll give me your love. Perhaps
you'll have ceased to believe that I'm a 'nice person' whom it
would be wrong to 'lead astray'. Perhaps curiosity – for my
body and what it can offer you – will have got the better of
you. If you had met me in a railway carriage, perhaps, for the
fun of it.... If I hadn't loved you, and had wounded you
or angered you, perhaps you would have done violence to me,
for the sheer pleasure of overcoming me and dominating
me.... (It's true that if I didn't love you I wouldn't want to be
yours.) I can still wait. A year or two more, perhaps.... My
youth is not yet over. I don't look my age, I've often been
told. If I hadn't admitted my age to you, you would think
me younger. All you can see in me is a black-clad provincial,
an earnest intellectual. Whereas, if I were at all happy, however illusorily, I would still be capable of so much playfulness,
such a blossoming out.

With you, as far as I'm concerned, it must be everything or
nothing. As I have told you, I no longer have any feeling for
you, nothing live, nothing that moves. But if you yourself
were to move, *it* would move. For what is latent beneath *it* is
not friendship but love. It could burst forth again, as a flame
springs up from what seemed to be nothing but dead wood
and ashes. If the worst came to the worst I could kill this
latent love, or at least stifle it, prevent it from coming to the
surface; what I cannot do is dilute it. In order to go on feeling

anything for you at all, I must have the certitude that one day you will be more than a friend. One evening we exchanged a lot of fine phrases, you and I – especially you – about friendship between men and women. Friendship between men and women is what music is to the instrument that produces it. Friendship between men and women is something totally disembodied and ethereal, something totally different from sensuality, but which can only exist through sensuality. Friendship is no longer possible between us without a pact, a solemn promise that one day it will be something else. One day? When? Whenever you like – in six months, in a year, if that is your whim. But what I must have is your firm promise, your promise on everything you hold most sacred. Then I can wait. Otherwise I can bear it no longer, not a moment longer. Unless I change the present, in which I am torn between hope and despair, into irrevocable past or potential future, unless I pull out the knife, I shall go mad.

A.

This letter remained unanswered.

The scene took place in a restaurant in the Bois de Boulogne. (Each of these restaurants in the Bois evoked contradictory memories for Costals: hours of intoxication when he was there with a woman he had not yet enjoyed; hours of deadly boredom when he was there with a woman who was already his.) Birds could be heard flitting from branch to branch, their shadows streaking the trunks of the trees as they passed. Above a lawless world, they flew to kill time.

He was saying to Solange:

'I'm not in love with you, nor you with me, and that's as it should be. For God's sake, don't let's alter it! So, you've never had any feelings for a man?'

'Never.'

'Never been kissed?'

'Sometimes, by surprise. And I fled at once. But never twice, If you only saw me snubbing people!'

'But look at those handsome young men. Why wouldn't you want them to love you?'

150

'I realize they have handsome faces. But what difference do you think that makes to me? What connection is there between my affection and a handsome face?'

'And yet I only fell for you because of your face!'

'Ah, but you're a man.'

'Never been deeply unhappy either?'

'No.'

'Never cried?'

'I don't know what it means.'

'Well, well!' he thought, 'here's the ideal cold fish.' At the same time he was surprised that she should allow him to stroke her hair and her legs and kiss her in public. 'It's all very inconsistent.... But what *is* consistent, except the behaviour of characters in novels and plays?'

As they were sitting down to table, a small child who was walking past with some other diners caught sight of Solange and stopped, entranced by her face. 'I don't know why children always like me,' she remarked. Costals, seeing the child's expression, understood why: because they were dazzled by her beauty. And this took him back, full of wonderment, to those days of old when beauty had a power of its own.

When the waiter said: 'As Madame wishes....' Costals frowned: this 'Madame' raised the spectre of the nuptial Hippogriff. 'What's at the back of her mind? And her parents'? Mistress? Wife? Bah! Never mind all that. If the Hippogriff rears its head there'll be plenty of time to try conclusions once more with my old enemy.'

Costals had always been struck, not so much by the (perfectly legitimate) tendency of girls to see matrimony wherever they go, and to want men to marry them, as by their obstinate belief that he might consider marrying them, even if such a contingency was so improbable as to verge on the grotesque. It seemed to him that each one of them was accompanied by a Chimera – remember, a Chimera has claws – which they mounted at the slightest provocation, or no provocation at all, to gallop around in an element in which they were so much at home that they seemed to be capable of anything – that is to say in a cloud of unreality. He had christened this Chimera 'the Hippogriff', and the word had become a familiar one on his lips and on those of the young ladies who did him the honour of having designs on him. According to whether the idea of a possible marriage gained or lost ground in their imaginations (for in Costals' it was always in neutral) the Hippogriff was said to be thriving or losing weight. Sometimes Costals would 'feed the Hippogriff', sometimes the Hippogriff was 'insatiable', and one of the most chaste of these girls had even gone so far as to designate a certain part of her anatomy, with which she was obsessed, the 'hippogriffic part'. Costals spent his time fighting against the Hippogriff, endeavouring to kill the monster – in other words to convince his girl-friends that nothing in the world would persuade him to marry them. But, like all good mythical creatures, the Hippogriff, brought low, had no sooner breathed its last than it came to life again more fiery than ever. Nothing is more difficult than to persuade a young woman that one has no desire – none whatsoever – to dedicate one's life to her.

After dinner, when night had fallen, they strolled down the avenue des Acacias. Hardly a bench there had not been turned into a bed for a couple glued together; yet nobody threw a bucket of water over them, as over rutting mongrels. 'Perhaps they'll teach me some new tricks,' thought Costals. But no; at each gesture they made he scoffed: 'Why, I know that one, fat-head!' Dismal how limited the register of caresses is. These couples, as identical in their reactions as in their postures, exasperated him in the end, with their apparent conviction that they were the only people in the world, and the smiles they gave you to invite you to admire their happiness, which would end up with the vitriol bottle and the intravenous injection. Truly a gigantic miasma of vulgarity (literature, films, newspapers, sentimental songs...) bore down on this unhappy man-woman combination. How bitter it was to be unable to escape it! After the tenth pair, Costals felt paralysed. 'In ten minutes' time, I shall be one of these puppets. Come on, I must take the plunge. Four or five more of these ecstatic couples and I'll no longer have the heart.'

He indicated a secluded path, making sure it was not one he already had memories of (no super-impressions – he was already too inclined to mix everything up).

'Shall we go down there?'

'If you like.'

They made their way through the trees, and came to a sort of clearing, where two iron chairs awaited them side by side, by special arrangement of the goddess Prema.

All at once he had her on his shoulder, her head thrown back, her eyes closed, offering her half-open mouth, not returning his kisses but letting him devour the inside of her mouth and her lips, never opening her eyes, never uttering a word. How was it possible that this slender form had become so solid and heavy in his arms? She was all corseted in rubber, armoured like a young Menelaus. At one moment she gave a little moan, as though she were about to burst into tears; from the way she clenched her lips against his, he guessed that she would one day have an aptitude for biting, and he felt her pointed nails scrape on his jacket, like the claws of a cat he had been holding in his arms thinking it was happy when in fact it was impatient to be off and would scratch him at any minute and escape. She took his wrist and gripped it more and more tightly, evidently trying to stop his embraces but failing to do so; and then a shudder ran through her. And all the time the paradise of her face lay open, motionless, and he was everywhere upon it with his mouth. She did not embrace him, did not even make the slightest show of doing so; she did not move her lips, never once returned a kiss. When he knelt down, she bowed her head completely, hiding her face. That she was his for the taking was patently obvious, but, as we have seen, he liked to proceed by degrees; besides, at that moment, sentiment was stronger in him than sensuality. And all the time he heard her rapid breathing.

From time to time he raised his head to recover his breath. A deep, protective silence seemed to have shaped itself to the very contours of their embrace. He caught sight of a stretch of water on their left that he had not noticed before; perhaps it had approached noiselessly so as not to take them by surprise. It glistened, motionless, beneath the thirsty trees. Fifty yards away from them there was a lighted car, with people who must have been picnicking on the grass, and children playing. Never would he forget her face when she opened her eyes for the first time and drew herself up – her eyes, normally rather screwed up, but now dilated, immense, staring at him without blinking. He scarcely recognized her; and she was seeing him for the first time; they were discovering each other. He said to her, as though she were really unrecognizable: 'Is it still you?' She said 'Yes', in a voice that was scarcely audible.

His watch pointed to half past midnight. 'We must go.' She got up without a word. Her hair had come undone, making her look like a little girl. She tidied it – in what a silence! It was he who handed her her hairpins, on the tips of his fingers. Then she stood in front of him, as she had stood the other day outside her house, smaller than he, her forehead bowed a little shyly, but her eyes still looking up at him without blinking, literally rooted in his. An unforgettable look, heart-rending in its directness. An unforgettable disharmony – or rather harmony – between her bowed, seemingly submissive head and this look of candour, almost provocative in its pride. She sought no higher than the face that was before her; her world stopped there.

He took her in his arms again, this time standing up, she with her head on his shoulder, he so intent on her mouth that he no longer knew who she was save by the taste of her mouth. He moved her from his left to his right shoulder with the same gesture – exactly the same – as that by which the matador transfers the bull from his left to his right side in the close *toreo*; with the same pose – exactly the same – as the matador adopts at that moment, feet firmly planted, slightly apart, back slightly arched; with the same grave expression – exactly the same – as the matador wears, and in his soul the same absolute mastery over himself and the other: intoxication and self-possession compounded in him as earth and water are compounded in clay. His domination over her was absolute, and he knew it. If he had said to her: 'Let's stay here all night', she would have stayed. If he had said 'Undress,' she would have stripped herself naked. She was subjugated. But if anything was equal to his domination over her it was his desire not to take advantage of it, or even to hurt her by pressing her too closely to him – for he could feel the play of his muscles, all that strength which, even if he were divested of intelligence, talent, money, would go on living within him for years to come, and tomorrow would make her happy. And his only precise sensations were the hardness of Solange's teeth, which he touched with his lips, and the scraping of her nails down his jacket, like one of those gestures people make in their death-throes.

They walked away unsteadily. He was holding her by the wrist. The lights had been turned off in the Bois; they had to go back as far as the Porte Maillot on foot, looking for a taxi. Now he was holding her left breast in the palm of his hand, and he felt it beat, as though it were the heart of creation beating in his palm. He made a few remarks, about the inconvenience of not being able to find a taxi. She made no reply. The impression she gave was of someone in a stupor, under some sort of spell. A little worried by her silence, he kissed her on the nape of the neck, as if to show her he still loved her. A young man called to them from a passing car: 'Not like that! On the mouth!' She did not laugh.

Still more worried, he asked her: 'What are you thinking about?' She replied: 'About this evening. . . .' O little girl!

At last they hailed a taxi.

From the avenue des Acacias to the avenue de Villiers, the taxi brought back a dead girl. No sooner was she inside it than she threw back her head. During the quarter of an hour the journey took she said not a single word, her eyes closed, her mouth glued to his, as though it were from there that she drew her breath and if she left it for an instant she would expire. Once, the taxi slowed down and almost stopped under the multi-coloured lights at a crossroads, and a face only a few inches away looked in at them through the rear window. He disengaged himself and brought her little bunched fist to his lips and kissed her nails and fingers. But then she lifted her face a little for him to take once more, and this slight movement was the only sign she gave to prove that she was not unconscious. In the avenue de Villiers he woke her. He said good-bye to her and added: 'I'll telephone you the day after tomorrow.' She got out without saying a word, like a sleepwalker, or like a ghost.

The taxi drove off. At the first bar that was still open, he said to the driver: 'Would you like a drink?' At the counter, he drank two glasses of white wine. He stopped the taxi before they arrived at his house, to get some air. It seemed to him that the terrestrial globe was rotating far below him, and that he walked stepping from cloud to cloud.

Pierre Costals   to Mademoiselle Rachel Guigui
Paris   *Paris*

23 May 1927

Well, dear Guiguite, this is it: we're going to drop you. We've taken up with an angel of heaven, and we've decided to concentrate on her, being no longer of an age when each one has her share of us but all have us in full.* We would come to her half-heartedly, our palate would be jaded – and we want to experience the sensation in all its glory. We expected a long night, pierced at last by the dawn of her consent, but this angel was carried off her feet forthwith: we scarcely had time to desire her. It's very serious; physically not perhaps pure gold, but emotionally pure gold, and if we make light of it that is because it's our way. In short, my dear, we are in the heart of the sublime, and since that is a region where you have no place, we will keep you in suspended animation, with your consent, until the day, which cannot be far off, when our angel in her turn will have to clear out: the sublime, alas, cannot be sustained indefinitely. Upon which, we send you our love, together with some cash (provision has been made).

                                                                              C.

P.S. We use the pronoun *we* because we're accused of being conceited when we say *I*. It's true, *we* sounds much more natural – one should have thought of it before.

---

*Paraphrase of a line from Victor Hugo's *Feuilles d'automne* (Part I) on the subject of mother-love: '*Chacun en a sa part et tous l'ont tout entier.*' cf. p.347 (*Translator's note*).

Extract from the Diary of
Mademoiselle Germaine Rival, Paris

Tuesday. – My last day here. Beautiful store-house dust that I shall inhale no more, behind these blocked-up, barricaded windows, amid the noise and disorder of crates being feverishly unpacked. And the little wooden staircase with its brass rail, that I shall descend once more but never climb again. It was like a companion-ladder in a ship. When I climbed it, I used to think the house was about to get under way and sail out to sea.

It was bound to come to this. When I took this job, C. did not reproach me in the least, although he must have been displeased: even when he's paying no attention to me, he wants to feel that I'm within reach. My new job was not likely to be more than a mild inconvenience to him, but the merest shadow of an inconvenience is for him a crushing burden. At the time he simply said to me: 'You won't stay a month. Imagine, a teacher! You're not one of them. They'll find an excuse to fire you.' He was getting at me through my pride. Three days later he became even more insidious: 'When they've thrown you out, I might perhaps take you to Italy.'

'Is that a promise?'

'A promise! Does *a man like me* ever promise anything?'

It isn't true, he promises all the time, but *a man like him* rarely keeps his promises. And never apologizes. 'I'm afraid I've changed my mind. You must take me as I am. Anyway, it comes under a statute of limitations.'

Even without promising, he put the idea of Italy into my head: that was all he wanted. Every time we saw each other he brought it up again: 'If you're sacked, and if we go to Italy, which, mind you, I don't promise. . . .' It was because of that 'if' that I eventually found a pretext and demonstrated with the others. I could have got myself fired for 'professional incompetence' (in other words, sabotage), but I couldn't face that: I, too, must be taken as I am. The motives of the demonstration were debatable. And anyhow I couldn't care less whether L—'s common law sentence was transformed into political expulsion or not. I didn't like L—'s face. Now I've been forced into giving the impression that I'm 'red'. Mummy is heart-broken. 'You who were brought up by the nuns!' and so on.

In this firm it isn't the manager who represents God for me, it's the cashier in his iron cage: deaf, dumb, blind – God personified. Another woman waiting on one of the benches in the hall, looking for a job, and there's nothing for her. That Renaud girl has just arrived with her narrow shoulders, her little face like a shrivelled lemon. It's hard at first, when you're only sixteen, and not used to it . . . She never stops thinking about her home, her pauper's lodgings, where at least she's not tied down and where she's sheltered from coarseness and abuse. That one over there has something wrong with her machine. She looks at me despairingly, appealing to me to come and help her.

'I don't know what's wrong, Mademoiselle.'

'Your driving-belt has slipped. I'll fix it.'

Now it's Lucienne, the one who says: 'I detest God.' (She'll get over that.)

'Mademoiselle, I've got a head-ache.'

'Go out into the yard, and come back in five minutes.'

'What if the manager sees me?'

'You can tell him I gave you permission.' She goes off. Then another says: 'Mademoiselle, Lucienne won't come back.' (Even the 'reds' are always sneaking on one another.) I reply: 'Of course, I hadn't expected anything else.' I can't get used to acting the part of a red. To show that I'm on their side, I should have to surrender my authority, but I just can't bring myself to do it.

(Yes, Andrée Barbot, you can stare at me, my girl. You won't get me to lower my eyes. You may drag a nervous smile out of me, but no more. You see, it's you who've lowered your eyes first. Nasty little beast!)

The five minutes are up, and Lucienne returns. I know quite well they're afraid of me. And I'm afraid of myself for having come to loathe these poor wretches. But apparently it's essential. 'Regard them as enemies. Be harsh.' They'll be talking for years about the hard-hearted overseer. As miserable as they. Perhaps even more so. Definitely more. But they don't rebel. What a flop, after all the drama! What a lot of 'no's' on the petition! Hardly a single 'yes', and a few signatures without either 'yes' or 'no'. And yet there were a large number of us who voted 'for'. What strikes one about nearly all of them is their lack of courage. Why should they rebel? Not only are they not shocked by tyranny and injustice, they actually like it: what they like is the fact of authority. And they don't like kindness either. If you're not unkind to them, they despise you.

I work with four men and sixteen women here. When I ask myself how many of them I shall say goodbye to, I can think of two men and three women. An interesting ratio.

Perhaps there's a password I don't know which would have made it possible for me to win them over. To be leaving without having discovered it.... To have received no help from anyone.... C., when I spoke to him about it, exploded: 'Me! Secrets of leadership from me! I neither give orders nor take them.' Of course, there's only one thing *he* wants: to escape.

Next day. – Worse than anything I had imagined:

'You know, we won't be seeing each other for a while.'

He could have told me anything he liked – that he was ill or something. But no, he always has to tell the truth.

'I've found a marvellous girl. Pure gold! I mustn't dissipate my energies right and left. I must come to her fresh. But when it's all over with her, we'll start again. It will be a matter of six weeks or so.'

He wanted to give me a thousand francs. His wretched money! I refused.

'You refuse? Just like an Arab!'

'What do you mean, like an Arab?'

'When an Arab is dissatisfied with the amount you give him, he flings it to the ground. And he doesn't pick it up again. But *you*'ll pick up the thousand francs. Because you're French. Because you're a woman. And because you have no reason to refuse it. I do something that annoys you. To make up for it, I do something that pleases you. What could be more reasonable?'

If he lied, I should feel strong enough to stand up to him.

But the way he puts things, there's nothing one can say. I didn't even mention Italy.

In the end I accepted. I shall buy a radio set with the money, and tell Mother I won it in the lottery. It's a 1,450-franc set, but I can get it for a thousand through Pierrette's boy friend. I asked C. to send me some records too, because he knows more about the latest music than I do.

No sooner had Costals and Solange sat down to dinner in the garden of this bogus 'hostelry' not far from the forest of Montmorency than Costals began to suffer. He hated all their fellow-diners, the men with their 'distinguished' airs ('Dear lady, doesn't this sky remind you of that Canaletto we saw in the gallery at Verona?'), the women with their faces set in a mould of boredom, stupidity and malevolence – all of them eaten up with self-esteem, and never more so, strange to say, than when they were apologizing to one another, all of them entrenched behind the barricades of their private language, their esoteric rites, their conviction of being a race apart, all of them irremediably exiled from everything natural and human, so much so that there were moments when they almost aroused pity, as though they were somehow cursed. There were a hundred and fifty people inside this enclosure, and the only sign of dignity was in the faces of the waiters, and the only sign of purity – a sublime purity – in a white greyhound.

It was not because they were rich that they disgusted Costals, but because they were so unworthy of their riches. Truly, it was a case of pearls before swine. There was not the slightest hint of envy in him, for the good reason that he himself either had what they had, or could have had it if he wanted it. But it was only by consorting with such people that he could obtain the things a writer of average talent can normally expect in France – honours, employment, 'position'. And he was incapable of consorting with them without feeling a disgust that was so painful to him that it was wiser to avoid occasions for it. As a result it was often said of him in those circles that he was aloof. And he was indeed aloof from 'those circles'.

There came a moment when his disgust grew so intense that the slightest pretext was enough to turn it into a physical revulsion. Seeing the expression of unbelievable stupidity on the face of one of these women, an expression intended to make it quite clear that she despised her husband (she was trying to look like Marlene Dietrich, and succeeding), Costals pushed his plate away and threw his head back....

'What's wrong?' asked Solange. 'Do you feel ill?'

He had turned so pale that she was frightened. He apologized without giving any explanation, and changed his place at the table so that he faced towards the forest and there were no longer any diners within his field of vision. It was not the first time that excessive disgust had caused this sort of revulsion. He had turned pale in the same way one day in the boulevard Saint Michel on seeing a parade of students, all wearing canary-yellow bow ties (a symbol?) and walking along with their arms round each other's shoulders bawling something, behind a placard on which the figure 69 was scrawled. They were escorted by policemen, with one of whom Costals had exchanged a smile of gloomy commiseration; he could not bear to think that these men of the people might suspect him of indulgence towards the demonstrators. How, incidentally, had the policeman managed to smile? In his shoes, Costals thought to himself, forced by the exigencies of the service to accompany these brats of the rich and to watch the obscene mummeries inspired by their idleness and stupidity, he could not have restrained himself from hitting them over the head.

He had always been surprised by the patience of those who, in 'good families', were charitably referred to as *the lower orders*. He had always wondered why it was that the humble people of Europe and the natives of the colonies did not hate more. For it was obvious that many of them felt no hatred; and he was touched by this, without understanding why it was. Periods of social peace, he thought, are neither natural nor logical, however agreeable they may be for some people; revolt is the natural order of things. Whatever its excesses and incidental injustices (lamentable though they be) the day of revolt is the day when the situation becomes normal again and therefore satisfying to the mind: the age of miracles is over.

If Costals had been alone in these surroundings, or with old friends, or with his son, he would have gone to dine with the chauffeurs. Even supposing their language was not particularly fastidious, which was certain to be the case, they at least had an excuse, having had no education, no culture, no leisure. Whereas these people, who were spiritually so impoverished, had had every opportunity. And moreover the chauffeurs were concerned with something other than making a good impression and repeating what they thought it was the smart thing to say.

From time to time Costals gave Solange a sombre look. It was because of her that he was here. This was the price he had to pay for his liaisons with women, unless they were women of the people – the necessity to take them to vile places, fashionable drawing-rooms, grand hotels, night-clubs, theatres, smart beaches. They knew, of course, that they had to affect to despise these places when they were with him. They repeated what he said about them himself, and went even further. Such splendid indignations. But you had only to see them in these pleasure spots, livening up at once, preening themselves, strutting about, to realize that this was what they loved, this was where they felt most alive – even the nicest and the most decent of them, even the simplest. There was nothing to be done about the equation: woman=chichi. And Costals' past was full of relationships weighed down, not to say poisoned, by the shame he had felt at having to belie himself in order to amuse women by accompanying them in a way of life which he despised. Just as a man, thirty years after having left his adolescence behind, no matter how loving and devoted his parents may have been, associates them first and foremost with infinitesimal grievances – 'They made me spend a year studying law for nothing', or 'They made me wear flannel vests at the height of summer' – in the same way, no matter how much pleasure a woman had given him, Costals could not help thinking: 'The days she made me waste (not to mention the money) doing shameful things! For instance, it's because of her that – I still blush to think of it – I spent a week at Deauville.' For the moment he did not hold it against Solange that he had felt obliged, because he was with her, to dine in a pretentious restaurant, but he carefully put aside this motive for resentment – a generous resentment, so to speak – to take it up again on the day he wanted to break with her.

Earlier that evening, as they drove through the forest of Montmorency (passing motorists laughed as they saw him kissing her like mad, and Costals laughed back at them in a youthful, plebeian complicity he enjoyed), he had said to her: 'After dinner, at the *hostelry*, supposing I took a room ... would you come up with me for a while?' She had answered 'yes'. Still the same *yes*! And now their dinner, begun in ill-humour, was coming to an end with a sort of secret melancholy. There were times when he had taken girls in a sort of Jove-like whirlwind which left no room for anything but the glory of rape. At other times, such as now, he felt a twinge of uneasiness at the thought that an act of such cardinal significance in the life of a virtuous woman was bound to have so much less importance for him. And then he thought: 'In an hour's time I shall know how she does it.' Thereafter curiosity would cease to sustain his feelings for her, and he wondered what would become of those feelings once they were left on their own.

'Did your mother ask you any awkward questions about what happened between us in the Bois the other night?'

'Fortunately, no.'

'If she had asked you: "How did he behave to you?" what would you have answered?'

She remained silent.

'I can see by your silence that you wouldn't have spared her a single detail.'

'I've never kept anything from my mother.'

'Well, well, that's nice! You really have been well brought up!'

'I've never kept anything from my mother because I never had anything to hide.'

'Which means that if.... Ah! I see you have a grain of intelligence after all.'

Now there occurred an enchanting scene similar to the one

the other night in the Bois. A little girl of about five broke away from a party of diners who were settling down to table and advanced towards Solange, gazing at her with an expression of wonder and delight. When her mother came to fetch her, she cried. Thereafter, they could not make her eat, because her eyes were steadily fixed on Solange. And Costals remembered what she had told him about the mysterious attraction she exercised over children.

She went upstairs to the room with great simplicity, without the slightest embarrassment. He was struck by this, and thought to himself (an ugly thought? no, the thought of a man who has lived): 'You'd think she had been doing nothing else all her life.' At first there were great photogenic embraces on the balcony, opposite the trees which glowed a sickly green in the lamp-light, while the sound of the orchestra rose from below. Costals applied himself. 'I must do it well. I must leave her a beautiful memory, worthy of this dear old moon and those rascally violins. Let's get it into our head that *éternité* is the anagram of *étreinte*.* Let's give her a whiff of eternity.'

Now she was lying on the bed, naked except for her shoes, which she had kept on, and her stockings which she had rolled down over them. She had undressed, at his request, without either coquetry or prudishness, with the same naturalness, the same simplicity which she had shown as she climbed the stairs under the noses of the hotel staff. Her legs were a little hairy – a charming trait in a young lady, provided she does not overdo it.

She embraced this gentleman awkwardly and without conviction, and the kisses she gave him – her first since they had known each other – were tight-lipped and decorous. She seemed to be saying to herself each time: 'I must kiss him. It's the thing to do.' But when, with his mouth on hers, he imparted to her the rudiments of the art, he sensed that, among all these caresses, she had at last found the one which suited her, which really gave her pleasure, and that now it was clear that her day had not been wasted. For minutes on end, in this unofficial intercourse of mouths, she gave herself quite as fully as in intercourse under its official form. When he

---

Etreinte = embrace (*Translator's note*).

asked: 'Would you like me to turn on the light?' (the first thing she had done on entering the room had been to switch off the light, but the room was flooded with moonlight), she said 'No, please don't', in a new voice, a voice transformed by emotion, the voice of a little girl, at once high and low, as though it came from far away, from a little Dandillot of another age who had remained in the depths of her being. Afterwards he was to call this voice her 'night voice', because she only put it on when they were making love – and the ship of love, when one is on it with little girls, always sails with its lights out.

Now he could no longer see anything of Solange's body, could see nothing of her but her face surrounded by her dishevelled hair, like the heart of a flower surrounded by its petals. It was as if the whole of this woman were concentrated in this great corolla: a woman-corolla. . . . At first she let him do what he wished, but soon she began to cry. 'No! No!' She cried for some time, with real sobs, while he fondled her without withdrawing from her, and he thought to himself: 'We know all about this.' Partly out of reluctance to hurt her, but mainly in order to keep some of the mystery and attraction for future occasions – while at the same time gratifying his fad of never taking advantage of an easy opportunity – when he let go of her he had not taken the decisive step. It is rare to be able thus to combine pleasure and virtue. Her sobs continued for a while after he had drawn away from her, then grew fainter, then stopped at last; in him, meanwhile, sensation was still as sharp as a fresh wound. They remained motionless and silent, lying there side by side, and he wondered if she was angry. Perhaps she was a false *ingénue* (it was a hypothesis which his mind could not entirely reject), piqued at not having been taken completely; perhaps, on the other hand, merely a little girl, vexed with him for having gone so far. . . . But suddenly, turning her head – cloc! – she kissed him on the cheek. The noise of a tree-frog jumping into the water.

He lay there for several minutes, silent by her side, and his thoughts began to take wing. There are elevations, religious or otherwise, which are provoked by fasting. Others – through

the identity of opposites – can arise from the digestion of a
rich meal, a process that transports us into a better world.
With Costals, such elevations often took shape as soon as the
carnal act had been accomplished, and they were all the more
intense the more wholeheartedly he had thrown himself into
that act. This was either because, having used up all his
sensuality in the act, only the spiritual part of him remained,
or because no sooner was he physically plugged in to a woman
than he was filled with light – as when one plugs in an electric
lamp – and this light was total : the absolute of sensation
followed by the absolute of sentiment (there are certain souls
that flow towards the absolute as water flows towards the
sea). Almost all his most inspired work had been conceived
during these post-coital periods. So now, as he lay by Solange's
side, his thoughts turned to Thérèse, and he saw her soul
threatened (from the Catholic point of view) without her suspecting it in the least. Yet he had had more than enough pity on
her, and was weary of it.

The orchestra had stopped playing. The windows were wide
open on to the warm night, and the dark foliage (the lamps
had been put out) made a continuous rustling sound as it
stirred, like the sound of rain. Now it seemed to Costals that
Andrée was standing at the foot of the bed with her tormented
face. 'I who feel, know, understand ! I who have penetrated
to the heart of your work more profoundly than if I were you
yourself ! And you refuse me what you offer unreservedly to
this insignificant little creature, simply because she was born
pretty !' Often the injustice of one of his actions would cause
him a kind of enthusiasm : the pleasure that God feels when
he contemplates his creation. This time, it weighed on him.
Nevertheless, he began caressing Solange once more ; since it
was understood that he was biased in her favour, why make
any bones about it ? But he made up his mind to write Andrée
a nice letter next day. (He did not in fact do so, being exclusively preoccupied with the religious thoughts evoked by
a letter he was writing to Thérèse.)

In the taxi, she was less stupefied than she had been on the
previous occasion. Several times she raised her head from her
lover's breast and gazed into his eyes in silence, as though,

after the event, she felt the need to get to know this person to whom she had given herself. And he, suffering her gaze, said to himself: 'My face is that of a man of thirty-four who thinks. How ugly people are who think, or profess to think!' He remained thus, under her scrutiny, like a soldier forcing himself to keep his head above the parapet: the terrible nakedness of a man's face, without powder, without paint, so brave compared with women's faces, which are always patched up. This lasted for what seemed to him a long time. Then she put her head back on his shoulder, as though she were surrendering for a second time.

As he felt he had the right to use the familiar form of address to her, whereas she still said *vous*, he asked, smilingly: '*Tu? Vous?*' And she replied, quite simply (without in the least meaning to be ungracious):

'I don't know how to say *tu*.'

He liked this remark, in which he saw a mixture of shyness and pride: the remark of an infanta.

Suddenly, after a silence, she asked him point-blank:

'Do you really love me?'

Rather foolishly, without thinking – and yet perhaps because he still had the feeling at the back of his mind that she might not be sincere – he said to her:

'It's I who should be asking you that question.'

She leapt up at this, and with a violence that he had neither seen nor suspected in her, she said:

'You have no right to say that to me! Haven't I given you enough proofs?'

She had drawn herself up like a little snake.

'You have no right!' Never would he have believed that she could use such a phrase. Might she be capable of passion? He also asked himself, with typical male cruelty, 'What proofs?'

'I,' she went on, 'I shall love you always, I know I shall And you, how long?'

'A long time.'

She made a face. Then he said to her:

'When I was sixteen – sixteen, do you hear – I had a little girl-friend of fourteen. I loved her as one loves for the first time, which is to say with a fervour one never recaptures.

And of course she said to me exactly what you've just said, which is a classic remark: "With me, it's for life. What about you?" And I replied: "For as long as possible." I loved her madly, and I was only sixteen; but I was as clear-sighted as that. I need scarcely add that six months later we had forgotten each other. You see, I like reality. I like to see things as they are,' he insisted passionately. 'People say one's unhappy when one sees things too clearly. I see everything clearly, and I'm very happy. But because I know what reality is, I know that one must never commit the future. What will your feelings be in a year's time? In six months? In three months? What will mine be? That's why I don't give you that "forever", which nevertheless I find quite natural on the lips of a young girl, and which touches me profoundly. I merely say "a long time", and I say it to you as a man who knows what "a long time" means. And it means a great deal. To know that one will love someone for a long time is a great deal, believe me.'

She did not answer.

When they parted, he wanted to give her some sign of encouragement, and said to her with a nice smile:

'I don't feel a bit tired of you, you know....'

Later, he felt sorry for having doubted her. Not that he had doubted her in the strict sense of the word. He believed her to be pure of heart; he knew her to be intact of body. But he found it impossible, when faced with the 'no, no's' and the tears, and even the night voice, that unforgettable little schoolgirl's voice, not to think of all the counterfeits of these that abound among the fair sex. He was so convinced that Solange was 'genuine' that he found it almost vile of himself to have occasional doubts about her, even if these doubts were, so to speak, forced on him. For Costals' past injected into the present a whole accumulation of knowledge and experience that modified his vision of Solange, and there was nothing to be done about that. Nothing could alter the fact that for him she was only the latest, whereas for her he was the first. Nothing could alter the fact that he had known a great many copies before he knew the original, and that the original seemed less original after these copies. And whereas his attitude towards

Andrée caused him no compunction, he felt guilty towards Solange, although he had done her no other wrong than being what he was. For it is a fact that everything conspires to the advantage of that which we love.

But there was another feeling that tended to make him doubt Solange a little: he was astonished that she could love him. Costals was devoid of literary vanity, and one of the things he liked most about Solange was that she never spoke to him about his books and never uttered the faintest word of admiration. His vanity as a male, on the other hand, ran to extremes. His first impulse was to assume that no woman he desired would refuse to give herself to him. But whenever one of them fell into his arms, at the same time surrendering something of her heart, he was taken aback, and repeated to himself the remark of Louis XV: 'I find it hard to understand why they love me so much.' In this way he savoured alternately the pleasure of believing himself invincible and the pleasure of proving himself humble: there is a time for everything, says the sage. That Solange could really love him he found hard to believe. 'She's incapable of appreciating what is great and superior in me. Poor darling, she has the brain of a water-flea. So what can she find to love in me? What is there about me, physically, that's worth loving? It's not at all clear.' This was to ignore the fact that women, unlike men, go from affection to desire. Thus two elements played a part in his distrust: one which could be *stigmatized* in these terms: 'the disillusionment of a cynic who corrupts simple innocence', and another which it is difficult not to describe as genuine modesty. So his feelings were partly good and partly bad. Like three-quarters of our feelings. Which is what society – which prefers people to be either black or white, so that one 'knows where one is' with them – will not have. But what nature – which loves nothing so much as confusion – will.

'Nothing can alter the fact that I am by nature clear-sighted – and clear-sighted *always*,' he said to himself as he thought of the 'long time' he had opposed to her naïve assurance. 'And moreover nothing can possibly make me want not to be. My clear-sightedness frightens people, but it never frightens me. I'm amused by it; it is a monster I've tamed.

But why "a monster"? Call it rather my tutelary spirit. It's thanks to this clear-sightedness that I lead a thoroughly intelligent life, doing only what I know I can do, and concentrating on that, never going off on the wrong tack, never wasting time, never being taken in either by others or by myself, never letting people cause me suffering and only very rarely being even put out by them. And as this lucidity of mine is combined with all the powers of imagination and poetry, through poetry I can enter the domain of dreams, and through the imagination I can enter the feelings of people who are not clear-sighted; and this allows me to take controlled holidays from my clear-sightedness when I think fit, and thus to win both ways. My life is not a superior life because, although my senses never fail me, my mind, my character and my heart are full of lacunae; but these elements are such that a superior life could be built upon them. As for my dear Dandillot, who is not me, I must see that she does not suffer on my account, and I shall do this sometimes by lying to her and sometimes by not lying to her, in short by letting myself be governed not by principles but by expediency, by flair and tact, with my affection as my guide. It is possible that in other circumstances I might muffle her up with illusions. But I had, at least once, to make her face up to things as they are, even though in future I may conceal from her a spectacle which it would be in the worst possible taste to impose uninterruptedly on a girl of twenty.'

Pierre Costals
Paris

to Thérèse Pantevin
La Vallée Maurienne

19 May 1927

Mademoiselle,

I have had great pity on you before God of late, as you requested me to, and a few hours ago, by virtue of some rather special circumstances, I saw your soul in a dream, and I saw that it was in grave peril. You are like those people who, on the eve of a revolution, believe they are safe because they are liberals. 'Afraid of the revolutionaries? Why should I be?

They know I'm with them at heart. And besides, if they condemn me, they'll have to condemn everybody.' The revolution
occurs; they are left in peace; they are exultant. Then they
are arrested and killed. You sleep in peace, seeing yourself
surrounded by such a crowd of petty sinners and false innocents that God must be obliged to spare them. But you ignore
the example of the Jews, who all perished in the wilderness
save two, and the whole of Scripture, which tends towards
the establishment of this doctrine. Jesus Christ tells us that
'few are chosen'; he warns that the way is narrow and rare
those who will find it. Christians read this with indifference:
they think it's all part of Christ's rhetoric.

A multitude of the damned can be seen in the churches at
eleven o'clock Mass, genuflecting and putting money in the
plate. Their extenuating circumstances are granted by the
Church itself, which has left them in their fools' paradise in
order to keep up the numbers on its lists. The contemporary
Church has no more right to invoke the example of a St
Augustine or the doctrine of a St Thomas without making
itself ridiculous than the dead humanism of our universities
has the right to claim descent from Greece or Rome: the
ancient world and the Middle Ages were tabernacles of a
spirituality which no religion or philosophy has been able to
continue or to transform.

The Church of Christ lasted a thousand years or so. I believe
(erroneously perhaps) that it survives only in monasteries and
convents. I dreamed of seeing you completely cut off from
the outside world, in a place where the affairs of the world
would revolve beneath your feet, as the affairs of heaven revolve above our heads. Even if nothing in Catholic doctrine
were true, you would have given me thereby a noble idea of
yourself, and that was not to be despised. If you were damned
in any case, it were better to be damned in a lofty and
singular quest than in the squalor that surrounds you now.
But you do not seem to have followed the advice I gave you,
to go and see a priest and let him probe your hidden depths.
I will not, therefore, pursue the matter. I cannot waste endless
time on you. The living, who merely pass by, can only interest
me in passing. And besides, if you yourself turn aside from

this path, so much the better : it is a sign that God did not intend you for it. There may be false stirrings of life in a dead soul : some people know this – from experience. I may have been mistaken about you.

You tell me you suffer. That could stand you in lieu of prayer, if you had no other way. Suffering is the prayer of those who neither think nor pray. I do not know the nature of your temptations, but I believe that to be tempted is a sign of God's grace; if you did not interest him, he would leave you in peace. Perhaps, in the state of peril in which I saw you, this temptation will save you. Even supposing that the temptation means not God's presence but his absence, there is probably not a single saint who doesn't feel God appear and disappear in his soul in rapid succession. The soul is like a sunny sky dotted with little clouds which veil it from one moment to the next.

I too have my temptations regarding you, and I am torn between them : the temptation to point you towards God, as one takes a dog by the collar and points it : 'Fool, that's where it got up', and the temptation to abandon you to your nothing-ness – which you will feel at last when I am no longer there.

Believe me, Mademoiselle, yours sincerely,

Costals

I must remind you that I am not a believer. . . . If I looked for God, I should find myself.

I reopen my letter to add this. I make no secret of the fact that last night, when I wrote the above, I intended to abandon you. You had let me down. But the other alternative remains. I shall have pity on you next Saturday at six o'clock in the evening; and I specify this hour because I shall be with someone from whom I can draw this power of pity. But beware – I shall have pity on you in a certain way, and in a particular direction. And you have no idea of the mysteries of pity. *I* know all about them.

Andrée Hacquebaut   to Pierre Costals
Saint-Léonard   *Paris*

1 June 1927

'Another endless letter! The girl must be mad! God, how mad the girl is! And how right Ecclesiastes (or Solomon) is when he speaks of the misfortune of falling into the dreams of an ardent woman!' That's what you're thinking, isn't it? Well, no, for once I'm not going to bore you this morning. I feel a little better.

Why do I feel better? I have the impression that in my last few letters I've rambled a good deal, and that now I see the situation more clearly for what it really is. First of all because I went to the hairdresser two days ago, which means that my hair now looks nice (it takes at least that long!), and looking at myself in the mirror with the thought that these horrible days must have added ten years to my age, I find my face more or less the same (indeed it's unbelievable how often I've been told since my trip to Paris how young and smart I look). And then because the weather has become overcast, there's no longer that intoxication of summer that seemed to mock my suffering – today's weather is like autumn, and next autumn, for me, will be *different*: I shall have other clothes than those in which I've suffered so much . . . a kind of superstition. . . . Hope has hoisted sail once more. Would you ever have thought that dull, grey weather could bring the promise of happiness?

Hope . . . promise. . . . That pact of hope constantly renewed with myself! That perpetual waiting! For four years now I've waited for a sign from you. I've given you everything, and had nothing in return. You haven't kissed me once in four years. If I were dead, would you give me a kiss at last? Why, oh! why, since it would cost you so little to leave me at least one souvenir which I passionately desire, when you have hundreds of such souvenirs and I shall never have another in the whole of my arid life? For one spontaneous kiss from you I would have given ten years of your friendship without a moment's hesitation.

There's an anomaly in your attitude: you love and yet you

give nothing. When one loves, one gives; it's a natural impulse. *Your* motto seems to be: 'Avoid giving at all costs.' It's so abnormal that I might be tempted to believe that you do not love me. But there's no question that you love me; I should have to be very blind not to have noticed it: women have an infallible instinct in these matters.

You tell me you do not love me. You try as hard as you can to persuade yourself of it. If I knew that you didn't love me, if I was certain that making love to me would be a penance for you, then I would give up of my own free will, for I'm too proud even to beg for anyone's love. But there it is. I'm certain that the opposite is the case. I know that, without having a devouring passion for me, you love me all the same. Was I dreaming when I read the tenderness in your eyes? Did I dream that the idea of our marrying crossed your mind when we visited the flat in the rue Quentin-Bauchart? Did I dream that you held my hand in yours on the 16th of May last year, that you held my arm and pressed close to me as we walked that day in the square des Etats-Unis, that you confided in me that same day, poured out your heart to me (about your regrets at not being a father)? Did I dream that once, when you were late for an appointment with me and I asked you why, you replied: 'Ask me rather why I came at all!' Do you know what made me aware of your affection? In May 1926, our legs touched in a taxi, and at once you drew yours away, sharply. I realized then that you loved me with your soul. 'The woman one does not enjoy is the woman one loves.' (Baudelaire)

If you are so sure that you do not love me, kissing me would be like kissing a stone. Why, then, do you resist so vehemently? Why don't you invite me to your house any more? Why don't you take me somewhere where we could dance and drink champagne? Then we would see what happened. It really is too stupid of you to pretend that you don't desire me, when you do everything in your power to exorcize this desire.

For four years, in your company, I have felt overwhelmed by your shyness. You want to make an advance, but you dare not. With women whom you don't love with your soul, you can dare all right. With me, you lose your head. Perhaps, too, you think me frigid! It was delightful for a time, but it has gone on too long. It's too absurd to be afraid of me.

If I were to take you at your word, if – however improbable it may seem – you did not want my love, there would be only one way of breaking it off, and that would be to convince me that you do not love me. But you couldn't because you *do* love me. You see what an inextricable jungle-growth you've got yourself entangled in! Inextricable for you – though a child of two could get out of it. You make me smile, you know. It just shows that a person of genius can be at the same time an idiot. Nothing could be more ludicrous than your attitude towards me – always on the defensive.... You poor, poor child!

Do, please, let yourself go at last. You hold yourself back, and you suffer from doing so. Is this wise? How can you allow the light I kindled in you to fade? How can you return to your barren, loveless solitude, when salvation is there, close by, with its naked arms outstretched, and its fresh face, and all the deep-down things inviolate? Never again will you find a woman like me. Never again will God hold out his hand to you.

Yours,
Andrée

P.S. My friend Raymonde has just left. I have always kept her informed – in a general way – about our *liaison*. She asked me how things stood. When I told her there was nothing new, she exclaimed: 'Don't you realize that he couldn't care two hoots about you?' When I explained to her that your reserve was a proof of your love, she laughed in my face. I'm ashamed of being a woman when I see women as coarse as that. However, I would like you to authorize me to write to her – after a suitable lapse of time – and tell her that at last you have made me yours. Thus I shall feel more at ease when I speak to her again. Yes, authorize me to say, not only to Raymonde but to one or two other *reliable* friends: 'Costals is my lover.' You would be giving me the shadow of that happiness of which you refuse me the substance. And after all, you owe me that much at least.

This letter remained unanswered.

Thérèse Pantevin   to Pierre Costals
La Vallée Maurienne   *Paris*

Sunday

Yesterday, Saturday, at the hour when you were having pity on me – six o'clock – I was seized with violent palpitations. The Angelus went, and I knew then, by an inspiration from you, that those who were ringing it were among the 'false innocents', that they were the Gentiles preparing to go through the pretence of celebrating Corpus Christi tomorrow with lying pomp, and I was horrified by the noise of the bell. I was seized with a violent shuddering – my body quivered like the withers of a horse – and fierce stirrings of the bowels. Then I gave a loud shepherd's cry – they must have heard it as far as Noison's. I began to groan, and lay down prostrate on the floor with my arms outstretched; I felt it was the only place where I would be at ease. I shook my head from side to side, as though dazed and befuddled by the state I was in. Meanwhile, as soon as I had prostrated myself, little Marcel (my sister's child, he's two) began to cry so loud that they couldn't pacify him, so I had to sit up and fondle him. Then I lay back on the floor, which made the child start crying again. I took him on top of me, and he stayed there quietly. But I went on groaning, I felt my bowels stirring, I said all sorts of things, about the spirit of Babylon, you, our marriage, 'Sigara, who is the symbol of thirst', Lucifer, 'created in rejoicing'. I pressed little Marcel against my breast, against my face, between my legs, I kissed him over and over again, he splashed about in me, he was our son, I was drunk with child. Mamma wondered if they ought to call the priest, but Barbiat said no. So then Mamma got the missal and read the prayers of the Mass, the *Te Deum* and the *Magnificat*. After a time

Barbiat took little Marcel away from me. Then I began punch-ing myself repeatedly and violently on both breasts at once, and that relieved me a little. I was still talking, but I can't remember anything I said. I hid in a corner. I crawled about on my knees. I clapped my hands. I asked Barbiat to breathe on me, which he did, and then the same thing with Mamma. All the time I was crying to myself and moaning: 'Ah, I'm dying.' I must have looked frightful (it's a pity you can't see how ugly I am). Eventually, when I had suffered enough, I told Barbiat to beat my breasts with a bundle of firewood. He did so, very hard, and I was delivered.

My beloved, I can say no more. Let me know when you have another great pity on me. Oh, how I long for it! But not for a few days – it's too shattering for me.

Marie

PITY FOR WOMEN

'God created everything for man's happiness. There's no sin in any of it. An animal, for instance, will sleep in the Tartar reeds or in ours. It makes its home wherever it happens to be; it eats whatever God provides.'

TOLSTOY, *The Cossacks*

(*Spoken by a Chechen peasant, the Chechens being at war with the Tartars.*)

In the town of N—, in 1918, there was a little girl of twelve whose family described her as a 'quiet little thing'. She had no friends, and played silently at home by herself for hours on end; she sat through whole meals, too, without saying a word. She was known as a tomboy because she liked going for long, solitary walks or bicycle-rides, and showed little enthusiasm for girlish things. Also because she was brave: in boats, in the dark, or left by herself in some lonely shed, she never showed the slightest fear. And yet she was shy. If the maid forgot to serve her at dinner, she made no complaint and went hungry.

At school she was a fair pupil, though this must be qualified by the fact that she was a year behind. From twelve to fourteen, attempts were made to teach her the piano, without success. From fourteen to sixteen she was tried on the violin: a waste of time. After these four years and the expenditure of thousands of francs, it was at last conceded that this child of silence had not the slightest gift for making noise; later, a wireless set had to be got rid of, so greatly did this machine exasperate her. Then her father, who could wield a pencil rather nicely, thought he would teach her drawing: soon he had to lay down his arms. The fact was, she had neither inclination nor aptitude for anything. M. Dandillot became worried. In order to get her to 'acquire a personality' he would leave her for a whole hour, her cheeks on fire, sweating over a letter to an old uncle or to her godfather: her instructions were to write something 'original'. 'Original'. . . . M. Dandillot himself was considered something of an original. The son of a public prosecutor, after a year at the bar he had abandoned pettifoggery and with it any idea of ever making money, although his own fortune was no more than adequate. From the earliest days of French athleticism (he had been twenty-one in 1887) he had developed a passion for these things and had founded a sports club in N—. He was particularly keen on swimming, of which he had become the apostle. In his middle years, since he was by no means unintelligent or uncultivated, he had given up sport itself for the wider problems of physical culture, and resigned the presidency of his club – which from then on he condemned as heretical – to throw himself heart and soul into the natural health cults which were then taking root in France: a photograph taken at the Institute of Athletics in Rheims and published in *l'Illustration* around 1910, shows M. Dandillot heavily bewhiskered and clad as a Greek shepherd. He solemnly broke with his worldly life, went so far as to get rid of his dress-clothes – symbol of all the sins of Babylon – and thereafter concerned himself solely with the open air, the sun, diets, measurings and weighings, immersed in terrifying charts of all the things man must and must not do in order to remain 'natural', and in what might be called the hard labour of the 'natural' life – in short, forever harping on nature, although he could reach it only through the most preposterous artifices, which would have poisoned the life of any reasonable person, even supposing they could be reconciled with the obligations of a normal existence, which clearly they could not. At the age of fifty, still pursuing the path of 'purity', M. Dandillot began to 'tolstoyize': man, in order to be truly 'natural', must also remain chaste, and love his fellow men; thus the hatred M. Dandillot had always had for his father, from being a simple filial hatred, became as it were sanctified by the heads which the prosecutor had been responsible for lopping off. Shrewd, deceitful, stubborn, naïve, with a mind dappled like a panther's skin with patches of luminous intelligence and patches of dark stupidity; a bachelor by vocation though a father and a husband, with the qualities and eccentricities of the bachelor; and singularly uncreative, to the extent of not having managed by the age of sixty to deliver himself of the modest little treatise on the 'natural life' which he had conceived before the war and which would have been a mere compilation of his favourite masters.... But we shall not describe M. Dandillot further; he will do this for himself in what is to follow.

In 1923, Solange's elder brother died in Madagascar, where he had gone farming, and the Dandillots moved to

Paris. Solange was made to take a domestic science course.

Nubile at fifteen years and three months, she had gone through puberty without any of the turmoil – the sensation of being physically sullied, the depression, the indignation, the secretiveness, the anxious, furtive glances at the parents, the hurry to get away from them when they are together, the vows to renounce love 'forever' – which one often comes across in pure and sensitive girls at that age. When she had asked her mother how babies were born, she had done so out of boredom, not because she was really interested. Her hair, once golden, had gradually turned black. Her eyes had narrowed a little, and they had a bluish tinge which appeared behind her dark lashes like the Mediterranean behind a curtain of pines. She was so pretty that hardly a day passed without her hearing exclamations from the men who passed her in the street. Like the two workmen in Toulon, for instance: 'Take a look at that! Isn't she a beauty?' It sometimes happened that Southern labourers would stop working one after the other as she went by. For it was in the South particularly that she was a success: she was too natural for the Parisians, who only like grotesquely 'dolled up' women. Yet she remained quite unspoiled. She was always in the back row at church, always a little in the background at family gatherings. And it was incredible to see this ravishing girl going out in the morning wearing an old, dowdy, worn-out dress. Never in her life had she bought a fashion magazine, though if she chanced to find one she would read it with apparent interest. It was not that she did not enjoy being attractive, but her enjoyment was not sufficient for her to go to great lengths in order to achieve it; when she had passed a damp finger along her eyebrows and her tongue over her lips, she felt she had done a great deal. She never went to the hairdresser, wore no jewellery, and did not use scent or lipstick – only powder, which she put on badly. And this was neither affectation – which would have implied pride – nor a matter of principle – for she did sometimes wear jewellery or paint her lips for a few days, or spend a whole afternoon doing her nails, carefully getting together everything she needed and then, when she had finished, scraping off all the varnish and going up to the attic to ruin her hands rummaging in old packing-cases. She always wore royal blue, and nothing would make her give it up: she was greatly praised for this. But one day she set her heart on a wine-coloured dress.

The *Lycée* at N— was strictly run. In the top form, only one in every six girls had a lover. Solitary practices were unknown and Solange did not even discover what they were until she was twenty-one. Only a few of the girls had 'crushes' on others, and all of them, without exception, were from convent-schools. When Solange, one day, had been caught letting another girl smother her with kisses, her 'But, Madame, there's nothing wrong with it between girls' had been the cry of innocence itself. Once she knew, she repelled the girl's advances. But she remained the ideal confidante to all her friends, who were soothed by her placidity and her good advice. She listened to everything they told her and never said a word about herself. If the truth be told, there was not a great deal to be said.

As for men, nothing. Purveyors of flattery were sent packing, often with a flea in their ears. She liked dancing, but regarded the men who held her in their arms merely as a means of achieving that pleasure: she would as soon have danced alone. In a little book with a rose-pink cover she kept a list of the houses where she had been invited to dances, but she did not keep a list of her partners, even in the cotillions; she merely noted down indiscriminately the names of the young men and girls of her acquaintance whom she met at such parties. When first one, then another confessor in Paris (the provincial ones had been most correct) asked her questions which displeased her, she stopped going to confession altogether. Her religion became that of most Catholics: going to Mass on Sunday. She had no faith, and her life was in no way guided by religion; yet if she had missed Sunday Mass it would have worried her, and she would have gone into a church for a few moments. The habit of not going to confession increased yet further the power she had of keeping her intimate thoughts to herself and also of pondering over everything she did; instead of casting it all into a dark corner, she held on to it and turned it over in her mind. From that day (when she stopped going to confession), she became more intelligent and more conscientious. What may seem strange is the fact that she realized this.

Her mother and father loved her dearly, and with some intelligence. She loved them too in her way, which at first they had found some difficulty in getting used to. No sudden bursts of affection towards them, never a charming word, never a thoughtful 'attention'. She even disliked the 'attentions' they had for her: 'I hate being fussed over.' If her mother stroked her hair, she would frown and narrow her eyes even more. Her 'No's' were as famous as her silences: she would wake from her dreams at night shouting 'No! No! No!' As a baby, if someone merely glanced at her without saying a word she would scream 'No!', and she used to throw a tantrum immediately on entering the street where her grandmother lived, because the old lady was liable to paw her with maniacal affection. At the *Lycée*, she had not remained a boarder very long because she pined for her parents so. Yet when her mother came to visit her, the child would sit by her side in the parlour for half an hour without saying a word: it was her way of loving her mother. Her father nicknamed her 'Miss Silence', or sometimes just 'Silence'. 'But why didn't you ever say anything nice to me in the school parlour?' 'It didn't occur to me.' Once, when her brother had tortured a kitten in front of her, squeezing its neck until it no longer gave any sign of life, she had watched it all with her eyes starting out of her head and made no attempt to save the little creature. 'But you loved Misti, didn't you? Why didn't you call somebody?' 'It never occurred to me.' It was true: nothing ever 'occurred to her'. However, once one had resigned oneself to her cold ways, there was nothing to complain of in her behaviour. 'She's cold, but she's gentle,' her mother used to say, 'and she has never given me the slightest trouble.' Indeed, it was not that she did not love her parents, but rather that, while she felt at ease with strangers, she was shy with those she loved. And if, when punished by her father, she kept out of the way and sulked, she was burning inside with the desire to go and kiss him. Only it wouldn't 'come out'.

She really was a 'quiet little thing' until the day when, her brother having slapped her, she had a genuine fit of hysterics (she was fourteen). But even at the height of it, still no tears.

'If you had cried, you would have felt better,' the doctor said.

'But I can't cry!'

'You mean you can't cry in front of other people? Or you can't cry at all?'

'I can't cry at all.'

During the thorough medical check-up that followed this episode (the unexpected violence of her nervous reactions had caused some alarm) it was discovered that her heartbeats were abnormal in number and intensity. Three years later, when she was about to be X-rayed and the electric light was switched off in the laboratory, she had another attack. The family diagnosis was altered. She was no longer a 'quiet little thing'; she was now a 'suppressed hysteric'. The description was not such a bad one: everything that came out of her seemed somehow damped down, like a noise stifled by a wad of cork or cotton-wool.

Whatever their experience to the contrary, men persist in believing that a character must be all of a piece. Yet it is only in artificially-created characters that unity is to be found; whatever remains natural is inconsistent. Mlle Dandillot's principal characteristic was her naturalness. There was great surprise when, an elderly young man having proposed to her, she showed both pride and delight: with the character attributed to her, it was assumed that she would send him packing. And so she did, but only after having granted him two interviews. Later, she refused two other proposals. She only wanted to marry a man who attracted her (she had at least discovered that!). The trouble was that none of them attracted her. Her parents did not want to force her. In this they were right; but they should have taken her out more. As it was, since they did not care for society, she met very few people. So the three of them settled down to wait for the husband the heavens would send. The fact that Mlle Dandillot had firmly and vehemently refused three good matches did not however alter the family's verdict that she 'lacked will-power', any more than the handsome fortune her brother was piling up in Madagascar altered the family's verdict on *him* – that he was not 'practical'. He had never been able to mend a fuse: therefore he was 'not practical'. In certain circumstances, Mlle Dandillot showed will-power, and in certain circumstances she was fatalistic. It is this 'in certain circumstances' that people always forget. And yet, having so often heard it said that she had no will-power, she had come to believe it herself. But if she exerted her will so seldom, it was perhaps because there was little she desired.

And thus she reached the age of twenty-one, which she had only just arrived at when she slipped into this tale. A good housewife, adept at dealing with the upholsterer or the electrician, an expert on food and liking only the best, thrifty in the house and a spendthrift on herself, squandering her small allowance on silly things that gave her no pleasure, she was nonetheless still very much a child, fighting with her brother, climbing trees, rushing down the stairs four at a time. Disliking dogs – too frisky – and birds – too noisy – she liked cats, being very cat-like herself, and above all aquarium fish, perhaps because they were silent like herself, and cold, with neurotic reflexes (watch them as they twist and turn). She had a continuous succession of them, for after a week they would be found floating belly upwards: she had forgotten to feed them. She read little – a few snippets – and in the forty-odd books that made up her little library there were only three novels, which were there by pure chance; as for poetry, the less said the better: she hated it as she hated music. Even then she was far from having read all her books, though all the pages had been cut and the volumes carefully wrapped in transparent paper. She went to a dance about once a month, and had to force herself to do so, such was her hatred of 'dressing up'. At the last moment she would hesitate whether to make an excuse and not go, but once she was there she was happy as could be, never missing a single dance and always the last to leave: it was enough to wear her poor mother out. Whereas on the days when she did not go out she was in bed by half past nine. In society, she was sometimes thought to be stuck-up, because she carried her chin a little in the air (on account of her very heavy bun, which pulled her head back).

Whereas her brother, at fifteen, had impatiently shaken off everything that reminded him of his childhood, and lived only for the future, she did not think of her future, but awaited it passively, huddling over her past instead, hoarding her school-books, her prizes, her volumes of the *Bibliothèque Rose*, filing away, as it were, the whole of her childhood, every relic of which she would have preserved in her bedroom had not her father from time to time impounded some beloved* toy-rabbit or porcelain Infant Jesus and taken it up to the attic. All of which will no doubt gratify the reader, for a woman without childishness is a horrible monster. And yet, though she remained so close to childhood, she was incapable of talking to children as girls of her age usually can, and felt bored and ill at ease in their company. In her state of romantic solitude, she felt peaceful and happy. Of course she realized that the day would come when all this would change (for, let me repeat, she was not guided by any principle and there was no 'theory' behind her coldness) but she did not yearn for that day, and could not in the least imagine what sort of change it might bring. 'One shouldn't organize one's life, it's unlucky', she used to say. If she had had any precise feeling about her future, it would have been fear, fear of being less happy than she was now, fear of being, as she put it in her typical little-girl idiom, 'disappointed'.

Thus Mlle Dandillot lived, in a placid key which the author has endeavoured to emulate in writing about her.

(We have omitted to mention that from the age of sixteen, that is some twenty years before the age at which a man, and a man of mature understanding, begins to have a few notions as to how he should govern himself, Mlle Dandillot knew how the State should be governed. Not being clever enough to embrace all political convictions at one and the same time, she restricted herself to one: she was madly right-wing. She even belonged to an extreme right-wing group, and had intended to work on one of its charity committees; but she had only gone twice, being too right-wing to be able to settle down to it. We shall not mention the group to which Mlle Dandillot belonged, since she has given herself to a gentleman.)

---

*'But you never talked to your rabbit!' 'I talked to him inside.'

Andrée Hacquebaut   to Pierre Costals
Saint-Léonard   *Paris*

7 June 1927

Dear Costals,

Status quo. The weather's too hot, I haven't the energy to suffer, at least to suffer acutely. I'm certainly unhappy, and prefer to be unhappy because of you than apply myself to being angry with you; but unhappy not with an unhappiness that tears me apart, but with a torpid unhappiness, always the same. The state of mind of one still anaesthetized after an operation, of a detached convalescent, of Lazarus rising from the tomb – a kind of indifference and meekness towards the world. 'Let them do as they like. All that's over for me.' Do not however mistake this meekness for benevolence. I no longer wish to be frank, nor to give pleasure. Thanks to you, I have become like you.

How strange it is, but I must admit it : failure can be satisfying, or at least can give one a feeling of repose not so very different, I imagine, from the feeling achievement brings. I summoned up my courage and took the plunge. And I failed. You denied me the only thing in the world I wanted. And yet, in spite of it all, something has been gained. Now, all that is being reabsorbed. . . . What difference is there, when all's said and done, between a body that has known pleasure and one that has not? Renunciation! The peace of the woman who has renounced. If you knew how simple it is, when one has renounced all one's life. How quickly one gets used to it. My love for you was always, *a priori*, counterpoised by renunciation. My only error was to believe that that impossible love was in fact possible, to believe that tenderness and pity were enough to waken desire in a man, to believe that love could be created in another person as water can be got by turning on a tap. My sacrifices have always been made in advance. And self-imposed suffering is almost ecstasy compared to the suffering imposed on one by others. And then (even though I haven't had my fill of memories of you, not by a long way), I have taken so much from you that it makes it easier for me to renounce it all.

I must add that if you came to me today and offered me the two months of plenitude I wanted, I should be afraid. I felt passionately that it would be better to lose you after than to lose you before. But now I'm frightened. Some enthusiasm on your part would have been essential. To obtain that from you as an irksome duty . . .

You made it clear to me that the greatest gift my love could offer you was to give you nothing unless you desired and asked for it. And I sometimes think that my love was not so much love as a desire for self-glorification. I regarded you, in fact, as an instrument of my pleasure and happiness. True love would have meant searching, not for what pleased me, but for what pleased you; and thus giving up what I wanted of my own free will. No doubt I must have loved you very imperfectly, since I could not bring myself to make this sacrifice. Perhaps you loved me better than I loved you, since you did not love yourself in me. And perhaps it is now that I am giving you the best of my love. But a lot you care about that . . .

For the first time, I can tell you that there is no need for you to answer me. You would be bound to hurt me, with your genius for sadistic phrases, whereas in your silence I re-create and re-discover you, such as I once loved you.

Yours,

A.H.

I should also like to put to you a rather difficult and delicate question. I should like to know whether it has ever occurred to you that you might perpetuate my love by transposing some aspects of it into one of your books. This desire has nothing to do with vanity. It's simply that it would give me the feeling that so much suffering had not been entirely in vain.

This letter remained unanswered.

On the evenings when Mlle Dandillot came to the flat in the avenue Henri-Martin, the first thing she did was to switch off the light. And a sort of ritual had developed. He would undress her little by little, while she stood there small and upright in front of him, in her habitual pose, her head bowed a little, gazing at him without an atom of false modesty out of her dark blue eyes which seemed even larger and darker – almost black – in the dim light of the room, as if they had absorbed some of the night's darkness (which was why this night hung so clear above the world). And thus, half-naked, she would seem like a new person, and he would say to her: 'My little one, is it really you?' And sometimes she would answer 'Yes', as though it were a question which demanded a precise answer. And already this 'yes' was in her night voice, her voice of love, that extraordinarily changed voice of night and love, veiled and high-pitched like the voices of those who are about to die – her little girl's voice, her baby girl's voice, the voice of a woman newly-born and the voice of a dying woman.

And now behold him, vibrant, enveloping her in his coils, while she remains standing, motionless, wordless, only turning her head to follow him with wide-open, unblinking eyes, as the cobra, motionless on its coils, turns its head according to the movement of the snake-charmer's face. He moves as in more ductile air, in the infinite power he has over her; he kisses her now here, now there, according to his whim or with no whim at all; he rests his eyes now here, now there, and each time, as if bewitched, she removes some flimsy garment from the place his eyes have pointed to. Now she stands naked and utterly pure, and still he enfolds her in his coils. Her legs are warm and fragrant as freshly-baked dough. Her belt has left a red weal at her waist, as though she had been whipped. He pulls out two tiny hair-pins from her chignon, the only two he can find (for he is such a fool). She pulls out the rest and hands them to him, one by one, in silence, and their number never varies. Now she stands with her hair over her shoulders, over her breasts with their soft, dune-like curves, more than ever sunk into her childhood; and sometimes it happens that her hair is still damp, like a forest after rain, because she has come to him straight from the swimming-bath. He takes it in his hands, and first he kisses the ends of it, where it is her without yet being quite her, almost foreign to her, like a river which, at the end of its course, no longer knows its mountain or its source. Tracing it back along its whole length, he at last comes to her and the faint odour of her warm scalp.

He comes back to her face and meets again – like an old acquaintance – the scent of her face-powder which he had forgotten. He wraps her hair around her neck. He spreads it over her mouth and searches for her lips through it. With one lock for the moustache and the rest for the beard, he turns her into a young lady of Saint-Cyr in the role of Joad. And now she is naked in front of the window, practically on the balcony. He warns her, but she does not stir. On crossing his threshold, she has entered a magic circle. . . .

Lying down, she did not seem very different from what she had been the first time. She lay there, innocent and peaceful, as natural as a little goat in the midst of the flock. Nearly always she kept her eyes closed, and when she opened them, light with dark flecks, she created both light and darkness at the same time; and then she would look at him with astonishment, her face so close to his it made her squint a little. And she would give him short, sharp kisses, like a bird pecking, three, four, five at a time, like constellations; and then a single one, sudden, violent, like a ball shot at goal, or like a lightning flash. In between long silences broken only by a half-hour striking or a towel slipping from the towel-rail in the bathroom, he would say:

'What are you thinking about?'

'How nice it is. . . .'

O little girl!

'How silent you are!'

'When I'm happy I never talk.'

O little girl!

(When I'm happy . . . Andrée had written the same thing, but he had not thought it to her credit, because he did not love Andrée.)

Then he would tease her.

'I'm going to switch on the light.'

Whereupon her 'No! No's!' would break out with unexpected violence. And he: 'What do you mean, no? Have we, by any chance, a personality of our own?' (The possibility did not seem to please him; and besides, caressing a woman in the dark is like smoking in the dark: no taste). But when after a moment he asked her: 'What would you do if I suddenly switched on the light?' she answered: 'Nothing....'

O little girl!

And oh! that night voice as she said it, the incredibly child-like intonations, rising from the depths of her childhood as from a tomb – that other voice that came to her as soon as she was 'horizontal', like those chaste dolls which automatically lower their eyelids when one lays them on their backs.

It was on one of these evenings that he wrote this poem for her:

> Since you love me, I you (that's understood)
> Since I am wholly yours today – agreed?
> Since it appears that either finds it good,
> For I suffice you, you are all I need,
>
> Then lay against my breast, sweet age-old child
> (Don't fear those other heads; their trace is light)
> Your scentless hair and your long eyes, beast-wild,
> More deep, more dark, for having drunk of night.

And so it went on, but we shall quote no more, for we do not think it is worth a tinker's curse.

He never failed to express a little more tenderness towards her than he really felt, to add to that tenderness a sort of halo which spread it further. For instance he would sometimes say 'My little darling' at times when the words did not spring spontaneously to his lips, or else he would clasp her in his arms with greater vigour than his natural impulse called for. He knew that women tend to think one loves them less when one does not love them more and more, and that men, being poor at loving, must keep a constant watch over themselves if they do not wish to disappoint.

There were moments when he passionately wanted to be the man who would reveal her to herself. There were other moments when he had no such desire.

He still did not take her completely, for he wished to go on picturing this unknown territory before him, as when on board ship one looks toward that part of the sea where land will appear tomorrow. He would stop at the precise point beyond which he would have hurt her, as a dog that bites its friend in play will check itself delightfully and take care not to go too far. But their kisses were so voracious that the tip of his tongue was split and he had to give up smoking.

He was always afraid she might catch cold while naked, and would willingly have sacrificed part of his pleasure to have her put on some of her clothes again. She would complain a little: 'You treat me like a child.' To which he would reply: 'A person one loves is always a child.' Often he reminded her of the time, but she did not seem to hear. Sometimes they would stay together in this way until that supreme hour of night when the cats settle down in the middle of the road to attend to their toilet. Clocks chimed the hour, answering one another like cock-crows. He had the impression that if he had not said to her, 'Time to go, little one', she would have stayed there all night, as though her mother and father did not exist. In all their relations, it was never she who took the initiative. And he praised her for it. 'I hate women with a will of their own, and that is why you were always made for me.' (And yet, if we are to believe Schopenhauer, who sees a connection between will-power and sexual passion, he would not have been sorry had she willed a little more. . . .)

Now she went off to the bathroom without being told, like a kitten that has been house-trained. Meanwhile he brushed the left shoulder of his jacket, where her cheek had left a cloud of face-powder like a milky way deep in the night sky. And now here she was by his side in the avenue, striking the echoing pavement with her short, mule-like steps. What had happened? Had anything happened? Here she was, exactly the same as she had been when she arrived that evening. Terribly womanly, when a moment before she had been such a schoolgirl. Terribly intact in appearance, and yet no longer intact. Terribly prim and proper.

He knew she never told them at home why she got back so late at night. The thought that she lied to her parents was infinitely pleasing to him. 'That way, we can talk.' He felt that this made her somehow more human.

Sometimes they walked hand in hand, like well-brought-up children who have been told to go and play in the park and be good – or like Tunisian gendarmes.

At about that time he had just published a new book, which brought him many flattering letters and reviews. He had taken as his motto Gobineau's phrase, which he twisted round to read thus: 'First love, then work, then nothing.' But his work was his writing, not the relationship between his writing and the public. To this he was more or less indifferent. He skimmed rapidly through both reviews and letters mechanically, without getting involved. Praise was to him like musical instruments being played in a silent film: he knew that they must be producing a pleasant noise, but he could not hear it.

He was saying to her:

'You really must try and see things as they are. Michelet says that it's most humiliating for the loved one to keep enough composure to be able to distinguish the truth behind the lover's fine words. *There's* a piece of nonsense worthy of the 'stupid' nineteenth century. To keep one's composure is never humiliating. And to see things as they are is always admirable. The fact, in our case, is that I am not in love with you. What I feel towards you is, on the one hand, affection tinged with tenderness, together with esteem, and on the other hand, desire. But all this does not constitute love, thank God. It makes up something which is my own particular formula, in which I am entirely myself, and which is wholly commendable: this last point alone would be sufficient to prove that it isn't love. For one likes a woman *because*, and one loves her *although*. Besides, experience leads me to believe that my formula pleases women, because according to my own observation they seem to need affection and tenderness more than love properly so called. You're not in love with me either, are you?'

She shook her head and shrugged her shoulders slightly, with an amused expression on her face – all this very young-lady-like and full of charm. And she said:

'Not exactly, no, I don't think so.... I mean I don't love you in a sentimental way.'

'There's one sure sign that you don't love me; you never ask me questions about my life. And you don't blush when your parents talk about me, do you? You've never looked me up in *Who's Who*? You never came round to the avenue Henri-Martin when we first met, to see the house I lived in? You've never scribbled my name on a sheet of note-paper for no reason at all?'

To each question she shook her head with the same gentle and amused expression on her face. True, the night after he had kissed her for the first time, she had gone to sleep with one of his books under her sheet. But that was right at the beginning; nature had blundered because it had been caught unawares. Never again had Solange done anything of the kind.

'It's true, isn't it? Before I brought you here myself, you never had enough curiosity to come and see where I lived? Then that settles it: you've never been in love with me. And that's how I want you to be. A loving girl, not a girl in love. I don't want you to get worked up about me. You would be bound to suffer, and it would be absurd for you to suffer on my account when all I want is your happiness. One must know how to handle the absurd, my dear, and I think I can say I'm a master of the art, but it should at least give you some pleasure. It's always stupid to suffer. To say that suffering is something great and remarkable is one of the worst lies spread around by the leaders of the masses (for political ends) and then taken up by the intellectuals (from sheer stupidity). At the end of your first fairly intimate letter you assured me of your 'tender affection'. I don't know whether it was a phrase you just happened to use by chance or whether you had weighed its meaning, but if it represented what you really felt, then it was magnificent, since it corresponds exactly both to what I feel towards you and what I expect from you.'

'I wrote that because it seemed to convey just what I felt.'

'Then, my dear, it's splendid, and I can see that we shall get on famously.'

And yet, that same evening....

That same evening, when he asked her: 'Will you come to my flat for a while, later on?' she answered: 'Not tonight if you don't mind ... Perhaps we ought to space out our meetings a little....'

And she added:

'When I come to visit you, afterwards I feel you're further away from me ...'

Although disappointed, he did not take her up on this. They were crossing the Place de la Concorde. He made a few remarks about the colour of the sky at that twilight hour. But inwardly he was turning to stone. Not only was he wounded in his male vanity, but it seemed to him as though she had locked the door on the future: how could he ever make love to her again after that?

There was a long silence, and then he asked her:

'Would you like me to take you home, or would you like to go somewhere?'

It was a terrible thing to suggest leaving her so early, contrary to all their habits, merely because of frustrated desire – terrible for a girl of Mlle Dandillot's temperament; and terrible for him too. He had hoped she would answer: 'Take me home.' How could she not have realized that she had made the evening untenable? He was surprised at what he deemed her lack of tact when she said: 'Let's go somewhere.'

The cinema is the cesspool of the twentieth century. Whenever there is something vile between two people, it always leads to a session at the pictures. In the cinema near the Invalides where they finally landed up, she tried from time to time to make small talk. He, as though the muscles of his tongue had been severed, found it literally impossible to say a word. He was convinced that they were meeting for the last time. No, never had a woman said anything so humiliating to her lover; he had thought his caresses brought them infinitely closer to each other, but they made her feel he was further away! Now he wanted to wound her in his turn. 'She may as well know what I'm really like?' During the two and a half hours the show lasted, he never once opened his lips. As it was very hot, she sometimes put her handkerchief (her minute little girl's handkerchief) to her forehead, to her nose – to her eyes perhaps – and he wondered whether she wanted to cry. He noticed that one of her hands was resting in a rather unnatural way on the arm of her seat next to him, and thought

she must have put it there so that he would take it and hold
it in his. He did no such thing. Once or twice, too, she turned
her face towards him without saying anything, as though
asking to be kissed. The more he realized how base and vulgar,
how petty and ridiculous – how bourgeois, in short – his
attitude towards her was, the more he stuck to it. During the
intervals he could read the thoughts on the faces of those
around him : 'Such an exquisite little thing, and such a ghastly,
sulking brute ! Talk about pearls and swine !' What sickened
him most about the 'scene' he was creating was that it seemed to
him the very image of a conjugal row.

At last, the torture came to an end. They went out, still
silent. Then she did something she had *never* done before:
she put her arm through his. He was touched. This gesture
seemed to say, with the utmost simplicity : 'Come back to me.
Can't you see I'm not cross with you?' Yet, touched as he
was by her gesture, at the same time he saw in it a way of
hurting her even more: simply by not responding to it. However, when they reached the avenue de Villiers and passed her
door without her showing any sign of stopping, he exploded.
In a jerky, unrecognizable voice he blurted out: 'You have
wounded me deeply. You have said the very worst thing a
woman can say to a man. Now I can never touch you again.
I shall always think that you let me make love to you out
of complaisance, when in fact you feel nothing but disgust. . . .'

'Of course not, you know very well. . . .'

'To hell with girls – especially winsome, frigid little French
girls who never know what pleasure is before they're twenty-
six ! After all, nobody has yet found any other way for a man
to show his affection for a woman. No, there's no way out of
it. I can't make love to you any more now. And as for playing
at brother and sister, frankly it's impossible; I'm not that kind
of man. You gave yourself, and now you've taken yourself
back; but you did give yourself, and the taste of it will always
remain. You opened the door on to a room filled with music,
and now you have shut it again. . . .'

She said nothing. They went on walking, going round the
block for the third time.

'And then, how can I dare talk to you again? What value

can you ever again attach to what I say? I told you a dozen times: "Above all, you must be frank with me." And it's by being frank that you've destroyed everything. You're being punished for being what I asked you to be. And so from now on I can neither talk nor act with you. It isn't your fault. It's simply that our temperaments are incompatible. But I repeat, there's no way out of it.'

Once again they reached her door. She would have gone on; it was he who stopped. He held out his hand:

'Since we're seeing each other at the d'Hautecourts' to-morrow, we're bound to talk to each other again. But in fact everything is over between us.'

He saw her raise her beautiful eyes towards him, full of surprise, sadness and reproach, as a bitch gazes at the brute of a master who has struck her for no reason. A taxi passed, and he hailed it. His voice was so strangled that he had to repeat his address several times before the driver understood it.

At home he found the bed prepared, and the armfuls of flowers he had arranged for her. He threw himself on the bed in an agony of suffering. Suffering from having made her suffer. Suffering from having made her suffer although he loved her. Suffering from having made her suffer for being honest with him. Suffering from having deprived himself of her body. Suffering because he suffered from having deprived himself of her body, although her body gave him so little pleasure. Suffering because he suffered only in the basest part of his male self (his sexual vanity) and because this male suffering was so very puerile. Suffering, not least, because the room was so hot (eighty degrees Fahrenheit). At intervals, a petal fell from a vase like the chime of the half-hour. The intimate odour of the girl's body came back to him obsessively, exacerbating his resentment, a wisp of fragrance that seemed to float about the room like seeds borne on the summer air. Finally he thought of going to the larder for a cold chicken which he knew was there. He ate it, and his anguish died away. He even felt glad that he had suffered a little. One must try everything once.

That night he had a dream. He dreamed of the old English governess he had had as a boy. Never in his life had he dreamed of her before. And try as he might, he could find no clue to what the dream meant.

He began to think about the woman, and a strange memory came back to him. He remembered his terror when, waking up in the early morning, he used to imagine that perhaps, during the night, she had gone away for ever. Then he would get up and go barefooted to the governess's room. Objects, clothes, everything would be in place: the Englishwoman had simply gone to Mass, as she did every day. But such irrefutable evidence was not enough to reassure him. He would tiptoe on to the landing and wait there with beating heart for the rattle of the returning governess's key in the front door (for, after all, he must have realized that she was at Mass). Then as soon as he heard the noise of the key, he would rush back to bed and pretend to be asleep. . . .

All this would have been easy to understand if he had had some sort of childish crush on his governess (he was then seven or eight years old). But nothing of the sort. On the contrary, he rather disliked her. She rapped his knuckles with a ruler when he made mistakes in his piano lessons, she left him – without a word – crying for half an hour at a time because he could not make head or tail of his arithmetic, she took the currants out of his fruit cake at tea-time, pretending they were bad for him when really she wanted them herself. . . He liked her so little that when she retired, although she settled in Paris, he had never once been to see her. No, however carefully he ransacked his memory, he could find nothing in his feelings for her except indifference tinged with resentment – nothing but indifference, with here and there those wild uprushes of passionate feeling, those torments of the tiny lover, at half past six in the morning, in the great, slumbering house. . . .

Costals began to wonder whether he did not love Solange.

The next day, a hop at the d'Hautecourts'. A few women's bodies would make it bearable. What would society be without bodies? One could see it wiped out without a murmur.

Arriving after her, he followed her with his eyes without letting her see him. He would have liked her discreetly to show her contempt for all these people; but no, she seemed at ease among them; was she, perhaps, one of them? She danced three times with a young buck. 'If they go and sit behind the buffet, or on the stairs, I feel – yes, I feel it as if it were happening at this very moment – that all the blood will drain from my face, will drain from my legs as if it were flowing away under the ballroom floor.'

He came towards her with an ugly expression on his face – an unwonted ugliness, a husband's ugliness. She greeted him, suddenly transformed, her face open, her eyes radiant with tenderness, as though nothing had happened the day before. He was touched by her unquestioning trust.

They danced. He was thinking: 'Am I going to be the ignoble male to the bitter end? Yesterday I was cruel and unjust because my petty sexual pride had been hurt. Tomorrow I shall debase myself by resuming my love-making, knowing that she merely tolerates it. This body in my arms in front of two hundred people – I have laid my head on its naked belly (an exquisite sensation); with my cheek against that belly, I have heard the rumbling of her intestines, like the faint sound of thawing snow.... In fact, by God, she's mine!'

And he let them see it all right. The dance over, an astonishing thing occurred. No sooner had they sat down beside each other than he put his hand on the girl's thigh (over her dress), and then let it rest on her midriff, as a lion spreads out its paw over the chunk of meat it has conquered.

Not in some secluded corner, but right in the middle of the room, surrounded by two hundred people. Not for a brief instant, but for a good half-minute, perhaps. Not in any dubious or 'advanced' company, but among well-bred, respectable people. That's what comes of inviting poets to your house!

He was deeply aware of the element of the grandiose in his gesture. Nothing licentious. The gesture of the couple. The primitive gesture of the lord and master, that of the ape with its mate: the essence of the couple. And he was also aware of the grandeur there was in the fact that she accepted it, that this reserved and modest girl did not flinch under his gesture, did not offer the least resistance, in the heart of that crowd, as though she did not care in the least, as though she were pleased even, that it should be demonstrated in this extraordinary manner, in front of everybody, what she was to the man she had chosen.

When he drew his hand away, yet another link had been forged between them. Invisibly, his hand was still upon her. That same evening she came to his house at the accustomed hour.

Andrée Hacquebaut   to Pierre Costals
Saint-Léonard   *Paris*

15 June 1927

Please read the whole of this letter.

Dear Costals,

I am far away, defenceless, sick with loneliness, crushed by such heat that it reminds me of that line of yours:

'The heat of the day sits, man-like, upon the earth.'

There was a big thunderstorm last night, and I was glad it woke me up since it gave me the chance to think about you. What was I saying in my last letter? I don't make a rough draft of my letters to you, and I'm afraid they must contradict one another terribly. I think I was telling you I had found a kind of peace ... Yes, I wanted, with genuine good-will, to safeguard our friendship through this ghastly business, although I know only too well how little a man cares for a woman's friendship when he cares nothing for her love. When you refused me, I thought: 'For him, of course, the woman who refuses herself is desirable, and the woman who offers herself is disdained. How childish!' But it has to be admitted: a disappointment, a refusal, makes what was desirable a thousand times more desirable. I can see it now with you.

Besides, how could I forget you? The fact that you are now a public figure (the same word for a 'public figure' and a 'public woman'! How appropriate. . . .) makes it *physically* impossible. In order to·be free of you completely, I ought never to open a newspaper or a magazine. And by the way, there's something I'd like to know.... Yesterday's *Nouvelles littéraires* (which I read – horror of horrors – in the deserted church,

because it's the only cool place here) brought me your poem:
'Since you love me, I you. . . .'
and I should like to know whether, when you wrote it, you
did not have me partly in mind. I very much doubt it, and
yet. . . . But no, of course not, it's addressed to someone else,
and I can just see you sneer: 'How naïve the girl is!' Naïve!
You have only yourself to blame: you could have made me a
woman, but you did not choose to. These amorous confidences
you spread around in the weeklies (isn't it nice to be able to
indulge one's exhibitionism in the sacred name of Art?) twist
the dagger in my wound, filling me with jealousy and desire.
It's too obvious: my love for you fills you with horror. But
what am I supposed to do about it? I think of you from morning till night. It oozes out of me. I was about to say like an
emanation, but the word is too pretentious; like sweat, rather.
You passed too close to me, you swept me, lonely little star
that I am, into your orbit, and you scorched me with your
fires. In all good faith, I still want to believe it is so. Man-
slaughter, not murder. You have annihilated me; I'm not
humiliated, I'm not torn apart, I'm stunned. You have made me
unfit for everyday life. I am like one of those antiques about
which dealers say to one: 'Yes, it's beautiful. It's worth a lot.
I can't buy it from you, though; they're not in demand just
now. But it's lovely, hang on to it.' I know I'm worth something, but no one has a use for me. And I shall end up by
hating myself, by destroying myself perhaps, as one ends by
hating and sometimes destroying those objects which antique
dealers find so beautiful but which nothing on earth would
make them buy. Yes, unusable. Because of you, I have nothing
to offer the man who might now come along expecting and
desiring someone intact; I would be giving him an empty husk.
It's *exactly* as if I had had a lover or a husband; my moral
virginity no longer exists. How can you not feel that all
this gives you a responsibility towards me, that you must
make amends? And by making amends I mean giving me the
satisfactions of the flesh to which I am entitled.

Your disinterestedness is a subtle form of perversion. You
told me once, parodying the motto of *l'Action Française*: 'We
stand for everything natural.' Oh, no! you are not close to

nature; that is perhaps your greatest illusion. It is saintliness you stand nearest to, but a sort of inverted saintliness, a diabolical saintliness. Ceaselessly preoccupied with you as I am, I learn a little more about you each day, in spite of your silence. I learn more about myself too. You once admitted to a certain 'curiosity' about me (and I have come to believe that it is the only feeling – a professional one at that! – you have ever had towards me). You might perhaps have desired me if I had not revealed so much of myself in my letters: it is the great misfortune of my life that, owing to my loneliness, nearly everything between us has happened by way of letters. But are you sure you really know me? Do you know whether, even *professionally*, a more intimate relationship between us might not reveal much more? Are you sure you don't actually *need* me?

You will never find me again unless, some day, you feel that need – but it must be total. I shall be your mistress or your wife, never again your friend. You will come back to me, if you do, knowing that I love you, that I adore you, that I have never wanted and do not want anything but your kisses and your arms around me. Are you satisfied? Is that clear enough? I feel a kind of wild relief in reaching these depths of self-abasement, in renewing the written proof of it, in giving you these weapons you will always be able to use against me.

Andrée

This letter remained unanswered.

'Just her legs alone, and I go mad!' he exclaimed, heedless of syntax. 'Look at that lovely little creature, old thing. Extraordinary how a pretty face can make you sit up. Suddenly, when you were sated to the point of not caring if you died, you want to go on living. Suddenly, if you had to write, you'd have forgotten how to spell. Eighteen, think of it! And arms even prettier than yours. And those vaccination marks! Enough to drive the archangel Gabriel to perdition. Quite frankly, my dear, I could gobble her up. She blows her little nose behind her newspaper (rather conservative in tone) so that

I shan't see her do anything so unbecoming. Then with her
rosy fingers she stuffs the handkerchief back into her bag.
Every time she catches me eyeing her, she moistens her lips
with the tip of her tongue. And the way her shoulders shake
when she laughs! And the parting in her hair, meandering all
over the place! And her ears – I bet they've never known ear-
ache! And there's a hint of poverty in the cloth of her dress,
in her little wrist-watch, that makes me swoon with desire.
What power on earth could prevent me from desiring her?
I'd like to know what her hair would taste like if I chewed it.
I'd like. . . . She's worthy of desire, and so I desire her: it's only
nature, after all, damn it! Oh, only *desire* her, you understand:
I'm not breaking things up. But when I see those rather heavy
veins on her pulpy feet in those sandals, then I tell you, old
girl, I begin to feel like a man. Am I being wounding? Yes, I
see I am. . . . I'm so sorry. . . . But what can I do, old girl?
I belong to a sex which is the complete opposite of yours; I
belong to the lecherous breed of men. What I enjoy is seeing
what women are like when they surrender, and then comparing. . . . What is happiness, for those of my race? Happiness
is the moment when someone surrenders. And incidentally,
mystics often change their women, because attachment to one
person is what is most contrary to the spiritual life. You too
are a tiny star among thousands of others. And at dawn you'll
fade away. . . . Ah! so I have wounded you? I recognize that
way you have of smiling when something's gone wrong. . . .
I haven't said anything unpleasant, though, have I?'

'Oh, no! Nothing at all!'

'And anyway, what I've been telling you was set to dance
music, so to speak. You're not much of a sport, are you?'

'What's the good of explaining? You refuse to understand
what you mean to me.'

'Yes, I do refuse. Because I ought not to mean too much
to you.'

She turned her face towards him sharply, with a look of
reproach. Then he said:

'I'm glad you love me, but I don't want you to love me too
much. I'm glad my desire pleases you, but I don't want it to
please you too much. For that would force me to exaggerate,

to go beyond what comes to me naturally; in both spheres it would saddle me with a duty to reciprocate exactly; and this I dread, not only because it's duty (and duty doesn't suit me) but because it would drive me to artifice, which for the moment I'm entirely devoid of. What I want is for you to love me and to welcome my desire precisely to the extent that I love and desire you. And believe me, that's a great deal.'

Written the next day by Costals in the Bois, on the blank page of *l'Education des Filles*, which he was reading:

Two ravishing little things, fifteen and sixteen, straight out of Meleager, sitting on a bench with their mother who obviously. . . . Well, with their mother who knows a thing or two. (They were each swinging one leg, like two little donkeys swinging their tails in unison. Oh, to spend a night with one of those feet in my hands!) And it seems to me that merely by looking at them as I do, over there in the avenue de Villiers, suddenly, without knowing why, while she is sewing, her heart is pierced and it bleeds. O Nature, spare me from desiring others as long as I love her!

Mlle Dandillot's predominant feeling now she was in love was the fear that Costals might not love her enough and might abandon her. Faced with her first man, she was like a bas-relief changed into a statue – deprived of its support, suddenly alone and threatened on all sides. Before she loved, her nights had been uneventful. Now each night brought its dreams, always unpleasant dreams, though they never developed into nightmares. For instance, she dreamed that, cycling down a slope, she lost control of her bicycle; but that was all: there was no fall, no precipice. Or she dreamed that a cow broke away from the herd and approached until it was almost touching her, but did not attack her. Costals, the cause of all these dreams, never appeared in them: he was the hidden demon behind them. Sometimes, however, she dreamed, not about him, but that she was thinking about him.

There are women who are invigorated by love, particularly

a first love. Mlle Dandillot, on the contrary, ever since she had been in love, had physically declined. And it was fear of losing Costals that had weakened her. Often she felt below par, tired out, needing to sit down; when she had been standing for a while, her thighs ached.

At meals, the need to find an outlet for her nervous energy made her chew rapidly and vigorously. Having thus finished each course before her mother, she took second helpings to fill the gaps, and found herself eating appreciably more than usual. Then she noticed that she felt stronger after these large meals, and that as soon as she started over-eating, it was again in her thighs that she first felt better.

From then on, whenever she was due to meet Costals later in the day, she systematically took second helpings, which brought a smile to the face of the maid serving at table, a smile to which Solange responded sweetly, not knowing quite whether Suzanne had guessed her secret. She also had two cups of coffee, and could easily have managed two breakfasts. She was to be seen chewing away at peach-stones till they were worn down and cracked, as a dog worries a croquet-ball with its slobbery mouth. And although she was normally a non-smoker, she would now sometimes smoke two strong cigarettes one after the other. Yet Mme Dandillot noticed nothing (and as for her husband! ...). Thus the servant saw what the mother didn't. It is said that mother-love is blind. Yes, indeed.

If Mlle Dandillot had not been such a good little girl, she would have known that a few drops of alcohol would have produced the same factitious vitality she obtained by ever so slightly stuffing herself. But she did not know this, or even guess it. And in any case the world in general does not know it either. Or rather it knows it *a little*, which is tantamount to not at all. A war-leader knows that, in battle, a good army is an army that is slightly the worse for drink. But he does not generalize from the fact as he should. A man who knew that there is no torment of love that a *really* good meal cannot dispel, at least for a few hours, a man who knew that physical and moral courage, poetic inspiration, devotion, sacrifice, may all depend on a good meal – that the most sublime flights of the soul may be due to the rotting flesh of dead animals – a

man who knew all this could never be fooled by anyone. But
the man who is on the brink of knowing all this shrinks from
the knowledge. And if he does know it, he behaves as if he
didn't. For man must live in the clouds.

On the other hand, Costals' meals before his meetings with
Solange were very light. He was naturally so healthy and
eupeptic that a little hotting-up would merely have decreased
his lucidity, which he prized above everything. At these meals
he even refrained from drinking, and thus weighing himself
down, and only drank on the days when he did not love her
so much. So that, when Solange was getting ready to leave,
the first thing he did was to go to the wash-basin for a drink
of water. And if Solange had failed to turn up at the rendezvous
he had given her, which was always a few steps away from
the house in the avenue de Villiers, his disappointment would
have been offset by the fact that, after waiting twenty minutes,
he could dive into the nearest wine-shop. He had elevated into
a philosophy of life what had at first been no more than a
delightful characteristic : to love (and to be capable of doing)
in everything its opposite. Thus fate, whether it gave him a yes
or a no, satisfied him equally. And he was always on velvet,
which was very pleasant for him, and even satisfied his mind,
for he held that only dullards and mock philosophers conceive
of life as a struggle.

She had said : 'Come and have tea with me on Sunday.
Mummy and Daddy are spending the day with some cousins
of ours in Fontainebleau, and it's the servants' day off. We shall
be alone in the flat.' The idea of making love to her in her own
house, in her own little-girl's bedroom, had set him on fire.

It was an exquisite sensation to find her alone in the empty
house and to see her switch off the front door-bell. But soon
he noticed a slight sore on her lip, and dark rings under her
eyes which intensified the depth of her gaze. She confirmed
what he had guessed; and his feelings took on a new note of
solemnity, as when the piano pedal is pressed down. These
were the times he always loved best in women, when he knew

them to be unwell: this weakness in them fanned his heart as much as his senses. However much they protested that they hardly felt it, he fussed and worried, convinced that they were simply being brave and really needed nursing. He had always had a tendency to pamper women, even sports-women, in spite of the impression they sometimes give of having more stamina than men.

And now they were in the drawing-room, sitting side by side on a sofa. The cloudy summer day seemed more like autumn. At first they had talked about trivialities (but how touching she was when, gazing straight in front of her, she would swiftly turn her head towards him whenever he said something particularly nice or striking). He had asked her to take him into her bedroom, but she, who usually agreed to anything he asked, had this time firmly refused. He had asked her to show him some photographs of herself, but she had not been photographed since she was fourteen – so lacking in vanity all these people were! Eventually he came to a subject which was very much on his mind. The last time she had been to his house, he had embraced her with an ardour so intense and so frequently renewed that at the end of the evening, while he was getting dressed, he had been overcome with a sort of nervous prostration: he had suddenly gone silent and numb, and heavy with weariness. He had to make a real effort to drag out a few commonplace remarks as he escorted her home. So now he explained that men, after having given too generously of themselves, are subject at times to such temporary diminutions of vitality, that this is a normal and recognized phenomenon, and that, assuming she had noticed it, she should excuse it in him. But had she in fact noticed it?

He had put the question almost casually, and was surprised and a little worried when she said 'Yes'. Did she notice everything, then?

'What about the other occasions?'

'Then, too.'

His surprise increased. On other occasions, either this collapse did not occur, or if it did, it was so slight and fleeting that he thought he had managed to conceal it under a renewed outburst of caresses. 'Goodness! The girl sees everything!'

'But how astonishing! You really did find me distant, those other times, when I was taking you home?'

'Yes. I wondered why. Whether I'd disappointed you. . . .'

He started explaining afresh, citing the *Omne animal post* . . ., offering to show her medical textbooks. Meanwhile he kept gently tugging at the little hairs above her elbow (a detail worth mentioning, after all). Suddenly he fell silent. It seemed to him as though his eyes were being opened at last.

'But then, when you said to me: "Afterwards you seem further away from me", is that what you meant?'

'Yes.'

He repeated the words to himself: 'Afterwards, you seem further away from me.' For the first time he realized it could be interpreted in two different ways: either that, after their love-making was over, Solange felt colder towards him, or else that she felt that he was colder towards her. An abyss separated the two meanings. How had he managed to see only the first and not the second?

'Look here, Solange, this is extremely important: did you feel you were further away from me after we'd made love, or did you, on the other hand, find that I was further away from you, colder towards you?'

'I found you colder towards me. I could sense in you the reactions which you've just described, as a blind man feels a Braille text with his fingertips. But I didn't know there was a purely physical reason for it.'

'What an incredible misunderstanding! I understood just the opposite. But why on earth didn't you explain? You let me sulk for hours and make a frightful scene, and all the time you say nothing, you just stand there gaping at me like a sick calf. . . . When all you had to say was: "It's *you* I find so cold, afterwards. . . ." '

She made a slightly impatient, rueful gesture.

'You know how hopeless I am at explaining. I've told you often enough. The more I saw you going off on the wrong tack, the more paralysed I became. Often when I'm with you, I feel stupefied. . . . The first time, in the Bois . . . if you had told me to jump into the water, I would have done it.'

'Yes, I know. And may I point out to you that I did not do

so. But still, I've never known such an incredible misunderstanding. You could never put anything like it into a novel. Nobody would believe that a twenty-one-year-old Parisienne, in the year 1927, could allow herself to be upbraided for hours by her lover for having said something which merely expressed her fear of seeing him grow cooler towards her, in other words for expressing nothing but affection, and all because she's hopeless at explaining? But you're crazy, my dear girl, absolutely crazy! A real little artichoke, on a railway embankment!'

'Why a railway embankment?'

'Because that's much nicer, of course!'

With a feeling of deep tenderness he took her in his arms. Never, no, never had she seemed to him so like a child, so defenceless, so vulnerable, so susceptible to the suffering which everything in life, and especially he, would ultimately inflict on her. He remembered the gesture she had made when, not knowing how to break down his moody silence, she had – for the first time – slipped her arm through his, as a scolded dog puts out a paw to obtain forgiveness. In that instant, a complete upheaval occurred inside him: he saw that she was infinitely weaker than he had imagined, and he realized too that he loved her far more than he had imagined – while at the same time the only complaint he had ever been able to make against her had lost its justification. In that short moment she came really close to him, to what was essential in him. What joy he would have felt in killing anyone who harmed her now! Then he bent down and kissed, not the top of her shoulder, which was bare (for this might have seemed like sensuality), but that part of her shoulder which was covered by her clothes.

Then the conversation drifted. With the same kind of feeling that had caused him to kiss her blouse and not her skin, he was now holding the edge of her dress. Eventually, prompted by their surroundings, the talk settled on Solange's family.

'My brother wasn't very clever: the only thing he was capable of was making money.... I don't love Mummy and Daddy in the same way. I love Mummy in an indulgent way: she's so superficial! Daddy has much more finesse. Besides, he's so ill. . . . ' (M. Dandillot was suffering from cancer of the prostate and his days were numbered.) 'The point about men like my uncle Louis is to get the maximum of approbation for the minimum of risk.' ('What a splendid definition of the bourgeoisie!' thought Costals.) 'My religion? I'm not a believer, but when I see a paper like' (there followed the name of a weekly with a particularly 'Parisian' tone) 'it makes me almost want to be a Christian again. I tell myself there must be more to things than *that*.'

And finally, this scrap of dialogue:

'None of the young men of my generation seem to have a sense of duty. Whereas a man like you. . . . '

'Seriously, do I look like a man with a sense of duty?'

'No. But you are.'

'You're a sly one! Yes, of course, as soon as one's in love, one can't help having a sense of duty.'

At first, Costals had seen Solange as a doll. He had taken her as one takes a woman for a waltz and then brings her back to her chair. Later, when he knew her better, she seemed the product of the kind of upbringing which teaches that it is impolite to express one's own opinion, and that one should always agree with the other person. He had snubbed her when she said, as girls so often do: 'I'm a bit of a freak.' 'You're not in the least a freak. You're exactly like any other girl.' He had snubbed her again when she said she was 'misunderstood': 'That's what all women say when there's nothing in them to understand.' He had regretted not being able to tease her to his heart's content, because she wasn't witty enough to answer back: 'She would only feel offended and hurt.' He had once paid her this compliment – a considerable one, though its limits are obvious: 'I have never heard her say anything either stupid or vulgar.' He had seen her as soft and self-effacing, in fact an ideal heroine for a French novel. And yet, confirming from his own observations in society that she was telling the truth when she said she had no friends, he was inclined to infer that she must be worth something, since solitude and worth are synonymous. This worth did not, however, go further than 'magnificent negative qualities', and he still thought of her what St Teresa says of herself: 'Thou art she who is not.' His predominant feeling towards her was admiration for her beauty.

But now it was as though he were watching a photographic plate in a bath of developer: gradually, as on the plate, new details of Solange's personality emerged; gradually her complete image was taking shape, and this image reflected great credit on her. Her qualities of perception and judgement, so shrewd and so sensible, were not in themselves so very unusual. But he did not expect to find them in her. He discovered how little he knew about her, and in particular how much better she was than he. Even her voice was a new discovery. Until then, he had known three voices of hers. Her society voice, rather affected, which she adopted not as a pose but on the contrary because she was shy. The voice she used when she talked to him, about which there was little to be said. Her 'night voice', full of pathos, a voice from another world, with its childish words springing from the depths of her past like birds from the bottom of a well. And now there was this new voice, calm, utterly simple and serious, with its soothing quality, its indefinable intonations which made him think: 'Exactly the way girls of the aristocracy speak.' He said to her:

'I'm talking to you as if I'd known you for years, and I'm glad. I'm ashamed of the coarse way I treated you at first. As though you were a tart. Forgive me. . . .'

'It doesn't matter. I would have overlooked everything, since I love you. As a matter of fact I did overlook everything. . . .'

'Overlook what, for God's sake?' he wondered. 'Bah! the fact of having given herself, no doubt.' It was clear that she had judged him – perhaps with the same 'indulgence' with which she judged her mother. At other times he would have found this rather irritating. Now it only raised her in his estimation.

'You're in a lower key today. What's happened?'

'Only that I feel more at ease with you now our misunderstanding has been cleared up. Before I knew you, I was afraid of the future. Then, when I was with you, I wasn't afraid any more. And then that misunderstanding occurred and, ever since, I've felt like a bunch of flowers tied too tight. Now you've loosened the string and the flowers can breathe again.'

'Oh! we're in full poetic flight, I see. . . . I'm sorry! Even

when I'm very serious, moved in fact, I can't help joking.
Besides, I love teasing you.'

'I know. I'm beginning to know you.'

'You said something a moment ago.... What was it that
you "overlooked" out of affection for me?'

'Don't you know?'

'I can guess. It's true: you, such a good girl, to give yourself to me like that, like a falling leaf.... When I think of the
moving speech I had prepared to make you give in! And lo
and behold! Like a falling leaf.... It must have been written
in the stars. You have every virtue, including the principal one
of having given yourself without any nonsense. For a woman
who isn't easy isn't a real woman as far as I'm concerned. And
I ask you, what would all those virtues have been to me if you
hadn't given yourself with such dazzling promptitude?'

'When I gave myself to you, I had already given you everything.'

'Così fan tutte.'

'To tell you the truth, it wasn't the act itself I "overlooked".
But ... all the secrecy ... that hotel, the first time....'

'Like a falling leaf,' he said again. 'Like a little artichoke one
picks.... And yet there are women who put up a show of
resistance even when they've made up their minds to surrender.
The last stand....'

'I loved you too much to resist you. That at least is not a così
fan tutte.'

'It's very extraordinary indeed,' he said gravely.

Languidly, with the sickness of the lunar cycle upon her, she
was half reclining in the crook of her lover's arm, like a small
strip of moss in the damp hollow of a rock. When Costals had
entered, two cats had fled: not all cats are heroes. Now they
kept coming back, walking across the room, going out again,
coming and going as silently as ghosts. At moments their presence could be guessed by the sound of a creaking floorboard,
now here, now there.

'You really ought to be taken in hand; you'd be well worth
moulding,' he said, after a silence. 'That's quite clear to me now.'

'That's always the way. The man shapes the woman as he
wants her to be, and she acquiesces.'

'Except that the man doesn't know what he wants. Is there anything more foolish than the male? And besides, he may not be interested. I love you, I want your happiness, and yet I don't feel like moulding you. Do you know why?'

'Yes.'

'What do you mean, "yes"? I bet you haven't the slightest idea.'

'You're not interested in moulding me because you have enough to do moulding your books.'

'Really, you are fantastic! You've hit the nail on the head. I have better things to do than to create individuals. The reason why Rousseau put his kids in an orphanage was that he wanted to write *Emile*. All the same, it's rather horrible. You've backed the wrong horse, old girl.'

'Oh! no, I haven't.' (She put her hand on his.)

'Yes, you say that now! We'll talk about it again in two years' time. . . .'

'But shouldn't love go on increasing all the time? That's the only way I can imagine it.'

'That sort of love isn't my line at all. Mine is more like a waterchute.'

He smiled as he said this, so she smiled, too. And they ended up in one another's arms.

'She lacks inspiration,' he thought to himself. 'Yes, I've put my finger on it. But she's a fine girl all the same.' How openly she had always behaved towards him! Trying to please him (changing her way of dressing, for instance, in accordance with chance remarks he made) but without a trace of coquetry; giving herself without affectation or artifice or pretended flight; so discreet (never asking him anything about his life or telephoning him first, or, on the telephone, saying more than was strictly necessary); not obtrusive or 'interfering' in the least, when there are so many women one eventually has to push away with practically the same gesture one made to pull them towards one; completely devoid of 'pose'; so far removed from the easy tricks used by others to captivate him, in an age when it is the men who are pursued by the girls; and even going to the unbelievable lengths of never – not once – making the slightest allusion to his literary work, whereas all the women who tried to worm their way into his life first tried to unlock the door with the key of admiration. He was grateful to her, too, for knowing nothing about the mediocre literature of the day and, knowing nothing, keeping quiet about it rather than trotting out the usual clichés, grateful to her for being so innocent of all snobbery, of all unhealthy – or even healthy – curiosity, of any wish to play a part or push herself forward, of any admiration for false values or false riches, for being so different, in a word – and apparently to her detriment, although she was infinitely superior to them – from all those bogus, snobbish, loud-mouthed, empty-headed bitches who were the flashy partners of so many prominent men in Parisian society. He was grateful to her for all this, and his spirit soared in an uprush of simplicity and trust.

'You see,' he said, 'the fact that you're a decent person is far more important than you probably imagine. For a long time now, a very long time, people have been working both inside and outside the country – and God knows with what calculated hatred – to make France a place where anyone with any decency must feel an exile. It's been a long and arduous business, because France was a good nation, basically sound. But at last it has been done. Dare I admit it? I who identified myself so passionately with my country in my youth and during the war, find that there are moments now when I not only feel no loyalty to it, but I even feel a violent need – which arises, and this is the serious part of it, from all that is best in me – to reject it entirely. Well, meeting someone like you, who are French, checks this impulse, and one thinks: "No, I can't desert"....'

'But there's nothing extraordinary about me. I can assure you that I know lots of girls like me, and there must be many more who are better.'

'It's possible – although, believe me, I tried a good many before I found you: "maiden trials", in racing parlance. But the whole effort of society – perhaps the whole effort of mankind – seems directed at showing off worthless women and making them appear interesting. Women complain of being misjudged. Why then do they allow the worst of their sex to take the limelight? And why do they swallow so easily every male suggestion that tends to make them appear grotesque and degraded? Why such a failure to recognize their own interests? Nearly always when women debase themselves – by some hideous fashion, some obscene dance, some idiotic way of thinking or talking, it's men who have put them up to it. But why don't they resist? Everyone knows that a woman's body, when it's no longer young, tends to become a ridiculous and often repulsive object, a joy for cartoonists, whereas a man's body, as old age draws near, keeps in much better shape. Morally it's the same thing. When a woman is morally not much good, she becomes abominable: it's either one thing or the other. When a woman is ill-bred, lacks decorum, she is a harpy.'

'I thought you only liked easy women.'

'I like women with a sense of decorum who are easy at the same time.'

'Oh, I see.'

'Do you know what a harpy is? Well, I should say bitch, if I were the sort of man who used such expressions. All the women who put on airs, the vamps, the flirts, the "Hallo, darling!" women, all the women who get their pictures into the glossy magazines, all the women I include under the heading of women-who-want-their-faces-slapped are harpies. It is the harpies that all the theologians, the philosophers, the moralists have been aiming at for thousands of years in heaping scorn and anathema on women; but they were wrong in not indicating clearly that it was those women, and them alone, whom they condemned. Which brings me back to my question: why don't decent, sensible women defend themselves against these harpies? Don't they realize the harm the harpies do to them? Women's worst enemies are women. I was telling you just now that, when I meet the sort of woman I take you to be, I feel more kindly towards my country. But it goes further: I feel more kindly towards the whole of your sex and ready to treat it more honourably. For if men behave badly towards women it's because they're afraid of them, because they're obsessed by the harpies. Most of the caddishness, the desertions, broken engagements, etc., that women suffer from are due to the fact that, however sweet and loving a woman may be, the man thinks he can detect the harpy in her, either hidden or potential. So he turns on her, or else he bolts: either way he treats his natural companion as an enemy. And that is why, among your sex, the good pay for the bad.'

'All the same, hasn't there ever been a harpy in your life?'

'Never. And I take no credit for keeping them at bay, as I can't stand them anyway. Me, have anything to do with people like that? Never! As far as they're concerned at least, I shall die intact. I have never loved and I cannot love – more, I cannot bear – any woman who is not simple and straightforward. When I was out in Indo-China, I saw most of the officers – men with the power of life and death over hundreds of their fellows – manoeuvred like pathetic puppets by the worst kind of women, sewers of shame, hideous, vile, ravaged, but full of airs and graces and the same grotesque poses one sees in film stars (ah! the female spy must have a fine time in the French army!). And now and then I would say to one of these men: "How could you?" And he would answer: "There's no one else; I have to take what I can find." And I would say: "Marooned on a desert island, with no other woman in sight, I'd rather make love to a Great Ant-Eater than to one of those pretentious bitches, however ravishing." If I'd had my way in one of those colonial outposts, I'd have had them all deported or clapped into jail. I'd let my men go with native women, with men, with kids, with donkeys, with the leaf of the prickly pear*, anything but those women. The harm they do in our colonies is un-believable.'

She saw that he was full of a sacred fire, and remembered reading in her history books how the revolutionaries, during the Terror, killed for the sake of virtue. Nevertheless she approved. Then, when Costals started joking again, she said she would go and make tea: such eloquence deserved it.

'Have you any idea how to make tea?'

'You don't know me.'

'Come on, then, I'll teach you. And you'll see the cats play-ing the cello.'

---

*The *raquette* of the prickly pear, much appreciated in the wilds of Africa (*Author's note*).

'Do your cats really play the cello?' he asked, for everything always seemed possible to him.

'No, but they stick a paw straight up in the air when they're washing, and then they look as though they're playing the cello.'

'That image doesn't seem quite accurate to me,' he said, like the honest craftsman he was in the art of writing.

He followed her into the kitchen. The cats had preceded them, but they were not playing the cello. The black one must have had cold paws, for she had covered them with her tail. While the grey one doubtless had a cold tail, for she had placed her paws upon it. The black one opened her eyes as they came in. The grey wondered whether to do the same, then kept them closed, to show her contempt. A deep silence reigned in the kitchen, punctuated by the disproportionately loud tick-tock of a huge alarm-clock, which emphasized the silence instead of breaking it. The silence was even deeper here than in the drawing-room, for the kitchen overlooked the inner courtyard and the whole building on that side was wearing its Sunday look, meaning that it looked uninhabited. The kitchen windows, open on other days to disgorge the wail of gramophones and the chatter of maids, were closed. The drawn curtains were marked at the level of the hasp of the window-bolt with a dark patch which showed they had been pulled back over it all week and gave them the special crumpled look of housemaids' Sunday dresses.

Solange put a kettle on the stove, and Costals picked up a volume of the *Bibliothèque Rose* entitled *The Holidays*, which was lying on the table. Solange said that she had lent it to the cook's daughter, who had come up from the country to spend a few days with her mother.

'The Comtesse de Ségur! You can't imagine how well this book fits in with what I was thinking about you a moment ago. Of course, the "model little girl" is you! "Marguerite de Rosebourg" is you! All my childhood comes back to me with this little red book, and this time you're in it. How delightful!'

Standing, they turned over the pages of the book which lay before them on the kitchen table.

'The holidays were drawing to a close; the children loved

each other more and more,' Costals read. 'Isn't it charming! I feel that you and I, too, love each other more and more.'

'Oh, yes,' she said childishly, turning her face towards him. Then she leaned her head against his, as people are supposed to do when they are reading the same book. He pushed the curtain to, lest anyone should see them. The room became a little darker. Solange read:

'Marguerite threw herself into her father's arms, and he kissed her so hard that her cheeks became quite crimson.'

They laughed, for one day he had remarked that her face was all flushed with his kisses. And they kissed madly.

'The divine Comtesse!' he exclaimed. 'Her books breathe the very soul of the nobility. They make one drink to the dregs the bitter draught of low birth. All the good characters have titles, all the bad ones haven't. At least one knows where one is. Ah, ha! Here's a sentence which seems to concern someone I know: "I shall now ask Sophie to explain to us how the accident happened".'

'Is it me that sentence is supposed to concern?'

'Dear Rosebourg, wasn't there ever, in your girlish life, a little accident?'

'Which one?' she asked, and he laughed, charmed by her innocence.

The water began to sing in the kettle. Solange was about to take it off the stove, but he stopped her.

'Let the water sing its little song; you can see it's enjoying it. It seems to me that I can hear a thousand different noises in this room which at first seemed so quiet, in the same way as one gradually begins to make things out in the dark as one's eyes get used to it. Can't you hear lots of tiny noises round you?'

'Why, yes!'

'What do you mean, "yes"? The cheek of it! Only writers are allowed to have any imagination. You deserve to be put to the test: tell me, please, what are the voices you profess to hear so clearly?'

He put his face in his hands. She said:

'There's the noise of the tap dripping into the sink – a dull, muffled sound. There's the noise of the water dripping from the

bain-marie into the metal pan below – a quick, sharp sound.'
('The *bain-marie*!' he thought. 'Oh, ho! isn't she knowledge-
able!') 'There's the noise of the water spitting from the kettle-
spout on to the stove – like a locomotive getting up steam.
There's the noise of the steam lifting the lid with something
like a big sigh of contentment...'

Smiling into the palms of his hands which still covered
his face, he repeated:

'...with a big sigh of contentment....'

'All these noises occur at regular intervals. But then there
are the free-lance noises. Can you hear the little tap-tapping
of the chair on the tiles? That's the black cat scratching herself. The table's creaking: it's as though it were stretching its
legs, lazily, because it's Sunday. In fact it's as though these
noises only exist on Sundays, as if all the household things
were having a day off. And the alarm-clock beats time for the
whole little orchestra, as potbellied and self-important as a
ballet-master from the *commedia dell'arte*.'

'Well, well, old girl!' said Costals, lifting his face. 'This is
certainly a day of revelations. Where do you get it all from?
The gift of observation and the gift of imagery: the two fundamental gifts of the craft of writing, you have them both. And
to think that I had quite made up my mind that you were
totally lacking in imagination.... Oh! here's something else....'

Catching a few drops from the tap in her palm, the girl
sprayed them over the hot-plate of the stove, where they
evaporated with the rustle of a silk dress. She said:

'They're running, running, as if to escape their impending
evaporation....'

Costals watched them with the look people have when they
stare into the fire.

'Yes, like soldiers running, running before being blown to
smithereens by exploding shells. How they hate to disappear!
And it's you who thought that up!'

She made as if to stop. He implored her:

'Please kill a few more for me....'

Again she scattered the tiny drops. And again she stopped.

'More! I could go on forever watching them vanish into
oblivion.'

'One would think you enjoyed it.'

'It reminds me of the remark made by a general in Darius's army in the middle of a battle. Every time one of his men fell, he said: "One more fool the less." It's true he was a philosopher-general – a breed that shouldn't be encouraged.'

Leaning over the table, she flicked through the book in the red and gold binding.

'I'm looking for a sentence in *The Holidays* which always used to move me when I was a little girl....'

In the silence, the genie of dripping water, the genie of boiling water, the genie of fire in the stove – a fire that never went out, as in the most ancient myths – the genie of the motionless cats and even the genie of this melancholy day, this strange winter day in the heart of summer, re-created the familiar world of Costals' early childhood, with its cats, its nursery rhymes, its kettle, its Hans Andersen's *Fairy Tales*, its musical boxes, its New Year almanacs, Humpty Dumpty and *La Tour prends garde*, Cadichon and Kitty Darling, all the magic fairyland of Old France and Old England adapted for the edification of rather strait-laced little boys. And it was she, the most silent genie of them all, even when she spoke, it was this unobtrusive Cinderella ('If I were to disappear for a week, I don't believe my parents would notice, I take up so little room in the flat'), it was she who, with a wave of her wand, had reawakened this universe for him. It was this stranger who had reopened his nursery door and given him back the savour of his past.

'There!' she exclaimed, 'I've found it! You know, the sentence I found so moving when I was a little girl. Paul says to Sophie: "So you had forgotten me?" And she answers: "*Forgotten you, no, but you were asleep in my heart and I dared not wake you.*"'

Costals glanced at the book and read the sentence himself. Why did he feel it was somehow familiar? He blinked in an effort to remember. Suddenly it came back to him, and a shiver ran through him. Long ago, his mother had said to him about those very lines exactly the same thing that Solange was saying now: 'When I was little this sentence touched me deeply. I used to whisper it to myself over and over again....'

224

He had always been happy to talk of his mother to Solange.
But this time.... To think that, at a distance of so many
years, his mother and this young girl had been moved by
the same words! He said so to Solange, without comment: his
heart was gripped by something too strong for words. It
seemed to him as if some mysterious sign had descended upon
her.

'What about the nightmare of the Maréchal de Ségur in the
haunted house! Could it have frightened a boy? It used to
terrify me....'

Silently they read the story together. Costals reached the
place where the Marshal, as the spectre puts the point of its
dagger to his breast, kisses the Star of the Holy Ghost on the
ribbon of the Order and the spectre, seeing this gesture, spares
his life. He reached that passage, and then a strange thing
happened: his eyes filled with tears, and he began to tremble.

Trembling, and his eyes full of tears, he said:

'When I was a child and came to this passage in the book,
the tears would come to my eyes as they have today. I cried
because the Marshal had been saved for being brave. And
because the ghost was not too wicked to be moved by his
courage. And I too, like the ghost, am not so wicked that I
can't still cry, even now. And I owe this to you! You have
transformed me into what is best in me. You have brought me
back into the atmosphere of my family, to the days when I
was a good person, living among good people. Whereas now
I live among literary men, and have become a humbug and a
rake. What would my life be worth, but for the time I spent
in the war? I should never have been a decent person, except
when I was a child.'

He bent down and placed his forehead on the open book.

'I'm doing as you do when you switch off the light, so that
you may no longer see this face of mine, this man's face with
all its unpunished crimes.'

Standing against the sink, she was stroking his hair. He
took her other hand and clasped it in his – so warm, like a

handful of sand. Then he raised his head. He felt a terrible urge to tell her the truth about himself. It was an urge that he felt fairly frequently. It was nearly always into base souls that he cast this truth, for there it was more likely to disappear. But it could be cast into a pure soul; there was no rule against it. So he said to her:

'If a certain lode in me were to be followed up, an unbroken succession of good actions would be found. If another, a succession of horrors. Not petty horrors, judged by this code or that – according to local customs – but really hideous things which the universal conscience can never forgive. Yet if I had not done these dreadful things, what an abyss of despair I should be in today, and above all tomorrow, when I am old. It is not from a desire for self-abasement that I accuse myself before you. It is because I want to see things as they are, and for you, too, to see them as they are, without flinching, because that is what is good. ... No, no,' he said, his eyes blurred, sensing that she wanted to speak, 'let me surrender to this spirit that sways within me. Let me be what I am!' he exclaimed passionately. 'What was I saying? Ah, yes, the lodes. ... Well, sometimes, these lodes run parallel, but sometimes they cross, and when they do they interweave in arabesques, twining playfully about each other. And sometimes, too, it happens that they dissolve into each other, the best and the worst blended together, indistinguishable from one another. And in the evil I do there is a part I like and a part I dislike, just as in the good I do there is a part that I enjoy and a part that leaves me cold.' (One of the cats sneezed.) 'Certainly I enjoy evil, but I think I enjoy good even more intensely. However, I'm not so sure about that. ... Do you remember greeting me one day with the question: "How's your morale today?" And I replied: "My morale is fine, but so's my immorale."* That's what you must understand. Beware of preferring your own image of me to the reality. You must take me with all my "outbuildings", the stables and the latrines. However that may be, it is this pleasure in goodness which you have reawakened in me. And what you must know is this: that I've enjoyed

*The pun works better in French, where the words are *le moral* and *l'immoral* (*Translator's note*).

226

and will go on enjoying the harm I have done and will do to others, but that never – and I say it in all solemnity – never will I enjoy the harm I may do to you.'

He slid on to his knees on the tiled floor, trembling all over with the effort of resisting the pleasure he would have liked to give her by asking her to marry him. As she was half-sitting on the edge of the sink with one foot dangling, he kissed the hem of her skirt, then removed her grey suede shoe, and taking her foot in his hands, pressed it to his lips at the spot where the stocking had a small darn. Often, he had kissed her face on the places where her features were a little defec-tive, thinking that, while in her perfection she belonged to all men, in her imperfections she belonged to him alone. Now he kissed the darn in her stocking because it introduced an un-expected hint of poverty into his idea of her, a faint possibility that the apparent affluence in which she lived might not be altogether genuine; and the thought that he would one day wrong her seemed to him more odious than ever. And the knowledge, underlying all his other feelings, that she was a little unwell today, added new warmth to these feelings and brought them to the boil, as the flame nearby had brought the water to the boil.

'You,' he said at last, 'you, so quiet and good, as though to appease the Fates. It's strange, I wish you well. What a mysterious thing it is to really wish someone well! What is essential is that you should always be happy. Once you are out of my hands, of course, because as long as we're to-gether.... I so much want to keep the damage I shall do you to a minimum.... Don't love me! Don't love me!' he ex-claimed vehemently. 'It's the only chance you have of not being unhappy because of me. Ah, yes, there's another: you must realize that I'm mad. I'm not *only* mad, but I'm mad *as well*.' (He felt her toes moving beneath his lips; at the same time, in spite of the intoxication of the moment, it struck him that her foot was rather thin, and he would have preferred it to be a bit sturdier.) 'Marguerite de Rosebourg,' he said, raising his head, 'I ask your pardon for the future. It is the divine part of my soul (though I don't believe in God, I have no reason not to believe in him), it is the divine part of my soul that asks your pardon in advance for whatever harm I may do you; and I ask you this while mentally kissing the glittering Star of the Holy Ghost which I, too, wear invisibly on my heart. Remember this well, Rosebourg: I shall do you harm, but the harm I do you will give me no pleasure.... Am I boring you?' he asked, seeing the grey cat giving a jaw-splitting yawn. And, because of this ludicrous association of ideas, his laughing self was reawakened and took over once again. Throughout this entire speech, it was as though he had been swept now right, now left by opposing gusts of wind.

He straightened up, and then, standing in front of him, she rested her forearms against his chest, either from some immemorial girlish instinct, or because she had seen it done in films. She had not raised him up when he was kneeling. She had not wept when he wept; the time had not yet come when he would know how to make her cry. With a confidence that nothing, then, could have shaken, she had listened to him as one listens to a child babbling in a dream. She said: 'I know you will never do anything to hurt me.' He was disturbed to think that she knew him so little, and said to himself: 'What can I do against such trustfulness?' Meanwhile the sky had cleared, she had opened the window (canaries were chirping in a cage which had just been put out), and their long embrace was visible to the outside world. He thought of this, but did not close the window, as if something new had occurred which gave them a right to embrace publicly. Thus they remained, merged with each other like the sky and the sea on certain days when the horizon is no longer visible in a great, smooth, even splendour. Then they parted, well pleased with each other.

That night, after the five hours they had spent talking with passionate truthfulness and sincerity, and with no caresses (he despised the very thought of them) – all of which was new in their relationship – Costals was unable to sleep. The esteem he felt for her kept him awake. This esteem had created in his body a tension of a wholly virile kind which he had not experienced during their chaste hours in the kitchen and which was not, even now, accompanied by the faintest lustful image.

'The *Précieuses*,' he thought, 'used to distinguish "tenderness based on esteem".* This is a case of tension based on esteem.' Till then he had never suspected that a feeling of a purely moral order could have such an effect, and he was greatly astonished.

He was perfectly aware that he had treated Solange that day as though he were engaged to her, and that it was impossible for her not to have noticed it. For the first time he envisaged the possibility of being weak enough some day to bestride the nuptial Hippogriff with her if she should ever decide to confess to such a desire. He knew for certain that it would be the purest folly. He knew that marriage – of which he had always said, in the words of Don Quixote: 'It is impossible that I should ever conceive of being married, not even to the Phoenix' – would wreck his future: as a writer, because of the obligations, the nervous wear and tear, the need for money, the time-wasting it would involve; and as a man, because his independence was for Costals a necessity as absolute as the air which kept him alive. The Hippogriff, once straddled, could only lead him to Hades. But the idea of marrying Solange was an abyss that had suddenly opened before him and might suck him down.

Supposing the marriage did take place, it was inevitable that a day would come when he would have to get divorced, both to *save his work* and to *save his soul*. But if Solange had done him no wrong (and he was sure she would not have), and if she refused to divorce him, how could he regain his freedom? All night long this prospect weighed him down like an incubus. At last he realized that the only solution would be to murder her. Not to murder her openly, and be condemned, for that would place him in a situation where he would be unable to continue his work and pursue his love-life. But to murder her in such a way that he would not be detected. For instance, by toppling her over the rails of a ship. Or by taking her out to sea in a dinghy. He had already thought it all out in other circumstances.

Le Tendre sur estime – from *la carte du Tendre* in Mlle de Scudéry's novel *Clélie* (*Translator's note*).

Of course, killing her would be a hideous crime. But what if there were no other way of recovering his manhood? 'Am I then a monster? No, I'm just like everyone else. Sometimes better than others, sometimes worse. I'm like seven people out of ten. And if seven people out of ten are "monsters", there can be no such thing as a monster. It may seem strange that, on one and the same day, I should not only love this girl enough to consider marrying her, but that I should also contemplate murdering her – not for any jealous motive, but simply because she would be in my way. But many other things in men's souls are equally strange. Of course, since it's the idea of marriage, and it alone, that is responsible for fathering this homicide plan, the simplest thing would be not to marry her. Alas, it isn't as simple as that. It's like an abyss sucking me down.'

He had thought that the night would dissipate these musings like evil phantoms. And, indeed, when he awoke, the possibility of marriage had lost a great deal of its substance. Not enough, however, to prevent him from taking an immediate precautionary measure, painful though it was.

He was due that day or the next to send to a monthly review a long story about a man who poisons someone for fear that he will 'talk'. All the emotions through which the man passes before committing the deed, and the technique employed, were minutely described over some sixty pages. It was a piece of documentary evidence which, should Costals ever fall under suspicion, would tell fearfully against him. 'A man capable of thinking up a murder with such hallucinatory precision cannot be far from committing it; he has already almost committed it in spirit.' He could just hear counsel for the prosecution! Regretfully Costals wrote to the editor of the review to say that he was unable to deliver the promised story.

At the same time he wrote to Andrée, for he felt sorry for her because he was happy.

Pierre Costals   to Andrée Hacquebaut
Paris   *Saint-Léonard*

21 June 1927

Dear Mademoiselle,

A small cousin of mine,* sweet and open-hearted if something of a rascal (thanks to his father who's quite impossible), was out on an excursion one day when he suddenly decided to telephone his father. 'Hullo, is that you, papa?' 'Yes, what's the matter?' 'Nothing, except that I'm happy and enjoying myself, and I just wanted to let you know.'

Yesterday I was happy. Happy in a kitchen. And, my goodwill having been awakened as a result of this happiness, I wanted to 'let you know', and also to ask how you were. Tell me *briefly* (not more than two pages). I have an idea you've been writing to me lately, but I confess I don't remember what you said in your letters; I must only have read the opening sentences. I won't ask whether you're happy, as I know it isn't your fate to be happy. But still, how's it going?

So long. You can't imagine how benign I feel at the moment. 'Opportunity not to be missed.'

C.

I had never seen the inside of a kitchen before. It's an astonishing place; all sorts of possibilities. And to think that it was there all the time!

If this novel conformed to the rules of the genre as laid down in France, the scene in the kitchen between Costals and Solange would have been placed at the end. Everybody would have been delighted: the pundits because, in a novel constructed in the French manner, that is to say a *logically* constructed novel, the culminating scene must come at the end, and the moralists because this scene seems to foreshadow a union between the principal characters. And thus the novel, by ending on a *vista of blue sky*, would have been edifying from beginning to end, for French novels, like Christian souls,

---

*Costals' bastard son.

always preserve the possibility of redeeming themselves *in extremis*.

But life, which knows nothing of living, foolishly presumes to ignore the conventions of the French novel. In the story we are here relating, as it really happened, that scene in the kitchen, in which Costals and his sweetheart discovered together some estimable areas of their souls, was indeed a summit, but with all the drawbacks of summits. For, the summit having been reached, one must perforce descend. That scene had no aftermath.

When they next met, Solange was taciturn, almost morose. Perhaps she had her reasons. Perhaps she had none. Perhaps, even, she was no different from her usual self, but they had climbed too high. A multitude of small signs made him doubt whether she loved him deeply. Her face did not light up at the sight of him. . . . A fortnight had elapsed, and she still hadn't had the snap-shots she had taken of him developed. . . . Whereas so many women overwhelmed him with solicitude, there was never anything of the kind from her. . . . Once she said to him: 'Neither you nor I are infatuated with each other. That's a sign of the solidity of our attachment.' The 'neither you' was an echo of what he himself had said to her about his not being in love with her. But the 'nor I' seemed a bit chilly.

He thought: 'She's like a shaded lamp. The light is there all right, but it lacks radiance.' And indeed, as soon as they were apart from each other, it was as if Solange's personality, after all rather frail, was, as it were, swallowed up by that of Costals. When he was with her, he believed in her integrity. When she was absent, all that was tortuous in his nature began to ferment again. Distrustful as a prince and always prone to believe that others wished him as much harm as he felt capable of doing them, he had unwittingly substituted his own turbulent spirit for that of the girl, and soon found himself confronted by a detached, blurred image of Solange, which was no more than a projection of himself. He had re-created her in his own image.

He had once asked her: 'What did you think of the way I made love to you that first evening in the Bois?' She had answered that she had been extremely surprised, though not shocked, and that the sensation had been disagreeable. He was inclined to exaggerate her physical coldness, and comparing the poor quality of her responsiveness to that of, say, Guiguite or certain others, he sighed; for sexual enjoyment, he could only give her five out of twenty. And he consoled himself with theories, all deriving from that tedious habit he had of drawing a sharp dividing line between the sexes: 'Men only love with the heart when they have first desired with the senses. With women it's the opposite: first they love with the heart, and from thence flows desire. Ugly men are loved, ugly women are not. A woman in love doesn't mind if her lover hasn't shaved for two days, whereas no man would kiss a bearded woman.'

At other times, this coldness in Solange did not displease him. It provided him with an excuse, opening the door through which he too would one day escape to undertake the divine conquest of some new little partner. Had she remained the Solange of 'Kitchen Sunday', he might eventually have married her. But if she were the first to show signs of wanting to break it off, then he would break it off himself with total indifference. The only person he ever missed was his son, and in any case nobody is irreplaceable. Hence one of the most significant traits in his character was that he was almost devoid of jealousy, which he characterized as a 'shopgirl's sentiment'. Whether the girl fell madly in love with him, or whether she threw him over, made no difference to him at all. He would adapt himself to either contingency with the same promptness and the same contentment: more passionate as she became more passionate, more forgetful if she chose to forget him. Such was the amplitude of his inner keyboard, and his mastery over it, that he could draw from it at will whatever he wanted.

Nevertheless, prepared as he was to believe that their liaison was on the wane, he decided that it would be unfair to her to postpone the regularization of their position any longer. The state of *demi-vierge* could not forever satisfy a soul with a thirst for the absolute. The time had come to bring Mlle Dandillot into a more clearly defined category.

With this end in view, they were at his flat one evening, in the room which he called 'the tomb of the unknown woman', when suddenly. . . .

> Who's that ringing at my door
> Said the fair young la-a-ady

Yes, who, well after half past nine? . . . The servant was out. He saw her start up suddenly from the bed, her eyes wide open, and tried to calm her down. An electric sign outside threw splashes of red on to her arms and shoulders, while the glow from the lights of the city, shining in bands through the slats of the shutters, streaked her face with light and darkness as if she were behind the bars of a prison (this figurative prison was her love for him, little though he realized it). The doorbell rang again, and then a third time, with insistence. She slipped out of bed and hurried to the bathroom.

He followed her, and found her getting dressed. He begged her not to. But she was shaken. A minute went by, while she sat, half-dressed, on a chair. And suddenly the bell rang again, and fists began to pound on the door of the flat.

This time Costals was worried. Solange was now fully dressed. There was no one there but a respectably attired young damsel, whose parents must be aware that she often visited him. But he did not think of this: he was simply a frightened man who has heard fists pounding on a door behind which he is in bed with a girl.

Meanwhile the banging had stopped. He tiptoed into the hall, to make sure no one was waiting behind the door. There, on the floor, lay a visiting card. Andrée!

'Your letter touched me so much that I felt we must talk things over and get our bearings at the earliest opportunity; so I caught the first train. I know you're at home, because the windows of one of your rooms are lit up. But never mind. . . . Please write to me express at the address below, tomorrow if possible.'

So this woman wasn't content with pestering him from a distance. She had to ring his bell at half past nine at night, and bang on his door like a drayman, and watch his windows like a spy. She, whom he did not love, had to disturb him in what he did love.

He told Solange that it was only 'some imbecile of a friend', but when he asked her if she wanted to call it a day, and she pleaded her shattered nerves, he said to her:

'Don't apologize. You'd hear bells ringing and fists banging the whole time.... Even I, after nine years of peace, I can't hear a knock on the door without being reminded of machine-guns. Let's finish the evening in the Bois. Tomorrow I'll pick you up at a quarter to four in front of your house, and we'll go to my country place.'

This was what he called a garden studio which he owned, off the boulevard du Port-Royal, where they sometimes went.

Then he wrote an express letter to Andrée, the Angel of Treachery reading over his shoulder.

Dear Andrée (*it was the first time in five years he had called her by her Christian name*):

I am so looking forward to seeing you again! If I could have guessed that it was you just now, I would of course have opened up, even though I was in night attire; but so lonely! Come tomorrow, 25th June, at four-thirty, to 96, boulevard du Port-Royal, and ring three times. It's a little 'folly' I've had there for some years. We shall be undisturbed.

Yours,

C.

P.S. In writing to you I am behaving treacherously to another woman. Sweet treachery.

They went out. The stars were dancing about like motes in a sunbeam. He stopped the taxi at a post-office, and handed the express letter to Solange.

'You post it, just to please me. You may read the address. You see it's to a woman....'

She gave him an anxious, questioning look.

'It's a woman I'm punishing.'

'What are you punishing her for?'

'For not loving her.'

Back in his flat, he wrote in his notebook: 'Here on my balcony, at a quarter to twelve, I savour to the full the exquisite tang of treachery. It is such a pleasurable state that I wonder how one can ever relinquish it without some grave reason. Above the town, the sky glows like heated iron. An emerald breeze gently fans my face.'

Next day, at four, Costals and Solange arrived at his Port-Royal studio. Situated at the end of a small garden, this studio was like every other studio, and so not worth describing (the bachelor apartment in all its horror). There was, however, one thing peculiar to it: a number of show-cards, which Costals had had made following an American fashion then becoming fairly widespread in France, were lying about on the furniture. One of them bore this inscription:

LADIES!
NEVER OFFER GENTLEMEN
MORE THAN THEY ASK FOR

Another:

THIS GENTLEMAN
DOES NOT MARRY

And another:

THIS GENTLEMAN
NEVER RETURNS LETTERS

It was not in awfully good taste, but youth will have its fling. And the highest moral altitudes are all the more pleasurable if one comes down to earth occasionally.*

'None of this is meant for you,' Costals said to Solange. 'Don't worry, I shall give you back your letters. And now, follow me.'

At one end of the studio was a staircase leading to a tiny loggia, which Costals called the dovecot because, perched high as it was, it did bear some resemblance to a dovecot, and because human doves did nestle there at times. He also sometimes called it his *columbarium*, by virtue of an old saw according to which funereal thoughts stimulate pleasure, though he himself had little need of such stimulants.

'Well, my pet, no more nonsense; now's the time for you to take the plunge. On this bed, shortly, you will become a

---

*Untranslatable pun here. The French is *pied-à-terre*, = .'feet on the ground' and also 'bachelor flat' (*Translator's note*).

woman. So you'd better get a good eyeful of the décor, if what they say is true, that the act still has some importance for a girl in spite of everything. And it has! A moment like that is like an oil-stain that will spread over a woman's whole life. So try and do it properly. For the time being, though, the only thing I ask is that you should stay here and keep mum. In a few minutes, I shall have a visitor downstairs. You see this curtain? Behind it you'll hear everything, and see everything too, if you draw it aside a little. without being seen. Goodbye for now. If you get restless, you'll find plenty of books on morals lying around. Here, for instance: Louis Ménard's *La Morale avant les Philosophes*. You'll see the progress morality has made since then. Splendid chaps, the *Philosophes*!'

He went downstairs and settled in an armchair. For a moment, his eyes vacant, he wondered how he would tackle the scene with Andrée. Then, with the touch of arrogance that woke in him at times, he decided that such a question was not worth his bothering about, that Andrée did not deserve to have a set speech prepared for her, and he made it a point of honour not to think about her any more. He flicked through a magazine and thought of Solange, hidden and yet present, like God perhaps.... Whereupon he plunged into a sort of lucid confusion, was seized with a gust of spirituality, and composed some lines, which he jotted down:

> O God! Hide then yourself but in appearance,
>   Not in reality.
> And when you withdraw deep into your silence,
>   Listen to me.

At four thirty-five, Andrée had still not arrived. At twenty to five still nobody. He was glad she was late, as it was further justification for the cruelty he was about to inflict on her. The fact was that he would cheerfully have suffered insults, dishonour, desertion, the loss of all his money; but he could not bear to be kept waiting. He always told his women, from their very first meeting: 'The chief qualification of a woman in love is punctuality. Everything else is secondary.' He had told Solange, too. He had a notebook in which he kept a

record of the number of minutes his girl-friends kept him
waiting, and when the total reached five hours, he broke with
them – at least in principle. Not without warning them three
times, at the end of two, three and four hours, in accordance
with an old Arab precept: 'Warn the snake three times before
you kill it.' To date, after six weeks, Solange's total only came
to one hour seven minutes. A very decent average.

At a quarter to five, the bell rang and Andrée appeared.
'Ah! there you are, my dear Mademoiselle. The burnt child
still risks the fire, eh?' On shaking hands with Costals, she
held his for a long time, which the writer found far from
agreeable. Mlle Hacquebaut, who was usually content with a
dab of powder and a touch of lipstick, had today really made
herself beautiful, but in a Saint-Léonardesque style: glaring
red lips and irregular blotches of dark powder. Her legs were
bare, which could have been explained by the heat, though the
real explanation lay elsewhere. Her face looked parched and
emaciated, like that of a literary gentleman who has had to
wait too long for a good review (a plant without water). And
there were dark rings under her eyes such as Costals had never
seen there before: blue, purple, glossy, huge, spreading out
like a fan, or the wake of a boat, nearly up to the temples –
terrifying in the broad light of day. He thought she must have
developed a taste for solitary practices.

She glanced round the room and read the show-cards.

'No, dear Mademoiselle, you are not really in a house of
sin. The worst that ever happens is that I occasionally shut
my cat up in here with some tom when she's on heat. But
one or other of them always seems to lack interest. The tom,
usually. Isn't nature odd? Some day I must shut the tom up
here with a mouse. It might sharpen his desire.'

'Yes, his desire to eat her up, after torturing her for hours.
And you would be watching them through the window, gloat-
ing. I can see it all!'

'What a lurid image you have of me,' he said with disgust.

Still, he had her there in front of him, completely at his
mercy, and he wondered what would be the best way of
making her suffer. For a sort of chemical reaction had taken
place in him since the day before. For nearly five years he had

restrained himself from wounding her, for five years he had
been waiting for the present moment. All that pity, that kindness, that forbearance had been transmuted by last night's
irruption into an element which was chemically their opposite:
cruelty. Like milk changed into blood. 'Milk or blood, it's all
the same. I love both milk and blood, like the *manes* of
antiquity.' And all the effort that had gone into his benevolence now went to reinforce his cruelty. 'I felt heroic, and
that's a feeling I dislike.' Now he could give rein to that other
self that had been stifled so long, now he could drop the weight
he had been holding up for five years. The strength to make
her suffer began to wake and stretch itself within him, and he
watched the girl as a wrestler measures up his opponent,
wondering what sort of hold to try on her. 'She once wrote to
me, paraphrasing Cleopatra's words about Antony, in Shakespeare: "For thy bounty, there is no winter in't." Why, in the first
place, should I show myself bountiful to her? Don't know.
And then, why should there be no winter in my bounty?
Winter's a very fine season, when you look at it in relation
to the others. Blessed are those who blow hot and cold
together. If the souls of the just are like good trees and good
pastures, as the Gospel says, they must love winter as well as
summer, drought as well as plenty, darkness as well as light:
it needs a little of everything to make a man. All the seasons
exist in me, one after another. I am a revolving cosmos that
presents every point of its surface to the sun, one after another.
One after another! Always one after another! Now she'll see
what it costs, five years of pity from a man like me.'

'I see you have bare feet,' he said nonchalantly. 'In Algiers,
when young Frenchmen of the upper classes want to seduce
a girl who also belongs to the upper classes, they take her by
car to the forest of Bainem. There, if she refuses, they wait
until nightfall, then take her shoes and jump into the car. She
gets back as best she can, barefoot. The forest of Bainem is
twelve kilometres from Algiers.'

'Poor things!'

'Well, it teaches them to stand on their own feet, no pun
intended. We must defend ourselves, mustn't we?'

'Defend yourselves! Poor helpless males! Either defending

themselves against women who refuse, or defending themselves against women who throw themselves at their heads.
But I,' she said (with sudden volubility, rushing the words to
the point of stammering, as though all of a sudden she had
started rushing down a slope), 'whatever you may have
thought, I never threw myself at your head : I never begged;
on the contrary I offered. You refused. Of course, to be loved
takes away part of one's freedom. But so does everything that
has to do with life. By simply going on living, you accept the
tyranny of time and space, the weather, the need to eat and
sleep. . . .'

'My entire life is based on one thing: getting rid of everything that isn't essential to me.'

'If you really had to be afraid of something, you could have
chosen something else to be afraid of besides love – mine, at
any rate. But however that may be, you can't say I've forced
myself on you. I went out of your life in silence, and so I have
remained. Shall I tell you? I was utterly fed up with you. With
you, and with this wretched love that has never fed upon
anything but itself. And then, just as I imagined you must be
thinking: "Now she's dead all right, and she'll never stir
again," you wrote to me, you shouted "encore" to bring me
back on stage, as if you had enjoyed my little tragi-comic act.
Oh! you know how to keep women in suspense all right. Why
did I come? First of all, to show you I wasn't sulking. And
then because, in spite of everything I wrote, I hadn't given up.
The only way you could have made me give you up would
have been to tell me you didn't love me. But that you've never
done. Not once, in four years and nine months. Not once.
You've always run away, but you've never really broken off.
And then, after running away, you return to the attack with
redoubled vigour.' ('My head! My head!' thought Costals,
putting a hand to his head in the gesture of Achilles tearing
his hair.) 'I came here in order to hear these words from you,
if that is what I am to hear. To hear them from your own lips.
Whatever happens, this abscess must be lanced.'

'Well, we'll see about that,' he said cheerfully, not yet clear
as to what he was going to say or do.

From her spotless legs, her made-up face, he guessed she

must have prepared herself with minute care. He could also guess why. Yet the seam of her dress had come unstitched in places, the lace edge of her petticoat, showing at her throat, might have been cleaner, and her nails – pointed and varnished – retained a thin streak of black under the artificial pink, which made him wonder whether she thought black finger-nails an additional attraction, as negro women do their lip-plates, or a measure of hygiene like the dirt on Arab babies which their mothers preserve religiously because it is a guaran-tee of good health. Slatternly people, in their occasional attempts at cleanliness, always overlook some detail that betrays them. And it is the misfortune of women that men can bear negligence in a man but loathe it in a woman.

Nevertheless, all this time, Costals had been smiling at her, and smiling so naturally that he was not even aware of it. He smiled at her (a) because he had a natural gaiety which ex-pressed itself in that way, a kind of artless vitality, like one of those electric currents, innocently blue, but deadly; (b) because he was grateful to her for the pleasure he was about to derive from making her suffer; and (c) because, in spite of everything, he still rather liked her. (Through all their debates and dis-cussions he had never stopped liking her, and that was no doubt one of the reasons why he tormented her.)

When he had taken a good look at her, Costals shifted a vase of flowers on the table in such a way that his face was hidden from the woman who loved him. She moved her chair sideways so that she could see him again. Once more he shifted the vase.

'Why don't you want me to see you?'

'Just to annoy you,' he said gaily. 'But there, I'll be nice.' He pushed the vase aside.

'I've really been an awful fool, haven't I?' said Andrée. 'If men only knew how stupid women can be, they'd pity them instead of torturing them.'

'Women keep on begging until one gives them something. But one can give them pretty well anything. Pity, for instance. In any case, men do give it to you, though without realizing it. They call their pity love. On the whole, what brings man and woman together is pity far more than love. How could one fail to pity women when one sees what they are? One doesn't pity an old man: he has reached the end of his cycle, he has had his day. One doesn't pity a child: its helplessness is but momentary, the future belongs to it. But a woman in her prime, at the peak of her development, look at her! Woman would never have conceived herself to be man's equal, if man hadn't told her she was, out of "niceness".'

'Sometimes, it seems, this pity turns into desire.'

'Of course. Everything changes into everything else. What people call "love", "hate", "indifference", "pity", are only momentary phases in one and the same feeling. And we must thank God that pity is only a momentary phase. Otherwise it would annihilate us. We should escape from the enslavement of love only to enslave ourselves to pity. One can make people do anything by exciting them to pity. Do you know one can die of one's pity? Consequently, everything that is done out of pity turns out badly, except perhaps what is done out of pity for greatness, and you won't find that sort of pity every day. Half the doomed marriages in the world are marriages in which one or the other has married out of pity. When I was wounded during the war, the more the civilians at railway stations pitied me, the more I despised them. I felt their pity put them so utterly in my power! I could have got them to sign cheques or hand over their daughters, anything I wanted, and all this without deserving it, or putting on an act. It was revolting! Still, one might as well take advantage of it, and it seems to me that now, if I coveted other worldly goods than those I already possess, I should be less inclined to acquire them by exploiting the stupidity or the vanity or the greed of my fellow-men than by exploiting their pity.'

A butterfly flew into the room through the open window and (ignoring Andrée) fluttered around Costals as though asking to be stroked. But it is not easy to stroke a butterfly.

'I'm beginning to understand,' Andrée said slowly. 'The only feeling you have ever had for me is pity. The only feelings you ever have for women are desire, irritation and pity – never love. So you arrogate to yourself the right to pity women! Do you realize how ridiculously nineteenth-century you are? "Poor unfortunate" women! Michelet! Oh, no! please, not

242

your pity! I've had enough of those life-belts of yours that hit one on the head and send one under. Please don't throw any more. Women don't need your pity. You're the one who should be pitied.'

'Why? Because I don't love you?'

'Because you love nobody. You have no wife, no home, no children, no object in life, no faith. And perhaps it's because you're ashamed of all that that you come and huddle close to those who do love – that you call them back to you, as if you were one of them. And you're not, oh no, you're not! A leper, that's what you are!'

'Yes, it's exactly as I said: because I don't love you. But really, Andrée Hacquebaut, take a look at me: do I look like an unhappy man?'

'It's a mask, a grimace.'

'The grimace of the literary man is intended to make him appear *un*happy. They all want to look like Pascal. "M. Thingummy's Pascalian anguish." There are two certain recipes for admission to the Academy: a book on Racine, and a book on Pascal."

'You admitted it all to me, don't you remember: "I lie all the time"?'

'I remember very well. I said that in order to give you a false idea of myself. And besides, what I say to you is of no importance. It's in their work that you must look for men like me, not in what they tell you.'

'One has only to look at your photograph in this week's *Vie des Lettres* to see that you're not happy.'

'One has only to look at my photograph in this week's *Vie des Lettres* to know that the photographer had disturbed and irritated me. Come, come, my dear girl, this is a perfect example of reaction 227a.'

'I don't want to know what reaction 227a is. It's sure to be something unpleasant as usual. . . . What *did* you mean?'

'I'll tell you – it's quite nice, really. As you probably know, all women react in the same way to a given stimulus. There's nothing mysterious about women. Men have led them to believe they were mysterious, partly out of chivalry and partly as a bait, because they desire them. And of course the women fall for it, and even improve on it. It's always the same: at first sight, in a gathering of women, when you see them all saying the same things, laughing at the same things, etc., you feel that they form a kind of interchangeable substance. Then if you get to know one of them and develop a warmer feeling for her, she begins to appear very different from the others, the others can tell you nothing about her, she is an enigma to you, and so she will remain until you have conquered her; for it was desire that made you believe all this. Once conquered, she soon appears exactly like the others again. So one sees that in reality all women's reactions are automatic and can be foretold in advance. These reactions can be classified, and that is what I have done, identifying them by numbers. Reaction 227a is the classic reaction whereby a woman, because she is unhappy, tries to convince the man she loves that he too is unhappy. Not only because she wants to comfort him and "mother" him, but because it exasperates her to see the man happy, and happy without deriving his happiness from her. Men too, of course, often exhibit reaction 227a, but in them it arises exclusively from desire. And then nearly all Catholics, both men and women, also have a similar reaction: they want to convince unbelievers that their situation is desperate. In that category, the reaction is numbered 79PC. PC stands for "practising Catholic" as opposed to the non-practising variety.'

'I don't know what women can have done to you to make you speak of them in such terms. They must have made you suffer dreadfully. Oh, of course, I forgot – I mustn't say that! It's reaction 227a. You just wait, though: one day you'll be rid of women for good. I've often wondered what you'll be like when you're old. Well, you won't be much to look at. I could tell you exactly what wrinkles you'll have: I can already see the first traces of them, like the light pencil strokes with which a painter begins a sketch. It's true, there are lines on your forehead which weren't there three months ago....'

He began to laugh, delighted by her naïve rudeness, and feeling slightly attracted towards her. He wondered which of his different selves to bring into play. After all, had Solange not been there, he would not have minded 'taking' Andrée. 'The nape of her neck isn't too bad. But is it enough? Six of one, half a dozen of the other, as they say. But even so!' For the first time, he felt a sort of desire for her, more especially, perhaps, because of the rings under her eyes. Perhaps also because he found her repulsive: 'The strong alone relish horror.' He watched a fly in the ash-tray on the table in front of him, which had been quietly feeding on the ash and cigarette ends for three minutes with as much apparent enjoyment as if it had been jam – so drunk with ash that one could have picked it up with one's fingers. So it was with him: everything was much of a muchness. This sudden upheaval of all his feelings, of his whole policy towards this girl over the past five years, would have had its comic side. He felt no hatred towards her, merely indifference with if anything a certain liking, and from this indifference anything might emerge. He did not mind making her deliriously happy: why not? She deserved it. He did not mind making her deliriously unhappy: she deserved that too. It was just as rational to make her suffer in order to compensate for all the unwarranted good he had done her, as to make her happy in order to compensate for all the unwarranted harm he had done her. And in any case, was there any need to behave rationally at all? Everything came easily and spontaneously to him, just as it did when he sat down at his desk in front of a blank sheet of paper. Costals' inhumanity did not arise from an inability to experience human emotions, but rather from his ability to experience them all equally, and at will, as if all he needed to do was to press the appropriate button. There are those who rebel against the arbitrary nature of the laws that govern human lives; others are not even aware of it. Costals was aware of it, but rather than suffer from it, he chose instead to worship it. For his whole existence was governed by this one thought: since the world offers so many reasons for joy, only a fool would choose to suffer (since suffering has to be paid for in this world and is unrewarded in the next). After having suffered for some years from seeing the decline of France, he had decided to enjoy this decline (for patriotism, not being inborn, can be lost as easily as it is acquired). He had reacted in the same way towards social injustice, and in general to the whole problem of evil. 'If I were to suffer because of all the evil in the world, my life would be a torment, and therefore an absurdity. So let's enjoy that too.'

He debated for a moment whether to arrange a meeting with the young woman next day in order to pleasure her? But would he be able to recapture the feeling he now had for her? Suddenly, Andrée's ridiculous remark came back to him: 'You've no idea what a woman's will-power can do,' and at once the problem was settled; for there still remained all the reasons he had had for the past five years against going to bed with her, with the added irritation of remarks such as this. Nevertheless he no longer felt the same desire to torture her. The idea of staging a melodramatic cat-and-mouse act ultimately repelled him as being too facile and vulgar. He decided, therefore, to bring matters to an end without more ado. 'Forgive this interruption, but it's now five thirty. I must warn you that my landlady is calling at six o'clock. If there's anything you particularly want to say to me....'

'But isn't it you, Costals, who have something to say to me?'

'Me? What would I want to say to you?'

He saw Andrée's face harden in an instant, like the faces of those women who, after swaggering into the police-station with their tawdry jewellery, are told by the superintendent that he will have to detain them. His good genius tapped him on the shoulder: 'Don't be unkind.' 'Why not? I'll be nice to the other one in a moment.' 'What about this one?' 'Another time.'

'Your attitude towards me is a perpetual insult, and there are times when I wonder how I ever managed to put up with it....'

'I've often wondered about that myself. But it's surprising what women will put up with from a man....'

'Of course, when they're in love. But you're only interested in abusing your power. The life of a man like you is dreadful, monstrous!'

'A writer worthy of the name is always a monster.'

'Taking advantage of certain people and thwarting the others. Never in tune with other people. Destroying everything in the germ. Your life is one long series of abortions – your own, and those you inflict on others. Have you forgotten what you once wrote to me? "It's too easy to make women unhappy. I leave that to the gigolos"?'

'That "once" was a long time ago. It was at the time when

you yourself wrote to me: "A girl is never the first to tire of platonic love." Besides, you're intelligent enough for it to be worth while making you unhappy. You can make use of your suffering.'

'No, no, don't you believe it! I'm not intelligent enough.'

'But to suffer because one loves: isn't that a kind of happiness? What if your suffering ceased? Wouldn't you miss it?'

'It's easy for you to talk.'

'I don't know, it's the sort of thing women say.'

Now she was afraid of him, with a sort of animal fear, the fear one has of a madman when one is locked in the same room with him and has seen a murderous glint in his eyes. Frantically she sought to placate him.

'Please don't try to be cruel, Costals. It doesn't come naturally to you – you have to force yourself.' (She was trying to persuade him that he was kind, just as other women tried to persuade him that he was 'a Christian at heart'.) 'Is having loved you my crime?'

'Why yes!'

'Why no!' she said vehemently. 'Why must you take revenge on me? I've never done you any harm, and I've suffered a great deal from you. My anger was only a form of inverted misery. I paid for it as I paid for my sulks – which you didn't even notice. I beg you not to destroy this pitiful peace of mind so painfully acquired after three months of struggles and tears. I said to you once: "Rather than this silence and this uncertainty, bludgeon me until I have the strength to escape from you." Now, I say: "No, for pity's sake, spare me these blows." What would I have left of you, if you were no longer even kind to me?'

That she was afraid of him gave Costals no pleasure. All he wanted was to be able to make her suffer with a clear conscience.

'You admitted the other day that your love was not up to much, since you preferred your happiness to mine. For once, I ask you to prefer my happiness. Let me make you suffer. Then I shall love in you the pain I have caused. In this way I shall become part of you, and so love you. For five years you have given me the pleasure of resisting you; now give me the pleasure of being cruel to you. Women always refuse to recognize the degree of falsehood, calculation, weariness and charity in the love men bear them. With me you will see it all. And it will do you good! It will teach you something about life. You see, the important thing is not to let life stagnate. Life is always kind to the virile.'

'But who said I was virile? Is it my business to be virile? I'm a woman, damn it, a woman, a woman!'

'Still, women have a sure way of preventing themselves from suffering.'

'What?'

'Looking at themselves in a mirror when they're unhappy. They'd change their expression at once. And there's another recipe for automatically putting an end to your suffering. That is to try and imagine what you will be like in five years' time. You know perfectly well that, in five years' time, you will have ceased to love me, and that the whole of this episode will seem to you as ludicrous as the items they print in the newspapers under the heading "A Hundred Years Ago". A new sand-hill piles up and buries the old one. Just put yourself in the place of Andrée Hacquebaut at thirty-five. It only needs a little imagination.'

She was about to answer – to explode – when a sort of centipede appeared on the table and began to saunter nonchalantly around. She had a horror of such creatures.

'Kill that ghastly thing!'

'Why? It hasn't done me any harm.'

'What about me? Have I done you any harm?'

She crushed the insect with a newspaper. He gave her a nasty look.

'Mademoiselle Hacquebaut, you exhaust me. The other day I was in a kitchen with a little girl who made me very happy. Being happy, I wanted you to be happy too, and that is why I wrote to you. Last night, at half past nine, you came and banged on my door like a drayman. I was with that same little girl: everything had been arranged so that I should make a woman of her that night. And you dislocated the whole thing. However, since you had come because of me, I did not want your journey to have been in vain, and I made this appointment with you. We might have had a good hour and a half in which to talk pleasantly, if you had not contrived to turn up a quarter of an hour late. Now I really don't know where all this is getting us.'

'What are you after? Are you trying to make me so sick of you that I shall leave you in peace? So that's why you brought me back! To tell me of all your filthy goings-on with a scullery-maid! It's just as I always said: you're incapable of loving your equals. . . .'

'I'm not interested in equality in love because it's the child that I look for in a woman. I can't feel either desire or tenderness for a woman who does not remind me of a child.'

'That way you'll end up in gaol as a satyr.'

'Satyriasis is only an over-developed form of masculinity.'

'And so this is your "goodwill" – the goodwill you spoke about in your letter! This moral trap you set for me, carefully prepared as you prepare everything. . . . Well, did you or did you not emerge from your peaceful existence to write to me: "Opportunity not to be missed"?'

'That was a joke.'

'When Nero hurled himself at one of his courtiers with a dagger, and missed, he used to laugh and say it was a joke.'

'Oh God! Have we got to Nero now?' He heaved an exasperated sigh, pressing his fingers against one of his eyelids. 'I can't help it if I like joking, can I? Life has infinite charm as soon as you stop taking it seriously. But you women are all the same; you always think I'm joking when I'm not, and that I'm not joking when I am.'

'Why won't you admit that what you wanted to do was to watch the effect of your refined tortures on me minute by minute, to watch my thoughts and feelings struggling inside me, just as you might watch ants or Martians devouring each other while you, with your horror of getting involved, keep well away from it all. You like to have me within reach, as a cannibal chief keeps his favourite white man, cutting himself a slice from time to time. . . . Oh, yes, it's a splendid thing, your pity for women! What would it be like if you hadn't any? The pity one feels for a chicken just before wringing its neck.'

'I admit that, on occasion, I've behaved like a bit of a charlatan towards you. But not now. A while ago, yes, I wanted to make you suffer, and I even asked you to allow me to do so. But not now. At this moment, I feel very sympathetic towards you.'

Then she saw something which seemed to her extraordinary. She saw an expression both deep and solemn appear in Costals' eyes, and the word 'fraternal', that once she had loved to repeat to herself in thinking of him, rose to her lips as the one word which could describe what she felt towards him at that moment. But the expression quickly faded.

'Do you believe I could ever be generous towards you?' he asked, wishing to give her a false hope.

'I can no longer believe in you or in anything that comes from you. You have deceived me too often, wilfully misled me. Oh, men, men! Pits of horror and mystery and utter inconsistency as opposed to women, even the least stupid and the least affectionate of whom can do nothing but love, can do nothing but spend their lives returning good for evil!'

'Perhaps rather less is demanded of them. As for men's inconsistency. . . . Men are more inconsistent than women because they're more intelligent.'

'Oh, you and your intelligence! All I say is this: if, as you pretend, you have the smallest spark of feeling for me, then save me. Save me, Costals. To you it means nothing, to me it means life itself. And surely I have a right to live!'

She was only a few inches away from him, and her eyelids were now closed. She stood thus, with lowered lids, like someone expecting a blow – a little wraith-like, with her great hollow eyes, and burning with the desire to abandon herself. The only sound was the faint patter of sparrows' feet on the sky-light. Then, as Costals said nothing (and although she had not seen him raise his eyebrows when she said 'Surely I have a right to live', as if to say: 'Is it so important?') she moved away a few steps, her head bowed, saying in an odd voice: 'I'm sorry, I've got a speck of dust in my eye.' She turned to the wall and dabbed at her eyes with her handkerchief, silently (no snuffling). Costals waited for her to stop crying, endless though it seemed. 'There's still time,' he thought. 'One word, and I could make her madly happy.' But he said nothing, and she came back to the table. Then he took a step towards her. Suddenly his eyes fell on Andrée's right hand, and he saw what he had not seen before: while all her other nails were long and pointed, the nail of the middle finger of her right hand was cut short. He looked up at the dark rings under the girl's eyes, and his eyelids flickered with the gust of desire that swept over him. But it was too late.

'Did you break your nail?'

'Oh no,' she said, 'it's nothing.' And quickly she closed her fist. Her head was bowed.

'Off you go now, my dear. I think we've come to the end of what we have to say to each other.'

He thought she might be armed, and was going to kill him, or at least slap his face, and in order to be able to ward off the blow, he moved still closer to her, as modern bull-fighters stick close to the bull's flank in order to be 'inside' a blow from its horns. She raised her head, looked surprised, and stared at him motionless, with her bruised eyes. He realized meanwhile that she did not intend to kill him, that the idea had not even crossed her mind, and he thought: 'Really, these Frenchwomen!'

'Costals, I shall probably never see you again. I just want you to answer one question: are you aware of what you're doing?'

'What, me? That's a good one. If I weren't aware, I wouldn't be guilty.'

'What do you mean by that? Am I to understand that you *want* to be guilty?'

Without answering, he took her gently by the arm, and opening the door, escorted her along the short garden path to the door that led into the avenue. (There was a wing-shaped cloud floating in front of them.) 'Shall I kiss her on the forehead before throwing her out?' The reasons for and against such a gesture were equally balanced. The door-bell had been out of order for some time: it was not supposed to ring when the door was opened from the inside, but in fact, about every other time, it did. 'If it rings, I shall kiss her.' He opened the door. Silence. A twittering of birds, weaving a trellis of song above their heads. She went away.

251

He closed the door. He had an intuition that she would come back, that she would knock, that something would happen. But no, nothing: he had never had any luck with his intuitions. Back in the studio, he listened a moment longer, then went upstairs to the columbarium.

'Well, my little one, what did you think of all that?'

Solange was still standing behind the curtain in the attitude she had adopted for eavesdropping. And she looked at Costals with perplexed and feverish eyes. Her cheeks were flushed, too, as when he switched on the light after covering her with kisses for hours (that face of hers, a little swollen by his kisses), although today he had only kissed her three or four times, and that an hour and a half ago. And her hair was somewhat wild, because she had not wetted it that morning.

'Well,' he asked again, 'what did you think of that little scene? A real performance, eh?'

'I wish I hadn't seen it. When you made me read some of that woman's letters, I felt sorry for her. But after seeing that, I have no pity left.'

When he had got her to read some of Andrée's letters, she had been shocked by what she considered a lack of delicacy on his part, although he had not revealed the name of his correspondent. She had told him so, and his reply was: 'I'm taking the hat away.'*

_____

*'To return to the conduct of the Comte de Guiche, the secretary also told me that, being present one evening at the Queen's card-table where the princesses and duchesses are seated around the Queen while the others remain standing, the Count became aware that the hand of a lady, his mistress, was busy in a place which modesty forbids me to name and which he was covering with his hat. Observing that the lady's head was averted, he maliciously raised his hat. Everyone present began to laugh and whisper, and I leave you to imagine the confusion into which the poor creature was thrown....

'He played similar tricks upon ladies daily, and yet they continued to seek his company.' — Primi Visconti: *Memoirs of the Court of Louis XIV.*

'What do you mean?'

'You'll be told when you're a big girl.'

Now again she was shocked, out of some obscure sexual solidarity, that he had made her a witness to the humiliation of one of her kind. But such was her faith in him that it never occurred to her to wonder: 'Will this happen to me one day?'

'It does one good to see you again. To see a woman who still lives in the world of reality. It's true, you're one of the few women I know who isn't crazy. Literary men attract crazy women as a lump of rotting meat attracts flies. We're landed with every kind of loneliness and repression: they want food for their dreams! You're the exception that proves the rule, and as an exception I love you.'

'But then why bother to reply to them?'

Ah, well! When I see flies on a piece of meat, I say to myself: "Everyone has to eat".'

He had taken her in his arms, inhaling the warmth and freshness of her face and sliding a hand under her shoulder-strap (he was a real terror with shoulder-straps: he had only to look at them for them to snap), hungry to get back at last to something he really desired, and with the same ardour as if he were returning to her after a long absence; and he was indeed returning from a distant country, from the nether regions where dwelt the people who did not attract him. And it was as though he were about to give voice to the sort of little strangled yaps with which a dog will greet the return of its master, be he good or bad. He said to her:

'I bring you my cruelty while it is still warm. This cruelty is my tenderness for you; they are one and the same thing. Kind? Cruel? It's all the same. As one quenches one's thirst with a cigarette. Water would refresh you, and the cigarette burns, yet they're the same thing. Don't try to understand. You saw that girl? There are masses and masses of them around! All the women I've refused because I didn't find them attractive. Drown the lot of them, that's all they deserve – like Carrier's executions in Nantes. And in fact that's how it usually finishes: rrrop . . . I open the trapdoor. Quite seriously, what she ought to do now is commit suicide, so that I'm really rid of her. I showed you that little episode so that you should

253

see what happens to women I don't care for. There's a girl who started from nothing, who brought herself up entirely on her own in the worst possible conditions, who is cultivated, sensitive, intelligent, extremely gifted, and who has been in love with me for five years. If I weighed her merits against yours, yours would be non-existent. But I don't love her. I've never given her anything, never kissed her, never held her hand. Because I don't love her. You, on the other hand, come along, you attract me, and I give you everything: my attention, my affection, my sexual vigour, my intellect. Remember that, if one day you have reason to complain of me, which you surely will. You have had everything, for no good reason. There's no reason why I should have given everything to you rather than to others, no reason for such a preference or such a partiality. Where did I read that line that always runs through my head when I think of you?

I know not why 'twas you I chose.

What are you? A little thing like so many others, a dewdrop in the meadow. You might have had all the "negative qualities" in the world: do you think that would have stopped me? All you had to do was please me, and you couldn't help that. Picked out almost at random. That's how life goes – everything a matter of chance. Why this rather than that? *In reality*, there is no reason, or what reason there is is absolutely unimportant. For you, everything; for the others, nil. There's a terrible injustice there, and that is what I like about it. Not that I don't love justice too; I enjoy them both in turn. I had to tell you all this. In any case, you know that I enjoy telling you unpleasant things. It's part of my love for you.'

She listened without really understanding, with a certain bewilderment that was natural enough. But she belonged to a world where writers were thought of as 'literary chaps, not to be taken too seriously'. As for him, he was glad that she did not answer, for whatever she had said would doubtless have been very different from what he himself thought. He went on:

'There are so many worlds that are foreign to you. The world of knowledge. The world of justice. The world of suffering. The world of responsibility. You do not even suspect their existence. And I am only aware of them in flashes. A rocket soars, lights them up for a moment, then they are plunged in darkness once more. My darkness.

'Yet I devote time and attention to you, I give you part of my substance, there are times when I speak to you as if I were speaking to some unknown world. How many of my words have reached their target? What a lot of wasted shots! Am I right, or am I wrong? A little girl. A little twenty-year-old bourgeois Parisian girl. There are those who will say: "So that's what you spend your time on! When the social structure.... When whole nations.... When empires.... Aren't you ashamed of yourself?" And there are others who will say: "This little soul is every bit as important as the soul of an entire nation. All the suffering caused throughout the world by the war weighs no more than the tears of this chit of a girl. If there was nothing else in your life but the fact that you treated her lovingly, you would have fulfilled your human role here below, you would have worked the tiny human plot that is allotted to each of us." Which of these two viewpoints is the right one? A vulgar and meaningless question. Both of them are right. You must immerse yourself in one of them until you have exhausted it, and then do the same with the other. They're two aspects of a single truth. Fancy writers tell us that truth is a diamond, but what they never stop to consider is how many facets this diamond may show. And now, quiet! Don't try to answer. There's no need for you to understand, as there's no need for me to know that you haven't understood.'

He went and closed the shutters,* drew the curtains, and modestly turned over a little card from a press-cutting agency which bore the legend 'WE SEE ALL' in large letters. His soul was still smouldering, as if under the influence of some life-giving spirit: this delectable brew was his cruelty to Andrée. He flung Solange, fully dressed, on to the bed, and straightened her legs out. From then on, he was like an apache trying to pin a man to the ground. Usually he dared not squeeze her too

---

*The columbarium overlooked the gardens of a convent (of which there were many in the district). The convent bells could be heard, and the nuns could be seen from the windows. The author has refrained from exploiting the too obvious contrasts.

hard for fear of hurting her: she was so young! Now for the first time he was brutal with her, and although this was partly from necessity, because she struggled, it was also calculated, for he was determined to leave her with an unforgettable memory. She screamed, 'No! No!' with her mouth wide open and her head lolling from side to side, and he drank in her breath which no longer had the odour he knew but an odour which came from deeper down, as though her cries drew it up from the depths of her being. He could keep her head still only by seizing her tongue between his teeth and clenching them when she tried to move. And with every limb he systematically manhandled this thing which was Mlle Dandillot. Suddenly everything became easy and he let himself sink into a new sensation. She closed her eyes, and her plaints ceased. Meanwhile he was absorbed in his sensation, mediocre though it seemed. It gave him no more than an intellectual satisfaction: 'Well, that's done!' And he sniffed vaguely at this woman's face, as a lion, tearing chunks off the meat it holds between its paws, stops now and then to lick it.

With one of the handkerchiefs embroidered for him by Andrée Hacquebaut, he wiped Solange's forehead and the curve of her nostrils, so divinely moist. Her head, having slipped between the pillows, was now tilted even further back, so that the long, pale curve of her neck and throat assumed more prominence than the face itself, on which there appeared a look of such complete surrender that he pressed her eyelids closed in alarm. Her lips were parted a little, disclosing the small teeth like those of a sheep's head on a butcher's stall. There are three smiles that have something in common: the smile of a corpse, the smile of a gratified woman, and the smile of a decapitated beast.

He scrutinized her thus for a while, attentively. He was trying to differentiate her, to see in what way she was more than a mere body, more than an instrument for his caresses, more than a mirror in which to observe his own pleasure.

He stretched himself out at her side. His soul, already clouded with intimations of sadness, took flight and hovered in realms remote from her. It was the primordial moment when man asks, as in the Gospel: 'Woman, what have I to do with thee?' The primordial moment of pity for women. Outside, the sky must have clouded over, for the room was now almost dark. He had visions of flabby, white-skinned women, women of infinite depravity, who lie in one's arms at nightfall as the lights spring up one by one around the city, and who say: 'Look . . . there's a light . . .' and whom one goes on holding, out of pity, making them believe that one loves them, out of pity. This memory brought back others: the whole of his life opened out like a peacock's tail, and all of it, past and future, was dotted with faces like the golden circles on a peacock's tail. He felt pity for this young creature alive at his side, her face nestling in the hollow of his left shoulder, where so many faces had lain. (If that shoulder had been a photographic plate, how many superimposed faces would have been visible there, and what a hideous monster the composite face that eventually appeared. . . .) He felt pity for her for having placed herself in hands such as his (and yet, had he detected the slightest little ruse or merely precaution on her part, to protect herself, he would have held it against her). He felt pity for her because he did not love her more, could not find more reasons for loving her – and because for him she was but one among many, whereas for her he was the only one – and because of what she believed he was giving her, when in fact it was impossible for him to give it. He thought: 'One spends one's youth loving people one cannot possess fully (through shyness), and one's maturity loving people one cannot possess fully (through satiety).'

One of his arms lay under Solange's head, but his face and body were turned away from her. There was a moment when he betrayed her so cruelly in his thoughts that he put out his hand to seek hers and comfort her, as if she must have guessed what was going on inside him (and also because, now that he no longer expected anything from Solange, he felt he must be doubly kind to her as though to counteract the suspension of his love). She turned and, without a word, kissed him on the cheek – still the same childish kisses, in spite of all that had happened. She had emerged from her stillness to do this, as a solitary wave rises above a calm sea. A cry burst from his heart: 'She can suffer because of me, but I cannot suffer because of her. I love her, yet it is not in her power to make me suffer. This game must end, this abominable one-sided game, so harmful to the weaker of us.' Then a voice rose: 'You say you love her, yet she cannot make you suffer: therefore you do not love her.' And he answered: 'Why must I always be lumped together with other people! I love her but she cannot make me suffer, because I am not like everybody else. I am not so easily hurt.' He was suddenly seized with a passion for truth that was either dazzling light or cloudy obfuscation, either a glory or a vice (one of his women had called it his 'catastrophic honesty'); he wanted to say to her: 'Little one, my darling little one, I had better warn you now: I do not love you enough. You too will have to stand aside for someone else. The day will come when I shall have even forgotten your face. I am of the wandering race of men. The day will come when I shall love other women, different women. Perhaps it has happened already!' (this was not true). 'Perhaps already I have stopped loving you.... Perhaps I have never loved you at all, my darling child....' But he knew that she was like all the rest, that she too, like the great ones of the earth, lived and fed almost exclusively on lies, and would soon die if the lies were to cease, and that Truth, anyway, is *ipso facto* reprehensible and punishable by law since, as everyone knows, she goes about naked. He said nothing, but squeezed her hand more tightly. 'The main thing is that she should be happy.' Then, with her face buried in his neck, she made a cooing noise which it would be feeble to describe as being like the cooing of a dove, for it literally was the cooing of a dove. He asked her what it meant. She answered, 'It means I'm happy,' in the same far-away voice, as of another self, the ghost of the little girl she had once been, speaking from the depths of her sub-conscious where it had sunk long ago.

Then he remembered that there had been other women beside whom, lying thus after the act, he had not felt the same impulse to escape – others beside whom at such moments he had thought: 'I could die quite happily, like this. Now I really wouldn't mind dying, like this.' But lying there beside Solange, he did not say this to himself; no, he did not say to himself that he was ready to die.

'The main thing is that she should be happy.' Once again, his lucid mind laid bare the underlying meaning of the words. And he saw that it hardly differed at all from what he had felt for many, many others, of the most diverse kinds (and what does it matter how a person behaves towards those he loves; his behaviour towards the rest is what really counts). He remembered the emotion he had felt on reading the words of that splendid old fossil Captain Hurluret in *Les Gaîtés de l'Escadron*, when he is eventually retired: 'I've been forty years in the service, and the only thing in all that time that really counts for me is the fellows I've stopped making fools of themselves and getting into trouble, the fellows for whom barrack-room life has been a little more tolerable thanks to me. And if, later on, there are some of them who remember their Captain and say: "He wasn't a bad sort, after all," I shall have had my reward.' On reading this, Costals had raised his head from the book. It had struck a deep chord in him, and he thought: 'I am the same sort of chap as Hurluret. Of course, there are other things in me, but I'm Hurluret as well.' And now he realized that underlying his words about Solange, his wish for her 'to be happy', was something not so very different from what he had felt towards his men during the war: 'Are the men happy? Is there anything wrong?' – or at home towards the servants, always going out of his way to see that they got their fair share of pleasure in this world – or towards the hired native in the colonies, getting up in the middle of the night to give him an extra blanket because he had heard him cough in his sleep – or towards the almost unknown vagrant he had sheltered under his roof as a guest, and with whom he identified himself through the mere fact of this hospitality. And so it was for all that race of men and women encountered by chance, to whom he had given more than any other man would have given in his place – given not for the sake of 'principle', not because he believed that good was preferable to evil – given without even any preconceived ideas about the world, for he had come to the conclusion long since that no definition holds water, that 'the people' are not this or that, that 'natives' or 'women' or 'Frenchmen' are not this or that, that all is in everything, that the good are also bad and the bad also good – given, finally, without the least thought that it might be counted to his credit somewhere, in the hearts of these men and women, who had promptly forgotten him, or in the eyes of public opinion, which knew nothing of his actions, either before those human tribunals where the riff-raff dispense injustice, or before that supreme tribunal in which he did not believe and of which all he could say was that if it existed, and if one day he were to appear before it (as he no doubt would, having always lived without giving much heed to the Law), hundreds of people would come and bear witness in his favour. And he saw that there, too, Solange Dandillot was one of a crowd, and he pitied her for not being more clearly set apart.

He lay there, no longer thinking about her. 'What are you thinking about?' she asked, a little alarmed by his silent day-dreaming. 'About you.' A slight, very slight and tenuous thread of boredom pierced his consciousness. Then he thought: 'One day I shall put that image of her teeth, like those of a decapi-tated sheep, in one of my books. I *use* her!' At the thought that he *made use* of Solange, his throat tightened as if he were about to cry. But suddenly another thought leapt up like a dolphin out of a calm sea: 'I've been told often enough that I was wrong, "criminal" even, in not taking a girl who offered herself to me. Nature, society, public opinion, are you satisfied now? Well? I bet I still haven't got it right.' Amused by this thought, he was encouraged to say some things which he found a bit difficult. He sat up, and leaning over her, said with a smile: 'Well, my little Dandillot, now you're my mistress! You see the way things happen.... Now see if you can get away from me.'

She frowned a little, and he smoothed out the furrows with his thumb.

'You said "no" when it happened, so your honour is safe. ...There's another thing, rather less agreeable. Do you know what a woman does when she....'

He gave her some pharmaceutical advice in a whisper. He would have liked the room to be darker still, as dark as night. Several times he repeated: 'I'm ashamed to have to tell you these things....' But it was not 'these things', or having to say them, which made him feel ashamed: he knew that there was nothing shameful about them, that on the contrary they were beneficent and therefore moral. But he was ashamed of having said them so many times before. Eventually she got up without saying a word, and disappeared into the next room.

He sat down in an armchair. From the bathroom came the familiar sounds of the different water-pipes. 'Now she's doing this, now she's doing that. . . .' The almost identical similarity between this moment and hundreds of others he had been through plunged his soul in melancholy. 'For her, it's something so new, so surprising. . . . For me it's all so stale.' His melancholy would have been less had his pleasure been really spectacular. But far from it; and he was well aware that Solange had derived no more pleasure from the act than he had.

She came back, and with her hands on the arms of his chair, leaned over him, compassionately, in a very 'womanly' gesture; they were like two castaways flung up together on the shore. But so completely did she seem to share his sadness that this sadness vanished. He went and sat on the divan, and made her sit beside him. Then he said:

'Yes, all this is very painful. And yet, when I showed you that woman just now, although it was indeed for the reasons I explained, it was also in order to show you what becomes of a girl who doesn't do the necessary when she should. You see, there's only one way of loving women, and that's by making love to them. There's only one way of doing them good, and that's by taking them in one's arms. Incense needs warmth in order to give out its perfume; women too need that particular warmth to give out theirs. All the rest – friendship, esteem, intellectual sympathy – is an illusion, without love, and a cruel illusion, too. For illusions are the cruel things: with realities one can always get by. You remember the words of St Paul: "The prudence of the flesh is the death of the soul." I know many unsatisfactory marriages where the trouble is entirely due to the husband's "respect" for the wife: a wife should be treated like a mistress, and not just in fits and starts but all the time; whether it's easy or not is irrelevant. That silly little get-together we had just now disappointed you, no doubt. as it did me; but it takes six months for a young Frenchwoman

to learn how to be properly excited. You've only got to touch
an Italian or a Spanish girl and she practically swoons; but
French girls are slow starters and it's the devil of a job to give
them any pleasure: I usually reckon six months to get things
right. Perhaps some harm may come from my having taken
you; but since you love me, it would have been just as hurtful
– to you – if I had refrained. And in any case you're twenty-
one. Of course I don't mean it's the autumn of a woman's life,
but all the same, the way things are going now.... Why, in
this year's Miss World beauty competition, the age-limit was
twenty-two.... Come, my beauty, let time work for you. The
day will come when you will sense my desire from afar, and
will welcome it. We shall be attuned to each other like a pair
of runners in a three-mile race – both working hand in glove.
We shall speak to one another in our silences. You will want
what I want, I shall want what you want. So you'll no longer
want darkness when you are in my arms; you will want broad
daylight, the better to see me with, and you will see me....
What will keep me going when I am old? The books I have
written and the pleasure I have given women.'

She stroked his hair, then clasped her hands archwise over
his head and rested her forehead against his chest, bowing so
low that all he could see was her hair, in a gesture of utter
submission.

They went out. An old man was sitting on a bench feeding
the birds, and she made a detour so as not to frighten them
away. In the streets, a few radiant faces were almost engulfed
by the repulsive, virulent magma of the unloved and the unloving (not to mention the notorious ugliness of the Parisians).
And he was filled, for the hundredth time and yet as freshly as
ever, with that regal sensation of walking side by side, as
though her legitimate owner, with a woman who attracts
stares and almost shouts of admiration. She still addressed him
as *vous*, though oblivious of the delicate pleasure he derived
from being thus authorized to say *vous* in return. With this
vous, Costals was able to deny the intimacy of their relationship, to create, alongside the reality, another order of things
that belied it.

From time to time he put his hand on her waist, for a second only, as if to make sure that she was still beside him. But soon she put her arm through his. It was only the second time she had done so, the first having been on the night of their great misunderstanding. On both occasions, it was after having seen him troubled: he was touched by this. Soon, however, he began to feel uncomfortable. For the fact was that ever since he had first gone out with a woman he loved at the age of nineteen, he had always obstinately refused to keep in step with his female companions; he found it ridiculous and humiliating for a man. So they jolted along for another fifty yards, and it seemed to him painfully symbolic that a man could not walk straight because the woman who loved him, and whom he loved, was holding his arm. Finally it was she who, breaking step as soldiers do on the march, fell into rhythm with her lover. He noticed this and was pleased. Soon, however, it wasn't enough for him. That weight on his arm seemed like a chain. The very gesture with which, poor child, she had thought to bring them closer together, had only made him feel impatience and scorn at being coupled. He took advantage of a traffic jam, as they were crossing a street, to detach himself gently. And then, having regained his freedom, he felt a wave of tenderness towards her.

She was dining with friends in the centre of town. They passed travel posters showing Algerian belly-dancers (for the benefit of French tourists) shoeshine boys (for the benefit of British tourists), all the symbols of that devilish human invention, travel, which for inconvenience, exhaustion, danger, time-wasting and nervous wear and tear has no rival except war (the only difference being that travel costs you the earth whereas at least one is paid for going to war). What they inspired in Costals was not so much a desire to be sea-sick in Solange's company as an urge to make a great splash on her behalf, which, now that she had given herself, would no longer look as though he were trying to buy her (this feeling comprised a mixture of delicacy and vulgarity, as is so often the case with questions of money): he could feel the banknotes quivering in his wallet like thoroughbreds at the starting-gate. He said to her:

'You know, old thing, I like squandering money on women;

it's one of the things I pride myself on. When I am old and poverty-stricken, with only a pension of eight hundred francs granted me by the Society of Literature and the proceeds of the subscription launched for me in the *Figaro* to live on, I like to imagine that all the money I ever spent on the women I loved will be reconstituted somewhere in tangible form and that I shall depart this world satisfied with what I have done, my eyes fixed on that mountain of gold – which, if you'll forgive the expression, I shall call "the gold of my loins". This is why I regret having spent so little on you when we were out together. I get the impression that I'm out with a decent woman, and that's a sensation I don't like at all.' (Since when this note of insolence with her? Wasn't it since.... Ah, wretched males, even the best of them!) 'Listen: those are bank-notes, made to be changed into happiness; and that's something I know all about, for I won't deny I've had my whack at God's creation. Do you want to come away with me somewhere for a couple of months? I say two months, because that's just about the time it takes to get through a good love affair, but it might be longer – until one of us has had enough.' ('One of us' was a charming euphemism. He knew perfectly well that he was always the first to break off.) 'Anywhere you like. Persia. Or Egypt. Or Transylvania. Or Pennsylvania. Or Mount Ararat. And I really mean it: you name the place and off we go. In my life as in my art, I'm ready for anything: what's difficult is to really want something, but this time I somehow believe I do. And so it's all right, because I love my desires. I have the impression that God has given you parents who want your happiness above everything else. You will come back armed with two months' happiness: a splendid weapon to face the future with. You will then be admirably placed for marrying. You are no longer a virgin – though, taking one of those linguistic liberties which are the privilege of great writers, I shall continue to call you a girl, for I am too fond of youth to resign myself to using the word "woman" unless I really have to: it sounds so old and pompous – you are no longer a virgin, but from what I know of men, and if you have any wit at all, your husband won't even notice it. Besides, even if he does, he won't say a word: we're not savages in France! Then, either he'll make you happy and you won't regret me, which is what I very much hope; or else you'll be unhappy, and then I shan't be far away. We'll get you a divorce if need be, and go back to good old Ararat. This trip can either remain a secret as far as you're concerned, or be made public. In the latter case, it will redound to your eternal credit. You never bother about your own glory, so one has to look after it for you. But it can also be kept very secret. I've been on a dozen honeymoons in my life, and nothing has ever leaked out. And I would go to gaol sooner than give away a woman I loved. All in all it's a plan against which no objection, social, moral or otherwise, can hold water. Of course there are always those who will say: "Sir, you're a revolting cad" – to which I would reply: "Far from being a revolting cad, I'm a spirit of the air. Of course it's not your element, etc...." You see, when one wants to give pleasure to somebody, one mustn't look too far ahead, or bother too much about the consequences. When one wants to give pleasure to somebody, it's the same as when one wants to produce a great work of literature – it must be done with a kind of studied insouciance: because if you thought about it too long you'd never do it at all....'

For a moment he dreamed of seeing the beauty of the world with her, unveiling it to her, becoming merged with her as part of that beauty. Then his day-dream disintegrated, wandered, took another path. And he realized that though he did want to go on such a journey, he wanted to go alone. And it was true that, when he remembered all the wonderful places he had seen – every one of which he had visited at least twice, once alone and once with someone he loved – or when he wanted to use them in his books, it was always the time when he had travelled alone that came to his mind most vividly, most magically and most potently. For it is a major law of nature that we are no longer entirely one when we are two. If God said 'It is not good that man should live alone', it was because he was afraid of the solitary man. And so he weakened him by providing him with a mate, in order to have him at his mercy.

But he quickly repelled the sirens of solitude: 'After all,

whatever I made of it would be for her. To give pleasure to someone who deserves it is not to be despised. . . . '

Under an archway he pulled her towards him. His lips hovered above her face and eventually came to rest on one of her eyelids, where they remained for what seemed an eternity.

As they were about to part, he said to her :

'You know, one day I'm going to put in one of my books an image that occurred to me about your teeth – "like those of a decapitated sheep".'

'How horrible!'

'But it's true. And so it has to be said. You don't mind my making use of you in my books, do you?'

'Not at all. On the contrary, I'm glad to be useful to you in your work.'

'Well said. . . . You're not the first, mind you. . . . But still, well said. . . . Now I shall be able to love you even more than I do already.'

He gazed at her fondly. But just then an expression crossed her face which spoiled her prettiness. And it struck him that if ever he allowed himself to be finally caught, and married her, it would again be out of pity. And he was afraid of his pity.

Back in his studio, he was tidying up the bed when he saw traces of blood on the top sheet. He reflected that the sheet would go to the laundry, whereas fifteen years earlier he would have kept it as it was, as a souvenir. He felt a pang as he realized once again that he was not sufficiently open-hearted towards her. As though to make up for this, when he went to bed he searched for Mlle Dandillot's blood-stains on the sheet and placed them against his heart. And he fell asleep feeling somehow protected by the affection he felt towards her.

During the days that followed, Costals awaited some sign of life from Andrée : a letter, a telegram or a visit. . . . The concierge, the servant, everyone was warned – a little ridiculously – to bar her passage. Ah, if only he could have had her deported to the Island of Dogs near Constantinople, or to some other equally God-forsaken spot! But nothing happened.

'Perhaps she's killed herself.' The thought filled him with profound satisfaction.

It is a peculiarity of most young girls to wish to show their parents to the man they love, even when these parents are total idiots who will alienate him at once. Costals was invited to lunch at the Dandillots'.

The advent of 'the family' invariably provoked three reflexes in Costals. Terror at the threat of the Hippogriff: 'I know what they're after!' A feeling of ridicule, this being for him a basic element in the concept of the family. And animosity, for he could not but detest all parents, who represented the potential enemy. On this occasion, these reflexes combined to put him in a state of excitement to which the thought of the risk he was running and the ordeal to be overcome contributed greatly.

Solange had sought to make the prospect more alluring by saying: 'You'll see, my parents are very likeable.' 'Likeable to whom?' he thought to himself. 'To her? What do I care! To me? How does she know?' It reminded him of the people who tell you on their invitation-cards, by way of encouragement, what you will be given to eat or drink: 'Tea, Sherry, etc.' (The vulgarity of European manners compared to those of 'savages' – the Chinese, the Arabs etc.)

Mme Dandillot had the dimensions of a horse and the aspect of a policeman. To reconcile the two, let us say that she resembled a police horse. She was a head taller than her husband and Costals. To his horror, Costals recognized in her a caricature of her daughter. The same nose, though misshapen, the same lips, though colourless, the same expression, though deadened. The resemblance could not be said to be frightful, since it was natural; it was nonetheless startling: 'At fifty, my mistress will look a similar fright. In fifteen years' time she will be as plump as a partridge already. It's a warning from heaven; there's not a moment to lose.' He was appalled to think that Mme Dandillot knew all about their liaison and that perhaps, in certain circumstances, she had dictated Solange's behaviour. The thought that Solange was incapable of lying oppressed him now like sultry weather.

M. Dandillot, on the other hand, had an appearance of such nobility that no one would ever have taken him for a French-man. Close-shaven, and with hair as thick as a young man's, though nearly white, he reminded one a little of the 'family Doctor' as seen in advertisements for patent medicines. His smile, which was delightful, revealed a row of perfect, gleaming teeth. But all his features seemed to be drawn with pain. Clearly he was a doomed man. At table, M. Dandillot said nothing except for a few polite words.

It has often been said that nothing reveals a man's character more than his home. The Dandillots' interior bespoke an absence of taste rare even for their social background and for Paris. A few quite handsome objects stood cheek by jowl with a mass of vulgar and pretentious junk – inexcusable for people in their circumstances: it was all fairly opulent-looking. Costals could have understood a bachelor engaged upon some great work putting up with such surroundings out of in-difference to externals and contempt for them. But a 'worldly' family, and this ravishing girl! That Solange had not compelled her family to have a decent-looking home, that she could tolerate this obscene décor, told heavily against her: there must be something of the same inferior quality in her that enabled her to feel at home in it all. And it seemed to him even more serious that she should have no hesitation in show-ing it to him, no suspicion of the uneasiness it might cause him, or what it might make him feel about her.

Mme Dandillot said that her daughter had never had a day's illness ('She's beginning to boost her wares'), and that she did not care for scent or jewellery. When Costals said he did not much care for them either, she simpered: 'Another thing you have in common.' ('She's already treating us as if we were engaged, blast her!') She also sang her husband's praises, pre-sumably so that Costals should not think she had married a corpse. If one were to believe her, M. Dandillot had more or less created French sport. He had run various sports clubs, encouraged the young, been 'a man of action'. Costals choked back the retorts that rose to his lips: that action is like an

itch: you scratch, and that's all; that the only action worthy
of the name is inside oneself; that all men of action, when
you press them about it, can ultimately think of nothing to
say, so little justification can they find for it, etc.

Solange, her nose in her plate, said not a word. She was
embarrassed beyond belief to see Costals in the midst of her
family. Embarrassment hardened her features, gave her a sly,
ill-natured expression. What family life can do to people! An
angel of sweetness transformed into a *femme fatale*. Anyone
who saw Solange now for the first time could not have helped
thinking: 'She's a perfect bitch. Beware!'

Costals and Mme Dandillot talked about nothing for an
hour. In order to be sure of pleasing the writer, and also to
avoid saying anything stupid, Mme Dandillot would repeat,
after a suitable interval, precisely what Costals himself said.
Costals having expressed the view, over the hors d'oeuvres,
that 'journalism does not prevent a real writer from getting on
with his work', Mme Dandillot declared with an air of wisdom
over the coffee, as if it were a truth which Costals needed to
be convinced of: 'You know it's quite possible to produce a
good book and also write for newspapers.' Costals felt more
and more ridiculous, and humiliated at the idea that he was
here as a possible fiancé. A fiancé! A 'son-in-law'! Braggart
though he was, he could not shake off this feeling of humiliation.

He looked at these people and despised them for not looking
after their daughter better. 'Whether out of vanity, or
immorality, or calculation, or irresponsibility, they have let
her go out with a man like me, and I find it hard to believe
that they don't know I sleep with her. Perhaps they think I'll
marry her, but how do they know? A girl who was obviously
cut out to be a virgin, who was the personification of the
chaste young girl, and they don't do anything to protect her
against herself, the swine. No religion, no tradition, no education, no self-respect, no backbone. My role is to attack, I know,
but it's up to society to defend itself! Yet whenever I try to
conquer people's bodies, or trouble people's minds and spirits,
it's always the same: no defences! Soft as putty everywhere.
I play my game, but they don't play theirs!' From then on,
the thought of having parents-in-law so lacking in decorum

made the possibility that he might one day allow himself to be drawn into marrying Solange even more remote than ever. Nevertheless it must be noted that had the Dandillots been high-minded people who would never have let their daughter go out alone with him, he would have railed against both them and her, and would promptly have discarded her with a jibe against prudery. Despising them for being high-minded, despising them for not being so, he held them as though in a vice, and Solange with them. He would screw it tight the day he stopped loving her. The machinery was ready.

After lunch, a visitor was announced. Mme Dandillot and Solange went to entertain her in the drawing-room. M. Dandillot asked Costals to join him in his study. Costals thought: 'If he says: "I entrust my daughter to your care" (he felt a lump in his throat), I shall reply: "She will be like a little sister to me." It's not a phrase that commits me in any way. For as my mistress she's like a little sister to me.'

In his study, M. Dandillot let himself sink into a low armchair. He suddenly seemed tiny, like a fly shrivelling up just before it dies. The outline of his emaciated thighs was visible inside the trouser legs. We shall refrain from describing the study, for we know that novel-readers always skip the descriptions.

'Monsieur Costals,' he said, 'I am not the sort of person you think me. If I hardly spoke at lunch it was because I have been eating my meals with Mme Dandillot for thirty-one years, and we have said all we had to say to each other. I have lost the habit of talking, or rather I've acquired the habit of talking to myself in my room. As for you, I prefer to talk to you alone, as I want to talk to you seriously. However, there's something about you that bothers me a little, and I should like to get it off my chest before I start talking about myself. May I speak with absolute frankness?'

'You can always try, and we shall see,' said Costals, who this time could feel the baleful Hippogriff literally breathing down his neck.

'Now, now!' said M. Dandillot with a smile, pretending to see it as a joke. 'I owe it to the man who wrote that great book' (he pointed to one of Costals' books which was lying on a table nearby) 'to be absolutely frank. Well, here goes: why do you wear that?'

He pointed to the red rosette of the Legion of Honour in Costals' buttonhole.

'I don't like making myself conspicuous. If I had refused . . .'

He was about to add: '. . . I should have appeared to be making a great deal of fuss about it,' but stopped short, sensing that he was about to put his foot in it.

'Well, if you had refused? I'd like to show you something.'

Solange's father rose, took a sheaf of papers out of a drawer, and handed Costals a cutting from the *Indépendant de N—*, dated July 1923. The headline read: *Our fellow-citizen, Charles Dandillot, refuses the Legion of Honour.* A lyrical, or rather cautiously lyrical, editorial introduction was followed by the letter written by M. Dandillot to the unfortunate custodian of the scarlet flood.

Sir,
I understand that you wish to propose me for the Legion of Honour.
I have dedicated my life unostentatiously to the youth of France. I did not do so in the hope of a reward which must be shared with all and sundry.
Furthermore, I am now fifty-seven. Allow me, dear sir, to express one wish: that in future the Government will employ men better qualified to select the people who have done something for their country.
Believe me, etc. . . .

Costals saw in this letter the resentment of a man who had missed being decorated at thirty, and nothing more. 'As a way of thanking a man who has had a kind thought, it's not too badly put together.' The fact that M. Dandillot had communicated his masterpiece to the *Indépendant de N—* also seemed rather significant. M. Dandillot then embarked on a lecture about 'purity'. Costals knew this one well, having delivered it himself on occasion. His real opinion on the subject of honours was that they belonged to the category of things designated by Epictetus as 'indifferent'. But it was obvious from this letter that M. Dandillot attached great importance to honours.

While the latter was searching through the folder, Costals had cast an author's eye on the cover of his book (writers throw surreptitious glances at their names in print much as pretty women – or women who think themselves pretty – glance at their faces in mirrors) and noticed that hardly more than a dozen pages of the 'great book' had been cut. It is true, of course, that one can perfectly well 'place' an author after having read only a dozen pages by him.

When he had finished his lecture on 'purity', M. Dandillot said: 'Has Solange told you that I haven't long to live? It's not absolutely definite, but I'm fairly certain of it.'

'Mlle Dandillot has never said anything of the kind.'

'I shall be dead within a month. The end of all illusions!'

'For me, death will be the end of all reality.'

'For me, the end of all illusions. I'm going to die at the age of sixty-one. And for a man who has been living for the past thirty years in accordance with certain natural principles which could reasonably have been expected to promote both youthfulness and longevity, it's a bit of a fiasco. Sixty-one! The age at which everyone dies. And yet, think of it: for over thirty years I've lived with all my windows open, never touched alcohol, never smoked. For over thirty years, do you hear, not a drop of hot or even lukewarm water has ever touched my face or body, even when I was out of sorts. For over thirty years, I've been up at six every morning doing my exercises naked. And only a year ago I was camping in the mountains, walking twenty-five miles a day with a rucksack on my back like a young man, my head bare to the sun and the rain. Even if my face is lined, my body, up to a month ago, was still that of a young man.... Even now,' he added, pointing to his stomach, 'you mustn't think I have a paunch. I have to wear a flannel belt, and that accounts for the thickness. Actually I have a very slim waist. In short, I've lived a *natural* life: you realize what that means, *natural*? And in spite of all this to end up dying at sixty-one, at the mere threshold of old age. When heaps of people who have lived the softest, most artificial lives, go on living into their seventies and eighties. So now I say to myself: it wasn't worth it, I've been had.'

Costals, too, felt that it hadn't been worth it. He remembered the words of the Scripture: 'I shall suffer the same fate as the foolish. Why then was I more wise?' He said:

'The main thing is to know whether it was a sacrifice for you to give up wine, tobacco, etc. . . .'

'Often, yes. Particularly getting up at six. But I was determined to conquer myself. If I had had to struggle for my livelihood and that of my children, I should have told myself that the effort was not wasted. But no, I've always lived on my private means. If I have struggled, it has only been against myself, a kind of luxury. And now I tell myself: I've taken all that trouble for nothing. You see, Monsieur Costals, there's no point in being brave about life. And yet I feel obliged to go on, to see it through to the end.'

He threw back his hair with a sudden jerk of the head – the gesture of a young boy, or a horse tossing its mane.

'Why see it through to the end?'

'Am I to betray the ideals of thirty years? Am I to deny everything I have stood for? I know too many people who would have a good laugh, or should I say a nasty laugh? To every one who came near me I presented the image of a certain type of man. It is my duty to maintain that image to the end, even if I was mistaken. Look, my eyes are dead, my heart is dead, my spirit is dead. I know what would buck me up: champagne. But how could I possibly ask for it? It would look as though I were ratting on the whole of my past life. No, I refuse to be a deserter.'

'What an aberration of conscience!' thought Costals. 'That's how one turns into a living lie, when one imagines one is "pure".'

'I'm going to die,' M. Dandillot went on, 'but if I make the slightest allusion to the fact, I'm told I'm an alarmist. But hush. . . .'

There was a noise in the next room. M. Dandillot said: 'Walls have ears, you know. . . .' His expression was that of a child caught red-handed. When the noise had stopped, he went on:

'Yes, I'm going to die, and they expect me to be cheerful. I have to pretend that I don't know I'm dying, so that my family can go on enjoying themselves with a clear conscience.

When I'm at my last gasp, I shall have to say something memorable that my family can pass on to future generations. What about you? Will you make a historic remark on your death-bed?'

'I trust I shall preserve some decorum on my death-bed, and that means no historic remarks. If I were positively compelled to say something, I think I should ask the public's forgiveness for not having expressed more satisfactorily what was in my heart. . . .'

'You're a public figure, that makes it different. *I* thought I had the right to stop acting now, after thirty years of it – the right to three weeks' sincerity before I vanish from this world. But on the contrary, the farce has only just begun, and it will soon be in full swing! Yesterday the doctor came, and he had to give me a very painful injection. I was longing to complain, just to hear them say "Be brave", so that I could shout back at them: "Be brave? Why should I? When I've hardly an ounce of energy left, because I've spent it too lavishly in the service of others, I'm expected to use it up putting on an act for your benefit. This corpse of mine must buckle to and step out smartly so that you should all feel better and not have to despise me. Well, go on, despise me then! What difference will it make to me where I'm going?" That's what I should have liked to shout at them. Instead of which, I acted the Roman, the man of iron – not a sign of fear, not a moan. And while they were admiring me (at least I suppose they were) I was despising myself for my absurd heroism.'

'And so,' said Costals, 'you lie to yourself, and worse still, you do it to impress others.'

'What do I care about the opinion of others! Perhaps if they'd shown some gratitude for the example I gave. But all they did was treat me as a lunatic. "Dandillot never eats tinned food because it's not natural . . . Take off your scarf when you see Dandillot, otherwise he'll pitch into you: don't you know he breaks the ice to go for a swim in winter?" My wife laughs at me openly. Solange pretends to take my ideas seriously, but I know she only does it out of kindness. My son used to do the opposite of what he knew to be my principles, on purpose, simply to annoy me. So the results have been negative all along the line. Not only have I set an example which nobody followed, but it's also possible that the example was not worth setting. And yet, it might all have been very different if, like you, I had written something.... Ah, yes, you've nothing to worry about!'

It occurred to Costals that the world would believe that M. Dandillot had died of cancer, but perhaps in reality he was dying from not having received the recognition he felt to be his due. As lamps need oil, so men need a certain amount of admiration. When they are not sufficiently admired, they die. The only way of softening the last days of M. Dandillot would have been to flatter his vanity. Costals was touched, too, to see the old man so naïvely, or so nobly, envying the achievement of a writer of thirty-four. The tragedy of not being able to express oneself suddenly struck him as being quite horrible.

M. Dandillot spoke warmly of Costals' future: 'You'll get everything you want, etc....' But there was a sting in the tail: 'Nevertheless, in spite of all this, your standing with the public is not what it ought to be. I don't know whether you're aware of the fact....'

'He's embittered,' thought Costals, 'so he's determined that I should have reason to feel embittered too. It would console him a bit. And yet he's obviously well disposed towards me. Ah, well! One mustn't expect too much of people.'

The whole thing seemed to him all the more exquisite for the fact, of which he was still firmly convinced, that M. Dandillot had never read more than ten pages of his work.

The writer went on:

'My dear sir, you must not think that your lessons have been in vain. You are giving me one this very minute which confirms my own way of thinking: that it's madness to restrain oneself except for the most powerful reasons.'

Moribund though he was, M. Dandillot was still sufficiently alive to contradict himself madly, which is the essence of life itself. The conclusion Costals had drawn was not at all to his liking. He protested:

'Everything that's good in the world was born of restraint.'

'I don't believe a word of it!' said Costals sharply, thinking

275

to himself: 'That's the sort of tawdry platitude with which poor old humanity tries to justify all its sweat and tears.'

'Let me go on believing so, at least,' said M. Dandillot. 'If everything I've done has been in vain, let me feel at least that I rose above myself in doing it.'

It was then that Costals realized the extent of the old man's defeat. And he felt a great surge of pity towards him.

It occurred to him that Seneca had written more or less what M. Dandillot had just said. He told him so. But at the mention of Seneca, M. Dandillot burst out angrily:

'Don't talk to me about those humbugs! I used to fill up whole exercise-books with quotations from the moralists: I'll make a bonfire of them all before I die. Where did I read that splendid expression the other day: "a dunghill of philosophies"?'* Really Monsieur Costals, you as a literary man must admit that you need a typist who can copy a manuscript intelligently more than you need a new conception of the universe. Those charlatans! I love life, I get nothing but enjoyment from it, and yet I'm supposed to be pleased at the prospect of leaving it for ever! Doctors probe my inside, and I'm supposed to find the pain enjoyable! I've known old men who talked with serenity of their approaching end, who, knowing that death was imminent, continued to go about their business as if nothing was the matter. Well, they were all blockheads, idiots. Intelligent people are afraid, paralysed by fear. Those scoundrels of philosophers should be locked up in padded cells if they believe what they say. And if they're just laughing at us, they should be made to laugh on the other side of their faces. Yes, I'm surprised no emperor ever thought of exterminating the whole brood of philosophers at one fell swoop, on the same grounds as the early Christians.'

For a dying man,' thought Costals, 'he seems a bit worked up. But perhaps it does happen that way.'

M. Dandillot closed his eyes for a moment with an expression of intense fatigue. 'That's what comes of walking twenty-five miles a day at the age of sixty,' Costals said to himself. 'Alas! one can't use up one's energy with impunity. But one mustn't

---

*Panaït Istrati (*Author's note*).

say so. We must go on playing boy-scouts!' His eyes still closed, M. Dandillot raised his forearms and let them fall on the arms of his chair in a gesture of resignation and sadness.

'What I want is sleep. But Mme Dandillot and Solange keep waking me up to give me medicaments. The medicaments don't help, and sleep does; but no matter, I must be robbed of sleep because of the medicaments. Right up to the very end, one must behave according to what's "done", and not according to reality.'

Costals, who had imagined that this lunch was a trap set by the nuptial Hippogriff, and that M. Dandillot had got him behind closed doors in order to enumerate his daughter's assets, was more and more surprised to see that there was never any mention of her, or rather that M. Dandillot included her in the group – his 'family' – of which he spoke with such lack of warmth. And he began to think that Mme Dandillot alone knew what was happening between himself and Solange. Either she accepted it, because it gratified her pride, and looked no further, in which case the Dandillots were rather odd people. Or else she wanted to give their liaison the flavour of an engagement, for the sake of appearances, but just the flavour, not the reality. Or she had made up her mind to see the thing through to the end. But in any case it looked as though M. Dandillot had been left out. And this was quite natural, since he would soon be dead.

M. Dandillot opened his eyes again, and with a vague motion of the hand (at about the level of the books) which seemed to take in everything in the room, said:

'What do I care about all this! Mere trifles to help the living to kill time. Now my eyes are open, and it's all lies. The clock shows the wrong time, because it's stopped. The barometer is out of order. That Corot there is a fake. I won't talk about the books. Everything is false, and yet it's so much a part of the atmosphere we breathe that, as soon as we discover what a fraud it is, we die, as drug-addicts do when deprived of their drugs.'

Suddenly he sat up straight, as though pulling himself together.

'I am grateful to you for two things. For not having tried to

277

delude me about my condition. And for not having tried to console me. You see, if anything could console me, it's the thought that I'm dying a natural death, that I'm not dying for a "cause"....'

Costals did not answer. M. Dandillot added:

'It's quite possible, though, that my death may be other than a natural death. I've something there' (he pointed to a cupboard) 'that will hasten the end, if the pain proves too much for me to bear. Two tubes of veronal. Dissolve, drink, and it's all over.'

'Yes, but supposing the dose isn't strong enough and you recover – think what hell your family would give you!'

'Do you think so?' M. Dandillot said with a small, child-like smile. 'Nonsense, with veronal there isn't a chance of recovering.'

'Why not use a revolver?' said Costals, adding, with a grin: 'Afraid you'll harm the family's reputation?'

'Yes, because of Solange. Besides, revolvers kick, and there's a chance of missing.'

'Not if you aim at the bone just below the temple. No, the real risk is that the gun might jam. I know all about that. Filthy guns. Worse than anything – false security. If one really wants to kill someone, give me a good knife any time. No one has ever found anything better.'

'Since I can't kill myself with a knife, I'll stick to veronal. Do you think it's cowardly to kill oneself?'

'The people who call it cowardly are those who are too cowardly to do it themselves.'

'That's exactly what I think.'

There was a silence, as if they were both aware of having exhausted a subject. Then M. Dandillot went on:

'I've spent forty years doing things I didn't enjoy, and doing them of my own free will. As a young man I sweated over law-books in spite of my wretched memory, although both my family and I knew quite well that I would only be a lawyer for appearance' sake, and only for a year or two. I married without love, or self-interest, or any particular taste for marriage. I had children because my wife wanted them: I don't mind telling you that Solange was not at all welcome.

I took a flat in Paris, although I loved nature and solitude, because it was "the thing to do". I went on taking the waters year after year, long after I'd satisfied myself that they did me not the slightest good. I did all this without any good reason, simply because everyone round me was doing the same, or because I was told I ought to do it. And now I'm going to die without knowing why I've led a life which I disliked, when there was a time when I could have made for myself a life I would have enjoyed. Isn't that odd?'

'Not at all. Men let themselves be dragged into things: it's the rule. Men live according to chance: it's the rule.'

Suddenly the door opened. Mme Dandillot appeared, and addressing her husband, said:

'I came in to see whether you needed anything.'

'No, thank you.'

'Don't you want the window open wider? You of all people!'

'No, the noise tires me.'

'I see your bottle of Eau de Cologne is empty. I'll send out for another.'

'No, Eau de Cologne's too cold. . . .'

'We can't heat up Eau de Cologne, I'm afraid. Well, I'll leave you to it.'

For a few moments, Costals and M. Dandillot remained silent. There could be no doubt that Mme Dandillot, behind the door, had heard all or part of their last few remarks.

M. Dandillot resumed in a lower voice:

'If only I could go to a nursing-home! If only I could see new surroundings, new faces, before I die, instead of those I've been seeing for thirty years. But it's a dream: even that is forbidden me. Do you know the only occupation I find tolerable in my present condition? Burning my correspondence. Forty-five years of correspondence. If one added up all the hours one has spent writing letters or doing other equally futile jobs, one would find one had wasted years of one's life. You are still young, so I'll give you a word of advice: never answer letters, or only very rarely. Not only will it not do you any harm, but people won't even hold it against you: they'll soon get used to it. As for me, by destroying my correspondence I'm saying *no* to the whole of my past life. And I find pleasure in doing so, and also in depriving Mme Dandillot of the pleasure she would have in rummaging through my affairs. . . . It's odd that I should talk like this to someone I don't know.'

This way of casting one's innermost secrets into the void was familiar to Costals: more than once he had done the same with Solange. Unwittingly M. Dandillot was returning the mysterious trust he had had in the girl; and the thought made him ponder.

'My wife,' M. Dandillot continued, 'my wife's religion is that of the average Frenchwoman: she doesn't practise, she doesn't take the sacraments, but she goes to Mass on Sundays. Solange claims to be an unbeliever, but goes to Mass with her mother, and would be upset if she missed it. But Solange doesn't really know.... You know her: she's still in bud. As for me I've always been a pagan. You can't love nature as I do and Jesus Christ at the same time. Besides, we have an infallible proof that Christianity was inferior to the great pagan philosophies: the fact that it triumphed. Everyone knows the kind of things and people who triumph' (with an embittered smile). 'It isn't that I don't admire Christ's teachings. Any religion will always redeem itself from ridicule by charity. But St Paul ruined everything. And so, one of the firmest tenets of my moral code was: not to have a priest at my death-bed. This is still my intention, needless to say. But after the inner upheaval I have recently undergone, I must confess that this "gesture" seems to me less significant than it did. And you, Monsieur Costals, may one ask where you stand in regard to religion?'

'I'm an "old Christian", an old Christian *de sangre azul*. But of course I have no faith and I don't practise.'

'Ah! I'm very glad. I couldn't shake hands altogether honestly with a man I knew to be a believer, whatever his religion. Here, give me your hand, will you?' (He clasped it firmly.) 'Well, now, in spite of that, do you intend to have a Christian burial?'

'I should like my body to be carried straight from my death-bed to the paupers' grave, and buried there not too deep, so that the dogs can dig it up and eat it.'

'Splendid. But what about the priest? Would you see a priest if you were about to die?'

'It depends. If I were dying in the bosom of my family I think I would. For two reasons. To please those around me at little cost to myself, since they would ardently wish it. And to be left in peace. It must be horrible to be pestered and persecuted at such a time, when all one wants is to be left in peace. Shall I tell you exactly what I think of this particular manifestation of religion? It has no importance whatsoever, and to struggle against it is to give it an importance it doesn't deserve. But if I were to die far from home – which is my dearest wish – if no one mentioned priests, I should certainly not call for one.'

'You're probably right. "It's of no importance": that's about the long and the short of it. Take this room, for instance: everything is in order, everything classified, labelled, easy to find. Well, if I had been untidy, what difference would it make now? Another example: I've always bought things of the very best quality, on principle. Yet a fifteen-hundred-franc suit or a seven-hundred-franc suit both fray at the cuffs after the same number of months. So that one needs a new suit just as frequently, whichever one buys. Which means that it's really of no importance whether a suit is good or bad, just as it's of no importance whether a man is good or bad.'

M. Dandillot pressed his right wrist against the bridge of his nose, between the eyes, as though to filter the light which he found so tiring in spite of the fact that the shutters were three-quarters closed, and his magnificent hand hung limp alongside his cheek.

'I used to worship the sun,' he said. 'I believed it cured everything. I believed that whatever was wrong with one – pneumonia, an ulcer, a broken leg – one had only to lie in the sun to be cured. Yes, I believed this, from the bottom of my heart: it was pure fetishism. And I taught the same thing to hundreds of youngsters. And now, whenever the sky is the least bit bright it hurts me. I can't bear it any more. If I went out I would stay in the shade. (To think that I may never again see a cloudy sky!) Is there, then, one truth for the living and another for the dying? I was intoxicated by the beauty of the world and its creatures, quite disinterestedly, I may say, for I was never a womanizer. Now every living thing seems to me offensive, and I feel ready to hate them all. I've given up reading the newspapers. What do I care about all that, since I'm leaving it? My wife wants to take me out for a drive in the Bois. Well, I refuse. I don't want to see the beauty of the world any more, since I shall soon be unable to enjoy it. It would hurt me, and I don't want to be hurt.'

'It's strange that your reaction to light should be exactly the opposite to that of the dying Goethe.'

'There you go again with your great men,' said M. Dandillot impatiently. 'What do I care about Goethe! Let him die as he wishes: no one can set me an example any more. Goethe also began to study natural history at the age of seventy-five, and one's supposed to think how admirable. Well, I'm with Montaigne: "What a foolish thing is an abecedarian old man!" '

Costals was a little shocked. Out of conformity he had hypnotized himself into believing that Goethe was one of the great beacons of the human spirit, though in his heart of hearts he considered him grossly overrated.

At that moment Solange came into the room, the lady visitor having departed. And Costals experienced the odd sensation of finding the presence of someone he loved importunate.

As M. Dandillot made no move to send his daughter away, Costals took his leave after a few moments. In the hall, he ran into Mme Dandillot:

'I can't understand what's the matter with my husband. He groans when he gets out of bed. He groans when he puts on his trousers. You'd think he was doing it on purpose. And yet he's a man who has had a great deal of character all his life.'

'You can't understand what's the matter with him? The matter, dear lady, is that he's dying.'

'In the first place, thank heaven, it's not at all certain. And even if he does believe his life is in danger, isn't that just the moment for him to show his mettle? When can he show it, if not in times of stress? But do you know what he said to the doctor yesterday? "Don't hurt me, doctor." "But you won't feel a thing ..." "Yes, yes, I know how you doctors talk. Well, *I don't want to be hurt*, do you hear me! Let others put up with suffering if they like, I won't!" It's rather painful for those who love him to hear him talk like that in front of strangers.'

Costals mumbled something and left. 'So,' he thought, 'he brings me here so that he can unburden himself, and he lies! He'll be dead within a month, and he lies! God, what a bunch!'

Andrée Hacquebaut   to Pierre Costals
Cabourg   *Paris*

30 June 1927

Read this or not, as you please. This letter, which will be my last, is simply to tell you that I KNOW.

Crushed by you, with a temperature of 101 degrees – the fever of grief, nothing else* – on the point of becoming seriously ill or going mad, I had to have an immediate change of air and came to stay with a friend in Cabourg. At the Casino here I met a whole group of women writers and poets, and among them Baroness Fléchier.

'Costals?' she said. 'Not only has he never held a woman in his arms, but never in his life has he even desired one! He admitted it to me himself.'†

Then she talked about Proust. I plunged into Proust, whom I had never read before. What a revelation! The scales dropped from my eyes. It's all blindingly clear. *M. de Charlus is you!* ...

It's all there, everything! You love strength – like him. You go for long walks – like him. You don't wear rings – like him. All the details tally, everything speaks against you. The other day in your studio, you wore a shirt with an open collar. And

---

* Pure invention. She had no fever but, because of her 'emotional upset', a boil on the thigh.

†See p.121.

then there was the time you drew my attention to your big, square-toed English shoes such as nobody wears in Paris. You mentioned your delicate feet! In fact it was an affectation of virility, an alibi.

And the contradictions in your attitude towards me! The same 'inconsistency' we find in M. de Charlus. And your ups and downs. 'The very ups and downs of his relations with me,' as Proust writes of Charlus.

You said to me in the avenue Marceau: 'See how much I trust you. I talk to you as I would to a man.' You bet!

And that 'delicacy of feeling that men so rarely show'. One can deny you all sorts of things, but never delicacy of feeling.

Again, you once said to me that young men were fools. Charlus says it too. 'What impresses us about this man's (Charlus') face is a certain touching delicacy, a certain grace, an unaffected friendliness. . . .' Just as I used to say to everyone about you: 'He's so natural and friendly.' Fool that I was! It's absolutely frightful to be plunged into this underworld. It has changed my whole vision of the world.

And what was it you said about your character Christine in *Fragility*? 'I transformed myself into Christine.' Those half-admissions, which Proust also draws attention to! You reminded me of Flaubert's remark: 'Madame Bovary is me.' But Flaubert was obviously a pansy: he never married, there was only one woman in his life, and above all there's that phrase in *Salammbô* about certain Carthaginian troops whose 'friendships' made them more courageous, so it seems. (At that rate, I'd rather have an army of cowards.)

And your complete lack of jealousy, which you have often spoken to me about and which you describe as 'an almost sublime common sense'. That cannot be called manly. Jealousy is one of the basic characteristics of the male.

Now I understand why you did not find me more desirable. And to think of the tortures I went through, the time I spent staring at myself in the mirror! Now I understand why you did not need me. Of course, you were half woman yourself!

You, Costals, possessed but not possessing! Dominated but not dominating! Seeking in love the same self-abasement that we women seek. The very thought of it sickens me. You have befouled the face of the earth for me, after having filled it with radiance.

Since I knew nothing about this form of debauchery, and the ladies in the Casino knew nothing about it either, judging by the questions they asked one another, I overcame my nausea and consulted a medical dictionary (Labarthe's) which I found in my friend's library. I discovered that members of this infamous sect 'paint their faces'. And I've been racking my brain trying to remember whether that fresh complexion of yours. . . . And the thought that you might be strolling along the boulevards with 'a handkerchief, a flower or some needle-work' in your hand, as Labarthe puts it. . . . And to think that I had my copy of *Fragility* bound in green morocco, now that I know that green is the favourite colour, the symbol by which these creatures recognize each other! Oh no! it's too frightful! It's stifling me, it's killing me. . . .

I have shut the dictionary, and I won't bother with any more documentary evidence. Even if these descriptions are a bit fanciful, they are quite enough for me and I shall stop there. You may well say that women refuse to face reality, that they are always burying their heads in the sand, etc. Well, have it your own way, but for me it's all very simple: there are a certain number of horrible things in the world which I prefer not to know about. My dignity as a woman, and eventually as a wife and mother, forbids it: I should be sullied for ever. Let the world do as it likes – I personally have the right to ignore as much of it as I please.

For five years now you have prevented me from marrying. Because of you my youth has been wasted – in fact my whole life has been wasted, for youth is all that counts in a woman's life. And wasted for whom? For the *wretched creature* you are! Can you imagine the tragedy of a woman who has made one of these people the very incarnation of manhood, and who suddenly, one day, has this revelation? And you haven't even the merit of being original, for there are heaps and heaps of them, and you're nothing but a pathetic snob, a slave of decadentism and putrefaction, a mere hanger-on of the Gides and the Prousts, those imbeciles, rotten to the core with intellectualism, sterility, aestheticism, instead of honestly ful-filling their duty as men, men who are useful to others and to their country.... And not only did I love *that*, but I also loved its work! And since your whole attitude both towards me and towards society is totally insincere, your work must be the same. I can no longer believe a single word you have written. Your work is mere empty rhetoric, a monument of bad literature. If there were a spark of honesty left in you, you would break your pen in pieces. The only thing left for you to do is to creep into your hole in silence, pursued by the jeers of normal men and healthy women.

The love I had for you, I have given to another. You have no right to it, for one does not accept a love of which one knows oneself to be unworthy, one has no right to cultivate the friendship of a pure and chaste young woman when else-where.... My letters were addressed to a semblance of a per-son. I demand that you return them to me: they have fallen into your hands by mistake. And I am ashamed of them. What I loved was the man behind your work, the man of your false creation. It is as if I had given myself in the dark to someone I thought I knew, and at dawn discovered that I had been caressing some nameless creature, some half-man, some hideous hermaphrodite.... Are you aware that this kind of horror could lead one to suicide? Are you aware of that?

But in this tragedy of mine, I have one consolation. The thought of what I have escaped. When I think, when I think that I might have been touched by you! Whereas now I could not bear you to touch my hand, even with gloves on. Yes, to think what I have escaped!

I despise you.

Wednesday

I don't want you to take me for a dupe, but nor do I want you to think me cruel. I want you to read what I wrote to you yesterday, but I don't want it to be your last impression of me.

I am writing to you with infinite sadness. But it is not for myself that I feel sad, today, it is for you. Ah! times have changed indeed! You have pitied me enough, now it is my turn to pity you. You loved me, let us say, like a sister; I feel today that I might come to love you with the compassion and forgiveness of a mother, and that makes me more serene.

Yes, how sad it must be to be a monster! It makes one's heart bleed. I beg you to try and extricate yourself if there is still time. You are unhappy, and no doubt it was because you were unhappy that you took refuge in these refinements of vice. And now you are doubly unhappy; though perhaps you are not entirely guilty. I implore you, in the name of all that is sacred in the world, in the name of our memories (for you did love me, after all; only you could not, for obvious reasons, go all the way, could you?), abandon the path you are on. If ever my letters meant anything to you, if ever they helped you, made you ponder, please consider this one serious-ly: it is a solemn adjuration. Drag yourself up from this Abyss. Get back to the world of real humanity. Become a *man* again!

If only for the sake of your talent as a writer. To think that *you have never held a woman in your arms!* How can you not feel that you are incomplete, that your whole outlook on the world is falsified thereby, and your art so much the poorer?

When one is ill, one looks after oneself. But one must have the will to be cured. You must acquire that will.

This very morning, I had a talk with one of the doctors here. He told me there were various kinds of treatment, both physical and moral, for gentlemen of the Charlus type. I enclose herewith the names of some Parisian psychiatrists who have apparently effected such cures. Put yourself in the hands of one of them. But first and foremost say to yourself, and repeat it, sometimes even *aloud*, after taking *a slow, deep breath*: 'I want to become a man.'

These recent events, though they have shattered me, have brought me back to religion. God at least does not let one down. You know that I had more or less given up practising. But for the past five days, I have started going to church again daily. I no longer say, as in the past: 'O God, make me happy.' Now I pray for you. And I shall continue to pray for you until you are *saved*.

Farewell. I forgive you. Believe in my immense pity.

A.H.

Pierre Costals   to Armand Pailhès
Paris   *Toulouse*

My dear Pailhès,

Epigraph to this letter; the words of the Scripture: 'A woman's love is more to be feared than a man's hatred.'

Object of this letter: A man's rage finds vent in violence. A woman's rage finds vent in stupidity. It is this second point we shall now demonstrate.

I am sending you, duly 'registered',* a document which seems to me quite remarkable. You can return it to me when I have the pleasure of seeing you in Toulouse ten days from now.

A woman rejected because she is not attractive enough welcomes with transports of delight an absurd allegation by an old literary crone about the man who has 'insulted' her. The allegation justifies her in her own eyes by convincing her that it was not because of her looks that she was rebuffed, and at the same time avenges her by showing her 'insulter' in an 'infamous' light. In other words, she is shown the portrait of a person unknown, who in no wise resembles the insulter, except, shall we say, that they both have two eyes, one nose, etc., perhaps even the same colour of hair. Blinded by her passion, she recognizes the portrait as that of her insulter; if she were before a judge, she would take an oath on it. But it is not enough for her to execrate him; she has been pitied, so she must pity in her turn: her scorn is transmuted into pity. And finally, since in spite of all this she still loves, and since reality, by deceiving her hopes, has thrown her back into darkness, she begins to pray for her insulter, and is thus enabled to crown her triumph by congratulating herself on her magnanimity, and perhaps to pursue her relations with the insulter, without damaging her self-respect, by means of bi-weekly letters twelve pages long in which she will continue to talk to him about himself under cover of the supreme Being.

---

*A pun in the original: *recommander* = 'to register' (a letter) and to recommend' (*Translator's note*).

For, on the labels of cages in zoos, the males are indicated by an arrow, which means that they pierce the hearts of women, and the females are indicated by a cross, which means that they take refuge in the Crucifix.

The case of Andrée is all the more extraordinary for the fact that Andrée is a very intelligent woman – really some-body.

You know my ideas about the automatism of female re-actions. All the reactions you will find here have long been classified and described. The reaction which causes a rejected woman to accuse her 'insulter' of being a M. de Charlus is No 174. The reaction whereby an unhappy woman tries to con-vince the man she loves that he is unhappy too is No 227a. The reaction whereby a desperate woman turns to Christianity is No 89. The reaction whereby a desperate woman pretends she is ill in a final attempt to arouse in her lover that 'pity for women' which they long for and disapprove of at the same time is No 214. This last, it must be admitted, is no more than adumbrated in the case of Andrée. And it must also be admitted that one of the most typical reactions, No 175, whereby a rejected woman accuses her 'insulter' of sexual impotence, has not yet manifested itself here. In spite of this lacuna, there is in Andrée's graph something so classical and so pure, in a word, so perfect – in its vulgarity – that the mind derives from it an equally perfect satisfaction, a satisfaction as delicious as it is possible for any sensation to be : the sort of satisfaction astronomers must feel when they contemplate the acrobatics of the stars. I can also see myself as the chemist who, having put two solutions in a test-tube, watches the vicissitudes of the combination; knows what the final result will be, though the layman does not, and knows that it will be very unexpected for the layman; and at last sees these elements assume precisely the form, the colour and the density which nature intended. But the most splendid thing of all is that the curve of Andrée's progress, classical though it is, is at the same time absurd. There is in it, at one and the same time, something both baffling and foreseeable. *And in this it is the quintessence of nature itself.* Andrée is not afraid to write that the fact of having recognized me in M. de Charlus has 'transformed her vision of the universe.' I daresay my own vision of the universe, if I had one, would be transformed for less. . . . To remain in the same key, and since nothing less than the universe is in question, I may say that the Cabourg letter inclines me to believe that a celestial economy *really* exists, – which up to now, *pace* the priests and *pace* Voltaire, I had been rather inclined to doubt.

All this might also provoke a few reflections on the lack of psychological understanding in women, which I have always found rather striking. Most of them are quite out of touch with reality. If one cared to go back over the whole of Andrée's behaviour one would see that time after time she makes the grossest blunders, with a regularity that is as startling as it is baffling. She believes she's pretty, she believes I love her, she believes I have no children, she believes I'm M. de Charlus, she believes I'm unhappy, etc. You'd think it was something to do with a bet. And I repeat, Andrée is a woman of almost exceptional intelligence. You will say, perhaps : 'It isn't women who lack perception, it's women in love.' But since they're always in love!

Mistaken about what men are and what they think, women are also mistaken about the way to go about winning them. A woman maddens you by coming into your room while you are working, or by giving you little presents, or badgering you too often, or bringing along her friends, who are not yours. You are on good enough terms with her to speak out frankly. Well, she stops for a while, and then starts again. A woman delights you by her lack of affectation. You tell her so again and again and you castigate all affected women. Well, sooner or later she herself begins to get coquettish and indulge in little wiles. All women without exception spoil their chances with you by their inexhaustible demands for money, and the time comes when the pleasure you derived from them has been poisoned at the source; and so you break with them. Demanding nothing, they would have had everything, one would have been so touched. But no, they can't help it : you might almost think there was something that forced them to be so clumsy.

And just as women deceive themselves about their men, they deceive themselves about their children (girls or boys, though much more so with boys, of course). That 'maternal instinct' we hear so much about is nothing but a fraud. No mother ever knows what goes on in the mind of her child, nor what ought to be done for it. I could write a book on the subject, composed entirely of 'true stories', a few of which were provided by my own mother, for there are exceptions to everything. Any man who dares to look life in the face, whether he be a moralist, a doctor, a teacher (religious or lay), or a psychiatrist, will tell you so. But they will only tell you privately. They will never say so in front of a woman, or in public. They would never print it either, being far too frightened of public opinion which is created by women. Even the great Tolstoy himself said to Gorki: 'When my body is halfway into the grave, I shall say what I really think about women, and quickly slam down the tombstone over my head!' To my knowledge, Herbert Spencer alone had the courage to write: 'A mother's intervention is often more harmful than her complete abstention would have been.'

And grown-up sons, too, are well aware of their mothers' delusions about them, their profound lack of understanding. But they too will never say so; they will hardly admit it to themselves. They are sorry for their mothers: always this pity for women.

As for me, I have a son, and he is what I love most in the whole world. That is why I was determined to *protect him from motherhood*. I arranged that his mother should have absolutely no rights over him. And I put him in charge of a woman *who is not his mother*; he stands a better chance that way. As you know, the 'maternal instinct' of cats does not always prevent them from devouring their young. There's a terrifying symbol there for you: I may well have preserved my son from being eaten up.

Such, dear friend, are my reactions to Andrée's little effort, on the purely general plane. On the personal plane, I find it almost unbearably funny. I almost feel inspired to do a burlesque commentary on the whole thing. For instance: Andrée says that in loving me she took me for someone else. But that's quite commonplace: when you kiss a cat, you think you've kissed a cat; well, if you look closer, you find you've kissed a flea. And so on. . . . This kind of thing doesn't get one very far, but I feel madly inclined to go on: the absurdity of it all is intoxicating.

I never had much faith in Andrée's friendship for me, because I knew she was in love with me. I pretended to believe in her friendship, in the same way that, as a writer, I pretend to believe in the demonstrations of friendship of some of my confrères, even though I know they hate me like poison. And now, how am I to behave towards her? I might have been able to put up with her insults: there is something in me that rather enjoys being insulted,* like that famous shark Alain Gerbault writes about, which, while being eaten up by all sorts of other fishes, 'seemed not in the least to resent being torn to pieces'. What I cannot stand is her stupidity. I love and venerate, in a truly religious spirit, stupidity in pretty women, so long as it is sweet and passive. But the braying stupidity of an ugly woman, no thanks. (Incidentally, have you noticed how her stupidity, born of her anger, has affected her style – 'decadentism', a capital A for 'abyss', etc. – she who nearly always wrote so naturally and powerfully? And the intoxication with which she writes the word 'pansy'! It's obvious that she learnt it only yesterday, and wants to show how up-to-date she is. Just as Brunet, at the age of four, when one taught him a new word that caught his fancy, would go round bawling it out for a whole afternoon.) Now it's my turn to write Andrée a similar letter, fifteen pages long, in which I shall tell her exactly what I've thought of her from the beginning.

But it isn't only stupidity. If I were eighteen and Andrée the first woman I'd come across, I might have said to myself: 'This is what love must be like. It's bound automatically to turn into something squalid. It's the nature of things.' But I can't think that any longer: I've seen so many women and girls who, disappointed, abandoned, even betrayed, have managed to retain their dignity (not to mention their critical faculties) and have gone on wishing their tormentors well.

---

*'My self-esteem has always increased in direct proportion to the damage I was doing to my reputation.' – Saint-Simon

So, no forgiveness. And besides, I've had enough of forgiving all the time. A fifteen-page letter.

This episode prompts three further observations.

The first is that I have never been insulted by a pretty woman; always by ugly ones. When some unknown woman writes me an insulting letter, I know she is ugly.

The second is that the sublime Andrée seems cut out to be a literary critic, by which I mean a Parisian literary critic, vintage 1927. The way in which, in identifying me with Charlus, she 'proves' that an object which is black, as black as ink, is white, as white as chalk, shows how well she is qualified for such a role. She would put her pen to delightful articles in which she would demonstrate how some purely lyrical novel was in fact a work of realism, or how some obviously euphoric writer was really a manic-depressive; she would show how Morand is a Baudelairean, Giraudoux a proletarian writer, etc. And she would soon be widely esteemed, since the important thing for a critic (I mean a critic in Paris in 1927) is not to write the truth but to write something that has not been written before; not to possess a sound judgement, but simply to concoct pieces which will be 'taken up' in other journals.

And thirdly. You know how fond I am of secrecy, and of covering up my tracks. The Arabs, who are experts in this form of sport, maintain that the lion obliterates his with his tail; and it is said that one of their sultans had his horse shod back to front. 'Hide your life as the cat hides its excrement,' says the Egyptian proverb. Let us be clear about this: the secrecy I like is not the kind of secrecy practised by the majority of people, but the kind that deepens the more one confesses and shows off. Next to the 'aristocratic' pleasure of displeasing, of which, God knows, I have amply availed myself, there is the pleasure of being taken for something one is not, provided that it is a little to one's discredit. I do not know whether this pleasure can be called aristocratic, but it titillates me. Well, the maenad of Saint-Léonard has given me an idea: I would not swear that some day or other I might not include a Charlus in my collection of masks. Nothing could be simpler: I would merely have to start abusing women from the *intellectual* point of view, and the public is so obtuse – and moreover so ignorant of my carefully concealed liaisons – that it will inevitably deduce that I despise them from the *carnal* point of view. And then ... then my horizons broaden. Can you understand how? Can't you see how much less distrust I shall arouse in parents, how much easier my parthenomachy will become, if I am classified as 'a gentleman who does not care for women'? Indeed, Andrée may well have injected a new dose of happiness into my life. This woman I rejected may well be worth twenty to me. God grant that she may hear of it some day!

I conclude, my dear Pailhès, by sending you my warmest greetings, and a quotation from Juvenal: 'A woman's resentment is implacable when humiliation spurs on her hatred.'

C.

All the same!

For fifteen years, to have been transfused with the power of women as an organ is with air, and to have reverberated with it; one's travels, one's comings and goings, one's disappearances, one's long 'literary silences', everything that appeared inexplicable in one's life, all that to have had no other cause but the erratic race of women; to have spewed forth the world (how often!) in everything that was not love; to have sacrificed everything but one's art to one's private life, and that private life to have been exclusively devoted to love; to have suffered, more often than not, only from the suffering one was forced to inflict on women, or rather on young girls, for every adventure with a young girl that does not end in marriage is doomed to end in suffering and unhappiness; to have had one's whole life constricted, weakened, slowed down by a constant preoccupation with not hurting them; to be unable to read the words 'little girl' without feeling in one's throat the first spasms of tears; to be unable to hear a girl admit to having failed her *bachot* without longing to worship her; to be unable to see a spelling mistake in a letter from an unknown girl without kissing it – and then to be taken for a M. de Charlus by an intelligent, cultured, perceptive woman who has the whole of one's work at her finger-tips. Mind you, it is not the Charlus thing that frightens me. 'What we call unnatural is merely unusual' (Montaigne). The 'unnatural' is nature itself, as a torpedo-boat destroyer is no more and no less than a torpedo-boat. The silly woman talks of my 'Abyss'; but our abysses are elsewhere. No, what frightens me is the darkness that divides one soul from another. In spite of all appearances, she has never understood me in the least, since she could be so utterly mistaken about me. And I haven't understood her in the least, since never, never, would I have believed her capable of being so mistaken. Baudelaire was right: there's nothing that is not based on misunderstanding. I knew it, but how one forgets, or rather how the mind forgets! Forgetting is so essential to it that the mind might well say: I forget, therefore I am.

Pierre Costals
Paris

to Andrée Hacquebaut
Saint-Léonard
(Please forward)
3 July, 1927

Well, dear Mademoiselle, that was quite a letter you sent me! But what of it! My gratitude to you still has the upper hand: a man who professes to study the human heart cannot but rejoice at not having missed that. For five years you have given me your friendship. You are giving to me still by withdrawing it.

I think we have nothing more to say to each other for the time being. But I know you: doubtless you will come back to me one day. And I know myself too: doubtless I shall welcome you as if nothing had happened. However, let us not rush things. You must need a breather.

Please rest assured of my warmest regard. I follow your various moods with interest.

C.

P.S. I am sending you by the same post the book on Cosima Wagner which you told me you wanted to read in one of your letters last winter and which I've just discovered by chance on a second-hand bookstall.

Madame Blancmesnil   to M. Pierre Costals
Avranches (Manche)   *Paris*

2 July 1927

My name will mean nothing to you, but the name Thérèse Pantevin possibly may.

Do you remember these words: 'Should I ignore those cries? I haven't the heart to.... Perhaps there are forces in you that might be consecrated....' And then: 'On Saturday next at 6 p.m. I shall have pity on you.' Then a month's silence, which you probably did not even notice: what did Thérèse Pantevin matter to you? For you this correspondence was merely a game. But what you must know is the result of your little game, and the reason for this silence: three weeks ago my unfortunate cousin was taken into the lunatic asylum at Avranches. Will she ever come out again?

Thérèse Pantevin, the daughter of well-to-do farmers, full of bestial pride ever since her childhood, thought herself a genius because of her teaching certificate. I too have my teaching certificate. Do not therefore imagine I am envious. Envious of a poor madwoman! Lazy, scornful of manual work, bigoted, full of absurd intellectual pretensions – how she despised us! Shutting herself up with her repressions in her farm at La Paluelle; and then discovering the works of Costals. Costals, the one and only man capable of understanding her! She breaks with her friends, with her dearest pupils, everything, in order to read you and meditate on your work for days on end in her room, poring over all the photographs of you which she had cut out of the newspapers, and which were found on her. ...Finally she writes to you....

And you who, even though you are young and know nothing about life, in spite of all your pretensions (I have only read one of your books, but that was enough to make me detest you), you, who cannot after all have been so blind as not to guess my cousin's mental state from her letters, instead of throwing these letters into the waste-paper basket, you answer them, you add fuel to the fire. Vanity or sadism – what other motive could have prompted you? You were safe, you knew perfectly well that the little peasant-girl with her hair pulled back from her temples (she had sent you a photograph) would never come up from the depths of the country to pester you in your marble halls and that in any case, even if she had the impertinence to do so, you would have had her thrown out by your flunkeys.

In April, she leaves home to catch a train to Paris to see you. Her mother stops her in time and locks her up. In May she escapes again: we have to have her arrested at Vire by the gendarmerie. She flung herself on her knees in front of them and said: 'Let me see him for just five minutes and then you can arrest me!' They were obliged to keep her in prison for the night until we came to fetch her. Then, in June, she has a fit of hysteria.... That, Monsieur Costals, is what you have done.

And then there is the poor, wretched mother who has had to sell her farm to pay for her daughter's keep and who, at the age of sixty and more, has undertaken to read all the books of Pierre Costals in order to find out what sort of man is responsible for the ruin of her daughter and herself.

And now, Mr Great Writer (!), now that I have forced you into an awareness of your responsibility in all this, what do you propose to do about it? In case there is a shred of humanity left in you, which I doubt, I should like to point out that your victim's boarding fees at the asylum are 15,000 francs a year. If you should feel it your duty to contribute towards them, you could deal directly with me. I would hand over whatever you sent me to Mme Pantevin, who is hardly capable of dealing with such matters herself. If, on the other hand, you choose not to reply, we have your letters to Thérèse Pantevin and we shall know what steps to take.

Antoinette Blancmesnil

Written by Costals on a blank page of this letter:

'For you this correspondence was merely a game.' Played with Andrée, yes, sometimes. With Th. Pantevin, never. The opposite of a game. Put her on her guard against confusing the sacred and the profane. Snubbed her so that she would take against me. Urged her, not to enter a convent, which would have been presumptuous of me, but to go and see a priest who might help her to discover herself. Tried to give her the impression that she was a real person (which indeed she was). Simply and solely pity. Pity all along the line, without an atom of malevolence. Pity, sympathy, understanding and respect.

Imprudence? Agreed. But *every contact with another human being is imprudence.*

The imprudence of generosity – that's more like it. Any action undertaken out of pure generosity always turns back upon its author as automatically as a boomerang returns to the man who threw it. *Without exception.* Anyone subject to generous impulses can, as a matter of course, and in advance, be classified as a victim.

This being so, the tragedy is not that the Pantevin affair should have earned me such a letter: that was but the logical consequence of the premises. The drama, the tragedy, is that Thérèse Pantevin is very probably not mad at all. She has been put away at twenty-five because she was in touch with the higher regions of the spirit: being different, she was envied, that is to say hated. Thérèse Pantevin has been put away by the people she lived among for having been superior to them.

And what do I care even if she was mad, seeing she was suffering!

If I believed in God, I would pray for her.

Andrée Hacquebaut   to Pierre Costals
Saint-Léonard   *Paris*

8 July 1927

Dear Costals,

I no longer know where I am with you, and I no longer know *what you are*, and I am writing to tell you so, although I am well aware how much I must lower myself in your eyes with these eternal 'last letters'. As if it wasn't enough to be crushed by you in Paris, I had to go through it again with

that revelation in Cabourg. And now, this : in my indignation
I wrote to several acquaintances in Paris, people in the know.
I asked them why they had never warned me about you, and
they wrote back calling Baroness Fléchier a lunatic and telling
me that 'nothing could be more grotesque than to believe such
nonsense'. So now I no longer know what to think. There are
still moments when I believe that the woman was telling the
truth, but they may simply be the moments when my suffering
is too great. At other times I doubt. I suppose this uncertainty
must be pleasing to one who once wrote to me that he liked
nothing better than 'the fringe of uncertainty where one thing
merges into another.'

However, something new has happened to sustain me. I am
no longer the thirty-year-old spinster whom no man had ever
taken in his arms, to whom no man had ever said : 'My little
one.' Now I too have my joys*, which are just as good as
yours, whatever they may be (oh! this frenzy to know what
sort of pleasures you enjoy . . .). Now I have other friends
besides you, and *they* don't invite me to second-rate restaurants.
So you needn't despise me unduly any more. Nevertheless you
must know that even if I get married, that night of love I
asked from you will always remain a hope for me. My life will
never stir again until you yourself make a move. If you are not
what I thought you were in Cabourg, if you should realize
one day that I mean something to you, that you want me in
your life, body and soul, that I am as irreplaceable to you as
you are to me, if I should ever seem worth the perturbations
and anxieties that love inevitably entails for the man who
loves a woman and considers her worth it all, then send for
me and I shall be yours, whatever man I may belong to at the
time and whatever the ties that bind me to him.

Good-bye. I have loved you very very much, and I love you
still. As for you, nothing can alter the fact that you allowed
yourself to be loved. I feel that if I heard you being attacked
as I did the other night in the Casino at Cabourg, I could not
and would not endure it at any cost. However cruelly you

---

*Pure invention. This 'man' who was supposed to be part of
Andrée's life did not exist (*Author's note*).

have wounded me, there is something between us which can never be lost or destroyed. And then, perhaps my name will live on in the character you will draw from me in that novel you promised me.*

A. H.

But to think that some day, perhaps, you will marry! If you were to marry a rich woman, I could at least console myself with the thought that she was giving you something I could never have given you. But if you should marry a woman no richer than I am! It's enough to drive one mad!

This letter remained unanswered.

'There is something divine in serious illnesses.' *Saint-Cyran.*

Costals received a note from M. Dandillot saying that he would like to see him two days later, at four: 'We shall be alone.' In the same way the daughter had said: 'Do come, we shall be alone.' What it is to belong to a family! Whereas many dying people write in a firmer, better-formed hand than usual, because they make it a point of honour to do so (as a drunk man will try to indulge in the refinements of calligraphy), M. Dandillot's handwriting was falling apart, and meandered all over the place: a corpse of a hand, preceding the other corpse. His letter was written in pencil.

M. Dandillot was now confined to his room. As Costals entered, a male nurse came out – a man with the sort of face one would not care to meet in a dark wood at night. The first thing M. Dandillot said was: 'Isn't there a bit of a sick-room smell in here? I get them to burn aromatic paper, but I don't know whether.... The only real dignity, you see, is health. And God knows I used to be a healthy man. But now!'

His voice had become a little shrill, and weak, like the voice

---

*Pure invention. Costals never promised her anything of the kind (*Author's note*).

of a man who hardly speaks any more, who no longer has the strength, and who has anyway lost interest in the sounds he emits. His eyes seemed to be veiled by leukoma. He was un-shaven, and proceeded to explain why:

'I've done enough for people. Why should I shave for them? Why should I be nice to them? I see now that one should never try to do good to people one doesn't love. Nothing requires more naturalness and spontaneity than doing good. There too I went wrong by forcing myself. And besides, the good we do is poisoned by the fact that we do it the wrong way.'

'One should never try to do good to people one doesn't love,' Costals repeated to himself, thinking of Andrée.

Costals had realized from their first meeting that M. Dandil-lot was only interested in himself, and he liked him for it. But now that death was drawing near, he saw him shrink even further into himself. He had always thought it natural for old men to be selfish. How the devil could they love the world after having endured it for a life-time?

'My oldest friend has just left,' M. Dandillot said, uncon-sciously picking up Costals' train of thought. 'We've been cronies for fifty years. Do you know what we talked about? For a quarter of an hour he described his plans for a trip to Egypt, India and Ceylon, going into ecstasies about all the won-derful things he'd see. He spent the next quarter of an hour asking me for letters of introduction for his son. And for the last five minutes – the last five minutes of our friendship, since I shall be dead by the time he returns from his trip – he scolded me very severely for living in a room with the shutters closed. That's what a man says to the friend of half a century who is on the point of death.'

'It's simply lack of imagination.'

In a dense cone of sound, the piercing cries of the swallows came surging in from the trees in the avenue.

'And the veronal?'

'Always ready.'

'You'll never take it. We once had an old cat at home, who developed an incurable sore by scratching himself. So we had him put to sleep. Then my mother felt remorseful. "Even with his sore he might still have enjoyed a few happy hours." When you're on the point of swallowing your veronal, you'll say to yourself : "Perhaps I might still enjoy a few happy hours".'

'I haven't taken the poison yet because the pain isn't bad enough. What I feel most of all is tired. Tired! And do you know what makes me so tired? It's having done too much good all my life, having obliged too many people. I was destroying my correspondence the other day. And do you know, I sometimes went through ten or fifteen letters in succession and every one of them was a request for some favour or other or to thank me for a favour I had done. And if you allow that only one person in two ever thanks you for something you've done, it will give you some idea of the number of people I've obliged – and for what, ye gods? Remember this, Monsieur Costals : the people we help *never* deserve it.'

'I'm lucky enough not to be obliging, so I'm not a good judge. But how a man of your calibre...? Only fools are hurt by ingratitude. Isn't generosity just another way of saying "Return to sender"?'

'What makes me tired is not the ingratitude with which my generosity has been repaid, it's the generosity itself. So futile! Such a waste of time! Ah! Be selfish, Monsieur Costals.'

'But I *am*.'

'Well then, the world is yours.'

Then M. Dandillot went on to say that he was so tired that he would be glad to die. He expounded, as if it were his own, Mechnikov's theory that a man dies only because he wants to. He proclaimed : 'I hate people who are afraid of death, like the Pascals, etc. . . . ' Costals was glad to find him in this frame of mind, since it relieved him of the necessity to put on a solemn face.

'That said, I wonder why I've lived at all,' M. Dandillot concluded with a gloomy stare.

'You've lived because you could not do otherwise,' said Costals impatiently. 'Nearly all men's lives are corrupted by the need to justify their existence. Women are less subject to this infirmity.'

'If I had been happy, I shouldn't feel the need to justify my existence : it would justify itself. But I have not been happy,

302

and I've discovered that that is why I'm dying at sixty-one, instead of seventy or seventy-five as I should logically have done with the principles on which my life has been based. Can you realize what it means to have lived for forty years without ever meeting an intelligent person? And I'm so tired of people who aren't intelligent. . . .'

'It takes a lot of searching to find an intelligent person. . . .'

'And now I meet you, just as I'm about to die!'

'It's better that way. We should never have got on together.'

'Why not?' M. Dandillot asked, shyly.

'Because I should have grown tired of you.'

'How can you say such a thing to me?' M. Dandillot said, flabbergasted.

'Because I know you won't understand.'

'Yes, I'm stupid, aren't I? And boring too.' (A terrifying expression of bitterness spread over his face.) 'Boring . . . people have made it plain to me often enough. I should have loved to know whether my wife really thought me an imbecile, or whether she merely pretended to, just to be disagreeable. It's true that I actually do become an imbecile when I'm with her.'

'Haven't you become more intelligent since you've been ill?'

'Yes, I think more.'

'If you'll forgive me, I don't believe you really think. Not real thinking. I myself don't really think. I've often tried to see things clearly, but the time goes by and I still don't understand a thing.'

'You consider that I think like an amateur, isn't that it? My family have always looked on me as an amateur. If I'd had a job of some kind, it would have been different. For ten or twelve years now, they've made a habit of ignoring what I say. It would be impossible to climb back up that kind of slippery slope even if there were still time. Even if the Minister came in person to decorate me in this armchair, they *wouldn't understand*. Did I show you the letter I wrote to the Minister refusing the Legion of Honour?' (With a scornful emphasis on 'Legion of Honour'.)

'Yes, you did.'

'Forgive me, my memory goes at times,' he said with an absent stare. 'Did I tell you the story about the man who was prepared to sacrifice ten years of his life for the sake of the Grand Cross of the Legion of Honour?'

Costals shook his head.

'A friend of mine has a brother aged seventy-two. This brother is unhappy because he considers that, according to the promotion schedule, he should have had the Grand Cross a couple of years ago. My friend said to him jokingly one day: "I believe you'd rather die in a year but be promoted at once than live another ten years without it." "Of course I would," the brother answered, without a smile. Isn't life wonderful?'

'It is. I couldn't have done better if I'd created the world myself.'

M. Dandillot smiled, under the impression that Costals was being blasphemous. He did not realize that Costals was in fact very fond of Catholicism. Then he frowned in an effort to re-focus his eyes, which had grown vacant again, and which now wandered from one object to another until they finally came to rest on a drawer of his filing-cabinet.

'Would you be kind enough to get that drawer out? It con-tains all the correspondence I had with my mother when I was a young man. I should like to give it to you. We'll make a parcel of it. If *someone* comes in and asks you what it is, you can say that it's press-cuttings about physical culture.'

'Someone!' Costals was still rather surprised at the way M. Dandillot 'annulled' his daughter, as it were, passed her over in silence, or let it be understood that she was one of the people he despised. And just as he had been irritated by Solange's irruption into the room the other day while he was talking to her father, he was now forced to the conclusion that any reference to her would have lowered the tone of their con-versation. She seemed so unimportant compared to the kind of preoccupation with which he and M. Dandillot were absorbed; even more, she seemed unimportant compared to M. Dandillot himself.

'This is the second time we've met, and yet you want to give me your mother's letters!'

'Who else can one trust if one doesn't trust strangers?'

'Give them to me some other day.'

'There may not be another day.'

'Of course there will!'

'So you really think I may live a bit longer?' said M. Dandillot, his face brightening, although not so long before he had professed himself happy to die.

M. Dandillot then asked for paper and string and began to parcel up the letters. They kept slipping from his fingers; he could scarcely move without dropping something or other.

'Everything falls ... everything falls.... Things run away from me. They can sense the corpse.'

And as Costals drew nearer to him to help him with the parcel, he said:

'I should be glad if you would tell me frankly whether my breath smells. I've changed so much since I've been ill. I looked quite a different man six months ago, you know. People thought I was only fifty-three or fifty-four.'

Among the letters, Costals noticed some press-cuttings. They were reports of social functions dating back to 1890, and M. Dandillot's name had been underlined in red pencil. He had repudiated his worldly phase to the extent of ostentatiously selling his evening clothes, and yet his vanity was such that he had kept these pathetic accounts of provincial parties for forty years, simply because his name was printed there. Ah, nature had indeed erred in refusing M. Dandillot the gift of expression. He was born to be a man of letters.

'What is your motive for giving me these letters? Am I to destroy them? Am I to keep them without reading them – in which case, what's the point? Am I to read them, and if so, on what grounds?'

'I'm giving them to the novelist. Read them, and you may find things that are of use to you in your novels.'

'Well, well! what a bunch!' thought Costals once again, rather flabbergasted in spite of himself. 'I knew of course that there were female readers one had never met in one's life who sent one whole notebooks in which they described their conjugal life in the most intimate detail "in case it could be of some use". But a man! And what would the late Mme Dandillot have had to say about it all? Would she have been pleased to know that her letters to her son would eventually be handed over to a stranger – for after all, I am a stranger to him – to be

"made use of"? Humanity? A swarm of thoughtless idiots.'
M. Dandillot's hand went up to his forehead.

'Those swallows,' he said, 'what a din they make! Swallows,
sunlight, everything that's good exhausts me. Just now there
was a workman singing on the landing: you may have noticed
that the staircase is being painted. You can't imagine how true
his voice was, and I thought to myself. "He's in overalls, he
doesn't wash, he's coarse and vulgar, and yet his voice is so
pure, so tuneful. . . . A voice from another world",'

'And that voice tired you too?'

'No.'

'I had the impression from the way you began that you were
about to tell me that the workman's singing tired you like
everything else. . . . '

'I'm sorry: I can't remember how I began. These gaps in
my memory. . . . '

He began to fiddle with the medicine bottles on the table
beside his armchair.

'In fact you don't know whether the workman's song pained
you or pleased you, any more than you know whether you
really welcome death, as you said earlier on, or whether it
horrifies you, as you have also given me to understand. You find it
both horrifying and acceptable, simultaneously. Just as the workman's song simultaneously exhausted you and did you good.'

'I don't know,' said M. Dandillot, like a schoolboy who has
been asked which way the Gulf Stream flows. Before saying
this he had clenched his fists (the nails must have dug into his
palms) as though he were making an effort to pull himself
together.

'I was wondering why I liked you,' said Costals with a sidelong glance at a pattern on the carpet. 'Now I know. It's
because you are like me. And you gave me your mother's
letters, because you know that I'm like you: I've only this
moment realized it. . . . O God! give him eternal life!' he added
in a passionate murmur, his eyes on the carpet. M. Dandillot
gave a start:

'What did you say? So you believe, then! . . .'

'Me, *believe*?' hissed Costals with withering scorn. 'The
words just came to my lips. It doesn't mean a thing.'

306

'The last time, you fortified me in my unbelief. And now you throw everything into doubt again. And at this late stage – when I am so weak! Men, like nations, never stop declining from the moment they start hearing about God. I can't help it if the moral dregs of mankind cannot do without religion. But you, if you have a religion, at least you should be ashamed of it and keep it dark.'

'You are about to die. Could you not concern yourself with something more important than God? You told me just now that you used to be a healthy man. A healthy man doesn't bother about God.'

'But it was you who.... You pretend to be an atheist and you think about God all the time.'

'What you say is simply ludicrous. I might have expected some such cheap psychological commonplace from you.'

'How you enjoy insulting me!' said M. Dandillot in a milder voice and with even a friendly gleam in his eyes.

'Yes, I like being rude to you. It's because you often say things which exasperate me. Here you are, on the verge of death, trying to brush up your conception of life, like a schoolboy mugging up his syllabus three days before the exams. But don't worry: even if I enjoy insulting you, it doesn't in the least affect my feeling for you.'

'I'm not worried. You don't worry me at all. Does that surprise you? But why do you despise me?'

'I have a right to, if I despise myself, as I in fact do. Just as I have a right to kill if I don't mind being killed myself.'

'You mustn't despise human nature so. You know it has some admirable virtues.'

'I despise it in its virtues too.'

'Why are you smiling?'

'Because I can see myself in the mirror,' replied Costals, who had just caught his own reflection in the mirror and found it amusing.

'My exams! That's exactly it,' said M. Dandillot, smiling a little in his turn. 'Will I pass or fail my entrance to paradise? Whichever way it goes, eternity is now opening out in front of me. You, I imagine, even if you believed, would distrust an eternity that hadn't been tailor-made for you....'

He was still fingering the bottles and tubes of pills on his table. One of the bottles fell.

'What I distrust above all is eternity as such. If God existed, he would by definition be intelligent, and in that case he would never have created anything permanent.'

'There's a brand-new proof of his non-existence.'

'I always thought "proofs" of God's existence were the last word in human stupidity, but I see that those of his non-existence can go even further.'

'No matter, I like your proof.'

'And I prefer dry port,' said Costals, hoping that M. Dandillot would offer him a glass. Perspiration was soaking through his shirt and moistening his face as though he had just emerged from a river. Life was oozing from his body, shamelessly, in this liquid form.

'Is it true, Monsieur Costals, is it really true that it was only a figure of speech?'

'I swear it. It would take too long to explain....'

It was on the tip of his tongue to say: 'In three weeks' time you'll be a dead man. Why should I bother to explain anything to you? My passions alone interest me.' He did not say it, but mentally turned away from him as the Greek gods turned away from corpses. And at the same time he had a horrible sensation of loving what was doomed in this man.

'Tell me you believe in nothing,' said M. Dandillot, convulsively seizing him by the hand.

'I believe in nothing. And it's because I believe in nothing that I'm happy.'

'The happiness of the man without God! Thank you,' said M. Dandillot, looking him in the eyes with an unbearable expression of gratitude. 'Oh! those swallows! Why swallows in July? It's in September that they congregate before migrating. But everything's at sixes and sevens, isn't it? You do agree with me, don't you?' he insisted. 'There are no laws governing the world. I find the thought so comforting.'

He was silent. But soon his face, which had relaxed, began to express discomfort. In a few seconds, he was deathly pale, and sweat broke out all over his forehead.

'Are you going to die?' Costals asked softly.

'No, but please ring the bell, quickly! I must go to the lavatory, at once. Yes, I'm subject to these ... Everything's going slack inside me ... Please go away. I'm so sorry. And don't forget the letters. ...'

Costals rang the bell, then went to the door and called the nurse, and as soon as he arrived, slipped away quietly. 'How much longer will he last?' he thought, feeling as exhausted as the dying man. 'When will I be able to stop suffering on his account, and to tell myself that it *really* is too late?' In the avenue, he sank on to a bench, and fanned himself with his hat. Then he lit a cigarette. 'He never even offered me a cigarette, on the pretext that he was dying.' Above him, the swallows still clamoured shrilly.

He opened one of the bundles of letters. He read the first ten, skimmed through the next twenty (there were well over a hundred). They were a cross-section of what is supposed to be the most sacred thing in the world: the trusting, tender relationship between a mother and her son. A cross-section of human love, in its purest and least questionable form. And yet the whole thing was triteness itself, not to say inanity; it was nothing, nothing, nothing. There was a drain-hole nearby. Costals tied up the letters and threw down the drain the love between Mme Dandillot and her son.

A week later, on the 15th of July, by means of a telegram from Solange delivered *poste restante*, Toulouse, Costals learnt of the death of M. Dandillot.

A natural death? Or had he taken the veronal? Presumably a natural death. In any case the question was totally irrelevant. He was dead: that was all there was to it.

For a long time he wandered aimlessly through the streets, holding the telegram in his hand. He felt limp all over; anyone could have jostled him without fear of reprisal. Soon his eyes were wet with tears. 'I bet there isn't a passer-by who doesn't think it's because a woman has let me down.'

He continued his conversation with M. Dandillot: 'Here I am weeping over you who, egotist that you were, probably never shed a tear over anyone. And yet you tried to give me a taste for the future, a future that you knew you would never see.'

309

In the restaurant, he was unable to eat. He sat there gloomily, unable to hide his grief: 'People must think I've got money troubles.' But he was thankful to be in Toulouse on the day of the funeral. Nothing on earth would have induced him to get mixed up with that sort of mummery.

Back at his hotel, he wanted to write to Solange and her mother. But he found himself writing 'Mons ...' on the envelope. So he took another envelope and wrote on it: 'Monsieur Charles Dandillot' and the address, and he kept this envelope in front of him. The thought that he would never have to write this name again brought the tears back to his eyes. 'Why weep for a man after he is dead? It's during his life, and *for* his life, that one should weep. It's better to be dead than to be only half-alive.' He remembered the tears he had shed, some years earlier, over the death of a great writer, tears that would subside for an hour and then burst out afresh as if their source had meanwhile been replenished, so much so that eventually his mother had observed testily: 'You didn't cry like that when your father died.' And he savoured to the full the words that now sprang to his lips: 'Never again will I make friends, because one suffers too much when one loses them.' They were the self-same words old ladies use when their little doggies pass away (but then, was M. Dandillot his friend?). He decided to send merely a telegram to Solange and her mother. They did not interest him.

In bed, incapable of sleeping, he jerked his leg up and down over the sheet in an incessant movement, like a dying horse pawing the ground. An immense community of suffering linked him with those dying horses, an immense chain stretching between him and them.

After a while he remembered something that had struck him in a letter from his son. One of Brunet's school-mates had just died of meningitis, and the child wrote: 'I feel awfully sad, but let us hope I shall get over it.' Costals, too, hoped that he would soon get over it. 'It's nature that has wounded me, and it's nature, too, that will heal me through oblivion. The day will come when I shall feel as indifferent to M. Dandillot's death as to the memory of his daughter. Since for the very same reason that I am weeping today I shall have ceased to weep tomorrow, then my weeping today is merely a game.'

At four in the morning Costals woke up and thought: 'A girl living alone with her mother is almost bound to fall. A boy likewise. So powerless is the mother, unless her power is evil. But Solange has already fallen. How stupid; M. Dandillot died for nothing.' He went back to sleep.

Solange Dandillot   to Pierre Costals
Paris   *Poste restante, Toulouse*

18 July 1927

Why this silence, nothing but that telegram to my mother, did you not promise when you left to write to me within three days? and can you not feel that I am all the time on tenterhooks waiting for the next post?

This intolerable existence has now lasted five days, I beg of you, put an end to it. I implore you to come to my help. I'm at the end of my tether.

Or else it means that you have gone away for good and are going to abandon me. Then you must say so, it's better than not knowing.

All my love,
Your
Rosebourg

I am enclosing a stamped addressed envelope with some paper inside, if you don't feel like writing, you only need to write your name on the paper, nothing more, and I shall know that you are not abandoning me.

My poor papa was buried this morning. What a void it has left for us! I shall write again to tell you how he died. We were so glad that he agreed to see a priest.

Costals' Note-Book

Well! So much for cold little Rosebourg!

With her letter in my hand, I wandered through the crowds, my eyes on the ground and biting my lips with emotion.

So she, too, in her turn has begun to howl like a beast, to screech like a cat locked in a cellar. She too has gone mad in her turn. It took Andrée four years to go mad. G. R. one. Undstein six. Claire one. But she has gone mad in two months. That's what comes of being a quiet little thing.

As Andrée's desperation subsides, hers begins to rise. Always these female lamentations, this music of flutes and tears that accompanies me all through my life.

(Her punctuation is inexcusable.)

Like the sorcerer's apprentice, I have unleashed this virgin love, this wild element of which I am no longer the master. At the Opéra-Comique, she was well behind me. Then she gained and gained, moving much faster than I, and caught up with me, and has now overtaken me. I have the feeling, almost, that she is starting again when I've only just arrived.

Is there, perhaps, some slight exaggeration in her letter? As I, at the age of sixteen, used to date my love letters two in the morning when they were written at two in the afternoon. This sudden outburst is so surprising! Had Solange been a little more 'demonstrative' with me, such a suspicion would never occur to me. Perhaps the poor child is paying now for having been so discreet and reserved. How unfair that would be. But what can I do about it?

I accept her love.

I agree to enter into the world of duty.

Sweet duty, since I love her. But duty all the same, and duty has never suited me.

However, I accept this love. With respect. With gravity – that intermittent gravity of mine which, in spite of everything, always comes into play when it is needed, if only at the eleventh hour. With ... the word escapes me; I meant to convey that her love does not displease me, that I do more than accept it: I welcome it.

And now, another matter.

Her indifference to her father's death! That postscript. She thinks of nothing but me, and I feel ashamed for both of us.

And yet she's a nice girl. Of course, fathers are not made to be loved by their children. Such is nature, and Brunet, tomorrow, with all his niceness.... But getting used to nature is always a painful process. We always expect it to be the extraordinary that takes us aback, when in fact it is the ordinary that is so terrifying.

Whenever I have visited the recently bereaved widow or orphan of someone I was more or less indifferent to, I have felt that I was more deeply moved – more sincerely moved – than was necessary: I seemed to be teaching them a lesson. It was *always* they who were the first to change the subject.

Pierre Costals   to Solange Dandillot
Toulouse   *Paris*

20 July 1927

Peace, my child. Peace, peace, peace everlasting to little girls. Why all this frenzy? An artichoke is always cool and collected.

You ask for reassurance: I give it to you. Peace, my darling little girl. Peace in the present. Peace in the future, as far ahead as it will please you to want me in that future. Total and absolute peace. Gaiety and serenity of mind in trust and in peace.

I have held you against my heart at the peak of my solitude, and you were alone there also, yet protected. You may remain there as long as you wish; I shall not go away from you. I love you, and what is rarer, I love the attachment you have for me. I shall never leave you until you have left me.

I have heard it said that a woman in a situation such as this should be put to the test. I do not put what I love to the test.

I have heard it said that one loses a woman by loving her too much, that an affectation of coldness, from time to time, brings better results. And so on. I shall play no such tricks with you. No tricks at all. I am not one of those people who see love as a battle; it is a notion I abhor. Let love be truly love – that is, let it be peace – or let it not exist at all.

Why this terror of my absence? What more could my

presence bring you? You are here, silly one, did you not know? In the daytime, like a little shadow, you glide quietly by my side. At night I go to sleep with you in my arms.

And my body thinks of you too. It wakes in the night and reaches towards you, as a dog stretches out its neck asking for a drink.

I have followed up your preoccupations in the order in which they appear in your letter. I have spoken first of you and me. Now a word about your father.

I do not know whether you loved your father, but I met him twice and loved him. I do not know whether you respected your father, but I met him twice and respected him. I had the impression that he was someone superior to you.

You think of no one but me, and yet you hardly know me. The casual way in which you refer to your father's death in your letter shocked me, although I understand it; exactly that: I understand it and am shocked by it. Granted, you are 'in love'. But I would have you know that love is not an excuse, but an aggravation. Precisely like drunkenness, which the insane justice of men treats as an extenuating circumstance, when it is an aggravating circumstance.

Must I be the one to make you realize what sort of man your father was?

I want you to be the person you ought to be. And you ought not to be *altogether* the person who wrote that letter.

There now, my little one, I send you my fondest love. Other men, perhaps, will love you more than I do. I love you as much as I can love you. I cannot do more.

C.

The punctuation of your letter is inexcusable.

Pierre Costals   to Mademoiselle Rachel Guigui
Toulouse   *Paris*

20 July 1927

Dear Guiguite,

Two whole months since we last met, and since I last wrote to you.

When I discovered the angel you know of, my first reaction was to drop you: one fancy drives out another. I gathered in my scattered affections from right and left in order to concentrate them all upon my angel and to make them into something powerful, like heat concentrated in a burning-glass. This adventure gripped me; I was full of it. In reality I was disregarding not only my own nature, but nature itself. Nature accumulates, and a well-endowed man does so too; in him, as in nature, there is room for everything. My angel is what she is; *you* are something else, and that is enough to make me want you as well. And so I trust that in your kindness you will see fit to resume your place among my delights.

Of course, as you remember, I had intended that we should eventually get together again. But I thought that would be when I had grown tired of the angel. Quite the contrary, my feeling towards her has never been so serious, so deep, and so strong: affection, supported by the twin pillars of esteem and desire. And it is on the tide of a great uprush of feeling that I have for her at the moment (as a result of a note received from her yesterday) that I am reverting to my natural instinct and the guiding principle in accordance with which I cannot have only one woman in my life.

Besides this, I love intelligence. And that is why, whatever my team of the moment, I must always have a Jewish mistress in the batch. She helps me to put up with the others.

I shall be in Paris on the 25th. Come on Tuesday, the 26th, the feast of St Barnabas, at 8 p.m., to Port-Royal. We'll have dinner, and afterwards you shall see what you shall see.

Goodbye, my dear; I stroke you with my hands, and even send you a kiss, for, as you know, my sensuality is of the tender kind. You, too, are a very sweet girl, and that is why my affection for you is so real. But get ready to make me happy, for I badly want to be. Thinking of you, I feel a spasm of fuliginous joy, comparable to the transports of the mystics or the final spurt of a flame. And lastly, after such a dose of the sublime, I yearn for a love that is not disinterested.

C.

Pierre Costals   to Mademoiselle du Peyron de Larchant
Toulouse   *Cannes*

               ('*to be given to Brunet*')

                                         20 June 1927

My pet,

I do not like doing things behind your back; what's more, I cannot. I must tell you therefore that I wrote to Mlle du P. five days ago asking her whether by any chance you mightn't have done something really naughty, and begging her to tell me the whole truth. She answered that there had been nothing out of the ordinary run of your day-to-day tomfooleries.

Now this is why I wrote to her. Not a day passes without my thinking of you at length, and the time I spend thinking of you is always the best part of the day, however good the rest of it may be. But this time it was a dream. I dreamt that, taking advantage of a moment when the chest of drawers in Mlle du P.'s room was unlocked, you poked inside it and took out some money. And this dream was so striking, so plausible, so coherent from beginning to end, that I could not help wondering whether it might not be a mysterious warning, and so wrote the letter.

This dream made a profound, almost overwhelming impression on me. I felt more forcibly than ever before what a terrible blow it would be for me if I were no longer able to think well of you.

There are several people for whom I feel a certain affection. But this affection, sincere though it is, goes only so far and no further. Like a motor-car which one knows has only so much horse-power in its belly. The affection which I feel for you, on the other hand, knows no obstacles, never reaches a limit. It belongs to another, infinitely higher category.

The affection I feel towards those other people does not preclude my being able to do without them, my being able to tease them, or wound them even, or see them in distress without suffering from it or doing anything to relieve them. The affection I feel for you would preclude all that. Not once in my life has it occurred to me to try to upset you, or to let you be upset when it was in my power to prevent it, or even to keep you waiting for a pleasure which it was possible for me to grant you at once. For this belongs to another, infinitely higher category.

When I emerge from the atmosphere generated by those persons and return to yours, everything, with you, seems so simple. That is because I really love you and nothing is simpler than loving, just as nothing simplifies things more.

Nevertheless, my affection for you is not altogether unassailable. The affection I feel for the various other people is at the mercy of those people themselves, who may cease to deserve it, but also at the mercy of my moods, my lassitude, the exigencies of my work and my need for independence. The affection I feel for you is at the mercy of you alone – by which I mean that in one eventuality only could it weaken: if you became unworthy of it.

It's a sort of miracle: for fourteen years (or let's say eight – since the age 'of reason'), I have never had anything to reproach you with, you have never done anything to offend me. I observe it all, as one observes the perilous feats of an acrobat, thinking: 'If only he can hold on to the end!' And I say to you, with all the force at my command: change, since in nature everything must change, and at your age especially one may change utterly within a fortnight; change, but in your essence remain what you are. Let there be a solid, steadfast nucleus in your nebula (ask Mlle du P. to explain what a nebula is; I would do so myself, only it bores me stiff, and I'd be at a bit of a loss to do so anyway). As you know, I allow you considerable scope for your idiocies, more so than any other father would allow his son; that is because, in my opinion, they do not affect what is really important. But in matters of importance do, I beg you, be on your guard. What I want passionately is to reach the point where *it would be inconceivable that I should have any anxiety on your account,* as regards your intrinsic quality; a point where you would represent complete calm and complete security to me; and that another living creature besides myself should represent complete calm and complete security to me is the most extraordinary thing I can imagine, since in effect it hardly belongs to this world. But it must be given to me, and by you and you alone: no one else means anything to me. You are the only person who has permanently engaged my affections, which are not easily engaged by other people. In fact, you are the only person I love, since the word can only be applied to that feeling which strictly extends to infinity, from which infinite demands can be made, with no more trouble than there would be in asking for water from the sea. Were the feeling I have for you to collapse or merely to fissure, it would mean the collapse or fissuring of the whole of myself. It would shatter me.

When one truly loves someone, there is no need to tell him so: that can be left to inferior people. And as you know, I never do tell you. But that dream frightened me, and I felt the need to set something of it down for you on paper. Keep it (this may be asking a lot), and let us now move on to the absurd business of your bike....*

Mlle Marcelle Prié
Rue Croix-des-Petits-Champs
Paris

to M. Jacques Picard†
chez M. Pierre Costals
avenue Henri-Martin
Paris
20 July 1927

Jacquot,

I am here in the café like last Sunday, alone of course, since you have deserted me. I've been waiting for you for six days. What does your silence mean, love? If you didn't want to see me again, then why did you call me back? So you were just making fun of me, were you? I'm not having you throw me over like this, my boy. We've got to meet again, do you hear. Come on Tuesday at 10 p.m.

Do you know when I first realized you had had enough of me? In the Underground, coming back from the boxing match. I wanted to kiss you and you kept turning your face away. So I said to you: 'Don't you love me any more, then?' 'Yes,

---

*The rest of this letter has no bearing on our story (*Author's note*).

†Costals' manservant.

but don't kiss me like that in the Underground. It's not right.'
'Are you ashamed?' 'Yes, I'm ashamed.' It was plain enough.

Please be straight with me. I'm the victim of my passion for
you. I wanted to love you, to guide you a bit in life. You're
twenty and I'm twenty-five, but really the different in our ages
is much bigger than that. Oh! I would have been prepared to
do without marriage, since you didn't want it, but we could
have been together, or just met on Sundays; it would have
been better than nothing. Now you don't want it any more.
You're free! But you'll regret it later. Your youth would have
been all my happiness. But you never understood me, and now
it hurts more than ever, my heart bleeds with loneliness and
with all this waiting and not being able to make you see.
Honestly, Jacques, do come one last time, and then I'll leave
you to do exactly as you please.

If you can't come tomorrow, I'll wait for you all week till
Sunday.

I kiss those eyes I used to love.

Marcelle

This letter remained unanswered.

THE HIPPOGRIFF

Nescio; sed fieri sentio et excrucior.

I do not know ... but I feel it happening to me and am racked
by it.

Catullus, 85

PART ONE

Scoronconcolo, bring me my cloak of light. I want to stroll in a garden, where the shade will open wide my eyes. But above all, no work – at any price!

On the way to Bagatelle we shall stop by the lakes to see the animals there. Animals we love, because they never lie. That was why man reduced them to slavery: they reminded him of truth.

Happy is the life that begins with ambition and ends with no other aspiration than to throw bread to ducks! Here they come, trailing long triangles in their wake, each with its individual geometry that intersects the geometries traced by the others, while the water swells gently beneath the pressure of their plump breasts. Some have little green lanterns in place of heads. How beautiful they are when they feel an impluse to be gay, when they rise up, and balancing themselves on their tails, flap their wings enthusiastically: they remind one of Members of Parliament putting on a show of indignation. Suddenly they dive, leaving only a quizzical rump in the air. This position is slightly indecent when swans adopt it. But with ducks it scarcely matters, because ducks are so much smaller.

Which reminds me, by the way, of the scoter-ducks on the Lake of Tunis. *They* perform a little pirouette as they float on the light swell. One feels what fun it is for them to let themselves go, just as one guesses the idea at the back of their heads, which is to imitate those celluloid ducks that are the pride of every well-bred bathroom.

But I haven't yet finished with the ducks. How charming they are when they fly! How can a man (unless he is starving) bring himself to aim a gun at them? The sight of their happy freedom would cure us of the pangs of love, if we suffered from them, but luckily we don't. How swiftly they fly, striving to catch up with the leader ducks, who have chosen and imposed a direction on the flight: I fancy they must be bringing good news to someone. Then, having caught up, they all fly in line abreast. Clearly they are proud of their impeccable alignment. They have too much sense to want to overtake one another. They leave that to men....

Bagatelle. These long hours in a garden are perhaps the best thing in our lives; there at least is something that takes the weight off your eyelids. And let me hear no more about adorable creatures; dream-land for me at present is to be rid of them. Today I abandon myself to the flowers and the foliage – they have the decency not to love me – and the milk of the day is warm in my mouth. It is that precious moment when the soul, having had its fill, dreams of the time when it will thirst again.

Such is evidently not the frame of mind of my dear confrère, Pierre Costals – the devil take him! I see him walking there, flanked by an extremely pretty girl in deep mourning. This young person has apparently just lost her father or her mother, a godsend for a gigolo: under such circumstances, what woman would not need some relaxation? Costals is holding forth, as though he were giving a lecture. And she walks on (what a ravishing gait! – long-legged, and so natural ...), with her eyes glued to the toes of her shoes. Here I am, three yards behind them; it would be nice to overhear a remark that I could use against him some day. But they stop under an archway of rocks. Embrace. I hear: 'Cloc ... cloc ... cloc....' I remember that line from a youthful poem of Costals':

The lovers' kisses like the sound of dropping turds.

The resemblance had never struck me before. Why, yes, dear confrère: that's exactly it.

Let us leave them. The weapons to be used against him are in his books. I admit he has some talent. But he irritates me, and there's nothing I can do about it. In the last resort, what do I feel about him? I am waiting for him to die.

Two o'clock. The garden is filling up again. A healthy organism suddenly invaded by microbes. I want to go down this way; a man is there already. Retrace my steps? People there, too. I'm surrounded. Even where no one is to be seen, someone is whistling at the top of his lungs behind a bush, and with this noise, invisible though he is, he sets up against me his own conception of the universe, which is vulgarity itself. People pour into the garden from every side. I am not of their kind. If they realize this, what will they do to me? I think of those small divinities of the woods and springs who remained on earth for a time after the advent of Christianity, always on the alert. No myth has ever touched me more.

Before leaving, as a souvenir of the garden I pick up a stone, cool as the necks of the young. But I do not know why I have picked it up, since I shall throw it away in a few minutes. Perhaps simply in order to be able to throw it away.

On the way out, I pass a pretty girl sitting by the succulent grass on the edge of a walk. She is smoking, and studying a list of share prices. My face, which had relaxed, stiffens again. Lines reappear which the glow reflected from the foliage had effaced. I must go back to the world of men, I must begin to hate once more. Scoronconcolo, take back my cloak of light.

After lunching with Solange in a restaurant in the Bois de Boulogne, Costals had taken her to the Bagatelle gardens.

At their second meeting, in May, he had told her how surprised he was that such a pretty girl should still be unmarried. Answer: she had had several offers, but would only marry a man who attracted her. Costals knew how rash it was to be the first to talk of marriage, and it was out of a natural tendency to rashness that he had done so. Seneca has a famous phrase for woman: *animal impudens*. Add one letter and you have man: *animal imprudens*. After that, the subject of marriage had been dropped.

Today, again, it was he who broached the subject point-blank:

'Marriage without divorce, Christian marriage, is a monstrosity for men. Completely against nature. Man's instinct is to grow tired of what he is accustomed to, and yet he's expected to remain faithful to a woman who loses some of her attractiveness every week. A husband of fifty-five who isn't a moron is still in the prime of life : how can he be satisfied with a woman of fifty unless he's a pervert? If he does it out of a sense of duty, nature rebels, and his health suffers. All the most intelligent doctors I know advise men of that age, if they are at all virile, to be unfaithful. Christian marriage is the basis for a whole multitude of offences against reason and nature – but then that is the very essence of Christianity : *quia absurdum*. You'd think the "jealous" god *wanted* man to be miserable, and created him stupid so that in his stupidity he would deliberately seek out the conditions that make for misery. As far as I'm concerned, I'll tell you this : the upper age-limit for a woman if she is to be considered desirable by yours truly is roughly twenty-six. As for the lower limit, better not mention it. An Arab naturalist of old, who has deservedly become a classic case as a result of similar characteristics, tells us that the hare changes sex every six months. For me, a woman changes sex at twenty-six or twenty-seven, and ceases to be a woman to become something one no longer desires. Do you think I would want to kiss you, let alone all the rest, when you're fifty? Not to mention the moral transformation : a woman, after marriage, can change morally as well as physically, can become a different person, as a boy of sixteen may become a different person from the one he was at fourteen. One would be venturing into the unknown.'

Suddenly, like a bird flitting from a branch, a little girl jumped down from a bench.

Continuously though she turned the idea of marriage over in her head, Solange could not have been less prepared to counter these observations with judicious arguments. She listened, with an air of some constraint, without saying a word. He went on :

'An average man can marry. But if a man who's at all exceptional marries, woe betide him. Great men's marriages are the part of their lives they hate to admit. A wife is a source of worry, and an exceptional man must have serenity of mind. A writer, for instance, must be able to regulate, measure out what he gets from life, turn on or off at will the

tap marked life and the tap marked work. One writer* has
said something to this effect: "What I need are flat, level days,
empty days, so empty that even love and friendship would
disturb them." Such empty days are essential for reflection,
conception and creation. And of course, there would be no
question, as Flaubert exaggeratedly demanded, of empty days
all the time. But empty days *in one's own good time*. For
that, a man must not be dependent on anybody else, must
not cohabit with anybody, and must have no business com-
mitments. A creative man should be able to *forget* his wife
and children. That is impossible, and besides, what is the point
of marrying in order to forget you're married? I've tried living
with women three times. With all three of them I quarrelled
almost as soon as our cohabitation began. It's as automatic as
falling out with a friend you've lent money to. Besides, I
cannot bear to feel chained. To go and live abroad, or join a
remote expedition, or withdraw into a religious retreat – all
these things I can very well do without, but I need to feel
that there is nothing to prevent me from doing them. Anything
that tied me down would kill me; there's only one thing I'm
tied to, and that is my work. I would put up with a thousand
times more from an unacknowledged bastard of mine than
from a legitimate child, from a mistress than from a wife,
because it's the legal, compulsory nature of the tie that drives
me mad.'

'I can see that a man like you might do without marriage
if need be. But the absence of children seems to me more
serious, especially for someone like you who has no brothers
and sisters.'

'If I wanted to put it a bit pompously I would say this: I
am wedded to life, and the books I draw from life are my
children. It was in a similar spirit that Barrès said of Napoleon:
"His victories were his daughters." And would to God
Napoleon had had no other family but that! Another thing:
one of the reasons why I wouldn't have a son today (let's not
even speak of daughters – that would kill me) is because I
believe that, in the world we live in, I couldn't have the kind
of son I wanted. Sooner or later the ignominy of the age

*Emile Clermont.

would be bound to rub off on him. And what would I do with a son I could not but despise? I would hate him, with an un-believable hatred. I don't want to run that risk.'

It was true that at the age of twenty, when he had had Philippe, he had not yet written anything, nor had he enough experience, nor perhaps enough self-discipline, to be deterred by the risks he was running. Chance had ordained that Philippe should turn out well. But it would be foolish to tempt providence.

'And yet,' said Solange, 'there are plenty of men who are quite satisfied with marriage, even famous men.' (She con-fused famous men and exceptional men.)

'The weak-willed and the simple-minded will always be satisfied with marriage. And remember this : those who defend marriage most vociferously are often those who suffer most from it. They feign marital bliss, for fear of being seen through and pitied.'

'You're young now, but don't you think that a time will come when you will feel the need for someone to comfort you in moments of depression?'

'What a very bourgeois idea of the world – to think that it's inevitable for men to have their moments of "depression"! Believe me, there are men who not only don't know what "depression" means, but haven't even the faintest notion of what it might be. Myself, for example, I never have the slightest need of support (unless of course I'm physically ill). I rely on my creativity; that is my health and my salvation; that is what relieves and refreshes me. I have no need to be two; or, more precisely, there is only one circumstance, one alone, in which I need another person besides myself, and that is for the purpose of pleasure. Otherwise, whenever I am, or visualize myself to be, with another person, I feel diminished. And in any case, supposing I did have difficult moments, I would find consolation either in myself or in the teachings of the sages. Or in the sexual act, the most potent consolation of all – but there's no need of a wife for that, as far as I know. I ask you, where could a young woman find the power to console me, otherwise than in her body? No, I'm afraid I have nothing but contempt for marriage con-

ceived of as a mutual insurance policy between two poor
devils who are incapable of standing up to "the difficulties of
life" on their own: two shivering paupers who need each
other's warmth.... If it is that, so much the better: we
oughtn't to sneer at anything that comforts people. But let
me repeat what I said to you at the beginning: that it's only
for second-raters. And let's leave the rest out of it.'

'Millions and millions of men, ever since the world began,
have found solace in a wife. You can't alter that.'

'Oh, yes I can – I can deny it by my actions. To every man
his own destiny; and that's not mine. I have always had a
brotherly feeling for Sisera, whose story is related in the Book
of Judges. He's a Canaanite general, and fleeing from the
Hebrews he takes refuge with Jael, the wife of an allied king.
Jael comes out of her tent and says to him: "Turn in, my lord,
turn in to me; fear not." He goes into her tent, and lies down,
exhausted, and she covers him with a cloak. And he asks for
a little water, for he is dying of thirst. The Bible actually says
"a little water", and when I think of the modesty of this
request, I weep a tiny bit (if you don't see me weep, it's
because I'm weeping inside). Sisera falls asleep, and Jael, taking
a tent-peg and a mallet, nails his head to the ground from
temple to temple. Sisera is a brother to me because of being
hated and because of having such a thirst, which for me is the
thirst of the triple tongue, my thirst, that is to say the thirst
of the three wisdoms, and his fate would be mine if I ever took
refuge with a woman: she would reduce my brain to pulp,
because women always hate men's brains, and there's a remark
of Mme Tolstoy's about her husband, so revealing of the female
attitude and so profound in both its terms that it is worthy of
holy writ: "I cannot abide him, because *he never suffers*, and
because *he writes*." The Catholic theologians, or at any rate
the Jansenist ones, in whose writings I came across it, claim
that Sisera is one of the forms of the Devil. Which may well
be, if one considers his thirst; though on the other hand I
doubt whether the Devil would ever have put his trust in a
woman, since he is the personification of Intelligence.'

'You couldn't help admitting that when you are physically
ill, you need help. When you are old and infirm, you'll be

very glad to have a wife to prepare your poultices for you.'

'I hope you said that like a parrot, and not after mature consideration. Because if you really meant it you would go right down in my estimation. What a splendid victory for a woman, to be called upon at last by a decrepit old man! On a par with the victory of the Church when the unbeliever in a coma agrees to see a priest. Well, yes, when I am old and tottering I may perhaps marry. And what then? It won't be a question of being united body and soul, and so on and so forth, but of giving a devoted nurse the satisfaction of an established position. And it won't invalidate anything I've said about marriage.'

Now they were among the rose-beds, themselves a bit decrepit in the late July heat. He went on:

'Whenever there is anything beautiful or successful, man somehow contrives to spoil it, even when it's his own creation. Just now I heard the murmur of distant water; we hurried towards it, and what did we see: a statue above the water – and a statue that isn't beautiful is something really horrible. If I see a bench, it has no back to it; and to make a bench without a back is to show very little knowledge of what real rest means. And now look at these roses, and then I'll tell you in what way they remind me of marriage. Each rose has an identity disc with its registration number, its French name, its Latin name, and a reference to a "plate", for we are still at school. I notice that none of these roses bears the name of a poet. But there's the "President Carnot" rose, as heavy as a soul in sorrow: it reminds me of those Algerian villages which used to be called in Arabic "Head of the Waters" or "Pigeon's Rest" and which were re-baptized "Ernest Renan" or "Sarrien". In this oasis which one thought had been created for relaxation and enjoyment, these labels plunge us right back into the social maelstrom. The "Honourable X" rose invites us to consider such delicate moral problems as the precise definition of honourability. The "Entente Cordiale" rose obliges us, in spite of ourselves, to indulge in such questionable gestures as investigating whether it (the rose) may not have withered a bit. The "Mme X" (a well-known actress) forces us to draw a comparison between Mme X and a rose. In my opinion, having started on this path, one ought to go the whole hog, and I suggest that the names of the people appearing on these labels should henceforth be accompanied by their honorific titles, their French and foreign decorations, etc., not forgetting, wherever it applies, the sign indicating ownership of a car which one sees in directories, nor the entry HP for *hôtel particulier*.'*

'But what's the connection between these roses and marriage?'

'Man ruins love by marriage, as he has ruined these roses by red-tapery. Love is spoiled not only by marriage itself, but by the mere possibility of marriage. The spectre of marriage clanking its chains – the chains of marriage, needless to say – poisons any relationship with a girl. The moment I say to myself that I might . . . no, I can't even bear to pronounce the words . . . my love for you begins to dwindle, as though under the influence of some evil spell. If I dismiss this baleful idea, it rears its head again and spurts fire. No, the only way of turning something as insensate as marriage into something at all reasonable would be to allow either party to divorce at will without any need for justification. A priest has the right to abandon the cloth after his novitiate if he feels he has no vocation for the mystic marriage. Ordinary marriage is a vocation too, and one needs to have had a taste of it to see whether one has it or not. I should certainly have married if I had been sure of being able to break it off without having to justify my decision, after a two-year trial, for example.'

'A two-four-six year lease. Or rather six-four-two!'

A child's ball landed near them, raising a little cloud of dust. 'Look, a shell exploding!' cried the small boy, who was about seven years old. Where had he seen shells? At the cinema? The things a little European will think up in 1927!

'There's one other contingency in which I might be prepared to marry. In the event of some catastrophe, war or bloody revolution. Then, since everything would be done for anyway, a little more, a little less hardly matters. If it's going to give so much pleasure to a damsel, we might as well call at the

---

*Hôtel particulier: a large private town house (*Translator's note*).

Registrar's before buckling on our swordbelt. If war broke out tomorrow, I might perhaps marry you.'

The ground was scattered with bamboo husks (at least, that is what I call them), smooth, white, polished, made expressly for profound thoughts to be inscribed thereon. There was a bird . . . (well, my little bird, do give me a nice simile! Ah yes . . .) a bird in the centre of a round tree, like the flame in the centre of a Venetian lantern. There was foliage drenched with sunlight, a blaze of foliage, and a man could be seen carrying it away in his arms. There were crows, self-important and cantankerous, not unlike humans. There was a sparrow gargling on the edge of the pool, and more sparrows lying in the dust like cattle. There was a sea-gull listening to its own cry (but was it really a sea-gull?). There were little frogs, the shape of whose bodies reminded one of the French athletes selected for the Olympic Games. Dead leaves covered the surface of the pond, under which the fish must have found it difficult to see, poor things. An artificial overhanging rock had been built for them to shelter under when it rained.

Solange Dandillot   to Pierre Costals
Paris   *Paris*

28 July 1927

Dear Friend,

I have made up my mind to write to you, despairing of ever plucking up the courage to speak. When you are there, I feel paralysed, I lose all initiative, and yet our frequent meetings, the fact that we are seen together, the indiscrete (*sic*) gossip that may arise from this, make it essential to have things out with you as soon as possible. You must be indulgent with me if I cannot express my feelings any better in writing than by word of mouth.

Surprising though it may seem to you, I am still a pure young girl. No doubt it's ridiculous, out-of-date, but there it is. If we are to continue to see each other, to go out together, people are bound to say that we're engaged (I refuse to en-visage any other explanation). If it were your sister, what would you advise her to do? What would you think of a man who had adopted such an attitude towards her?

What are we to do? Stop seeing each other? That would be very hard. Could we not find a way of reconciling your repugnance for marriage with my scruples? Why could we not try a sort of legalized relationship, with a civil ceremony only, and without informing anyone (except my mother and my grand-parents, naturally), a temporary marriage, since you cannot bear the idea of permanency? No religious ceremony; I have too much respect for the Church to involve it in a travesty of matrimony. And I promise you that I would go out of your life as silently as I came into it, as soon as you began to find me a burden. A two-four-six-year lease, nothing more.

There! I don't know what else to say to you, and I shall await your reply with trepidation, though I feel certain that, honourable man that you are, you will not put it off too long. I leave you, my dearest friend, with the assurance of my tender affection.

Solange

Ever since her first meeting with Costals, at the Doignys' on the 1st of May, Mlle Dandillot had been thinking of marriage. She had never conceived of marriage except with a man who attracted her; on any other terms it seemed to her repellent. No one had attracted her up till then, and she awaited her Prince Charming with tranquillity. Usually, a woman starts by loving love, the universe, nature, God, and then she realizes that what she needs is a single human being. Solange had never loved anything, or anybody – except her mother. Neither her heart nor her senses being in need of sustenance, she was perfectly happy in this state, and quite prepared for it to last forever. But she saw Costals, and sensing that he was attracted to her and feeling drawn to him herself (oh! no question of love at first sight!), she thought to herself: 'Why not?'

She had discussed it with her mother at once – yes, from the very first day, such was their mutual trust. Mme Dandillot was delighted: 'At last she's attracted to a man, and since that was all she was waiting for. . . . ' It was worth overlooking the drawbacks : the difference in age, the fact that Costals was a writer and so might draw Solange into a world to which she would not be entirely suited either by her tastes or her comparative lack of culture. Though not at all snobbish, Mme Dandillot had nonetheless been flattered by the fact that a famous man . . . (and vanity had also played its part in her daughter's preliminary reaction, though it was soon to give way to the opposite feeling : regret that Costals was a writer, and regret that he was famous). Utterly remote from the literary world, and never having read anything of Costals', Mme Dandillot was unaware that he had a somewhat dubious reputation in sexual matters.

On the way back from the Doignys', he had complimented her on her simplicity : 'That little girl's ring !' Solange was indeed simple and natural, but she had always taken it for granted. The following week, having been invited through Costals to the Piérards', and 'dressing up' more than she had done for the Doignys', since it was a much more elegant party given by people she did not know, she decided not to wear a handsome family brooch which normally went with this particular costume. And whereas at the Doignys' she had worn a little make-up, this time she used none, but simply bit her lips to bring the blood to them, and remained for a full minute on the landing with her head down (pretending to fix her stocking) before going into the flat. From then on she had always kept a close rein on this capacity for simulation, in big things as well as small. The advantage of this inconsistency of hers was that, having a little of everything in her nature, it was easy for her to externalize only what was pleasing to Costals, and to keep the rest in abeyance.

In the box at the Opéra-Comique on May 11th, she had hardly opened her mouth she was so paralysed with shyness. But if Costals had made an advance it is doubtful whether she would have demurred. From then on she had ignored the impertinence of his first letter and his habit of treating her as a bit of a tart, partly because she was fond enough of him to put up with it, partly because she wanted to bind him to her, and partly because, like her mother, she was lacking in pride.

She had not shown the letter to Mme Dandillot, for fear of the bad impression it might make, but had agreed with her the sense of her reply – that she should telephone her willingness to see him again. She pretended not to understand what he meant. But she understood perfectly well, though in a rather vague way : for she liked vagueness, like all women, who feel more at home in it.

In these circumstances, Costals' advances during the concert, straightforward though they were, had come as a surprise to her. He had embraced her in public; he had kissed her thigh through her skirt, had lifted her skirt and stroked her naked thighs. This girl, who until then had never been kissed without putting the man in his place, who would never have tolerated even the mildest advance, had been bowled over by all this. On returning home that evening, it will be remembered, she had had a sort of nervous fit, and vomited : from that evening (16 May) she loved him. It had taken her a fortnight to work up to it.

And so, in the Bois de Boulogne, on the evening of their first kisses (22 May), she was already entirely his, though a little shocked (contrary to what she told him later) by some of his caresses. She told her mother that he had kissed her, and kept quiet about the rest. It was from that moment that she decided on the policy she would adopt in order to get him to marry her : never to speak of marriage, but to wait until he did, so as always to be able to say to him : 'But who was the first to mention marriage?' She was ingenuous enough to have no doubt that he would do so one day – a day which she believed much closer than it was in fact – and knew herself to be patient enough by nature to be able to await that day without too much anxiety.

As is usual in such cases, the two women waited as long as they could before breathing a word of all this to M. Dandillot. For a fortnight the name Costals was never mentioned in his presence, but eventually he had to be told that they were going out together. M. Dandillot pricked up his ears. Plans were discussed. Costals was invited to lunch.

M. Dandillot had hit it off with Costals from the start, and given his blessing to the women's plans, but for various reasons

said nothing about them to the writer during their two conversations. This born bachelor, who had married 'because
everyone does' and who had had nothing but worries as a
result, who moreover was by far the most intelligent of the
three Dandillots, sensed that Costals was not the marrying
sort. In addition, he had no great love for his daughter, who
had been conceived by accident at a time when, being extremely worried about his son, he had sworn never to have
another child. The fact was, he considered her stupid, which
was untrue, or at best insignificant, which was equally untrue:
no one is insignificant. If he had broached the subject of
marriage to Costals, he would have said to him: 'First of all,
you're not cut out for marriage. Secondly, even supposing you
were, my daughter would be wrong for you. Thirdly, I shall be
dead in a few weeks. My family have given me enough trouble
for the past thirty years: I wash my hands of what happens
after I've gone. My wife and my daughter want this marriage.
You are old enough to know your own mind. You can sort it
out yourselves.' This 'thirdly' had overridden the first two
reasons, and so he said nothing.

M. Dandillot had died without a word of any consequence
to his wife or daughter; no supreme adjuration; no final piece
of advice; no outburst of tenderness; no posthumous letter.
Entrenched behind the solitude and silence into which he had
withdrawn twenty years before, he had left no indication even
as to the state of his affairs, so that it was only by chance,
when going through his papers, that Mme Dandillot learnt
of the existence of a safe-deposit box containing some gold.
When Mme Dandillot had asked him two days before his
death: 'Do you still agree to Solange's marrying Costals if he
proposes to her?' he had simply said: 'She can do what she
likes', just as, two days later, when she had begged him to
agree to see a priest, he had merely raised his arms and let
them fall back on the bed in a gesture of resignation, too weak
to say a word.

From the day of their first embraces in the Bois, through the
day he had made her *demi-vierge* (25 May) and the day he had
made her a woman (24 June), to the day at Bagatelle when we
have just seen Costals, for the first time, admit that in certain

circumstances (war or revolution) he might marry her, Solange had stuck to her policy of never mentioning marriage. She had been astute enough to grant him without fuss or affection everything a woman of easy virtue would have granted, while at the same time remaining what she was: a rather old-fashioned little thing. In this way she had satisfied not only Costals' sexual appetite but also his 'austerity'. She had shown herself to him in a dual role – tart and young lady – and people only interested him if they were dual (at the very least); she had presented herself to him as something of a contradiction, which was the best way of exciting him: he had thought of her as someone after his own heart.

What she felt for him seems to have been not so much love as the possibility of love. Abhorring anything irregular or underhand, she was waiting, before giving free rein to her love, to see a path open out in front of her along which she could venture wholeheartedly. It was from the same sort of feeling that she had not been able to bring herself to say *tu* to him: she did not want to say *tu* to a man who might abandon her any day and become a complete stranger to her; she would not say *tu* to him until he had slipped the engagement ring on to her finger. She had given herself to him out of affection, and also in the hope that it would bind him to her. Which was wise of her, for if she had played hard to get in order to inflame him the more, he would have slid out of the whole thing: he was not the sort of man who allowed himself to be manipulated by women. At first she had experienced an overwhelming pleasure from his caresses, when they were more or less chaste, though the pleasure grew less intense when she realized that his tenderness was usually but the prelude and, as it were, the froth of desire. From the caresses of his sensuality she had experienced no pleasure at all: she was frigid by nature, being a young girl, and frigid by heredity, so to speak, since both her father and mother were frigid. Thus she kept her love as it were in abeyance. It was to some extent Costals' own attitude towards her at certain times, when he told himself that he would willingly become more ardent if she became more ardent too, or more indifferent than she if she chose to withdraw.

She was convinced that the marriage would take place. Her mother had her doubts, being more experienced and having meanwhile read Costals' books. Not all of them, however, such is the frivolity of humankind. This woman was prepared to give her daughter to a writer, and yet did not take the trouble to read, and ponder with the utmost gravity, the entire literary output of this writer, who put the whole of himself into everything he wrote.

'If he doesn't mention marriage, you'll have to do so first. Things can't go on like this. There's sure to be gossip sooner or later.'

'Don't worry, he'll mention it.'

'If he hasn't said anything by next week, I shall invite him round and ask him what his intentions are.'

'No, please, don't interfere. In that case I'll write to him. But we must wait a little longer.'

'And what if he answers your letter with a firm "no"? You'll have to stop seeing him.'

'Obviously. . . . But I assure you that even if he does answer "no" it won't be a firm "no". The main thing is not to pester him. If one does, he digs his heels in, and then. . . . He likes to make people fume with rage. He reminds me of Gaston (her brother) at the age of fifteen. You think he's serious because he writes books and all that. He's a kid. He does things only kids do, like running his hand along railings or shop-fronts. The sort of thing you only see errand-boys do, not men. In fact, there's a guttersnipe side to him which is what I like least about him. . . . '

That 'obviously' of Solange's took a great weight off Mme Dandillot's mind. How sensible her little girl still was, after all!

Mme Dandillot did not interrogate Solange too closely. 'You've been to his flat?' 'Yes.' She knew quite well that if she added: 'Have you slept with him?' looking her straight in the eye, Solange was not the sort of child who would say no if it was in fact so, or at any rate would persist in the lie. And she loved and respected her too much to want to make her tell lies. Nevertheless she had been unable to resist asking her: 'You know there are certain precautions to be taken?' – to which Solange had answered 'Yes' without raising her eyes.

Since she had no girl-friends, and since Mme Dandillot could not for a moment imagine her seeking enlightenment on such matters from books, it must have been Costals who had instructed her. For the future? For the present? Mme Dandillot was fairly sure that her daughter was the writer's mistress, and let it go at that, being a woman of her time and of her country, not to mention her social position. In fact she thought to herself: 'If he gives her a child, he'll marry her.' Be it noted that not the slightest suggestion of blackmail crossed her mind.

Holding that the notion of ambivalence is the key to psychology, Costals had spotted at once that in these two women honesty was mixed with a certain amount of calculation. Yet, though capable of a just appreciation of the general picture, time and again he found himself debating whether in such and such an action they were being true or false, and often proved to be mistaken. And this uncertainty was to be one of the factors in the mistrust which he never ceased to entertain towards the plans of the Dandillot family.

'I received your letter. It surprised me a little. But before tackling the main issue, as they say in the law-courts, I should like to make one observation. You tell me you are a "pure young girl". Words must after all have some meaning. I might call you a pure young girl because as a writer I am entitled to some poetic licence. But you, when *you* tell *me* that you're a pure young girl.... I really cannot understand how anyone could put that in a serious letter. Now let's get to the point.

'My first objection is that you have raised this dilemma much too early. I hardly know you, I haven't had time to put you to the test. And how could you yourself agree to marry a man you've only known for three months? You need to know a man for three years.

'Let us assume that there's one chance in a hundred thousand that I might marry you. By breaking with me now, on the grounds that I haven't made up my mind at once, you would lose that chance. And that chance does after all exist, infinitesimal though it is. You talk of breaking off, whereas, on

339

the contrary, the more we see of each other the better I shall get to know you and therefore the better basis I shall have for making a decision.

'Like you, I should like to reconcile "my repugnance and your scruples". But the solution you propose is not at all, whatever you may say, a "travesty of marriage". You know perfectly well that it makes no difference whether the Church comes into it or not. It is the civil ceremony that makes a marriage, and there's no way out of it except by divorce. If I want a divorce without having any complaint against you legally speaking, and if on the other hand you refuse to accept divorce, there's nothing I can do about it, I'm trapped.

'A word about your "respect for the Church". You "respect" the Church "too much" to wish to involve it in what you call a travesty of marriage. In my opinion that "too much" is very little, and you don't respect the Church at all, since you're prepared to dispense with it in order to get married.

'Briefly, what I suggest to you is this: that our relationship should continue as before, but with greater regard for secrecy than in the past: absolute secrecy, in fact. (If I have not kept it as secret as I might have done up to now, it's because I thought you might acquire some reflected glory from showing me off a bit.) Let me make you happy in an atmosphere of liberty, spontaneity and vigour, which is my natural element when nothing trammels me, and not in the atmosphere of the kitchen sink. After a certain time, when I have tested your feelings and mine, I shall consult a man of law and get him to work out how one of the parties to a marriage can get out of it without the other's consent.'

All this, which occupies two pages of a book, was gone into in elaborate detail for two hours and ten minutes, with passionate sincerity and seriousness. He also made known the conditions, all *sine qua non*, he would lay down for any marriage, no matter who with: separate maintenance; a quiet ceremony in some remote spot, with only the witnesses present; no religious ceremony, so that they should be spared the grotesque formalities of annulment in Rome; no children; and three months' conjugal holiday per year, during which he could go away wherever he liked and the couple would be strangers to each other, for, he added, 'a home ought not to be a place one stays in but a place one goes back to.' The rejection of a single one of these conditions would entail the immediate abandonment of the whole scheme.

Solange seemed rather stunned. She said she would think it over, and might perhaps agree. She said 'perhaps' in a bird-like voice, a thin, high-pitched voice, as women say it when they are about to yield. She would discuss it with her mother.

'What exactly are you afraid of?'

'Becoming too attached to you.'

'And then my leaving you?'

'Yes.'

'Well, then you'll suffer! Frankly, I think you're being rather cowardly. And how would marriage put your mind at rest, since I shall never marry anyone unless I find a means of getting out of it whenever I want to? A sensible man going off to war thinks out ways of getting himself evacuated when he has had enough. In marriage too one must foresee how to get oneself evacuated.'

'You're not much of a one for taking risks. . . .'

'You can say that to me, of all people! That's a good one! I take risks in order to get things I want. But to take a risk for something I don't want. . . .'

She was staring at the ground, but at these words she lifted her face towards him (as though in reproach?). Touching her lightly on the cheek with the tip of his gloves, which he was holding in his hand, he turned her face away, as though he did not want her to look at him at that moment.

'I want to lend you some books: Tolstoy's journal, and his wife's. You'll see what would happen to us if we committed that act of madness.'

'What a lot of notes there are in the margins!'

'They're the notes made by the various girls I've lent these books to. You'll find at least five or six different hand-writings. For these volumes are a veritable breviary for any young lady who wants to marry me.'

He turned over the pages of one of them, and read two or three hand-written observations.

'Look, here are some intelligent notes. In pencil – so it's

impossible to recognize the writing. It's rather moving, this message from someone I can't identify, someone who loved me, and of whom these notes make me think: "Perhaps, after all, I might have been able to marry her without much damage." ...'

Solange's eyes were glued to the margins, and Costals was struck by the hardness of her expression. So we're jealous, are we? Ridiculous!

'Are you satisfied with our conversation?'

A silence, then:

'Yes. . . .'

'So, for the time being, we carry on as before?'

A silence, then:

'Yes. . . .'

'And you'll come to my flat the day after tomorrow at six?'

A silence, then:

'Yes. . . .'

'My little darling, I can see you're unhappy. From now on you'll have to settle down with that unhappiness, while I, who am the cause of it, do my best to soothe it and gradually cure you of it.'

When he kissed her hand on leaving her, he felt that it was as cold as ice.

Costals' Diary

3 *August* – Looked at in cold blood, this marriage seems to me absurd and impossible, which it undoubtedly is. But in moments of exaltation I see it as:

1. An ordeal worthy of me. It is a great thing to make a success of something one despises, because one has to overcome not only the obstacle but oneself too. It always takes courage to challenge life. Not that I'm afraid of life, damn it! I've overcome adolescence and all its horrible miasmas, I've overcome war, I've overcome long-distance expeditions, I've overcome solitude, pleasure, success, and all the various dangers which surround the private life of a man who is ready for anything. There is only one monster before which I've

always flinched: marriage. And now it's up to me to over-
throw the Hippogriff! Or rather to turn it into a saddle-horse.
I want to astonish myself, to prove to myself that I can be
just as daring, just as free and easy in marriage as in celibacy.
Of course I should have to behave like a braggart flexing his
biceps: 'We shall see what we shall see,' followed by a roll of
drums. Such an attitude is farcical, seen from the outside. But
is it my fault if I'm obliged to whip myself up into a frenzy
in order to face what terrifies me so? Even to the extent of
calling to the rescue, for example, the Roman knights whose
order, under Augustus, comprised more bachelors than married
men? Those who braved the enemy most valiantly dreaded
finding themselves alone with a missus. I'm no exception.

2. An experience necessary to my knowledge of life, and
hence to my work. A means of renewing the human substance
of my art, fertilizing a new patch of earth, opening a new
water-course. An unknown land to be annexed, or at least to
fly over proudly. That's it, fly over, glide over, as I glided over
the war, as I have glided over pain, as I glide over fatherhood
– barely wetting the tips of my fingers. To go through marriage
as one goes through the midsummer fires. Will there be crises?
So much the better. A writer will always pay cash down for a
crisis, no matter what.

And then, it would be amusing to learn what duty is.

4 August – She came. She gave me back Tolstoy's diary, and
his wife's, without a word. Aurel's saying: 'There are women
to whom one lends a marvellous book and who return it to
you without a word as though they were handing you the
sugar-tongs.' If Dante were to reappear and give a public
recital of an unpublished canto of the *Divine Comedy*, there
would be women, intellectual women at that, who could think
of nothing else to say but that his trousers were not very well
creased. To all my questions she replied with feeble variations
on the theme of: 'Why do you think what happened in
Tolstoy's case will happen in yours? There's no reason to
believe it wouldn't work....'

Everything is made more difficult by the fact that these
people are totally lacking in wit.

In just a few days, she has managed to mess up my Tolstoy, sticking the cover together with adhesive paper. She must be rather slovenly.

Nothing on earth can persuade me that I need her presence. There is absolutely no reason why I should marry her.

I don't love her. I should like to find more reasons for loving her, but I can't. I don't love her, and yet I'm prepared to commit this folly for her sake.

The fear I used to have as a child when I was taken out in a boat. The impression of someone embarking.

I feel drawn towards the story of the Tolstoy marriage as one is drawn towards an abyss. The story used to haunt me even before I had the slightest thought of marriage. *Deteriora sequor.* I see where evil lies and I head for it.

I marry you not to make *myself* happy but to make *you* happy.

If one talks about it enough, it will happen. The feeling that a machine has been set in motion, and henceforth it will be impossible to stop it.

5 August – I am going into this adventure as I went into the war, and perhaps as I go into everything else: obsessed, from the moment of entering it, with how I shall be able to get out.

Worse still, thinking of the leap of triumph I shall give when I get out – in fact conceiving it as a preparation for this.

And then, for ever after, this wrong vis-à-vis Solange, not only to have gone into the marriage as into something one will escape from, but to have considered it as a sort of foil intended to make my subsequent life more deliriously happy.

6 August – She comes, but informs me that she is unwell. Women, always ill, always unhealthy, never absolutely wholesome. I inquire when her indisposition will be over: tomorrow. But when I ask her if we can meet the day after tomorrow, she says she cannot. The following day she can't either. Three days! How unloving she is! A brief good-bye. A limp handshake. Her coldness frightens me. What has happened? Have I offended her in some way, either morally or physically?

This has happened. When she first broached the question

of marriage (in her letter), I resisted. Now that she's cold, the idea keeps running through my head, and I see myself demanding this marriage which four days ago I rejected. I who thought I was master of my own will now see myself submitting because of her. At the moment of writing, I do not feel inclined to lose her. And yet she is so cold, so capable of running away (like a little gazelle), I can sense how certain she is to make me suffer.

You have given me everything, happiness and suffering. You have been mingled with all the things of this summer, like rain mingled with the branches of a tree.

You have disillusioned me with solitude. I can hardly believe in it any more.

Baudelaire: 'I can understand how one might desert a cause in order to know what it will feel like serving another. It might be pleasant to be alternately victim and executioner.' Pleasant perhaps to be the victim, after having been so often the executioner.

I am always going from one extreme to the other.

10 August – I told her flatly that I had come closer to the idea of marriage, and that in the meantime *she* had moved further away from me. 'No, I haven't. On the contrary, I think I'm becoming more and more attached to you.' – 'Why were you so cold the other day?' – 'But I wasn't cold!' When I insist that she was, she goes on protesting she was not, with a look of anguish in her eyes, as though imploring me to believe her, which immediately makes me feel that *I'm* in the wrong.

On leaving her, I am convinced of her sincerity. Convinced that everything is moving towards *it*. But a moment after leaving her I ask myself: 'Why she rather than another? Why she, when there are so many others more this and more that than she?'

Even if I were presented with the Queen of Sheba's daughter, fourteen years and three days old, on a golden platter, I would think of the unhappiness it would cause you, and I could not do it.

11 August – Here is a girl for whom I feel affection, esteem, and physical attraction. And the prospect of marrying her is like a waking nightmare, as bad as a declaration of war.

Will she get on with Brunet? She doesn't like children. She doesn't like small boys ('Their ugly little mugs. . . .'). She doesn't even like young men ('They're so *stupid*! . . .'). She won't like him. Not to mention the silent reproaches: 'How could you have brought him up like this?' (To be censured by Mademoiselle Dandillot! . . .) Perhaps she will want to exert her authority over him. That I shall never allow. I did my damnedest, God knows at what cost, to keep him away from his mother, and now to think that he might have to reckon with a step-mother! Someone coming between him and me! Fifteen years' work destroyed!

As for him, I know he'll say at once (before he knows anything about my plans): 'Couldn't you fix me up with her? No? How mean you are!' With anyone else but her, yes, it might have been a good idea to allow him to take the plunge with his step-mother. But S. is absolutely the wrong person for that: much too stupid. He'll hang around her the whole time. He'll know I sleep with her. She'll be the object of his repressed desires, the harbour of his solitary voyages. He'll be tossed about and will suffer because of her. And I don't want him to suffer through anyone – woe to anyone who lays a finger on him! – and above all, above all, not through her.

I ought to arrange a meeting between them right away. But I know so well what will come of it: one more reason for not marrying her. And what I'm looking for is a reason for marrying her.

Another thing: what if I give her a child? The very thought of it nearly drives me mad. If it's a girl I shall be certain to desire her eventually: a lot of agitation, complication, responsibility, in spite of my education* – the whole machinery of

---

*Costals is referring to the tuppence-coloured picture books (*Images d'Epinal*) which were the earliest reading-matter for French children at the beginning of this century. They depicted kings enamoured of their daughters, cats in love with princesses, giants addicted to little boys, etc. It is not surprising that Costals retained from all this a tendency towards sexual confusion (*Author's note*).

trouble grinding into action, as it does whenever a man has anything to do with a woman. And then, desired or not, a girl commits and ties one much more than a boy; one can't leave her to get along by herself: an Everest of worry and time-wasting. If it's a boy, I shall love him, and I don't want to give to another son what I've already given to the one I have. There are words that cannot be uttered twice, even inwardly. I can, at a pinch, repeat the same words to a hundred or a hundred and fifty women and mean it every time, because women only affect the surface of my life – and even so, I've suffered often enough from this sort of reiteration. But to repeat everything to a second Brunet.... No, not that. *'Chacun en a sa part et tous l'ont tout entier.'** Perhaps mothers can really divide their maternal love without weakening it; but I'm not a mother. And besides, all have it in full – I'm sure that's a hoax. They're boasting once again.

Moreover, I have already taken the insane risk of creating a human being, and this human being, in my opinion, is a success. I love him, I think he's fond of me, I have never had any fault to find with him, he enjoys my company and I enjoy his; that sort of miracle doesn't happen twice.

There are powerful reasons why a woman should marry. For a man there are none: he does it out of gregariousness. (And it is therefore natural enough for the law to give men a better position in marriage than women.) 'But then, why do men marry?' I once asked the Abbé Mugnier. His answer was: 'Out of a taste for disaster.' Yes, it really is a love of risk, of danger, the dark and unhealthy attraction of trouble, which drives the male to bring this hornets' nest about his ears. If he jibs in the slightest, people accuse him of 'cowardice' – cowardice in this case being synonymous with that form of intelligence known as the instinct of self-preservation.

Truly it is an urge towards tragedy that makes me contemplate marrying her....

But no! I am seeking excuses in order to disguise from myself the only motive that inspires me, and that is charity.

---

*Each has its share, and all have it in full. See footnote, p. 156 (*Translator's note*).

13 August – When you are waiting for a woman you very much desire, when she is an hour and a half late and you have given her up, and then she rings the door-bell, your first impulse is not one of joy but of annoyance. Your imagination had gone off in another direction, and had got used to it, and this sudden reversal is disconcerting at first.

I don't know whether I was awaiting S. very passionately, but when, half an hour after the appointed time, she has still not arrived, I hope something may have happened – some revulsion on the part of her mother? – which will prevent her from ever coming again.

Here she is. I go over the same old arguments again:

'By not marrying you I shall be safeguarding our love. Marriage is the end of love – as has been known ever since Methuselah. I should grow tired of you. You would get in my way. You would see me at my worst. Good-bye to rapture. Whereas in a love affair there's none of all that, or very little. What difference would marriage make to you? Children? You know in any case that I won't let you have any. Material interests in common? Well, honestly, do you need that? Being together all the time? But that's precisely what would undermine our love. In a love affair, each of us retains his freedom. Love is not bound by a code. Loving you is not a conjugal 'duty'. Seeing you is not an obligation but a pleasure. And the secrecy in which our relationship is wrapped makes it all the warmer – that too has been known ever since Methuselah. . . .'

I tell her all this, but what's the use? Her mind is made up.

Girls entangle you in the spider's web of marriage. Whores wear you down with their demands for money. And respectable women give you a dose of c. . . .

14 August – On waking up this morning it seems to me as though all the reasons 'against' have sunk to the bottom like lees in a liquid; I can find nothing but reasons 'for'. Decide to marry her. Then, halfway through the day (four o'clock), a sudden decision not to. Is this the beginning of a stable attitude? Await her arrival with boredom.

(Later) The smell of her eyelids. Her skin, as soft as flour. During our love-making, that succession of deaths and resurrections, she is like a string being plucked and then allowed to slacken. Lay beside her for a long time, filled with tenderness, and loving her. Her hair, which always comes undone at the same time – ten minutes past midnight – as though to remind us that it will soon be time for her to leave. Then, when she goes to the bathroom, I am on the point of telling her not to give herself a douche. If I get her with child, well, that will settle the matter.

The unforgettable look in her eyes as she leaves – standing upright in front of me like a little soldier. 'You cannot possibly be false with a look like that.' 'I am not false.'

I asked her what she would do if I told her categorically that I should never marry her. At first she did not reply. Then, after struggling a little, something the gist of which seemed to be that she hadn't considered such a possibility. Her confidence irritates me a little. Nevertheless, determined to marry her.

Costals thought about the marriage only for a few moments each day – on waking – and then dismissed it from his mind, as though laying down a too heavy burden, postponing a decision one way or the other. Having a horror of action that amounted to a philosophy, he acted only when pushed to the limit. It was also a matter of principle with him to put off painful decisions, not out of weakness of character but because he wanted to allow for the possibility that the circumstances might change and he would no longer have to decide. Moreover he knew that apprehension makes people vulnerable to whatever it is they apprehend. This policy had always stood him in good stead.

Two days after he had noted in his diary: 'Nevertheless, determined to marry her,' he suddenly thought of writing a long letter to Mme Dandillot explaining the reasons why he would not marry her daughter. This corrective measure seemed to him appropriate; he had come to feel a certain sympathy for this woman in the cruel suspense from which she must be suffering because of him. Moreover, he wondered whether she might not take him at his word. With what impatience he would await her reply acknowledging that 'under the circumstances, perhaps....' Or simply a reply in which he might detect a certain insolence, which would allow him to break it off there and then.

Costals wrote this letter with much gravity and a touch of complacency. An excellent way of spending the feast of the Assumption.

Pierre Costals   to Madame Ch. Dandillot
Paris   *Paris*

15 August 1927
Dear Madame,

I am writing to you from an empty flat in a deserted building, looking out on an avenue in which there is not a car, not a passer-by, not a sound; I had almost said not a cat, but in fact there is one, and very nice he is, with his tail as straight as a ramrod. I feel that if you are in Paris today, and Solange too – at a time when the ordeal you have just been through makes a rest and a change of scene more than usually necessary for both of you – it is partly my fault. And many other things are also my fault. It is for this reason that I feel moved to speak to you at some length, with deepened sympathy; to explain myself to you; and to ask you also to understand and forgive me.

If I write you this letter instead of coming to see you, it is not only because, as a writer, the form of expression that betrays me least is writing, so that with this letter you will have a very *precise* testimony to my feelings. It is because I feel sufficiently secure, as far as my conscience is concerned, to want you to possess, against whatever contingency may arise, this document signed by my hand.

Do not be surprised if the feelings I am about to describe sometimes seem strange to you. I am indeed strange. Far from priding myself on it, I have always sought to smooth the sharp edges of my nature, to emphasize whatever brings me closer to my fellow-creatures rather than what separates me

from them, just as I seek to pass unnoticed in my private life.
As a novelist, God knows the efforts I sometimes have to make
to imagine the feelings of the ordinary run of humanity, feelings
of which I have little spontaneous experience. However, I have
never suffered from this singularity of mine until this moment,
when I find myself suffering from it for the first time.

This marriage must not take place.

* * *

I can see what would happen as though it had already
occurred, as though *I were remembering it*. I can see it because
I know myself, because I have a long and subtle experience of
myself and of my relations with other people, because I have
always had a premonition of how I would react in any given
circumstances and how, for instance, if I tried to go against
my nature, nothing but disaster could come of it. It is as
though it were not so much my soul as my constitution which
rejects certain things to which it is ill-adapted. (When I went
to Indo-China, I knew in advance that I should fall ill there
because of my reluctance to go; and indeed I did fall ill. I
could give you a dozen other examples of the same kind. . . .)
The satisfaction of duty done? As far as I am concerned, it
would be more suitable to talk of the satisfaction of duty
left undone.

This is what would happen if I married Solange. From the
very beginning, the moral obligations which her tenderness and
devotion would create for me would destroy whatever pleasure
I might derive from that tenderness and whatever comfort I
might derive from that devotion. I should be anxious about
what she thought and what she felt. I should be afraid all the
time that I was not giving her enough. I should be afraid of the
harm I might do to her and that she might do to me. I should
have to reckon with her, and an artist ought not to have to
reckon with anything except his work. She would blunt some
of my strength, and rob me of my concentration. I should have
no right to complain, and yet she would be a nuisance to me,
and a source of weakness. I should feel that she was giving
herself entirely to me, and I should be unable to give myself

entirely to her. I should be unhappy, whereas in my solitude I have never been anything but happy. As for her, living with a man who was pining away, how could she herself be happy?

The outcome? Divorce. But divorce from someone with whom one has no fault to find? How could I reject a young creature who is all sweetness, affection and good will? 'Go away! You've done nothing wrong. Your only crime is existing, and loving me. But your presence weighs me down, and your love imprisons me. Take your things away, I'm giving you your notice. You can sort things out with your mother.' No, that I shall never say. Why pretend that circumstances could arise in which I might say it and she might accept it? To do so would be to build on sand – deliberately.

What then? We would remain stuck to each other, gnawing away at each other, like the two damned souls in Dante's *Inferno* – an infernal tête-à-tête until the bitter end.

Another reason, a minor one in the eyes of the world, but not in mine. I am a volatile creature: I like people, I like possessing them, I have them in my blood. It is inevitable that a time will come when I shall desire other women. What then? Secrecy, constant lies, squalid deceptions with someone you love and who loves you? I shut my eyes and see that girl and imagine myself 'double-crossing' her. No, that too is out of the question. What remains? Collusion? With certain women, perhaps: not with her. But the fact remains that I shall want other women. Not after months or weeks of marriage. Not after a few days of marriage. The day after. The very day. 'But you must fight against it ...' I do not fight against what I desire.

This marriage must not take place.

The future also must remain open to us.

*　*　*

Two solutions. The commonplace solution, the lazy solution: never to see each other again. If you should choose that, I shall leave for Morocco, and you will be rid of me for ever.

But in that case Solange must know the tenderness of the affection I feel for her, must know that she will always remain for me a memory undimmed by any clouds other than those I myself created, must know that this tenderness has never been stronger than at the moment when I conceive of cutting myself off from her, and that it is precisely the strength and constancy of this affection which compels me to bring about this rupture, since without them I should have no scruples about giving her less than she gives me, or lying to her, or divorcing her.

The alternative solution is less bourgeois. But you yourself have shown me, Madame, by being prepared to accept a marriage as bizarre as that which we have contemplated, that you have no hesitation in leaving the beaten track when your daughter's happiness is at stake. This solution is that Solange and I simply continue as before, but without the slightest intention of marriage.

Let us not talk about 'social conventions'. What is at stake? Once more, your daughter's happiness. One does not talk in terms of social conventions when one's daughter's happiness is at stake. Let us be realistic. Your daughter finds pleasure in contact with me, and I in contact with her. Must we forgo this pleasure on the pretext that we are not going to marry? Personally, such an attitude seems to me worthy of the Ice Age. Is there no middle way between estrangement and marriage, those idiotic solutions? Whatever is human is made up of all sorts of complexities and nuances. So, the *status quo*, with a new arrangement in the practical sphere to guard against gossip: she will come to me, but we shall no longer meet out, in Paris at least; and I shall never again mention her name in public. Morally and materially I shall give her everything, as in marriage; but outside marriage. In fact I shall be giving her much more than if we were married. For the feeling I have for her, which, when I see marriage ahead of me, advances painfully since it is aiming towards castastrophe and knows that it must decay and eventually be shattered, leaps forward and expands freely as soon as the prospect of marriage is dispelled and no more obstacles stand in its way.

I remain, etc. . . .

Costals

Next day, at a quarter past eleven, the telephone rang, and the somewhat raucous voice of Mme Dandillot asked if Costals was there. 'No, I'm not here,' Costals was on the point of answering: symbolic words, for indeed he never was (morally or intellectually) where people expected him to be. 'Speaking,' he said in a weak voice, but silently he exclaimed: 'Hurray! She's going to blow me up.'

'My dear sir, I was extremely touched by your letter, which was so honest and straightforward. But the matter is too important for us to go into in writing. Will you come and have tea with me this afternoon at five o'clock? We shall be alone.' 'Hum, five o'clock, I'm engaged,' said Costals: his first impulse being always to dodge – it was second nature with him. Then he changed his mind and accepted: just as well to get it over. He hung up, and at the same time hung up the idea of marriage, as one hangs a coat on a peg. Since they would be chewing it over for two hours that evening, he could well give it a rest in the meantime.

Every death is an occasion for renewal: out of the corpse spring pungent flowers. M. Dandillot's death, coinciding with these marriage plans, meant that everything in the Dandillot household for the past three weeks had tended towards the future. The dead man's room had been disinfected, all the paraphernalia of disease cleared away, as though no one would ever fall ill again between those walls, the windows everywhere thrown wide open, after being kept shut against noise for weeks. And, Solange having repeated some remarks of Costals' on the insane obsession of the French – much derided by foreigners – for cluttering their interiors with bric-à-brac, no small quantity of junk had been disposed of.

Mme Dandillot's soul had undergone a similar airing – a desire to slough off the old skin. If she had weighed heavily on her husband, he too had weighed heavily on her. The thought that her daughter was in love, then the certainty that this beloved child spent every other night in the arms of a man, had reawakened and rejuvenated Mme Dandillot, who was then in her fifty-second year, a difficult age for a woman. The vague yearnings that possessed her were not in the least directed towards men; they represented no more than a feeling that as soon as her mourning was over she would do some of the things she had never done, would 'get about a bit', travel, in fact would become what people call 'emancipated' – in other words look after her own happiness for a change.

Meanwhile, in the middle of August, the two women were still in Paris. Mme Dandillot might have had to stay there in any case, because of the lawyers she had to see about her husband's estate. Solange, however, could have gone to stay with friends at Etretat. But apart from the fact that it would have been difficult if not impossible for Costals to see her there without giving rise to gossip, the latter had refused to leave Paris. 'It's the only time my friends and relations are not here, and I can have some peace and quiet.' He did not much miss the beauties of nature. The older he grew, the less susceptible he was to nature and the more susceptible he was to people, or to himself. 'I don't object to a tree here and there, but I don't feel the need for a whole eyeful. As for the sea with its idiotic surface, crinkled like an elephant's behind, I don't want to hear of it at any price. I have more interesting things inside myself.'

In these circumstances, Mme Dandillot had been touched by the writer's letter. Its somewhat brutal frankness had shaken her, but without annoying her – on the contrary. The words 'with deepened sympathy' had not escaped her. Strange as it may seem, Costals' arguments had glided over her without making the slightest impression. And she awaited their conversation with a feeling of great serenity.

Costals had a hang-dog look about him as he rang the bell. However much he indulged himself in the avoidance of boring duties (he almost never did anything that cost him any effort), whenever he was forced into it the slightest thing crushed him, took on catastrophic proportions in his mind.

They began by beating about the bush in a state of mutual embarrassment. In the extravagant desire to gratify him which she shared with Solange, Mme Dandillot, who had understood from a remark of her daughter's that he was infatuated with Italy, observed incidentally that he was 'rather Italian looking', which was pure fantasy. Finally the tone changed, and at once things livened up as our hero leapt out of his trench without even a glance over his shoulder.

He repeated all the arguments he had gone over so often with Solange since the day at Bagatelle. Mme Dandillot listened with affectionate sympathy, almost with amusement. No, no, dear reader, set your mind at rest! Mme Dandillot is not going to fall in love with Costals. But after weeks and weeks spent looking after a dying man, then visiting one lawyer after another, it gave her an agreeable feeling to see a lively young man in this renovated flat; in this drawing-room where she had so often been snubbed by her son, had so often felt herself despised by her husband, socially and intellectually her superior (and class distinctions exist even within families), she enjoyed being spoken to by a distinguished celebrity in this tone of respectful inexperience, enjoyed hearing him talk such charming nonsense on a subject which she flattered herself she knew so much about.

And which she did indeed know about. She was well aware of what a normal marriage amounts to (there are admirable exceptions, of course): the classic music-hall duet, Nénette and Rintintin. 'What did I feel when I got married?' M. Dandillot had once replied – to someone who was not even a friend. 'Nothing. But a woman who brings you four hundred thousand francs is worth catching. I didn't love her, but I told myself that it might come with habit.' It had not come. After the first three weeks of marriage Rintintin had never again kissed Nénette on the mouth. From the outset he had made her feel his superiority. 'He loves me!' she used to think in the early days when he told her she was an idiot. Soon she began to take his remarks – 'You're off your head!' or 'What? You must be mad!' or 'How boring you are!' – at their face value. She hoped that the birth of Gaston would bring them together. Nothing of the kind. Rintintin refused at first to kiss the newly hatched infant (might not the latter's odious character as a child and as a young man have arisen from this sort of parental malediction? Mme Dandillot believed so), and could not bring himself to do so until a week later, with repugnance and dread, and blushing profusely. He did not like his son, although he was devoted to the boys in his sports clubs – perhaps because with his son this formidable egotist felt that his responsibility was engaged and that he had duties towards him, whereas with other people's sons.... Besides, it was not them he liked but his theories, which they were supposed to illustrate. Nénette buried herself in her household chores and hobbies, absorbed in the running of a big house with a garden, in the country. Truth to tell, she had little need of her husband's love (and even less, dear God, of the drudgery of sex, happily less and less frequent. Only when he told her that such and such a woman he had met was ravishing, or that he had been accosted by a street-walker in the rue Saint-Lazare, did she feel a faint gust of passion for him). All she wanted was to be 'understood'. Normally, when a woman complains of not being 'understood', it is because she is not loved at all, or because the man she loves does not return her love in due proportion. For Mme Dandillot, being 'understood' was more modest: it meant that M. Dandillot should give credit where it was due, that he should not leave her with all the burdens and responsibilities (the children, the house) while retaining the right to complain (everything tiresome that occurred was Nénette's fault – he treated her worse than the maid, which was logical enough since she could not hand in her notice), that he should take his nose out of his newspaper when she spoke to him, and that he should take an interest in something else besides the pentathlon, or 'natural' man, or whether it would rain on Sunday, in which case his cross-country race was done for.

When Solange – unwanted – was born, Rintintin, this time, did not go to see Nénette for two days, and left her crying alone in her bed: he was punishing her for his own clumsiness. There was no longer any question of a new child bringing them together. 'Anyhow,' she thought, 'I shall no longer be alone. If those spiteful beasts' (her husband and her son) 'make me suffer, I shall have one consolation at least.' And Solange was indeed in every respect a consolation. Besides which, as he approached his fifties, Rintintin began to realize that he had wasted his life, and grew embittered, and his wife, sensing this, took a leaf out of his book. It was her turn to make wounding remarks, to create scenes, which always had the same finale: she would break them off brusquely by going up to bed (at two o'clock in the afternoon), and did not re-appear. She was making up for twenty-five years of restraint when she was beastly to him. At certain moments of crisis she would go so far as to burn a newspaper that M. Dandillot had touched, or wash her hands with soap and water after he had shaken hands with her, or hesitate before kissing Gaston because he had just kissed his father. When he died, she would have liked to shed a few tears, but she could not manage it.

Such was Mme Dandillot's personal experience of marriage, at a time when she desired the union of her daughter with Costals to the point of submitting to almost any humiliation to ensure that it took place. Costals' intellectual superiority over Solange, his egotism, his eccentricities, the gap in age, their different attitudes to life, Solange's quasi-frigidity: all these circumstances were very similar to those which had clouded her own marriage. But it never occurred to her that anything but happiness could come of it. She was sincere in the apologia for marriage she was about to make to Costals, as sincere as one of those sublime fathers who say of their sons, if the head-master of the boarding-school informs them of some 'distress-ing' episode: 'I'd prefer him to be dead than to think he had such habits as that!' when they themselves at school were notorious little monsters. The irresponsibility of young people who marry is excusable. But what are we to think of the irres-ponsibility of those who encourage them to marry and who know, or should know, better? It is as though the urge to marry were as much a basic human instinct as the urge to copulate.

Mme Dandillot interrupted Costals' reasoning from time to time. She was full of arguments which carried little weight, and did not even conceive of those – numerous enough, after all – which might have shaken him. Costals spoke of the exigencies of his work, without false modesty, like a man who knows he has the upper hand.

'What work of art could be purer than a simple human

heartbeat?' said Mme Dandillot. 'Besides, that solitude of yours is no life at all. Marry, and at least you'll have warmth and good food and light and noise around you, and of course a few anxieties – life can't exist without them, but at least it will be life.'

'Noise!' thought Costals. 'So that's what they want. Their frightful inner poverty demands "noise" and not solitude: otherwise they would become conscious of their emptiness. They think I'm unhappy because I'm alone. "Good cooking"! They think their abject idea of happiness is the same as mine. And they think my life is no life at all!'

Mme Dandillot must indeed have thought that Costals' life was no life at all, for she went on about it, with many a jeer at old bachelors. Yet there are bachelors and bachelors, and it is comic to hear people harping on the 'solitude' of some of them, when this 'solitude' is peopled with ravishing creatures in a way that marriage can never be; there are ways of being married in celibacy, as there are ways of being celibate in matrimony. As for the attitude which sees the old age of a Flaubert, a Baudelaire or a Nietzsche in terms of bachelordom, it had best be forgotten.

Naturally she trotted out the cliché about 'companionship', and the cliché 'Someone to look after you when you're old', and then the even hoarier one about 'doing what everyone else does'.

'Surely you're not afraid of a bit of discipline? You've always been your own master, followed your own inclinations, but some day you'll have to go the way of all flesh. If you don't marry, you'll end up hankering for hearth and home when it's too late. Seeing some nice little bank-clerk on his way home to his wife and family and a hot supper, you'll sigh: "If only I were he!"'

Costals thought of Schiller's remark (in *Joan of Arc*): 'The gods themselves are powerless against stupidity.' He had once quoted this in an article for an evening paper. The article had been published *in extenso* except for the aforesaid quotation, which had been cut. One must never speak ill of stupidity in a French newspaper.

Then this respectable bourgeoise proceeded resolutely to

boost the virtues of her daughter, like a slave-trader his negress
or a horse-dealer his filly.

'She's utterly straightforward.' (Costals wondered whether
to be pleased or displeased that she should be utterly straightforward.) 'She's very neat and tidy; she'll keep your things in
order.' ('What's the point of having servants?') 'She doesn't
care about luxury. Oh no, she's not the sort who'll cost you
a fortune in clothes. A motor-car? She said to me herself that
she didn't want one. She's told me dozens of times that her
vocation was to be subject to a man, like an oriental wife.'
('Yes, when she's dug herself in.') 'She'll help you. She's no
fool, you know. She'll type your manuscripts....'

'She'll go and see your publishers for you, and as she's,
ahem, pretty, she'll get you some splendid contracts,' Costals
finished off for her, sourly. The friendly feelings he had had
for this woman the day before were melting away like snow
in the sun. And the fact that Solange could be so intimate with
her relegated the girl to a remote corner of his estimation.
And tomorrow Mme Dandillot would have rights over him –
the right to ask him to show her his accounts, the right to
know all about his life, the right to enter his house any time
she liked and poke about among his things. (His eyes fell on
her very unfeminine hands with their prominent veins, gnarled
hands like the claws of a bird of prey.) He remembered the
title of a novel that had just appeared : *Strangers in My House*.
'One family is already too much for me, and now I've got to
have two! If one simply married an individual, well and good.
But one has to marry a whole flock of strangers, the obscene
tribe of mothers and fathers, sisters and brothers, uncles and
aunts and cousins, who also have rights over you, if only, to
put it at its best, the right to waste your time. No, society is
mad. The whole thing is monstrous. If I had to marry at any
cost (if the law were to compel me to) I would ask for a girl
from the Public Assistance. Seriously.'

Costals proceeded to talk about the 'heaviness' of women.
He recalled an incident that seemed to have made a deep
impression on him : one day he was alone in a canoe not far
from the shore when suddenly the frail craft seemed to have
become weighed down, he had to paddle furiously, it was as

though the boat were paralysed by some evil spell. Then he
heard a laugh: a swimmer was clinging to the stern, being
dragged along behind, and this swimmer was a woman he
loved.... Another time, he had seen a frog coupling with a
fish and holding it clasped between her legs for a whole day
until the fish suffocated to death....

Costals made such a funny face – so horrified – as he told
these stories that Mme Dandillot thought him 'too sweet': the
language of the shop-girl seemed to come naturally to her.

'So you're as frightened of women as that?' she asked with
a rather triumphant air. Costals would have liked to point out
that the strongest of the strong can lose the fight because of
a speck of dust in his eye, that the lion justly fears the
mosquito, and that 'dead flies cause the ointment of the
apothecary to stink', as the Scripture says. But it is not easy to
say such things in drawing-rooms, even a drawing-room with
a dancing faun in imitation bronze, duly fig-leaved, and a palm
decked out in pink ribbon like a pug-dog; in a word, a
drawing-room much like a dentist's waiting-room, the only
difference being that you are waiting to be married instead of
waiting to have a tooth pulled out. But this difference, our
hero thought to himself, is negligible.

'Let's get down to brass tacks,' Mme Dandillot said at last.

She told him what she would agree to. What did she agree
to? Everything. She agreed that the wedding should take place
in the country, in total privacy except for the four witnesses.
She agreed to separate maintenance: she would give Solange
an annual allowance, and would settle a dowry on her only
after a few years, when the marriage seemed solidly based.
('She'll have stopped paying the allowance long before that,
and the whole thing will end up with solicitors' letters',
thought Costals.) She agreed that there should be only a civil
ceremony; they could go through a church ceremony later,
when the marriage had shown signs of lasting. 'There's no
point in dragging the Church into a travesty of matrimony.'
At these words, Costals gave a start: they were the very
words Solange had written to him. Had the letter been inspired,
dictated perhaps, by Mme Dandillot (in which case Solange
had lied in protesting the contrary)? Or had the daughter, like

a child, simply repeated something she had overheard at home? And once again Costals was revolted by this despicable conception of Catholicism. 'The religion of Europeans is worse than no religion at all.' He could not resist pouncing on it.

'My dear sir, I hardly expected after reading your books to receive lessons in religion from *you*,' said Mme Dandillot, pursing her peasant's mouth. She was one of those women who make you laugh when they put on a severe look and whose laughter gives you the shivers. She did not feel in the least shocked, but judged it only proper, since religion was at stake, to look as though she was. The Church serves as a pretext for the worldly, just as Jesus Christ serves as a pretext for the Church.

It was Costals' turn to protest a bit, but he at least was sincere:

'If I prided myself on being a Catholic, I should be a proper one. And if the Pope offered me a cardinal's hat, as he did to M. de Turenne, who had no better title to it than I have, I should accept it gladly. I say it without boasting: I'm sure I'd make an excellent cardinal.'

There was a noise of a hen laying an egg – a strange thing in the avenue de Villiers. It was Mme Dandillot laughing. She put her hand in front of her mouth when she laughed, as little girls do. She did not understand that Costals had spoken seriously, and that if he had entered the Church he would have been as stout a prelate as the Borgia Alexander VI, who was a bit dubious as regards morals, but never wavered an inch as regards dogma.

The good lady opined that, the civil ceremony completed, they could later, on the way through some out-of-the-way spot, get themselves blessed by the local *curé*, just like that; they could let him think they were already joined according to the rites of the Church, but that an extra benediction would be a comfort to them. Thus they would be able to announce in the *Figaro* that 'the couple were blessed by M. *le curé* of ...' etc., without lying. Costals recognized in this suggestion the true genius of the upper middle class.

He asked for a little more time to think about it. Mme Dandillot agreed with alacrity. If Costals felt he was on a

slippery slope, so, too, was she: the slope of infinite complaisance. 'What a lack of pride!' he thought. But, after all,
there is really no difference between people who are proud and
people who are not, since the proud pocket exactly the same
number of insults as the rest. There are no proud people; there
are people who talk about their pride, and those who do not.

He said he wanted to think it over. In reality, he wanted
to consult his lawyer on a point which he had not dared to
raise with Mme Dandillot: how a man can get a divorce if
his wife refuses to give him one and is guiltless? For Solange
had emerged from this conversation intact. She had even
survived maternal assistance. She still held firm in him.

Outside: 'Well, all this is very odd. Am I dreaming? What
a business!' He felt as though he had got into a train to say
good-bye to a friend, and the train had started up without
warning and was now bearing him off to some unknown
destination.

Women were wont to say of Maître Dubouchet that he had
a disagreeable look. This is what they say of a man if he looks
grave, or dignified, or just serious. Maître Dubouchet was a
Pyrrhonist who took the utmost pains to look serious; such
an effort is essential in the law-courts; without it, everyone
would burst out laughing. Dubouchet compensated for this
effort by making the most of the voluptuous pleasures of the
court-room. To be able to bellow and fume and choke and
mop one's brow and insult and weep and throw oneself around
as though one had St Vitus's Dance, with a view to proving
the innocence of an individual who has already admitted his
guilt to you; to twist facts and falsify documents, to make
fun of the victim, to crack jokes at the expense of witnesses
– all this with the approbation, nay (here a flourishing of
sleeves) nay, the enthusiastic approbation of society – is worth
a few sacrifices to a man whose whole philosophy is based on
the spirit of derision. Bald, glabrous, with a noble jowl and
gold-rimmed spectacles, Dubouchet had the air of a thinker
who does not think – a serious betrayal of Pyrrhonism, which

deserves better than that. All this is nevertheless to imply that his appearance was nothing if not respectable, except of course when he was threading his way through the trams in the boulevard du Palais, dressed in black peplum and bib, not to mention his decorations. Dubouchet was unpopular, because he had a little too much money, and showed it. And anyone with money is a monster to those without it.

'The hero of my novel,' Costals was saying to him, 'is a sort of idiot who allows himself to be dragged into marriage out of charity for the young lady. After a time he sees that the marriage is obviously harmful to what he calls his opus – I forgot to tell you that my idiot was a literary idiot. He wants a divorce. But he has married an absolute nincompoop of a girl who has no desire to be unfaithful to him, has given him no cause for complaint, and refuses to divorce.'

'I'm afraid there's nothing to be done for your literary idiot if the wife is guiltless and refuses a divorce. Divorce under those circumstances is impossible. They could live apart, but they would still be married.'

'Come, come, Maître Dubouchet! You're not going to tell me there's such a thing in France as a restriction that can't be got round! My so ... my young cousin told me one day that a school-friend of his to whom he had remarked: "I wonder what parents are for?" had answered in a flash: "To be lied to, of course." The same might be said about laws: what are they for, if not for people to sharpen their wits on?'

'Of course there might be a way ... rather an improbable one, but since we're dealing with a novel.... A divorce is granted if the husband can produce in court some document which provides a strong supposition of the wife's infidelity; for example, a letter in which the wife told the husband that she had "had enough of this existence, that it cannot go on, etc." would suggest that her affections are engaged elsewhere. Your idiot could ask the girl, when they're engaged, to write such a letter, which he would keep in his possession and simply put in the post as soon as he had had enough. But is it likely that a fiancée would consent to write that sort of billet-doux? She'd have to be devilish keen to get married, and personally, I should have some qualms about the character of the young lady in question. But perhaps your heroine is like that?'

'Whichever way it is,' thought Costals, 'whether it's love or a frantic desire to see the thing through, she'll write the letter. I can't see her jibbing at an extra genuflection. What will she think? Probably what is in fact the case: that I love my destiny more than I love her. Once again I shall have put her in the position of knowing where she stands; which is to say that I shall have behaved honestly towards her.'

'Is it a parachute that opens or a parachute that fails to open?' he asked.

'In the normal course of events, it should open.'

'In that case, will you be so kind as to draft such a letter for me. And please weigh your words carefully. I want my idiot to land safe and sound in the luscious meadows of freedom regained.'

'Have you a fountain-pen? I'll dictate. "Dear friend . . ." No, don't let's put "dear friend". Let's begin *ex abrupto*: "If I write this to you it is because in your presence . . ." '

' ". . . I feel I scarcely exist." Perfect, you've hit the right note straight away. Leave a space and I'll fill it in: etcetera, etcetera. And then?'

' "We must face the fact that our experiment has failed. It is true that you always warned me that I should have to take second place in our life, after your work. But I had no idea how that would turn out in reality. I realize now that I mean nothing to you, and . . . and . . ." '

' ". . . and, although you try to conceal it from me, with that generosity which I have always admired in you . . ." Forgive me, I'm so used to drafting articles about myself that flattering epithets come naturally to me – it's an irresistible tic . . . "you cannot help showing it, because of your natural irritability, with an unconcious cruelty which often stabs me to the heart." I've spelt *unconscious* wrong, because the young woman is supposed to be in the throes of passion. Besides, one of her principal endowments is not being able to spell.'

'New paragraph', said Dubouchet.

'No, in the throes of passion one doesn't make new paragraphs.'

' "I confess that I can no longer endure this life in which, in order to be a writer's wife, I must cease to be a wife at all." '

'That's too good – people would think at once that I had written it. But leave it : I'll make gibberish of it. Now what we need is for her to insult him a bit. How about this? "You have always thought that my presence would eventually be a burden to you, but I did not imagine that yours would become such a burden to me...." '

'And now the crucial sentence : "... or that I might one day contemplate a life in which the presence of someone other than you would be capable of making me happy. Do not answer this letter. My sole object in writing it is to ensure that you are not taken unawares if what you no doubt wish for were to come about." '

'Do you think that will do?' asked Costals, with the expression of an aeroplane passenger glancing at the frail form of his parachute in its bag.

'If that doesn't work, nothing will.'

'Wait,' said Costals. 'I must sprinkle it with a few womanly spangles.' He put three dots at the end of every other sentence, and an exclamation mark at the end of each of the others. He concluded the final sentence with: 'So there!' Dubouchet laughed.

'Congratulations on the "So there!" It's quite true, when a woman doesn't know how to put her meaning into words, or simply when she has nothing to say at all, she puts "So there!" There are infinite depths in that "So there!" '

'Allow me to disagree. In my opinion, women write "So there!" when they are particularly proud of having succeeded in expressing what they think or feel. "So there!" is a shout of triumph analogous to the cluck ... cluck ... cluck ... of the hen that has just laid an egg, and at the same time a childish challenge : "That's what I think, do you hear? Full stop. That's that." '

They argued the point a bit, but both were agreed that, however one looked at it, 'So there!' was pregnant with the *unfathomable mystery of the fair sex.* The *bewitching smile,* etc., etc., of the eternal Sphinx, etc., glowed adorably, etc., etc., on the face of 'So there!'

Before parting company, they gurgled a bit longer over their superiority, real or illusory:

'So you too,' said Costals, 'refuse to believe in the unfathomable mystery of womanhood? It's funny, all men, when they talk about it in private, are of the same opinion: there isn't a grain of mystery in women. But if they have to write about women, or speak about them in public, in other words if they have to express themselves officially on the subject, they all trot out the same old dithyramb about *mysterious Eve*. I suspect that on these occasions, acting as social animals, they unconsciously assume the role of heralds and recruiting sergeants for the species. Obviously the species requires women to be overestimated. Where should we be if men began to see women simply for what they are? As I see it, just as man does not desire woman because he finds her beautiful, but proclaims her beautiful in order to justify his desire, in the same way he does not idealize woman because he finds her "mysterious", but proclaims her "mysterious" in order to justify his ideal, an ideal which society, far more than nature, inculcates by every possible means with a view to propagating the species!'

'For thirty years, women have been coming to see me in these chambers, and these are women at the moment of making a clean breast of things. Well, I can tell you, a perceptive man can read the mind of any woman like an open book. He can see all her feelings stirring inside her, like fish behind the glass walls of an aquarium. But however much even the most perceptive woman may hang around the male, watching him furtively, listening at doors, he remains impenetrable to her. One proof of this is the fact that however feebly drawn female characters may sometimes be in novels written by men, they are never as grotesquely feeble as male characters created by lady-novelists.'

They went on gurgling a bit longer, but enough is enough. Whatever the truth may be, whether or not there is a mystery about women, there is certainly a mystery about men. The mystery about men is how women can ever love them.

A quarter of an hour later, back in his flat. A sudden shift from the sordid to the ethereal, from juridico-burlesque foxiness to the head of this woman thrown back in abandon and her love-tormented face.

Afterwards:

'I've seen my lawyer, and he said to me: "There is one way in which your hero might escape" (I pretended it had to do with the hero of a novel I'm writing) "if the experiment fails. But your heroine would have to be a girl who loved him deeply and trusted him implicitly, the kind of girl you never come across nowadays, a virgin of antiquity, a Corneille heroine. Is that what she's like in your book?" I told him that although the girl in my book was not strictly a Corneille heroine, there was nothing grand and generous that she was not prepared to do. "Well then," he said, "this is the way." '

He explained the whole thing to her and showed her the letter. He felt a little ashamed, and as they were sitting in armchairs, he leant back in his so that she should not see his face at that moment, or perhaps so that he should not see hers. But she turned towards him with a smile:

'I get it: it's "on appro".'

'On appro?'

'When something's delivered to you which you've bought in a big store, and you no longer want it, you can send it back. That's what they call "on appro" – on approval.'

'What a sublime girl you are,' he said, touched that she should take it so calmly. 'I called it a parachute-letter; so now let's call it an appro-parachute. Do you love me enough, are you really Cornelian enough, to write me such a letter?'

'Yes,' she said in her composed voice.

'Thank you. You *are* a docile person, and that's how I like women to be. That's how I should like you to be always. I want you to be like a *cheich* to me. *Cheichs* are Arab scarves which can be folded in all sorts of ways and which you can do whatever you like with. The Arabs are never without them: their *cheichs* serve them alternately as scarves, hats, towels, ropes, veils, filters, bags, fly-whisks, belts, handkerchiefs, underpants, or pillows. I haven't brought you up to my level so that you should be anything else but me. I want you to be me, and nothing else. So that I shall never have occasion to mistrust you. So that I shall never grow tired of you.'

The draft of the letter lay on the table. 'I ought to get her to write it at once.' But although he had dared to take the first step, he did not dare take the second, his supply of effrontery having run out for the time being. It would recharge itself, but it needed a bit of time, as when men expend their vital fluid. Moreover, he had only his own note-paper there, or the typing paper on which he wrote his manuscripts, and these would be recognized as his by the court. What was needed was either her own, or any recognizably 'feminine' – i.e. flashy – note-paper. So they talked of other things.

He said to himself: 'Is she doing it out of love for me, or simply out of hippogriffic passion? Is she amorous or ambitious? In any case it doesn't matter; I'm not going to kill myself prospecting a human soul. If it's love, it's admirable, and it might almost make me decide to marry. If it's ambition, she's a monster, and it would be interesting to live with a monster.'

'Things are going well for you,' he said to her on the door-step.

Costals' Diary

23 *August* – The situation I've got myself into in the past five weeks is truly hellish: not loving her enough to take the plunge, but enough to suffer from not taking it. Yesterday, as we parted, I said to her: 'Things are going well for you.' When I woke up this morning everything was in the melting pot again. For five weeks, no peace of mind, no taste for anything. My life at once frittered away and blocked up. Every morning in a different mood, and at the mercy of the most trifling influence. If I go to the window and see a pretty face in the avenue, I cry: 'Abandon the pursuit of wenches? Oh, no, it's too frightful!' An item in a newspaper about a young peasant who in answer to the mayor's fateful question: 'Do you take this woman. . . ?' replies 'No,' thus, the reporter adds, 'avoiding the irreparable', reminds me of the extent to which 'universal wisdom' finds that it really is something irreparable. Now I am at the *no* stage. A moment later, I remember

something she said, or her plush rabbit, and I turn round and zoom back towards *yes*. This perpetual see-saw is killing me. My mood changes literally *from minute to minute*. One moment I'm frightened of her, of her mother, of all her family, of the whole horrible network; the next I'm puffed out like a spinnaker, thinking how happy I can make her. (I used to have mistresses to make *me* happy. I shall be taking a wife to make *her* happy. Tit for tat.) At the moment of writing, what I should like is to clear out without seeing her again, go to Morocco, spend three or four months there with my beloved Rhadidja, and on my return take Solange as my mistress, nothing more. The multiplicity and confusion of my desires and impulses, the speed with which they succeed one another, are such that I find it impossible to express them.

Whatever the final decision, doom is upon me for a long time to come. If I marry her, this doom is an absolute certainty. If I don't, I shall have regained my freedom but will always be plagued by remorse for having made her suffer, by the thought that I might have been happier with her, by an uneasy feeling, as long as she remains unmarried, that it is still not too late....

The train is carrying me off.... The same mixed feelings – apprehension and attraction – that I had in the train which carried me for the first time to the battlefront.

This is the most bourgeois of dramas. If I turned it into a novel, it would be appallingly dull and prosaic, without the slightest relief. It could not be otherwise, since it is in the nature of the nuptial tie to be sordid. The crisis of adolescence, the crisis of war (should I do the decent thing?), the crisis resulting from a surfeit of pleasure, the crisis arising from my duty to my work when all I wanted was to live, simply to live – all my crises have been in a sense honourable. But this one? This one is *Triplepatte*.* Precisely, I am Triplepatte. And yet this drama too has a certain nobility: on the one hand, because it is my work that I want to safeguard, and on the other because all the trouble arises from my reluctance

*A famous comedy by Tristan Bernard. Triplepatte is the personification of the man who cannot make up his mind (*Translator's note*).

to hurt Solange. This does not, however, lift it above the level of the sordid. The fact of marriage corrupts everything.

24 August – I want you to forget me and I want you not to forget me. When you are not tender, I am hurt; when you are, I think you calculating. Because you are placid I call you cold; if you were warm I should call you gushing. It is I who am the element of torment between us, and it has never been anything else but me.

I, whose only desire is to be like the close-cropped grass on which the cows lay their muzzles without grazing.

One always falls ill on a Sunday, when chemists are shut and doctors on the spree. One always needs urgent legal advice in August, when Paris is empty. Horrible August of 1927! In the Jardin des Plantes – one of the disgraces of France – the bear pads to and fro without a moment's respite, and the lion stands with lacklustre eyes swaying from paw to paw. Like these beasts that confinement and monomania have turned into neurotics, Costals too, cooped up in the cage of a love he does not feel, sways from side to side. Our swaggering hero, to put it bluntly, is now a poor devil who needs advice, who needs to be given a lead. That's what the idea of marriage has done to him! But why blame the emptiness of Paris for his failure to find people who might help him? His pride alone is to blame. Even if Paris were full, his plight would be the same. Expose his ridiculous situation to a friend or relation – never! Allow himself to be seen in this state, he who has always been so much his own master – never! Out of pride, he would rather commit an act of folly, perhaps irreparable, without involving anyone else, than avoid it by taking advice from someone he trusts. This marriage is only possible in one form: instantaneous marriage. At one go, as one gulps down a purgative.

However, at the end of the month he weakened. He felt such a need to discuss it all with someone, anyone.... To go and say to Maître Dubouchet: 'I've got a hero for a novel who ...' was no longer enough. He must say outright, to a man of experience, 'Look here, I'm contemplating getting married in such and such circumstances.... What do you advise?' And then, childishly, as believers confess to a priest because of the secrecy of the confessional and also because they believe him to be a kind and helpful man, Costals told himself that he must 'confess all' to Dubouchet, who would also be bound by professional secrecy, and was accustomed by his profession to 'lend an ear' to people's troubles. He struggled with himself, decided to telephone him, was delighted to find that the barrister was out till one, which gave him two hours' respite, telephoned again at one, to be told by the maid that Monsieur had gone away on holiday and would not be back for three weeks.

Loneliness closed round him again. At all costs he must break out of this circle! If a man of law confirmed that the parachute-letter would automatically get him a divorce, what risk would he be running? A few months of tribulation. He thought of his own solicitor, telephoned him, and made an appointment for five o'clock. Then remembered that his solicitor acted for the whole family, and if he were to hear in a few months' time that Costals had married, he would spread the story of the parachute-letter all over the place. Costals telephoned to cancel the appointment.

Then he remembered a lawyer whom he had button-holed in connection with some literary litigation, and who did not know his family. Telephone. The lawyer was on holiday. ('Always loafing around,' grumbled Costals, who spent the whole year on holiday.) But the head clerk could see him. Appointment.

Custom demands that the chambers of French solicitors should always be extremely dusty and ill-kept, as if thereby to guarantee the soundness of the firm and to warn one not to judge by appearances in these slum-sanctuaries. Maître S.'s chambers conformed to custom. In a wicker armchair, a relic, perhaps, of some third-rate boarding-house, where it had been worn down by the backsides of generations of governesses, Costals awaited his turn, glowing with humility.

The head clerk in Maître S.'s chambers, fifty-eight years old (fifty-four to the ladies), was repulsive from head to foot – or let's say from head to navel, for, sitting at his desk, he was visible only thus far. His hair was outrageously dyed and curled and heavily parted in the middle, his moustaches, also dyed, were turned up in the old style. Behind an ill-fitting steel-rimmed pince-nez, his eyes oscillated continually between petty tyranny and fear. His nose was repulsive, both bulbous and snub. His mouth was repulsive, warped at the edges, shiny and wet with kissings and suckings and lickings – a mouth doomed to cancer in three years; with a cigarette butt dangling from it. His flesh bulged over his collar, which was of celluloid, cracked at the corners. His chin had such dimples, my dear! There was a tie-pin stuck in the very knot of his tie. He was wearing two waistcoats (in August). He had a peevish, shifty, sidelong look, suggesting servility with superiors, ferocity with small fry, and cheap restaurants where people stuff the two remaining nuts in their pockets because nothing must be left, and where they furtively paw the waitresses and threaten to have them kicked out if they refuse to co-operate. He had the air of a minor official in a government office – one of those government offices no self-respecting person would be seen dead in.

Costals gave him the whole rigmarole about the hero of his novel and the parachute-letter. When he had finished, the fellow burst out laughing:

'The letter your barrister friend dictated to you belongs to the realm of fantasy. Far from being of any use to your character, it will tell against him. It's obvious that the wife, if she doesn't want the divorce, will make a clean breast of the whole thing and explain how the letter came to be written.'

'But wouldn't the court find it an improbable story?'

'They wouldn't find it improbable, because your hero is a literary man,' said the head clerk, who knew who he was dealing with. 'In any case, their suspicions would be aroused. They would institute an enquiry, from which it would emerge that the wife's putative lover does not exist and that the whole thing was fabricated in advance. Then the famous letter would be pronounced invalid, and the court would refuse to grant a divorce, if only to teach this too far-sighted husband a lesson. Indeed, the latter might well be charged with contempt of court. No, sir, with all due respect to your friend, the whole thing doesn't hold water. Imaginative, I grant you – barristers are never lacking in imagination. But otherwise. . . .'

Costals was shattered. If there was no emergency exit from the marriage, there could be no question of proceeding with it. And he looked at this wretched creature, who was nevertheless *the man in the know*, the man on whom the *yes* or *no* of his destiny hung, the *yes* or *no* of Solange's; he looked at him, and he felt very humble in front of him, humble and sad as a Friendly Society badge.

'But can I rely on what he says?' His doubts were justifiable, for there was no lack of errors in the head clerk's observations (it would be tedious to enumerate them). 'After having checked the barrister's statements with the solicitor's clerk, I now ought to check the solicitor's clerk with the solicitor himself. Then I should get Counsel's opinion on what the solicitor says. Oh, yes, we've got plenty of people to fall back on.' In the same way, the man who has just been told by Dr A. that he has cancer, goes on to consult Dr B., who tells him he is perfectly healthy. Then he rushes off to consult Dr C., who tells him it isn't cancer but TB. Such divergences are in all probability part of the harmony of nature: three thermometers on the walls of your room, consulted simultaneously, will never show the same temperature. 'Allah alone knows the truth.'

Then a strange thing happened: our hero, who was always more or less intoxicated with himself, always more or less of a firebrand, stooped to an unparalleled humiliation in his need for his problem to be taken seriously and for someone to come to his rescue: he put himself entirely into the hands of this unspeakable creature.

'Listen, monsieur, I might as well tell you the truth: the person concerned is not a character in a novel, it's me.'

The head clerk moved his pince-nez and stared at Costals.

'This letter business must seem to you in rather bad taste. But the young woman, I assure you, is beyond reproach. I imagine she agreed to it out of love for me; people are so strange! And the young woman's family, too, is an excellent one. The grandfather was a public prosecutor. The father was one of the founders of the Olympic Games, and a Commander of the Legion of Honour....'

The head clerk bowed slightly, as though to say: 'Congratulations. I see we're moving in the best circles.' In spite of his distress (the word is not too strong) the old Costals, Costals the rake, had been unable to suppress a secret smile on conferring the red ribbon on M. Dandillot.

'Mind you. I have no desire to get married,' continued the writer, to whom the very idea of marriage seemed so ridiculous that he could not help pleading extenuating circumstances, even in front of this shifty stranger. 'I'm doing it to please the young lady....'

'Beware!' the head clerk broke in severely. 'I tell you: beware! I consider that I should be failing in my duty if I didn't put you on your guard against a marriage undertaken in such conditions.'

'Ah, don't I know it! You've no need to tell me this marriage is sheer madness. I never stop telling the girl so. And that is precisely why the question of the efficacy of this letter is so important to me. Mark you, the young lady is prepared to make a solemn promise that she will agree to a divorce – by whatever farce we can think up – if she sees that such a life is unbearable to me.'

'Well, of course, any girl will make such a promise, *beforehand*. But *after*? ... Aren't you aware of the female talent for constantly going back on what has been settled?'

'Woman aren't all as bad as that,' said Costals, who disliked hearing women spoken ill of, as though he considered that his own special province.

'And don't you know the old adage: "All's fair in marriage"? There's no such thing as a marriage in which one of the partners hasn't been more or less unfaithful to the other. In this business the worst is possible, and without ever going beyond the bounds of perfect respectability.'

'Insolent swine!' thought Costals. 'Did I come here to listen to this? Those horrible maxims! I came here to be encouraged to marry.' He glanced at the chief clerk's ring-finger, and saw that, like Dubouchet, he was wearing a wedding ring. 'Ah, so they're all married! They speak from experience! Besides, one has only to look at them to see marriage written all over their faces.'

'So, no precaution is guaranteed effective. One has to set sail without a lifeboat.'

'No precaution is guaranteed effective. But wait, it's quite simple, I'll show you the Civil Code. . . .'

'Oh no, not that! If I put my nose into the Civil Code I'd go completely mad. I'm well on the way already: that's quite enough.'

'Moreover, believe me, it's always those who take most precautions who are the first to be gulled. Anyone who wants to get married should blindfold himself and dive in without a second thought.'

'Do you mind if I make a note of the information you've given me?'

'Not at all. Here's pen and paper.'

Costals jotted down: 'Repulsive from head to foot. Hair heavily parted. Eyes continually shifting between petty tyranny and fear. Wet, slobbery mouth. Flesh bulging over his celluloid collar.' He would put the character into one of his novels.

'Forgive me, I'm keeping you,' he said with genuine affability.

'Not at all! Take your time.'

Costals looked the man over once more, and noted: 'Hideous nose. Peevish, shifty look. Mouth doomed to cancer in three years. And such dimples on his chin, my dear!'

'Thank you. You're kindness itself. I don't know whether I shall follow your advice, but in any case as far as I'm concerned our short meeting won't have been a waste of time.' Then he left.

'Blindfold oneself, and dive straight in regardless,' he thought to himself. 'It's exactly as I said: instantaneous marriage.' What was the point of seeing these lawyers, who only tormented him? It was as though he only sought advice once his mind was made up. It was no use his summoning up every possible reason 'against' (seeking them even in Solange's face, her body, her way of making love); none of it made any difference; all that had been transcended; it was as though he had gone beyond the decision stage. It had come about by an imperceptible train of circumstance, as everything happens, as war happens: one wakes up to find oneself already embroiled. On 3 September he noted in his diary: 'It is absolutely incomprehensible why I am marrying her.' And on the 4th: 'The longer it goes on, the clearer the reasons for not marrying her appear to me to be. And yet it is more and more certain that I shall.'

Next day he was invited by Mme Dandillot to another prenuptial cup of tea.

The moment he entered the Dandillot drawing-room, Costals was struck by the smell of Virginia tobacco – to him rather repellent – which hung there, and he remembered something Solange had told him – that her mother did not smoke, except when her nerves were particularly on edge.

'I should say the situation looks fairly promising from your point of view,' he said forthwith. 'In fact, assuming that *the thing* is to happen, one might aim provisionally at October.' (He never pronounced the word *marriage* in her presence, partly because of the absurdity of the word and partly in the same spirit as certain primitive peoples are afraid to name their gods, and only refer to them periphrastically.) 'It could be done at Perros-Guirec, where I once had a shack. I shall have to find out if the two witnesses per partner can be reduced to one apiece.' (He had no idea whom he would ask to be his witness, appalled at the thought of being seen in such a grotesque situation by someone he respected.) 'You, for instance, if you absolutely insist on coming....' (He felt magnanimous, and entered the sacrifice he was making in the debit and credit account he was already keeping with the Dandillot family.) 'Do you think any inhabitant of Perros-Guirec would do as a witness for me? When I had to declare my father's death at the town hall, I went to the nearest bar to find a witness, and gave him a few francs....'

Mme Dandillot's face had lit up, exactly like a room when one switches on the light on entering. She had been so afraid he would say to her: 'My dear Madame Dandillot, we must drop the whole thing.' She at once began galloping into the future.

'Perros-Guirec is most amusing.... Afterwards, you can retire to some secluded little spot to hide your love.' (At the words 'hide your love', Costals shuddered; supposing he had loved Solange, they would have deflated his love on the spot, like a pin-prick in a balloon.) 'At the end of the month, you'll come back and settle in Paris.' ('So, she's giving the orders already?') 'During your absence I could find a flat for you.' (Costals, who had been looking for a flat non-stop for nine years without finding one that was strictly adapted to his needs, his fantasies and his idiosyncrasies, contemplated the abyss that separated him from Mme Dandillot, and indeed from the human race in general.) 'As you'll be on the system of separate maintenance, Solange will bring her own furniture.'

'Would they be things belonging to you, or things newly bought?' the writer anxiously inquired. Solange might want to bring the laughing faun. He would refuse to have it at any price. A first bone of contention. But not, alas, a ground for divorce.

'Everything would be new,' said Mme Dandillot, who had not forgotten Costals' remark about 'French bric-à-brac'. 'And besides, you could choose it with her. A man must have an interior that pleases him.'

'I shall wear a lounge suit at the Registrar's,' said Costals, who had forgotten this detail. Like all of his kind, though vague about the general picture, he was meticulous about trifles.

'I don't even think there's a law against your getting married in a soft collar,' said Mme Dandillot, laughing. Her face was exultant.

'Solange must have told you we agreed that I should have three months' conjugal holiday a year, during which I would go far away and relax.'

'Yes, so she said. At first I thought it a bit odd. But after all, lots of women are separated from their husbands for long periods. Naval officers' wives. . . .'

'And the sort of liveliness of imagination which prompts me

to strike up acquaintance with every attractive woman I
meet....'

'I'm broad-minded. I can well understand that a man, when
he's travelling, for instance.... But provided, of course, that
the dear child never gets to hear of it.'

'Adultery and deceit are lawful and commendable!' Costals
thought to himself. God knows, he liked easy-going mothers.
But at this moment he felt a bit disgusted.

'There remains one very important point; that Solange should
agree to a divorce if it becomes absolutely necessary. She gave
me a solemn promise that she wouldn't oppose a divorce.'

'She has said to me time and time again : "Do you think I'd
foist myself on him if I knew it made him unhappy?" That
she would never do, she has too much pride. In that event, she
would simply leave the conjugal home and come and live with
me : a case of automatic divorce.'

'Is it a case of automatic divorce?' asked Costals, in whom
these words inspired an uprush of joy, as if Solange had just
left the conjugal home, taking the laughing faun with her.

'Of course. Haven't you ever read the Civil Code?'

'Someone tried to make me read it the other day. But I
thought that would be an absolute disaster.'

'Yes, indeed, I can't quite see you struggling with the Civil
Code!' said Mme Dandillot with an affectionate laugh. This
famous man, whose opinions people sought, who was said to
be hard and an 'awkward customer', was an absolute child!
She did not think precisely : 'I shall be able to lead him by the
nose', but she thought so vaguely. And, in her mounting
euphoria, she poured him another cup of tea. Meanwhile he
was thinking : 'Neither Dubouchet nor the head clerk ever told
me there were cases of automatic divorce. How frivolous
people are! Not for one moment did they realize that these
things were vitally important to me....' He also recalled Mme
Dandillot's remark about her daughter's 'pride', and he smiled
at the thought, convinced as he was that Solange had not an
atom of pride, or anything approaching it. But women boast
of their pride, real or imaginary, while men hide theirs. Because
women like to be envied, whereas men fear to be. Nevertheless
he felt the need for additional guarantees :

'May I have a solemn promise from you too, that you will not try to influence her against divorce?'

'I give you my word of honour.'

'Saadi, although in love with his wife, abandons her in order to devote himself to his work, and writes to his father-in-law such a beautiful letter on the subject of freedom, that the latter forgives him. I shall write you such a letter.'

'The Corsicans have always had very distinctive ways,' said Mme Dandillot, who assumed this Sadi must be a Corsican. There was Sadi Carnot, and everyone knows that the entire administration of the Republic is Corsican.

'I had various other important things to say to you, but I've forgotten them. . . . Ah, yes, this for example. . . . If the husband refused the mother-in-law entry to the conjugal home, would that also be grounds for automatic divorce?'

'Well, well, if we've already got to *that* stage!'

'Shouldn't one always be ready for the worst?'

'I've never heard of a marriage taking place under such conditions,' cried Mme Dandillot, without acrimony, but showing signs of having reached the end of her tether.

'You're the one who wants *this thing*, not me,' said Costals somewhat drily.

'My dear Monsieur, if this marriage is really such a cross for you to bear. . . .'

'No, no,' said Costals, staring at the floor. 'I'm simply pointing out your responsibilities.'

There was another silence. Mme Dandillot's face had clouded over.

'We are also agreed,' said Costals, 'that I shall not be obliged to accompany her when she wants to go out in the evening.'

'If you don't want to go out with her, she can come out with me or with friends.'

'And there'll never be a wireless in the house.'

'She loathes them.'

'We shall entertain very little. I'm sick and tired enough of my own friends. . . .'

'We shan't impose our friends on you, and we shan't try and get to know yours,' Mme Dandillot interjected humbly.

'I refuse to go out to dinner parties, in other words make

polite conversation to some strange woman in a diamond necklace I find sitting next to me, whose name I don't even know,
who wants me to talk about God, and who has the mentality
of a housemaid, a stupid housemaid – the whole thing lasting
a full four hours, which means five counting the time it takes
me to dress – five hours that might be spent re-reading the
classics (for I only read the masters, nobody else matters), or
thinking, or taking the air in the Bois, or simply sleeping, which
is innocent, whereas making small talk to imbeciles is not.'

'But isn't life bound to involve a certain amount of voluntary time-wasting?' said Mme Dandillot. Like all people who
waste their time (ninety-nine point nine per cent of humanity),
she instinctively resented those who did not, suspecting that
they were superior to her. And then, the woman with the
diamond necklace – had she not played that role often enough
herself?

'What appears to be time-wasting can sometimes be rest,
or even work. No dinner party has ever been that. . . . But what
if I wanted to get married in Naples?' he asked out of the blue,
as though this new prospect settled everything.

'Legally there would be no problem. Provided, however, as
far as I know, that one of the parties has lived in Naples for
some time. It would delay things. . . . And . . . isn't Naples rather
far?' she asked hesitantly.

'Would you come?'

'I don't know. . . . You've taken me unawares. But still, if
you absolutely insist on Naples, you shouldn't bother about
me. The main thing is for Solange to be happy.'

'I wonder if the wedding could take place in Persia. We
might have it in Isfahan. . . . '

'All that can be looked into,' said Mme Dandillot, with sudden weariness. She swallowed several strong mouthfuls of tea,
and said in a firmer voice, as though she had stoked up the
engine:

'I presume you have a lawyer?'

'Oh yes, several.'

'Ours is Maître Vignal, rue de Miromesnil, an old friend of
my husband's. Perhaps the one you decide on could get in
touch with him?'

'In order . . .?'

'In order to draw up the contract, of course.'

'Oh, there's no hurry.'

'But, dear Monsieur, Solange — not to mention myself — Solange urgently needs to go to the country for a rest. She's put it off long enough, and I suppose she could put it off a bit longer. . . . Still, you must agree that the sooner it's all settled the better.'

'Nothing can be settled until a decision has been reached.'

'What! Hasn't a decision been reached? We've been settling the minutest details for the past half-hour!'

'Excuse me, dear lady, let us be precise. I said to you at the beginning: "*If* the thing happens," "*assuming* that the thing happens." That's clear enough.'

'So you haven't decided?'

'I've decided in principle. In practice, I can't yet give you a firm promise.'

Mme Dandillot's body drooped and sagged.

'Listen, dear Monsieur, I'm convinced of your good faith. But you're putting a strain . . . such a strain . . . on Solange and me. It's been going on for six weeks now. . . . I'm quite upset by it,' she added, the accents of the cook piercing through the upper middle class exterior.

'I know, Madame, I know!' said Costals with feeling, putting his cup down on the table. 'It must be a very painful ordeal for both of you. But after all, if Solange is suffering, it must be admitted that she herself asked for it. Whereas, if there's an innocent victim in all this, it's me. *I* never asked anything of anybody. It's you who have put me in this frightful dilemma. And besides, if I hesitate, I have every cause to. There are as many reasons *for* this marriage as *against* it. How could one not hesitate? Anyone who didn't would be a nincompoop.'

'You'll never decide!'

'I *have* decided.'

'Are you speaking seriously?'

'I'm speaking solemnly.'

'Well then?'

'I repeat, I have decided to marry Solange. But as for putting the decision into effect, that calls for a renewed effort on my part, which I beg you to spare me for the moment, because I'm at the end of my tether.'

'Do you consider yourself engaged, at least?'

'Of course not, I ask you! An engagement is the second stage. Besides, I don't understand these rites. What exactly does it mean, to be engaged?'

'You make a firm promise to the girl, you give her a ring. . . .'

'Solange and I have already agreed that there won't be any rings. "Rings for birds", what! With me, there'll be no rings beforehand. But I might give her a ring when we divorce, for instance. That at least makes some sense. It means that we remain good friends.'

Mme Dandillot stared at Costals with consternation. She rang the bell. 'Is she going to show me the door?' he wondered But no, it was to tell the maid to close the kitchen door, from which, indeed, there drifted an appetizing, too appetizing smell of Brussels sprouts. Ah! all hope in life was not yet dead!

'What am I to say to you? I suppose we must wait a bit longer. And you can't give us even an approximate date when you think you. . . .'

'Oh, no dates please!' cried Costals, stiffening. 'Fixed dates, fixed hours, are like dust in a machine – that's the way to throw a life right out of gear. One morning or one evening I shall telephone you and say, "Well, dear Madame, it's settled".'

'Do give the poor child this chance of marrying someone she likes,' said Mme Dandillot in a tone of supplication. For some time now she had been looking right and left and making nervous gestures with her hands – with her jaw, too, like an old horse chewing its bit. 'We realize perfectly well that you could marry anyone you wished. But do give her this chance! If after two years you find that she interferes with your work, well, at least she will have had two years of happiness.'

'I want to give her a whole lifetime of happiness, not just two years,' said Costals vehemently.

' "In principle" or "in practice"?' Mme Dandillot inquired with a faint smile.

'In principle. In practice, it will have to simmer a bit longer.

383

But don't worry,' he added, getting up, 'things are going well for you.'

She escorted him into the hall with a sad smile on her face. But he was so eager to get away that, before Mme Dandillot could stop him, he had boldly made his way to the kitchen door, mistaking it for the front door, and opened it. Whereupon the smell of Brussels sprouts emerged and hurled itself upon him with all the joy of a locked-up dog released by its master, and much denser, more powerful, more aggressive than before.

Left alone, Mme Dandillot went back to the drawing-room and collapsed into an armchair. Her face, which had been set in a worldly grimace for the last hour, loosened and sagged, but at the same time hardened, giving her an almost wild appearance because of her staring eyes. She massaged her cheeks in the direction of the ears, to smooth out the wrinkles that ran down from her nose.

Costals, meanwhile, rushed down the stairs four at a time like a schoolboy escaping from prep. five minutes before time and skedaddling as fast as his legs will carry him, imagining the beak is on his tail. When he felt he was out of range, an expression of amusement spread over his features. 'Before I was merely a Triplepatte. But after the kitchen gag, I'm Charlie Chaplin as well.' At various times in his life he had thought himself Julius Caesar, Don Quixote, Jesus Christ, Gilles de Retz, etc. Which may sound ridiculous, but is not, since each of these great men also imagined himself to be a character he was not, and actually drew his strength from the illusion: Caesar believing that he was Alexander, Don Quixote that he was the Knight of heaven knows what, Gilles de Retz that he was Tiberius, and Jesus Christ that he was God. The shame Costals felt at the thought of being a son-in-law, or on the way to becoming one, he tried to get rid of by exaggerating the farcical side of his situation, in such a way as to be able to go on turning life into art. Although he had been perfectly natural throughout his interview with Mme Dandillot, he could not help feeling, after the event, that he had enacted with her a scene in the best traditions of classical comedy; and this to some extent *saved* him, in his own eyes, from the nuptial tragedy. With his feet turned out a little, in imitation of Charlie, he strolled down the avenue, appalled and delighted.

They met the following day at the entrance to a picture exhibition – masterpieces of modern art. As neither of them had
the slightest feeling for these pictures, and as they were both
natural and honest enough to admit it to each other after a
quarter of an hour, they left the gallery and walked aimlessly
through the centre of Paris, very peaceful in these early September days.

'Did your mother tell you about our talk yesterday?'

'Yes.'

'Things are going well for you. I'm convinced that *this thing*
will take place. Leave it to me. But, my poor girl, what must
you think of these shilly-shallyings?'

She turned her face towards him and said simply:

'I just wait. . . . '

Poor little thing! Such submissiveness! Yes, she was patient,
as patient as. . . . (Costals almost always thought in similes) as
patient as a mare.

He stopped her in front of an interior decorator's window.
'That's a nice carpet. Liable to show the dirt, unfortunately.
. . . Do you like that kind of lighting?'

It was the first time he had spoken to her about such
matters. They went in, and talked to the salesman for some
time. It gave Costals a feeling of gratification, not only because
it committed him further ('Now I can't possibly turn back.')
but because this future he was preparing was attractive to
him. He took a little sketch out of his wallet and showed it to
her: it was the plan of a flat. One of the rooms was marked:
'Sol.'s room.'

'I've put your room and mine at opposite ends of the flat,
for days when I can't stand you any longer.'

She did not reply, but he felt her hand searching for his.

During the next hour, in a tea-room, he recaptured once
more the atmosphere of that Sunday in the kitchen, when he
had thought her so serious. But what giant strides had been
made since then! They spent this hour chatting about their

future, and about the flat, which was to be 'as pale as Parian marble', and the servants, who 'mustn't be too intelligent', and the food, which should be 'plentiful, but decidedly mediocre' (he had noticed she was something of a gastronome, and disapproved), etcetera, etcetera, the whole thing cosy, familiar, cordial – and so simple! Impossible to treat her more like his wife. (And that soft voice of hers, that was so well bred.) He found that, in everything, she met his tastes more than halfway. 'She won't disturb me,' he told himself, with some amazement. 'Perhaps she will even help my work, by keeping my friends at bay.' For a moment he thought of hastening the celebration of *the thing*. From time to time she would turn towards him suddenly, and, being smaller than he, raise her eyes a little, smiling, with an expression of radiant tenderness, as though to thank him for giving her his love – which was not love but a sincere attachment.

'You happened to be there, so it was you I chose. Yes, if this thing takes place, I shall have picked you more or less at random, so that it should really be like life, since most marriages happen by chance. I wanted to place myself in the normal circumstances of marriage, and that is why, quite voluntarily, I shall have married in absurd circumstances. I also wanted not to give it too good a chance of succeeding, because I was curious to see what mutual sympathy and goodwill could make of it. You notice that I still say "If this thing happens." I'm not making any promises. You would lay yourself open to the most horrible disappointments if you got it into your head that we were engaged. When I consider we're engaged, I'll let you know.'

He asked her what she wanted to do – whether she wanted to come back to his flat (with all that that setting now usually involved), or go somewhere else. She said her mother had seen a film which was partly set in Chatelaillon, where they used to spend the holidays when Solange was a little girl, and that she had even recognized their villa in it. She would very much like to see this film. Costals could not help thinking that she did not have a very pressing desire to yield to his embraces.

The pen jibs at having to describe, however sketchily, the depths of stupidity, vulgarity, imbecility and baseness of this comico-lachrymose film, which was of course French. Five hundred half-wits licked up this pus with ecstasy. There was the Supercretin and the Supersucker, the pure-bred Degenerate, the unadulterated Subman and the quintessential Innocent; and beside each of them, one tenth of a virgin, meaning eight and a half virgins for the whole assembly, if our count is right. Our friends had been there for half an hour, and Costals noticed that not once had Solange retched with disgust. She did not laugh, but she swallowed the worst without turning a hair, whereas it had happened to Costals, sometimes even when he was at the cinema with a woman he had just picked up and was therefore in a good mood, to have to leave the theatre because he was physically at the end of his tether. On the contrary, when the action of the film switched from Chatelaillon to the Côte d'Azur and he said to her 'Shall we go?' she answered: 'Couldn't we see how it ends?' So she liked it! Crucified in his seat, Costals had to swallow this French film to the dregs.

'Well, I might have known,' he thought, 'but even so.... This is what she makes me a party to. And whenever one sees men at such squalid shows, they've been dragged there by women. I dislike anything that brings out the stupidity in men, and that's why I dislike woman. If it were Brunet, I'd say to myself: "It's his age." The eternal superiority of kids over women! *They* can't irritate us, or at least it's wrong to be irritated by them, since there's only one answer to everything they do: "It's their age." It's exactly the same with the proletariat: we forgive them what we cannot forgive the bourgeoisie.'

Afterwards they dined in a restaurant. Try as he might, he could not bring himself to speak to her. He wondered why: they had talked with perfect ease before. At first he thought the cinema had frozen him up; then he realized that it was simply because he had nothing more to say to her. He racked his brains, but nothing came. 'We're not yet engaged, and already we've nothing left to say to each other. The marriage of the young carp and the old rabbit.' Solange did not seem surprised at his silence: she herself was so used to that condition....

He had chosen a rather common restaurant, to punish her for being a gastronome. All their fellow-diners looked revoltingly healthy: must one, then, be tubercular, in order to look at all well-bred? As soon as he entered the restaurant, Costals had felt capable of murdering the lot of them. Characteristically, he at once envisaged the most extreme act: with him, there was none of the sort of protective padding that Europeans normally interpose between irritation and the thought of acting on it. He looked at each of these men and wondered which of them would get the better of it if it came to a fight. Everything else was nonsense. At table, he was to all appearances extremely quiet, and even had a slightly dopy look. And yet, at the slightest provocation, he would have grabbed a knife from the table and struck.

Their immediate neighbours were a party of eight – father, mother, daughter, son-in-law, muchacho, little girl and *babour** (the count is wrong: that only makes seven). The father, a realist. With dazzling intuition Costals guessed that he was a realist from Oran (a settler?) on holiday in the 'metropolis'. Blond, energetic-looking, with a tooth-brush moustache and aggressively untidy hair (no comb had ever passed through that mane), for a realist must be untidy: it proves that he is no aesthete, that he is of the earth earthy. A certain resemblance to Benda, which sounds a bit steep but is nevertheless so: if Benda, instead of having a few wisps of hair, had a proper thatch, he would look like a realist from Oran. The mother, perhaps calving under the table, just like that, simply by opening her legs, like a true realist from Oran. The daughter, short-arsed, a swarthy young she-goat, and ditto the little girl. The muchacho, from whose agreeable physiognomy one could tell at once that he was called Albert. And the *babour*, musclebound, a show-off if ever there was one. These seven persons (or eight) vied with one another as to whose nails should be most deeply in mourning – perhaps mourning their lost illusions about French colonization in Oran.

But we haven't mentioned the son-in-law, and it was on him that Costals' attention was mainly concentrated: already in

*A word used in the author's family on the maternal side, meaning baby. (*Author's note*)

his eyes all sons-in-law formed one big family. Moreover, this
one was a Son-in-law with a capital S, the prototype of the
species. Dumb as a carp. Sitting there smiling at everything
that was said by his father-in-law – his mother-in-law – his
wife – and the muchacho – and the little girl. And lines had
formed on his face, already deeply ingrained, in spite of his
youth: the lines of perpetual approbation. He even turned
towards Costals from time to time, doubtless so that Costals
should also approve of the father-in-law – or the mother-in-
law – etc. No one ever addressed a word to him, or even
glanced in his direction: he really was the ideal Son-in-law.
Whenever he opened his mouth, rather than look at him they
lowered their eyes – that is, when they didn't start talking to
someone else. Only the muchacho showed the slightest kindness towards him: when the Son-in-law spoke to him, the
good-natured boy would offer him a few words in reply. The
agony of being a son-in-law! But then, why was he a son-in-
law? And yet he had had his day of triumph, dressed in tails
cut like a waiter's, with bridesmaids got up like sugar-plum
fairies. And to think that Socrates, Goethe, Hugo had been
sons-in-law. Costals' faith in humanity trembled.

'Miamiamiam!' said the *babour*.

'Yes, my little one. Didiadodoadoda,' said the mother.

'Dodoadidi?' queried the realist from Oran. '*That's* right,
dodoadidi,' he affirmed.

'Diddums want to go walkies,' said the she-goat.

'Diddums want to go walky-walkies,' said the son-in-law,
going one better, to get a share of the limelight.

'Meueueueuh!' howled Pipicaca, who saw the effect he was
producing.

'Yes, my little precious one, yes, bibiabobo,' said the mother,
putting her hand under its bottom, the instinctive gesture of
every fond mother.

'I think that child wants to be sick,' said the realist from
Oran, who, like a true father, wanted to show how competent
he was.

'To be *sick*?' screamed the mother. 'You're seeing double ...
oh! It's because Paulette was holding him. He wants me to
hold him, doesn't he?' She sucked the baby's cheek (kiss), then

shook it like a plum-tree, then sucked it again, ferociously, then slapped it. She was almost beautiful, as everything is beautiful when it is a perfect specimen of its type – and she was the incarnation of maternal hysteria. Finally she bore the child away to the lavatory. And the entire family, rid of the mother and the baby, gradually reverted to a semblance of dignity. Another twelve years, Pipicaca, today so beloved and so important, and you will be almost a little stranger at the family table. You will no longer be stupid, so you will no longer be interesting.

Costals and Solange left on foot, and went round to the avenue Henri-Martin. He felt so acrimonious towards her that he bought her a bunch of roses. She insisted on carrying the box. This quasi-oriental self-effacingness pleased him rather, although he wondered if it might not be part of her pre-nuptial strategy.

'I cannot offer you these roses without accompanying them with an amatory quotation,' he said to her. ' "Do not expect fidelity from the nightingale, for every moment it sings on a different rose," we read in the Gulistan.'

Inside his flat, they stood for a while leaning on the window-sill : he did not want to appear impatient. Clouds sped across the nocturnal sky above the Bois, so dense and so low that they might have been taken for a trail of smoke left by a loco-motive. Popping open the press-studs on the side fastening of her costume, he had slid his hand in next to her skin, im-prisoning one of her breasts. But anxiety about the future nullified the enjoyment he would have got from this contact if they had had a future of freedom before them.

'Would you mind undressing?'

As though she were incapable of anticipating his desires!

'Would you mind taking off your stockings?'

As though she did not yet know that he loved putting the sole of his bare foot on the bare arches of hers, like a crucified man on the foot-rest of his cross.

She had to go to the lavatory, and Costals remembered the Arab mare he had once had, so proud and so delicate that she would never urinate or dung when he was on her back.

We read into the sensations of physical love what the soul,

planing above it, puts there. Something immense, when a
sensation of this sort is powerful enough to be sufficient unto
itself. Mlle Dandillot was not the woman to give a man a self-
sufficient pleasure. Moreover, did she perhaps feel Costals'
aloofness? One has only to see the word 'French' on a box of
matches to know that they will never light. The same is true
of French girls, and it was true, that evening, of Solange. In
bed, she clasped him limply, as if for form's sake; as he did,
too, feeling the grain of her skin with his finger-tips, and
savouring every last drop of boredom this odourless body, these
flaccid legs might contain. There was absolutely nothing in
this girl that could rouse him. From a distance, her face gave
the impression of being clear-cut; close to, in the act of love,
it seemed rather blurred and flabby, without a hint of pathos.
(And how passionately he loved the faces of women at the
moment of satisfying them. There were women he passed in
the street whom he would have liked to have just once, for ten
minutes, simply to see what happened to their faces at that
moment. He would have liked to have a little camera on his
forehead, like a dentist's lamp, to film their faces at that
moment. Quite apart from the fact that it would have provided him with a 'collection' which, if offered to a few of the
more venerable academicians, would appreciably have hastened
his progress to the Quai Conti.) Almost the whole of Solange's
body, even her arm-pits, was as odourless as a sheet of paper:
there was nothing but the slightly sour smell of her mouth, the
faint, insipid smell of her hair, and another, sweetish smell.
(Why was Costals reminded of the lively, wholesome smell of
his son's hair? He was unaware of the fact that it is the rule
for a boy's hair to smell stronger and better than a woman's.)
They were folded in each other's arms, but still she did not
clasp him, and he would not have known she had moved her
arms but for the ticking of her wrist-watch which he could
hear in different positions, like some importunate insect that
had crept in between them.

Costals' body was dead, too. It was the first time it had
happened to him with her. That was the last straw! Suddenly
he thought – perhaps because of the stormy sky they had just
seen, which reminded him of a similar sky, highly dramatic,

above the Gharb, flooded as far as the eye could see – of the little Moroccan girl whom he met out there every year, and whom he called *Terremoto** because, in the way she seized and gripped and shook a man to bring the marrow through the whole length of his body from the distant cerebellum, she was like a little earthquake trying to uproot him. ('Oh, the paradise in that girl's body!') At this memory, his body awoke, came to life, like a snake hearing the snake-charmer's flute, and throbbed to the rhythm of his blood. And he clove the woman, as one opens up an artichoke to get at its heart, and he knew her. Nevertheless the whole thing was so drab that he scarcely knew it had happened until he heard Solange's impatient cry:

'You're hurting me!'

'What! Don't you realize that's part and parcel of your pleasure?'

'But I don't want you to hurt me,' she insisted querulously. He threw her a sombre look.

As soon as it was over she got up, almost with a bound – it was her only manifestation of energy during the whole evening – and made for the bathroom: how obvious it was that she had been in a hurry to get it over! Costals got up too, and met his image in the looking-glass, the tense features, the narrowed eyes of an enraged tom-cat. The face of the disappointed male, full of exasperation, malevolence and brutality – ugly and ridiculous, above all ridiculous. He flung himself back on the bed. And yet, on this very bed! ... There were plenty of others! ... Others with whom his sensuality was such that, glued to their bodies like an insect drunk and motionless in the corolla of a flower, not even a knock on the door would have budged him, as an insect will allow itself to be crushed without trying to escape. Faces rose up before him.... 'What I ask of a woman is to give her pleasure. The rest comes of itself, so to speak.' But perhaps, with this sex, everything was fake. Now to arouse a little tenderness, now to obtain marriage, now to earn a few pence. Perhaps there was not one woman in a hundred who felt anything in the arms of a man unless she had first been 'prepared'. They were not made for each other morally; they were not even made for each other

---

*Earthquake, in Spanish.

physiologically. Man enjoyed, woman did not; man had to teach her that, too; nature, already miserly enough where she was concerned, had failed to provide for it. When Dubouchet had said to him: 'No matter how much women may hang around the male, listen at his doors, he remains impenetrable to them,' he might have added: 'And first and foremost – how symbolic! – in the primordial act: in the orgasm. She tries to guess what it is, but cannot begin to visualize it, and envious of this male endowment, feigns to possess it herself in order to excite the male and in order that he shouldn't pity her.' The simulation of passion, the sad nightly comedy, year after year. And it was this fundamental incapacity that women sought to compensate for when they took refuge in 'pure love', set it up as an idol, tried to force men to worship it when men had an instinctive loathing of 'pure love' as of everything that is against nature, and finally, representing their infirmity as a virtue, and the health of the male as an infirmity, belaboured the poor fellow with their bogus commiseration and their sublime indignation, accusing him of being too 'selfish' and too 'coarse' even to glimpse the splendours of 'pure love'. Costals thought of all this, and all the time he remembered that sweetish, almost sickly smell and that soft, nerveless body, like a white slug. . . . And he dreamed of embraces that would be worthier of his mettle, heroic embraces, mighty minglings as of a pair of wrestlers on the mat, in which it would be no longer a question of conquering a miserable consenting ewe-lamb (all said and done, what a farce to talk about 'victories' over women!) but of strength overcoming strength and for an instant turning it into sweetness. That would be real sport. That would be man's work. . . .

He got up and looked at himself in the mirror once more. Now it was not so much his disappointed face he was ashamed of. He was ashamed of having been humiliated by *that*, of having wasted his vanity and his appetites on that sort of 'exploit'. The mirror reflected his vigorous, half-naked torso, and he gazed at it with satisfaction. 'I'm worth more than that.'

A blank sheet of paper lay on the table in front of him. He scribbled on it: 'Once more, that terrible thought runs through my mind: I do not know why I chose her. And once more I ask myself: "Why, oh why, am I doing this?"* And once more I reply: "I am doing it for her. I am also doing it in order to have experienced all the disparate savours of the world. I am also doing it in order to submit myself to the conditions of ordinary life. I wanted to be no longer aloof. I wanted, through her, to find, as it were, the subterranean water-level of what is most human and to bring back a bucketful, however bitter. I put my trust in her, in myself, in nature, in my destiny. May it not recoil on my own head." '

She came back. He could not help looking at her with a hint of derision at the thought of her lack of response. They stood at the window again for a while. He would always remember that stormy sky. He said to her:

'I suppose you would think me a swine if I were to leave you now.'

'I don't believe I could ever think that of you.'

His esteem for her came flooding back, heart-rendingly.

'You once told me you were afraid of the future. Now it's I who am afraid.'

'And *I* have complete confidence.'

His pity for her came flooding back, heart-rendingly.

He took her home in a taxi, incapable of banishing his forebodings, incapable of saying a word to her. Every time she had felt something crack between them, she made some affectionate gesture towards him: this time, she had taken his arm. He would have liked to make her understand that this gesture made him gloomier still. 'She does it like a dog putting out its paw.' On the threshold of her house he said, looking up at the sky:

'My heart, too, is full of clouds.'

'And mine is full of stars!'

These words shattered him.

Costals went home and took a sleeping-draught.† O healing

---

*Marrying Solange (*Author's note*).

†What Mme Dandillot, little versed in Latin, daringly called a *dormifuge* instead of a *somnifère* (*Author's note*).

waters of oblivion! As he lay in bed, he summed up his
dilemma for the hundredth time: 'I love this girl *up to a
certain point*, no further, as I've had the honesty to say to her
in writing. Why "no further"? Let's say it's because, socially
and intellectually, she is too remote from me. Let's say it's
because, sexually, she is pretty well rock-bottom. Or rather,
don't let's "say" anything. I don't love her more because that's
how it is. Obviously, such a marriage has no *raison d'être*. And
yet I love her enough to suffer from her suffering, in particular
the suffering that a break would cause her now that I have
allowed things to go so far. But the suffering she would undergo from a rupture at this stage would be as nothing compared
to what she would go on suffering for months or even years if
we married. So that this immediate suffering must not be a
bar to breaking it off now. No, the only serious objection to a
rupture – who would believe it? – is this: when all is said and
done, there is still a chance, a chance in a hundred but a
definite chance, that the two of us may find happiness in this
marriage. So the sole question at present is this: should one
gamble on this minimal chance, or should one refuse to gamble
on it, at the risk of regretting it later on in one's moments of
depression? But am I the sort of man who ever has moments
of depression? Etc.'

He woke up at four and heard the rain trickling down his
windows: those famous storm-clouds had burst. Summer rain,
always so strange. . . . Nocturnal summer rain, full of portents,
according to the Ancients. Nocturnal rain in July, on the night
when, at eighteen, he had had his first woman. Nocturnal rain
in June, in the war-time forest, on the eve of his being
wounded. Nocturnal rain in August, in Naples, the night before
he was stabbed. Nocturnal rain in September, after all hope for
Brunet had been given up (cerebro-spinal meningitis) but at
dawn the fever had abated. The strong man, the lucid man,
on his tormented couch, abandons himself to higher powers.
From then on he knows that the coming day will be marked.

He fell asleep again, and had a nightmare such as he had
never had before. A body was weighing him down, horribly, a
viscous mass covered him, stuck to him, enveloped him, and
he struggled to throw it off. A small child who had fallen

asleep with a huge cat lying on its chest might have such a nightmare. Although asleep, Costals had the feeling that he was awake, that it was not a dream, and that therefore he must be going mad, or rather that he was possessed, diabolically possessed; and it was a new and terrible thing for him, who had never been possessed by anyone except himself (the most disturbing aspect of himself).

The anguish of his awakening was somewhat similar to an unforgettable awakening he had experienced at the age of eighteen. On that occasion, he had fallen asleep beside his mistress – his first mistress – an Italian girl of sixteen. He knew she wanted to kill him, having heard her express the intention of doing so one night in her sleep. As he emerged from unconsciousness, he felt something cold and hard pressing against the nape of his neck. He guessed that it was the barrel of a revolver. The girl's hands were resting, gentle and motionless, on his head and on his neck. His gradual return to consciousness had been terrifying. His own hands were under the sheet; he would not have time to get them out before she pressed the trigger. But perhaps she was asleep: he could not see her face, which was higher up the pillow than his. What was he to do? He thought for a while, impossible to say how long. Then he murmured several times: 'God bless you, Maria, God bless you' and quietly turned his head. She was sleeping, or pretending to be asleep. He took the revolver. They went on seeing each other for four or five months, but he searched her whenever she came into his flat.

His awakening now, after his night of 'possession', was accompanied, like that other one, by palpitations and a feeling of oppression that lasted for some time. There was no escaping the meaning of his dream. It was crystal clear. The weight that had been smothering him was Solange and the life they would lead together. The 'possession' was Solange, devouring his soul and then creeping into the place where his soul had been. He remembered Dante's lines about 'the dreams of morning, more truthful than those of night'. He remembered the rain, full of portents. He remembered the premonitory dream. And the animal in him shuddered. And fear, which had been prowling round inside him ever since he had been haunted by this marriage, now took complete possession of him, submerging all else – no longer a rational and justifiable fear but the obscure, mysterious fear that makes wild beasts cringe and brings heroes to their knees. And under the impact of this salutary funk, he at last took the decision which his reason and his will had been incapable of taking for the past six weeks. That very day, without seeing Solange again, he would leave France for several months.

'She won't hold it against me. When I asked her "If I were to leave you now, would you consider me a swine?" she said she would never think that of me.' That's what men are like: give them a weapon against you, and they'll use it there and then. No one would have dreamed of regarding Flaubert as a minor writer had he not openly confessed that he sweated blood over every sentence.

In the eyes of the world, Costals' flight must seem the height of boorishness and cowardice. And yet the gods applaud him. Through the path of irrational panic, Costals had regained his reason. His flight would deliver him from the sort of magic spell whose hold over him he had been able to gauge that night, and under which he might have foundered utterly if he had not reacted in time. It would give him a chance to pull himself together. It would put his feelings, as well as those of Solange, to the test of absence. And finally, it answered to that supreme law which men do not take sufficiently into account – to wit, that inestimable advantages can accrue from the mere fact that one has moved from one place to another* – that

---

*When someone is run down the doctors advise a 'change of air', even if (they admit it themselves when pressed a little) the air of the place they recommend is of no better quality than that in which the patient is now living. A shy man, no matter how much he tries to summon up his courage, cannot bring himself to accost an unknown woman he covets in the street. He walks away, makes a detour, lets her walk on for a bit, and then, the locale of their meeting having changed, he accosts her with ease. A bull refuses to respond to the matador's pass. The capes draw it a few yards further on, and there the matador can do what he likes with it. The same is true of a horse that refuses a jump, or a wild animal that refuses to obey its trainer, etc.

what was impossible becomes possible simply because one has moved from one place to another. Costals' flight, 'cowardly' and 'boorish' as it undoubtedly was, from a narrow point of view, was from a higher point of view the right thing to do, however incompatible it was with honour, worldly opinion, and everything else.

Costals booked a seat on the 8.45 to Genoa that evening. Why Genoa? Because of Mlle Carlotta Bevilacqua, of Genoa, a little Latin sister who could refuse him nothing: in no matter what sphere, our brilliant novelist was never at a loss for positions to fall back on. Then he wrote to Solange and her mother. He told them he was going to Lausanne; he would not tell them he was in Genoa until he was sure, from the tone of their replies, that there was no risk of their turning up. This was the only insincerity in the two letters, which otherwise expressed nothing that he did not genuinely feel at that moment; in fact, he could not get through them without tears. Later on, he was to wonder how the joy of escaping from that inferno had failed to dry up these tears; why, indeed, he had wept at all, since he did not really love Solange, and knew it. He had wept, then, and wept for some time, because of the pain he was causing to someone whom he loved only *up to a point*! He concluded that tears must come easily to him, a fact of which he was not unaware.

Usually, when his inner life was going through an interesting phase (and this was certainly one of them: one does not weep for a woman every day), he would describe it in his diary. But today he was ashamed of his emotional turmoil, and was reluctant to dwell upon it. In his entry for 7 September he wrote furiously: 'Suffering. The bristles of my clothes-brush have turned white overnight.' It was the only trace of that entire day that remained in his diary.

Pierre Costals   to Solange Dandillot
Paris   *Paris*

7 September 1927

Dear Solange,

During the war, one of my parents' maids whose husband

had been home on leave, went to see him off on the train that was to take him back to the front. As the moment of parting drew near, before going through the ticket barrier, the man said: 'Wait here while I buy some cigarettes.' He slipped away, and joined the train by another gate, leaving his wife stranded there: he had fled from emotion. By the time the Armistice came, this man had won four citations for bravery in the trenches. Such is the courage of the male.

By the time you read this, I shall have left Paris, fleeing, in the same way, such useless and treacherous enfeeblements. This violent break was necessary to extricate me from the inferno of my uncertainties and my perpetual tergiversations.

I am not impervious to your fate. But if you suffer you are not alone in this. I shall say no more, for fear of showing weakness. Let us move on at once to the consolations.

You suffer now. It will be over in no time. If I had married you, you would have suffered long and deeply. Divorce would have been inevitable. Think of everything that would have preceded and accompanied it. God alone knows what I am capable of when I feel chained: like an old tom-cat, a friendly enough soul who will nevertheless scratch your face to shreds if he feels you are holding him forcibly in your arms. Be grateful to me for sparing you all that. It is my love for you that dictates this separation.*

Another consolation. Everything I have just said applies to me just as much as it applies to you. For six weeks I have suffered continuously. Great as were the joys I drew from you, the pangs I have drawn from myself because of you outweigh them: you love me, I love you, and my summer has been poisoned. I am putting an end to this suffering. You should be glad of it.

Another consolation. If you love my work, I want you to know that you have already done much for it. There is a corner of my work, as there is a corner of myself, where, whatever may happen later, you are lodged for the rest of my life. Nothing can alter that.

I want you to know that my affection and regard for you have gone on increasing ever since we met. I want you to

---

*This is going a bit far (*Author's note*).

realize that if, every time I saw you, I had not become more and more conscious of the extent to which you were worthy of this affection and regard, I should never have wavered in my hostility to the plan for us to marry; that it is because of this affection and regard that I have continually fluctuated; that it is because of them that I got to the point of awakening and nurturing your hopes; that it is because of them that I have now reached the point of appearing to behave badly towards you. And finally, you must forgive me because, whether culpably or not, I nevertheless did raise these hopes, and raised them only to shatter them.

I want you to know that my affection remains ready to play whatever part in your life you may wish. I am not abandoning you; I am simply breaking off in order to give myself a breathing-space. I am ready to give you everything you want of me, in whatever form you wish except marriage.

It is up to you, then, to choose either to forget me or to call me back to you on my return (two months hence). I shall know by the choice you make whether you merely had a hankering for the state of marriage or whether you really loved an individual.

Write to me poste restante Lausanne.

I cannot bring myself to end this letter with the usual form of words. I kiss you – you can guess how. A last embrace.... My eyes are filling with tears.... No, I cannot go on.

C.

Pierre Costals	to Madame Dandillot
Paris	*Paris*

7 September 1927

Dear Madame,

By the time you read this I shall be in Switzerland for several months.

I feel shattered – to an extent that you cannot possibly be aware of – by the inner struggle that I have been waging for a month and more in connection with Solange. I could not face the prospect of another painful and futile conversation with you, and a leave-taking with Solange that would have been more painful still. I have not the same mastery over myself that she has: I am a sentimentalist, which she is not. And I have already overburdened her with the spectacle of a man torn asunder.

You know my reasons. Too many risks of such a marriage turning out badly, and of my being a cause of suffering to someone for whom I feel a real affection. And, in such an event, the moral impossibility for me to ask for a divorce from someone who would have done me no wrong. Consequently, bondage – and bondage *to a person one loves*, which is *the worst* form of bondage. As well as all the other reasons which I have already explained to you. No, when one is perfectly happy in a particular state – celibacy – one does not strain oneself to perform a deed so fraught with menace.

I had never seriously had to debate the problem of marriage with myself. No doubt it is to your daughter's credit that she was the first to bring me to do so. But she is also its victim. Had I been more confident in my objections, I should have given Solange a firm *no*, irrevocably and at once, instead of nurturing her hopes. Allow me to point out, however, that there was never any promise on my part.

I bitterly regret having raised these hopes in Solange and in yourself; woe to him who arouses false hopes! But after all, if I hesitated it was because I had good reason to do so, and besides, hesitation is of the essence of intelligence. I have wounded her, yet I am not guilty: that is life. If the situation were the same today as it was four months ago, I would not behave any differently. When I told her that this marriage was possible, I believed what I said. Oh no, I have nothing to reproach myself with.

Both you, Madame, and she have treated my idiosyncrasies with the utmost tolerance, and with an intelligence that touches me and adds to my distress.

My deepest desire is to maintain my friendship with Solange. Is that so impossible? I have spoken to you about this.

I remain, etc.

C.

In the train ... and, as always, untarnished by habit, that gust of emotion, almost anxiety, that accompanied all his departures: 'Will I come back? And, if I do, will this journey have brought me all the happiness I expected of it? Will it have brought me more happiness than the last one?' He imagined the little girl settling herself in a corner, then coming to his help because he was struggling with his baggage.... He spoke to her, and she answered him in a whisper.

He had posted the two letters at the station, so that they would not arrive until the next morning, when he would be far away.

Next morning at eight o'clock, at Modane, he said to himself: 'The postman has just been ...' and his thighs began to tremble. And he made a heartfelt wish – that one day she might be entirely happy, and that he might find in himself the inspiration to help her to be so. And he conceived something which, had he been a Christian, would have been a sort of prayer for her. And he told himself that he owed her an eternal debt, for having made her suffer.

Thus was fulfilled, after an interval of four months and a day, the presentiment he had noted in his diary on the 6th of May: that one day he would leave France in order not to hear her voice again.

PART TWO

As soon as he arrived in Genoa, Costals proceeded to organize what he considered to be the ideal life.

He rented a bachelor flat (near the Piazza Fontane Marose), and engaged a daily woman. His lunch was brought in from a near-by restaurant.

He got up at five, and worked from six till noon, then from 12.30 till four. At half past four he went out, and roamed the streets until midnight, doing a great many things he enjoyed doing, each one more outrageous than the last. Whatever he coveted, he took. He had his own special code. This code, indeed, on certain points, was extremely strict. But these were points on which conventional morality is indifferent. Whereas he was lax over points on which conventional morality is strict.

He knew no one in Genoa except women. Only women crossed his threshold. His life was divided into two parts: work and pleasure. The only things that seemed important to him. As his day contained *nothing* else at all, he had all the time he needed for work and for pleasure, both of which require a great deal if one does not want to botch either.

He had worked the character of Solange into the novel he was writing. The plot bore no relation to his liaison with Solange, but the character was copied as faithfully as he could manage. 'Ah ha, my girl, so you wanted to devour my soul! Now it's my turn to devour you. This will teach you that a writer always has the last word.'

After four days, letters arrived from Solange and her mother, forwarded from Lausanne.

Solange wrote: '... You tell me you are shattered. I am completely overwhelmed. Your suffering may be great, you poor thing, but how much less than mine! Yours was active, so to speak; you are like the man who tears the dressing off his own wound, whose will-power to some extent annuls the pain. I am the one whose dressing is torn off by someone

403

else, and that's worse. . . . And God knows you operate without anaesthetics!'

Mme Dandillot, for her part, took up some of the arguments
against marriage in Costals' letter. She opined that a formal
liaison with Solange would be a much heavier tie than marriage.
She ended thus : 'Believe me, I have the utmost regard for you,
but it hurts me to see my little Solange suffering so. Write to
us. Best wishes, etc.'

Costals considered these two letters eminently reasonable.
'Really, what sensible people they are! Far from complicating
things, they lubricate them rather. I might even go so far as
to say that they were a bit easy-going. A great compliment in
my eyes, however much it may be decried.'

Extraordinary how, after a few hours, the whole episode had
become part of the past! His pain had been as it were overridden by relief. How often, dead beat, his muscles reduced to
pulp by over-indulgence in sporting or cytherean exertions, he
had said to himself : 'A couple of days and I'll be myself again.'
But in two hours all trace of it had vanished. In the emotional
sphere he recovered just as quickly. A few days of this Genoa
régime, under which he did absolutely nothing he did not
enjoy doing, were enough to put him on his feet again. The
first round of his fight with the Hippogriff had been won by
intelligent retreat. No doubt there would be a second round,
but since it was not yet imminent, it was wiser not to think
of it. Consequently, his euphoria was untroubled except by the
thought of Solange's suffering.

This characteristic ability of his to achieve happiness to the
full on the spur of the moment, was accompanied by another
characteristic : the desire to share it with someone he loved.
How often had he wired Mlle du Peyron, asking her to send
Brunet post-haste to wherever he, Costals, happened to be,
because he was in the seventh heaven in such and such
mountains or such and such forests! This time, too, after a
week of euphoria, he thought of bringing his son to Genoa.
But the boy was staying with some friends in England and he
had just written to his father saying he was 'perfectly happy'.
One cannot disturb someone who is 'perfectly happy'. So
Costals abandoned the idea of bringing Brunet to Genoa, and

contented himself, in order to make him even more 'perfectly happy', with sending him a nice little chunk of pocket money. On the same impulse, he sent presents to two young ladies for whom he felt a solid attachment.

In ten days he received four letters from Solange. (Her hand-writing, he thought, was beginning to look a little like his.) The first three were melancholy, but not excessively so. A touch of gaiety broke through from time to time. However, after he had neglected to answer the third by return of post, the fourth was an explosion similar to her 'geyser' in July:

'Our separation.... I am sucked down, as it were, by a force independent of my will, and this state of prostration from which I drag myself only to sink back even deeper leaves me gasping. If you ever doubted my feelings towards you, and if I myself perhaps was unable to guage [sic] them with absolute accuracy, I can no longer delude myself about their strength and profundity; I measure them by my suffering.'

Pierre Costals   to Solange Dandillot
Via Carlo Felice, Genoa   *Etretat*

19 September 1927

My darling,

I don't want you to be unhappy. It's quite simple: come.

Come and spend a fortnight here. You don't understand? I fled from you, and now I want you back! But you see, with me the absent are always in the right. Your absence in particular always does me good. The thing is, for the past ten days I've been working like a buffalo (or rather like half a buffalo, since I only work half the day). Now, there are two great sedatives in my life: a certain act which means little to you but which I find a great release; and work. On the 7th of September I had not written a single line for four months because of you. Now that I've unstopped myself, there is room for you once more, and I feel in the right vein to make you happy for a fortnight. I say a fortnight, because after that there is every likelihood that I shall start persecuting you again.

I shall take a suite in a hotel. You will sign yourself in as my wife.

And besides, for a girl who is as 'virginal' and well-brought-up as you are, there is something extremely improper about this plan of mine, which is an additional reason for you to give me the pleasure of agreeing to it.

With my fondest love,

C.

Beware! There are no hippogriffical implications in this plan of mine. I simply want you to have the 'fourteen days of happiness' of the *Bibliothèque Rose*. As you would stay for fifteen days, you see I give myself the right to make you un-happy for one day.

Written by Costals in his notebook the same day:
Charity commits one. If you write to a woman 'My darling', you must admit to yourself that it commits you. That you will never again be able to write 'Dear Solange' without causing deep despair, staring eyes, murmurs of 'Why has he changed?' and cow-like ruminations.

Costals had written this letter under the impact of the SOS from Solange. As soon as he had posted it, he began to feel uneasy. Not that he was afraid that his hesitations with regard to marriage might start up again : he felt that he was now firmly anchored in the negative. But a fortnight of Solange's continual presence would be a heavy burden. And moreover, in order to devote himself entirely to her, he would have to stop seeing Mlle Bevilacqua....

He had no need of Solange. No need at all. Neither his senses, nor his heart, nor his intellect nor his imagination needed her. He was calling her back simply because of the happiness his letter would give her. The difficulty would be to sustain this happiness. And for a whole fortnight. If only he had suggested a week. When he had written 'My darling' (it was the first time he had used the expression in a letter to her), he had asked himself : 'Why am I writing "my darling"? Pure affectation, that's all. In fact there's no reason.' The reason was that he loved her less. No doubt about it : it was because he loved her less that he called her 'my darling'.

He vaguely hoped that she would reply saying she was unable to come. He even thought of writing to tell her he had fallen ill. Only the pettiness and dishonesty of this stratagem prevented him. He had caused her enough disappointment without that. No more hot and cold showers !

Solange's reply was a little late in coming. He imagined that she had cooled off towards him, and was relieved at the thought : it would be easier for him to break with her. Then the reply came :

'My dearest love − your letter has given me enormous pleasure. The joy I feel is such that I can hardly contain myself from shouting it to the housetops. Mummy jibbed a bit at first. But when she realized the immense pleasure it would give me. . . . You've no idea how sweet she is. We spent last evening thinking up all the lies we shall have to tell our cousins here, to explain this trip to Italy. I shall arrive on the 27th at half past two. But I make one condition : that you should continue to be a semi-buffalo, in other words that you should in no way change your working hours or your way of life for my sake, and that I should not disturb you in any way.'

The letter went on, full of expansiveness and affection. Her happiness communicated itself to Costals : he was glad, and resolved to make this fortnight as nice as possible. Nevertheless, when he had to look for a hotel, and pack some of his things to move them there, etc., he sighed : what a lot of his time the girl was wasting ! He dreamed of the day when she would be gone, and notched it on his calendar : October the 12th.

On the 25th he realized he had forgotten something very important, and wired Solange : 'Bring plush bunny. Important. Love.'

On the 26th, another telegram : 'Bring diary Tolstoy and Mrs Tolstoy. Important. Love.'

At 2.2o, Costals was heading swiftly towards the platform at which Solange's train was due to arrive. Never before had he so badly wanted all the women he saw. Was he not about to

be Solange's prisoner for a whole fortnight? Suddenly, in front
of a newspaper kiosk, a seventeen-year-old girl. . . . 'Oh God,
that girl inflames me. And to think that she's only one of my
ribs! A *supernumerary bone*!* I can't help it, that bone inflames me.' He panted. In a few seconds he had turned crimson,
as though the blood was about to burst in droplets through
the skin of his face. She had black hair and almond eyes; the
long line of her forehead and nose receded, rushed back, as in
the profile of Lionello d'Este by Pisanello; the Aztec type:
yes, that was it, she was a Genoese Aztec; her chest was flat
like that of a boy, a boy without an ounce of spare flesh
(Costals hated this in a woman; it was indeed the opposite of
what he liked, and that was why he liked it now). 'I'm mad
about that girl . . . I'm mad about that girl . . .' Their eyes met.
Costals began to zigzag in his course, like a wounded beast,
then half-stopped. He had six minutes to spare, just time enough
to approach her, to start something up. This passionate
desire, this desperate need to escape from Solange at the very
moment when the cage seemed to be about to shut on him,
drove him to try and bring off this capture at any price. The
girl headed towards the platform. Costals overtook her, stared
at her again, intensely, and once more she turned her eyes towards him. Whereupon a train entered the station. Could it
be Solange's? His watch said 2.26, but perhaps it was slow.
Still, he could not allow his 'darling' to get off the train alone,
and have to look for him. . . . horrible thought! But it was
horrible, too, to lose this woman, when all that was needed,
perhaps, was for them to have met ten minutes earlier. He
moved away from her to interrogate an official (no, it wasn't
the train from France), then went back to her, almost at the
double. At that moment another train appeared at the far end
of the platform. How many seconds would it be before
Solange's carriage stopped? Thirty-five? Could one, in thirty-
five seconds, accost an unknown girl, of the Aztec type, and
say to her: 'In heaven's name, let me see you again, tell me
where we can meet,' with enough authority, supplication,

---

*Woman, according to the Bible, is supposed to have been created
from one of man's ribs. It was Bossuet who called woman 'a supernumerary bone' (*Author's note*).

sincerity, trust, etc., etc., in one's mien to etc., etc.? This he would like to do (perversity had now taken a hand in it) while Solange was there, two hundred yards away, a hundred yards, within eyeshot. 'Oh God! Oh God! How I long to make love to her! Oh God, inspire me! Oh God, help me!' (Inwardly he was on his knees.) 'All my life,' he murmured to himself, 'all my life will be devoted to making her happy.' The train glided along the platform. Costals lost his head. 'To think that I shall never have her!' Something akin to tears rose to his eyes. Exasperated, in despair, furious with Solange, he wheeled round and walked away from the unknown girl. Let him never see her again, at least! Let him never see that face again! Let him be allowed to forget her! Here, at a carriage door, was another face, once a promised land as that of the Genoese had been, but now too available and too familiar, too everyday.... Mlle Dandillot would never know how she had been deceived, betrayed and almost cursed at the very moment when, over-flowing with trustfulness and joy, she was reunited with the man who had summoned her there.

In the midst of the crowd, he gave her a swift peck on the cheek, a husbandly kiss. Then he bustled around for a porter – quite unnecessarily, for she had only a small, schoolgirl's suit-case – as though he were looking for an excuse, because he could think of nothing to say to her.

As they entered the hotel there was an atmosphere of chilli-ness, of huddled whispering, in the foyer. From the moment he had appeared there the other day, simply because of the way he had asked: 'Can one hire a suite here?' they had hated him.

Solange bent over the registration form. 'How I love to see her lying!' he said to himself. He knew she was writing Solange Costals. The girl's face was grave and beautiful. The manager watched her intently as she wrote. The porter and the bell-hop muttered something to each other.

'You lie like an angel,' he murmured approvingly as they went upstairs. 'I was afraid you wouldn't know how to – and it's a real disease, not to be able to lie.'

'I can lie to people I don't care about. I couldn't lie to some-one I loved.'

'No, nor could I. But I could lie to someone I only half-loved.'

Not for a moment had Mlle Dandillot suspected that Costals had invited her to Genoa out of 'niceness', in other words out of charity. 'Well,' she had thought, 'only ten days have elapsed and here he is calling me back!' What better proof that he could not do without her? How, after this, could there be any doubt of the outcome of their struggle? She came to the conclusion that Costals' flight had been providential. Mme Dandillot, too, was impressed. Lying on the bottom, belly upwards, on September the 8th, the Hippogriff was back on the surface again, more full of beans than ever, on the 21st. After some hesitation, she agreed to let her daughter go. She told herself: 'He will have lived with her, abroad, for a fortnight. Up to now I could pretend not to know the precise nature of their relationship. After this, impossible. Will he have the nerve to slink off again, when this time it will be tantamount to an insult?'

Mme Dandillot and Solange were agreed that it would be more than ever advisable for Solange to avoid the subject of marriage. She should give the impression, after Costals' two letters and his departure, of having given up her dreams of matrimony and of having come to Genoa simply for a final fling with him before resigning herself, so far as her mourning would allow, to grappling with suitors. Mme Dandillot thought of an even better idea, which involved arousing Costals' jealousy by means of these suitors. This was her plan.

Two years earlier, Solange had refused the hand of a young civil engineer, M. Jean Tomasi. But Mme Dandillot, attracted by prevarication as the magnetic needle is attracted by the North, had emphasized, in transmitting Solange's refusal, that 'the door was not finally closed', that her daughter was very young, and that 'later, perhaps. . . .' Once a year, then, the tenacious engineer had paid a visit to Mme Dandillot: everything still remained in the air, but the door was still kept half-open. Mme Dandillot therefore suggested to Solange that she should tell Costals that, since she had given up all hope of marrying the man she loved, her mother was about to reopen negotiations with M. Tomasi, and no doubt she would have no alternative but to accept the engineer.

At first Solange protested. When, a week later, she said to Costals: 'I could never lie to someone I loved', it was the truth. With a determined glint in her eyes, which she kept glued to the carpet, she repeated to her mother: 'No, I won't lie to him.'

'But, darling, it isn't lying to him. You know quite well that Tomasi comes to see me every year, and, as it happens, always in October. He'll be here in a month. It wouldn't be lying to tell Costals: "This young man is coming to see my mother at any moment".'

'That I can say, but I don't want to say that I shall agree to marry him, because I won't. I didn't marry him when I had no one close to my heart, and I won't marry him now. Now it's Costals or nobody.'

'You can say: "Since I've definitely got to give you up, you might as well realize that this fortnight in Genoa is the epilogue to our relationship. Mummy thinks that, after everything that's happened, the only solution is for me to marry as soon as possible. She's determined to get it over and done with this winter." Is that lying? How do you know I won't do that if Costals goes on shilly-shallying any longer?'

'I'll see,' said Solange. She turned it all over in her head, and much of it remained there.

Their suite in the hotel in Genoa consisted of two spacious rooms, separated by two bathrooms and a lobby. Costals had intended to show Solange round the town as soon as she had had a bath. He imagined her to be much more avid for the sights and smells of Italy than for love-making which, after their last encounter, he had every reason to believe might safely be postponed until the evening. He was therefore very surprised when, her ablutions completed, he saw her reappear not in outdoor clothes but in deshabille – completely naked, in fact, under an almost transparent garment. The centre of her body made a dark patch under the pale material, like a tuft of submarine moss under a light veil of water. What followed may easily be guessed. He performed it with the same avidity with which he sought to lay his hands on posterity.

In the Antwerp *cancionero*, Tristan and Iseult remain on the bed 'clasped, mouth to mouth, as long as a sung Mass'. Costals and Solange remained on the bed an hour longer than the office of *Tenebrae* at Solesmes. They had lain down at half past three. They rose again at nine o'clock.

He had drawn her out of the well of sorrow to make her live beside him, no longer for a few hours at a time, but night and day, he alone with her alone, closer still to each other in the heart of the foreign multitude. He had told her to sign in at the hotel under his name, and she had written this name which was her soul-name: Solange Costals. And now here she was, 'Madame' in the eyes of all, in the very circumstances in which she would have found herself on honeymoon, and in the traditional land of honeymoons and orange blossom. Never since she had known him had she had such utter faith in what she hoped for – a sense of absolute security. And her love, which had been waiting to see a stretch of clear road in front of it before giving itself free rein, burst forward with all its strength, like a sledge launched down a slope.

Never had Costals seen her as she was that afternoon. Her indescribable tenderness. Her indescribably blissful face, radiating happiness, in the midst of her loosened hair, which was like a third being lying between them, full and thick in his hand. In fact, the third person was chiefly the plush rabbit lying on the pillow beside Solange's head, rather moth-eaten and dusty – it would be ungallant to say 'grubby' – with one ear flopping over its snout, and one eye replaced with a boot button. Frequently Costals would kiss it instead of Solange, or else the mouths of all three of them would meet. Costals, who knew his own propensities, was well aware of why he had asked her to bring along the rabbit. (On the other occasions he would make his women wear carnival masks representing animal heads during their love-making. How he outsoared them then, leaping beyond the narrow limits of their sex!) So violently did he involve the rabbit in their love-games that there came a moment when it completely took possession of his imagination to the exclusion of Solange. Then his sensuality took on a quasi-religious character; but soon, no longer in control of the myth he had unleashed, and in the grip of all that was most unbridled in his nature, he was overcome with a kind of terror, and, his eyes dilating, he took the rabbit and placed it on a chair, hiding it under his pyjamas. Whereupon he was restored to reason.

Every few minutes Solange would draw back a little to gaze into his eyes; then she would kiss him, stroke his face, give him more kisses than he gave himself (he was like an overmatched boxer), and he could feel her long hands on his body in new and unexpected places, on his hip, or his shoulders, like those antique statues with severed marble hands still clinging to them from statues once joined to them but now lost. She thrust her head at him, cat-like, then nestled it in his arm-pit, and she had a way of suddenly pressing herself against him with a brief little moan – literally, a death-rattle of tenderness. As he took her for the second time, he thought he glimpsed a wild look in her eyes, and asked her : 'Well, are you beginning to feel something at last in this confounded puppet-show?' To which she replied : 'I feel less indifferent to it than at first.' Since a great deal was not to be expected from her on this score, Costals considered this reply so forthcoming that he was inflamed by it, and proved it to her a third time. She hung out her tongue like a dog, offering it to him.

When he got up, feeling hungry, and said to her : 'Come on, then, up you get! *Ogueff!** Time for grub,' she gave a little sigh, almost a cry, and then said to him : 'I love you so much!' as though to imply : how nice it would be to stay here for ever. Costals' lip was bleeding, from a bite by his shepherdess; his face was swollen and discomposed by her kisses; and he felt a bit groggy. He opened the door of Solange's bathroom by mistake; and he saw, imprinted on the wet bath-mat, the marks of her bare feet. He remembered that, although he had kissed every part of her body, he had nevertheless omitted to kiss her feet, and the thought saddened him.

----

*'Get up!' in Arabic.

Costals had always felt an obscure affinity with animals. In his day-dreams as a twelve-year-old, he used to see a bear advancing towards him. Whereupon he would smile at the bear, and the bear interpreted the smile as saying: 'Not only do I wish you no harm, but I wish you well, because I understand you perfectly.' (Already perhaps, in this 'I understand you perfectly', there was the intuition of a paranormal knowledge.) And the bear did not attack him. They even became pals, and helped one another. It may be worth noting, incidentally, that the child had despised the *Jungle Book*. No passionate person can tolerate, on a subject close to his heart, a way of feeling which differs at all from his own. The young Costals would have found it quite natural for the animal world to be completely closed to Kipling. But since this world was not completely closed to Kipling, he was irritated by the writer's superficial interpretation of these beasts, and by the superficial character of the relations between them and Mowgli.

The performance of 'stopping the bear with a smile' had never, as he grew older, vanished from Costals' mind. If, at the age of thirty-four, he happened to meet a stray dog with a savage look in some lonely wood, it never entered his head to pick up the nearest stone, or even to make the sign of the cross at it, which – animals being always full of hatred for Jesus Christ – would have made it run howling away. He would say to himself: 'If it passes by without looking at me, I won't look at it. If it does look at me, I'll simply look back, and it won't bite me.' There was a mystical faith in all this, and Costals recognized it as such: he knew, therefore, that the whole thing was absurd. In confronting a savage dog he was savouring a triple pleasure: (1) the pleasure of the absurd; (2) the pleasure of putting his trust, not only in the dog (love) but in his own power (pride); and (3) the pleasure of risk (for, after all, he knew he was taking a risk by trusting to his smile).

When he came back from the war, Costals had struck up an acquaintance with an animal-tamer, Monsieur B—, from whom he had learnt that training by kindness, originating in Germany, had recently caught on in France. Between German trainers and their beasts, male as well as female, bonds of affection would often develop, which sometimes went quite far and by means of which the animals performed from love what the old methods made them perform from fear. Costals had gone into the cage with Monsieur B. and, after four or five sessions as an observer, had learned to handle the animals under the trainer's supervision. He believed that if he had had the time to practise regularly, he would have acquired some skill at it. The taming of felines, in so far as he understood it, was a work of domination based on a mixture of courage, intelligence, 'pure' sympathy and sexual emotion (an emotion that innocently revealed itself in its physiological manifestations), all of which, being liable to turn to violence at a moment's notice, admirably suited his temperament.

Costals' power over animals extended also to young people, but stopped there: he had no power over 'mature' men and women (such a pretty word, 'mature' – like cheese!). In his business relations he had no other faculties but will-power, cleverness, brutality and duplicity, which are the usual ingredients by which a man succeeds in doing what he wants and avoiding what he doesn't want. In his pursuit of women, only prestige, persuasion and patience came into play – nothing out of the ordinary. And moreover, his failures in both spheres were legion. Finally, it must be added that, even with animals and young people, his power subsided like the wind on certain days. Melancholy lulls! He was reduced to being a normal man, and felt totally at a loss.

In the vast world of the living, animals and young people were the only creatures to whom Costals never wished harm, to whom indeed he always wished well. Perhaps, partly at least, that was the secret of his power over them: they sensed that he wished them well. The reason for this benevolence doubtless lay in their sweetness and grace, but also in the fact that they were the quintessence of naturalness: how could one be angry with them, since they were devoid of pretension? 'Mature' men and women put on airs, and nine times out of ten lower themselves in the process – hence they are a source of justifiable irritation to those who still have some regard for the human species. But one cannot hate, one cannot despise, either animals or children, because one can never accuse them of being unworthy of themselves: they are miraculously exempt. Costals was so grateful to them for enabling him to experience what sympathy is – that quality which, according to him, had been the characteristic of the golden age – so grateful for being able, with them, to relax from the harsh mistrustfulness which was his normal attitude towards his fellow-men, that he tended to express it in somewhat excessive terms. 'They redeem humanity,' he would say of animals and young people. It was because of them, *and them alone*, that, if he had had the power to do harm on a grand scale (bombing a city, for instance), he would have done it with reluctance, and perhaps could not have brought himself to do it at all. The redemption of humanity by animals and the young was one of his favourite myths, and (which was even odder) had been so ever since he himself had been an adolescent.

It has been necessary to expatiate a little on this subject, to prepare the reader for the scene which follows.

No sooner had Costals and Solange ordered a table for lunch in the garden of a little suburban *trattoria* than a squad of cats came trotting out of the house towards them. They advanced in extended order, one of them stopping dead right in the middle of the manoeuvre to lick a paw. Although there were other people having lunch, it was they who had been picked out at once. The pink cat didn't think twice: at one bound it was on Solange's lap, then it scrambled up over her bust, settled on her shoulder, nuzzled her toque and knocked it askew, raised its tail in the approved style (resisting Solange's efforts to lower it) to show her its bottom, like a tiny full moon, and in fact seemed to have no other objective than to place the aforementioned under her nose.

As for the yellow cat! A feline prawn. A prodigy of emacia-tion and virulence, with affinities to the flea, the prawn and the spider. Standing on its hind-legs and wiping its nose on Costals' dangling hand. Jumping on to the table to get nearer to his face. If Costals moved away to take a look at the scenery, balancing itself on the edge of the table, its fore-paws stretched out, waving, as though to hold him back, and proving *ad nauseam* that, unlike mystic love, feline love does not lend wings, otherwise it would long ago have flown through the air to nestle against his cheek. And all this with such an uproar of purring that Costals' own throat seemed on fire. But every time a noise was to be heard from the inn, the creature would turn its head and stop purring. 'Animals, too!' thought Costals. 'They too have only to be reminded of *home*, and at once their happiness is over.' (Incidentally, it really is an astonishing thing in cats, this gift of being able to stand on their hind legs exactly like goats. That they should do it when one calls them or strokes them, well and good, but to rear up like circus cats ten yards away from a man simply because, having lost sight of him, they have just spotted him again – what sensibility, with an engaging tinge of hysteria!)

When the pink cat nuzzled Solange's neck, Costals noticed that she shivered slightly. She said that it smelt of vanilla, as all cats do when they are young, healthy and well-groomed. And her understanding of cats was demonstrated by the conversation she carried on with it. Every time she said something, it answered with a miaow. If she was silent, and then spoke again, it would reply. What else could that be but speech?

'I've always been like that with animals: a big sister to them. When I was small, I never made any distinction between them and humans. I used to say to my brother: "If you drum against the aquarium like that, you'll make the fish cry." I maintained that horses didn't like their faces, and that was why they stirred the water they were going to drink with their hoofs, so as not to see their reflections in it. At Toulon, where we had a villa for a time, the days when the sirocco blew used to put me in the same state of electric excitement as the animals, who used to go a bit mad. I simply had to run, and I used to drag Gaston along with me. . . .'

'I've noticed this animal side of you for some time – from the way you stare at the flame when someone makes us a rum omelette, or the way your voice changes when you talk about your cats, whose names, incidentally, I don't yet know. . . .'

'They haven't any.'

'No names? What do you do when you want to call them, then?'

'I don't call them. They come when they want to.'

Sublime words, thought Costals. There's the guarantee of my future freedom, if I marry her, as I may well. And the hardest thing to get people to do, even one's friends, is to leave you alone. I'll 'come when I want to'.

Alone of the four, the blue cat crudely begged for food; the others no doubt were there with the same object, but they disguised it admirably (and what an age the blue cat took to decide whether it wanted what Costals offered it or not!). When Costals held out a bit of mustard at the end of his finger, what a look of disappointment, of irritation, of reproach, and also of snootiness! Monsieur fancied himself, Monsieur felt insulted. But when he was offered a piece of orange peel, that really was the limit: Monsieur fled at once. Now he was sulking, sitting a few feet away from the table, looking the other way when one said pss ... pss ..., like a bourgeois when a beggar approaches, and yawning. As for the mauve cat, which had climbed on to the table, it simply devoured Solange with its eyes, opening its mouth from time to time and emitting a miaow that was more potential than actual (not a sound could be heard): it looked like a cross between a seal and a bear-cub. Solange said:

'How much more moving the silence of animals is than the verbosity of men!'

'Yes, but the silence of men is more moving than the silence of animals. . . . Forgive me, but the more I hear people talk about the intelligence of animals, the more I am struck by their stupidity.'*

Meanwhile the yellow cat had buried its head roughly in Costals' half-closed hands, where it had remained for some while, like a child crying into its mother's hands, or a lover into the hands of his beloved. And Costals, when his food was brought, at first did not have the heart to touch it, for fear of disturbing the cat. Fortunately the latter, raising its head and catching sight of a little boy who apparently appealed to it more than Costals, jumped down unceremoniously and ran off to rub itself against his bare calves, leaving our author to resume his lunch. Whereupon the mauve cat, which had

---

*There is an untranslatable pun here: *bête* = animal, *bêtise* = stupidity (*Translator's note*).

awaited its turn like someone waiting to go into the confessional, performed its act, which Costals might have described as follows:

'Pussy right in the middle of a ray of sunlight, like a dancer under the spotlight, while everything else remains in shadow.

Pussy shakes a paw.

Pussy, one ear up and one ear down, like a roisterer. (Why a roisterer?)

Pussy pushes me away with a paw. Ah! so we have a mind of our own, have we?

Pussy bites my shirt-cuff with the utmost violence.

Pussy lifts its dangling ear with its paw, but this time turns it inside out: bad luck! Pussy cannot get it back into place, and gives me a dirty look.

Pussy sucks the handle of my fork.'

Etc.

To get rid of the mauve cat, Costals spread out a newspaper on the ground for it. The pliability and dryness of this newspaper, and the crackling noise it made, played marvellously on the mauve cat's nerves. Now it would sit on its posterior, playing with the edge of the newspaper with its fore-paws and then, of course, losing its balance, falling over backwards, catching sight of its backside in the process, whence an irresistible temptation to lick it there and then. Now it would sit on the newspaper, with the tip of its tongue, which it had forgotten to draw in, sticking out like a bit of ham sticking out of a sandwich, without its knowing – and even if there had been twenty people there, not one of them would have drawn its attention to it, as one would to a gentleman with some bird-lime on his jacket. And yet this forgotten bit of tongue gave it a not very intelligent air. When the mauve cat made as if to leave the newspaper and come back to the table, Costals gazed at it sternly, and the cat stopped with a paw in the air.

'The way you stopped that cat reminds me of the way I control our black tabby. I may tell you I don't like her at all, because she's always been everybody's pet, especially my father's. I only have to look at her and her face falls, she lowers her ears, and slinks away at once, sensing that I don't like her.'

A slight pause, and she added : 'I don't like her!' with such passion that Costals felt that she could be dangerous one day.

'I'll show you something even better.'

Placing his hand over the root of the mauve cat's tail, he took its hind-quarters in his palm. Whereupon the mauve cat, which was obviously a female, completely lost its head. Erectile and vibratile, stretched to snapping-point, in a really sensational nervous paroxysm, frantic, snarling, its eyes like those of a Russian woman (bright green and popping out of its head), it twisted and writhed like a serpent-cat, offered itself right and left, all its dignity (which had never been great) gone to pot, 'came' and 'went' like an 'easy' bull, covered Costals' ankles with hairs – unimpeachable evidence, an examining magistrate's delight – fawned on his shoes, and reminded him in a thousand ways that it was high time it was exorcized. Costals himself was seriously affected by the Spirit. In front of the mauve cat, as in front of a bouquet of flowers, he would have liked to dance, prostrate himself, bang his forehead on the ground, and finally eat it – this last impulse being that which inspires believers to eat their God, lovers to kiss and bite the person they love, which is an adumbration of the act of eating him ('devour with caresses'). He contented himself with uttering cries and mimicking; his face had become cat-like, he had adopted their infantile ways, their look of wild innocence, and even purred, with such a realistic purr that Solange, leaning towards him, listening, was quite taken aback. Soon – as with the plush rabbit – he had to break off, feeling that the moment was coming when there would be nothing for it but to slash his own flesh and crunch ground glass.

As they were leaving, after touching farewells to the charming squad, he said to her :

'In Provençal, a young girl is known as a *chatouno*. From now on I shall call you the *chatoune*.'

From this lunch he took away two profound impressions, left by (1) Solange's animality, which brought her much closer to him, and (2) the strange look (jealousy?) she had given him

when he had gone on holding the two warm little hands of
the yellow cat in one of his.

Afterwards they took a taxi to the harbour. The sea was sea-
green, the sky was sky-blue, the steamers – their hulls painted
with minium – bled into the water. The quays smelt of hemp,
tar, wood and brine. In the scorching barges kohl-eyed dockers
lay sleeping. A liner was getting under way, and as it headed
for the open sea it gave a little toot, poor thing, to keep its
pecker up, and made water behind: piddling with fright.
Clearly it was a boat that was new to the job.

They walked along the jetty, then stopped and sat down on
a pile of rope. A delicious compound of cool breeze and warm
sun! From time to time a wave struck the base of the jetty
with an explosive thump. A fishing-boat called *Dignitas*
(imagine a French trawler calling itself *Dignity*) was bearing
off, and its hawser, unwinding along the quayside, was the
image of a sea-serpent sliding lazily into the waves. Along its
beams the sun lit up a flickering patchwork of flames and
flowers, and the shadow of the boat, beneath it, was absinthe-
green. Gulls rocked up and down on the swell, with an air of
acute discomfort, as though they were about to be seasick. And
amid the slow, ponderous movements of the harbour, a single
motor-launch alone added a touch of speed, leaving in its wake
a wide Neptune's trident of foam that lingered on the water
long after it had disappeared. On the other side, towards the
open sea, the waves surged and tossed like a woman having a
bad dream.

Solange said that the boats at their moorings, with their
heart-shaped sterns and their perpetual rocking motion, made
her think of hearts in torment. Costals said that, swinging
against each other, they reminded him rather of a row of
dervishes. Then he delivered a poetic speech about 'boats with
women's flanks which are like steeds beneath you, like mares
taking a jump when the waves lift them and one feels them
rippling beneath one with all the life that is theirs, and one
helps them on with the complicity of love.' He confessed that

whenever he was in a boat on a sea furrowed by waves, he could not help falling prey to a certain sensual perturbation. Solange refused to admit defeat: she compared the gentle motion of the moored boats, drawing slightly apart, then coming together again, to that of prams being rocked to and fro by seated mothers to send their infants to sleep.

Costals said that their combat with images on a given theme was like the alternating songs of the herdsmen of ancient Greece, and that she deserved the laurel wreath for her image of the prams.

'I won the wreath for the taming of the cats. You've won it in the image tournament. What will the decider be?'

'Which of the two of us can stare longest at the sun.'

Costals flexed his biceps: the sun and he (or 'he and the sun'): they were pals! He'd show her!

Solange raised her head and her pupils widened. She gazed calmly at the sun.

'You looked sideways!'

'Sideways? Oh, how can you be so unfair!'

'Let's begin again.'

He glanced towards the sun, then, with the air of a photogenic dictator, focused his eyes. . . . In fact he focused nothing, for no sooner had his gaze struck the fiery zone than his head sank, his eyes filled with tears, his eyelids clenched tight like those of the aurochs when Ursus breaks its neck.

'Ah, the dirty dog!'

The *chatoune* turned tranquilly towards the zenith. Her features stiffened, her pupils became so immense that they devoured the cornea almost entirely. And she stared at the sun.

If Costals did not fall on his knees, it was because, in spite of everything, he was a fairly civilized man. And if he did not say there and then 'I'll marry you', it was because he still retained a modicum of good sense. But he had to make an effort to prevent himself from doing so. He was certainly determined to marry her. Could any man but he be the lord and master of She-who-stares-at-the-Sun? (Surely there must be a hieroglyph which meant just that: He, or She, who stares at the sun.) He had thought her an ordinary little bourgeoise, but no, she was someone of his calibre, even superior to him. She had proved it with a supreme sign. He imagined her sculpted in granite, seated, her hands on her knees, with the head of a cat. And he seated at her side, his hands on his knees, with the head of a lion. And their tails were entwined. And two rays of sunlight, carved in the rock, descended upon them both. They would take a Coptic priest with them from Cairo, and their union would be blessed on the ruins of Heliopolis. To celebrate the marriage, he would give a great public feast in Alexandria, at which he would do battle with a lion. Yesterday there had been no question of having children. Now all that was changed: they would have fourteen sons. Yes, from the moment they moved on to the superhuman plane, all values were changed. From the moment she had stared at the sun, Costals' literary work retreated to the background; their reign was all. For it would be too stupid if they could not find some tribe to reign over: since already, for her beauty alone, Solange was adored by the children of Europe, there must surely be a child-race that would adore her. And the strength he would draw from her would be great enough to enable him to deal simultaneously with his realm, his work, and his fourteen sons. Before the scene on the jetty, Solange had been a curb on his wilder flights. Now that he knew she was worthy of them, he would make her participate in these flights; she would be one of the ingredients of his poetry. Before, he could find no place for her in his life. Now she had one. Once again he realized that it was not marriage that had made him hesitate so much as Solange's presumed mediocrity. Now that she had given proof that she partook of the superhuman, he thought of their marriage: 'It would be madness to let it slip.'

Costals had not drunk more than a glass of wine the whole day. But when they returned to the hotel, he was so intoxicated with her, or rather with his own idea of her, in other words so intoxicated with himself, that he hastened to wrap a wet towel round his head to ease the strain of the laurel wreath. As the reader himself may equally feel the need to wrap a wet towel round his head, let us pause for a while.

They were at the window, after dinner.

On the suburban hills, rows of street-lamps bordering

avenues invisible in the darkness made a diadem of pearls about the city. Houses full of modest angels each playing with its little paradise. A stretch of beach against which the surf lapped contentedly, rising here and there like a horse tossing its head to show its rider its white-flecked forehead. The high places of silence above them, and the stars, each named after some erotomaniac God, the stars recumbent like cattle in a meadow, a few of them apart from the rest, as a bull stands apart from the herd, waiting to attack some young passer-by who ventures off the road. To the left, the Milky Way seemed to rise from a hill, like smoke from some dying sacrificial fire.

'I love big cities,' he exclaimed passionately, dreaming of all the human material waiting to be corrupted there. And, like an electric current, he felt the three 'phases' of his relationship to the world pass through him: (1) how to enjoy it; (2) how to guard against it; (3) how to make game of it.

'I love any city when I'm there with you,' she said. 'I'd like any provincial hole, or the country, or the desert just as much, if I were there with you.'

Continually, now, she sought physical contact with him, which was something quite new. She had put her arm round his waist (a thing she had never done before) and laid her head on his chest. From the open window on the floor below them rose a 'heady' female scent. She kissed his hand, his mouth, his forehead. He laughed. 'Why do you laugh?' she asked, her face a little anxious and abashed. He did not answer. He was laughing to see her so amorous, she who had always been so cold. But it was she who laughed when, having slid his hand inside her clothes by complicated routes, he plucked the hairs at the base of her spine.

For the first time in her life she had wanted something. Thereto she had dedicated a new-found will, a fresh strength, unused for twenty-one years. She had wanted this stranger to be hers for ever, and she felt that after all their torments he was ready to be at last. How normal, how natural it was, this life they had lived in common since yesterday! It was as if she had never lived in any other way. How quickly her past had closed up behind her! And the more aware she became of it the more her love grew, as a torrent swells gradually more

and more. It was really the thought of marriage that was the
cradle of her love, as it was, or had been, the grave of love
for Costals. And she leaned against her man, with all the
primordial heaviness of her sex, heavy as a rain-sodden tree,
murmuring a confused prayer: 'O God, make my happiness
last! I shall never grow weary of it. . . .'

'Look at that light-house,' she said. 'Wouldn't you think
there were people inside it following one another perpetually
without ever catching up? That's something one mustn't do
in life. . . .'

And indeed there were shadows flitting across the illuminated
beacon of the light-house, always equidistant from one another.
'The waves also go on chasing one another without ever
catching up,' said Costals. 'It's an interesting reflection, though
I distrust metaphors with philosophical pretensions. Metaphors should just be metaphors, and not try to pass themselves off as something more.'

For a long while they gazed at the nocturnal city and the
commonwealth of stars, and then he said:

'These houses, already full of youthful sleepers, torment me.
They remind me that there are things that I do not possess. As
far as my eyes can reach, and well beyond, across the whole
face of the earth, my people stretch: all those to whom, as
a writer, I have brought something vital, and who are ready
to offer me a token of their gratitude. This brings me no joy,
for I have no use for their tokens: I know that what they
are ready to offer me is never what I want. There are as many
unknown women as there are stars in sight as I speak to you
now who have written me page after page assuring me of their
gratitude, their admiration, their friendship, and what have
you. But if, one night, I were to knock at their door and say:
"I am he whose name is alive at the other end of the earth,
and yet it is as a supplicant that I have come to your door.
I have come to receive my reward for what I have given you.
You who said to me one day, with such fervent simplicity: 'I
would like to give you pleasure', you who so far forgot yourself as to kiss my hand, lead me now to that room where the
flesh of your flesh lies sleeping, and let me know her. I shall
not harm her, I shall not turn her against you, I shall cover

her with my riches and she will flower beneath my riches; she will flower beneath the riches of my rain and of my summer. Woman is the warrior's reward, but the children of men are the reward of the poet, and mothers who shut their eyes are the dew of the human species" – if I said all that to them, I should doubtless be met by closed faces and mouths full of insults. And the thought pains me. But what pains me even more, perhaps, is the thought that there are mothers who would be prepared to offer me the flesh of their flesh, for love of me and my works, but who do not know that that is the only thing I want of them, that I spurn the incense of their praise and the smoke of their sacrifices.'

'You ought to slip a veiled appeal into your next novel, in the style of an advertisement: "Mothers wishing provide tangible proof admiration M. Pierre Costals by putting him in touch daughters requested communicate. Utmost discretion. Please send photographs." And perhaps you might even add: "Tokens M. Costals' gratitude will surpass all expectations".'

Solange's jocular tone failed to conceal her underlying acerbity. People who know nothing about life (and pride themselves thereon by calling themselves 'particular') are always rather acid towards those who have some human experience. She did not at all approve of Costals' bringing home to her the extent of his appetites at the end of a day when they had come so perceptibly closer to each other. To which he might have retorted that old father Zeus, in the *Iliad*, is no more tactful towards his ever-loving when, inviting her to share his bed, he enumerates all 'the others' on the pretext of attesting that he likes her best of all; and enumerates no less than seven, with a suitable encomium for each.

Nevertheless Costals replied with the utmost seriousness:

'It's a good idea, and by giving it to me you improve your own prospects. Yes, I shall launch an appeal on those lines in my next book. Let them understand who may. I'm tired of being loved so inadequately, in a sterile and pointless way – it makes me sad and reproachful like a dog whose master, with stupid persistence, goes on offering it a piece of meat it doesn't want, when there's some vanilla cream on the table which would make it burst into speech with joy.'

'If I remember right, the Minotaur needed seven boys and seven girls every year. Is that your ration?'

'I have no ration. People say a lot of things against lust. They say it's disappointing – that it makes one sad – that it prevents one from working – that it prevents one from being an entirely moral person. But what they don't say, and this is one of the most striking things about it, is that it's never-ending. In the act of love-making one thinks to oneself: "What riches I'm storing up for myself. With this, I'm well provided for." But no. Your mistress gives you pleasure and happiness, and you feel desire, affection and esteem for her; but at the same time you go on chasing, and one day in three your pursuit brings you someone new. Well, if you're suddenly deprived of all that, it's as if you had never had anyone at all, you're as starved, as *empty*, as if you'd never had anyone. It's like water through a sieve. During the dog-days, we're irritated because science has failed to tap some of that excessive heat in order to return it to the atmosphere during the excessive cold of winter. Happiness is like summer: it doesn't go on radiating. There is nothing to be got from the memory of it when we feel cold. There are sensations that write in indelible letters. Happiness writes white.'

She felt sorry for him. She was always so glad when she had an excuse to feel sorry for him. And whereas a few minutes earlier she had felt herself to be of very little account in his life, now she felt indispensable once more, *to protect him from the cold.*

'Dear Minotaur, may I suggest that if you need this per-petual renewal of fresh bodies, there could be no better proof that none of the women you've known has fully satisfied you.'

'Perhaps, on the contrary, it's because a woman *has* fully satisfied me that I feel such a desire to begin again with an-other – with all the others.'

They went back into Solange's room. The only light came from the pink lamp above the bed. This pink light was a novelty: there was no pink light in the avenue Henri-Martin; and there was something virginal about it. It was also the first time (apart from the 'hostelry') he had seen Solange in a bed-room that had not done duty for others of his women.

He asked point-blank :

'But after all, why do you want to marry me?'

'To be happy, of course!'

How she had blurted it out! 'To be happy.' O wise response! He always liked people who spoke without shame of their 'will to happiness'.

'I do so want it to happen!' she said fervently.

And he, sincere but prudent :

'And *I* so want you to be happy!'

Yet, since the previous day – and above all since the scene on the jetty – he had begun to think of them as 'we'. Their harmony was complete, and his trust in her immense. What she said and what she did left an impression of ease, of familiarity, of absolute naturalness; they were on a footing of equality; they had only to let their souls give forth their emanations without in any way constraining them. It seemed to Costals that already he had fallen into the habit of thinking of the future in relation to her. His erstwhile exaltation having spent itself, he nevertheless found that it really was marriage that he now fundamentally desired. But what he was physically incapable of was saying the word that would bind him.

'In Athens, the betrothed girl dedicated her childhood plaything – your rabbit – and a lock of her hair to Artemis. In Boeotia, when she arrived at her husband's house for the first time, a wheel of the chariot that brought her there was burnt, to show that henceforth she could never leave this house again. In Rome, when they had reached that point, the bridegroom took his wife in his arms and carried her over the threshold. . . .'

'I wonder if you're strong enough to carry me. . . .'

He sensed the naïve challenge behind the remark, and did not like it. He lifted her up, and she clung to his neck, glueing her mouth to his. Carrying her, he crossed the two bathrooms, but stopped on the threshold of his own room and put her down. The corners of her mouth drooped, and her eyelids fluttered.

He suggested that they should finish the day by reading together.

'Shall we read Tolstoy's *Diary*, for instance – "waiting for each other at the foot of the page", as the saying is? We could begin at the page where he writes: "For fifty years, without a break, woman has been going down in my estimation." Unless you'd prefer the passage which begins with that graceful quotation from Gogol: "Lord, there was already enough filth of every kind in the world. Why did you have to add woman?"'

One may guess what these pleasantries led to: much romping and playfulness. Nevertheless, that night he did not go to her, for fear of spoiling, by sensations which she was liable to reduce to mediocrity, a day that had passed off so successfully. Perhaps also in order to show her that she sufficed him without those sensations. Alone in his bed, he turned over, half-laughing to himself, and murmuring: 'My little girl!' And he thought: 'It would be a *crime* to reject her now, and it's already almost wicked of me to leave her in uncertainty as I'm doing. Yes, now that I've brought her to such a stage of love and hope, it's my *duty* to marry her.'

He woke up in the night and heard the sound of raindrops. He remembered that the window of her bedroom had been half-open when he left her. He was afraid she might catch cold, and crept stealthily towards her door – curious, incidentally, to know whether she had locked it. But no; he went in. He did not look at her asleep: how was he to know? – since she did not want to be seen naked, or to be seen dressing or having a bath, perhaps she would be angry if she learnt that he had seen her asleep.... He merely noticed that she was lying curled up, and promised himself to tell her next day that it was bad for the circulation. Between rounds in the boxing gymnasium, he was always told: 'Stretch your legs well out....'

He closed the window. On the way back, he kissed the foot of her bed.

Costals' Diary

29 September – Enchantment of fascist cats, challenge to the sun, nocturne at the window.... Yesterday was a day of wonders. After these two radiant days, today we get down to the prose. Five years since I cohabited with a woman. Reapprenticeship.

Palazzo Rosso, Bianco, etc. Luckily I know it all. Better not to have seen a museum at all than to have seen it only once in the company of a woman, unless she's exceptional. *Margaritas. . . .*

Anxious about her all the time. Is she bored? Does she think I'm nice enough to her? Was she embarrassed by my shouting at the curator? Have I been idiotically extravagant enough for her to consider that I'm a man of the world? If she says to me: 'Don't bother about me,' is she sincere or merely being tactful? (a woman's ideal being to be served in small things and to serve in great). When I get back to my room an hour before dinner, having been alone with her without a break since ten o'clock in the morning, I feel an absolute physical need to lie down, heart thumping, convinced I've got a fever. A feeling of nervous exhaustion. A feeling of dispersion. A feeling of losing grip. It is three quarters of an hour since I left her, and the nervous vibrations inside me have not yet subsided. My handwriting has been quite changed by it all.

And all day long, in a country where looks are outstanding, being scorched by every face I met, while I was stuck to her. Naturally, I had never seen so many. (The one with the plaits round her head, like the ring round Saturn. . . .) Oh, to let nature go to waste like that! If only I had been alone! As dismal as a horse that senses that its pals are out at grass while the bit is still lacerating its chops. One person can deprive you of the whole immense world, can steal the world from you, put a screen between the world and you. Everything is devoured by that one person; the resplendent universe ceases to exist.

(Written before going to bed.) These three days, the first two of which were flawless, and spent with a girl whose character is ideal, who is the soul of tact and docility, have nevertheless reduced my personality to a state of deliquescence. This evening, while preparing for bed, I go from one object to another without finding what I am looking for although it is under my nose. The dilution of my personality shows even on my face, which seems washed out; my eyelids are so heavy that I can hardly lift them. Inordinate intensity of my reflexes. 'I scarcely belong to myself', sigh the weak-willed. Exactly, but I want to belong to myself all the time.

Title for a novel about marriage: *The Man Who Lost His Soul*.

During the first years of his marriage, Tolstoy thinks he is happy. In fact he is in a daze. He has been knocked over the head.

I am a snake that has been knocked on the head with a bludgeon. It can no longer move.

30 September – In the morning I stay in my room, on the pretext of having letters to write. In the afternoon, a walk in the old town (Sottoripa, San Lorenzo, etc.). Easy, pleasant conversation: all is well. And yet something she said disappointed me in the extreme. As she continues to refrain from questioning me about my life, I congratulate her on this. And she explains: 'But what if I found cause for suffering in your life, in your past! I would rather cherish the illusion that your happiness only began with me. . . .' So, what I assumed to be exquisite tact was nothing but feminine hatred of reality! Trust deriving from ignorance – *there*'s something essentially feminine. They prune away from a man, from an author, everything they don't like, everything that doesn't conform to their 'dream'. The atheist, for them, is presumed to be a 'seeker', the hard man a tender plant, the happy man a prey to anxiety, the scoundrel a man of honour. They don't like real people, but phantoms or archetypes, and they know it. And people are surprised at the blunders they make! And *they* are surprised to find themselves 'let down' in the end!

After dinner, fearing that she might feel deserted, went to read Renan in her room, my armchair next to hers, my left hand slipped under the hollow of her knee, which is moist as a runnel that has recently contained water (this method of reading him would have delighted Renan). She reads Michelet's *La Femme*, rearranging her hair continually. Then I write this, having moved a bit behind her, in such a way that I have only to raise my eyes to see her. Spelling mistakes, words skipped, as a result of the absorption of my personality by hers. I am bewitched by this cohabitation, exiled from the world. I try in vain to read and write; my mind is elsewhere. In fact, it has been turned inside out. . . . S. pumps me dry, as hysterics do when they take on the nervous strength which they have sucked from those they come in contact with.

She asks me: 'No shadows? No misunderstandings?' I fondle her. But she must have read my thoughts.

She said something rather silly: 'Perhaps you don't love abundantly enough. . . .' Why should one love a lot of people? A handful of attachments is enough. Four or five people – the piles upon which one builds one's bungalow. The beasts of the jungle may prowl and roar below, but one is safe. Unshakeable devotion to the members of the clan, but for everyone else, hm . . . like those savages who, though tigers where society is concerned, have a brotherly pact with one particular species (snake-charmers, elephant-tamers, etc.). But why even a 'handful' of attachments? Fewer still: a single attachment is enough. A single attachment would be enough to justify one's exist-ence, if existence needed justifying. A single person whom one loves more and more, from whose body and soul one draws ever more profound harmonies, like the violin of a master, which grows better and better the more he plays it. And this is why, contrary to what is believed by those I do not love, who judge me only by my non-love for them, I am a faithful person, absurdly faithful; only it is to those I love, not those I do not love, that I am absurdly faithful. Ah! when one loves, fidelity is not very difficult. . . . I should like to say all this to her, but if I say it like that, in the abstract, she will be con-vinced that she is one of the 'handful', and one fine day, what an awakening! And if I told her in so many words: 'I'm not talking about you', I should be stabbing her to the heart. So let her go on thinking me 'heartless'.

Going into her room later, find her with playing cards laid out in front of her. 'You're consulting the cards to see if I'll marry you?' She blushes. 'Not at all. I'm playing patience.' Even assuming she was telling the truth, to have caught her in the act of playing patience produces the same effect on me as if I had caught her pleasuring herself. That she should have brought a pack of cards in her suitcase! One degree lower, and we shall be at the crossword stage.

Cohabitation with a woman one 'loves' makes a man of one, because of the continual necessity of coming to terms with her, being on one's best behaviour, keeping a watchful eye both on oneself and on her. The spontaneous outpouring of love gives place to another feeling, by no means ignoble, in which one's affection for another person arises from constant self-scrutiny and self-discipline. But when this woman is only 'loved' (in theory) and not truly loved, and moreover bores you, such an effort is exhausting, especially if one is unaccustomed to putting oneself out for anyone or anything.

Living together is said to be an art. True enough. A state in which one needs constant therapy with a view to forgetting the other person, with a view to protecting oneself from the other person.

I, by your side, will find my solitude again – *Géraldy*.

Agreed, but that being so, the question irresistibly arises: in these conditions, what is the point of living together?

She pines, droops, looks distracted if I do not clasp her lengthily in my arms. As soon as I do, her face becomes transfigured: a dried-up garden in which a hose is turned on – or a dog that was whimpering because it was left alone too long. She is always imperceptibly reminding me of her presence, as a cat does in order to be stroked, or a dog to be played with. I think of that Siamese cat I was rather fond of, but which had such a need to be stroked that it roared ceaselessly – thirty raucous, agonizing miaows per minute – whenever it was not on someone's lap. As soon as it was, and being fondled, it stopped. Since I could not hire a special man-servant to stroke the cat, or have an electrical apparatus specially designed for the purpose.... If I want Solange to purr, I have to pay heed to her the whole time: a little cajolery, an affectionate word, an 'attention' of one kind or another; she must feel continually *propped up*. To be somebody's oxygen flask is not much fun. No doubt, as I say, to remain in control of my work while being continually wrapped up in her, to carry through my life's task while comforting others, is a manly thing to do. But it exhausts me.

Let me live at the summit of my being. Let me drink myself silly on the exaltation I experience from the complete and perfect harmony between what I am and the life I lead. Let me walk on the waters. But no, she burns less ardently than I do, and more slowly. She does not and never will belong to the race of half-madmen to which I belong and which is the only ambience in which I feel at ease. I was on fire: she extinguishes me. I was walking on the waters; she takes me by the arm: I sink.

Lord Byron: 'It is often easier to die for a woman than to live with her.'

Lord Byron, to X: 'It seems you've married a pretty woman. Hm. . . . Don't the evenings sometimes seem a bit long!'

I am not condemning *her*, for she is blameless. I am not even condemning communal life, married or otherwise. I am condemning charity, which forces one to behave towards people as though one loved them, when in fact one doesn't (or at least: when one doesn't love them *deeply*).

1 October – Night with her – agreeable enough. But this morning she is sad. Women, eternal Penelopes, who unravel during the day what they have woven during the night. Evidently she senses that her presence does not make me happy. It is as though both of us were suffering from the *accidie* of people who have just entered the conventual life. I do my utmost to see that she is not unhappy, and in doing so I am unhappy myself, and she remains so: it is the moral of all works of pity. Is she also perhaps disappointed that I have said nothing definite to her, after those first two days when we were so near to marriage? Does she realize that I am at the same stage as when I took the train? Those strange words of hers: 'Mummy is absolutely determined that I should be married before the spring. We must soon give an answer to a young engineer. . . .' There follows a long story about some engineer who has proposed to her. 'But you've never spoken to me about this engineer. . . .' 'I didn't want to worry you.'

Well, let him marry her, and take her off my hands. And yet

at the same time it does affect me, not in my pride, but in the affection I have for her. And then, I can't help wondering whether this engineer really exists. I believe that, if I discovered they had concocted the story in order to fool me (who knows, perhaps a *combinazione* with her mother), I should never see her again for the rest of my life. I may be this and I may be that, but I am not a person who can be fooled with impunity.

At five o'clock, as I was going out to do some shopping, she asked me to post a letter. It was to her mother. Young Dr F. once told me that he used to force the letter-box of his fiancée's house, to intercept letters addressed to her. When I told him: 'You're a real skunk,' he laughed and said: 'Well, at least it shows I've got some personality.' I was holding this letter in my hand, and I thought that if I needed to prove that I had 'some personality', like Dr F., perhaps the situation would be cleared up once and for all, and I should be released and cured. If I had read: 'I've told him about the so-called engineer....' I should have asked her to leave Genoa that very evening, and the future would have been washed clean. It is disturbing to realize how often it is the shabby thing one should rationally choose to do. When I fled from Paris, it was not a glorious gesture, and yet it was the right thing to do.

I strongly suspect that these letters she writes to her mother and receives from her (she does not correspond with anyone else to my knowledge. How lonely she is! I feel sorry for her) are full of me. I don't like it. All kinds of advice and diplomatic instructions must arrive from Etretat.... These two women intriguing away together.... How pure my life was when I was far from the gynaeceum! When I took what I wanted from it in my own time, without ever going into it myself. And fooling fathers and mothers for days on end instead of having to reckon with them.

And yet, even if the engineer is a myth, have I the right to blame her? Isn't it natural that, in the situation I have placed her in, she should try to hasten, to force my decision, even by falsehoods? If, discovering her fib, I had put her on the train back to France, wouldn't that have been odious of me?

It is a horrible thing to feel for another person nothing but that hybrid sentiment, half-way between love and indifference, which is pity. A sentiment that makes it impossible to enjoy them unreservedly, or for them to enjoy you (for people sense pity, and who has ever loved the pity of which he is the object?), that makes one fret and wear oneself out, and all to no purpose, because pity always ends with an explosion which hurls the two people, bruised and panting, in opposite directions, back to where they should always have been.

Rule: Never pity those you do not love (more or less what old Dandillot said to me).

Rule: It is pointless to be really nice to someone, unless one loves them a great deal. For one must love someone a great deal in order to be satisfied simply with having given them pleasure.

Rule: Do good, but at the same time wound the person to whom you do it, so that he will hold it against you. In this way you will gratify two vices at one blow – your love of being charitable and your love of being hated.

2 *October* – The school year begins tomorrow. In every city in Europe, as here in Genoa, all the kids with the same parcel under their arms: the new shoes they have just been bought. Brunet makes a scene, insists that unless he is bought a frog-green scarf, he won't be able to work properly. He also wants Old Mother Hubbard to buy him a tie: 'You're a woman: you know about such things. . . .' He loves his frog-green scarf so much that he cannot be persuaded to take it off in the house: he eats his meals in it. He has not written to me since the 25th.

When he lived with me, he used to irritate me too. But it wasn't the same as with Sol. It would take pages to explain all the subtle differences. Or perhaps only a line. He distracted me from my work, because I was too busy loving him all the time.

(Written in the evening.) Interminable day with her. Nothing serious: simply the fact that we have nothing to say to each other. I imagine myself having made up my mind to marry her, and soliloquizing thus: 'To think that we're going to have nothing to say to each other for thirty years. Not only that it's just beginning, but that it hasn't yet begun. . . .'

'You're gloomy. What's wrong?'

'You know quite well, it's always the same thing.'

'The future?'

'Yes, I'm haunted by the thought of being dispossessed.'

'Dispossessed of what?' I persist, determined to probe the wound thoroughly.

'Of you.'

'So you think you possess me?'

Without answering, she presses herself against me – a gesture which maddens me. Her remark has turned me to ice. Three possible interpretations of this idea of 'possessing me'. She possesses me in the sense of forcible seizure. She possesses me in the slang sense of the word: I've been *had* by her, gulled. She possesses me in the sense of diabolical possession: the dream in which she was lying on top of me like a fungus, and everything I have observed about the way she eats up my life.

Later, seeing a train pass by, she sighs: 'Think of all the shattered hopes and unrealized dreams it's carrying away with it.' A woman will never believe that a passing train may also be carrying away realized dreams. For melancholy is the luxury of the poor in spirit. In the West, dominated by women, the cult of suffering; in the East, where man is the master, the cult of wisdom. But I, by the side of this silent and dejected woman, become soured, and turn over in my mind phrases that are unworthy of myself and of her. So then I take her by the arm and put her hand in mine. Every time I sense that there is something irremediable between us, I perform some little act of endearment intended to lead her to believe that I still love her, as though I felt she had read my thoughts. And in the end I come to have a horror of these lying caresses, which dishonour true affection, of which they are the simulacrum, as charity dishonours love. O God, do not let me give in to all the ugly feelings she arouses in me! Help me to hold out for the week that remains. . . .

Living together consists almost entirely of waiting for the other person. Solange not being ready, Costals had gone down and taken his seat in the hired car which was to take them to San Cassiano. The village of San Cassiano is a target for excursions, in other words a place totally lacking in interest, since the sole object of excursions is to try and kill time. Solange appeared at last.

'You've put too much powder on.'

'That's because I hurried.'

He looked at her malevolently. Simply because she had put her powder on badly, because she wasn't looking her best. He saw what she would be like at fifty: a frightful, bloated little bourgeoise.

They drove off. The sky was greenish-blue like the bellies of certain monkeys. From time to time the countryside opened out to disclose the hard outline of the sea, and from this infinite, dazzling expanse of azure and sunlight there rose a chill as from a well.

Solange said not a word, and when you are a couple, neither has the right to look absent or preoccupied without being made aware of the other's anxiety or disapproval. As always when he did not know what to say to her, Costals slipped his arm through hers and took her hand, as a matter of form. She pressed close to him, still silent, and he caught a glimpse of her expression of dumb reproach, with its eternal question-mark: 'Why, why don't you marry me? You know how much I love you, and you pretend to love me.' But soon, at the slightest jolt the car made she began to make faces and cling to the door-handle. Costals did not mind these jolts, which he would not even have noticed had he been alone. Gradually he became aware of them, and suffered likewise. Living together induces a process of osmosis. If one of the pair is bored, he forces the other to be bored too. If one suffers from some discomfort or other, he forces the other to suffer from it too.

Thus the journey, which lasted an hour, was ruined for Costals. Then they arrived at San Cassiano. The red and white village lay drowsing in the innocence of morning. Urchins, rather lumpish, snotty-nosed, their shouts tailing off, were playing at persecuting one another. A man was asleep in the sun, covered with flies like an open wound. Worried-looking

438

dogs trotted briskly about their business, obviously with important engagements to keep. A tourist motor-coach, whose occupants had just visited the church, was driving off again. A pretentious-looking little woman sat in it with a tiny dog on her lap. Costals exchanged an extremely roguish wink with the dog as they passed.

'You made eyes at that old hag!' said Solange in a very unfriendly tone.

'Not at all, I made eyes at the dog. And how very saucy he looked!'

Now they were climbing up to the church, Mlle Dandillot's eyes glued to the tips of her shoes (a fine way to visit 'beauty spots'), in other words sunk in her hippogriffical stew-pot. They went into the church.

She remained for a long time on her knees. 'Did you ask the god of the Christians to persuade me to marry you?' he asked on the way out. 'I simply said: "My God, make me happy",' she replied, quite unselfconsciously. 'So you have faith?' 'No, but I have something. . . .' Costals had expected an answer of this sort, and it was in order to receive it that he had asked his second question: so that she might flounder a little more.

The torture of having eternally to reckon with another person whom one does not love! When one does love someone, it is pleasant to have to reckon with them; of the time they make one waste one simply tells oneself: 'After all, a certain amount of relaxation is always necessary.' Before the war, Costals had had a German sheep-dog, and often this dog, seeing him go out, would accompany him without being asked, and then make it blatantly obvious that Costals was expected to devote his time to playing with it. For two hundred yards Costals would make it chase after stones, or else, pretending that the dog was a lion, and roaring on its behalf, he would tame it. After which, since he had come out to read, if not to work, he had had enough. 'You damned monkey, this is the very last time I throw your stone for you.' Faced with the dog's imploring eyes and its irresistible sadness, this 'last time' was repeated over and over again. And Costals' walk was ruined. Fortunately, Hesiod's words can be applied to gods, beasts, children, savages and Costals (this recital is a key, though it may not appear to be one): 'The mind of Zeus passes easily from one thought to another.' Thus it would happen that the dog, its whim changing, and suddenly no longer 'loving' Costals, would abandon the game and go back home alone. And Costals, delivered from the demon of charity, could open his book again.... Walking beside Solange, he remembered these little scenes. 'Although nobody would suspect it, no doubt it gives her pleasure to go out with me. There's no accounting for tastes.' But if, changing her mind with canine suddenness, in other words no longer 'loving' him, she were to return by herself to the car, leaving him alone if only for ten minutes, what a sigh of relief he would have given!

On the way back she was even more silent and morose. And her silence continued in Genoa while they lunched in a restaurant – surrounded, as it happened, by five or six other couples none of whom unclenched their teeth except to eat. 'We are the Eternal Couple, who spend their lives sulking at one another. And if one wants to plumb the depths of human abasement, one must never seek them in the individual, however abject he may be, but always in the couple.' However, towards the end of the meal she tried to start a conversation, but this time it was he who did not answer. He was on the point of ordering his dessert in advance, paying the bill, and going back to the hotel alone, leaving her in the lurch. But they left together, he lashing his calves with his tail (it being understood that, ever since the 'challenge to the sun', he regarded himself, more or less, as some lion-headed Kronos). No doubt he had now earned the right to be alone for a few hours, but he would still have to see her again towards the end of the day. The prospect of meeting her again seemed an ordeal, and the thought of the girl's idleness – which rubbed off on him – a torture.

As soon as they arrived at the hotel, the storm broke.

'And now I insist that you tell me precisely why you were sulking this morning.'

'But I wasn't sulking! On the contrary, it's you who never really let yourself go when you're with me....'

'I know you too well to let myself go with you. I only let myself go with people I don't know, and when it's dangerous to do so.'

'You trust people you don't know, but not me?'

'I don't trust anyone.'

'Don't you trust me?'

'I trust what you are now. I should be lying if I said I trusted what you may become.'

She shrugged her shoulders convulsively.

'You always think I'm sulking when I don't talk. Have you forgotten *Miss Silence*? I always feel much better when I'm not obliged to answer.... What I want is to be understood without having to explain myself.... But after all, doesn't everyone, more or less.... When you went out with your mother, didn't she remain silent some of the time?'

'Please don't bring my mother into it. I never had the slightest difficulty with my mother. I was always happy with her, and she was always happy with me. So you weren't sulking this morning? You didn't say more than twenty words in three hours, and you weren't sulking?'

'No. I was thinking about the future.... I was so happy to be with you....'

'Well, anyone who had seen you would have sworn you were having a fit of sulks. If you look as though you're sulking when you're happy, it's rather serious. Because I've got better things to do than spend the whole day asking myself: "Did she get out of bed the wrong side? What's the matter with her? Is it my fault? How? Or is she simply feeling happy?" To have to hang on everything that goes through a woman's head! Let's say it's a misunderstanding on my part. Let's admit I'm impatient, irascible, impossible; nevertheless it's a fact that there are dozens of men and women with whom I never quarrel. And with you I have a quarrel after a week of living together. If it had happened after five years of marriage! No, believe me, a situation in which by loving each other we can't help hurting each other is not a healthy one. For I love you, and yet I feel capable of hurting you, although it is my misfortune not to have the courage to take the plunge and be frankly cruel to you.'

'If you're unhappy because you can't be nasty to me, then go ahead, get it out of your system.'

Agitated and distraught, she paced up and down the sun-speckled room like a wild beast prowling through the sun-speckled jungle, lashing her calves with her tail. Yes, it was true, there was something wild about her, this girl who normally lived with all her lights dimmed. Her expression was hard, her eyes had darkened and grown strangely bloodshot, as had her cheek-bones, which were now slightly blotchy; and her nose gleamed in the middle of her powdered face. Costals realized the extent to which she had become a woman, the extent to which he had made her a woman with all his manipulations. Ah! she had been well worked over. From her very first day here, even when she had been so tender in her caresses, he had noticed that she had lost her school-girl's voice, that voice from another planet, her lunar voice of old. Her face, her expression, had become sharper. And the energy with which she stuck the hairpins into her hair and combed her thick tresses was fraught with menace for that peace of mind so dear to the man of thought. Before, she had been a little artichoke. Now she was a woman. A bad business. Like the sea, which the timorous traveller goes out to examine at seven o'clock in the morning and finds calm, but which at ten, when he goes on board, has turned rough. Her hard woman's face. He was afraid of her. Afraid of what she was about to become. Afraid of what she might be capable of doing to him, if he were mad enough to shut himself up in the cage with her. And as there was always a dormant ferocity in him only waiting for a chance to show itself, it was fear that awoke it (the mechanism is always the same, with wild animals as with men : fear engenders the ferocity by means of which one may eliminate what makes one afraid, and ferocity engenders fear – fear of reprisals). And she, pacing up and down, glowing with beauty and life in her emotion, had the air of a caged panther; while he, seated, drawn in on himself, bent forward (so that his back suggested a bristling spine), his eyes narrowed, his mouth cruel, tense with cowardly malevolence, irresistibly recalled a hyena.

She went on :

'If you feel that this experiment has proved that you can't live with me, you have only to bring it to an end. I can simply go away. I didn't impose myself on you. It was you who sent for me. . . .'

'I've been waiting for you to say that for a long time. I sent for you, yes. And why did I send for you? Because I felt you were unhappy. I had no need of you; on the contrary, you were bound to get in my way. I brought you here out of charity. The demon of charity, which is always disorganizing my life. . . .'

Mlle Dandillot collapsed into an armchair and began to sob. Costals flung back his head, like a boxer who has just floored his opponent. 'Well, there it is at last! At last she knows what crying is.*

'It's always the same. I struggle against charity, then I give in. But charity is a double-edged weapon, it turns back not only on me, but on the person to whom I've dispensed it – for charity always misses its target; that's axiomatic. Then I suffer, that's to say I turn nasty, for with me suffering is never passive and inert, it at once becomes aggressive. Most of the cruel things I've done have been the after-effects of charity. With women. With men. That woman I showed you in my studio at Port-Royal. . . . And lots of others. . . . Always charity or pity at the bottom of it. Charity upset things. Cruelty restored them to normal. In fact I don't know why I say "charity"; it's much broader than that; it's good itself that's at issue. The "good" should mean living life to the full, without bothering about others. Your warmth should rekindle them, set them in motion. Alas! it doesn't work out like that. This frightful temptation to do good. Try as I may, I succumb to it the whole time. It's a vice. And doing good knocks me out. You know, the way rockets shoot up and then reach the summit of their marvellous ascent and fall back again, or rather vanish, cease to exist. Sometimes, too, they fall into the crowd, and people are wounded. And there would have

---

*Solange never cries, has never cried. 'You can't cry when some-one's looking at you, or you can't cry at all?' the doctor asks her. 'I can't cry at all.' Cf. *Pity for Women*, p 190 (*Author's note*).

been neither that fall to earth, nor that sinister dying away, nor those wounded, if there had been no marvellous ascent. Or again, think of a wild cat, its eyes popping out of its head, making a mad rush to the top of a tree. But once there, it can't get down, it miaows, and one has to climb up and get it. I too, when I've done good, or simply when I've done what the mob would call "my duty", when I've rushed to the top of the tree, I too am caught and start to cry. Such sadness.... As after the carnal act. Only, after the act, it's physiological, it's over quickly; and besides, it's exceptional, at least in my case; in fact one's extremely happy; in any case it's not in the least important, and those who use it as an argument against sex are fools. Whereas the depression I get after doing good happens every time, and it lasts, and there are reasons for it, or at least so I suppose. Perhaps the knowledge that it was useless: apparently useful, but useless in fact, and that I've been duped. Or the feeling that, where others would be happily aware of having done good, I feel only remorse, and the realization that one's so different.... Why should I feel pleasure in being so different from others, on occasions when that difference implies no superiority over them?'

'You said ... that day in the kitchen : "I enjoy evil ... but ... I ... I think I enjoy . . . good even more",' Solanage hiccoughed through her tears.

He began to laugh.

'I told you that because it was the opposite of the truth, to tease God (metaphorically speaking, since I don't believe in God).'

A silence.

'I've had a fairly adventurous life. Out of two hundred battles fought, let's say I've lost a hundred. Out of this hundred, I lost fifty out of cowardice; I broke off and fled under full sail. But it wasn't only cowardice. I have too much contempt for the world's opinion not to enjoy running away. Someone once made a very witty remark about me: "He's only capable of making up his mind when it's a question of beating it." The other fifty battles were lost because of a momentary hesitation. One moment's hesitation, and my opponent got the upper hand. Well, in those fifty battles, my hesitation was always the result of charity. I was overcome with pity, and although in a position to strike the final blow, I didn't. Result: it was I who received the blow.'

'Have I struck you many blows?'

'Yes, many, without realizing it.'

Solange sobbed into her hands, her body shaking convulsively. Then with one hand she began rumpling her dress, and one of the seams split open. Ought he to shut up? Pity again! Besides, he was enjoying his anger against her, especially because today (as we have seen) Solange was not looking her best. Achilles in the *Iliad* says that anger is 'sweet as honey'. And anyone who has never felt himself quivering from head to foot with anger or hatred cannot be called a man: there is no merit in being kind if one lacks the power to be cruel. Moreover, he had never relented towards someone who was crying, simply because they were crying. Not even his son. He had a horror of tears. When his son was small, he had made him promise never to cry. (And sometimes Brunet would hide his face in Mlle du Peyron's skirts and say: 'Hide me, because I'm going to cry, and I don't want papa to see me.') One day, when he was thirteen, his father having given him a fifty-franc note to buy some ink for his fountain-pen and told him to bring back the change, Brunet had come home looking crest-fallen. 'It was the boy at the stationer's, not the boss. He cheated me out of fifteen francs. There's fifteen francs missing from the change. He said he'd given them to me. Oh, if only there'd been a policeman about!' Costals had never caught his son out in any dishonesty. But the disappearance of the fifteen francs struck him as suspicious. 'It's annoying, because I don't know which of you is lying, you or the stationer's boy.' Ten seconds went by, during which Costals made a few commonplace remarks about how irritating it was to lose fifteen francs, and at the end of those ten seconds his son's face turned scarlet, his mouth swelled up, and he looked like a frog: he was crying. 'Why are you crying?' 'Because you said it was me who took the money.' Whereupon he believed that Philippe was telling the truth, but did not embrace him or console him in any way. He let him go on crying, still saying nothing but vague and banal remarks.

It was not until the boy's tears had dried that he said: 'You know, I believe what you say.' And another ten seconds later, the child resumed his frog's grimace and started to cry again. 'You've got nothing to cry about any more. Why are you crying?' He did not answer, but heaved a great sigh and moved nearer his father (they were both sitting on a sofa) and put his cheek against his. And Costals, though convinced of Brunet's double grief, at being robbed and then suspected, and having witnessed his extreme sensitivity, since it was the assurance of having been believed that had made his tears flow a second time, Costals, his face in contact with that of his son (which was as fresh and cool as the body of a trout), had still resisted the temptation to embrace and fondle him. He had simply touched his hand, and then they had talked about something else. All this because he wanted to train people to understand that their tears would never persuade him to relent. (In fact Brunet's tears had not been entirely in vain, since it was through them that he had proved his innocence. But that is another matter.)

Costals went on:

'I began to pity you the day I realized that I didn't love you enough. That is to say from the very beginning. Ah, if only I loved you! If only I had been able to take you out of the hell of charity and bring you into the paradise of love! Everything would have been so marvellously simple. I know what it is to love: you would have been my wife three months ago. But I don't love you. I mean I don't love you deeply. And there's an abyss between loving deeply and loving otherwise than deeply. To love otherwise than deeply is not to love at all. My life is elsewhere. My life is where you are not. You were a mistake. . . . '

Mlle Dandillot leapt up, quivering, with the force of a billiard ball quivering at the edge of the pocket, and rushed to the door. He caught her, took her by the arms, forced her to sit down again, and knelt on one knee in front of her. He soothed her, letting her cry against his breast while he kissed her eyelids sadly. Sadly, because he knew that soothing her did not alter in any way the situation he had just described; and once more he was revolted by the caresses and cajoleries by which one tries to disguise some irremediable ill, he fought down the clichés that passed through his head: 'Cruel only to be kind,' etc., he fought down the vulgar impulse of lovers, whereby a 'scene' can only end up in bed. He did not speak, he had the honesty not to say anything to her: what could he have said that would have consoled her? He would have had to retract his last remarks and that he could never have done, even if she had begged him to. 'The desire for sincerity, that sort of turbid passion which justifies every crime.'* She stopped crying at last, and kissed his face, the palm of his hand, even his hairy fore-arm. These last two gestures, which she had never indulged in before, seemed very extraordinary to Costals, and little to his taste. Her mouth in those hairs, especially. Obviously women must be very different from the rest of the world, to take pleasure in touching a 'mature' man. (Perhaps, after all, they were merely following the instinct of their sex. But still, a man after the age of eighteen was not exactly appetizing.)

And then, always these gestures, when it was words that were required. However, the words came:

'I who try to do everything I can to make you happy. But you know yourself that I've always remained a little girl. I've never left the shadow of my parents, I've never had any friends. How do you expect me to be anything but awkward in my relations with people, especially with a man like you? I've got to get used to you. It's all a question of adapting oneself. You say it's more serious that we should have these clashes before marriage than five years after. It would be much more serious then. A day will come when habit....'

'But I don't want life ever to become a habit with me.'

'Still, at the moment we're living in rather abnormal circumstances. You feel you have to look after me all the time; if we were living a normal life we'd only see each other for a few hours a day. If it was up to me, you could have the greatest freedom even now. Do you think I haven't learnt how to keep myself busy and amuse myself, over the past fifteen years?'

He went on fondling her. He stroked her forehead to smooth

*Jean Cassou (*Author's note*).

447

away her frown. 'Have I got wrinkles?' she asked. He teased
her a little: 'Didn't I warn you in writing that I reserved the
right to make you unhappy one day out of fifteen?' Pointing
to the little stains made by her tears as they fell on her sleeve,
he asked her if ordinary stain-removers were effective against
tear-stains – unless she would prefer to leave them there as a
souvenir, and her costume thereafter be christened, in the
language of the fashion houses, 'Fountains of Italy' or 'The
first time I cried'.

'I told you just now that I didn't trust anyone. Do you
remember?'

'Do I remember!'

'Well, it wasn't true. I was lying. I *want* to trust people, just
as Christians say one has to *want* to believe.'

'I trust *you*.'

'And there you were, pacing up and down the room like a
jungle cat ... or at least a jungle kitten....'

She smiled, and he was mean enough to think that she had
cheered up remarkably quickly....

'You're always making the most execrable jokes, but for
once you've thought up a nice one ... And you're afraid of a
kitten?'

'Yes, of course. Kittens can scratch your eyes out.'

However, he could not let himself go as he would have
liked, clasp her wholeheartedly in his arms, because his anger
had exploded as soon as they returned, before he had had a
chance to change his shirt (a tennis shirt which he wore without a jacket), and, the day being extremely warm and humid,
sweat had seeped through under his armpits, so that he was
afraid Solange would notice the smell if he brought her too
close. This fear of his modified the whole aspect of their recon-
ciliation, made it somehow stiff and cold, which distressed
Solange: she would have so loved to bury herself in his arms!
For her part, she was embarrassed by her red-rimmed eyes and
flushed face, in spite of the fact that she had quickly powdered
it again. Both of them hesitated to admit to themselves that
if they were to carry through a scene that would figure
honourably in their sentimental annals, they would first have
to go next door to spruce themselves up.

He said to her :

'I've twice made you a woman – the day I took you, and the day I made you cry. Now I've really set my seal on you. Nevertheless I ask you to forgive me for having made you cry.'

With the utmost solemnity she replied :

'Yes, I forgive you.'

He went into his own room, and, after a moment, lit a cigarette. After another moment, she knocked on the door, and he threw his cigarette out of the window : no, this was not the moment to appear nonchalant! She said to him :

'I've just put a stitch in my dress – the seam had come undone. While I've got a needle threaded, is there anything of yours that needs sewing?'

He saw that she in her turn wanted to be forgiven, and to obtain forgiveness by making herself useful – materially useful, since she had failed to make herself spiritually useful. He was partly touched and partly embarrassed. Embarrassed chiefly.

'No, thank you. Besides, there's the floor-maid. . . .'

Lovers' quarrels are said to cement love. In reality, they cause cracks that nothing will cement. When one looks back over one's past, one finds (especially if one is a highly-strung person) that the people one has loved most deeply are those with whom one has *never* had a quarrel. And there are some : the miracle exists.

The next five days passed so-so, with walks in the town or on the sea-shore, and a few excursions. Solange was more and more certain that nothing positive would come of her stay; she found Costals stiff and evasive, with already a whiff of absence; and she put on her ugly 'What's the use?' expression. 'It was too good to last,' she sighed on one occasion, after a long spell of mutism. The remark brought a sharp rejoinder : 'What do you mean by that? Personally, when something is going well, I say to myself : "It's too good not to last." And it lasts.' Costals thought that what she ought to have said when he had caressed her after her tears was : 'Well, since you don't

love me, and since you've admitted it to me, God knows how
forcefully, I had better give up the idea of marriage.' But she
had not said this. She would put up with anything. She was
stuck to him like a cupping-glass, and she would not unstick
herself until he tore her off and threw her away, at the risk
of breaking her. She was in love, not with him, but with
marriage, or else simply with the idea of seeing her obstinacy
triumph. He wanted to have it out with her once and for all.

'Do you still think, after what I said to you the other day,
that this marriage should take place?'

She lowered her eyelids before answering, with a slightly
superior, big-sisterly look, as if to say: 'Come, come, the
question hardly arises,' and then she said:

'Of course. It will all come right in the end.'

Why hadn't she at least thought of advancing her departure,
if only, in order to avoid explanations, by pretending that her
mother had called her back for some reason or other? But no,
far from it; a remark of hers – 'Venice must be magnificent in
autumn. Is it very difficult to get there from here?' – showed
him beyond a shadow of doubt that she wanted him to take
her to Venice. 'I only half-give to her, and half-giving is useless: one must give all or nothing. I put myself out a great
deal for her; but in her heart of hearts she reproaches me for
having brought her here to moulder in a rather ordinary town
like Genoa. A town where no one is ever heard singing *O sole
mio*, pooh! She bores me to death without getting any satisfaction herself: we know all about that. Take her to Venice! I'd
rather die! Have her ruin all the exquisite memories of the
time I was there with a woman I loved *deeply*, and the pure
memories of the time I was there alone. She's unhappy here,
and she sees that I'm unhappy because of her – so why does
she stay? Because her trip's been paid for, and Genoa after
all is a bit better than Etretat?' (For Costals, anyone who did
a thing he had no particular desire to do, for the simple reason
that he could do it for nothing, was condemned out of hand.)
He asked her several times, almost reproachfully: 'So, in spite
of that scene, you continue to love me?' She answered with a
fond look. He was disappointed. Ah, if only she could have
brought herself to break away from him!

He was already so immunized by habit that when she wandered round their suite half-naked he no longer even raised his eyes to look at her, pretty though she was, with that figure worthy of a 'Miss France'. Rather any unknown woman, however plain, than the most beautiful body in the world that one can have every night. In spite of this, from time to time he found himself wanting her, and hovered round her like a hawk above a hen; ridiculous no doubt, but not more so than cats or dogs that feel randy, and they, poor things, make no bones about it. She was slow to understand what he wanted. That endless rigmarole of caresses, with nothing to back it, that viscous sentimentalo-sexual mush – how loathsome it all was!

During the course of one of their conversations, she said to him:

'I admire you for having a moral code of your own, so totally non-conformist, and for remaining a decent man in spite of it. But you would do well to keep it to yourself, because if it fell on certain ears.... It's lucky you haven't a son....'

Costals felt himself turn pale, and was disturbed by it. So all the effort at dissimulation and pretence to which he submitted himself could be ruined in a second, and by whom!... A wretched little female had the power to prise him open, as one prises open a box.

'And why is it lucky that I haven't a son?' he asked in a strained voice.

'Because if he heard all these theories from your lips....'

He threw her a glance full of hatred. Ah, so she would be against him in front of his son, if ever....

'If I had a son ... I would passionately want to make him ... like me, towards and against everyone.... (His voice came in jerks, misfiring like an engine.) 'And his morality would be *my* morality ... towards and against everyone. And he would be a fine son. A miracle? But I live in expectation of miracles. I expect a miracle to happen every day. I wait for it, I challenge it, for weeks on end. For months. There have been times when I have waited for it for years. But it always comes. And I see it the very moment it comes – that is my gift – I see it as God could be seen when he appeared in the burning bush.

Sometimes I grow tired of the miracle. Then I wait for another. For weeks. For months. You say to yourself that it must always be the same. But I've been at it for fifteen years and I'm still not bored with it. I'll never be bored with it. I'll croak in the middle of it. I'll croak with a miracle issuing from my mouth – like a fire-eater in a fair, puffing fire.... Now let's talk about something else. You and I are tired of this subject.'

An hour later, looking at his watch, he saw that it had stopped an hour before. He thought it must have been the violence of his rage when Solange had said to him: 'Lucky you haven't a son', which, affecting the mechanism by bodily contact, had thrown it out of gear. It had happened to him several times.

The two days preceding Solange's departure passed fairly lightly for Costals. The loss of nervous energy to which she had subjected him was such that everything inside him seemed to be happening in a sort of vacuum peopled with ghosts. In Algeria, he had heard of a kif-smoking Arab who, when in the last stages of stupefaction, was in the habit of repeating (was it a sensation peculiar to him, or a dictum?): 'Inside the kif-smoker's head there is a little bird breaking dry twigs.' Inside Costals' head there was a little bird breaking dry twigs. But where had it gone, the strength she had drained from him? When he thought about it, a strange smile appeared in his eyes, as though he knew where that strength had gone.

On the last night they spent together, a stormy night, he had made love to her mightily, and had gone back to his room, when a thought struck him which he was amazed not to have had before. He had asked her for a 'solemn promise' not to oppose a divorce if he married her. But he had not asked for a solemn promise about what the French language, with sybilline modesty, calls *la suppression de part*.* We know how strongly he felt on the subject (there was no longer any question of the fourteen sons). This omission disconcerted and

---

*Abortion (*Translator's note*).

appalled him. He could not bear the uncertainty for another half-hour (the time it would take him to go to sleep), so he got up and went back to Solange's room.

She was asleep. He lay down beside her, above the sheet, without switching on the light. He could hear the rather unattractive noise of her grinding her teeth. He could hear the shrieks of the steamers in the storm-tossed harbour, the frightful shrieks they uttered when they went adrift, shrieks that might have been uttered by beasts or men. He had no desire to touch her, or even to look at her asleep, although there were so many others whom he had watched endlessly as they slept, full of frowns and sighs, like dreaming dogs, or with their mouths half-open and a thread of saliva strung from lip to lip.

'Solange!'

No answer.

He thought she might be dead. Oh, what a dawn! He remembered the night he had sat up beside his dead mother and had ended up by stretching out, exhausted, beside the corpse, above the sheet, as he was doing now.

'Solange!'

'Is it you?'

'Wake up.'

'What's the matter?'

'I have something important to say to you. Are you properly awake?'

'Yes.'

'I once asked you to make me a solemn promise. I now want you to make me another solemn promise. I emphasize the word "solemn" because just a mere promise. . . . For instance, when I give a promise. . . . Having "given" it, how can I possibly "keep" it? Whereas, a solemn promise is quite different.'

'What do you want me to promise?'

'If I married you, and you became pregnant, would you do whatever was necessary not to have a child?'

'Yes.'

'An abortion is always dangerous. If the child was born, would you do whatever was necessary to see that it didn't live?'

A flash of lightning lit up the room, a dazzling thought from on high: Nature, too, when she is angry, has infinite thoughts. And there followed a vast, long drawn-out roar, like the roar that the sea must have made when it closed over Pharaoh's host. 'Pharaoh, Pharaoh,' thought Costals. 'The hardening of Pharaoh's heart.... But it was Jehovah who hardened it, and afterwards punished him for it. So, which of the two, Jehovah or Pharaoh, behaved like a swine?' And his soul continued to call through the night, lovingly: 'Pharaoh! Pharaoh!'

When the trance was over, and silence had returned, he said to her:

'Do you remember what I asked you before the thunder?'

'Yes.'

'What is your answer?'

' "Yes".'

'Your answer is "yes"?'

'Yes.'

'Is it a solemn promise?'

'Yes.' ,

'How naïve it was of me to think: "What sort of a world am I dragging this little girl into?" ' Costals said to himself. 'Why, she has been in this world for ages!' A wave of affection swept over him: yes, they might well get on together.... 'I love this sinister world we live in: we suit each other. Innocents are not in my line.' He put his hand on her knee, above the sheet.

'Don't mistrust me,' he murmured, using the familiar second person singular.

'I shall never mistrust you.'

It was the first time he had used the familiar form ever since that distant day when, after their first kisses, he had ventured an occasional *tu* which she had promptly put a stop to by saying: 'I don't know how to say *tu*.' Supposedly a young girl, yet a woman. Supposedly respectable, yet travelling with a lover. Supposedly Catholic, yet prepared to by-pass the Church to get married. Supposedly honourable, yet ready to kill. And indeed, this is what a man likes in a woman. Mme X 'says' nothing to him. But suddenly she takes to robbing and killing, and at once he begins to desire her. Ten minutes earlier

– supersaturated with the flesh – Costals had been loath to touch the body lying at his side. Now, suddenly, he slid under the sheet and covered her. He was embracing the child-killer.

Next day Solange was due to leave, and Costals gave an extraordinary proof of his exhaustion. Since it was still raining, they remained in his room, and after a while, as though by mutual accord, each of them picked up a book. Costals' eyes began to close ... He was re-reading, without noticing, the pages he had read the night before ... Suddenly, with a start, he saw close by him Solange's amused smile.

'Well, do you feel better?' she asked.

'What?'

'Yes, nature's sweet restorer ...

'Did I fall asleep?'

'You've slept for exactly twenty-five minutes.'

He never slept in the day-time. Never. Not even in the Bibliothèque Nationale. Who do you take me for! He had only done it during the war. So this was what she had driven him to! He who was in the prime of life and the pink of condition, he who was always on the alert, always so keen never to waste his time, he had fallen asleep in an armchair at four o'clock in the afternoon, like a decrepit old man. He felt humiliated, and took it out on her. The new-found warmth he had felt towards her during the past two days vanished in an instant, like the warmth of a room in which one opens the window in winter. Ah! if only she had realized, she would never have given him that amused smile. Small victories are dearly bought.

But Costals was never to know that Solange, next day, herself exhausted by the nervous tension of that fortnight, would lie down fully dressed on the bed in which Mme Dandillot was having her after-lunch siesta, and fall asleep too, curled up and snuggling against her mother, who dared not get up for fear of waking her.

At seven o'clock in the evening, after seeing Solange off, he left the station, went back to the hotel, and ate. It was the first time for a fortnight that he had eaten wholeheartedly. For when he was at table with Solange he was preoccupied with what to say to her, what she was thinking, whether she was bored, how they could kill time that afternoon, etc., and could not eat wholeheartedly. Afterwards, no sooner was he undressed than he drifted off into a sleep as opaque as wine (the sort of wine he loved).

He slept until two o'clock the next afternoon. And from three o'clock until nightfall he lay stretched out on his bed, his eyes closed, trying to recuperate his strength and bring back his soul, which the woman had devoured.

And when he woke up next day, before he had even washed he had himself driven back to his flat. And he felt the pressure of his creation knocking inside him to be let out, for his strength had returned. He was himself once more. He was a man once more.

And no sooner had he arrived, without opening his suit-cases or anything, than he picked up from the table all his notes and drafts and files, and scattered them over the floor. And he said: 'Now I'll show them!'

And his work-room was the smallest room in the flat, so that its exiguousness might concentrate his thoughts, send them back to him, so that he should really feel cornered. And it was in a state of disorder worthy of the gods.

And he stripped off his jacket, his waistcoat, and his shirt, and threw them on the floor as well, and remained in his aertex vest. And he took off his shoes, and remained in his stocking feet. And he ruffled his hair with both hands. And thus, neither washed nor shaved, he sat down at his table. And with one deep breath he filled his lungs with air, like the big bad wolf in the *Three Little Pigs*. And whatever he may have looked like, he certainly looked a brute; and he was one. And he uttered his war-cry, his 'Montjoye and St Denis!' at the top of his voice: 'B— the lot of them!' (For is not the creation of novels a violation of nature?) And he bent over the blank sheet of paper. And he plunged back into his work, hungrily. And his integrity was restored to him.

And the first sentence took shape, sure in its sweep, its curve and its aim, rejoicing in its promised length, with the coruscating coils of its *which's* and its *what's*, with its parentheses, its grammatical errors (deliberate), its commas and its

semi-colons (he scanned it aloud: 'comma ... semi-colon ...':
it was the text breathing; if the text did not breathe, it would
die, like a living thing) – took shape, coiled and uncoiled its
spirals, its rugosities, its softnesses and its iridescences, with
sacred deliberation; and when it had satisfactorily exercised
its *which's* and its *what's*, and its parentheses, and its grammatical errors, and its commas and its semi-colons, it raised
itself up for the final image, as a king cobra, with lazy strength,
glides at its leisure one way and another, though always with
a single end in view, then raises its glittering head above the
rocks and strikes.

He wrote for nine days running, at the rate of twelve hours'
work a day. He dipped his pen into himself, and wrote with
blood, sperm, fire and sweat. He drained the girl dry, as one
sops up a dish of food, as one dredges a silted pond. He
pumped her dry and disgorged her into his novel. She was far
away and thought herself safe. But from afar he drew off her
fluids and depersonalized her by the intensity of boredom
that emanated from her. And he doubly depersonalized her, by
distributing her traits among several of the characters in his
book. She ceased to be an individual; she ceased *to be*. 'Ah!
so you wanted to devour my soul, did you!'

And on the evening of the ninth day he received, with the
author's compliments, a little book that had just been published,
by a colleague he admired and detested. He would have
admired and loved him if this colleague had lived eighty years
earlier, but he detested him because he was alive and in his
way. And he read:

EBLIS

'Jesus came to a city at the hour when the heat of the day
is at its strongest, and the city was deserted. And hearing a
noise of flutes that sounded fearsome in this light, he asked
what it was. A stone answered him: "It is Eblis weeping for
himself."

'Now Jesus, some time after this, met Eblis, and said to him:
"Prince of Delights, it is said that you weep. Is it true?" Eblis
answered: "Men have a strange idea of what they call the

gift of tears. Demons weep too. And what does that prove? And I too weep, at times." Jesus said: "Why do you weep?" Eblis said: "I weep for the ingratitude of men, to whom I reveal evil and who do not love me the more because of it. Now I know that men do not love happiness." Jesus said: "Is that all you weep for?" Eblis said: "I weep because I, the demon, am forced to believe in God, and I suffer from it." "I too am forced to believe in you," said Jesus. "But is that all you weep for?" Eblis said: "I weep, too, for myself."

'Eblis said: "I have flown above battlefields, and urged on the combatants, for my contempt for them was great. I have pierced with my caresses the flesh of human bodies so tender that they were torn apart. I have crouched beside warm beasts, and killed them by marrying them. When I withdraw to my caverns in the depths of the perfumed desert, I have commerce with no other creature but the objects of my fornication. I need only them. They alone cross my threshold: it is known only to them; I never hesitate when they knock. They do not love me, nor I them. We mingle in silence, like shadows. That is all I do, and it gives me no pleasure."'

'What a fool!' Costals exploded. 'He "has commerce" and gets no pleasure from it! A neurotic devil! From everything we know of God, from the words, the sentiments, the acts which all the religions have attributed to him *in saecula saeculorum*, we know that God is stupid. The demon being his antithesis, one might therefore expect him to be intelligent; and indeed he gives plenty of proofs of this. If he is stupid too, whom is one to trust!' He went on reading.

'Eblis said: "There are also things about me that are known only to myself. Often I help a stumbling child to carry the burden that weighs him down. I whisper in a girl's ear that her flatterer is deceiving her. When a sleeping man is threatened by his enemy, I bark and he awakens in time. I lie down beside a shivering old man and warm him with my great wings. I love men, strange though it may seem. And I love my round-headed damned, crawling along on top of one another like worms, their hearts beating precipitately...."'

Costals stopped reading, and his own heart-beats quickened at the electric contact of this sentence. He felt an affinity with these round-heads, as with children and animals.

'Jesus said to him: "You are full of the heavens, and that is why you are the Tempter. But can one believe you?" Eblis said: "Why should I not be believed?" Jesus said to him: "Do you not know that it is the punishment of demons not to be believed? I thought that you spoke out of pride." Eblis said: "I have no pride." But Jesus thought to himself: "Do not let us give him his due, for that would give him pride."

'Jesus, having withdrawn a while, began to weep. He returned to Eblis and said to him: "I wept, because I believed you at last. O Lucifer, you who were created in rejoicing, you who were so beautiful in the heavens, offer up a prayer to my Father, that he may recall you to those meadows of grace where once you shone so resplendently." But Eblis said: "That cannot be." Jesus said: "Why? You have said that you did evil and that it gave you no pleasure. You have also said that you did good." Eblis said: "When I do good, it gives me no pleasure either." At this, Jesus left him.

'The beasts came out of the woods and drew near to Eblis, to see him suffering. When it was the hour at which men leave their houses, because the heat subsides, those of the beasts who pray for demons (they are like flowers without stems) said to Eblis: "Go away, for men will see you, and might stone you." So Elbis went off to the cities, and did good and evil there.'

Costals closed the book, placed his fingers on his eyelids, and began to write again.

And he wrote for twelve days, at the rate of ten hours' work a day, full of creative naïvety and coarseness, and full of creative amusement. And what he wrote was good.

And then he wrote for four days, at the rate of fourteen hours' work a day. And then he rested, and went hunting woman for three days, and had two adventures.

And then he wrote for fifteen more days, at the rate of twelve hours' work a day. And then he rested: he hunted for two days, and had no adventures.

And then he wrote for fourteen more days, at the rate of thirteen hours' work a day. And then he rested: he hunted for three days, and had no adventures.

And then he wrote for six more days, at the rate of nine or ten hours' work a day. And on the evening of the sixth day, he snorted like an ox. And looking at what he had done, he laughed and said: 'Well, that'll show them!' It was his own substance that he had poured forth, and yet it remained intact in him: in work as in pleasure, he was always full of what he had given out.

And then he wrote for eleven more days, at the rate of fourteen hours' work a day. And on the morning of the twelfth day, which was the seventy-first day of his creation, he had had enough, and returned to Paris.

THE LEPERS

PART ONE

I

If the dead, in the Beyond, were not entirely absorbed in jockeying for precedence (ditto the heavenly hosts – the Thrones pushing themselves forward to become Dominations, etc.), the late M. Dandillot would have squirmed and twisted himself into knots during that month of October 1927. Ever since their return from Etretat, his widow and daughter had been engaged in altering everything in the flat, and their efforts were almost entirely directed towards counteracting the tastes of the dear departed. It was chiefly his bedroom and his study that they were determined to transmogrify – that study in which M. Dandillot, catching his wife 'meddling with something' one day, had said to her: 'Here you're only tolerated.' Three months after her marriage, Mme Dandillot had not yet unpacked her personal belongings, imagining that she would not be staying long, that she would soon be returning to her parents; and when she had eventually resigned herself, she had not so much mingled them with as added them to those of her husband. Now it was the turn of M. Dandillot's belongings to be withdrawn from the communal hoard. Even his sporting files and his photographs of athletes had been burned (in spite of the fact that Mme Dandillot felt some gratitude towards sport, convinced as she was that physical culture had accelerated her husband's death by ten years). The sober grey wallpaper had been replaced by something pink with a pattern of nightingales. M. Dandillot having been anti-Christian, the mantelpiece now sported a Virgin, flanked (in order to 'soften this austerity') by a pastel drawing of some mimosa and a charcoal sketch of a King Charles spaniel – products of Mme Dandillot's girlhood – and a 'pretty thing' cut out of *l'Illustration* and framed: *Exquisiteness* – a woman in a cloud of muslin, signed Domergue. And Sacred Hearts and Calvaries and First Communion cards: for Jesus Christ was everywhere in a place of honour in this household ready for civil marriage, divorce and abortion. Not to mention innumerable other more or less unspeakable objects, mostly presents – for it was a household so lacking in personality that every present they had ever received was kept and displayed in a prominent position. In the same way a French literary man invited to Morocco will admit that although he has no desire to make the journey he will go nevertheless because 'he likes free trips'. Doing something one has no desire to do because one can do it gratis, making use of an object one dislikes because one has got it for nothing – and this when one is very comfortably off – is a characteristic, and infallible, sign of mediocrity.

Solange Dandillot had returned from Genoa rather down in the mouth. Genoa should have settled matters. What had come of it? Nothing. And now he was out of range, and for how long? A man who has just received a severe blow, and needs to think about all sorts of urgent and important matters, is often inclined to fling himself into any mechanical chore: even sew on buttons or clean his shoes in order not to think. In the same way Solange tidied and tidied, 'finishing' an old dress, wearing gloves in order to protect her hands (though in fact it gave the impression that she did not want to touch anything that had belonged to her father), glued to her task, which she complicated unbelievably, in accordance with the natural propensity of the female of the species; at once meticulous, niggling and disorderly, in accordance with that same propensity. Apart from the distraction it provided, she experienced from this tidying the sort of voluptuous pleasure one feels on seeing a void take the place of the objects one has eliminated – an intellectual gratification, one might say. The thing became an obsession. More! Still more! Now let's have a go at this corner! Reducing whole sectors of bric-à-brac as passionately as a general reducing an enemy pocket. And, by evening, overwrought, with circles under the eyes as after a sleepness night, but conscience at rest in a way one rarely experiences after having performed a good deed or some high and arduous duty. With certain women it is a good sign when they start tidying: it means that the crisis is over, and they have begun to cherish their home again. With others, however, it means that they need to find an escape in some meaningless task. Solange dreaded the day when everything in the house would be in order. To put off the evil day, to draw out her task, she invented household errands in every direction, going out, coming back and then going out again : more parsimonious, however, than before the trip to Genoa, as though something inside her had tightened up. Finally, vegetative by nature, she had always slept a good deal, but now she was in bed with the light out by nine o'clock.

Meanwhile, the physical space occupied by M. Dandillot in the establishment went on shrinking until in the end, of all that this man had woven round himself in sixty years, there remained no more than the equivalent of a small packing-case, which was relegated to the attic : similarly, of an incinerated corpse there remains nothing but a handful of bones. If the dead take possession of the living, as they say, the living repay it with interest.

Solange participated in this operation against her father largely unconsciously, though not entirely so. In diminishing her father's physical traces, she was not unaware that she was diminishing his moral traces in the process. Women always want to diminish a dead man, as they diminished him when he was alive. If a man has been a free-thinker, a mother, a sister or a wife will climb on to his grave and relentlessly seek to prove that he was a Christian 'without knowing it'.

When Solange received Costals' first letter, in which he complained of the weather in Genoa, spoke in pathetic terms of his solitude, and, without saying precisely that he missed her, recalled her presence with a touch of nostalgia, she had a feeling she had never experienced before : she was rather glad that he did not seem happy. It did not even remotely cross her mind that Costals, in Genoa, between his work and his amatory adventures, might be as happy as a king. If he had adopted a slightly pathetic tone, it was because, guessing that she was discontented, he did not want her to think him contented – partly out of charity, and partly because, like the Athenians of old, he often made sacrifices on the altar of Envy. Solange's reply was consolatory, and ever so slightly patronizing; mention was made of 'a taste of ashes in the mouth' – the pity men feel for women is matched by the pity women would like to

feel for men. Costals guffawed when he read this shop-girl's
cliché. It was the taste of Mlle Bevilacqua's saliva that he had
in his mouth.

She thought of him now with a touch of acerbity. Her
fervour had been crushed, the spontaneity and integrity of her
love corrupted. No longer, she told herself in her still rudimen-
tary parlance, was she willing to 'trust to appearances'. She
deliberately made him wait two days for her reply: she must
not appear too eager. . . . Perhaps, too, since living alone with
her mother, she had become morally less sound. Whether man,
woman or child, a person always changes for the worse by
living only with women.

The author pauses. . . . Describing mediocrities always gets
you down in the end. 'And now, Madame Baudoche, back to
the kitchen!' cried Barrès, exasperated with the principal
character of his novel. If only these two Dandillot women
were sufficiently highly developed in one aspect of their mediocrity to be caricatured. But they even elude caricature; and
besides, photography is better than caricature. Costals had
often thought what a sad and pitiable subject for a writer a
young girl was. True, her face and her body, if they are beautiful, are at their best at that age. But underneath! . . . 'To introduce them into his work, look at the treatment Shakespeare is
obliged to put them through. He remakes them. He invents
them. He forces himself to romanticize them. A young girl has
to be idealized in order to make her possible at all as a subject
for poetry. Byron admits it quite openly.* And Dante's
Beatrice is pure Theology. When a writer does not transfigure
a young girl, she is a failure. Molière's are failures. . . . Balzac's
are failures. . . .'

The author has made no attempt to transfigure Mlle Dandillot. A failure? True to life, at any rate. If she bores the reader,

---

*I have always had a great contempt for women; and formed
this opinion of them not hastily, but from my own fatal experience.
My writings, indeed, tend to exalt the sex; and my imagination has
always delighted in giving them a beau idéal likeness, but I only
drew them . . . as they should be.' (Medwin's *Conversations of Lord
Byron*) (*Author's note*).

it must be because the author has reproduced her faithfully, since she was by nature boring.

One Sunday in November, as they were preparing to get eleven o'clock Mass 'over and done with', Mme Dandillot stared at her daughter:

'Why are you putting on such acres of powder?'

'No more than usual.'

'But yes, my child, look at yourself, you're like a clown.'

Solange rubbed the powder off with her handkerchief. Her face remained deathly pale. Mme Dandillot's clouded over.

Some days later, leaning her elbows on a table, Solange noticed that her wrist-watch had slipped two or three centimetres further down her fore-arm than usual. Only then did she realize why, for some time past, she had felt that her hands were literally swimming in her gloves. She said nothing: she was ashamed. But soon afterwards Mme Dandillot saw the light, and a bottle of tonic appeared on the dining-room table. The Dandillot household thus became even more representative: a bottle of patent medicine is a feature of the armorial bearings of the bourgeoise. (They need a doctor to tell them to eat less. They need a doctor for their 'rest cures'. They consult the doctor if they are putting on weight. They consult the doctor if their child starts playing with himself.) Solange also bought some rouge. And she altered her hair-style, because the existing one was very 'young girlish', and with her drawn features the 'young girl' style gave her a look of an overgrown virgin, while the new one made her look rather more the 'young woman', and a young woman has a right not to look all that fresh.

Costals' letters went on arriving two a week, still full of tenderness. 'But is he sincere?' wondered our neophyte of mistrust. She had some difficulty in answering these letters. Since she expressed herself awkwardly when she was at her most fervent, it may be imagined what it was like when that fervour had waned. 'You have carried away a part of my being, a fairly recent me which you yourself created, which had taken a predominant place, and which now leaves a great void. . . .' That was true enough, but she remained too detached not to

end up with a bit of literature: '... like finding oneself alone
in a house in the evening, when the child has gone.' Or again:
'My plush rabbit awaits you, still the same, with his boot-
button eyes and one ear drooping like a weeping willow.'
Excellent, but then she added the following, which was pure
invention, designed, it would seem, to titillate both the sentimental streak and the satyr in Costals, always prone to be
aroused if ever she evoked her childhood: 'I took him in my
arms and laid him on my pillow, as I used to when I was a
little girl, not so long ago.' (Every woman up to the age of
fifty likes to pretend she is a little girl; there is not one woman
in a hundred who has not said at least once to a man: 'You
know I'm only a little girl.') Solange had deliberately waited
before answering the first letter from Genoa. Now it was
because these answers had become almost a drudgery that she
often put off writing them for several days. Mlle Dandillot
belied the cliché that a woman becomes more attached to a
man who has made her unhappy, and also that other cliché
according to which a woman expects the man she loves to
yield to her in small things and resist her in great. The truth
is that every human being has a certain capacity for love, hate,
suffering, application and patience. In Genoa, Solange had
launched the longest wave of her love. Now that love was
imperceptibly withdrawing, like the tides.

In these circumstances, how are we to account for her not
throwing in the sponge? Let us try. She was a girl who, up to
the age of twenty-three, had desired little, and had never had
to exercise her will. But now at last she wanted something, and
it was as though all that unused will-power had gathered itself
together for a single onslaught. Ah! so I haven't any will-
power, have I? Well, I'll show them! Her lack of desire in
all things was taking an enormous revenge. She was as tenacious in clinging to this marriage as she was docile in submitting to 'impossible' behaviour in order to keep the man who
was the master of her fate. She had committed herself totally.
Obstinacy is not so far removed from morbid indecision: weak-
willed people are as slow to stop as they were to get started.
And then there is the feminine addiction to chimeras. What
could be more different, at the outset, than an Andrée Hacque-

baut and a Solange Dandillot? Yet both ultimately arrive at the same point: a belief that sheer obstinacy must prevail. For obstinacy is the blind and crude opposition of the self to a reality which it fails to grasp; and this opposition is a feminine thing. People talk of diseases of the will. The will itself is also at times a disease.

And yet, beyond all this, the desperate persistence of these two women in wanting something so obviously foolhardy remains incomprehensible. But why write novels at all unless to show adults as they are (and as children see them), that is to say arbitrary and incomprehensible? The intrigues of women to get themselves or their daughters married usually spring from self-interest, ambition, etc. They can also be simply the result of stupidity, and this was perhaps the case here. But what a betrayal of life, so desperately to want a loveless marriage!

Solange was not suffering from unrequited love; she was suffering from frustration, and that uncertainty from which women suffer so much more than men. Her resentment some-times had a touch of rather sly aggression: the fighting bull is especially dangerous at the end of the fight, after he has been wounded. When Costals wrote her an enthusiastic letter about the beauty of Italian women (at a time when she herself was wilting), she felt the lack of a private life of her own, a past which she could use as a weapon against him. Having come across an unpleasant article about our hero, she took a great delight in sending it off to him. She needed both to hold on to him and to punish him.

In mid-November Costals announced that he would be re-turning on the 25th. In the following letter he postponed his return, without specifying a new date. Solange took this letter calmly, but a little later, caught sight of her typewriter and burst into tears. She was feeling unwell at the time, and her imagination was always more impressionable at such moments, as with those men of the people who start writing poetry when they are ill. She had bought this typewriter three months before. Convinced that she would type Costals' manuscripts when she became his wife, she had wanted to learn to type. On her return from Genoa, the machine had been relegated to a corner.

Exasperated by the knowledge that he did not need her, she began to wonder if he had not falsely announced his return with the sole object of making her feel how self-sufficient he was by later postponing it. And also to see how much she would put up with. Would there never be a day when it was she who called the tune? How tempting it would be, if ever he made the first move, to take a step back herself and play with him a little!

Often she had the sensation of being bereft of all feeling; it was as though she had ceased to exist since no one was paying any attention to her: scenes, contemptuous remarks, insults – anything would have been better than this nothingness. She was even more silent than ever, or left her sentences unfinished, as though speech were a futile waste of effort; and she no longer wanted to see anyone, starting involuntarily and even turning slightly pale whenever the door-bell rang.

'I know perfectly well why I no longer want to come out of my shell. No, no! relations with other people are too difficult! Altogether too wearing. To think that, even with those one loves most, everything has to start again from scratch. . . . '

'There's always me, darling, you know that,' Mme Dandillot had replied. Solange must have thought: 'Parents, that's not the same thing. . . . '

Mme Dandillot's efforts to interest her in lectures, in a political group, were met with remarks such as: 'What for?' or 'Why complicate one's life?', etc. And it was true that the slightest little effort created a vacuum in her brain, like an air-pump: tidying a cupboard, unravelling a ball of wool, were things that *occupied* her completely. Her handwriting began to disintegrate: she scribbled the ends of her words, skipped accents and punctuation. The maid's presence exasperated her, as though it distracted her from her obsession and her ruminations, and because it made her think up orders to give which she would never have thought of if she had had to ring for the maid, and she was incapable of giving orders without endlessly verbose explanations. Her lips were dry and her breath smelt. Finally she developed two boils on one of her buttocks, and then another on her thigh. Cold weather had always stupefied her; her whole character changed in winter; how much more so now that her vitality had dwindled. Sitting side-ways on the radiator, her sick buttock in the air, beside *Madame Vigée-Lebrun and her daughter* (the two tabby cats, who always slept entwined), she spent hours knitting sweaters for some charity (Costals had indignantly refused her offer to knit one for him), not so much because she was interested in making garments, or out of sympathy for the poor, but for the sort of distraction which the manipulation of the needles provided. So absorbed was she that she would fail to hear Mme Dandillot speaking to her, or fail to understand what she said. The wrist-watch had moved no higher up her fore-arm, in spite of the tonics. But from time to time her eyes would come to rest on the veins of her wrist which Costals had once told her he loved, as though to re-assure herself, with astonishment, that there was still something about her that he had loved.

In Genoa, Costals went on writing the novel into which he was putting Solange. (Feeling all these things as he did, he would have gone mad had he not written them down there and then.) Everything of her that he put in the novel he took away from her: that was a hold stronger than any carnal hold. The day he dotted his final *i* and crossed his final *t*, Solange did not die, drained dry, but she felt, at the dinner-table, something hard in her mouth, and spat into her fingers the crown of a broken tooth: she was so run down that she was becoming decalcified. 'Madame de Chateaubriand, whom I made to spit blood at will....' (Chateaubriand, *Mémoires d'Outre-Tombe*).

Costals announced his return for the 2nd of January, a date chosen in order to 'skip' the New Year celebrations, and made a date with Solange for the 3rd. But on arrival in Paris he found a letter from Mme Dandillot. She wanted to see him urgently, before he met Solange.

Also a letter from Andrée Hacquebaut, which he did not open, but put away. He had a file for letters which he kept without having read. And a file for letters which the (female) senders had marked: 'To be destroyed'.

Andrée Hacquebaut   to Pierre Costals
Saint-Léonard (Loiret)   *Paris*

30 December 1927

I have been sulking for six months. I am obliged to acquaint
you with the fact, since you refuse to do me the honour of
noticing it yourself : you ignore my very indifference. But I
cannot let this date pass without wishing you a happy New
Year, Costals. Is it undignified of me to write to you again
after six months of silence, now that I no longer ask anything
of you? You have *bled* me of my love – there is no other word.
You will never know what you refused : I would have given
you Love with a capital L – something full, round, compact,
glittering, like a loaf, or a cake. But don't let's go back over
all that.

I am writing to you. The door of the mirror-wardrobe, in
which I keep everything that concerns you, is open, and it is
as though I were in a tiny little room face to face with you
alone. One can scarcely see, because of the gloomy weather. It
was inevitable that I should start writing to you again on a
Sunday. There is such a piercing sadness about a rainy Sunday
in Saint-Léonard. So many Sundays wept away outside my
window !

I am calm but I am not cured. A little music (I now have a
wireless set), a little insomnia, a little rain . . . or, on the other
hand, a ray of sunshine, is enough to cast me back, body and
soul, into everything that hurts me. I am bored to distraction.
Waking up dejected, with one thought alone : getting through
the day as fast as possible, like holding one's nose as one
swallows a dose of medicine. Ever since my sinister 'holidays'
in Cabourg last June, I haven't been away from Saint-Léonard
except for twenty-four hours in Orleans. I no longer want to
go anywhere. No one awaits me anywhere. No one, anywhere,
wants to see my face. If one knew that one's face pleased
someone – how one would be reborn ! If one knew that one's
face existed for someone in a world full of dead men who
neither look nor love – what a fragment of immortality !

I am not in the least embarrassed to be writing to you. I still have the impression, as strongly as ever, that we ... how shall I put it? ... that together we know things that others don't know, things that you have not even said to me but which nevertheless you've said to no one but me.

A.H.

This letter was filed away by the recipient, unopened.

3

The great French novelist said to one of his fellow-writers one day:

'I've had fourteen books published. And if I were a bachelor, I should only have published seven.'

'In other words: one book in every two to keep the pot boiling. Don't you think the proportion ... ?'

'Ah, but I've got three children.'

And yet the great French writer is rich. . . .

Everything they do that is vile or second-rate is blamed on their families. One would think they only married in order to have this excuse, just as there are people who only volunteered for the war in order to be able to boast of the gesture for the rest of their lives. Mme Dandillot, in the taxi that was taking her to Costals' house, felt sustained by her clear conscience as though by a steel corset. Her clear conscience was her love for her daughter; in the name of that love, she would have been prepared to rob. We know, moreover, that her love was firm and true. When a boy reaches puberty his mother's love slackens: she can no longer go near this monster, about whom she understands nothing. The metamorphosis of the little girl into the adolescent, on the other hand, makes maternal love blossom and develop into friendship. Later, the transformation of the adolescent girl into a woman brings a new blossoming. Since Solange had become a woman, Mme Dandillot loved her more than ever.

What she wanted from Costals today was a 'yes' or a 'no'. If he continued to prevaricate, she herself would say 'no'. But when Costals appeared she felt intimidated. It was the first time she had come to his flat, and she felt disorientated, like a football team playing away. Moreover, the absence of worry in the past three months had given Costals a healthier appearance (he had also drawn sustenance from Solange – whence, perhaps, those full round cheeks). Outwardly calmer and more assured, he over-awed her a little. For some while, keeping her most telling arguments in reserve, she confined herself to repeating what she had often said before.

'You hunch yourself up, instead of bracing yourself against the wind. You balk at the hurdle. You're afraid of making a mistake, afraid of failure. One must throw oneself into the water to learn to swim.'

'Don't you think that if a man who can't swim throws himself into the water, the chances are that he'll drown?'

'The truth of the matter is that you don't love Solange enough.'

'Exactly, I don't love her enough. Don't turn that against me. Heart! One needs a great deal of heart to love even a little.'

'But love will come, I tell you. It always happens like that. . . .'

'So you want a man for a son-in-law who admits he doesn't love your daughter enough.'

'I appreciate frankness more than anything,' said Mme Dandillot. She was thinking what all women think: 'Let him keep his frankness to himself; it only diminishes and degrades him.' How often had she not said to Solange: 'A man's frankness is a trap that makes us drop our guard. When he tells you he doesn't love you "deep down", beware!'

'There's no need for a great romantic love,' she went on. 'You love Solange enough, it seems to me, to provide her with the help and support which every woman has the right to expect from her husband.'

'Excuse me,' said Costals firmly, 'I don't live for other people. I am, if I may say so, perfectly natural. And nature does not demand that we should devote ourselves to others. It only demands that we should live.'

'Solange is natural too. And yet I can assure you that if ever you found yourself in trouble. . . .'

'I'm never in trouble.'

Mme Dandillot laughed. The more embarrassed she was, the more relaxed and cheerful she appeared. She thought: 'I shall go away without having done what I came to do, without having delivered my ultimatum. I can see it already.' She also thought it would be a mistake to emphasize Solange's determination, because that would make Costals dig in his heels, and so, before each sentence, she was careful not to draw attention to it. But she was so intent on what she ought not to say that eventually she blurted it out: 'She has a will of iron, that child. She's told herself: "This is the man I want".' She had gone slack, as an organism in the last stages of debility no longer retains its faecal matter: Solange had infected her mother with her own exhaustion. Costals' riposte was immediate: 'I like refusing,' he said. She fell silent, checkmated. Through the silence, from the floor above, could be heard the noise of children rolling a ball about, and a dog scampering across the floor-boards. Mme Dandillot massaged the pouches under her eyes with her fore-finger. The telephone rang. Costals went to answer it.

'...'

'Do you think the novel is an outmoded literary form? No, monsieur, it's lack of talent that's outmoded. Talent can sustain any literary form. Besides, you know as well as I do that the novel's in splendid condition. So don't you think we're wasting our time?'

'...'

'Meet you? Why? I've just answered your question. But will you allow me to ask you a question in return? I should like to know whether, in your opinion, the telephone interview isn't a journalistic form that should be considered outmoded?'

'...'

'A gentleman whose opinion is presumably of some value, since he is asked to state it with a view to benefiting the human race, must be engaged in doing something important: thinking, or having a rest from thinking; or deciding things, or controlling someone's fate, or making love, or having a rest from love-making. The telephone hails him brutally, doubly disturbing him – in his mind, by interrupting its train of thought, and in his body, which has to move in order to get to the receiver.

And it turns out to be a total stranger, who wants to know if he thinks the novel is an outmoded form and who, as likely as not, will not even publish his reply, because he already has too many contributors, or because the enquiry has been dropped in the meantime. Well, my dear confrère, I say this sort of behaviour is – I'm searching for a mild world – is unworthy of savages. . . . '

From time to time there was a rattle of machine-gun fire from the adjacent flat (water-pipes?). Mme Dandillot played with her necklace, her mind a blank. She stared at the globe of the table-light, which Costals had switched on while telephoning – the glowing kernel at the heart of this nebula – or at the windows of the neighbouring house, lighting up one after the other in the gathering dusk, like people's faces when something nice is said to them, or when they are spoken to about themselves. She could not have explained why these interiors, revealed for a few seconds between the switching on of the lights and the closing of the shutters, made her dreamy: it was because they suggested to her that unknown interior in which Solange, in the company of this man, would spend her life in happiness.

Costals, having hung up, went on where they had left off.

'I cannot understand why custom, which demands so many precautions, signed and sealed, in defining the material rights of intending couples, and their property, demands so few as regards the respective rights of the mind and personality. Today, every government in Europe has adopted a code of morality under which everything you and I understand by morality is trampled underfoot the moment the good of the State is in question. Personally, I consider a work of art as important as a State, and deserving of equally great sacrifices. *Salus operis suprema lex*. I'm behaving badly to you by leaving you in suspense, but I'm justified in behaving thus, because this suspense saves me from marriage, which would be detrimental to my *opus*. Citizens allow their rulers the morals of highway robbers in the interests of the State. Allow me, then, in the interests of my work, those departures from commonplace morality which I permit myself when it is at stake. Loving an artist must, for a girl, be as though she loved death. . . .'

('Fie, madam Nurse, how you do prattle on!' But he had not finished yet.)

'There are two categories of men: those who lead, and those who are led. The first are the creators – literary, artistic, scientific, political. In short, the conquistadors: the conquest of thought by the writer, of beauty by the artist, of truth by the scientist and the philosopher, of power by the politician. Conquistadors need peace of mind, which marriage dispels. Let other men marry. Let them have children to make up for all that they fail to contribute to the patrimony of the human race. But let the conquistadors take from coupling, and from paternity, only what may be of use to their economy.'

'Allow me the last word,' said Mme Dandillot. 'Besides, chivalry demands it,' she simpered, with a forced smile (this simpering, at a moment when she was deeply moved, was somehow monstrous; but it too had materialized in spite of her). 'You, my dear sir, you have your work. It is, if I may say so, your tether, you who loathe being tethered. But I have my daughter. Happy women are fond of their children; unhappy women love them desperately. And moreover, all the affection M. Dandillot failed to give his daughter, I have had to give her myself; I have had to love her enough for two. And now look what's become of my daughter, thanks to you.'

She took from her bag one of those slips which chemists give their customers after they have been weighed, and handed it to Costals. He read:

9 December	–	59 kg. 100
16 ,,	–	58 kg. 100
23 ,,	–	57 kg. 200
30 ,,	–	56 kg. 300

She saw him raise his head. His expression was grave.

'Do you know what it means to have boils? People get boils when their blood's gone wrong. Solange has had three boils since last month. Do you realize . . . do you realize what this means?'

She took a folded piece of tissue paper out of her bag. Costals put the chemist's slip on the table, and took the piece of paper and opened it. It contained the crown of Solange's broken tooth.

'You know what's meant by decalcification? You can imagine the extent to which an organism must be affected to produce all these symptoms: loss of weight, boils, and decalcification. And when the only disease it's got is moral rather than physical ...'

'Have you a good doctor?'

'From the fees he charges I presume he's a good doctor.'

'And she told me nothing about this in her letters!'

'I can see you don't know her.'

(How to stifle the voice of conscience, as one stops a woman from screaming. . . .)

There was a ring at the front door. They fell silent. The manservant brought in an express letter. Costals sniffed it.

'Excuse me, but this missive has the little crooked look of a blackmail letter. . . .'

He read it, and handed it in silence to Mme Dandillot, who read it in her turn:

Dear Sir,

You must surely feel, as we do, that the time has come to reconsider the Universe. *Studio 27*, a team of young people, has taken upon itself the most delicate of these essential investigations: to take the measure of mankind. Our Council has therefore decided that the first pre-requisite is to open an immense debate on that most urgent problem: *God, the Revolution, Poetry*. A Congress, to which the thinking Youth of the entire World will be fraternally invited, will be organized by us in March. At the end of these sittings, during which we shall have compared our conclusions and weighed up our desiderata, we shall make proposals – and if necessary demands.

A preliminary enquiry is needed to provide us with the tools for our task. We would ask you therefore to reply to the following questions (N.B. since *Studio 27* is so far able to appear on a limited number of pages only, you are requested to confine your replies to not more than four typewritten pages.)

Questions:

1. What is God?

2. Do you not think that God is the permanent message of the revolution? If so, what place does this thought occupy in your life?

3. Are the gratuitousness of God and the gratuitousness of the revolution inter-dependent?

4. Does the doctrine of *Studio 27* – God begins where poetry ends – seem to you calculated to condition your vocation as a European?

5. Reasons for your despair.

We remain, dear sir, etc.

P.S. We go to press at nine o'clock this evening. May we hope to have your reply in time?

'I must confess I hardly understand a word of it,' said Mme Dandillot, handing the letter back to Costals.

'But Madame, there's nothing to understand.'

'Ah! good. Perhaps they're schoolboys?' she asked, remembering that her son used to write stuff of that sort at the age of sixteen.

'Oh no,' said Costals. 'I know some of the signatories. They're men of between thirty and forty. But there are certain intellectual circles in Paris that can hardly be called precocious.'

He put his hand to his forehead.

'So you see, we haven't been able to devote half an hour to serious matters without being twice interrupted by those whom I shall call the Fools, because they are people who, first and foremost, lack that decidedly cardinal virtue: common sense. French life is continually shot through by the Fools. Women living fantasy lives, semi-intellectuals for whom words are everything, bourgeois blinded by the blinkers of class, proletarians blinded by their ignorance, students blinded by their stupidity – all of them, for one reason or another, out of touch with reality. Yet all of them having a say in the tragicomedy, and – you sense the Shakespearian grandeur of the thing – the Hero, he who holds all our destinies in his hand, whatever he may think in his own mind, not daring to decide without their approval. But the ones who astound me most are these Fools of the intellect who have just burst in on us and buzzed around our ears while we were having a serious discussion. Their race is ours through and through. They are the descendants of the *Sorbonagres* of Rabelais, the *Précieuses* and the *Médecins* of Molière, the *Idéologues* of Napoleon : intellectual quackery is one of the eternal characteristics of France. With us, they say, everything ends in a song. Everything also ends in a students' jape, but a jape that takes itself for something extremely important. . . .

'Where were we before all that? Ah yes, decalcification. . . . Well, it's agreed, I marry your daughter.'

Mme Dandillot had swallowed with equanimity the reading of the express letter, the digression on the Fools. . . . She had reached a stage where it seemed to her that the verdict had been given long since, and given against her. She did not leap at Costals' words; it was as though she were henceforth beyond reach. She simply said :

'For the past half-hour you've been maintaining to me that you couldn't marry because of your work. Have you changed your mind once more, then?'

'That attitude was thoroughly sound. But other attitudes towards that same subject are thoroughly sound, too. Nothing is easier for me, therefore, than to switch from one to the other. Like the different rooms of a house : the furniture is different, the exposure is different, but it's the same house. To know how to use a house is to know how to live in one room or another according to one's mood, the time of day, or the season. Now, why have I changed? Because that (he pointed to the broken tooth) is not a jape. A girl pining away because a man keeps her in suspense, it's anything you like to call it, but it isn't nonsense. Solange is faced with a real problem, unlike those nincompoops who want to *reconsider the universe* but stand in mortal terror of their concierges (he tore the express letter into tiny pieces). The reason for her suffering is not a laughable one, as are the reasons for three quarters of the moral sufferings of humanity. And as for your being sad because your daughter is losing calcium, nothing could be more reasonable than your sadness. Whereas I, when I reply *salus operis*, though I know *salus operis* is a powerful and respectable position, I know, too, that there's a side to it which is also a jape. So I stop japing, and I marry. I'll telephone my lawyer first thing tomorrow morning, and tell him to get in touch with yours.'

The telephone rang. Costals flung himself at the cut-off switch, which was in the hall. 'Hold your tongues, you idiots!' he bellowed.

Mme Dandillot had followed him into the hall. Like a cat with a bird in its jaws, all she wanted was to enjoy her prey on her own, in the depths of the family den. Anything she said would be superfluous; the only thing to do was to go. The water was still gurgling indefatigably in the neighbouring WC (the flush being out of order), like a fountain in a Moroccan patio. Mme Dandillot took Costals' hand and gave it a squeeze: 'You're a real brick,' she said. Her agitation was such that she added: 'I hope you have a nice evening.' 'So do I,' said Costals, aware of what he had let himself in for. To cut short their mutual embarrassment, she departed hurriedly: 'I'll telephone you tomorrow.' The moment Mme Dandillot had told him he was a real brick, Costals realized he had let himself be duped.

4

Andrée Hacquebaut   to Pierre Costals
Saint-Léonard (Loiret)   *Paris*

10 January 1928

I wanted to take up cycling again, not having done any for more than a year, and I went slap into a bench. My knee hurts, and I'm afraid I may have water on the knee. That's what comes of trying 'to come to terms with the outside world' when one isn't made for it.

You have left me to stew in my ignorance, my uselessness, my cerebralness, my desiccation, whereas true intelligence should broaden life, not constrict it, fertilize not sterilize it. Under the umbrella of our love I would have branched out, spread circles around myself, like a stone thrown into the water. And yet you needn't feel guilty: my misfortune both pre-dates you and post-dates you. The fatal thing about me is, at one end of the scale, that encounter with the bench, and at the other end my inability to encounter other people. I have lived too much alone, lived too much in books, to know how to make contact with my fellow-creatures. I keep telling myself that I shall know tomorrow. I make resolutions: 'After my thirty-first birthday.... Yes, after the 23rd of April.... Between now and then there's no point in trying, because I've made up my mind that in three months' time I shall start being a new woman.' In my cowardly way, I give myself this extension, this respite. But I know quite well that on the 23rd April I shall feel the same impotence, the same inhibitions. And I'm young and healthy, my face – whatever you may think of it – is not repulsive. What will it be like when I am withered and infirm!

People tell me I should get married. But I'm not marriageable unless my love can be boundless. I shall never be dominated physically except by a man who has first dominated me in every other way. The phoenix of these phoenixes having fled, I shall not seek another love. To build up from scratch, to work oneself up over nonentities, to feel one is always the senior partner, not to know why one loves except out of a need to love – the very thought of it fills me with nausea. People say to me: 'You don't know what to do with yourself. Go to Orleans, or even Paris, and get a job.' Having no training, I should have to work in an office, and life in town, having to pay all my own expenses, wouldn't leave me with any more money than I have here; and on top of that a less healthy life, less leisure, and a soul-destroying job. And meeting more human beings wouldn't in itself teach me how to break the ice, or, if by some miracle I did break it, how to manoeuvre in such a way that there would be a *second time*. 'Attempts at a break-through' was the phrase they used during the war; I can never manage to break through this hellish circle of loneliness. I wander on the perimeter not only of the world of men but of the world in general; I look around furtively, I eavesdrop. My awkwardness is such that if there's someone with whom I'm 'on good terms' but whom I don't often see, I avoid a meeting because there's a good chance that if we met I'd manoeuvre so successfully that I should alienate him for ever.

Women? They find me antipathetic. Besides, they don't interest me. Men? I don't know how to attract them, so that settles that. If a man is middling, and by chance does not disgust me, I seem to him too intellectual; 'affected', one of them put it (me, 'affected'! . . .). Last year, during the summer holidays, I happened to say to the young brother of one of my girl-friends, a schoolboy: 'You do nothing from morning till night. Why don't you read, take notes, improve your mind.' This phrase 'improve your mind' was a great hit; it appears it's a typical blue-stocking's remark. As the only intelligent man I've ever met, you know better than I do. . . . Children? They don't attract me. I belong to the race of lovers, not to the race of mothers – two very different races in my opinion: a woman can be a mother several times over, and yet be only a lover, whereas another woman or girl who loves a man may in reality only love the children she hopes he will give her. So I am not of the race of mothers, but there have been times when I regretted not being a mother. What maddened me far more than being deprived of children was not having experienced all those things that go with it, among others that immense revelation about life – life seen from an entirely new angle – which maternity must be.

But that was no more than my old regret at *not having had*. What is new is something I experienced in October. I had to spend a day in Orleans with my uncle, in order to sign some documents in connection with a great-aunt's estate. And there, in the square where I had sat down for a while, I found myself surrounded by toddlers who came up and gazed at me with an affection and trust that quite bowled me over (after all, I might have been a wicked fairy!), putting their grubby little paws in my lap. So, they had not sensed the curse with which I am afflicted, and I was so touched. But I had no idea what to say to them, or if I did say something they promptly went away: I couldn't hold them, any more than I can hold anyone else. One of the mothers, who was sitting beside me, was longing to start a conversation, but I slipped away. I should have been ashamed to admit I was a spinster, and if I had lied, if I had said, as for a moment I thought of saying: 'I too have a child', I should soon have given myself away by

my ignorance of things maternal: I'd be no more capable of
talking about nappies and feeding than you must be. (Indeed,
what *am* I capable of talking about, apart from books and
love? Just as I can't swim, or drive a car, or ride, or sing, or
play the piano, or cook, or dress-make, or even ride a bicycle
without attacking benches: I know nothing about anything.
To understand Bergson is to believe oneself to be on a level
with Bergson, but to make good jam is quite another matter.)
So I got up quickly and went away in despair. And now, when
I hear the kids calling 'Mum!' it's like a dagger in my heart.
All these women who are not a patch on me, most of them
stupid, yet to whom these children *belong*, whilst here I am
perpetually hovering on the periphery of closed Edens, exiled
from all that is human, carrying around with me wherever I
go an atmosphere of chilliness and suspicion and absurdity....
Woe betide homeless women, who are obliged to pursue other
people's husbands, or other people's children, to fulfil their
need for love! Or stray dogs and the neighbours' cats. Our
neighbour's cat, when I smother it with kisses, looks at me in
surprise, and seems to understand.

One fine morning in the middle of all this my uncle and I
each received a most unexpected cheque from the lawyer, a
legacy from my great-aunt. Fifteen hundred francs for myself,
out of the blue!

This money arrived just at the moment when I was most
preoccupied with my regrets at not having any children. And
immediately I had an idea: to give it to the day-nursery run
by the nuns of Sainte-Opportune here. Fifteen hundred francs
is a tidy little sum for Saint-Léonard. I would become the
'benefactress'. I could go into the day-nursery as I liked; they
could no longer refuse me anything. Incapable by myself of
finding a place among normal human beings, I would buy my
way in. I would be paying for the right to take an interest in
these children as though they were my own. I would be paying
for something to live for. It was a horrible idea, if you like,
but since there's no other way....

And then, after thinking it over, I saw what would happen.
They would accept my money, and gradually I would be eased
out. Why? Because I would be out of place in that little circle,

awkward, useless, in fact an embarrassment. They would say to one another: 'What's she doing here, what does she want?' They wouldn't know what to think. . . . Oh, I saw it all so clearly! The embarrassment of the good nuns, torn between the respect due to the 'benefactress' and the aversion they would feel towards me, a justifiable aversion, since I am indeed not one of them, since I do not and cannot belong to any human community. So I gave up the idea. When I try to fasten on to other people, in order to draw my happiness from them, and they resist me, it's bad enough. But to be rejected when I try to make *them* happy, ah! that would be another dagger in my heart.

Let's be honest. I know perfectly well that it wouldn't have been the happiness of those wretched kids I was after, but my own, always my own. They would simply have been the means I used to get away from myself. I'm well aware that self-sacrifice is not in my nature. At thirty years and nine months the best thing one could do would be to be a big sister, to help others. And apparently (it's something one hears people say) when one's unhappy it's a way of becoming less so. But to do that one would have to have one's life behind one, one would have to be a woman who has experienced life, who is throwing into this second-rate existence, into these petty responsibilities on behalf of second-rate people, the skin of a well-sucked fruit. . . .

This little episode has taught me one thing at least: to understand a certain category of people, and to pity them – those who have lots of money and throw it around without ever succeeding in finding happiness. That must be even worse than being penniless and unhappy. If one is penniless and unhappy one can always console oneself by blaming one's unhappiness on lack of money; one's self-esteem is not affected. When one is unhappy *with* money one has to admit to oneself: 'There's something in *me* that alienates people and life.'

Of the fifteen hundred francs, eleven hundred are still intact. Four hundred have gone on a dress, some bindings and some books (I've bought the whole of Sainte-Beuve!). I wanted to exchange money for life, but there's nothing doing: I can only exchange it for non-life. One makes an effort to be something other than what one is, then one gives up; being oneself is least difficult in the long run. The dog returns to its vomit.

A.H.

This letter was filed away by the recipient, unopened.

5

After his 'yes' to Mme Dandillot, Costals returned to the drawing-room and fell into an armchair. His first thought as a fiancé was an optimistic one. The door into the hall was open, and the lavatory cistern continued its Moroccan gurgle. 'Lavatory cisterns – that'll be *your* pigeon, Solange, old girl.' The weight slip was still lying on the table. He re-read it, and was touched. 'Poor little thing! Now we shall see her swell up again, as though she were being pumped full of air.'

The struggle between his intellect and his heart was constant. Every time (or almost) he was generous, he felt sad about it afterwards. The consciousness of duty done had spoiled a lot of fun for him. He had done something decent seven years ago, and for seven years he had regretted it. He had done something decent twelve years ago and for twelve years had regretted it. One night he had dreamt that war had been declared, that volunteers had been called for, and he had offered himself; and as he marched off with the columns, tears ran down his cheeks. But these tears were not prompted by the horror of going off to the front; they arose from dismay at having chosen to go when he could have lain low; it was really *goodness* that he was suffering from.

Once the nuptial 'yes' had been pronounced, Costals therefore expected to undergo a fit of depression. Nothing of the kind. The die was cast. With the uncertainty, the disease had evaporated. There was a difficult situation; but now it was simply a question of facing up to it, manipulating it, making the best of it. That was a man's job. And his folly left him strangely calm. 'One way or another, this parenthesis will be closed in two years. I'm thirty-four (the age at which Jesus Christ died; tradition says thirty-three, but I imagine that, following the general practice, Jesus knocked a year off). At thirty-six I shall be free once more. And it wasn't till the age of fifty that Tiberius began to lead a really agreeable life.'

He ate a hearty dinner, to build up his strength for the coming ordeal. He waited all evening for a telephone call from Solange. How her voice would thrill at the other end of the line! He smiled in anticipation, and the words he would say to her sprang to his lips: 'Well, my little one, your obstinacy has triumphed! The "fireside mule", so dear to shoe-shops, that's you.... And now I shall have to start hiding my manuscripts from you, like Tolstoy....' But no ring came. He was surprised, and somewhat disappointed. 'Perhaps she wasn't dining at home.'

Next day, when, at half past nine, he telephoned his lawyer to make an appointment, Solange had still not rung. After lunch, the same silence. 'For eight months she has been intent on this "yes". I come out with it, and it gives her no pleasure. If I had twopence worth of knowledge of the human mind, I might have guessed it. But I haven't. We know what the "psychology" a novelist puts into his books amounts to: sheer bluff from A to Z. Whatever happens hereafter, this can never be wiped out: that when I gave her what she so frantically desired, it never entered her head to pick up the receiver and say a word to me.

'She, so unromantic, finds herself sucked into a romantic adventure. And I, so wary, allow myself to be taken in. Waverers shilly-shally for months, and then, exasperated with themselves, make up their minds at random, and usually take the most dangerous course. Flight into danger is the reaction of the weak. Yet everything I know of myself convinces me that I am neither weak nor indecisive. But she has lured me on to a terrain which is not mine, and that is her great advantage. Put the bravest infantry officer into an aeroplane or submarine, and he will probably lose his head. Each of us has his element, from which he must not be drawn.'

The stupidity and incompetence of certain famous generals or marshals of France (outside their own speciality) is a source of amazement to intellectuals who have had occasion to meet them; but this suffocating secret must be kept, otherwise it's good-bye to the Academician's uniform: such is the intellectual's martyrdom. Gallieni, according to Lyautey, seems not to have been of that stamp. Lyautey cites one characteristic of his from which all of us should profit. Once while they were on the march in Tongking on the eve of going into battle, Lyautey was talking shop: 'Do stop fussing about all that,' Gallieni said to him. 'The orders are given, the necessary steps have been taken. What good will it do to ratiocinate about it? You've just as much need as I have to keep your grey matter in good condition. Let's talk about John Stuart Mill and we'll see what happens tomorrow morning.' And he took out from his great-coat pocket a John Stuart Mill and a d'Annunzio. There's a man for you, and I bet he organized his troops well, seeing how well he managed his personal economy: master of events as he was master of himself. Costals was to see Solange that evening. Since the decision was made, let it at least offer him the benefits of decisions made: that of leaving one's head and one's time free. From two o'clock till seven, Costals worked on the revision of his novel as though nothing had happened. Remembering his way of loving women, he even found a title for it: *The Contemptuous Lover*.

When Solange appeared in Costals' flat he was taken aback. Her clothes hung loose over her bust and hips. And her face! The neck too thin, the skin clinging to the jaw-bones, the features drawn. On top of all that (one realized why she had felt the need for it), heavily made up. It was the first time he had seen her made up. And what make-up! A 'foundation' of dark powder badly put on – in slabs, and her ears full of it – which in taking off her hat she had smudged over her forehead, so that her forehead was partly yellow and partly white – the papal colours! And her new hair style; so much 'the young woman' already! He kissed her with a sort of tender pity. They sat down side by side on the sofa, and he gently pinched the skin of her elbow. Embarrassed, he said jokingly: 'My poor pet, what has become of you! But we'll soon see you fill out: a real Jewish fiancée from Tunisia – they fatten them up like poultry over there. . . .' She smiled wanly, and they fell silent. He did not know what to say to her. Yet it seemed to him that the words should have gushed from them both. But nothing came, and he felt stiff and shy in front of *his wife*, as he had not been since the beginning, in the box at the Opéra-Comique. 'Well, are you pleased?' he asked at last, awkwardly. She did not answer, but he felt her cold hand sliding into his, as a reptile slides into the snake-charmer's sack.

She stood up.

'Do you mind if I fetch my coat?'

'Are you cold?'

'It isn't very warm in your flat.'

'I worked here from two till seven, without moving, and I didn't feel cold. . . .'

'I'm not in very good health, I'm afraid, you must excuse me. As for you! Superb! The whole of Italy in your face.'

Before he could forestall her, she had reached the hall. He sensed the reproach in her last remark. Yes, she was cold, in blood as in heart.

They sat down to dinner, and he sighed:

'What a difficult and perilous bit of coastal navigation we're undertaking together! To sail our boat along the shore of life without foundering. . . .'

She turned her face towards him with a look of pity, of slightly weary disdain:

'I'd so like to have convinced you that it won't be so terrible.'

'Of course it won't be terrible. In any case we've talked enough about that; we've nothing more to say to each other on the subject. One last word only. I want you to give me your solemn word, I appeal to all that is best in you, never to seek to harm me, and I hereby promise you the same. If there are solemn words on this earth, this is one of them. . . . But after all, is it a solemn word? How many solemn words must have been given ever since the world began!'

'I've already given you that solemn word, and I give it to you again. And now, you're right, let's drop the subject.'

They ate in silence. The silence went on and on.

'Unforgettable first engagement meal,' he thought. 'Obviously my "yes" hasn't filled her with joy. I turn my life upside down for her sake. And it doesn't make her happy. Of course I always knew it; it's the rule. If, risking one's livelihood, one's job, etc., one carries off a minor, the moment one clasps her in one's arms after weeks of anxious scheming, she "resumes" so simply, so coolly, that one is rather put out by her apparent failure to appreciate all that this moment has cost you.... After all, our honeymoon being over and done with (in Genoa), it's true that the daily grind is all we have left. And it has its good side : the less we have to say to each other, the less she will need me, and the more time I shall have for the cherished things which aren't her.'

Mlle Dandillot ate in silence, shading her eyes with her left hand from time to time as though the light hurt them, but in reality to hide the decline in her looks. No, she did not feel happy : it was a wingless victory. First of all, naturally, because she had left the paradise of the thing coveted and entered the limbo of the thing obtained. But mainly because for the past eight months she had propped herself up on the resistance of this man; and now this prop had yielded, she was thrown a little off balance. Yielded! He had yielded! And now, how shy and unsure of himself he was in front of her! How weak he was, this man whom the newspapers always described as a 'strong man'. Would he be capable of defending their home, their interests, if he let himself be manipulated like this? She had perhaps ended up by respecting him because she had been unable to do what she wanted with him. And doubtless she respected him still, for a different reason : because she saw that he had acted out of generosity. But it was a dubious respect. The constant duel in the male's psyche between his generosity and his egoism, between his blood and his sperm, creates an atmosphere of confusion in him that terrifies and fascinates women and moves them to pity. At this moment Mlle Dandillot was rather at the pitying stage. And she turned it all over in her mind as she ate in silence, making an effort not to scratch her hands and wrists, since for several days now the nervousness born of her anaemia had given her an itch on her wrists, her thumbs and between her fingers, which were covered with the scratches she had inflicted on herself.

Thus did their first (unforgettable) meal as an engaged couple go by. Like the statue of the Commendatore at the banquet, a spectre was seated opposite them, a hydra-headed spectre : the head of Boredom, the head of Embarrassment, the head of

Duty, etc. Casanova tells us that princes are always bored in the company of their mistresses. Is this trait peculiar to princes?

That evening, Costals felt no desire to possess this dismal, emaciated, furunculous and faded girl (even though, from time to time, she showed a sudden and delightful gleam of life). Nor did she herself have any inclination in that direction, not only because it gave her no pleasure, but because she foresaw Costals' disillusionment; and now she was beginning to calculate, to try to be clever: after two cold showers, the icy water had opened her eyes a little. When she excused herself because of her boils and suggested the cinema instead, he acquiesced willingly enough. The everlasting cinema. But which film? Well, they would buy *la Semaine à Paris*.

People go to infinite pains to kill time hour after hour. Even so, they are incapable of managing it alone – they need guidance. A magazine has been created with this end in view: to call the attention of Parisians, in a methodical way, to the opportunities available to them for wasting their time. This magazine is incidentally extremely well conceived: when one sees that it is edited in a thoroughly *practical* way, when one sees that one can really *find what one is looking for* in it, one is amazed that it should be run by Frenchmen.

'There's *The Admirable Mr Fane*,' said Solange, flicking through *la Semaine à Paris* outside in the street. 'It's being talked about a lot.'

'An American film! Do you want me to bring up my dinner! Technical perfection in the service of cretinism – what greater sin against the mind?'

'What would you say to *Brigade Mondaine*?'

'How often must I tell you that I refuse to go to a French film at any price? Isn't there something English?'

'Here's one: *Rainbow*.'

'Let's go.'

When the taxi dropped them at the cinema in Montparnasse, Costals first of all sniffed around outside it.

'H'm. It looks a bit sentimental. And when the English start getting sentimental.... I'd better find out what it's about.'

He asked the cashier to let him look at the programme.

'Are you taking tickets?' she asked.

'That depends on what I see in the programme.'

'We only give programmes to people who've bought their seats.'

'I'm not asking you to give it to me, I'm asking you to sell it to me.'

'The programme isn't for sale, it's gratis. Buy your tickets and you'll be given one. You only have to do the same as everyone else.'

Foaming with rage, Costals spun round and left, dragging Solange after him.

'Isn't there an exotic film of some sort? At least the scenery would help one to swallow the plot.'

'There's *The Sorcerer of Sacramento* – that must be South American. . . .' [sic]. 'Then there's *Waikiki Night.* . . .'

'That'll do. Driver! Take us to Waikiki.'

They drove towards the Champs-Elysées. From time to time he took her hand in a rather convulsive way. But no sooner had the taxi stopped than he shouted:

'You didn't tell me that filthy whore was in it! Ah! that'll be really something. In disguise, striking plastic poses in the virgin forest. No, Solange, I don't care what you think, but it's literally more than I could bear to watch that female ape for a full two hours. Have another look at *la Semaine à Paris*. Isn't there a single Russian film? I promise you, if there's a Russian film, we'll go and see it and stay to the end.'

'*The Volga Boatmen*, on the grands boulevards.'

'That's the thing!'

The taxi drove off again. Solange hummed the song of the Volga Boatmen, as in Genoa she had hummed *O sole mio*. Costals thought that in every woman there was a tart waiting to get out, and who did get out whenever she hummed.

On the Boulevard des Italiens they got out and examined the posters: all the actors were French. It was indeed a film about Russia, but shot at Joinville.

Solange had stopped in front of one poster, Costals in front of another, a few yards away. He whistled to bring her across to him, like a pimp.

'Are we going in?' asked Solange, who had given a start.

Weariness made her features look more drawn than ever.

'Not on your life! ... All that French riff-raff! ... Tramps disguised as Russian princes....'

He stamped his foot with rage. It quite often occurred to him to stamp his foot – literally stamp his foot – like a small child or an oriental potentate.

'Let's go to a cafe,' she said. The boil on her bottom, after being shaken up by the taxis, was throbbing painfully. And she was weary of this man, weary to death of his spoilt child whims – or were they bachelor eccentricities or aesthete's poses? And of his punctuality: Phineas Fogg! ... And of the cigarette ash he dropped all over the place – on *her* coat, on *her* gloves – like bird-droppings. And of his coarseness.

'No,' said Costals vehemently. 'We haven't driven round Paris in order to end up in a café. Let's walk up the boulevards. There are cinemas every fifty yards. We're bound to find something.'

She took his arm (horrible gesture: 'I've got a good grip on you.') and he closed his hand over her wrist. He felt no more pleasure in touching her skin than if he were touching the smooth surface of a rubber cushion, whereas had he but touched the wrist of any one of these passing women! ... He never looked at her; he looked into himself, and outside himself, at the women he did not possess. It was not Mlle Dandillot he loved, it was a moment of Mlle Dandillot's life he had loved.

The neon sign of an Austrian film brought them to a halt. But when they drew near they saw there was a queue – a dense queue – at the box-office. Costals declared that he would gladly have seen this film but that he absolutely refused to queue. 'Queue for a theatre or a concert, well and good, but I absolutely refuse to queue for a film.' (We know how dear class distinctions in the arts – some being more noble than others – are to the French.)

They walked on again. Costals' exasperation vented itself in laughter and joking. Here he was, a man who believed in ordering his life, a man who believed that every hour must give proof of something gained or accomplished, and look how he had spent the last two hours! Yes, one had to laugh at it if one didn't want to lose one's temper.

On the boulevard Bonne-Nouvelle, a little cinema was showing a Russian film with Russian actors. But it was a three-franc flea-pit. 'After all, I can't take you to a three-franc cinema.' He hoped she would say 'What does the price matter, if we've found a film that interests you at last.' But she merely gave a little laugh, in obvious agreement. So she too suffered from that base love of luxury, that base subjection to the 'done thing.'

'Let's go back,' he said.

They walked back along the boulevards. Costals became more and more desperately animated : the evening could only be made bearable by turning it into a gag. Every true artist at times develops more of a liking for the personality he puts on than for his real personality. And it is at these moments that he should say, like the stage Marseillais: 'Hold me back!' For, with 'the wittiest people in the world', an author cannot sacrifice his solemnity without sacrificing his prestige, despite Victor Hugo's line :

L'Olympe reste grand en éclatant de rire.

They passed a news cinema close to the Madeleine :

'Well,' said Solange, 'what about this one? Newsreels are harmless enough !'

'It's half past eleven,' said Costals, pulling out his watch. 'And you've got a bad backside. It would be a sin to put that backside to bed at some unearthly hour. It's quite pointless to go to a cinema for half an hour.'

This remark was so superbly typical of a husband that it took Solange's breath away. Ah! he was cut out for it far more than he thought! She dragged herself along for another few steps, and then flopped down on the stone ledge that runs along the foot of the railings of the Madeleine.

Costals sat down beside her. The passers-by, numerous at that hour, turned and looked with astonishment at this respectably dressed couple sitting among the crowd on this freezing January night at the foot of the Madeleine railings, like exhausted provincials on the stairs at exhibitions. They both burst out laughing. Costals took off his hat and held it upside down between his knees.

'I hope they'll start throwing coins into it.'

> A penny,
> A penny,
> To set up our home!

They sat there for a while. Their laughter had subsided and they no longer spoke. Solange began to tear *la Semaine à Paris* into little pieces, which she carefully arranged on the ledge beside her. Costals felt that at all costs this scene must be prevented from turning to melancholy. He burst out gaily:

'A literary man, yes, a nice present to give to a little girl! You see, almost without thinking, I've been turning our first evening as an engaged couple into a scene from a play or a film. You must admit my gags have been a success. And now you're joining in the game! It was your idea to sit here, and then tearing *la Semaine à Paris* to shreds like that – the sentimental note after the comic turn.... We were made to get on together.'

'Why, of course, we were made to get on together,' she repeated, tenderly.

He escorted her home. As he was about to leave her at her front door (he no longer accompanied her up to her landing – ah! how remote they were, those long conversations of theirs on that landing, while the time-switch for the electric light had to be pressed three or four times), she asked him: 'When shall we be seeing each other again?' And he thought what torture this question can be when it is asked by somebody one does not care for. Oh, how sweet it is to be able to leave a person without having to arrange a 'next time'!

Back home, he noticed in his bathroom mirror that there were red smudges round his mouth. He wiped them off, leaving the towel stained pink. So, not content with wearing lipstick, which he loathed and despised, Solange was still schoolgirlish enough to buy a cheap brand. Not only did she do something stupid, but she did it stupidly. And for four hours she had let him walk round with lipstick all over his mouth! Either she did not see it, in which case she was a fool. Or she did not dare tell him, for fear of annoying him, which was worse still. 'To think that this mouth has given thousands of kisses which

never showed. And a single kiss from a clumsy girl betrays it!'
He heard again the little laugh she had given when he had
spoken to her about the flea-pit, that laugh that was so profoundly revealing of her mediocrity, the little laugh of the
woman-who-doesn't-go-to-three-franc-cinemas. He saw again the
pink smudge on his mouth, like that of a wounded soldier who
has just vomited blood. And he felt like a wounded soldier
himself – badly wounded.

6

> And he goeth after her straightaway, as an ox
> goeth to the slaughter. *Proverbs* 7, 20

> 'Is there anyone with whom you have as little
> conversation as with your wife?' – 'Almost no
> one.' Xenophon, *Oeconomicus*, 3, 12

And now, religion and myth, literature and history, help me!
Let's really get ourselves worked up, for God's sake! How
can one still complain about culture when it helps to gild the
pills of daily life? In the Bibliothèque Nationale, while the
guardian angels of the establishment discharged enemas of
sweet perfumes into the atmosphere (impossible, though, to
counteract the organic fetor of the thinker), Costals devoured
tome after tome, sheathed in dust like bottles of vintage wine,
describing the customs and legends of marriage in antiquity, in
the Middle Ages, in the East, etc. Methodically he squeezed the
phenomenon of 'marriage' to extract from it the last drop of
true or false poetry it might contain; pen in hand, and making
copious notes, for the foundations of every 'working up' need
to be as solid as rock.

Afterwards he went to see his solicitor. The latter, who had
already received a telephone call from the Dandillot lawyer,
could not refrain from observing that Mme Dandillot was
proving very generous in this matter (she too, with her
'magnificent negative qualities': neither ill-natured, nor conceited, nor self-seeking). Whereupon Costals realized that, if
Mme Dandillot had never asked for details as to her future
son-in-law's means, *he* had never asked for details about the

496

family he was about to join. For all he knew, Mme Dandillot might have been fished out of a brothel and the late lamented brother might have skipped to Madagascar because he was in trouble with the police. On both sides they were marrying in the dark. But it was a little annoying that Mme Dandillot was being so 'generous': a man of quality, when striking a bargain, must ensure that he gets the worst of it.

On the advice of his solicitor – appalled by his ignorance about the married state – Costals called at the town hall, where he was handed a yellow leaflet: 'General information concerning marriage'. But this leaflet, a masterpiece of French administrative prose, was incomprehensible: it reminded him of an income tax form. The only thing that was clear about it was that marriage must be regarded as a 'bond issue'. Costals would go back to his solicitor the following day for an exegesis of the yellow leaflet.

On all these matters he could seek advice. But there was one question on which he could not seek advice from anyone: the question of his son.

Solange, who was irritated by boys, would not like Brunet. Brunet would take a dislike to Solange. Or, on the other hand, would take too much of a liking to her, and it is too great a blessing to be able to think well of one's child for one to endanger it in such a way. In any case, how horrible it would be to have this outsider coming between father and son!

Why had he kept his son's existence secret? Because he loved him. Because he did not want him criticized. Because he did not want his way of bringing him up criticized. He clung to this secrecy inordinately, irrationally, as Arabs cling to the secrecy in which they guard their wives. Once he was married, everything would change. There could be no question of Brunet appearing to be kept at arm's length. So he would be prostituted to this rabble of mediocrities, this vapid, brainless young woman, that ludicrous old hag, and all the cousins and aunts. He would no longer be *hortus conclusus*. . . . And then, what was the use of having resolved the difficulty foreseen by the sages*, what was the use of having succeeded in having

---

*'Must one then agree to subject oneself to woman in the hope of having children?' – Djâmi, *Beharistan* (*Author's note*).

the child without the woman, only to take on the woman after the event?

And how was he to break it to him, how was he to foist this 'mother' on him? To Solange, Costals would say bluntly: 'I warn you, I have a son.' If she didn't like it, she had only to give up the marriage. But to him? Write to him and say: 'I'm getting married. She's this, that or the other. You'll be delighted, etc.'? Monstrous and impossible. So he would have to go and see him. With Solange, perhaps. How painful the interview would be! The idea that finally kept running through his mind was this: that he should never have committed himself until after having *consulted* his son.

Costals had leapt the hurdle of decision. He no longer wavered, no longer suffered from it, scarcely thought about it. But he had not yet taken this other hurdle: the Brunet-Solange problem. And faced with it he wavered and suffered. Since Solange was near at hand, he would begin with her. Tomorrow, under the pretext of showing her his family, he would run through his photograph album with her. When he came to the photograph of his son, he would first pass him off as a young cousin. According to her reaction, he would either speak or not.

Every other day, the fiancés spent the afternoon and evening together. Costals gazed at this stranger, at this face which, in Genoa, he had seen as though diluted by love, this face of a sleeper awakened, now cold, hard and dry (the girl's handwriting, too, had become more angular). He had forgotten Mme Dandillot's words: 'She has no will-power, you'll be able to do what you like with her', and remembered only that slightly different version: 'She has a will of iron, that child. She's said to herself: "He's the man I want".' He concluded that he had been *had*. Thyroid glands, injected into a sheep, will make it bite the bars of its cage. Hippogriffical glands, injected into a vigorous man, will make him as weak as a lamb. By dint of harassing a man, stuffing him with worries, responsibilities, obligations, scruples, decisions to be taken, self-questionings, one can stupefy and wear him down to such an extent that he no longer offers any resistance to another's will, even when he knows it to be inimical. Women know this, and that is why to introduce a woman into anything is to introduce strife and confusion: like warships, they proceed behind their own smoke-screens. In the past Costals had been 'bewitched' by the pall of boredom that emanated from Solange. Now he felt equally bewitched by her will, more potent than his own. He felt a sense of inferiority, as with a dangerous chance companion, a tough customer who seems more mobile, more vigorous, more active and aggressive than oneself. And the fact of being armed, when he is not, only adds to one's shame the shame one feels at cheating. Costals no longer dared to say to Solange what he had to say to her, particularly on the subject of his son; day after day went by without his saying a word about Brunet. He was continuously obliged to make an effort in her presence. When she looked him straight in the eyes he no longer thought: 'What magnificent honesty!' but 'She's challenging me. She wants to get the whip hand.' It seemed to him that the way he looked at her was softer, that his very features were softer, and that she must be able to read in them how dominated he felt – at times almost annihilated, for she made him sleepy. In certain parts of Moslem Algeria – and in the South of France, too, apparently – custom demands that in the course of a ceremony the fiancé should step lightly on the tips of his fiancée's toes, to indicate that he will keep the upper hand in the household. 'The opposite happens too,' he thought to himself.

Since the decline in her health, Solange had been more pre-occupied than before with her creature comforts. And she ate more, thinking to build herself up, the more so as she had been forbidden wine and coffee because of her boils. Perhaps, too, soured by a sense of disappointment, although victorious and moreover full of confidence (whereas her mother was still doubtful, she no longer feared a new volte-face by Costals), she was more or less unconsciously taking her revenge by lolling about, by being a dead weight, by forcing him to over-spend. Costals became exasperated by the fact that she could not get through an afternoon without wanting to go into a tea-room. Whatever they might be doing, however important, everything had to be dropped there and then while they went and had tea, like cats that stop dead in the middle of an apparently determined gallop in order to lick their behinds. Having tea would be stretched out over an hour: it was probably just a way of killing time. No sooner was tea over (so it seemed) than they had to start looking for a restaurant for dinner. Out of politeness, as in front of the scruffy little cinema in the boulevard Bonne-Nouvelle, Costals pretended to find such and such a restaurant not 'good enough'. And Solange would never say, any more than she had in the boulevard Bonne-Nouvelle: 'What does it matter! Let's go anywhere.' He could tell that she preferred luxury restaurants, or so-called luxury restaurants; and in his view, with few exceptions, only people of doubtful quality can like luxury. 'The waiter pisses in the soup, the bellhop spits in the oysters, not to mention the scullion, who cleans his fingers with the lemon; the service is inefficient and interminable; the prices are scandalous; but there is plenty of fake gilt and fake marble, a basket for the wine, pretentious music, menus on which the names of dishes are embellished by the unemployed definite articles laid off by literary gentlemen who have no more use for them in the titles of their works (no! no! there is nothing more grotesque than a smart restaurant!), and given all this, she purrs, she is in her element. She would happily spend the whole afternoon there. . . . But at least the music allows us to be silent. Orchestras in restaurants must have been invented for the benefit of couples.'

And how she ate! Choosing, too, as though deliberately, nearly always the most expensive dishes. 'She orders expensive drinks. One can tell she comes of a good family, that girl,' Costals had once heard a man naïvely remark of a woman at the table next to his in a café. Costals, on the contrary, when he saw Solange peel her banana with a knife and fork so that her precious fingers should not touch the coarse substance, thought: 'Bogus refinements by which vulgar people try to make believe they are arch-dukes, when in fact they only proclaim the gutter.' She, so slender and light, whose weight 'would scarcely hold down the flap-seat in a cinema' (so she said), the amount she could swallow! Mockingly, to see how far she would go, he tempted her: 'You'll have another Peach Melba, won't you? Don't you fancy the rum pancake?' Then he would see a look of hesitation on her face, a struggle between her greed and her awareness that he was teasing her. She would push out her lips in a pout that signified 'no', while her eyes said 'yes' and always ended up with: 'All right ... just to please you.' At these moments, she filled him with such disgust. As she did when she would say apologetically: 'I have to eat a lot to feel completely myself.' That's it, he thought, she has no reserves. . . . In the end he would fold his arms and stare straight in front of him in silence, while she swallowed and swallowed, his tongue itching to reply to her interrogatory look: 'I'm waiting for you to eat the rind of your cheese.' He thought despairingly that all the money he would ever draw from his intelligence, his skill and his hard work would flow down into the intestines of a woman. 'Can one be both greedy and worthy of respect? I almost think I would have preferred the money to be wasted on clothes and cosmetics.' Thus did the hours go by, annihilating the inestimable boon of time. And Costals parodied the words of Alexander swept away on the waters of Hydaspes: 'O Society, the things one must do to merit thy praise!'

'It is often said against Donjuanism: "Ah! one sole woman, whose depths one plumbs ever more deeply, from whom one draws ever more marvellous harmonies!" And this is indeed tempting, provided one is given the recipe for finding a woman in whom there are depths to plumb, and from whom these stupendous harmonies can be drawn. Because one sole woman who is a void. . . . I'd much prefer a thousand and three voids. Look at this one, clinging on to me, although she loves neither me, nor my work, nor making love. What has she done to adapt herself to me? How can one love a person if one doesn't modify one's own life, add to or subtract something from it because of that person? She sullies me by condemning me to so-called gourmet's food, which I don't want and which I disapprove of, by dragging me to so-called luxury establishments, which I dislike and disapprove of, in fact thoroughly abominate. This tartishness that potentially exists in almost every woman, even the best (like her humming in the taxi)! Eating, always eating. Sprawled in armchairs for hours on end. She wants to turn me into a typical French capon, a pot-bellied bourgeois with his aperitif, his brandy, his cigar, his motor-car, his "good living". Frigid herself, she wants to emasculate me, out of jealousy. Lacking vitality, she wants to devitalize me. Then there are the shops, the buying of useless objects, the cinema, the theatre, anything as long as it's idiotic, for the only object is to stupefy me here as it is to emasculate me there. All this with endless precautions to avoid being seen, because one's in deep mourning, because one's joyously trampling on the grave of dear sweet papa; civilization run by women: everyone watching everyone else, guided by others, inspired by fear of what others may think. And always ingurgitating. Now she's really getting down to the job of sucking the life-blood out of her prey. Women always claim to give, when they do nothing but engulf. Think of their position in the sexual act (such a ridiculous posture, too: froglike). She sees me as a being specially created for her (every woman's dream!), destined to make her happy, to bring her, together with a "position" and material security, something to keep her occupied and distracted; charged by Providence to prevent her from being bored. How much of my strength, my substance, my time, my money, has this once so simple, or fake-simple, girl already forcibly sucked out of me! The engulfment of valleys.... The woman-valley.... A valley in her embraces, a valley in her organs, a valley in her very essence, cut off from the world, seeing no further than the end of her nose, surrounded, hemmed in by walls which sometimes may be the walls of her love, and sometimes not even that. And the enervating climate of valleys....

'Not knowing what to say to each other. Not knowing where to go. Dragging from place to place, desperately trying to dredge something up out of one's brain and one's heart. And always by taxi, because of course no woman can go anywhere except by taxi. (All that putting on of airs: the simplest of them is the Queen of Sheba for life. They can't understand how much good they would do a man by allowing him to treat them casually – and how much they would gain thereby.) And always with the same one: "Always the same one! Always the same one!" like the baby pelican's "Tripe! always tripe!" And always that snap of the clasp of her hand-bag when she closes it, which irritates me in the same way as did the rustle of that Spanish *amiga*'s fan when she closed it at least thirty times a minute (for which, in the end, I had to get rid of her). And each of these wasted, deadening, soul-destroying days costing you several hundred francs, money with which so many persons . . . so many things. . . .'

It was at the end of one such day, eaten up by chatter, vacuousness, sterility, by the futile and exhausting task of trying to work up some enthusiasm for insipid remarks which he would have condemned as such had they issued from other lips than those of a 'beloved' woman, of trying to make someone intelligent and lively when she was neither, a day when all the meaningless words he had uttered had left a kind of dough in his mouth, that Costals, in one of his notebooks, came across the following reflection by his beloved Abbé de Saint-Cyran : *Any converse he may have with a man without due necessity, or without appreciable purpose, is ample cause to prevent a priest from sacrificing the next day.* Ah! fellows like that were capable of reconciling a man with Christianity. However little store one set by Christianity, the cloister was after all a bit better than a fiancée.

As though to make up for all this, he began to treat her with less ceremony. Sometimes, when they left each other, he would proffer her his left hand, as though he were withdrawing at the same time as giving himself. And he no longer looked at her, in fact he avoided looking at her : there are women with whom one lives, with whom one sleeps, and yet whom one never looks at, about whom one knows no more than a passenger who has spent the whole crossing in his cabin knows of the sea.

She had kept her make-up and her 'young woman' hair style, although he had expressed his irritation with it, and had even said one day: 'Go and wash your face before I kiss you' – because she liked herself so, and because she thought it was high time she had her own way a little. He no longer desired her physically, and he knew that she did not desire him, nor ever had. Marriages, for a time, are sustained by desire ; a day of scenes and silences is balanced by twenty minutes in the dark. But if there is not even that? Nevertheless, on no account would he have had her believe that her boils and her drawn

face were the cause of his coldness. Besides, he was a little
ashamed of loving her less because she was less pretty; he had
been moved by the gesture she had made once when he was
looking at her closely : she had put her hand over his eyes to
prevent him from seeing the decline of her face from so near.
So he took her, he caressed her, with his nerves severed, as it
were, like those of the '*énervés*' of Jumièges.* To beslobber
each other's mouths, when one isn't particularly keen to do so,
is no joke. (And outrageous thoughts came into his head, such
as this, when she threw back her head and opened her mouth
during the act : 'Does she want me to pull one of her teeth
out?') How exhausting it was to simulate desire! To what
extent would his body lend itself to the farce? One day, like
a stubborn animal, it would simply refuse. The camel remains
on top of the she-camel for a quarter of an hour thinking of
something else. The cameleer belabours it with his cudgel. The
camel gives a thrust or two, grunting the while, then relapses
into contemplation. Another whack. Another burst of passion.
And more contemplation. After the fashion of this absent-
minded beast, Costals. . . . Drudgery for them both, enough to
disgust you with the flesh for ever – or else plunge you into
every sort of frantic debauchery. But Charity demanded it,
Politeness demanded it, Duty demanded it. One can hear the
derisive laughter of the Daemon of the Good as he presides
over these sublime and sinister gymnastics.

During the hours when he was not with her, he flung himself into his work as others fling themselves into alcohol or
drugs. He was hungry for his work; it was his life-line. He
gathered up and filtered into it everything he was living
through with Solange : art is a quintessence of life, it purges
it of its waste products and offers only the undiluted blood.
Had he not worked in the morning, he might not have been
able to endure Solange in the afternoon and evening without
falling really ill himself. His lucidity, his creative power, were
what they had always been. As soon as his fiancée ceased to

---

*There is a tomb in the Abbey of Jumièges, Normandy, which is
said to be that of two sons of Clovis II, King of the Franks, who
were punished for having rebelled against their mother Bathilde
by being hamstrung (*Translator's note*).

exist for him (otherwise than in his art), he became a man again.

He constantly put off showing Solange the photograph album or mentioning his son. He put off writing to Brunet. The preposterous idea he had toyed with for a moment – flying to England with all Solange's letters and photographs and the diary entries he had written about her, and spreading them all out for his son to see, talking to him about Solange for two hours, and then asking this youngster of fourteen and a half, whose character was that of a thirteen-year-old: 'Do *you* want me to marry her? If you don't, there's still time' – this idea had evaporated. In becoming engaged, he had reached the limits of his will. Now he had given up the struggle.

The two of them were sinking, as though drowned, their faces already those of another world, into ever darker depths, a few feet from each other, without touching.

One day, however, a shaft of light pierced momentarily through the gloom. Some cad (a man from the sixteenth *arrondissement*, as might have been expected) asked Costals with a playful wink: 'Who's that ravishing girl I saw you with in the avenue du Bois?' Whereupon Costals realized that people would find his wife ravishing, and preened himself on it, and was ashamed of doing so. Everyone speaks against the world, and everyone has it in his heart.

7

Andrée Hacquebaut   to Pierre Costals
Saint-Léonard (Loiret)   *Paris*

22 January 1928

All alone! Yes, yes, come quickly. I'll open the door. Oh! how cold you are! You have a nice wintry, frosty smell. I must warm you up. Get rid of your overcoat, your hat, your scarf, and let me get a good look at you, you whom I've merely imagined for so long. How I love it when you stretch out all five fingers at once in your big fur-lined gloves! Such a man's gesture. . . . But look, a ray of sunlight on the snow! Let's go out. Go and wait for me for a few minutes by the fountain, while I change. Which dress shall I put on?

My little town, so calm and peaceful. I'm glad you've seen it at last. And it's so sweet of you not to be afraid of people seeing us together. Let's go for a long, long walk, until I beg for mercy. Me, cold? You keep me nice and warm. Me, annoyed because you ogled old Bernardeau's daughter? Jealousy's a shop-girl's emotion. Don't talk; you'd only talk about yourself, and what more could I learn? I know you like the back of my hand. I don't feel the need to talk to you either. I'm going to keep you with me for a while, just breathing you in and feeling myself throbbing with life close beside you. Let's walk in silence. You are the only man who never bores me. How could I ever get bored with this soul-to-soul between us?

You make me happy, very happy, and so you should: I've deserved your kindness. And then, this certainty that at last you have understood. You realize at last that you love me.

Life is wonderful.

They're celebrating the return of one of my cousins from his regiment at Didier-le-Petit, and I have to be there with my uncle on Wednesday and Thursday. For two whole days, no more Sainte-Beuve, no more wireless, and cousins by the score. The restfulness of being with simple people, oh yes, I'll say! Before I loved you, all this drudgery was somehow bearable, but now it seems beyond my strength. On Friday I shall be back, and we'll go for another walk together.

Much love,
A.

This letter was filed away by the recipient, unopened.

8

Costals was due to have lunch at the Dandillots'. In the ten days since he had become engaged, he had met Mme Dandillot only twice, both times at her solicitor's: they had only talked 'business'. This morning, he was confronted with a tiny prob-

lem which, greeted at first in a light-hearted vein, had gradually taken a serious turn: what to call his mother-in-law when
he had to address her? 'Call this stupid and rather vulgar
stranger, this Pulcinella, this police horse, "mother"? Not that
I subscribe to the convention that regards the word *mother* as
sacred. There are women of every kidney; and as the majority
of women are mothers, there must be mothers of every kidney.
But I personally had a very nice mother. To give this stranger
the name I gave *her* is something I will not and cannot do –
it wouldn't come out. "Dear Madame" is insulting. "My dear"
– we haven't reached that stage yet. The only alternative is
not to call her anything at all. Very convenient!...' The
thought of this luncheon was torture to him. Incapable this
time of taking refuge in creative stupefaction (work), he ended
up by stretching himself out on his bed – the bed in which, a
few hours earlier, while asleep, he had dreamed of these two
women: it is not the ghosts of the dead that haunt us, it is
the ghosts of the living. 'It's also essential to fix a date for the
wedding. It's also essential and urgent to come to some decision
about Brunet. And all this *for what*, FOR WHAT? Because
there's no sense in this marriage.'

At first, the idea of the fiancé prostrate on his bed also
seemed rather a joke. His laughter subsided when he felt himself in the grip of a real physical malaise (occasioned, no doubt,
by his mental distress but also perhaps by the cigarettes he
had been nervously chain-smoking for three hours – *Caporal*
cigarettes, which taste as if one were smoking arse-hairs). He
got up to fetch some Eau de Cologne, poor fellow, and saw
himself in the mirror. In ten days his face had aged, and had
taken on a permanent expression of melancholy. 'I shall grow
thin while she grows fat: communicating vessels.' He thought
he looked ugly. 'No, she can't love me. It's all a ridiculous
farce.' His head really began to spin; his face was as pale as
death; he lay down on the bed again. 'I shall have to get drunk
before going to the registry office with her. The instinct of self-
preservation might easily arise *in extremis.*'

'If I could only say to myself, as I've sometimes done: "It's
only a parenthesis. A bore with whom one finds oneself in a
railway compartment, and one thinks: ten hours to get

through." But no, she'll refuse to divorce me. One can see it in her face – in everything she's transformed herself into today, her new hair-style, her new handwriting. Perhaps I shall end up by becoming attached to her, because of what I've given her. I've nurtured the little feeling I had for her, which God knows what would have become of (nothing at all) if I had left it to itself, if I hadn't fed it with charity, as one metal is fed with another at the mint to make the coins more durable. The disease is in me – this charity – and that is what's getting me down.'

By noon he had neither washed nor shaved nor dressed. He got up once more, and once more was quickly obliged to lie down. Dramatic! To have to spend one's life with people the anticipation of whose mere presence for the space of a luncheon was enough to nail him to his bed with a face like a corpse – and when there was still time to say no – yes, that was no joke, it was really dramatic.

He telephoned to say he felt unwell and would probably be late. (Mme Dandillot thought he would fail to turn up. She herself, often enough, had feigned a stomach-ache at mealtimes when she was in a fit of sulks with her husband.)

A splash of cold water on the temples, a sniff of Eau de Cologne. . . . At half past twelve he managed to get to the bathroom, and at half past one he was ringing the bell at the avenue de Villiers.

'From now on, consider this house your own,' said Mme Dandillot as he entered the drawing-room. These are words to which it is pretty well impossible to reply when one's heart is not in it.

On a table there were photographs of Solange and Costals, jointly framed. The day after his *yes*, Mme Dandillot had asked the fiancé for a photograph of himself 'which hadn't appeared in the papers'. Faced with these likenesses, so full of idealistic implications, Costals was reminded of the 'He' and 'She' whose effigies were discovered in mosaic among the ruins of Pompeii: She, a goose, He, a nincompoop – so ineffably the Eternal Couple, even then. Representing, more or less, for the Couple, what Goya's *Family of Charles IV* represents for the Family.

Oh! as far as the grub was concerned they had certainly put

themselves out. It was the betrothal feast to end them all. Caviare, duck, truffles, and extremely enticing bottles. Materially perfect, morally lamentable, like American films. The police horse caracoling as gaily as one could wish. Solange with a look of severity and constraint as on the day he had visited the Dandillots for the first time, when they were still pretending to be semi-strangers: 'Good morning, Mademoiselle,' 'Good morning, Monseiur.' And as for Costals: 'If only a trapdoor would open and swallow me up.' However, he soon perceived that the watchword was not to broach *that subject*, and was duly relieved.

After lunch, there was a period of embarrassed silence. To have nothing to say to one another, but never to show it, is the whole art of the drawing room. The wireless and the gramophone were invented for just such circumstances: it is then that the hostess puts on a Mozart record, casts a withering eye at anyone who dares to venture a word, and a dozen puppets hold their breath in the interests of musical conformity; for to *feel* anything for Mozart is of course inconceivable in a man of 1928, but the humbugs of society get together on Mozart as intellectual humbugs do on Racine. But there were none of these machines in the Dandillot house. So Solange, to keep herself in countenance, stroked the grey cat (and a rasping purr reverberated through the flat), gazing at it as one gazes at a flame, though this did not prevent her from darting in Costals' direction, from time to time, one of those furtive glances characteristic of little girls and bull calves. 'Do leave that cat alone!' Mme Dandillot burst out, and one might have imagined oneself back in the days when Mme Dandillot, who detested her husband, nevertheless became hysterical whenever he stroked one of the cats too fondly. At last Mme Dandillot had a brainwave: still at a loss for something to say, she picked up one of Costals' books and began to read aloud a passage she 'adored'. 'Is it going to go on for ever?' he wondered, his eyelids drooping with boredom: there are writers who find something indecent in their prose being read aloud. Mme Dandillot closed the book with cries of 'Admirable! Prodigious!' She made such a din one could have sworn she was a real society lady.

'Now will you allow me to ask you what you meant by this sentence, which I don't quite understand?'

She re-read a sentence. Hearing it out of context ten years after having written it, Costals could not immediately recollect what he had meant to say, and admitted it frankly, as though he were talking to intelligent people. Whereupon the two women shrieked with laughter. And he realized that neither of them had for a single moment assimilated the air he breathed and lived by. He remembered a remark Solange had made to her mother and which the latter had repeated to him without any suggestion of malice : 'I would love him just as much if he were a wholesale grocer. And besides, he'd have fewer women clinging to him. . . .'

Mme Dandillot had to go out. They remained alone. If the question 'When do we meet again?' is destructive, 'What shall we do?' is its brother. Solange volunteered that she would gladly go to his flat to look through an album of Egyptian sculpture he had told her about. 'Of course she doesn't give a damn for Egyptian sculpture. But she has to kill time somehow. And pretend to be interested in what interests me.'

She went into her room to change. She continued to forbid him entry to it because she was ashamed of her little girl's things, which she thought ridiculous but *could not* bring herself to throw away. Ashamed, too, of the perpetual mess the room was in. Costals had constructed a theory on the subject : 'No doubt she considers that room more sacred than herself. Just as a man may not respect himself, but respects an object of worship. Transferring on to an external object what should be dedicated to oneself alone. It has happened to me, having worked out a routine for myself, to become such a slave to it as to detest anything unexpected, however agreeable.'

As they leafed through the album at the avenue Henri-Martin, Costals suddenly felt tempted to pass from this album to another. The temptation grew, like the noise of a shell approaching. Then the shell burst, the decision was made : he went to fetch his photograph album.

As she looked at the pictures of his parents, of his grandparents, of his childhood, she spoke nicely about them, with sweetness and tact. As they went on turning the leaves, Costals felt a strange calm take possession of him, a most mysterious calm. It was the sort of calm that grips a runner in the hundred metres, during which he stops breathing. He turned a page, and two photos of his son appeared.

'It's a little cousin of mine. They say he looks like me at that age. Don't you agree?'

'Oh, no! You must have looked nicer than that.'

'Don't you like him?'

'Frankly, no. He has a rather bumptious look that I don't care for.'

Costals turned the page.

Peace. It was no longer a calm, it was unutterable peace. Sudden peace, like the outer harbour for the liner once it has crossed the bar out of a heavy sea. He remembered also the remark she had made in Genoa: 'It's lucky you haven't a son.' Anyone observing him then would have seen his face, tightly drawn ever since waking, relax and light up, like the face of a martyr in the midst of the flames, at the moment when, expiring, he imagines he has seen his God. For the first time since his return from Genoa, he took Solange in his arms with genuine feeling.

9

Next day, at about five, Costals awaited Solange. He had sent her an express letter that morning: 'Come to my flat at five. And be brave, my sweet. I have some extremely unpleasant news for you.' Afterwards he had switched off the telephone.

Each time he recalled her face, it was as if it were reappearing above the surface of the water with an imploring look: 'Save me!', and each time he thrust her back under with an oar. 'Yes, it's true, I'm murdering her' (he caught sight of himself in the mirror) 'and *I look it*. What I'm doing is abominable. Nevertheless I'm right, a hundred, a thousand times right to do it. I'm right to prefer myself to her, since I don't love her.'

She rang. He went to the door. He was moved, and yet he had great difficulty in repressing a desire to smile – not a smile of affection but the smile of someone who is amused – so much so that he paused behind the door to compose his features.

He opened the door. She was without make-up or powder. He knew she had understood. There was that tiny moment of immobility that occurs immediately after one has been wounded and the blood has not yet begun to seep out.

In absolute silence – no greetings – he led her to his bedroom. The lights were off, he did not switch them on. She-who-stares-at-the-sun collapsed into an armchair; her hand-bag slid down her legs and fell on the floor. He knelt beside her and kissed her frozen hands, her deep-blue veins, flowing like a river with several tributaries under the bridge of her wrist-watch. The cat whose kittens have just been taken away from her, and whose neck one scratches to make her purr. He noticed that some of yesterday's dust still clung to her black suede shoes: 'Slovenly – and an ill-kept house.' He kissed her face a little, too. She did not return these kisses, and he wondered whether it was out of ill-humour or because she was prostrate with grief. Her face was white in the darkness, like a glacier at night; the blow she had just received gave her a vague, cloudy, sunken look. Several times, in a touching, silent gesture of despair, she raised her fore-arm and let it fall again on the arm of her chair (when a man makes this gesture of discouragement, he does it with his fist clenched). He had always had the knack of retrieving painful situations, of making an angry woman smile in spite of herself; but faced with this gesture of despair he was left speechless. Presently he began to feel that her eyelids were moist under his lips, and he spoke for the first time: 'If you want to cry, you mustn't stop yourself.' Whereupon, springing up suddenly, she threw herself on the bed, face down, in that little girl's posture she loved to adopt, and sobbed.... Suddenly she cried: 'No, no! I don't want to lose you.'

Now it was she who was kissing him, running her hands over the contours of his face, stroking his hair, thrusting her hands between his jacket and his shirt, and always, when he said, 'My little darling ...' she answered with one word only: 'Yes....' Just as a cat which you talk to answers each of your sentences with a single brief little miaow. In a voice that was

barely perceptible she murmured: 'My heart's overflowing
with tears. . . . ' All her recent hardness had melted; she was
full of gentleness, like a dying dog that wags its tail in a final
farewell. She knew it was all over now. And she loved him as
she had not loved him since his return. She loved him because
it enabled her to plumb the depths of her despair, she loved
him because he was no longer a bewildered chicken, because
he was resisting her once more, because he had become her
master again. When he had stopped enumerating – as in a
dream – his never-ending reasons 'against', she said:

'Do you remember what Paul says in *The Holidays*: "Whatever you may do against me, I shall never do anything against
you"? Well, that's what I say to you. Try as I may, I can't
bring myself to blame you. I can't do anything against my love
for you. You would have had to be very nasty to me, and
you haven't been. . . . '

'I don't blame you either,' he said. He knew what he meant,
but Solange did not, and drew herself up:

'That would be the last straw!'

'After all, when you think of the power you gave me, I
could have used it more harmfully than I have. I've given you
seed for the dreams of your old age: you'll see how splendid
they will be when you see them flower. I've taught you to
live, I've provided you with a destiny. Thanks to me, you've
discovered yourself, you've plumbed the depths of your nature.
So many women never go more than half-way.'

'Being where I am now is staying half-way. And to think
that it might have worked, that we didn't try, that we suffered
in vain!'

'You haven't suffered in vain. A man may suffer in vain, not
a woman. I have tormented you: what more do you want?
Women need suffering. Take their suffering away from them
and you kill them, more or less. There are women who go mad
because they haven't suffered enough, *normally* suffered. If,
some day, women come to have their babies painlessly, they
won't love them. Which is why almost all women are unhappy, and it's right that it should be so. And anyhow, what
does your despair amount to? Think of the eight million war
dead. Think that it might be your mother dying, instead of a

man you didn't know eight months ago disappearing from your life.'

'So I haven't been hurt enough yet. Do you want to hurt me more by speaking about the death of my mother?'

But her actions belied her reproaches: she went on kissing and stroking him; and there was that same way of turning her face towards him every so often with a look of tenderness still, but which he did not quite understand.

'When I was a little girl, it shocked me that St Martin should only have given half his cloak to the beggar. What could one do with half a cloak? You've never given me more than half your cloak. And you shouldn't do that. You should give the whole of it or not give anything at all.'

'I gave what I could,' said Costals. He was not being fair to himself. He had given what he could, but only to the extent that she seemed to him to deserve it.

'With you I should have had a personality that otherwise I shan't have. Without you I'm nothing much, I know. . . . But all the same, I'm worth something,' she added.

'What would you like me to do for you? Whatever you like, I'll do it. Would you like me to relieve you of my presence by leaving France once more? Would you like us to go on seeing each other? Look, here's what I suggest: that we go on with everything that was decided as to our future, with the exception of the registry office. In other words, I fix up a room for you in my flat, and you come and live there several days a week. In fact, marriage without a zero hour.'

'Become your mistress! Oh, of course, that would suit you. But it would ruin my life. I find it hard to believe you're seriously suggesting it.'

'But . . . haven't you been my mistress for the past eight months?'

'I've never lived with you, at least in Paris. In Genoa no one knew. Here! . . . And besides, at that time we could have said we were engaged, which we can't any longer. I'm sure there are lots of women who would accept your proposal gladly. I suppose I must come from a different background. And I can't see myself repaying my mother's affection and understanding by agreeing to a way of life which would make us both outcasts, would close all doors to us, those of the family as well as those of society.'·('What society?' Costals wondered, contemptuous once more.) 'Furthermore, uncle Mercadier would disinherit Mummy on the spot if he heard I was living with you: the situation of the gentleman would make no difference. It's odd that you don't think of all that. What sort of women can you have known, you poor dear?'

Ready to flout conventions when she thought it necessary in order to get herself married, Mlle Dandillot was very much the bourgeoise when it was merely a question of flouting them for love.

Costals was rather pleased to detect in her a hint of self-interest.

'This sort of talk seems to me a bit new on your lips,' he said gently. 'But one cannot help approving. In that case, there's nothing left for you but to get married. Would you like "the gentleman" to try and find you a husband?'

'Are you mad! It will be years and years before I get married now. To ask me to marry would be like asking me to turn my head back to front – an appalling outrage.... Marriage with you was the only marriage which didn't seem like death to me. For the tragedy is not so much that you don't love me as that I can't love anyone else. How many women have *never* met an intelligent man? Where shall I ever find again such maturity combined with such freshness? Where shall I ever again find someone who understands me?'

This last heart-cry, which might have been uttered by an Aristotle or an Einstein, on the lips of a sort of shop-girl, froze Costals, who up to then had been moved. He plunged into that well of sadness into which men are forced by women when they would so much like to be able to take them seriously, and cannot. Although nothing was more foreign to him than the desire to 'mould' a woman (he had never thought of 'moulding' anyone but his son, and even then only rather desultorily), Solange's remark had touched him at first: 'With you I should have had a personality' (it was extraordinary that she never flattered him, incredible in fact). Now the remark irritated him, reminding him of those comic articles in the women's pages of weeklies, in which *Sylphide* or *Cousin Annie* provide their 'sisters' with the recipes for 'developing their personalities'. These efforts to inject a semblance of life into what has none are the most astonishing and depressing thing in the world.

'But . . . would you say I had understood you, then?'

'Of course,' she said. Costals was a bit flummoxed by this, thinking that there was so obviously nothing to understand in Mlle Dandillot.

'Are you then so different from the rest?' he asked treacherously.

'Haven't you ever noticed?' Every woman, so cruelly similar to her companions, believes herself to be different.

'The important thing is not to be different from others, but to be different from oneself. And you are always like yourself.'

There were flowers shedding their petals in a vase, like a man dropping women from his life.

'All the same, it's stupid,' he went on. (Like all men, often unexpectedly modest, he thought that since she had given herself to him she must be prepared to give herself to anyone.) 'Women only become attached when they're not intelligent. Come, be a little intelligent, like a cat that pushes a half-open door with its paw, in order to get out: *learn how to get out.* There are plenty of Costals in the world who are made for you, whereas it's obvious that we weren't made for each other. Quite apart from the fact that your experience with me will have stood you in good stead; now you'll be on your guard; until you met me you let other people think for you. Besides, what you want is not love but marriage. We'll deceive your husband as much as you wish.'

'What if I'm incapable of leading a double life? You know perfectly well I shall never be unfaithful to my husband, whoever he is. I'm not made that way.'

'Well, what do you want? What can I do for you?'

Suddenly he had an idea, a typically masculine idea, in the worst possible taste, but the outcome of which proved that it was an excellent one.

'As you know, I've never doubted that we'd get a divorce, and I wanted it to be as solemn as our marriage would have been clandestine. Divorce is the cardinal instrument of mar-

riage, it's there that the emphasis ought to be put, and I could
even wish that the Church would make it a sacrament. . . .
But no doubt that will come one of these days. . . . '

She smiled, and he was pleased to see this first ray of sunshine. Oh! there's nothing more stupid than a psychologist. As
if one didn't smile when one suffers!

'. . . Which is why I told you that I'd give you an engagement ring when we divorced. Let me offer it to you now. The
diamond on it is a solitaire: symbol of the destiny of your
friend.'

'I'm not going to accept a ring from you now!'

He went to a jewel-case and took out a rather handsome
ring which had belonged to his mother. Shortly before she
died, his mother had said to him: 'As for my rings, you can
give them to your girl-friends.'

The room was still in darkness. But when Solange, with the
ring in her hand, switched on the light in order to examine it,
he knew that she was feeling better.

She made as if to give the ring back to him.

'Don't you want it?'

Silence.

'Please!'

She pouted her lips as she had done when 'refusing' the
Peach Melba:

'All right, I accept. But not as a present – that wouldn't be
very dignified of me. As a souvenir of you.'

'Of course! I never meant it otherwise. It isn't at all a
present.'

She flashed the ring in the light.

'It's a pity the setting's a bit old-fashioned.'

'I'll get a modern one put on for you.'

'She's a pathetic little tart,' he thought. 'The girl who didn't
like jewellery! Prostituting herself in order to get married,
and when that goes phut, quite ready to accept the price of
her disappointment. Just like all the rest of them, in fact, for
there isn't a woman who doesn't prostitute herself. And a
sponger, too; in the eight months we've been going out together, she's put her hand in her purse only once – to buy
herself a reel of cotton. All that remains for me to do is to

write out a testimonial for her, with her five out of twenty for
sexual capacity, and the dates of enrolment and departure. But
what could I want better? Now we're quits.' As a potential
wife, then as a fiancée, she had dragged him into a 'sublime'
element, which was not his. As a tart, she put him at his ease
once more: they were back in the world of reality. And he
had paid her, as a prisoner bribes his warder in order to escape.
One pays women to come, one pays them to go; it's their
destiny. His old rakishness reappeared. Besides, he was incapable of taking his misdeeds seriously for long.

'When you marry, you can tell your bridegroom it's a
diamond you inherited from your grandmother, who used to
wear it at Napoleon III's balls. Warn your mother, so that she
doesn't betray you.'

'Betraying is your *forte*, it seems to me.'

'In my family, we've always betrayed. Betrayed for the sake
of betraying, as we waged war for the sake of waging war. For
five centuries. It's in our blood. But if you had been a daughter
of the house of France, I should have treated you differently –
because you would have been different. You like to think
you're a phenomenon. It's now that you'd be a phenomenon,
if a man hadn't betrayed you.'

Somewhat brutally, he asked her to undress. For the first
time since Genoa he wanted her. Because he no longer feared
her. Because she was no longer his wife to be. And because
he saw her as a tart.

'Do you want me to undo my hair?' she asked, as though
nothing had happened.

He took her twice, buoyed up by the excitement of the whole
scene as though by a wave. And she too, for the first time
since Genoa, seemed to find some pleasure in it. Unresponsive
when he was an absent-minded lover and a pusillanimous
fiancé, she warmed up a little when he was once again force-
ful in his decisions and his caresses. And besides, they were
nothing but lovers now: they might as well be good ones.

As she was leaving, Solange slipped the box of Abdullahs
Costals had just finished into her bag – a final souvenir of her
engagement! But he had spotted it.

'People who keep my letters or my old packets of Abdullahs

for sentimental reasons exasperate me, in the same sort of way as people who pray for me. You have the ring, dear Solange, that's enough.'

He took back the cigarette packet and threw it into the waste-paper basket.

On the telephone, after dinner, Mme Dandillot was 'perfect'. How easily they had given up, these women! How quickly they accepted everything (the docility of Frenchwomen)! Where was that determination which women talk about so much and which wears out so soon? Four times the mother forbids her child to do something, but after the fourth time she gives up, and the child can break his leg in peace. To Costals' question, 'Shall I go on seeing Solange?' Mme Dandillot, with apparent firmness, answered in the negative.

It was the answer Costals had hoped for, and he had planned in that event to go to Morocco to join his little girl-friend Rhadidja, whom he had not seen for eighteen months. There was a boat leaving for Casablanca in two days' time. The next day he took the train to Bordeaux without having seen Solange again. 'Not only have I always known how to escape, but I've always known how to escape in time.'

He was closing the brackets.

10

Andrée Hacquebaut
Saint-Léonard (Loiret)

to Pierre Costals
Paris

27 January 1928

I've brought back from an antique shop in Orleans a sheet of Chinese rice paper with a bird painted on it. It's the only original work of art in my room and even in the whole house (the rest are reproductions). I gaze and gaze at it.... And I think: it was a man who painted that. I remember a little wood carving in the Musée Dennery: a snake coiled round a tortoise. The snake's body was slightly flattened where it rested on the edge of the shell, and that single detail was enough to give it life. Thousands of miles away, hundreds of years ago, it was also a man who had carved that. Brought up in uncultured surroundings, for a long time I believed that art was superfluous, fit only for women and school-children, and elementary education was hardly calculated to change my ideas. When I began to realize that art was almost exclusively male, and the highest form of masculine activity, I was so dumbfounded that I probably haven't got over it yet. So, when I see a work of art that moves me, when I read a passage that makes me turn pale, I remember that it was a man who did it, and I am filled with respect and gratitude, and feel that we women ought to keep our mouths shut. The Virgin in the sculpture museum at Autun, Andromache holding Hector's son, the Jungle bidding farewell to Mowgli, Chartres, the Parthenon – all these, in the last resort, were born of love, of that love of other men which men are capable of giving otherwise than by taking someone in their arms. But for art to transmit to me fully the love with which it was conceived, I should have to have been in those arms once at least, to know what it means, to be able to take it or leave it. Once I had experienced this, the world of art, which at the moment I have only an inkling of, would really be mine, I should be swept into the vast, slow current that circulates between the artist, his fellow-creatures and the world of things, instead of being condemned to remain on the edge of it. By your pitiless and unjustifiable veto, you have thwarted me of a whole world, and yet at this moment I do not bear you any grudge.

Next day.

You know how it is with me: I have to get things off my chest. So I will not try to conceal from you the fact that you have hurt me. Already, last autumn, I knew from the papers that you were in Italy, and I realized that you wanted to put an even greater distance between us. This time, you deliberately choose to speak on the radio on the day you know I shall be with my cousins, who have no wireless set. I remember quite clearly writing to you and saying: 'Wednesday and Thursday, no books, no wireless – that's going to be fun.'

My uncle has just come in. Good-bye for the moment....

Listen to this. Just now, on the way home with my uncle, exactly at the corner of the rue de la République and the rue des Tanneurs, I had the impression that someone had kissed me. The illusion was so strong that I actually blushed. It was the wind, a little puff of wind, but since I'm one hundred per cent woman, that is to say ripe for the loony bin occasionally, I believe more or less in telepathy. I come back home and what do I find in the newspapers? An announcement that your radio talk did not take place on Thursday but has been postponed until the day after tomorrow. Can I assume, am I too presumptuous in assuming, that you had a fit of remorse for giving it on the very day I couldn't listen? If so, slip the word *remorse* into your first sentence the day after tomorrow. For example: 'Ladies and gentlemen, the date of this talk has been changed, but I should have felt too much remorse had I not found it possible, etc.'

Having written my letter, quickly, quickly, I hurry to the post, as though it must get to you forthwith. In fact you will no doubt receive it tomorrow morning, and it will be a crumb of pleasure to start the day with.

A.

P.S. I enclose a sample of the material of the costume I'm having made, so that you can choose the same for your lady friend of the moment.

A.

This letter was filed away by the recipient, unopened.

I I

Andrée Hacquebaut   to Pierre Costals
Saint-Léonard (Loiret)   *Paris*

29 January 1928

Costals, dear Costals, ah, no, you're not much of an orator! How I waited for your 'turn to sing'! I was so afraid you might begin five minutes early. By seven o'clock I was already listening in, and that's how I learnt that the Lapps eat cod seasoned with paraffin, that M. Claude Farrère is a 'great writer', and that *Febo* shoe-polish 'would put a shine even on a ball of wool'. You see the things I learn, thanks to you.

I waited to hear the word *remorse* on your lips. I didn't hear it. But it's possible I may have missed it, you articulate so badly. On the other hand, when you quoted – *when the quotation did not seem to me to be relevant* – the remark of the mother to her daughter in *Purple* : 'I love you so much that I never think of telling you', I took it as being addressed to me, I thought you had perhaps said it on purpose.

Yes, you articulate badly, you get nervous, your voice becomes strident and your delivery hurried. Do you know what the best moment in your talk was? When you whispered to the producer : 'Am I talking too fast?' Whispered! A hundred thousand listeners must have heard you. Afterwards I thought I oughtn't to have told you I'd be listening in. Perhaps it was this that disturbed you. I upset your life. My letters waste your time. My thoughts, perhaps, injure your love-life (for I love you for myself; others can give you *your* pleasure). Forgive me.

But it's funny. I saw you as a splendid intelligent brute with rough hands. At last I could get rid of the wretched feeling of superiority which I was forced to get used to in my dealings with all those weak men, the only kind I came across before you. And yet, every time you make a mistake, how my heart goes out to you. I am happy when you are happy, it consoles me for having to kick my heels waiting, but happier still, I think, when you do things that bore you, or when you are bored, because then I feel more of a sister to you. That heart of yours that is continually deafened by the roar of its victories, perhaps it deigns to listen a bit when they fall silent. There can be no doubt that your somewhat feeble talk on Radio-Paris will have disappointed your admirers. Throughout the length and breadth of France people will have been saying : 'Why does he talk, since he talks so badly?' Perhaps, even, some will have felt, as I myself felt, that even the substance of your talk was not up to much. I feel I ought to warn you that you're beginning to repeat yourself a little, my friend. So much so that at the moment I have the impression that thousands of men and women must have turned away from you slightly. And because of that, I feel closer to you than ever. I at least am faithful to you. How cosy we are, huddled together, aloof, in the midst of that crowd of deserters! (Blast! My uncle is calling me to dinner. 'Dédée!' Dédée, at thirty years and nine months! If only it were you who called me that!)

9 p.m.

I have switched on again to tell you this: when the light went out in my room, my arms went up as though to encircle a beloved form, my face became transfigured, and I said: 'I am near you.'

1 a.m.

My beloved love, I write to you now, while I wait for the infusion which will bring me, perhaps, a little sleep, to tell you how much I love you. My love, my darling.... For I cannot possibly die without having said those words once, die without having said anything or done anything, die without having experienced what the poorest of the poor have experienced, and which would cost no one a penny, would do no one any harm. You can so easily find happiness in anyone's embrace, whereas I can find it only in yours – and you know this, you who love me and are yet so dishonourable as to give me *nothing*! And yet tonight my room is full of you, of your voice, of your presence. It was you who came, it was not I who called you. You came out of that wireless set, like a genie out of a magic box, looking a little crestfallen (your colleagues had made catty remarks to you: 'No, no, it wasn't bad at all! You'll find it easier when you get used to it....'). I was so hungry, so terribly hungry for you. When I gave no sign of life, I was waiting for you. When I wrote to you, I was waiting for you. When I hurled insults at you, I was waiting for you. And here you are at last, your presence is not an invention of my mind. O my God, may I prove worthy of it! There's an electricity breakdown. I've lit two candles as in

the last act of *Werther*, and they make everything look so
fantastic in my room. It does not seem like my room, but like
a completely strange room. I'm in pain. If you only knew the
pain I feel. You have shaken me to the core. If you only knew
how she strains towards you, this woman whom you wanted
thus, whom you created thus, for, before you, she did not
exist. Sit down here, and let me stay motionless against you,
simply telling myself that it's you, that these are your clothes.
Now lift me up, lay me on this bed which I no longer recognize, which is not Dédée's bed, which is not the bed on which
I used to twist and turn as though I were pinned there by an
arrow. You take my head between your hands, burying your
fingers in the hair on my temples (how cold your hands
are . . .). How gravely you unstiffen my legs! Why doesn't the
electricity come on again? We need bright lights : I'm not
ugly at this moment, as you can see; and I want to see all of
you, now that you are identical with the man I dreamed of.
It is no longer that imperceptible infiltration of you into me
which has been taking place until now, at once ineluctable and
acquiesced in. I feel that you are bearing down on me, you,
Pierre Costals, with your whole body, your whole work, your
whole life. Your caress, so deep, deep, seeming to search
beyond me, to seek me out I know not where. How it fulfils
me. How well it calms this flesh that you have bruised in
exorcizing. Just like those little cuts one gets on one's fingers
and which one only has to squeeze hard for the pain to
subside. Hug me, crush me, until I scream and beg and moan
with so much happiness. And you listen to my moans; you
know that you make me happy, and you are too. And you show
no sign of exhaustion. You stay as long as I waited for you.
Now, my friend, you know what it is to love.

And afterwards you will speak to me the words I ascribed to
you, dictated to you so often in a whisper, in solitude, words
which bind the future a little, words you used to speak to me
long ago when I loved you before I knew you, as the mother-
to-be loves her unknown child in advance. And I shall remain
at your side, all limp with happiness, I shall protect myself
from myself against your flank, as a little ewe, to protect itself
from the sun, presses against the flank of the ram of the flock.

And then I shall lie back again and say to you : 'More! I'm not cured yet.'

I'm closing the envelope of this letter quickly. I no longer wish to know what I have written to you.

My happiness deserves some punishment. I inflict upon myself that of not writing to you before next Saturday.

A.

This letter was filed away by the recipient, unopened. However, the stamp not having been cancelled by the post office, M. Costals removed it.

PART TWO

1 2

'How did that happen?' he asked.

'The heat.'

'The heat! In February, in the Atlas, with snow all around!
And when even in this heated room you can see the vapour
coming out of our mouths!'

'At noon, the sun is hot.'

There were neither shutters nor curtains on the window (if
that small aperture deserved the name) of Costals' room in this
old military post of Tighremt which was now a shabby
fondouk* run by a retired sergeant-major. Costals had draped
his big travelling coat over the pane (a window-pane in the
Atlas, wonder of wonders!), through which there came an icy
blast. And they raised it now to look outside.

Three hundred yards below them, the bushes were ablaze;
a belt of fire, some fifty yards wide, beleaguered the village,
with its houses of pale mud, in tiers, like giant steps mounting
to an altar. At the edges it was gaining ground, advancing like
a wild beast, with the same life-like appearance as the clouds
yesterday on these slopes, as Costals watched them crossing
the track a few yards away from him, skimming along
the ground with the speed of a car. From the extremity of the
cordon, the smoke was rising to an absurd height, veiling the
flotillas of stars, until finally it was absorbed by the vast
absence of light that created a void in the upper sky. Above
the snow-capped peaks the sky was lighter, as though a halo
emanated from the snow.

'Is your house outside the kasba?'

'Yes, over there.'

'Do you think it's in danger?'

'Oh, no!'

('If I had to save Rhadidja from the flames at the risk of my
life, would I do it? Answer: "Yes".')

---

*An Arab inn (*Translator's note*).

She was draped to the calves in two lengths of grey wool, tied at the waist by a girdle of blue wool and fastened at the level of her 'salt-cellars' by two heavy brooches of wrought silver. Her neck, bare from the throat, and her arms, bare almost from the armpits, emerged freely from it. Costals smelt her spicy odour, that odour of another race which had greeted him, spellbound, on the quay at Alexandria the first time he had landed in Africa. He would have liked to sink his teeth into the dense heart of that odour, like a mad dog into the dense heart of a jet of water.

And all the words he addressed to her in solitude, but which, when she was there, she rendered stillborn by her silence and inertia. . . . Thus, he would have liked to tell her what the cordon of fire reminded him of. He remembered that other cordon of fire he had faced one day in 1924: Abd-el-Krim's men firing. He was blazing away with the French. A civilian, he had followed them into the front line, as Peter, on the Mount of Olives, had followed the soldiers taking Jesus away, 'to see the end' (Matthew VII, 58). And he had taken a gun simply because a gun is man's second *membrum virile*. In fact, he did not give a damn for the French. Nor for the Moroccans either. He was more on the side of France because he understood the French language, and life was therefore easier and pleasanter for him in that country than in another. Now, at moments, he wanted to talk about that time to Rhadidja, and about the feelings he had had. Then he realized that it was pointless. Words are pointless, and the Rhadidjas of this world are right to remind one of the fact.

She let the overcoat fall, and sat down again on the only chair in the room. Costals poked the wood fire, which responded by hurling itself at him, like an animal provoked, in the shape of a billow of smoke that enveloped the room. Then he sat down on the bed. Rhadidja snuffled continuously, like a child. 'Got a cold?' 'Yes.' She blew her nose; he saw that it was bleeding.

She was a girl of sixteen and a half who looked nineteen or twenty. Her complexion was light, her eyes slightly slit, her nose small and rather flat, her mouth fleshy: a face with pure and regular features, more Indo-Chinese than Moroccan. She had left on the bed the red and green scarf with which she covered her hair; this was light-brown, very fine and silky: altogether European. Although they exchanged few words, Costals was wont to prolong this expectation of pleasure. Nothing in the world would have persuaded him to fail in this courtesy, just as Rhadidja herself, when she had dressed after leaving the bed, never failed to sit down again. Indeed, one of the reasons why he loved her was that he did not feel obliged to carry on a high-flown conversation with her. He had a cast-iron belief that all conversation is futile. And especially high-flown conversation.

He had met Rhadidja four years before in Casablanca, where she was then living with one of her uncles. She had sat down beside Costals on a beach in Lyautey Park. At first he had not dreamt of desiring her, but she began picking a tooth with a safety-pin, he saw her tongue, and that was it. White-skinned and rather skinny, he had defined her as 'a chicken wing in a cheap restaurant'. Her pale complexion and hieratic features suggested Asia, the subtle smile of the *bodhisattvas*. He had taken her; she was a virgin. Thereafter, having acquired the taste, she gave herself right and left – or at least such was the rumour that reached Costals – provided the man was a European. Mademoiselle had always professed highly non-conformist opinions in front of Costals: to wit, that she did not like the Arabs, that she did not respect her parents, and that she did not believe in God. At first he had thought all this (leaving aside the Casablanca 'atmosphere') was simply a way of making up to a Frenchman, but gossip confirmed Rhadidja's dissident attitude: for instance, it was said that she delighted in making love during the forbidden hours of Ramadan. But in other ways her behaviour never deviated from the tact and decorum which are characteristic of the Moslems in these matters. With Costals she was always reserved, keeping her place, perfectly brought up, if one can say such a thing of someone who has not been brought up at all; a full moon of calm, dignity and deliberation. Incontestably un-Arab in her discretion, her gentleness, her immobility (hardly a gesture), her punctuality, not to mention her physiognomy: a stranger among her people. Often it is stupidity which gives a woman a hieratic look; but she was intelligent, though it was an intelligence without glitter; having taught herself to speak French, which she did very well, and to read it, and even, gradually, to write it sufficiently well to make herself understood. Of more than modest birth, and a courtesan, she had none of the reactions, nor the coarseness, that might have been expected of her station. Nor, needless to say, did she have the comportment of a cultivated Arab. She belonged to a region somewhere in between, a no-man's-land similar to that which (according to Costals) must have been occupied by the Greek demi-gods and the Hindu djinns. Having got over her puberty when she had given herself for the first time, she had spared Costals the agony of witnessing the change, the paroxysms, he would doubtless have seen in her had she been a European. Equanimity and permanence, as in semi-divine creatures. And their security. Rhadidja's motto was: calm and security.

And her absolute honesty. And her extraordinary disinterestedness. For four years Rhadidja had taken the money that Costals pressed into her hand without ever glancing at it. Even if he had given her only a five-franc piece she would not have complained, he was sure of it. She never asked a favour, never asked for money, never even asked for an 'advance'. There was never that unbearable glance of the European courtesan at the man's wallet whenever he opens it. Once she had even said: 'You spend too much money on me.' (But she never thanked him. Or rather she thanked him if he handed her a pencil or a pin. But never thanked him if it was a tidy sum.) Such was Rhadidja. No affectation, no clinging, no Christianity, no greed. And it had lasted for four years.

What was the nature of their tie?

A man to whom a woman has once said 'It does me a world of good' is really hooked. Our pleasure is the pleasure of the other person. Rhadidja had never said anything of the kind to Costals, nor the bogus equivalent of the phrase ('You make love like no one else', etc.). Nor had she ever made the slightest allusion to her relations with him or with anyone else. But her face, and her famous 'earthquakes',* proclaimed her

---

*Cf. p.392: 'Terremoto' (Author's note).

pleasure in the act. Her face lit up instantaneously when one went into her, as, in the telephone booths of some cafés, the electric light switches on automatically when you open the door. Costals travelled over a thousand miles to see her face at that moment.

The writer, as we know, had no great desire to be loved, and even preferred not to be loved, because this non-love left his heart, his mind and his time free. With Rhadidja he was well served. She was apathetic in everything that was not sensual pleasure. Costals thought she had no feeling for him. Perhaps an affection born of gratitude, but even then very superficial. And no pretence of tenderness. He found this to his taste, since he hated to be pawed. (As a child, when a little girl wanted to kiss him, he would say: 'All right, then, go ahead. But be quick, and not too hard ...' and he had taken a dislike to his grandmother because she kissed him too much.) Rhadidja was a catalyst; he reacted, and that was enough for him (not forgetting that she too reacted physically). He was, however, perplexed by her apathy, which incidentally extended to everything, for it was so extreme that it seemed to him almost inhuman. It was as if he had picked up a stone and fondled it, decked it with flowers, covered it when it was cold, put it in the open air when it was hot, washed it, smothered it with perfumes. Rhadidja, except in bed, was that stone. And it was perhaps this inhuman quality in her, and in him too, in feeling this attachment for her under such circumstances, that kept the attachment alive. The ways of men are various.

Attachment. From the second day, trust (she wandered alone round his quarters with every drawer unlocked). From the third day, respect. Then liking. Then something between attachment and affection, where it had settled down. No love, of course, and not the slightest jealousy of his numerous rivals. Was she capable of making him suffer? Yes, but only from the fear that some harm might befall *her*. This was the only tremor in the stillness of his affection, like the quivering of the sea in a flat calm. He did not love her, but she was the preference of his heart and marrow.

Of his brain too. She gave Costals what he wanted from women: mutual pleasure, embedded in indifference and remoteness. Wherefore there was something pure in their relationship which it is almost impossible to achieve with a European. It is not the sexual act that is vulgar and impure, it is everything people surround it with. There is less stupidity in a man's flies than in his brain and in his heart.

'I die at those hands of pale bronze, so pure.' He took them in his, which in comparison seemed like the hands of a labourer. He noticed then, on the ball of one of her thumbs, a brownish patch surrounded by a circle paler than the skin of her hand. 'Syphilis? Since it's taken for granted, according to the medicos, that eighty per cent of the Moroccans of these parts have it. But benign: family syphilis.'

'You've got a funny spot there.'

'It's *el djem.*'

'What's *el djem?*'

'I saw the doctor when he came by. He gave me a bit of paper....'

From the pocket of her white under-skirt she drew out a wallet, and from the wallet a sort of leather scapular containing a little papyrus on which some Arabic characters were inscribed. She smiled her delicate smile:

'A marabout gave me that.'

'You told me you didn't believe in God.'

'Yes, but he gave it to me.'

Costals had received the same answer from one of his friends, a notorious unbeliever, when he had expressed surprise at seeing a St Christopher plaque on his car: 'Someone gave it to me.' Universal flabbiness. People talk about 'non-resistance to evil'. There is non-resistance to stupidity, too.

The scapular also contained a folded piece of paper, which she handed to Costals. He read:

Name:	Rhadidja ben Ali.
Age:	16 (?).
Place of birth:	Ait Sadem, Tighremt.
Disease:	Leprosy. Haemorrhagic coryza. Macula on left thumb.
Treatment:	Specimen nasal mucus taken. Send Rhad. Marrakesh if confirmed.

Observations: Genl. condit. satis. No sympt. syph.
Date: 29-1-28

Signed : DR MAYBON

He re-read the document. His heart began to throb so vio-lently it was as though the wall of his thorax had grown thinner, as though each heart-beat must lift up his ribs like a lizard's.

'But, Rhadidja, it's a very serious disease! And you never told me....'

'The doctor said that it could be cured nowadays. He will bring some injections the next time he comes.'

'And you just sit there as though it was nothing!'

Costals knew nothing of leprosy except the commonplace images and schoolboy memories the word conjures up for the man in the street. The flesh coming off in strips, the 'leonine facies', the contagion, the isolation. Also – he remembered from an illustrated book of his childhood – the monstrous devices of the Church a few centuries ago, more monstrous than leprosy itself, which is at least natural : the leper assisting at his own Requiem Mass under a pall, having a spadeful of graveyard earth sprinkled on his head (sometimes in the grave itself), being declared dead to the world and led outside the town after his house had been reduced to ashes.

'And the doctor didn't tell you to take any precautions?'

'Yes, not to let my family eat where I have eaten.'

Costals remembered the famous doctor, the director of a TB centre, who, when he asked him what the centre did for patients who remained at home, had replied, with some em-barrassment : 'We give them a spittoon.'

'What do your parents say?'

(Emotion was making him idiotic.)

'Nothing.'

'Have you any other patches on your body?'

'No, only this one.'

'So you've been in contact with lepers?'

'Our uncle was one. Not the one in Casablanca, one who lived with us. But he died three years ago.'

'He lived with you! ... No special precautions?'

'No.'

'No treatment?'

'Twice a year he went to the Mosque of Sidi Bennour, in Marrakesh.'

The eternal instinct of humble people to believe, for preference, the one who lies. Between the Pasteur Institute and the bone-setter, one chooses the bone-setter; if one doesn't actually go to the priest.

'I'll speak to the doctors at the hospital in Marrakesh, so that you're properly looked after when you arrive there.'

For the first time, Rhadidja's face, so serene until then, showed alarm.

'No, don't do that! If they know that you know me, they will tell my father.'

'The doctors in Marrakesh don't know your father. And I'll ask them to keep it absolutely secret.'

'No, no!'

'I won't let you be looked after just anyhow, when a word from me will make them take an interest in you. I want them to do everything they possibly can to cure you, you understand? We'll send you to France if necessary.'

Still seated, she had bowed her head so low that he could only see her hair. He tried to lift it up again, but she resisted, like a sulky child. Completely indifferent to her horrible disease, but petrified by a non-existent danger. And there is no need to go to the Atlas to see this in a young person. . . .

'All right, I won't say anything about you,' he said at last, determined to intervene but anxious to calm her down.

He looked at the document again. The fate of this beloved creature in the seven letters of a word scribbled in pencil. And perhaps his own fate too. His desire for her had subsided. Not that he felt horror or even disgust for this poisoned body; but he was overwhelmed by his emotion. And perhaps this was a good thing. Perhaps it would be wiser to abstain from intimate contact today, and tomorrow to go to Taoud, four kilometres away, where there was now an infirmary with a native attendant (for the men who were building a bridge not far from there). At least he would get some idea from the attendant of the degree of contagiousness of leprosy – enough to judge whether or not it would be sensible to risk it tomorrow night.

He informed her of his plan. The look of terror, which had vanished from Rhadidja's face, reappeared.

'If you mention leprosy to Haoucine and he knows you are from Tighremt, he is sure to guess that you came about me. And he will tell my father. . . .'

'Then I won't go.'

This time he was sincere: Rhadidja's fears seemed justified.

Well then, he would make love to her. He could not see himself making a journey of four thousand kilometres there and back to meet a woman he was fond of, and not going near her because she had a touch of leprosy. It was not physical desire that prompted him. Nor a sense of duty, towards her or himself. Nor even, strictly speaking, the feeling that it was the 'right' thing to do. It was a feeling that it would be at once pusillanimous and inelegant not to do it. Send her away like that! Besides, any man in his place, unless he were a total wet, would do the same. As for the risk, quite apart from the last war, or the next, in his everyday life, at the mercy of all the fathers and brothers and lovers of his mistresses (mostly minors, to boot), he was perpetually running risks; and he had slept hundreds of times, without any precautions whatsoever, with syphilitics and consumptives. So it was only a risk like all the others, not exactly alluring, but necessary. Another one more or less!

'Undress, little one. Will you?'

It gave him such pleasure to say this to her. His heart began beating furiously again, but calmed down after a moment.

He had intended to examine her body. But she immediately felt cold, and quickly tucked herself into bed. How could he get her out? 'Turn round. To the right. Now to the left,' while she shivered: just imagine it!

'The medico examined her nine days ago, and only saw one patch. Very unlikely that another will have appeared since. As for her genitals, he must surely have taken a look at them since he suspected syphilis.' Nevertheless, as he undressed behind the back of the bed, he had something of the sensation of a soldier adjusting his equipment just before going over the top.

He dived under the sheet, as one might dive into one of

those greenish stagnant ponds in oases, traversed by a snake swimming with terrifying speed.

But when he was in her warmth, all his uneasiness evaporated. What was there was Rhadidja, the faithful, the excellent Rhadidja. (And he felt the outline of a recent tattoo on the inside of her arm, the ink still new on the surface of the skin.) She whom he knew to her very bowels, the sack of flesh into which he poured his seed. The haven of his security, even the security of his flesh: not once had he deigned to protect himself from her (one cannot *possess* by *protecting oneself*!), although she had twice infected him with gonorrhoea, in 1924 and 1926; the fiction of security governed – he wanted it thus – his relations with this woman who consistently poisoned him. The towel he had wrapped round the dangerous hand as a safeguard came undone and was lost between the sheets: well, let it stay there! However, he avoided her mouth.

Scarcely had he begun to caress her than Rhadidja's face drifted away into a dream-world. Sensuality took possession of her instantaneously, overpoweringly. Her eyes moved while her face remained immobile, her nostrils flared like those of a rocking-horse. And when, her eyes glazed, dead, like dead planets, she sought his mouth, he seized hers – hers, that mouth which yesterday was lined in so supernatural a pink, like the calash of a pair of newly-weds in Algiers, and which tomorrow he visualized with the palate perforated as though by syphilis. He took her mouth, and worked on it slowly and attentively. He was sucked in by this woman as a river is sucked towards the sea. His love of danger, absent until then, now entered him. Clinging to this mouth, so close to the 'haemorrhagic coryza', he felt like a parachute jumper during the moment of his fall when the parachute has not yet opened. But there was nothing more to it, after all – and he was aware of this – than when he drank at lengths from the mouths of advanced consumptives, and drew life from their death. (How he loved to kiss them in that depression in their cheeks that was reminiscent of the gentle hollow between two dunes, and on their sweating temples with the damp locks clinging to them! How he loved to see their pleasure weaken them a little more each day! How he loved to take them as they coughed, like those perverts who take ducks as they decapitate them! Edmonde, her mouth hideously dry ... holding Edmonde's tongue between his lips, it seemed to him that he was holding in his mouth a reptile's tongue, and he liked it.) And just as, then, he used to say to himself: 'Consumptive, me! So what?' so now he sneered: 'A leper, me? Nonsense! I'm well known to be a lucky dog. As lucky as the Devil.' He had an almost mystical confidence in his constitution, like the airman in his pitching bus, or the skipper in his old tub, rolling, shipping water, but always making harbour.

'One would think you hadn't done it for a long time,' said Rhadidja naïvely.

Later, he was ashamed at not having given her his greatest proof of affection – that kiss on the mouth – until carried away by sexual excitement. He took the tainted hand and kissed it devoutly, not far from the leprous spot. He experienced no sensation (of horror, audacity, etc.); his only feeling was the affection he had for her.

When she had gone, in the utmost silence, he waited for a long time, half dressed, his ear pressed against the door, to make sure that she was not coming back, that there had been no trouble with anyone in the *fondouk*. Finally he gave up listening. Another clandestine assignation that had gone off successfully! For fifteen years and more, his life had been a constant succession of risky ventures that had gone off successfully....

He went and drew back his overcoat from the window-pane. Men and children passed by, all in their big hooded jellabas, a little reminiscent of monks and monklets. The fire had spread. Visibly. As leprosy spreads. Under that sprinkling of stars.

Then he flung himself back into bed, still half-dressed, the room was so cold. The bottom sheet had kept a fold, a *cif*,* where it had been caught between Rhadidja's thighs.

A feeling of contentment crept over him then, as though he had performed a good deed. He remembered an anecdote he had read in some *cancionero* in which the daughter of the King of France and 'Queen Constantine', abducted by a knight and

---

*Crest of a dune, in Arabic (*Author's note*).

wishing to preserve her maidenhead, tells him that she is a leper's daughter, so that he does not molest her. Costals despised this knight, and this added to his contentment. Motionless, his eyes fixed on the undulating pattern of the ceiling, it seemed to him that he could feel the poison she had injected into him already stirring in his blood. He had two clear feelings. First, that if he had caught the disease, well, he did not regret that hour of tender pleasure in spite of it all. And secondly, that the horror of the disease would be mitigated because it had come to him from her. He thought: 'Ah! let her give me leprosy!' as a woman thinks of the man she loves: 'Ah! let him give me a child!'

Meanwhile his fate was in the lap of the gods.

I 3

Andrée Hacquebaut   to Pierre Costals
Saint-Léonard (Loiret)   *Paris*
[*Letter forwarded from Paris to Marrakesh.*]
20 February 1928

I have recovered my balance, and I'm glad of it. A bit disconcerted, though. A woman restored to equanimity always feels as though she were missing something. Don't think I'm embarrassed by my last letter. After all, if you don't want to disturb women, you shouldn't come and seek them out in their homes through the radio. It's as simple as that.

Yes, a bit sad. Reaction, no doubt. And they've delivered a dress which I thought would be nice (I never see you, and yet I dress for you alone) and which makes me look such a fright! I dress badly, but at least I know when something doesn't suit me. And I feel crushed. And then there were the fittings, and seeing one's face repeated in half a dozen mirrors. My face always surprises me in the mirror, and I try to recapture the other, the one I used to have, my first face. My passion – my passion for you: I dot the i's and cross the t's because you might not understand – my passion exhausts me and ages me more than a dull and empty life would have done. What was the use of changing! Oh, to be able to age peacefully, having laid down one's weapons with good grace. The day when one will at last be at peace with one's face.... But for that, one would have to have obtained something, however little....

You destroy everything for me, everything. But I insist: I want nothing else but you. And yet at the same time weary – weary of you: once more I dot the i's and cross the t's. Often, now, when I feel the urge to call you, I put my head in my hands, I close my eyes long enough to faint a little, and it goes. The feeling I have for you will die; it will die, as all useless things die. Gradually the determination not to write to you again is building up inside me. What have I to lose from you that might not just as well be lost immediately? (Reflection of a woman who has an occasional glimmer of sense.)

My sexual springtime was put back ten years by my mother's exaggerated frankness. One wonders which is better: to leave children in the dark about sex, or to show them things as they are before 'guilty conversations' have yet corrupted them. Both ways end in disaster. When the revelation comes too early, as I know from experience, it retards sexual development. Between the ages of fifteen and twenty, the couples I met filled me with repulsion because of the act. The mere thought that a man might speak to me made me bristle. Already solitary by nature, this revelation increased my shyness. If that was what all the hand-kissing, all the simpering, all the social whirl was for! Dances, social calls, casinos, I refused them all. I even pretended for some time that I was engaged, so as to keep people at arm's length. On the other hand, until I was thirty I was ignorant of the psychology of sex. My mistake about you (M. de Charlus!...) started me thinking, and in the past six months I've bought a whole heap of books on psychology and psycho-analysis. Well, now that I've read these books, I cannot help thinking that there's a certain anomaly in your life, which is the price you pay for your talent, as there is in mine. Wagner, as you know, told Liszt that if he had been happy he would never have written a note. One puts into one's art what one has been incapable of putting into one's life. It was because he was unhappy that God created the world.

Before I knew you, I attended a lecture at the Lamartine Society in Issoudun by an obscure poetess with nevertheless a certain talent, Claude Violante, who is in reality Mlle Marie-Alix de la Roche de Villebrune, a youngish spinster of some forty-two or -three summers. The title was somewhat ridiculous: *Must a great writer necessarily be a virgin?* But the idea was not. This woman maintained, with plenty of scientific proofs to back her, that the more eloquently an artist spoke of a thing the less he knew about it, that many famous laureates of women, Stendhal, Baudelaire, Poe, Pierre Louÿs, were impotent, that d'Annunzio had certainly remained a virgin until an advanced age, that Byron was repressed, and preferred young men to women, as is evident from his odd friendships with Eddington, Niccolo Giraud, Lord Clare, etc. ... and that the real Aziyadé 'was a small boy' (the remark, it appears, is Mme Juliette Adam's); in short, that the more splendidly a writer celebrated women, the safer it was to assume that he knew them very little in the flesh. I thought of all this again as I listened to your talk on Radio-Paris. The obvious embarrassment you felt at speaking in public made me think that you were shy, and that this shyness must extend to many spheres. And this confirmed what I have always thought, guided by that feminine intuition that seldom fails: that your insistence on emphasizing the carnal act in your work was an indication that your experience of these things was limited. And as I have never understood why you persisted in denying us both an innocent pleasure – which is sheer lunacy.... Perhaps that might help me to understand a little: not only have you never dreamed, in making love, of giving pleasure to the other person* (which is why you cannot imagine that to desire a woman is to give her a proof of love), but you yourself do not like pleasure, *you do not like sex.*

There is no need for me to tell you that the less you *have*, the closer I, who *have* nothing, feel you are to me. My theory about you helps me to live. Therefore it is true.

A.H.

---

*In one of the preceding volumes, Costals says: 'Our pleasure is the pleasure of the other' (*Author's note*).

Perhaps you try to pray, and cannot. Poor, poor child, it's fantastic how unhappy one can be. All the same, how much happiness one would create, when one has nothing, with the non-happiness of one who has everything, like you!

This letter was filed away by the recipient, unopened.

14

For the next five days Costals, each night, when darkness fell, received Rhadidja and knew her.

Save for that blissful hour, a trying time. Appalling weather, and telling himself all the time: 'Rain, disturber of assignations. She won't come. It's raining too hard.' The little room was sinister, with its walls decorated with ornamental patterns (native) almost invisible under a layer of dirt, with its pillar carved with a knife, unconvincingly supporting a battered ceiling, doomed to collapse under the first heavy snowfall. The sea of clouds floated past at window level, like waves at the level of a port-hole; above them the snow on the peaks, like foam above a raging ocean. He always hoped that one morning the mountains would have disappeared, as mirages did not far from there; but no, there they stupidly remained. Sitting in this room which the *kanoun* entirely failed to heat (never within living memory has a fire been known to give out any heat in North Africa), a blanket over his legs, a scarf round his neck, Costals tried to work; and eventually, tucking himself up in bed fully dressed, he continued his paper-work there. ('Nothing but mistakes! Nothing but mistakes!' Rhadidja would exclaim on arrival, looking at all his crossed-out drafts.) His relations with the landlord, a great patriot and a certified brigand, were an additional ordeal for him, because of the efforts at cordiality he had to make. For although the *fondouk* had the advantage that one could come and go without anyone being the wiser, Rhadidja was liable to be noticed. Hence, to avoid a fuss – she maintained that her parents knew nothing of her behaviour – the necessity to soft-soap the patriot a bit. If the price of pleasure can never be too great, it is nonetheless fairly steep. If it sometimes forces us to restrain our arrogance, if it teaches us to make a concession or two, that is the measure of its power.

As soon as he arrived in Morocco, Costals had written to Solange. He wrote to her again from Tighremt, a letter which he would post in Marrakesh in a few days' time. Generally speaking, as regards letters, he was exactly like a child – sweating over them as he never did over a page of one of his books, because he never knew what to say in them; or else putting down anything that came into his head as long as it filled up space; dropping them and taking them up again, like a cat with a mouse; and finally giving up the ghost on the pretext that he had told enough lies for one day. What, then, is one to say of his letters to Solange? He wrote them out of a sense of duty: already the torrent of oblivion had begun to flow through him. He had reached the end of this woman as one reaches the end of a cigarette; she had served her time. Whenever he thought of his bad behaviour towards her, it was as though he were pulling at a dressing: it 'pinched', and began to bleed again. But the rest of the time, no pain at all. However, he had made up his mind to soothe Solange, conscientiously to keep that little flame alive.... He affected an extreme tenderness in his letters: protesting too much, like a husband; alas, 'a long speech is not a long love' (St Augustine). In the event, these letters were not so long. He cut one of them short on the pretext that the bus was waiting to take it to the post. In the middle of the other his fountain pen ran out of ink, and it's so tiresome writing in pencil. In both of them, full of self-congratulation, like a businessman paying his debts, he emphasized how astonishing it was that he should be writing to her at all, pointing out that he was writing to no one else at the moment, that he had put all his friends into cold storage. With marvellous disingenuousness he wrote: 'And yet you complain!' He felt some regret at having had to do what he had done to her, but no remorse. Why had she wanted him to marry her? (Why had Andrée wanted him to take her?) He was like a motorist who is grieved at having run someone over but cannot help saying to himself, in all good faith: 'Why did he throw himself under my wheels?'

On the day of his departure for Marrakesh – he planned to

stay six or seven weeks afterward in the Sous, and then in
another sector of the Atlas – a few minutes before Rhadidja
left him, he said to her :

'You know I'm very fond of you.'

'I know.'

'I think I've said everything I wanted to say to you. And
you, have you nothing to say to me?'

'No. . . .'

There was no ill intent in this 'no', which was merely a
simple and sober expression of the reality – that she could
think of nothing to say to him. During these six days Costals
had heaped kindness (and money) upon her. He had given her
a proof of no ordinary kind, if not of love at least of 'something', by not allowing himself to be put off by her disease. He
had promised her that he would do whatever was necessary
to see that she was given the best possible treatment by the
doctors. Nevertheless she had nothing to say to him. When
she had left, he gave a sort of shudder; not a shudder of grief
but a shudder of amazement: 'Incredible . . . incredible. . . .'
Yet it is better to receive no gratitude for something that
deserved it, than to see someone (nothing is more embarrassing)
show gratitude out of all proportion to the little one has done
for them, and that with bad grace. Then he sighed – a sigh
of relief that their meetings in the *fondouk* should have gone
off without a hitch. The inveterate clandestine lover, each time
he leaves a love-nest, each time he is finally parted from a
mistress, each time a further stage in his life comes to an end,
is wont to sigh : 'Another flagrante delicto avoided!' A bitter-
sweet compound of melancholy and relief, like cool wind and
raw heat on the seashore. And his motto might be : 'As long
as it lasts!'

'Are you Pierre Costals the writer?' asked Dr Lobel, physician
in charge at the Marrakesh hospital. 'Do sit down. You'll forgive me, I hope, but my profession is all-absorbing . . . and then,
we become such savages here . . . anyhow I must confess that
I've never read any of your books.'

'That's all to the good,' said Costals, with an insolence that
was for once unconscious.

'But one of your friends has talked to me a great deal about you.'

'H'm. . . . In that case I foresee the worst.'

'M. Richard, a professor at the lycée in Rabat. But you mustn't think I haven't read anything of yours. I remember a particularly stimulating article, in which you made an eloquent defence of the Eiffel Tower.'

'What! . . .' said Costals, outraged. 'I've never done any such thing.'

'Come, come, don't you remember? Three or four years ago. There was a press campaign at the time in favour of the demolition of the Eiffel Tower. You wrote an article pointing out that, whether one liked it or not, the tower was part of the common inheritance of Paris.'

'It's possible that in the course of an article I may have remarked incidentally that these sudden journalistic indignations against the Eiffel Tower, or the Trocadero, were nothing but snobbery, sheer ballyhoo, if not rather suspect. But I've never *devoted an article* to the Eiffel Tower,' said Costals with restrained vehemence. That he should have published eight books, forged out of his flesh and blood, and that he should be known only by a casual sentence in a newspaper column, and whose sense was distorted, at that – how typical of the relations between writer and public! And yet it was quite natural that a doctor should not have read his works; doctors have other things to do. Nevertheless everything would have gone better if Lobel had had the slightest idea who Costals was. As it was, the latter glided gently, by a familiar process, from the fact that Lobel had not read him to the presumption that Lobel was a dismal nincompoop. The power of doctors, not only over our bodies but over our minds, is so great that we have a tendency to consider them unworthy of it. Our whole life depends, or may depend, on them; this makes us judge them severely; it is as much as we can do to allow them different tastes from ours, whether literary, political, erotic or gastronomic.

Dr Lobel was a man of about fifty, with the hair of a photographer and the moustache of a drawing-room actor; that is to say rather long hair – though not long enough for a bad painter's – and a few close-cropped hairs on the upper lip, like one of those actor-counts whose whole life would be ruined if he did not have the sensation of being hairless, but who keeps a few hairs to appease the countess. The beauty of Lobel's face lay neither in the intelligence nor the character it expressed, but in its heredity: it was the face of a man of the end of the reign of Louis XIII or the beginning of that of Louis XIV; one was moved by this if one noticed it. But if one's eyes, descending from these fine features, fell on his hands, they were held there startled: those pink and podgy fingers, those thick, coarse wrists, were the hands of a man whose father must have wielded a plough for half a century. The disharmony was similar to that which one sees among certain working-class adolescents, who have the faces of angels, and the hands of old blacksmiths. But the most striking characteristic of Dr Lobel was that he wore a bar of the Legion of Honour pinned to his hospital overall, which created the same effect as if a footballer were to wear one on his jersey.

Costals, having extricated himself from the Eiffel Tower, said what he had to say. When he had finished, Lobel said:

'I once knew a French official, in a remote spot where I was the only doctor, who, when his native mistress fell dangerously ill, did not send for me because he was afraid I might find her unprepossessing. I always tell this story to Europeans who consult me on behalf of their Moors. That said, I shall now come down to brass tacks.

'Throughout Morocco, leprosy is vastly on the increase' (he said this with a rather triumphant air, as though to suggest: 'We have a nice little nest-egg tucked away.'). 'But first of all I must correct your ideas about this disease. There are diseases which the public takes lightly, but which can have very grave consequences: bronchitis, gonorrhoea, measles, jaundice, etc. And there are diseases (or actions) which are less serious than people imagine. Syphilis, if treated at once, is no longer dangerous nowadays. Sitting in a draught is not dangerous, unless one is in a sweat. Masturbation, with which we terrify poor kids, is "no different from the normal sexual act" – so Janet tells us. As for Hansen's disease' (this was a comforting euphemism for leprosy, as far as Costals could gather) 'I won't say it's not serious, since people die of it. But it isn't quite what people think. For one thing the incubation process is slow: it can last from eight to ten years. And the development, too, is slow; the disease can be, if not cured, at least alleviated. Your little Moor may have ten years of more or less normal life, without pain, in front of her – there are outbreaks, followed by long periods of quiescence – and twenty years at least before she succumbs.' ('That's the vital thing for me,' thought Costals, 'if I catch the disease. I only need another six years to finish the essential part of my work.') 'Finally, and this is what I especially want to draw to your attention, it is nothing like so infectious as people think. Much less so than TB, since it cannot be caught by chance. You're surprised that Rhadidja and her uncle aren't isolated. But not all lepers are isolated. We have special hospitals, of course, but in many places lepers are put in communal wards, when they aren't left in complete freedom. There are three hundred lepers in Paris, of whom only twenty are hospitalized (at Saint-Louis); the rest wander around quite freely. Even at Saint-Louis they have always been, and still are, in communal wards, and there has never been a case of infection. Furthermore, married lepers may have sexual intercourse for years without their partners being infected. In short, it's not medically impossible, though it's extremely improbable, that, in the six contacts you have just had with this woman, you may have contracted the bacillus which, a few days before those contacts, was not detected on her genital organs.'

('One's always right to take risks,' thought Costals. 'I knew already that, with modern prophylactics, the pox had become a pleasure. But leprosy....')

'Let's assume the worst,' he said. 'If I caught it, when would the first symptoms appear?'

'In three or four months or three or four years, that's all I can tell you.'

'Should I start taking preventive treatment right away?'

'Your preventive treatment must, in spite of everything, be to give up your relations with this person. You can't play around with mucous membranes! I'll have her brought here as soon as possible. I'll carry out another examination, although Maybon is quite categorical: nasal examination, and so on. She'll be given chaulmoogra oil injections. Afterwards, she'll have to go back to her village. We only hospitalize advanced cases here. There's a plan for an isolation hospital in Marrakesh, but it won't be ready for two or three years. Maybon will visit your protégée regularly at Tighremt; I shall see to it. The clinician at Taoud will look after her, and see that she doesn't drop all treatment at the first sign of improvement; a typical Arab dodge.'

Lobel offered to show Costals some of the lepers in the hospital. 'Many visiting men of letters, and all ladies of letters, have themselves photographed among the lepers,' he said with a wounding smile. Costals refused. 'It wouldn't do anyone any good for me to get worked up. Besides, it's something exotic, and the exotic doesn't interest me.' But he accepted the doctor's offer of the loan of a technical manual, one chapter of which was devoted to leprosy. He wanted to know, but to know without the risk of losing his composure.

However, he had to face some 'exotica', whether he liked it or not: photographs of the 'leonine facies' – wild-looking eyes, crushed noses, missing eyebrows and eyelashes. Patients whose fingers, feet, or genitals had dropped off, having rotted away. 'It would be a great blessing for me if I could stop loving her,' he thought, reasonably enough, instinctively seeking the position in which he would suffer least. 'But perhaps, when she starts being disfigured, nature will come to my aid. . . . Though that's by no means certain.'

It would be a week before Rhadidja arrived in Marrakesh. He debated whether to wait for her, and finally decided that it would be pointless. Next day he left for the mountains.

15

Back in the mountains, Costals nevertheless saw to it that every Thursday he was in a place with a postal service, in order to collect the airmail letter which his son wrote to him on Sundays from the little town near London where he was at school. Of the two hundred or so letters which reached him every week, only Philippe's mattered to him; the rest, according to the mood of the moment, were either impatiently skimmed through or torn up and scattered without ever being opened. One letter that you really look forward to, one letter that really gives you pleasure, out of two hundred – isn't that the usual proportion?

During the autumn term of 1927, Brunet, at the lycée in Cannes, had protested that there was nothing he wanted more than to attack once and for all the imposing mass of ignorance which had accumulated inside him, but that it was 'this rotten hole' which prevented him from working. Costals had therefore had the idea of sending him to a private school near London : England had come to mind since Brunet had been 'as happy as a king' there in September, staying with friends of his father's. Moreover, it would be a way of escaping the warping pedantry which French secondary education imposes on young minds; Costals had been thrown into a state of nervous prostration for twenty-four hours when Philippe had told him with great excitement that the subject of his French homework was : 'Racine depicts men as they are, and Corneille as they ought to be.' The Ancient has truly said that those who have children are beloved of the gods, but 'schooling', when it expresses itself in these absurd debates on questions devoid of any importance, is enough to make one regret having a son.

Meanwhile, fresh laments had been arriving from Bradborough. In Paris, Brunet had memorized in the right order all the stations on every line of the underground, more or less; he had that awful memory of bright children which registers everything, so much so that his father often felt paralysed when about to say something in his presence, for fear that it might impress itself too deeply. In spite of this, Brunet's memory rebelled against the English language; the boy realized that he would never be able to speak it, and was distressed about this, not because of the social advantages he stood to lose, but because he had boasted to his chums at Cannes about the superb knowledge of the language that would be his when he returned. At first Costals had not taken these moans very seriously. He remembered Brunet, aged twelve, weeping so bitterly over a dead rabbit that one wondered if he could possibly be suffering as much as all that, and Brunet pretending to have hurt himself one day when he had been playing the fool, in order to get the expected reprimand transmuted into endearments; so he was a bit suspicious. But when he looked at some photographs his son had sent him and noticed he was thinner, he said to himself: 'It's because he's worried about his English that he's lost weight.' Besides which, since little of the boy's charm and liveliness and fantasy appeared in his letters, he wondered: 'Is he unhappy? And if he is unhappy, isn't it my fault for having neglected him?'

'When I was a kid and we were separated from one another, I only thought of you when I wrote to you, and sometimes in bed at night. But now I want to see you again so much.' With a view to re-reading this one sentence, Costals searched his pockets for his son's letter – one of those letters which were now so regular, whereas in the past it had always been such a chore for the child to write one (childish letters, with margins and lines ruled off in pencil). And he thought (in spite of his phobia for being alone with another person, as others have a phobia for being alone with themselves): 'When one wants to cheer someone up, one should do it at once. Oughtn't I to bring him to Paris at Easter to live with me once and for all?' And again: 'How silly people are to say life has no meaning when there's always a possibility of making those one loves happy, and at the same time drawing sustenance from their happiness. . . .'

He thought about his son's thinness, real or imaginary, and was worried by it; about his happiness; about his quality; about his future, in face of which he was like a wrestler weighing up his opponent, wondering which 'hold' to try on him; for he knew that he himself was too unordinary for his view of life to be automatically valid for someone else. His son, in fact, was the touchstone by which he distinguished, in what he believed right, what was right for everyone, or at least for those he loved; he was the stimulus to a constant re-consideration and readjustment of his value judgements (for instance: 'For me, a knowledge of Latin is indispensable. But for Brunet? And, if so, why?')

It was in the midst of these anxieties that, one day, sitting on a stone in the snow, he jotted down these thoughts:

'St Teresa cries out about Satan: "Poor wretch, he does not love!" Agreed, the man who has never brought a woman a bunch of violets, or removed the stamps from a letter he has received from abroad to give them to a child, will always be missing something. But it must also be said: "Poor wretch, he loves!" Where love is (and here we are only talking of love as affection), no more freedom, no more peace, no more taking wing. If a man is ruined or "disgraced", he will take it philosophically if he does not love, but if he has a wife or a child whom he loves, his ruin or "disgrace" becomes a torture. If a man is about to die, all the stoicism with which he would face death if he loved no one falls to pieces if he is leaving loved ones behind, because of the anguish of losing them and the dread of what may become of them. Loving embitters and corrodes (and I repeat, there is no question here of passionate love, but of conjugal or parental affection, etc.). There can be no philosophic wisdom in the man who loves; there can be no wise men without egoism. "God is love", say the Christians. To which the unbeliever might reply that, if God loves, God is weak, God is dependent on his creatures and is therefore no longer God. A God who loved would be a slave God, and a slave God is inconceivable. Look at the smile of the Buddha and don't talk to me any more about his love for humanity: people only smile like that when they do not love.

'And yet, if non-love means freedom of mind and soul, the anxiety one feels when one loves can sometimes be one of the props of the mind and soul. A heed for the health, happiness and well-being of another human being, not continuous but constantly returned to on re-emerging from other preoccupations, is a kind of cement that finds its way into all the interstices of a person's life, binding together its more or less disparate elements and giving it cohesion and solidity. It gives unity to so many scattered lives (maternal love in widows), as well as plenitude.

'Plenitude! How *occupied* one is with somebody one loves! It could be enough to occupy one exclusively. But the cruel law, "art against love", does not only govern passionate love; it isn't only with Solange and other women that I have experienced it: if I have not given the best of myself to my son, it's because I have given it to my work, and there are moments when this troubles me to the point of acute anguish. "What!" you will say, "can a life be exclusively occupied in thinking of and wishing for another person's well-being?" I who have spaced out my meetings with him to keep myself fresh, to want to see him again and to look forward to seeing him again, to avoid getting too accustomed to him, or to loving him, I reply: "Yes, why not?" I can perfectly well imagine myself having done nothing else for the past ten years except devote myself to bringing up my son (his schooling, of course, remaining in the hands of specialists), and *that* would have been an education, in the only valid sense of the word, *that* would have been loving him, in the only valid sense of the word. I had a choice between creating a man and creating a body of work; I chose the latter – as Rousseau abandoned his children to write a book about childhood. With ordinary fathers, it's earning money, or position, or playing cards, that keeps them from their children. In my case, it's my work that has kept me from loving and educating my child, that has made me betray my child, made me "put him off till to-morrow" – whereas at other times, on the contrary, I find him dissipating my energies, making me devote by fits and starts to the perishable what my most imperious instinct tells me I should devote exclusively to the eternal (for every artist worthy of the name should behave as though his work must be eternal). Like the sea upon the shore, now my son gains ground in me, and now he withdraws. But is this not the motion of all love? And ought one to complain about it? How intoxicating to live on those restless waters, which never run dry, which are never constant, never beyond hope! As for the discrepancy between art and love, it's probably just a particular instance of a universal discrepancy. If one wants to do things seriously, one cannot – in my case, for example – create, cultivate one's mind, pursue adventure, pursue glory, and love, all at the same time: there is always one of these activities that will suffer.

'... It isn't the ties of blood that speak in me when I love him, or rather it isn't only the ties of blood: such ties alone could never be enough for me. Nature gave me this child, but in such conditions that I could have refused him had I wished, as I refused F.* He was given to me, but I also chose him; just as I loved him, but also *wanted* to love him – *wanted* to love him as the (intelligent) Christian *wants* to believe. When he was still in the insubstantiality of childhood, I took a gamble on him: I gambled on his being worthy of my love, and of the time this love would cost me....'

Thus he reflected, amid the beauties of nature, so insipid to whomsoever has seen into a human soul. And he smiled to think that the literary world spoke of his 'solitariness' – solitary, because I don't mix in *that* society! – when there had never been a period in his life when he had not been completely taken up with a person he loved – when he had spent the whole of his life loving, just as one spends the whole of one's life dying. Solitude? Yes, sometimes. But a solitude always illuminated by the affection he gave, as the solitude of these highlands was illuminated by the soft sunlight on the snow.

16

He used to meet her every Sunday evening on the train coming back from her Aunt Charlotte's. One day he had told her who he was, and said that he had noticed her long before. He had asked for permission to write to her, and had accompanied her to her door. He had written to her several times. She had thought he wrote well; his letters enchanted her. The enchantment subsided when she saw him, every Sunday evening: her 'dream' was so much more beautiful from a distance! Finally he had proposed to her. His proposal was centred not so much on himself as on an exquisite little eighteenth-century house which was about to become available.... It was this house that had brought things to a head. That evening, he had sat down beside her in the train, instead of in his usual place on the opposite seat. After having inquired whether the gesture

---

*Another bastard of Costals', whom he had refused to recognize (*Author's note*).

would displease her, he had kissed her on the forehead. She had felt nothing, literally nothing, and had not flinched. 'Won't you kiss me?' he had asked, with a rather constrained look. She had turned her face towards him, brought it closer.... and then, when it came to the point, had been unable to bring herself to take the plunge: her face had turned away. Her hands lay inert in her lap, and she had begun to cry (tears came easily to her).

When Mme Dandillot recalled this scene, she always thought that at that point M. Dandillot 'had turned very pale'. Let us not exaggerate: M. Dandillot had simply looked as all gentlemen look in such circumstances. He had promptly regained his original place, on the seat opposite. He had said a few banal words. They had parted. Next day he wrote to her: 'I realize that you do not love me,' and withdrew his proposal. Whereupon she wept more than ever: she imagined she had been happy. It was not this man she missed, it was his letters – so tender and so respectful. She had no need of him; she needed to wait for the post. Her disappointment went through two phases, both equally familiar: one phase during which she wrote poetry, and a second phase during which she took to religion. The day she spoke of entering a convent, her father rushed round to the Dandillots. At first Charles Dandillot stood on his high horse: he did not like sourpusses, and his desire had waned. But the little goose's golden eggs smelt good, and a few weeks later one more 'eternal couple' was born. Nénette and Rintintin for ever!

Her youth whisked away, and her life as a woman completely null. But how our love can sustain us! If a person's life, however null, embodies a love for his children, that is enough: his life is fulfilled and justified in his own eyes. The person is never more poignantly aware of this than at the crucial hour, in the face of death. At that moment, all the great problems and pretensions of his existence, all that he has built up, his 'message' if he had one, seem to him derisory. But the fact that he loves, and the object of his love, do not appear derisory. They endure terrifyingly, with all their power for good and evil, while the pillars of the temple crumble. Mme Dandillot loved her daughter, and was saved. At the summit of the hierarchy of love, one would doubtless have to place the love of a father for his son, if such a love existed. But it does not exist, or rarely : men are usually too preoccupied, and moreover too dense, to pay attention to their sons otherwise than in a rough and absent-minded way; boys are only really loved by a few born educators and a few pederasts of the better sort. So that it is in a mother's love for her daughter that we see the most perfect form of human love.

For the third time that night, Mme Dandillot awoke. And instantly, with a sublime impulse, her dawning consciousness pounced upon the person of her daughter, as though some sort of right of occupancy were at issue there which it was vitally important to establish. It was not total consciousness, however, but those confused moments wherein, like river and sea at the bar, those two equally formidable adventures, sleep and wakefulness, meet and mingle and grapple with each other. Her heart was beating with morbid violence. The memory of some family keepsakes she had found in a cupboard the day before came back to her, moistening her eyes : they had reminded her of desertion and loneliness, harbingers of the desertion and loneliness of her daughter. And her whole day had been filled with a sense of inferiority : a visit to the hairdresser for another of those perms that never stayed put; a visit to the dressmaker for one of those two-thousand-franc outfits that never suited her. Suddenly, from this gelatine of bitterness, something broke loose – a certainty, an absurd, blazing certainty : Solange had gone. Gone? . . . Where? Why? Between the moment when the two women had kissed each other goodnight ('If you get into a sweat tonight and want to change, call me. If you change all by yourself, you're bound to catch cold') and now, Solange had dressed, hurriedly collected her things, and left the house. Mme Dandillot switched on the light, got up, and walked distractedly to her daughter's room. On the way, she kissed one of Solange's coats which was hanging on the wall, burying her face in it for a moment.

Solange, too, was awake in the dark. (Both needed a little happiness to bring them back their sleep.) She recognized her mother's form. The form came up to the bed :

'Is that you?'

'No, Mummy, it isn't me! ...'

'I thought you'd gone.'

'Gone?'

'Yes, that you'd got up and dressed and left with your suit-case.'

'Mummy! Are you going a bit mad?'

'I think I am.... Let me kneel beside your bed without saying anything, just touching you with my hand to make sure you're there.... Why are you putting on the light?' (smiling) 'Yes, it's you. I recognize you now. You're my only daughter.'

'But of course!'

'What would your father have said if he'd seen a light under your door at this hour? When I used to read after eleven, I was sure to see him come in and ask: "Can't you sleep?" Since you're awake, won't you make room for me beside you? I'd like to be warm.'

'You know I haven't enough warmth even for myself.'

'It's not really to be warm, it's just to be near you.' (She settled in.) 'Have you been awake long?'

'I don't know. I woke up once at a quarter past twelve, then at two o'clock, and then just now.'

'I woke up at exactly the same times. I've noticed before that we nearly always wake up at the same time. It's strange. ... You haven't got a pain anywhere, have you?'

'Of course not! Oh, please don't worry about me the whole day long. A few minutes ago I'd "gone"; now I'm supposed to have a pain somewhere. ...'

'Your father used to say that the whole world would be full of milksops if one always imagined that the people one loves are about to be run over. Personally I think that if anyone who loves another person stops imagining they're about to be run over, well, it simply means they don't love them so much.'

Slipping her hand under her daughter's arm, she felt the crook of the elbow, in which the nocturnal perspiration of sickly people (which had seeped through the night-dress) stagnated like damp in a fold of the ground where the sun never penetrates; looked at the veins of the fore-arm which had exactly the same contours as her own, as though they had been traced from hers; and placed her other hand over Solange's forehead, as if to gather up and expel the evil spirits. 'To think that, behind this forehead, nothing has ever been or will ever be conceived against me!' This person – this face and body – who for her was the most precious thing in the world, was the same person who made Costals yawn with boredom; the same person whom thousands of men and women passed or jostled in the street with indifference; the same person for whose body other men would have risked damnation, without loving her soul: all and nothing, supreme and defenceless. Solange was in the habit (which is that of all Arabs and many Spaniards) of sleeping always with her mouth covered, even in summer. Mme Dandillot recognized from its dampness the place where the sheet had been resting on her daughter's mouth, and buried her face in it with a little moan. She was 'Nénette', she was the 'police horse': and yet at this moment she reached the summit of all that was truly strong in her, all that was most valid. Solange looked with pity at this face, slightly swollen by sleep, in which the pouches under the eyes had sunk, like the pouches under the eyes of cocka-toos, and the lines of which were criss-crossed by the creases of her pillow – and the pathetic expression of avidity and ex-haustion which that gesture had suddenly given it. It is well known that desire, in the instant of gratification, assumes the mask of death; it must be said that maternal tenderness, on occasion, can assume it too. Mme Dandillot let her head fall back on the bolster (her daughter was on the pillow) and lay silent. Then she said: 'My little darling.... What else need I say to you when I've said that?' After a while she must have come down from the heights to which love had borne her for an instant, for she said (her eyes raised towards the arch of the ceiling):

'There are flaws in the wall-paper.* Your father would never have allowed that. He may have been this and he may have been that, but as a hanger of wall-paper he hadn't an equal. At Limoges he hung a frieze in the drawing-room that took

---

*It was new wall-paper put up during the alterations made to the flat after M. Dandillot's death (*Author's note*).

up a whole roll of it, all in one piece, and without a hitch.'

'Your father,' always 'your father'. Alive, he counted for nothing. Now that he was dead, they spoke of him constantly. To contradict him, of course. But often to praise him too.

Mme Dandillot took her daughter's hand and raised her arm, and the two fore-arms, joined, swung together with melancholy grace.

'If life could be just that – lying beside you without stirring, without having to go out, or order meals, or dress. You know I went round to Janine. But, it's funny, the older I get, the more difficult I find it is to choose. I used to look all right in any old thing more or less. I remember a blue satin blouse I made for myself in '16, which suited me so well. I was so proud when people asked me: "Where did you buy that blouse?" I always remember how pleased I was when the Curé of Pontorson asked me if I lived in Paris – and I was wearing my blouse that day! To be taken for a Parisian! And with no make-up!'

She laid her head on Solange's shoulder, with another little moan. Her head rose with each breath, like a boat lifted by the gentle respiration of the sea. At the other end of the room, beside the radiator, the two cats, mother and daughter, slept in one another's paws.

'I would like to give my life for you.'

'But, Mummy, what good would that do?'

'To think that that pig is chasing chamois in the Atlas.* while you....'

'Why do you call him a pig now? Three weeks ago, you said he was a "likeable brute". That was much better.'

'I call him a pig because he makes my little daughter unhappy.'

'Oh! please don't let's talk about that.'

'This afternoon I was looking for some curtains in the big cupboard, and I opened some boxes. Goodness, what gloomy things I found! Your grandmother's wedding ring, my wedding veil, your first tooth.... But to cap everything, I came across your baby clothes. The size of a bottle, you were, when you were born; yes, just about the size of a litre bottle. Your father used to say: "The only thing to do is to call her Flea.

---

*Chamois in the Atlas? ... (*Author's note*).

Flea Dandillot." We had to buy your clothes in a toy-shop:
doll's clothes. Did you tell him that, the chamois hunter?'

'Yes.'

'What did he say?'

'Nothing. . . .'*

'That doesn't surprise me; Southerners have no heart. I
always remember the day of your christening. They were celebrating downstairs, and they'd forgotten all about me, in bed
in my room. I cried. After all, not to have even thought of
bringing me a glass of grenadine! So I sent out for a bottle of
champagne, so as not to have to ask your father for anything.
A little later he came up and found me in tears. "God, how
stupid you are! We thought you were asleep".

'The day you came into the world I was also abandoned like
a poor old dog. Your grandmother hadn't wanted to make the
journey because of the snow! Always some excuse! Your
father said: "All will be well." What did he know about it, I
ask you? When your Aunt Charlotte arrived. . . .'

Suddenly she was silent, like a little musical box which has
jammed, and stops dead in the middle of its refrain. 'Are you
asleep?' she asked. No answer. She switched on the light.
Solange was sleeping, a little saliva at the corner of her mouth;
while her mother had been meandering on, fleet-footed sleep
had brushed across her face. How vast the darkness of the
night is, how silent the earth, when one watches a loved one
sleep! He who is obsessed by the disparity inherent in every
object, and who seeks to discover therein one of the keys to
the mystery of nature, must be moved to meditate on human
tenderness, which is at once the height of anxiety and the
height of repose. Mme Dandillot reposed in Solange, as Costals,
at the end of his wanderings, always came to rest in thoughts
of his son; now there was no difference between Costals and
Mme Dandillot. Had they but known, they might have smiled
at each other across their barriers; but they were searching
elsewhere. Their two tender melodies drew near to one another, ran side by side, without ever meeting. Mme Dandillot

---

*In fact Costals had said: 'I see. It must have been a *walking*
doll' (*Author's note*).

looked at her daughter's hands, so thin that they seemed
scarcely wider than her wrists, like a monkey's hands. She
had an impulse to join her own hands in a prayer: 'O God,
make my daughter recover from all this!', but by a not un-
familiar mechanism of substitution (which would be worth
expatiating on), it was Solange's hands that she joined. No
sooner had she seen her daughter with her hands joined on her
breast, than she imagined her dead. She put her hand on that
breast, and felt it rising and falling faintly. Then she turned off
the light and lay back on the bolster. Her daughter had heard
all these stories a hundred times – the doll's clothes, the bottle
of champagne, the grandmother who would not put herself
out because of the snow – and yet the fact that she had fallen
asleep while her mother was talking to her took on a sinister
significance in Mme Dandillot's mind: yes, Solange really had
'gone', as she had feared; yes, she had indeed been abandoned
once more. Mme Dandillot no longer dared lay her head on
her daughter's shoulder, for fear of waking her, and yet she
was filled with an immeasurable hope that she *would* wake,
that she would 'come back'; and she had to struggle with herself in order not to provoke that wakening. A few minutes
went by in this way, and then she thought of her recent tears.
They were waiting. Her throat tightened, her eyes misted over,
and they began to flow again.

17

During February and March, Costals nomadized and hunted
in the Fez region and in the Atlas. An Arab proverb says: 'A
lone traveller is a devil'. He is also a saint. The long solitude,
the manifold ordeals, the faces and landscapes that brush past
you without ever sinking in, the enforced submission to
nature's ever-disquieting dictates – what a retreat!

Lobel kept him posted. The new examination of the nasal
mucus had confirmed the original diagnosis. Rhadidja was
having treatment at Tighremt. She wrote once to Costals
(through an Arab café proprietor in Casablanca, as she always
did, so that no one at Tighremt should know she was writing

to a Frenchman). The letter began: 'I am writing to let you know that I am in good health.' There's nothing like knowing, as they say. The letter passed on forthwith to other matters.

Costals still wrote regularly to Solange. Unlike most men, who are prepared to assuage all the sorrows of the world except those they themselves have caused, he wanted her to suffer as little as possible. He wanted her to make a soft landing in a smiling landscape: that of her new life, her engagement and marriage to another man – Tomasi no doubt. He was reluctant to tell her a truth she would be unable to bear. He sought to persuade her that his affection was still alive, when in fact it was not: sometimes it is this that is called fidelity. 'The greatest proof of love I ever gave you was to leave you.' (This was pure humbug, and he knew it.) 'My love for you has blossomed in an extraordinary way now that there's no longer a zero hour' (the hippogriffical hour). 'What can I do for you?' (Certain savage tribes honour the heads of their decapitated enemies.) He wanted her to believe that he was unhappy ('I cannot find the peace and freedom for my work which I came to seek here'), when he was not suffering at all except from acting this part. This play-acting did not come easily to him, and at times it gave him a slight feeling of disgust. As he filled his letters with endearments, it sometimes struck him that the paper ought to tear under his nib in protest against the abuse of these fine phrases, and to emphasize the chasm that exists between one and the same sentence when it springs from the depths of your soul and when it is an imposture. At the end of these letters, his writing quickened, became almost joyful: the horse scenting the stable. One day, however, having changed pens, he found that the sentiments came to him much more easily.

At all events, these letters – the drafts of which he filed in a portfolio marked *Flute for my fiancée** (doubtless in allusion to Muslim weddings, which are always celebrated to the sound of flutes) – were the most touching he had ever sent her: it is well known that the most beautiful love-letters are those that have not been written sincerely. Nothing is less eloquent than

*Untranslatable pun. The phrase, in French, can also mean: 'To hell with my fiancée' (*Translator's note*).

real love. When Brunet flung his arms round his father's neck and covered him with kisses, saying: 'Do you love me a lot? More than last year? Do you think of me every day, or only every other day?' all Costals could think of in reply was: 'Of course I do, stupid.' Aware that this was not sufficiently warm, he tried to think of something more affectionate to add, and eventually embraced the brat with an 'I've never met such a stupid boy as you.' Such were this writer's powers of expression when he loved with all his heart. But when he did not love, the words came gushing out. 'How well you lie!' says Athene to Ulysses.

Toiling over these missives, not only did he have to struggle against his indifference towards Solange, but, mesmerized by his desire to do her harm, to punish her for the 'season in hell' which she had made him endure, he also had to struggle against this desire. Holding her thus at arm's length was killing. How he suffered, whenever he acted out of kindness! When future biographers of this author discover all he did when driven by the Daemon of the Good, they will include him in the Golden Legend, and since at that moment he will be in hell, it will be his greatest punishment to see himself beatified. He will roast twice over.

At the end of April, once more in the Atlas, he was the guest of the kaid of the Aït Arouen, a little fellow with a goatee beard, an Auvergnat mug, a crop of hair as wiry as his own sheep's wool, a bear-like gait; jovial, lecherous, an attacker of farms and adorer of planets and fire; in short, one hundred per cent *bled-es-siba.**

One morning, as he was washing his hands before lunch, he suddenly stopped dead. On the outer surface of his right forearm there was a little patch. Exactly the reverse of Rhadidja's: a macula of discoloured skin, and around it a brownish halo.

He stripped, and examined as much of his body as he could (with a travelling mirror!). As far as he could see, there was nothing sinister.

---

*Bled-es-siba: that part of Moroccan territory occupied by unsubdued tribes, outside the effective authority of the Sultan (*Translator's note*).

He was surprised his face had not changed. How treacherous, to have leprosy without its showing on your face! He was also surprised that he was not more agitated.

Decision : get himself examined by Lobel as soon as possible. At lunch, on the pretext that a stupid oversight had made him forget that he was due in Marrakesh two days hence, he asked the kaid for a guide and a mule to take him to Souk et'Tnine, sixteen kilometres away, where he would no doubt easily find a bus or a car. That done, he ate, drank, talked, smoked, and belched as if nothing had happened : life must go on, after all. As if nothing had happened? Not exactly, for, exchanging dirty jokes with the kaid, he showed off a bit. This attitude was his first reaction to the threat.

Two hours later he was on his way. Then he began to think. Up to then he had not had the time.

'The spots begin mainly on the face and *the extremities of the limbs.*' This was a sentence he had noted in the medical manual.

What did it matter that only two months had elapsed since his last contact with Rhadidja – too short for the incubation period? It was perhaps two years earlier that she had infected him.

'How tragic it would be if one couldn't kill oneself. The absolute futility, the irreducible wickedness of physical suffering! But when I'm in a really bad way, and suffering too much, I'll kill myself. (That revolver I was so keen to lend to old Dandillot!) Say I have four to six years of lucidity in front of me – and getting them must be partly a question of will-power and organization. The only problem will be to balance, during this given period of time, my pleasure (as long as it remains possible), my work, and what I owe my son. On the work side, I shall have to conclude my *opus*, not where it would naturally have ended, but within the framework of the second chunk which is now in progress and which I should be able to finish if I organize myself properly; that would be the only way to conclude it without skimping it. As for Brunet, he'll be twenty when I die, so he can shift for himself. No, there really isn't any problem, except that of arranging my time even more carefully than I have up to now. I must ration myself with extreme care.

'I used to say, thinking of the next war: I must learn to dominate the war. Now: I must learn to dominate my disease.

'Unquestionably, it's painful to die at forty. But I might have died at twenty, in the war. I might have died a hundred times since the war, with the sort of life I lead. Leprosy makes me a condemned man, but no more immediately so than I already was without it.

'In another sense, this disease is a renewal of my life. A new element of interest in my life. My life loses in duration, but will gain in richness and variety, as well as being cleared of the dross which still encumbered it, in spite of my vigilant hunt after dross. Sudden death would have been fine. Death in six years' time is fine too; it gives me time to turn around. The awkward compromise would be death in two months' time: two months of useless consciousness, since two months is not enough time to sort oneself out.

'A good test. Enrichment of my experience of adversity, which was inadequate. I shall need all my humanity to face up to it.

'As for death itself, that is even less of a problem. If only they would stop bothering us about death. What will become of us after death? Sensible people don't ask such questions. They make an act of faith or they don't, and that's the end of the matter. Besides, even granting that death is something to "think" about, it will be time enough to think about it a week before I polish myself off. A healthy man doesn't think about his death until it's under his nose. Children talk of death as of a joke that never happens. There again, we should take a leaf out of their book.

'How right I've been to get a lot done! How right I've been to enjoy myself!

'During the war, I knew that from one minute to the next I might be killed, or disfigured, or maimed, or go mad. And yet, on the whole, I enjoyed myself in the war.

'This landscape is symbolic. Behind me, my life and all the people in it, like this animated valley. And in the background, my work, like the mountain. And I, a traveller hurrying against the night.'

His mule stumbled and recovered its footing on the steep track, battered by thousands of hoofs and buttressed by beams sunk into holes in the rock. The nag was led by an old man with a pale skin, a round, snowy head, and the calves of a ten-year-old child, while a younger man, unbelievably gorilla-like, pulled its tail with the utmost energy. It was impossible to tell whether its tail was being pulled in order to encourage it or to restrain it; the whole secret seemed to be to pull the animal simultaneously forwards and backwards, and it was this that made it advance. O thou, Creator of the universe, how inscrutable are thy ways! The two guides worked themselves up with shouts full of vowels, which echoed and reverberated at every bend in the track. The whole landscape around them recalled those book illustrations for which the stingy publisher has instructed the artist: 'Don't use more than three colours.' The reddish pink of the soil. The white of the snow. The blue of the shadows on the flanks of the hills, and of the soft sky. On the slope of the mountain above them, forests of young trees were mirrored in the clouds. On the slope below, wadis had forgotten their mission in life ('wadis that have betrayed,' thought Costals, haunted as always by the act of betrayal) and had become tracks, littered with boulders and only distinguishable by their ribbons of oleander; and then a stream of red ice, like a stream of red-currant jelly or a trench full of freshly coagulated blood. Flocks of sheep, which were the very colour of drought, passed above their heads, flitting by like shadows, and the sheep-dog crunched the hardened snow. There were mummified shepherds who had been there for five thousand years. And grasshoppers, motionless too, and marked down by pneumonia, on the snow-clad bushes. And great white falcons wheeling and gliding with the grace of Egyptian dancers.

After an hour, as the sky changes, his inner sky changed too, clouded over a little. He felt a little afraid, not of his leprosy, but at seeing how he functioned in the opposite way to other people, in not being afraid (perhaps it was out of mere contrariness that, in circumstances where everyone would have been afraid, he had not been). He compared himself to that patient of Revault d'Allones, who seemed to see his life unfold without him, who no longer reacted, and went to ask the doctor to restore his lost feelings. Always out of line, always the dissenter, always *bled-es-siba*, like the old kaid. 'Inhuman?'

Aware, too, that in not being more afraid, he was being cheated of something. No doubt, as regards 'character', his insensitivity was a gain. But still, the fact remained that he was cheated of fear. (As he was cheated of jealousy with women, not being jealous by temperament: which was honourable in terms of reason, but was also a loss, after all.)

His spirits began to warm up a little – was it an instinctive reaction, to make good this deficiency?

'We laugh, we play the fool with Nature. She lets us be. We tease and provoke her some more, we pull the tail of Cybele's lioness. Whereupon, with one blow of her paw, she splits our heads open, and it serves us right. We provoke the sea by showing off with all our ships and submarines. It goes on like that for years, and then one day we sink to the bottom, and it serves us right. The airman provokes the sky, and one fine day, without fail, the sky will lose patience with this infant and his puff-puff. His aeroplane crashes, and it serves him right. Nature has punished me in whatever sphere I have provoked her. My passions have always been of the kind one pays for in one's body: war, adventure, love affairs, dangerous company. I pay. When Mephisto, in *Faust*, bursts out in sores all over, it's because he has gazed too long at the backsides of the angels.

'From that point of view, it was really rather scandalous that I hadn't had a dose of the pox, considering the way I live. From another point of view, it was clearly an inadequacy in my personality. Two lacks: the pox and the law-courts. Now we have something much better.

'If I'm cured, what a lesson it will have been for me! A lesson? My life will go on exactly as before.'

They passed the ruins of a massive *kasba* of red earth, full of the melancholy of power that is no more. Screeching like tom-cats, crows wheeled above the sleeping forests as though they took them for fabulous herds. The silken beat of their wings made a sort of rhythmical hissing sound, very like the sound of a panting dog.

'Leprosy. Like the kings and the Popes. And like the conquistadors. It's odd, the ancestry of an anomaly is always a fine one.

'*Morbus sacer*, that too. The Greeks, who in certain epochs tended towards the neuropathic, used to render divine honours to disease, "provided it was really powerful". Leprosy would have merited these honours.

'Trace all the great lepers in history.

' "*Without the camp*" – the curse upon lepers, as formulated in the Bible. But have I ever been anywhere else but without the camp?

'A heart painted on my tunic, like the lepers of the Middle Ages: symbol of the heart I lack, according to women. And the anaesthesia of the skin, symbol of my so-called (partially true) moral anaesthesia.... But all this is literature, unless I'm utterly mistaken.'

Urchins went by, hooded like the infant Harpocrates depicted on Hellenistic terracottas; and sturdy, impudent-looking little girls, unveiled, but putting their hands vaguely over the lower half of their faces as they passed.

'Pack of trollops. Not Rhadidja. Nor Jeanneton, nor Marina, nor La Fleur. But the rest of them. Now we'll have some fun: I'll bung the whole lot of them full of leprosy, the sluts. For we must still enjoy our pleasures. So kiss my spots, sweetheart: they're birth-marks. "Lepers seek oblivion in an intense sexual life" – another sentence from the medical text-book. Infect the entire globe – that would be something to be proud of. Where did I read about a consumptive who spat in his wife's soup, so as not to be the only one to croak?*

'I was surprised I wasn't more upset. It's the memory of the evil I've done that prevents me from suffering.

'If only the human race could perish with me! To be able to tell myself on my death-bed that in dying I'm not losing a single person!

'*Malebolge.*

'I'm sure that after a time I shall wonder how I managed to live without it. One gets used to everything. I'm sure one gets used to hell.

'And let's not forget our work, damn it! Job, leprous on his

---

*Cited by Dr Fiessinger (*Author's note*).

dung-hill, joins Mme Roland in the tumbril* when he cries:
"Who will provide me with the wherewithal to write my dis-
sertations? Who will give me the means to transcribe them in
a book?" That was Job's ultimate regret – not having a fountain-pen. He ought to be the patron of men of letters. We'll
write a novel about leprosy, if we have a little time to spare.
And our *ultima verba*, of course. Besides, writing one's *ultima
verba* is enough to prevent one from dying. And our complete
works bound in sterilized leper's skin – the skin cuttings were
such pretty colours in Lobel's book. And I trust they'll write
theses about us – lepers stimulate literary men. Maistre and
le Lépreux de la cité d'Aoste, Huysmans and *Sainte Lygdwine
de Schiedam*, and that prototype of the bogus masterpiece by a
bogus genius, *la Jeune fille Violaine*.'

He saw that dusk was falling, and thought: 'What do the
changes in nature amount to compared to the change that is
taking place in my body at this moment?' On the horizon, the
mountains grew blurred and disappeared; now there was
nothing to be seen but the snow on the summits, like shrouds
suspended in the sky. Then everything changed again; the
mountains reappeared, grape-purple and pink in colour, and in
those high places dedicated to nature-worship there began the
daily sacrifice of the Sun. The silence was total. No more
beasts, no more birds, no other life but that of the immeasurable winds; or the tiny sounds of the snow or of a stone coming loose and rolling down the embankment of the track, or
of a dead branch breaking off like a warning. For a moment,
through a break in the clouds, a ladder of gold descended on
to purple rocks. For a moment, in a valley, a lake could be
seen, of a violet so intense it might have been a vast bed of
violets. Then, suddenly, all was shadow, and the spirits emerged
from the dark mountains.

Sure, now, of arriving before nightfall at Souk et'Tnine, no
more than a kilometre away, Costals dismounted and dined off
the fruit, cakes and milk which the kaid had given him of his
poor riches. These substances, having reached his belly, helped

---

*In the tumbril taking her to the guillotine, Mme Roland asked
for paper to write down her impressions (and was refused) (*Author's
note*).

to modify his attitude to life. His first reaction to the threat
had been one of calm, partly because his lunch had bolstered
him up. Then, exhausted and weakened by the hard journey,
and his stomach having emptied, he had indulged in a bout of
confused exaltation: his defence against the terrible reality
had then been the one we all turn to – the impulse Andrée
Hacquebaut had had when she decided he was an invert, or
when she persuaded herself that he loved her, the impulse he
himself had already had when he sought to gild the pill of
marriage by systematically working himself up in the Bibliothèque Nationale. It is our natural bent that saves us from
everything. In times of trial, the man of pleasure takes refuge
in pleasure; the man of imagination, if he can convince himself that the ordeal he is living through was once faced by men
who inspire him, takes a liking to it. 'Men are troubled, not by
things, but by opinions about things,' says the Ancient. Yes,
but what saves them, too, are opinions about things. Costals,
with his romanticism, had attempted to construct a world in
which he would not suffer unduly, and he had succeeded, for
human nature is extremely well adapted; one has only to
manipulate it with a little intelligence. Now, fortified by rest
and food, he had recovered his original serenity. The supposed
benefits of his disease had reinstated themselves in the fore-
ground of his consciousness: an interesting experience, a better
use of the time that remained to him, his life concentrated on
essentials. 'That which is noble in my nature is safe,' says
Mephisto, while his body bursts with sores.

Meanwhile they were descending the last slope of the mountain, returning to the human world, the gentle world of
humanity, and Costals felt the same emotion he had once felt
on a scorching August day in Paris (in the place de la Bourse)
when an itinerant pedlar had proffered some violets: violets!
an evocation of cool winter in the midst of this furnace! Unleashed waters resumed their course, with the delicious roar
of distant artillery; the night was full of invisible running
water. Invisible? Here was a stream whose sinuous coils, as of
a bludgeoned viper, shimmered in the darkness; here were
waterfalls, grandiose by virtue of the rocks and heights from
which they fell, charming because they looked like long

sparkling oriflammes or the unfurled tails of Arab horses. The moon had appeared, flanked by tiny Venus (like an ox flanked by an ox-pecker bird), and the constellations glittered on the further slope, like snow crystals in the sun. A vast sky inlaid with bright forms, a night wreathed in whispers and voices. In sight of the first lights of Souk et'Tnine (there was a dog running behind him, whose course down the slope he could only guess by the noise of the stones it sent rattling down); in sight of the first lights of Souk et'Tnine (there was an insomniac bird that uttered a shriek of connivance); in sight of the first lights of Souk et'Tnine, Costals had a thought that was a little strange, but full of peace: 'After all, it's only me who's dying.'

18

Costals arrived at the front door of the Marrakesh hospital, and went past without entering. He was funking it. 'It's five past nine. At twenty past nine I shall know I'm done for.' Then he rapidly retraced his steps, and with a smile of resentment and fortitude, went in and asked for Lobel.

When Lobel arrived, they went into his office. Costals took off his jacket, rolled up his shirt-sleeve, and showed his forearm without a word. He was still smiling, but it was a different smile, a quizzical smile as if to say: 'You must admit it's genuine all right, and that you didn't expect it.'

Lobel bent down and scrutinized the spot, while Costals watched him intently. 'This is the moment when he'll lie to me. I wouldn't be a writer of psychological novels if I couldn't see through him now.' But the doctor's face remained sealed.

'No other marks on your body?'

'Not so far as I could see.'

At the hotel, he had not dared to examine his body for fear of discovering more marks, like a consumptive who does not dare examine his spittle.

'You haven't been blowing your nose more than usual? No tingling sensation at the tips of your fingers?'

'No.'

A pause. Ah! this was the moment of truth. 'How is he going to break it to me? Probably he'll say: "No definite symptoms, but you'd better have some treatment, in case...." What! he's putting his hand on my arm. That must mean that he's about to come clean. He wants to give me courage.' Costals felt himself turn pale inside. Passionately he murmured the prayer from his childhood missal, giving it a human meaning: 'Say but the word and my soul shall be saved.'

Lobel said:

'The thing is, you see, you're a very nice chap...but you haven't an appointment, have you?'

Silence.

'I wouldn't want to keep you waiting. And I can't see you for another hour. Have you anything you need to do in Marrakesh?'

'No, I haven't anything to do in Marrakesh,' said Costals, glum and icy. At the same time he was thinking: 'The brute makes soothing noises, like all doctors; only I've got leprosy. If the spot wasn't suspect, he would already have laughed in my face. And if it is suspect, then that's that.'

Lobel calculated aloud, and then: 'I can see you in forty minutes. Wouldn't you like to look around the town. Marrakesh is quite picturesque, after all.... Oh, of course, it's not the same sort of thing as the Eiffel Tower....'

'He'll drive me mad with his Eiffel Tower.' Costals allowed himself to be led to the door, and went out.

'Would he talk about sight-seeing to a man when in forty minutes' time he was going to tell him he had leprosy? Why not? Before telling D. he had cancer, the doctor made him sign some limited editions of his books.

'So I'm a "nice chap"! And if he had read a eulogistic article about me by the most stupid academician, he'd be calling me *cher maître*. But he's never heard of me, and so, as he can only judge me by my face, he tells me I'm a nice chap – in other words that I'm a half-wit. And indeed that is what I must be. "Nice" to Solange. "Nice" to Andrée Hacquebaut. "Nice" to Rhadidja.'

Never would Costals forget those forty minutes killing time in Marrakesh: they were enough to cure him of Africa for the rest of his life. 'Sometimes it's the world that is the theatre of an imminent unknown: the eve of a revolution. This time it's inside my body that the catastrophe is brewing. And there's nothing I can do but look on – until the revolver shot. But can I even count on that? X. and Y., who tried to kill themselves while there was still a tiny glimmer of hope for them, and failed, never dared make another attempt – they both admitted it to me – when they knew the game was up.' As the appointed hour drew near, his anxiety increased. He remembered a friend who, telephoning to hear the result of a Wassermann test, took care to put the call through from a café, with a glass of rum at hand which he could gulp down at once if the result was 'positive' and he felt himself about to pass out. After thirty-five minutes, Costals could bear it no longer and returned to the hospital.

He was led through a room full of terrifying appliances. 'What a waste!' he thought. 'One would be enough to make me confess.'

Lobel stuck a bit of tin-ware up his nose, pawed his hands knowingly, and gave him a few of those taps on the knee with a hammer that children find so comic. Then he examined the *macula*. 'Close your eyes.' He tickled him on the spot and all round it with a sort of pin. 'Can you feel anything?' The man who knows. Who may be coarse, vulgar, ignorant, dishonest. But who knows. And the man in front of him, who may be a man of the highest intelligence and refinement, but who nonetheless says to him: 'I am in your hands.' Religion demands that this should also be man's attitude towards the priest. But the priest is a charlatan, whereas the doctor really knows. Costals, standing there, grave in his surrender and passivity, had already gone beyond. Beyond what? Beyond his will. He was no longer master of himself.

More tickling. 'Can you feel anything?' Costals in his agitation answered a little haphazardly. It seemed to him at times that it was his body that was insensitive whereas the *macula* was sensitive: surely that was not how it ought to be. In the same way, when Lobel tested the patch for heat and cold with some scruffy little tubes, Costals at once confused hot and cold – just as, long ago, as a boy, when the riding-master

commanded: 'Right!' our young genius forthwith pulled the
reins to the left.

'Undress.'

A little laugh.

'If you were a Spanish lady I'd tell you to keep your under-
clothes on. I never make Spanish women undress. I don't want
my native attendants to see how dirty a European woman can
be.'

When the examination was over:

'Are you obliged to stay in Morocco?'

'Not at all.'

'Well, go back to Paris without delay. The more detailed
examination I should have to give you would take several days.
But there's no point in starting anything here (*starting*, noted
Costals), because if you require treatment – which, I hasten to
say, is highly unlikely – you would have to have it in Paris.
Here, we're not all that well equipped for research.'

'He didn't tell me that when we talked about Rhadidja,'
Costals thought. 'Although I asked him to treat her as he
would treat me. No, Arab, in other words *anima vilis*: nothing
to be done about that.' He did not realize that, in advising him
to leave, Lobel was mainly concerned with getting rid of somebody who might be a nuisance. Then, shamefacedly, like a
man asking his mistress, 'Do you love me?' he asked: 'Well?'

'It's quite impossible to make a diagnosis. As far as I can
judge after such a cursory examination, you have none, I
repeat, none of the primary symptoms of Hansen's disease.
Only that spot is suspect. But that could be dermatitis, it could
be vitiligo, it could be all sorts of things. Marrakesh is the
paradise of skin diseases. It seems most improbable to me that
leprosy should declare itself three months after a contact. I've
never known a case, I've never heard tell of a case, where
incubation was as rapid as that. It's true that we're rarely confronted with first symptoms. In fact we only have fairly
advanced cases to deal with.... And then, if you have contracted the disease, it could have been from an earlier contact.
Rhadidja might have been in incubation all these last years.'

Costals told himself that there must surely be important
questions to ask, but although he had been alerted for

twenty-four hours (if not for three months) he was caught off guard and did not know what they were.

An assistant came in and murmured something to Lobel. The door remained open, revealing European patients waiting outside, huddled together on narrow benches like prisoners in a police station – Spaniards holding black caps between their hairy fingers, Italian women who seemed to have three or four breasts, with infants sucking at each of them like rivers sucking at the sea.

Lobel picked up an X-ray photograph from the table and held it up to the light.

'Look at that!' he said. 'What a beautiful picture!'

'What is it?' asked Costals, outraged that Lobel should take an interest in someone other than him, and leave him so quickly.

'A cancer of the stomach.'

'The chap's done for?'

'And how! But you must admit it's a fine picture.'

'Medicine's all very well,' said Costals, pulling on his trousers. 'Saving lives! But what for? A plaintiff or a defendant in a criminal case has scarcely finished wringing our hearts by the justice of his cause before we discover that he too isn't worth bothering about. It's the same with patients; how many of them are worth curing? When they're sick they're likeable enough; the virulence of their stupidity is abated. But when they're cured! And what will they do with that precious life you restore to them?'

'Oh! if we thought like that! Besides, the job keeps us on our mettle.'

'It seems to me that medical murder must be a terrible temptation. . . . It has sometimes occurred to me during a rough sea voyage that if the ship sunk I should die more easily if I knew that a hundred and fifty human beings were perishing at the same time.'

'Seriously?' said Lobel. For him, such sentiments existed only if unexpressed. 'No, no, really, that won't do at all,' he added with a smile. Costals was trying to do up his tie without much success, there being no mirror in the room. 'Come to the window,' said Lobel. One of the shutters, closed to keep out the strong sun, made a foil behind the window-pane.

'Once when I was staying in a strange town I had to have some injections from a doctor I didn't know. After these injections, I discovered that he was a devout Catholic, a member of the St Vincent de Paul society, and a regular communicant. I may tell you I hesitated whether to let him give me the rest of my injections.'

'I don't understand. . . .'

'Yes, if he had discovered that I was a sworn enemy of the Catholic Church. . . . He could have put anything he liked into the injections.'

'You certainly have a flattering idea of doctors and Catholics!'

'St Paul, having cited one of Jesus' sayings, adds ". . . for he knew what was in man". I too know what is in man.'

'Believe me, doctors often know it far better than literary men,' said Lobel, rising to his feet. 'That's it, he's showing me the door,' thought Costals. 'And yet we were just moving into a territory where we might have touched on important things. But there it is, he doesn't take to me; and between doctor and patient there must be some degree of mutual sympathy.' Ah! where were the beloved doctors of the urinary tract, who were always so cordial, who slapped you on the back and called you 'Old boy' the very first time they had dealings with you, who told you dirty stories and saw you off with the time-honoured jokes of eternal France : 'Only the third time? . . . Now if it had been the sixth or the seventh! . . .' or else : 'Now all you have to do is go and catch it again' (and even the humble eight-hundred-francs-a-month assistant, opening the door when you rang, would insist on telling you then and there : 'I must put your mind at rest at once. It's negative . . .'). With all those people, disease became almost a feat; there's something about a dose of clap that reminds one of a citation for gallantry. But as for Lobel, Costals took his leave of him with that sensation of being of no importance, of being abandoned, that he felt whenever he came away from his publisher's office.

As the thought that 'they can put what they like into injections' had stuck in his mind, and Rhadidja would be remaining in Lobel's care, he took out his cheque book. 'I should be glad if you'd accept, for the hospital. . . .' There are times, when one gives away money, when something inside one weeps. Not at 'forking out', but because it is so useless.

Costals came out of the hospital visibly affected. He felt physically incapable of smiling even had he wanted to; there was sweat on his forehead although the heat was moderate and very dry. No longer were there Europeans, Arabs, Negroes in the street, no longer any differences of nationality or race or class; only one great difference – between those who were diseased and those who were not. However, as he was being driven to the post office in a barouche to pick up his mail, he fell into one of those pointless rages with the native driver that are proper to a man in good health. 'Even if my body was falling to pieces, by God! *that* wouldn't prevent me from being the boss.' Which, translated into *imperial* language, came out as: 'I've got one foot in the grave, but that still leaves me one to kick you up the a— with!'

But back at his hotel, suddenly, it was the moment when the sick man panics – a moment as easy for the doctor to discern as is for the spectator the moment when a boxer is groggy or the moment when a runner cracks up. A horrible temptation to bury himself in the book on leprosy, and at the same time a fear of doing so. 'I'll open it again when I'm feeling better, when I'm strong enough to face the awful things I shall read in it.' He stood at the table, his eyes staring blankly, suddenly dumbfounded, shattered by the thought that he was not immortal. Was it he who, yesterday at the same hour, had greeted the discovery of the spot with equanimity? Was it not a dream? How could he have? How had he functioned at that moment? As astounded at having for a moment been serene in the face of death as he was astounded, these past few days, at having been able to live with his son far away. The fact that man is incomprehensible we know, not from other men, but from ourselves. How can one welcome the end of earthly enjoyment with equanimity? Yet those who do so – 'heroes', 'sages', 'saints' – are legion: dying 'well', the supreme vulgarity. Why, they're simply unhinged. After all, they may perhaps be men for whom life is insipid. The tragedy is not the loss of life but the loss of happiness. If there were no

happiness there would be no fear of death. That is the ultimate
punishment of the happy, the ultimate revenge of the 'vale of
tears' school: the infallible prescription for dying without
horror is to have been sick of life. Costals was paying for
having enjoyed life madly, and for wanting to still. It was the
existence of beautiful creatures that made him a coward,
divine faces that gave him such horror of non-being. 'To think
that I shall never see all that again!' Then he remembered a
sentence he had written in one of his books: 'I shall not die,
for my passions hold me to the earth.' It was his passions that
were casting him out of this earth, yet it was to them still
that he turned to keep him there. It was from them, and them
alone, that he wished to receive all that was good and all that
was evil.

His thoughts drifted towards his work. 'I bequeath to the
world something that is dear to it,' said the dying Byron. As
for him, he would bequeath to the world something against
which the world had never ceased to protest. Yesterday he
had thought that four more years of life would give him time
to finish at least the slice of work on which he was at present
engaged. Illusion! Under the shadow of death and physical
pain and gradual debilitation, a man may write a few scattered
pages, but he cannot produce a finished work. Thus, for
want of a few years, he would leave behind an incomplete
and unworthy picture of himself. (And what joy his disappearance would give to his fellow-writers! Ah! that
alone should be enough to keep him alive!) However, this
regret tormented him less than regret for lost pleasures –
and one other regret.... For at this moment his mind turned
towards his pleasures, towards his work, and also towards
his son: the only three things that had mattered to him
in life.

His son! 'What will become of him? What happens to someone who has no one to love him?' The blow was so sharp that
he put his hand over his eyes. It was always the same: a life
in which reason was supreme, that is to say a life of non-
suffering; but it was enough for him to care for a single being,
and his soul was plunged into anxiety and servitude. 'It's
horrible to love someone,' he blurted out aloud. 'Ah! why did

I bring him into the world! Without him, and without him alone, I would have gone through life like an invulnerable dragon. . . .' In accordance with his habit of jotting down there and then every emotional experience, he wrote on a blank page of one of the letters he had just collected : 'I remember that day last April when I went to see my son in Cannes and stayed at (*the name of a grand hotel*) because there were builders working in the house. I remember that beautiful morning when we sat on a bench in the garden of the hotel. Everything was in flower; a hose fluttered its quavering comet's tail over the red tennis court; the blue distances flaunted their villas hanging there like apples of power and happiness. My son was sitting on my left, reading a booklet describing the eleven scientific ways of drowning oneself according to the rules with a skiff one has built oneself – his feet on a garden chair, his head resting on my shoulder, and from time to time butting me like a young goat. When a breeze blew a cloud of spray over his face from another near-by hose, he shut his eyes and smiled. I said to him : "Do behave yourself! The gardeners can see you." And he, pouting like a badly brought-up child of the rich, replied : "Well, you pay enough here." ' Costals stopped writing. In evoking this memory he had been trying to clutch at something that would show his son in a bad light, looking for an escape hatch through which to escape from the prison of loving him. And he could see that there was indeed a slightly vulgar side to him; but it was no use, he still loved him. It was him he would take to the grave with him, like one of those stone knights on their tombs with their little pages at their feet. 'No, no, I don't want to lose all that!'

Who would believe it? Those horrible tentacles and suckers he had grown in order to cling on to life eventually lost their strength and slackened their grip. One cannot sustain even the fear of death for long at a time; that subject, too, exhausts itself, like all the others. Then Costals opened his letters (all except one, from Andrée Hacquebaut, which he put away in his suitcase unopened) and sat down to answer them all conscientiously. He noticed how firm his handwriting was. 'For how much longer?' He caught a glimpse of his face in the mirror, and was astonished to see how hard and energetic its expression was. He thought of what was behind it, and sniggered.

Next day he sailed from Casablanca.

19

Andrée Hacquebaut   to Pierre Costals
Saint-Léonard (Loiret)   *Paris*
            Letter forwarded to Marrakesh.

                                                    17 March 1928

What childlike joy some women would retain until their hair was grey if they felt they were loved! You were so sweet four days ago, when we walked to the La Mutte crossroads together, that I feel quite revived. You forgave me the pain my last letter had caused you: the mistletoe reproaching the oak for preventing it from living its own life! In the three months since I started writing to you again, you could so easily have shown me, had you wanted to, that you were bored by me. You have not done so; therefore.... Anyway, heaven alone knows the pleasure I get from writing to you, the joy I've experienced through you during these three months. I watch over you as you watch over me. But watch over me well, I haven't yet had my full share of happiness. Perhaps, this time, you have accepted me for ever.... By the way, what is the significance of the heart I have only just noticed stamped inside the cover of those of your books which you sent me and which isn't on those I have bought?*

I saw that you used one of my recent letters† in your short story in *Candide*. I'm glad to come across myself in your writings, to think that, in creating them, you must have lived with me. And when you live with me like that, it makes me better, more of a woman.

---

*This mark, made by the publisher, indicated that these were complimentary copies and could not therefore be sold (*Author's note*).

†This letter had not been opened by Costals (*Author's note*).

A publicity van from the X store in Orleans came to Saint-Léonard the other day. What a mad desire I had to buy everything. I bought some boots. I'm crazy about my little boots. Booted and hacquebooted! And so rejuvenated! And you, when I took them off, you sat there holding one of them between your feet so caressingly, as though my foot were still inside it.

I've just been singing at the top of my voice a slow pre-war waltz, *Amoureuse*. Nothing releases me more than to sing madly some old refrain like that, in the most refrainish way possible.

Life is wonderful. Have I not got what I wanted? I wanted a unique place in your heart. Ah! how delicious it would be if I were a young widow with a flat in Paris and .... Oh, fiddlesticks!

This letter was filed away by the recipient, unopened.

20

On arriving in Morocco, Costals had written to Solange: 'I must pay tribute to the excellent behaviour of the sea during the crossing.' No tribute on the return journey: it's a real calamity, this element.

The sea blotted out three quarters of the port-hole – sometimes the whole of it – and it was simply unbelievable that it did not shatter it: perhaps it recoiled from the human stench that accumulated in every cabin of a French liner. Costals drew the curtain over the port-hole: no submarine life for me. But the curtain had been designed in such a way (a thoughtful touch) that its swaying to and fro ensured that you were fully aware of the degree of the ship's roll. Costals roused himself from a bout of nausea and lurched to the notice-board where the number of his lifeboat would be indicated. But it was a French ship, so the number had not been filled in. As for the lifebelts, no question about it, they could be relied on to keep a man afloat – but upside-down, because the tapes were too long. However, all was well. A pity about that tenacious fly, though: a fly that hasn't paid for its passage, and isn't sea-sick either – ah! no, it's too much.

There was no question of thinking, but of hanging on, with a glance at his watch every quarter of an hour: 'Only eighteen hours more. In twenty minutes, only seventeen hours. No, we're bound to be late. To hell with these calculations.' Costals, his nose blocked, sneezed and snuffled and blew. Was it rhinitis, one of the symptoms of leprosy? Then, a little later, an armpit and the inside of one of his thighs began to itch. And pruritus often occurs in the early stages of leprosy. . . .

The woodwork groaned. From time to time the whole ship quivered like a horse twitching its skin. At one moment. . . . that icy hand, it seemed to have lost all feeling. Costals pinched one of the fingers, and felt nothing. Sweat drenched his forehead. The anaesthesia of leprosy. Then the feeling in his hand returned. He realized that he had gripped the edge of the upper berth with that hand, and the blood had ebbed from it. But the cold in his head and the pruritus were still there.

At ten o'clock in the evening the sea calmed down a little. The agony ceased, and consciousness returned.

Consciousness.

It is difficult to appreciate the poets when your shoe is pinching. And the vast edifices of the soul come toppling down over a pitching ship, like a palace over an earthquake. Costals, having risen from that pocket of physiological misery, now collapsed into another pocket – of spiritual misery. There he found Christianity.

For anyone who has spent his childhood among Christians there is a good chance that later, whenever he feels frightened, Christianity will rise up in him again; until the day when, fortified by the power of ripe old age, he has finally eliminated the poison from his system. Costals did not hate Christianity. In order for him to hate this religion, it would have had to contaminate someone he loved. And everyone he loved was untouched by it. As for hating it as the religion of the 'enemies of the human race' (Tacitus), he was not sufficiently infatuated with the human race for that. He despised Christianity, nothing more. But, having been brought up in it, his memories enabled him to evoke it easily. And as a novelist he needed to make very little effort to put himself under the skin of a Christian: we have seen this with 'Marie Paradis'.

In the past few days he had contemplated his disease in a more detached way. Much good it had done him: now he was dreaming of how he might Christianize it! Oh! of course, there was no question of 'believing' – although he envied priests, whose faith must make them happy to die (assuming they *have* faith), but envied them as he envied animals, who he presumed (quite falsely) to have no fear of death. No, there was no question of believing. 'I wept and I believed' (Chateaubriand) remained in his eyes perhaps the most stupid remark in the whole of French literature. It was a question of toning up his ordeal by infusing it with a new kind of poetical substance. He would enter a lay order, retire to a monastery. A leper in the world is pitiful and horrible. But a leper who, thanks to his disease, rediscovers 'the path to the old altars', was both photogenic and elevating: a proved recipe, one of those clichés of the bogus-sublime, sure in its effect. The absurd respect manifested towards the histrionics of monasticism even by the majority of non-believers would reach new heights if the monk's cowl were to cover rotting sores. (It is worth noting that a consumptive who rediscovered 'the path to the old altars' would be of no interest at all.) Costals worked himself up over all this bric-à-brac. No, it could not be said that he was thinking of making a career in Catholico-Hansenian romance, as others in Judaeo-liturgical gush or in Pederasthomism. But he toyed somewhat complacently with a possible 'persona'. It was the same process as at the Bibliothèque Nationale, when he had sought out stirring images about marriage which would make his own bearable. When he had gone skirmishing against Abd el-Krim as a volunteer, it was because he had worked out a formula for himself whereby the taste for adventure prevailed over the fear of death. Now he was working up a formula which would allow him to feel that it was a good thing to die of leprosy. In creating a *persona* for himself he was taking a hair of the dog that bit him; he was sinning through literature, but he was saving himself through his sin. And if a man as remarkable as Goethe, after having written 'There are four things that are as hateful to me as poison and snakes: tobacco smoke, bugs, garlic and the crucifix', could nevertheless dare to say later 'I would rather that Catholicism did me harm, than that I should be prevented from using it to make my plays more interesting', who could throw stones at one who dreamed of using Catholicism, not to make his works 'more interesting', but to make a leper's life more liveable? He was taking a dose of religion as one takes a dose of quinine.

There were also moments when he seriously believed his passion for coition would prevent him from having leprosy! 'When I get back to Paris and hold Guiguite in my arms, the disease that was taking shape inside me will be nipped in the bud. No, it's inconceivable that such a love of life should fail to get the better of death, it's inconceivable that a certain intensity of joy should fail to repel death.' At other times he thought (still quite seriously) that when he had made love to Guiguite or another once, once only, he would be ready to accept death. He remembered what a nurse had once told him about a badly wounded soldier who tore off his medals and yelled at her with a terrible look in his eyes: 'To hell with France. To hell with medals. All I want is one more f— before I croak.' (Might there not be women who would perform that function as a duty, for men doomed to die? Could not a charity be created for such a purpose? Or better still, why not an order of nuns who would specialize in this sublime form of charity?)

And here he was back in shabby old antiquated, ill-equipped France. No bootblacks, no taxis at the stations, no one to carry your luggage, cigarettes that go out all by themselves. Picard, his manservant, was not at the avenue Henri-Martin. Having gone back to his home in the country during Costals' absence, no doubt he had failed to receive in time the letter asking him to return to Paris. There was a hideous fusty smell in the flat, and a hint of stale tobacco (Picard must have been smoking there and forgotten to open the windows). And another atmosphere: that of a house in which someone has died and which has not been occupied since. And the same old neighbour behind her window. 'Another one who hasn't yet croaked!'

In these empty, dusty, funereal rooms, with their dirty window-panes and rolled-up carpets, another wave of cowardly weakness overcame him, as though the spectres of all the weakness and hysteria that for five months had plagued him here were now assailing him : here, the spirit of Solange took possession of him again. He did not have the heart to unpack, to add to the clutter in his study ('Mind you don't move anything, Picard'). He was cold : it was the 27th of April, the heating was turned off, and the season was hanging back. As was his habit, he stretched himself out on his bed.

It must be borne in mind that at this moment (1) he was a man faced, as far as he knew, with ten years of horrible and incurable disease; (2) his resistance had been lowered by the shock he had received in the Atlas and a day's journey over the mountains, partly on mule-back, followed almost immediately by an eight-hour bus-ride, by seventy-five hours of raging seas, and seven hours in a train; (3) that this cold and dilapidated flat oozed depression from every cranny; and (4) that the shade of Solange, which was omnipresent here, was for him a baleful presence. Small wonder, then, that, lying on his bed, he should give way to self-pity once more. And his cowardice, which on the boat had flowed quite naturally towards religion (whose phantasms had since been dispelled), here quite naturally flowed in the direction of woman. Woman the 'consolatrix'! Woman the 'guardian angel'! Absurd and pernicious preconception of the male, when all it amounts to is this : a defeated man – even if only momentarily defeated – taking refuge with the eternally defeated : the female. (In antiquity, defeat was equated with womanliness; certain peoples, to humiliate their vanquished enemy, branded him with a triangle representing the female organ.) And in what woman did Costals seek refuge? Aberration! He sought refuge in Solange. He turned towards the woman who had done him so much harm, as a dog that has been struck by its master seeks refuge by crawling at its master's feet.

He remembered a notice he had read mechanically in the corridor of the train : 'Admission to the compartments may be refused to persons whose infirmities are of such a nature as to inconvenience other passengers.'

Like a stone dropped into a well, he seemed to hear himself fall into the bottomless pit of eternity.

An absurd idea was germinating inside him, like weeds that spring up from impoverished soil. To support, help, nurse this man whose body would soon be in the throes of decomposition, who better than Solange? With Solange, no more necropolis-flats, no more of this solitude which terrified him at such moments as this: she had freed him from the spell of solitude. Oh, there was not much nobility in this impulse of his: Costals was giving Solange the look of gratitude he had given to a sympathetic steward when he was sea-sick; but a sick man puts nobility second. Would Solange be prepared to marry him now, knowing his condition? In any case he would put the question in a vague, hypothetical form: 'Would you marry a leper if it was a man you loved?' And he was convinced that her answer would be yes.

On this pillow-case where his head was now resting, surely their heads had touched. Solange was there, and he spoke to her: 'I fled from you twice after giving you hope, and you forgave me. I broke my word, and you forgave me. I mistrusted you and your mother. Now I am making an act of faith in human nature. I am putting myself in your hands. Do what you like with me.' And he ended with a typical invalid's phrase: 'I want to live with my head in your lap.'

For a moment he had a passionate desire for this marriage to take place, and as soon as possible. He got up and rushed to the telephone. She must come tonight! If she delivered her 'yes' that evening, how much stronger he would feel when he heard the other 'yes', his doctor's: 'Yes, you have the disease'! But the telephone was dead. It must have been cut off during his absence, because, away in the Atlas, he pretended not to know where to pay his bill. So he would have to go out and send a telegram. Solitude, at other times so dear, now wore the face of desertion.... Well then, having dressed and gone out, he would take the opportunity of fleeing from the necropolis. His bags were still unpacked. He would go to a hotel, at least until the following day.

At the hotel he wondered what to do. And then his strength reasserted itself (perhaps it was also because the room was clean and tidy). He went back to his work, as a cat goes back to the mouse to tease it a bit more. He settled down at a table and took up his manuscript again at the point where he had left it in the Atlas the day he had discovered the spot. As in the avenue Henri-Martin, when he was working serenely between two pre-nuptial affairs, everything else was obliterated. A man will believe that, were he to see hand-cuffs on his wrists, he would faint. When he has them on, not only does he not faint, but he realizes that it is perfectly possible to enjoy a drink with hand-cuffs on your wrists. In the same way Costals – convinced that sooner or later this writing hand would be a shrivelled stump, that pus would flow from his nostrils, that his genitals would rot away and drop off – scribbled and scratched out and devoted three minutes of his short life to finding the 'exact word'. When the telephone rang (Solange saying whether or not she was going to come), he made an impatient gesture.

After all, there are women, too, who take up their knitting, just like that, after a great upset. . . .

2 1

Solange had resigned herself without any reservations to the fact that Costals was not going to marry her. Unfulfilled desires become reabsorbed – as we shall see presently with the other heroine of this tale. Resigned : but she nevertheless retained for him, incoercibly, an affection tinged with love. 'Like iron to a magnet. . . . I'm attached to him like iron to a magnet.' The letters she received from Africa, so tender, so regular, convinced her that this affection was reciprocated. 'No, no! I don't want to lose you !' The cry that had burst from her went on echoing still. 'No matter what, as long as I can remain on the same terms with him as when he left.' The loss of their physical relations did not bother her. The loss of his kisses and attentions, or merely his presence, for good, was unthinkable (losing them for a time she could bear without too much pain). If, from Morocco, Costals had renewed the proposition whereby she would spend part of each week at the avenue Henri-Martin (but he was careful not to do so, only too pleased that she had failed to grasp that life-line), she would not have reacted with the indignation she had shown when he had suggested it three months before; she had not taken long to knuckle under. She melted at the thought of Genoa, and quite shamelessly had asked in one of her letters whether they might not return to Italy. He had excused himself on some pretext or other. Not long afterwards she had returned to the charge, but her ambitions had lowered: could they not, in the spring, have a little escapade of three or four days on the outskirts of Paris. He had replied evasively.... Of course, Solange was not unaware that she would lose him altogether when she married – but there was plenty of time to think of that. Girls are always convinced that 'it' will happen of its own accord.

Mme Dandillot had received Costals' 'latest' without too much distress. And with even less surprise, for she had never shared Solange's confidence in the solidity of their engagement. Perhaps, too, her widowhood enabled her to withstand the blow more easily: she was put out, but she did not let it get on her nerves, as it would have done if M. Dandillot had been a third party in the affair, and it is nerves, above all, that are women's undoing. Thus, ten years before, she had felt much stronger, much more mistress of herself, from the day she had started sleeping in her own room (*her* bed, in which she could shift about as she liked, *her* sheets, which were only used for her!): marriage is hell with a communal bedroom; with separate rooms it is no more than purgatory; without cohabitation at all (simply meeting twice a week), it might be paradise. Incapable of vindictiveness, except towards her husband, Mme Dandillot bore Costals no grudge. She was content to take refuge in platitudes, which are the haven of all women. A woman has too much need to feel protected to stray very far from platitudes. 'Disillusionment is all one can expect from men. Such is life. The best thing to do is to love . . . a Dream. Illusion is best because it forms the basis of our poor human loves. . . . ' With such vacuous nonsense she lulled Solange, and lulled herself, as one lulls infants to sleep with stories about elves.

She was, as we know only too well, defenceless where her daughter was concerned. She sought in Solange the justification of her own existence: as often happens, mediocrity in her case

expressed itself in unselfishness. She had advised Costals to
'travel', but she had not forbidden him all relations with
Solange. Their mutual correspondence was not much to her
liking, because it kept alive in the girl a feeling which it would
have been wiser to suppress; at the same time, seeing the
happiness it gave Solange, she refrained from asking Costals to
disappear for good and all. These muddled women wallowed in
ambiguity, a state to which they were suited by nature. When
Solange alluded, as though to something that went without
saying, to the relations she would resume with Costals on his
return 'on a footing of simple friendship', Mme Dandillot did
not turn a hair. She realized that one day she would have to
insist that the situation be brought to an end, if she was to
get her daughter married (for she did not, any more than
Solange, imagine them continuing once Solange was married).
But she put off this decision, vaguely hoping that one or other
of them would tire of it all and break it off without her having
to intervene.

Solange, therefore, on her way to Costals' hotel, had the
impression that she was taking up her life again more or less
at the point where she had left it three months earlier: one
simply stepped over the corpse of the Hippogriff and carried
on. She had even, though she still wore a little make-up,
reverted to her pre-engagement hair style. The permanence,
the immutability of all these women: Andrée Hacquebaut,
Rhadidja, Solange.

Costals awaited her in the hotel lounge, in order to have
an excuse for not kissing her, for fear of contagion. When she
held up her face and he said: 'Not in public. Later on,' she was
a little taken aback. But his words were at once so sweet and
tender. How simply everything picked up again! And this
time, if there was the melancholy of transitory things (a
transitoriness that might perhaps last a long time), there was
also the restfulness of no longer having to try, of no longer
being tense and strained. And of no longer having to torment
him, of seeing him happy, now that things were at last as he
liked them and as he always wanted their relationship to be: a
liaison, nothing more.

Costals had decided not to talk to her seriously until after

dinner. Dinner, in a restaurant, was full of ease and gaiety. He
told her about his travels and his work. He rummaged in her
hand-bag as of old, making amiably disobliging remarks about
the absurd objects he found in it. He teased her, for he teased
even the women he did not love. She told him that her boils
and her decalcification were over. 'It was a foregone conclusion : I had only to tell you I'd never marry you for you
to be restored to health. And I'm sure our urine is no longer
pale !' (It was true that in the past three months all her 'little
troubles' had vanished, although logically they should have
increased after the final blow; but the body is no more logical
than the soul. Unless patent medicines.... But that would be
too simple, wouldn't it ?) He refrained from swearing at her
when, every time he turned his head, she took the opportunity
of extracting her various appliances from her bag and touching
up her face. He talked very loud, as very young people do,
and since whatever he said was always 'impossible', she
(sitting on her gloves – one of her idiosyncrasies) had to reprimand him : 'Not so loud !'

'Everything's so like it was a month ago,'* she exclaimed.
'The same table in the same restaurant.... I'd never have
thought, when you went away, that one day we'd meet again
here.'

A little rashly, for it is always a mistake to rub people's
noses in their defeats, Costals said :

'But something in you has changed. I have a feeling that if
I suggested that you should come and live with me from time
to time, you'd accept. And yet you jibbed at the idea in January.'

'I've already told you that people would get to know, and
the scandal would rebound on Mummy. But there might be a
compromise solution. Without *living* in your flat, I could come
and spend part of the day there a few days a week, breathe
the same atmosphere as you, take part in your daily life. I'd
be taken for your secretary, and besides, I could be in fact :
I'd so much like to do something for you, for your work. And
why shouldn't you say I was your cousin? Surely we could
find a vague family link somewhere.'

---

*Pardonable inaccuracy (*Author's note*).

'You know quite well you ought to be thinking about getting yourself married. And yet you'd be prepared to spend part of your life with me, more or less as a recognized mistress (who do you think would be taken in by the "secretary" or "cousin" business?), and at the same time play the part of the pure young thing with your future husband!'

Her face took on the disconsolate look of a little girl faced with an insoluble problem in arithmetic.

'How could you think for a moment that it wouldn't be painful for me? But since it has to be. . . .'

'What do you mean "It has to be"?' asked Costals (who understood perfectly well).

'It has to be, because I love you. But you've never wanted to believe that I loved you.'

'It's true. Perhaps because, usually, that solution – that a woman loves me – is one I don't care for. Nevertheless at this moment I'm touched that you should love me, after all I've done to you. We'll come back to your plan later on. It depends on something I must tell you after dinner.'

A little later she said a terrible thing. She had written to him while he was in Morocco to tell him that a Norman pig-breeder had proposed to her.

'Perhaps I shall settle for him one day,' she said now.

'Rather than Tomasi?'

'Yes, you see, *I don't know* the Norman one.'

In the cloak-room, she helped him on with his coat. He found this fitting. *Ancilla domini.*

On the way back to the hotel, he said to her: 'Now I must tell you. . . . I'm not absolutely sure, but I'm almost sure that I caught a serious disease in Morocco. It's not a very contagious disease, contrary to what people think, but there's a risk that it may be if one doesn't take certain precautions. We can go on seeing each other, but our intimate relations must cease. I'll tell you about it in my room.'

She walked on in silence, her eyes focused on the toes of her shoes. Finally she said:

'I think I can guess.'

'You can't have guessed. You think, don't you, that it's one of those diseases that are called venereal?'

'Yes.'

'It isn't that.'

In the lift she looked at him in silence, visibly nervous and perplexed. When they were inside the room he said:

'Sit down there.'

He had not switched on the light. She switched it on. He switched it off again. Through the shutters and the curtains, the red glow from a neon sign on a near-by cinema penetrated the dark room. The glow of hell. Just the thing for Mephisto and his sores.

She was sitting on a chair. He sat down on another chair beside her, facing her. He put his hand on her fore-arm. She took his hand, he drew it away. 'If you wish, you can put your hand on my fore-arm, on the sleeve. Not on the bare skin.' They held each other thus, with the 'hand-clasp' of ancient Rome, which was in fact a 'fore-arm clasp'.

'Don't be afraid. No emotionalism, please. If I really have this disease, and I'm convinced that I have, I might still live another ten years, with a great deal of nursing and a great deal of pain. I should end up as a hideous object, but there's no question of that: I shall kill myself when I have to. In the meantime, I shall remain more or less normal, and we can go on seeing each other for some time, provided we don't touch each other ... except through our clothes, as we're doing now....'

She showed no impatience, did not press him: 'But tell me what it is, for God's sake!...' Always Miss Silence. Petrified, waiting. Always waiting. Beneath their window, the bell of the cinema began to buzz. A voice yapped: 'Continuous performance. Big atmospheric hall. A film of love and adventure. All the latest news.' What was an 'atmospheric' cinema? Costals wondered. This gibberish threatened to break down his composure.

'Do you know what Hansen's disease is?'

'No.'

'Do you know what it means to be a *lazar*?'

'Lazar? I don't know.... It means to be poor. What do you....'

'Do you know what leprosy is?'

She took her hand away from Costals' arm as though she had had an electric shock. Whatever might happen subsequently, nothing could alter the fact that she had taken her hand away.

'But you haven't. . . . '

'Yes. At least, very probably.'

'No, no! It isn't possible!'

Beneath the red glow, he saw her terrified face. A perfect setting for 'hell'. With a burst of volubility he sought to bring himself back to human reality.

'You don't know anything about it. People imagine all sorts of things. There are three hundred lepers in Paris, only twenty of whom are hospitalized – and in public wards, too. Perhaps the waiter who served us. . . . There are women who've lived for thirty years with a leper husband without being infected. All this isn't a lot of guff I was given to reassure me. It *was* told to me, of course, but I've also read it in a medical text-book. You can buy one yourself.'

'But how did you catch it? If you *have* caught it, because I can't believe you have.'

'From a woman.'

(Truth is tantalizing as death.)

'Was she a bird of passage, or had she been your mistress for a long time?'

'She was my mistress for four years. A native girl.'

She stared at him, her eyes dilated, with that red glow upon her, like a night-bird nailed to a wall and covered with its own blood. And he stared back at her, like a small furry creature of the fields stiff with terror in the face of a bird of prey. Not even the imbecilities of the cinema, that prostitution of pathos, could diminish the pathos of those two faces : life held its own.

'If I frighten you, you can go away at once and never see me again. I should find that perfectly natural.'

'I'm not afraid. I believe everything you've told me. I know very well that if there were any danger you wouldn't have brought me here.'

What trust! And as though to give him a proof of it, she placed her hand on his fore-arm once more. Then she smiled at him.

'You told me not to get emotional. That warning was unnecessary. I shall be upset when the doctors have made a positive diagnosis. Until then, I don't believe in your leprosy – or I only half believe in it.'

Costals was not very pleased that she did not believe in his leprosy. If he had had to choose at that moment between having leprosy or not, perhaps he would have chosen to have it, simply in order to show her that he was not bluffing.

For a long time he talked to her about his disease. The bell from the cinema buzzed intermittently. Each time it began to buzz it reminded him of the door-bell ringing in some clandestine lodging when he was there with a woman and their liaison was threatened. In these casual lodgings he often forgot that he was not in his own flat. And he would go into the hall in his bare feet with a revolver in his hand to see if there was a shadow under the door: the shadow of the man who had rung the bell, who was waiting there, who would bang on the door with his fist, interminably, if you did not open. You and he, six inches from one another, separated by a mere plank. And you, with your bare feet on his shadow.

As he talked, Solange's face was calm, calmer than when she had entered the room. Calm and thoughtful. Putting the accent always on the *if*, she produced a string of consoling observations, all of them sensible. 'If you've got this disease, it might have been worse. You might have died suddenly, and you've told me often enough that your affairs were not in order. Ten years! How many people in good health are certain to live ten years, the way things are these days? Then there's war.... In ten years you'll be forty-five, and haven't you always maintained that by the age of forty-five most writers have said their say and simply go on repeating themselves?'

'How she hits the nail on the head!' thought Costals. 'I've often had proof that she didn't understand who I was. Now she seems to have understood perfectly. And so wise! She's a real brick, after all.' It was then that he put to her the question which the whole evening had been leading up to:

'Would you rather marry a leper you loved than a healthy man you didn't love?'

'Yes.'

After a brief silence she added:

'Of course.'

He asked her to lie down, if she would, fully dressed on the bed. 'I won't kiss you on your bare skin. Only on your clothes. Or rather I won't even kiss them, I'll simply put my face against them. And I'm going to wear my gloves.' 'Why gloves? You've got nothing on your hands.' He put them on, and stretched out beside her in the darkness that enveloped the bed, which was out of range of the red glow. The bell still buzzed from time to time in the cinema, but the barker no longer barked. She lay huddled in his arms, curled up as in her mother's womb. He remained thus for a long time, his cheek resting on her breast, groping for her face and her hands whenever he moved so as to avoid touching them with his mouth. He felt an inner peace, and a sort of sweetness which he did not know was the false sweetness of the sea as it laps against the shore and gleams there before dying away for ever. The noise of people coming out of the cinema told them it was time to part.

She sat on the edge of the bed, plaiting her hair which had come undone, like the little school-girl of old.

Next day, more in control of himself – because his fatigue had evaporated – Costals took the decision not only not to go ahead with the crazy project of marriage which he had conceived the day before, but also to space out his meetings with Solange until finally he put an end to them altogether, whatever might be the doctors' verdict on his condition.

There were two reasons for this. No, he would not marry, in order to turn her into a leper's nurse, the girl he had not wanted to marry when it was a question of making her his companion. Furthermore (and this was perhaps the more powerful reason), he refused to allow himself to be dragged into that perilous sphere in which one noble gesture is capped by another. The sublime must not be allowed to be omnipotent. The world would fare even worse than it does already if, in order to tip the scales to the baneful side, one had only to add an ounce of the sublime. Dying for a cause does not make that cause just. Solange had been sublime; that did not make marriage with her a solution any less absurd and fraught with dangers – quite unjustifiable. The watchword must be: 'Hold out against the temptation of nobility.' 'She was sublime, and I too must have been sublime, though I can't quite see in what way. So if we went on, it would be sure to end badly, for when one plays at being sublime. . . .'

Five days later, when they met again, they went neither to the hotel nor to his flat (he explained that this was because of his fear of contagion). They went to a concert like old friends, or rather like strangers to each other. It was all dissolving into indifference once more, as wadis dissolve into the sand, where they end up by ceasing to be altogether.

2 2

Ah! make the most of what we yet may spend.
OMAR KHAYYAM.

Every intelligent being cast on to this earth sets
out each morning in pursuit of happiness. STENDHAL.

Six days later, in the place Saint-Augustin. Half past five. Costals crossed the square in the direction of the Madeleine. Heavy spring weather, almost sticky: a fumigation of asphalt. The sun hidden behind a white haze so as to be able to work its mischief undisturbed, as in the Sahara. And fellows with silk scarves in a temperature of 18 degrees Centigrade, because silk scarves look 'rich'.

Costals had just come from seeing Dr Rosenbaum, after four days of consultations and examinations with various big-shots. There was nothing wrong with him. The spot was lichen, which is not serious. The nasal catarrh was the result of having caught cold on the deck of the liner in the sea-wind. The pruritus (which anyhow had gone) was caused by the change of air between Morocco and France – something that often happens. Costals having once told Rosenbaum that the mere fact of having bought some medicament, even before opening the bottle, made him feel better, Rosenbaum tended to assume that with Costals any illness was imaginary. (We really must firmly resist our inclination to make fun of ourselves.) So the doctor had teased him a little: 'You have a lively imagination.' Costals had flung him one of those looks of superb contempt which cured patients reserve for their doctors, the look he had given the lifebelt the other day when they were in sight of Bordeaux. 'He also told me I was as healthy as an ox. But perhaps that was because he's going to send me his bill within a week. He wants me to like him for a week, so that I'll pay him pronto.' It was true that Dr Lipschutz had also told him he had an iron constitution, while Professor Lévy-Dhurmer opined that he had the constitution of a Bolivian general. Costals, who liked to have things in writing, had replied uniformly to them all: 'Send me a certificate to that effect.'

Happy? Of course, happy. One hundred per cent happy? Let's say ninety per cent. But just as it is well known that a writer, reading a dithyrambic article about himself in which there is one word of reservation, sees only this one word, so it was the ten per cent of non-happiness that set the tone for Costals. Lazarus emerging from the tomb must also have had his ten per cent of non-happiness, and railed a bit against Jesus Christ.

For a fortnight, Costals' entire future had been based – and solidly based – on this disease. And now everything had to be turned upside down again. Moreover, this disease represented grandeur, and grandeur acquired on the cheap. Now grandeur would have to be (1) invented, (2) conquered, (3) organized. In the meantime, back to the humdrum and the prosaic: it was as though a door had been slammed in his face. Rosenbaum had been right when he had made the classic remark of the doctor to the cured patient: 'You're no longer interesting.' And Costals caught himself murmuring a phrase that he regarded as blasphemy, a phrase he repudiated, spat upon – and yet a phrase that in spite of himself had risen from the depths of his being to his lips: 'Nothing but life....' Did he not love life? Of course, but leprosy had seemed to him an opportunity for a fuller life.

Not to mention the various inconveniences of perfect health. Since he had believed himself to have leprosy, he had cancelled all the lectures he was to have given that spring, had made up his mind to default on his contractual engagements – in short, had relieved himself of all obligations towards society. And now.... Well, no! He would pretend to be convalescing from a serious illness, pneumonia or suchlike, and give himself a rest. The moribund state has too many advantages to be relinquished just like that.

But enough of this nonsense. Spotting a pimply passer-by, he had shuddered: it reminded him of *something*. Besides, if he was so keen on leprosy, all hope was not lost: the incubation is so slow.... At the centre of his ninety per cent of happiness, there was normal life with his son, back with him again. One of the drawbacks of illness is that it forces us to pay attention to ourselves rather than to those we love. During the last week he had made up his mind that if he was given a clean bill of health, he would bring his son back from England; Philippe thenceforth would live in Paris. *Vita nuova*. The cry that had burst from his lips in the hotel room in Marrakesh: 'What will become of him? What happens to somebody who has no one to love him?' – that cry that he could not repeat to himself without being overcome with emotion (it often happened to him to be shattered by something he himself said, or by a sentence in one of his own books) – it was that that had clinched his decision. 'When one wants to make someone happy, one must do it at once.'

And at the centre of his ten per cent of non-happiness was the fate of Rhadidja. He would look after her. Already he had spoken about her to Rosenbaum, who wanted her to be treated in France, in Paris, or rather at Valbonne. He would write to Rhadidja to this effect. He would do everything that could be done.

The Madeleine.... The step on which he had sat with Solange on the first night of their engagement.... That nightmare, like the other, was over, and he was rediscovering the fresh joy of his sixteenth year. 'Freed from these two leprosies, O primal purity! May I now prove worthy of this purity!'

The temple known as the Madeleine, although exaggeratedly

filthy, is one of the rare monuments in Paris which may be said to have some majesty. Costals felt an urge to go in. For he was a religious-minded man. If he had never raised his head towards the sky in supplication, he instinctively raised it in thanksgiving. In thanksgiving to whom? The Spirit who ruled over his destiny. Which was tantamount to thanking himself.

The Madeleine was the only Christian sanctuary in Paris which Costals could tolerate. Was it in memory of this doughty deed: as a little boy, in this holy place, he had once stuck his tongue out at an unknown young woman praying? (The young woman complained to the child's English governess, who recounted the doughty deed at home: 'He's a tiger.' Mme Costals had recalled this story years later when she said to her son: 'You're so naughty.... Some day you'll become the Anti-Christ.' To which the fifteen-year-old had replied: 'I couldn't be bothered.') Was it the memory of Mgr Rivière, once curé of the Madeleine, a Diocletian who was wont to flourish his over-scented hands under the noses of the little girls in catechism class, all of whom were in love with him? Chiefly it was because the Madeleine was the only church in Paris in which there was practically no trace of Christianity. For nine years the Temple of Glory under Napoleon, to Costals that was what it remained: the Temple of Glory, that of the individual and that of the nation. But it was also many other things.

A temple of syncretism, in particular. A temple of the disparate – the disparities of the world, the disparities of each of its creatures. On the pediment, to the left of Zeus-Sabazius-Christ, a naked young Dionysus with disquieting hips; to the right, another naked ephebe, the Spirit of the Dance, or some other brother of Carpeaux's bacchic dancer. Inside, a temple devoid of mystery and devoid of humbug: nothing in its pockets, nothing up its sleeve – in other words the opposite of Christianity. Behind the altar, beautiful winged urchins bringing forth from a shell, like Aphrodite of old, the modern Aphrodite, Magdalen, the holy *puta*. The sinner, with downcast eyes and a charmingly bulging nine-month belly, half opening her arms in a gesture of resignation which seems to say: 'It was bound to happen to me one of these days....' What a pleasure not to be in a temple dedicated to the Virgin – that Virgin of whom the gospel hardly speaks, of whom we know nothing except that her son abandoned her; that Virgin who was not a virgin, and who as a mother is non-existent; that Virgin who was simply an instrument for making the Word incarnate, as terrestrial virgins in the last resort are no more than instruments for reproducing mankind. A temple of the Nation, of Glory, but also a temple of the Courtesan, erected on the threshold of that 'right bank' which is the courtesans' playground (whence the fact that its façade at night is symbolically illuminated with potassium permanganate*), Costals was in the habit of visiting it whenever he had made a conquest on the boulevards. Pick-up and up-lift. He went there to give thanks.

Today, once more, Costals gave thanks. But he also besought the unknown Presence to give him the strength and the audacity to think of his happiness unceasingly. He made a resolution to remind himself continually that his happiness must come first, that he must not allow himself to be put off by anything or anyone. Solemnly he made this resolution. Then, on the way out, he halted for a moment on one of the steps.

Paris ... white, grey, black, dirty, polluted, like sheets after a night's coupling. Nothing beautiful in what lay before him, except perhaps, under the milky sky, those buds of such a tender green one would have wished to protect it. They heralded the spring, season of purity and impurity, that great vessel which could be seen looming on the horizon, after the long wait, bringing the perfumes of unknown lands. And nothing strong, save this unscrupulous crowd and its infinite possibilities. Once, as an adolescent, walking with his parents on the Grands Boulevards, he had heard his father say: 'On the Boulevards, everybody's for sale.' As a result, he had conceived for the boulevards a respect arrowed with hope: already the river of his concupiscence was overflowing its banks. Later a doubt came to him: 'But I too was on the boulevards that day. And my parents. And we're not for sale. So there are exceptions, alas. ... ' Nevertheless, he had never forgotten his father's words.

---

*In 1928, the façade of the Madeleine was illuminated at night with violet flood-lighting, a masterpiece of bad taste (*Author's note*).

Beneath him, on the viscous pavement, flowed the race of men, of sub-men and of women, a vast stream of liquid manure which split in two at the foot of the temple and into which it was his destiny to discharge his male liquid, the purest of the substances secreted by the human organs – the only pure substance – innocent and pure as a grain of wheat. The baseness of this Parisian crowd, how he had hated it in the past! There was a time when he used to lower his eyes when he passed these women of Paris, for fear that some passer-by might think he desired them: he would have been ashamed.* Now he loved this baseness: 'It's my raw material.' The Latin gorilla, the Parisian marmoset, the fish-complexioned *pétroleuse*,† the *sans-culotte* with his foul mouth and girlish voice, all those grey people intent on evil-doing – stealing, cheating, f—ing, wangling, skulking – all this (external) Judeo-Latin licentiousness which horrifies and fascinates the decent Nordic, because it testifies to the licentiousness within and promises that here all things are possible – it was this sun-beaten dung (dung of body and soul) that he spread over his soil and that made it sprout so thickly. He knew, too, that there were plenty of pearls in this dunghill – and 'does one disregard a diamond because one has found it in the mud?' (Fénelon) – and purity in this filth, like the white teeth in the jaws of a dead dog.

As it happened, today he felt disposed towards the hunt, for he had not shaved that morning. And when he went hunting women he liked to be unshaven and rather scruffily dressed so as to make the sport more difficult and in particular to make it clear that he despised his quarry and, so to speak, dominated his subject: put myself out for them! let them take me as I am! there are plenty more like her! His beard increased his self-confidence – 'To hunt with a beard I must be really good at it!' – and at the same time provided him with an excuse in case of failure: 'Not surprising, when I'm as

---

*'They [Parisian women] are at most passable-looking, and generally plain rather than handsome.' – J.-J. Rousseau, *La Nouvelle Héloïse* (Author's note).

†A reference to the female incendiaries who, during the Paris Commune of 1871, emptied paraffin into the basements of houses and set it alight (*Translator's note*).

hairy as an ape!' For the first time since his return, he was also without either overcoat or hat: relieved of these symbols of respectability, a man is reborn, like a woman who has had her hair cut short: a light-infantryman without *impedimenta*, he can pursue the adversary more easily, as brisk and lively as the people one said good-bye to on the boat at noon, crumpled, haggard and dishevelled, and meets again at three o'clock parading along the harbour front all spick and span. Then he lit a cigarette. Then, with the same instinctive gesture as the caveman 'girding his loins' before venturing forth, or the soldier tightening his belt before zero hour, or the matador pulling his cape tight to his waist as he enters the ring, he buttoned the middle button of his jacket and plunged into the jungle. Just as wild beasts emerge from their lairs each day in search of food, so he resumed his regular way of life, which was to set forth each day in search of fresh prey. Less from a need of prey than from a need of the hunt: as Lessing said, if God offered him the truth he would refuse it, loving the search for it so much; and a shell that has burst is no longer interesting, it's the one on the way that excites you. Today, Costals had no great hunger, but he was taking the plunge because he thought: 'So those swine would like to stop me doing what I want to do, would they!' When other motives were weak in him, this one would decide him without fail.

Worshippers of love should draw the following conclusion from all this: that every man who falls ill becomes good and forgives all, while the first impulse of the man who has recovered is to run amuck. The nurse, almost before she looks at the thermometer, knows that the patient's temperature has dropped: he looks a regular shark again. Evil becomes identified with life (whence the fact that a man in good health always wants war, his life force demands it, even though his reason shows him how much good might be done in peacetime with the virtues expended in war). Thus all the forces of society are pitted against life, which is apt to cause far too much trouble; unable to attack life directly through men's bodies, which they need for the strength of the nation, they attack it through men's souls, inoculating them with morality and religion. Costals, strolling along the boulevards, amused himself by jostling people (especially old trouts of both sexes), or charging straight at them to see if they would step aside. And they always did, with never a protest : they were French-men of the 1928 vintage (just try and play rugby in the streets of Algeria or Spain or Italy !). True, he had no illusions about these billowing women with their generous backsides and their faces smeared with cream like tumours smeared with oint-ment, and he recognized that they hardly deserved to be coveted. His desire was simply to set his seal, his P.C., on each of them, and never to hear of them again – this for the pleasure a farmer feels as he surveys a flock of sheep all marked with his brand.

On he went, sizing up each passer-by at a glance, the women to see what there was to be had from them, the men to see what to guard against. He interrogated each face, turning away from one, following another, half tracker, half tracked, half savage, half coward – exactly like a beast of prey. He took a terrifying pleasure in this jungle, as much from being himself on the alert as from putting others on the alert. Fear swept over him in waves, like a thin film of spray over a rock ; this rock was his belief that he bore a charmed life : *Gott mit uns.* With his youth, his health, his effrontery, his writings, his charming son, his string of young mistresses, and all the advan-tages of power without any of its disadvantages, he felt himself invulnerable : stronger, more supple, more resistant, more malevolent than they. With his head jutting forward like a snake's, sniffing danger and prey from afar, and a slight thick-ness in the neck like the ox which Rosenbaum had seen in him, he was both ox and snake ; and the life force, the urge to take, to hurt, to corrupt, to deceive, stood out on his face not in a sweat, but in a sort of glowing veneer – glittering like Moses descending from Mount Tabor. And all this time he was creating, in the course of this feral prowl. And he would create better still, once he had offered up a sacrifice. The more he sacrificed, the more he wanted to sacrifice : his finest captures were always made when he had just finished sacrificing, was almost on his last legs, but nevertheless all set ; and he was the better fitted for it then, for the rails over which many trains pass are clean and shining, whereas little-used tracks rust. Doctors tell us that the sexual capacity of living organisms is far more considerable than people suspect. Costals had never perceived the slightest difference in intellectual or physical vigour, in lucidity and self-control – everything, in short, that makes a man's worth – between those periods when he indulged in apparently excessive delights and those during which (in the war, at sea, or in the mountains) he was forced into total abstinence. On the contrary, the more he sacrificed, the better his form, both in mind and body. When he was on his last legs – quick, a sacrifice! And he came out of it renewed, as delighted with himself as a doggie that has just done its business and immediately rushes round like a madman. Literally, a copious amorous excretion was necessary to his health.

Resuscitated from that other world – the world of disease and death, the world of despair and absurd projects to avoid being engulfed by it all – he was coming back to life, to *his* life, like a convalescent on his first outing, or a colonial officer who finds himself in a town for the first time after the dangers and hardships of two years in the desert. Whence the element of frenzy he injected into such a trivial act as walking along these drab boulevards. Whence, after ten minutes' walk, his almost unbearable nervous excitement, his abnormal anxiety – anxiety about the impending catch, anxiety about possible failure, anxiety about a possible *cogida*.* There was the dragon of Disease, which he had eluded, the Hippogriff which he had slain, the monster of Work, which he laid low each day; now there was also this Gorgon to be flung on her back without too much compunction. Already his eyelids ached, already his cheeks were hollow with fatigue, for his constant chagrin had come back to him – the chagrin of being unable to 'tumble' the whole youth of this city without a single exception. Just before he arrived at the corner of the rue de Richelieu (where there is a house with a double exit: pirates please note), he withdrew into a courtyard for a moment and closed his eyes to calm the palpitations that rose inside him – and also to allow his face to relax; a face so tense, so avid, so cunning, so give-away, that it seemed to him it must mark him out to

---

Cogida: goring of the torero by the bull (*Author's note*).

all as someone to be distrusted, when there was nothing he wished more than to pass unnoticed and to lull suspicion.

Faint voices, ridiculously feeble, voices from another world, from a world of shadows and ghosts, broke out above the crowd with the sour tinkle of a broken clavicord, or perhaps, rather, the cantilena of a foetus: 'Bibles for sale!' The monstrous ugliness of these Nazarenes explained everything. Costals turned his head away. He suffered from his outbursts of anger and loathing, as far as possible avoided anything that might occasion them.

At the corner of the faubourg Montmartre, he debated whether or not he desired a passing woman; there was an indefinable shabbiness about her footwear that was full of promise; in fact it was a very near thing. He took out a coin and tossed for his desire, heads or tails, in the palm of his hand. He let the woman go.

Opposite the rue Rougemont, having given an old man a light, he felt he had performed an act of altruism. One does what one can.

A little further on, he shuddered. The sun, traversing the five figures stencilled in the turned-down roof of a bus, above the platform, traced a number on the back of one of the passengers. With this number in large, garish figures on his dark jacket, the man suggested a convict. 'Hm!' grunted Costals. After a pause he added: 'But is there anything that is not worth experiencing?'

At the faubourg Poissonnière he slipped into a urinal. He had seen an ex-mistress of his approaching, and trembled at the thought that the end of such a promising day might be ruined by charity. He had no desire for her, but out of kindness would feel himself obliged, if they ran into one another, to spend the evening with her in some place of entertainment instead of getting on with the chase. 'No, God will not abandon me,' he repeated to himself in the urinal. Which was not blasphemy, since he did not believe in God. God did not abandon him: the ex-mistress vanished.

Then once more he plunged into the jungle.

And already he thought of the coming night reposing on his peaceful face, a night without demons and without dreams.

And already he thought of the first streak of approaching day, when the lights of the city tremble pitifully, as though they knew they had only a few minutes more to live, while the highest star, which knows that it too must soon be extinguished, stiffens and does not tremble. Early morning, an unappreciated hour compared to those literary sunsets, like a fastidious person who does not seek the limelight. And the solemnity of dawn: what will this day bring? Uncertainty in face of the day, as in face of a young life. And already he would be at his desk, lucid and pure and tenacious, his eyes soothed with sweet sleep.

And the first noise would be the jingling of the milk-cans brought by the milkman's boy. And he would go to his window, his chest all honey-coloured with the first rays of the morning, and he would feel the sunlight vibrating against his person. He would go to his window, so that the first face he saw should be a youthful one, a greeting and a sign of hope for the day to come.

And there would be the joy of water, the ancient joy of Triton and of Rome, *ludus matutinalis* (he had made one huge bathroom of his life). And the perpetual astonishment that a glass of cold water did not cost six francs in a restaurant, so much better is it than all their alcohols; the perpetual astonishment that our minglings with our aquatic partner are not a 'sin', so good they are, that one is not liable to four years' imprisonment without remission for getting into a bath; the perpetual astonishment, too, that one does not risk getting GPI by letting water flow over one's skull. Oh, the certitudes of sensation! And unpunished, too! And whose only limit is satiety!

And he would go out and walk into the Bois, where the birds would still be singing for themselves alone, his manuscript and fountain-pen in his hand, working as he walked. There would be the *insulae* of the ignoble rich, and soon the humble race of early morning people, drudging in their midst without hating them: the paper-pickers, all of whom he knew, and to whom he would say 'Good morning'; the rustic, dawdling roadmenders; the keepers, who are incapable of showing you the way to Bagatelle; the butchers' boys on their carrier-tricycles who, on seeing him, would show off by speeding along on two wheels, as a dog, the moment it sees you, lifts its leg in order to impress you; the night-watchman going home after having protected the rich, who will never be killed because they pay men of the people to be killed in their place, just as they will go to heaven because their relations will have paid for plenty of Masses for them.

Then, one by one, the sporting cranks, in sweaters, running, stopping, making rhythmic movements. And then the rich, who dig in their heels to avoid paying their divorced wives alimony, and shove their only sons into boarding schools, but walk the spaniel in the Bois every morning, not because it wants to walk but because it cost two thousand francs. And the little bourgeois boys, floating along in the air, lightly, like soap-bubbles. And the wan-faced satyrs, with their swift and restless eyes (underlined with pouches), affecting a supreme off-handedness.

And, in the background, the blueish Seine, blueish hills, a blueish mist, a pointed steeple evoking all the spirituality of France, etc.... (if I can't think up a flowery phrase for the steeple, I'm not a man), little boats which lower their funnels when they are covered by a bridge, with a gesture that somehow smacks of a woman succumbing. And the show-offs, male and female, in the riding alleys, and the little, shining, well-polished horses, waggling their bottoms in the most improper way, but above all proud of the veins standing out on their foreheads. And the little crosspatch urchins (you can tell from their faces that they're fuming inside) on bikes the colour of dragon-flies and poison, colours never seen except in oases – astonishingly serious urchins, pedalling in a dream (that they're doing the Tour de France), bunched together and jostling the uncomprehending butterflies out of the way. And the religious silence of the bunch as it goes by.

And everywhere he would recognize places where he had bored or debased himself with women, and at each of them he would shy internally, like a horse that passes a crossroads where it once saw a viper. And he would reject these places, but the pleasure of rejecting them would be such that it was as if he were going through the experience again. And passing in front of the thicket where he had kissed Solange for the first time, he would think to himself: 'Dead men tell no tales.'

And he remembered that in a week's time his son would be with him here, in this very place, on his bike with its emerald wings, insisting on doing a balancing act in a forbidden alley, and putting his hand on his shoulder every time the bike gave up the ghost. . . .

And off they would go, amid the laughing birds, in the grace of the morning.

2 3

I drive thee on pitilessly, knowing thy suffering.
Song of the Bedouin of Southern Tunisia (the rider
is talking to his mare.)

A life that stirs further than you wish, like those enormous chains which you set very gently in motion and which soon drag at your hands, and would drag you with them too if you did not let go. . . .

A has an old school friend, B. Since B has been living in Chartres, and comes to Paris for forty-eight hours every fortnight, he has taken it into his head that one of his two evenings in Paris must be spent with A. A finds this a bit much, and considers that an evening together every two months should be enough to satisfy the demands of his old friendship with B. He would like to be able to say to him, as Mohammed said to Abu Hosairah: 'O Abu Hosairah, visit me more rarely, and my friendship for you will increase.' (Saadi). He does not say this, but twice running he makes an excuse, and that is enough. B understands. He makes his invitations fewer and farther between.

The old school friend may be a little dull, immersed in his business and his money-grubbing, but he is a man, or something approaching a man – that is to say that there is not only a sort of dignity in him but a sort of intelligence which enables him to put himself in another's place. He accepts the fact that he gets more pleasure from these evenings than his friend, recognizes that this after all is the latter's right, and does not allow it to affect his friendship.

On the other hand, it is always a very laborious process to get a woman to realize either that one does not love her, or that one no longer loves her, that her presence, for you, means nothing but gloom and wasted time, and that all you expect of her is to clear out. Trying to drown a woman gently is like trying to drown a cat: one comes up against a terrible vitality. Which is why the only really agreeable love-affairs are those where one is jilted oneself.

Costals felt the sort of embarrassment one experiences on a liner drawing away from the dock, when one has waved one's arm and smiled at one's loved ones who are remaining behind, when one can no longer speak to them because of the distance, and when one is not quite sure what expression to put on. To all intents and purposes he had said good-bye to Solange, and now they stood there exchanging vague smiles, while the space between them went on widening until the moment when they could see each other no more. Every other day, at ten o'clock in the evening – because she knew that at that hour the servant was never there and that Costals would answer the telephone – Solange rang up. 'When are we seeing each other?' Good God! How he had to restrain himself in order not to send her packing! But his constrained, chilly, crepuscular voice ought to have warned the importunate girl. These telephone calls invariably ended with: 'I'm overloaded with work at the moment. I'll get in touch with you in a day or two.' Once a month he would say to her: 'I have an appointment on Tuesday at half past eleven. Would you like to meet me at half past ten outside the gare de la Ceinture?' (That mania of his for arranging to meet women on the pavement!) 'But that will give us so little time!'

At first she had made excuses (such clumsy ones!) for her telephone calls: 'Just a word. The bookseller in the rue d'Antin asked me to ask you if you'd be prepared to sign some of your books in his shop.' The bookseller had certainly never asked her anything of the sort, for he had received Costals' reply on the subject at least a week ago. Now she did not even bother with excuses: 'When are we seeing each other?' 'But we saw each other a week ago!' 'A week!...We saw each other on the 24th, so it's exactly seventeen days. And you know how I love seeing you and talking to you.' 'Allow me to say that this pleasure of yours seems to me incomprehensible. And for two pins I might say...the tiniest bit pathological.' He really thought this, for he was so gloomy when he was with her, and so 'ungracious', that it really seemed to him abnormal that she should get any pleasure from his company. They talked almost like strangers, holding hands out of habit. Now she only wanted to marry a friend of Costals, so she said, in order to be able to maintain relations (of pure friendship) with him which otherwise would be impossible.

Costals resigned himself to unplugging the telephone every evening, at the risk of missing important calls. She telephoned at eight in the morning. He unplugged the telephone in the morning too. Whereupon the notes began to pour in: he did not answer them.

He was inexpressibly weary of her: the last hours of a journey always seem the longest. He put his head in his hands: 'No, no, there's nothing in the world more boring than a woman. And especially an unhappy woman....We don't need their love, which they try to foist on us. As for their need to be loved....really, I'd a million times rather a person had a craze for money than a craze to be loved: that's what they bring us to. Women refuse to understand that they're a nuisance, refuse to understand the impatience they arouse in a man. Definition: "Woman: a person who solicits, a person who badgers." A woman who does not badger is an object so rare that I should like to see every woman of that species decorated – after due research and testimony – with the Legion of Honour.'

It was his custom, on spring mornings, to go and sit in a corner of the Bois near his house, and work. Unfortunately, he had confided this to Solange. One morning he was sitting on his favourite bench when she arrived looking bright and jaunty: 'Please don't think I've come to see you. I'm going to the so-and-so's in the rue Michel-Ange, and I made a détour to get a whiff of greenery.' He put away his papers (anyone can imagine the mood of a writer interrupted in his work). He

talked to her for ten minutes, then dismissed her without ceremony : a tactless woman makes a man a boor, *genuit indiscreta
muflum*. She left with a 'When do we meet again?'

Costals chose another bench, a long way from the first. And
he worked there apprehensively, convinced that she would
discover him there too.

Then she began to stick to him like a back who marks you
at football and keeps bobbing up wherever you move. If Costals was leaving a meeting of some literary panel, at the corner
of the street he was sure to run into Mlle Dandillot, full of
surprise : 'You here !' She had read in the papers that he would
be sitting on the panel, and had been waiting for him on the
pavement for an hour. If he called at his favourite bookshop,
Solange would be there ostentatiously browsing. The bookseller had told her the previous day : 'M. Costals is coming in
at ten o'clock tomorrow.' Whenever he saw her, his face fell.
But she, noticing nothing, or appearing to notice nothing, went
on imperturbably doing everything that was most calculated to
make him loathe her.

The author has often remarked, in the course of these books,
that such and such a trait he had come across in one of his
characters exceeded his powers of psychological analysis, and
that he preferred to admit it rather than throw dust in the
reader's eyes with some bogus explanation. So he will shirk
a decision as to whether Mlle Dandillot failed to see that she
was boring Costals to death, and was blinded by the rendezvous he vouchsafed her every three weeks to the point of
regarding them as a proof of affection; or whether she did
see it but persisted nonetheless, not because she wanted him
either to marry her or possess her, but because she wanted to
see him and talk to him, even though she was aware of the
drudgery she was inflicting on him.

However that may be, for Costals it was as though he were
watching a monstrous transformation taking place before his
eyes, like the processes of nature as revealed in cinemato-
graphic slow-motion (the caterpillar turning into a butterfly,
etc.): *Solange was being metamorphosed into Andrée Hacquebaut*. Solange, once so reserved that she never telephoned first !
The same frenzied scrabbling at one's trouser-legs to get the

piece of sugar, the same determination never to see what stares you in the face, the same desperate clinging, the same obtuse optimism and the same futile stratagems : the same masterpiece of vain perseverance. The truth was glaringly obvious : all women were Andrée Hacquebaut. Andrée Hacquebaut loomed up like a sort of gigantic idol – larger than life, like the Athene of Phidias, and, like her, terrifying, ridiculous and grandiose – made up of the entire female sex, millions and millions all swallowed up in it and now peering out from it with all their different faces. Andrée Hacquebaut was *Woman*.

One morning, Costals was dressing in haste and some agitation. He was lunching in town at one o'clock, it was half past twelve, and he calculated that he could not be less than half an hour late. The telephone rang. And there was that bright, cheerful voice, that voice which alone was enough to show how little she understood the real situation : 'Well, still alive?' This time Costals could stand it no longer. Six months of enforced courtesy and charity were destroyed in an instant : a branch one has been holding bent and which one suddenly releases : 'Listen, Mademoiselle Dandillot, I should be extremely obliged to you if you would refrain from telephoning me every other day.' 'Forgive me, I'm disturbing you ...' said the voice, stammering, and falling, like a bird that has just received some shot, and drops like a dead leaf. 'Yes, you're disturbing me. Let's arrange, if you like, to meet once a month, and telephone me therefore once a month. We saw each other last week. Telephone me in three weeks. Good-bye.' He hung up.

Mlle Dandillot telephoned no more, and wrote no more. When we introduce a person into our lives, we have qualms about how we shall ever evict them. But such qualms are more often than not superfluous. More often than not, life contrives to detach people without any open clash, simply by mutual consent (except in a few cases where people get themselves murdered).

KO of Mlle Dandillot. Technical commentary. – In the first and second rounds, Costals had the upper hand. In the third round, groggy, he had gone down (the hippogriffical 'yes'). If she had then followed up, if her mother had said, 'It's the registry office next week or good-bye for ever,' Costals would have been out for the count. But she had allowed him to recover, and he had come back at her, for he was tough; come back to administer the knock-out, failing which she would have won on points. Costals soon began to believe it was he who had dictated the fight. 'I was keeping myself for the third round. In the end, class told.'

More profoundly he thought, seeking to exculpate himself: 'It wasn't as a woman that she made me suffer; I don't allow myself to suffer through women. It wasn't through her that I suffered, but through myself. She was only a pretext for me to work out my anxiety about marriage. I could not suffer through her, since she never did anything against me. What I suffered from was the "fiancée as such". More precisely still, I suffered from the idea I had formed for myself of the "fiancée as such".'

After that, life came surging back. 'Every time I break with a woman, life begins again.'

I

Pierre Costals   to Andrée Hacquebaut
Paris   *Saint-Léonard* (Loiret)

17 September 1928

Dear Mademoiselle,

Between 1925 and 1927 you sent me some two hundred letters. I made no objection, and even replied to you several times.

Since your letter of 30 December 1927, which was your epistolary come-back after six months of quiet sulks, you have written me twenty-one more letters. Not one of these was opened on receipt. They remained in their envelopes just as I received them, carefully filed in a special file. To be frank, this file was a shoe-box; but since it came from a London shoe-maker, your honour is safe. I wanted to see how many letters a young lady could write to a gentleman without getting a reply. Twenty-one is by no means excessive.

I find it difficult to explain the strange impulse that prompts me to reply to you today, after having taken it into my head to open all your letters; or rather, alas, I understand it only too well. Let us, if you will, call it on this occasion a respect for the human person − for that human person I respect in you. Please do not misunderstand me : I am always half-involved − as a novelist, if not as a man − even in what I do not like; thus, willy-nilly, there is something of me in you. The other day, I came upon your earlier letters (those of 1927). Blackmail you? But there's nothing I want from you; and besides, you never gave yourself to me, or at any rate I never took you, if I remember rightly. I flicked through these letters, and dipped into them here and there. Do you remember the one you wrote from Paris, at the beginning of a distressing week, the 'solemn' letter which begins : 'The fire is roaring, and down below Paris stirs beneath the rain'? I cannot prevent this simple sentence from setting up a certain vibration in me. I saw you again, in your little room in the little hotel (where someone had stolen your bottle of scent), frozen, your overcoat over your shoulders, and writing to me frenziedly under the too-high electric bulb. Three years have gone by since then, and three years of my life are the equivalent in richness to another man's entire existence (if not several of them; but let's be modest). And yet there are certain images there which have become embedded in me – forever, it seems to me.

Again, don't misunderstand me. I have never had the smallest droplet of desire, or love, or affection, or tenderness for you. Nor have I today. But I have had, and have, some sympathy for you. Why this sympathy? The fact that you loved me could only irritate me, since I did not love you. The fact that you suffered through me was a matter of indifference to me, since I did not love you. I think this sympathy comes, as the word suggests, from the affinities that exist between us. If people were to read your 1927 letters, they would say you were a trollop; if those of 1928, a crackpot, and if all of them, from the beginning until now, a bore and a clinger worthy of immortality. These are judgements that I do not share. I have often been criticized for being too familiar with you. I have been told that it was *unbelievable* that a man like me should waste his time with a person as unimportant and uninteresting as you, and that it must be either irresponsibility or vice. But I know what I'm doing. There is an element of grandeur in you about which I feel I am not mistaken. And I like very much your last batch of letters, that lonely cantilena as of a child crooning a little story to itself. You cannot see straight? Well, who could have taught you to see straight? The whole education of girls is distorted. You have been a little indecorous? Believe me, others offer themselves as you did, only they're more circumspect about it. 'You'll end up by getting yourself killed, sir: you're too frank!' my batman used to say to me during the war. And besides, we all know that solitude has its unchastities. There remain the insults you wrote me. But for me it's fun to be insulted.

Finally, I was about to forget my great pity for women,

well known to you by its effects. When I think of all those skirts that nobody ever lifted, I feel like apologizing to the women who remain unloved.

I should rather like to see you again. There would, of course, be no change in the relations we have always had. Let's say it's a sort of divine curiosity on my part. . . .

C.

P.S. 1 – I also lit upon a passage in which you describe your feelings about the sculpted snake in the Musée Dennery, which flattens out when it touches the edges of the tortoise's shell. Somewhere in China, centuries ago, a man was enchanted to see a snake flattened against the edge of a tortoise's shell, and in 1928 a young lady of Saint-Léonard (Loiret) looks at it too and is moved. It would please me to think that the words in which you described to me your emotion should be among those that bring me back to you. What a long chain, right back to the moment when the artist thought of flattening the body of his snake a little, and how splendidly he is justified now!

P.S. 2 – As for your remark to your girl-friend's young brother, advising him to do something – to read, pencil in hand – do not be put off by mocking. Even if the whole universe guffawed at you, you would still be right.

P.S. 3 – As for your letter of the 29 January, expressing your desire for coition with me, it's perfect. Who does it come from? Mlle de Lespinasse? Adrienne Lecouvreur? Marie Dorval?

P.S. 4 – And no boils, no decalcification, in spite of all your troubles. A sound constitution. Bravo!

2

Andrée Hacquebaut   to Pierre Costals
Saint-Léonard (Loiret)   *Paris*

20 September 1928

Dear Costals,

You certainly have the knack of breaking the spell: I realize

for the first time the full meaning of that expression. For
fifteen months you have given me no sign of life, for nine
months you have not even answered one of my letters, and
today you are gracious enough to inform me that you had
kept them without opening the envelopes. Neatly filed, one
little rectangle beside another little rectangle, I can see them
from here: the cataract transformed into a salt-marsh. It makes
me laugh.

So, you've come back. You want to bring me back to you,
to chain me to your chariot once more. 'Go further away....
Come closer.... Love me a little less.... Like this, like that....
No, that's still not quite it....' Like a little dog being taught to
jump through a hoop. 'In love, I like to keep the initiative.'
And yet this time it's you who are giving ground. Your letter
is full of veiled whining – for after all, be honest: if you
emerge from your retirement after more than a year's silence,
it's because you feel you need me. But you've recalled me like
this once before, and having got over your fear of losing me,
you made me submit to those insults in your studio in the
boulevard de Port-Royal. I'm beginning to know you. You're
an illusionist. You give the illusion of being many-sided, constantly changing. And you're always the same, desperately the
same. You always fall back on the same chord, like Mozart's
music. You return with the same old tricks of two years ago.
Stupid you are, and stupid you'll remain. I've given up trying
to convert you.

Well, you delude yourself. The habit of writing to you was
so powerful that I went on – that's all there is to it. I wrote
to you as I used to write in my diary before I knew you; as I
might have written a novel: I have never been able to live
without a confidant. I've told you more about myself than my
father and my mother ever knew: you have had before you
a woman in the state of nature. But for the past year you
have been no more to me than a witness to my inner life.
Something had died. I was like those mystics who continue to
love God in a latent way, but no longer feel anything. Before,
whenever an article of yours, however unimportant, was
brought to my notice, I would order the number in which it
had appeared (often in the name and address of a friend, for

fear that the 'young lady from Saint-Léonard' might become famous in the book-shops); I would throw my head back as I read your sentences and gargle with them; I would cut out the article; occasionally, even, I would slip it inside my bodice, sometimes to gladden my heart, sometimes also so that my heart might transfuse it with a little of that tenderness you lack. But in the past year, I haven't even read those two limited editions you've published. Before, when I asked for one of your works in a book-shop in Paris or Orleans, I pretended to have forgotten the author, so as not to have to pronounce your name; I never pronounced your name except to myself. Today I pronounce it without the slightest emotion. I haven't removed your portrait from my wall; but it was enough that it was there; I never looked at it. In June '27 you wrote to me that if you did not wish to be my lover, it was in order not to 'sink' in my esteem. You wanted to remain on a pedestal. Well, you haven't remained there.

I was happy in that state. Formerly, absence was the rodent that gnawed our relations to shreds. This time, your absence and your silence have been a boon to me. They have been my occupational therapy. I embroidered on them, and i needed you only in order to recreate you in my own way. If you only knew how much I've put into your silence! how much I've achieved so simply in that way! I've made a life for myself beside my own life. For we *were* lovers, were we not? How romantic everything will have been in the existence of this little girl!

And no longer to receive those letters from you which I never opened without my heart beating, no longer to expect anything from you, no longer to have to beg, to insist, to strive to understand. To give up. To know that one has done everything one could, that it no longer depends on you. No longer to seek anything, and to tell oneself that perhaps it's because, in a certain sense, one has found what one wanted. Peace in despair (despair, naturally, in the literal sense: absence of hope). Peace with an obverse of anguish. But when one realizes that everything in this world has two sides to it. . . .

In these circumstances, to meet you again, unchanged except for this extra year (which shows very clearly on your face, if your latest photograph in *Vu* is anything to go by)? The very thought of it makes me weary. I have used up all too much courage and self-confidence in this affair. Seeing you again would mean the deflation of the prodigious balloon I have blown up during your absence. Already your letter has awoken in me a sort of wounded beast which was dozing there and which it would have been better to let lie. Go back to that unbreathable atmosphere of aridity in which you made me live for six months, as in a wood during the frost, when the ground is hard and crackly? And all that familiar routine of teasing and boorishness combined, of affectionate rudeness and irritable compassion, of which your letter is a reminder? And that famous lucidity, which only seeks to desecrate what decent people regard as sacrosanct, which in fact disqualifies you as a novelist, for how can the vision of a man who rejects normal values be worth anything? Well, the answer is no. Stendhal says that the great test of a friendship between a man and a woman is love, and that one can only survive it with the utmost honesty of feeling. I don't know which of us two was lacking in this honesty, but we did not pass the test.

If you care about me, as your return proves, but at the same time are flailing about without having the slightest physical desire for me, as you make no attempt to conceal (what a godsend for a man is a woman he does not desire! He can revenge himself on her for all the others. The un-desired woman has her role to play in God's creation, just as the rebel has a role to play in the social scheme), well then, marry me or something, give me a son, find something other than friendship, another bond. Anything rather than friendship. I am no longer capable of that. My dead love would poison it, like those dead flies in the ointment, of which the Scripture tells us, which ruin its sweet scent. Has it never happened to you, on a train journey for instance, to have a ferocious desire to sleep, and to close your eyes for a few minutes only, and, when you open them again, to find that these few minutes have sufficed to cure your desire for sleep? My unanswered letters this year have been those 'few minutes': they have sufficed to cure me of my desire for you. Now everything has been re-absorbed. What difference is there, in the last analysis, between a body that has known enjoyment and a body that has not? Things that one thought one loved fade away, and suddenly, one day, one decides that one has seen enough of them and they might as well disappear. I used to say to myself : 'How shall I ever be able to live when I've nothing left?' Then, once I was there, I realized that I could perfectly well live with nothing. Remember that, my child. It will come in useful for your novels.

The silence of a little country town at nightfall, the lights from the kitchens and stables, the clanking of chains, the heavy footsteps of the farmers, and then the electric lamp which lights up your table alone and leaves all else in darkness, all else ... so utterly the same, so utterly familiar after thirty-one years.... In such an atmosphere everything is reduced to essentials, and one can see deep inside oneself if one allows oneself to do so.

And what I see in myself is this : that I have loved you very badly, since I have never made the sacrifice you asked of me if I wished to keep you – in short, I have only loved myself and my own pleasure. Even today, I only lay down one condition for my return : that you raise your veto.... But I know perfectly well that you will not raise it. So that, in the last resort, *it is I who will not have wanted it.*

Farewell, dear sir, and be happy. Always remain exceptional in your quest for human happiness. For, if you were not happy, with the methods you use to achieve it....

A.H.

Perhaps, too (my letters in the void) ... a desire to maintain in you, at all costs, the life of the soul....

3

Andrée Hacquebaut   to Pierre Costals
Saint-Léonard (Loiret)   *Paris*

24 September 1928

Dear Costals,

You must think I'm mad. But I've just re-read your letter while the radio was playing softly in the background, and everything I wrote to you no longer holds good. You want to see me again, and I haughtily refuse! That would be a bit much! I'm taking the train tomorrow morning. Write or telephone in the evening, about eight o'clock, to the Hotel R., rue de Verneuil. I shall have done all I could for the beauty of my fate and for its plenitude.

Yours,
Andrée

4

Pierre Costals   to Andrée Hacquebaut
Paris   *Hotel R., rue de Verneuil, Paris*

25 September 1928

Express letter.

Dear Mademoiselle,

Do you know the Armenian Restaurant, 4, rue de la Chaussée d'Antin, near the corner of the boulevard des Capucines? I have eaten there fifty times with a woman I 'loved', and it would do no harm to disinfect the place by eating there with a woman I don't. I shall expect you there tomorrow, Tuesday the 26th, at one o'clock. I see from the calendar that it's the feast of the beheading of St John the Baptist. This anniversary bodes no good. But, as God wills! If it's agreed, don't bother to answer.

Yours,
C.

5

Andrée Hacquebaut   to Pierre Costals
Paris   *Paris*

26 September 1928

Express letter.

So, *as I suspected*, you only brought me to Paris to play a vindictive hoax on me. I was in the restaurant at 4, boulevard des Capucines from one o'clock till two, without seeing you. I didn't dare sit there for an hour without ordering a meal, and I had to pay thirty francs or so for one dish! All I can say to you is this: your behaviour makes me vomit.

A.H.

P.S. – I've just looked at your express letter again, and I see that the rendezvous was 4, rue de la Chaussée d'Antin. But as you went on to mention the boulevard des Capucines, I muddled the two (I hadn't brought your letter with me), and as ill luck would have it, there was also a restaurant at 4, boulevard des Capucines. Forgive me. Could we have lunch tomorrow or the day after instead?

6

Pierre Costals   to Andrée Hacquebaut
Paris   *Paris*

26 September 1928

Dear Mademoiselle,
   I waited for you from one o'clock till a quarter to two in the restaurant where I had arranged to meet you. I am a person who doesn't forgive but who forgets – who really forgets – the gravest discourtesies. But I am not the sort of person who can be stood up, even out of stupidity. Good-by, then, this time for good.

Costals

This letter remained unanswered. Costals never heard from Mlle Hacquebaut again. All's well that ends well.

1929

7

Solange Dandillot   to Pierre Costals
Paris   *Paris*

2 October 1929

My dear friend,
   You will give me credit, I hope, for not having exactly

forced myself upon you in the fifteen months since we last met or corresponded.

And indeed, I am not writing to you now to tell you about myself, assuming that if the subject interested you, you could easily have asked for news of me. I am writing to you about our housemaid. As you know, even at the time when you used to come to the house, she was not in good health. Now she has TB, and must go into a sanatorium. And I remember you once told me that your mother had left you a bed in a sanatorium, the name of which escapes me. Could you possibly do something for this girl who has served us loyally for six years? Thank you in anticipation. Telephone me, if you'd be so kind.

All the best,

Solange

8

Pierre Costals   to Solange Dandillot
Paris   *Paris*

3 October 1929

Dear friend,

How pleased I am that you should have thought of me to ask me a favour! Send me your housemaid any morning between eleven o'clock and midday: I'm very fond of consumptives. If I cannot find her a bed in the R. sanatorium, no doubt I shall find her one elsewhere (*honi soit qui mal y pense*). The only question is to know if she is to be kept alive or not, for TB is a question of money when it's caught in time.

I wonder what can have made you think that I'm no longer interested in you. If it's because I've given you no sign of life for fifteen months, you can't be serious. I don't feel the need to see even my dearest friends more than once every three years.

All the best, as you so nicely put it.

C.

9

Monsieur Alphonse Groger, Engineer-in-Chief at the Iron and Steel Works of S., Chevalier of the Legion of Honour, and Madame Alphonse Groger, and Madame Charles Dandillot, have the honour to announce the marriage of Mademoiselle Solange Dandillot, their grand-daughter and daughter, to Monsieur Gaston Pégorier, Member of the Institute of Engineers.

And invite you to attend the nuptial Mass which will be celebrated on 20 December 1930 in the church of Saint-François-de-Sales, rue Brémontier.

Avenue de Villiers

1931

10

Madame Gaston Pégorier
Paris

to Pierre Costals
Paris

8 October 1931

My dearest,

In a moment of distraction I mechanically dialled your number on the telephone, certain in any case that I should be told you were out or that the famous cut-off switch would be on. If I had known that you yourself would answer, I don't think I would have rung. In fact your 'Who's speaking?' at the other end of the line, harsh, peremptory, disagreeable, threw me into a panic. Had you or had you not recognized my voice? I shall never know. I began to pant into the telephone, and the shame I felt at panting there like an animal at bay – especially as it must have reached you amplified – together with my panic ... in short, I hung up.

And so, as in the old days when I was too nervous to speak to you, I am writing to you instead. As I used to with my husband, too, at the beginning. He would find the letter on his napkin when he arrived at table. I didn't appear until he had read it. I would look at him, he would not look at me, and the meal would go by in total silence. I would be screaming inside, but outwardly nothing showed: petrified and passive. You can just see me, I imagine. Still the little artichoke.

I'm afraid that this may appear to you (quite wrongly) as the thin end of a wedge. But how can I go on concealing the fact that your interminable silence causes me pain? It is true that I myself have been equally silent. Do not attribute this to coldness; it's simply that I hate badgering you; you know me well enough to remember how terrified I am of disturbing those I love. Clearly, you have no great desire to see me again. I trust that nothing I have done has injured me in your esteem, which I would like to feel is still intact. As for your affection, I wonder how much remains of it. Yet I should be sorry to lose you completely. Could we not meet from time to time at your flat? Don't you at least owe me that? My husband is at present in the Haute-Saône for six weeks. It is your friendship alone that I would like to preserve or renew. But I would be to you whatever you would like me to be. You know that I will only do what you would want.

My husband is an excellent sort and a man of great ability, but he does not understand me any more than Papa understood Mummy. Mummy tells me, to console me, that 'all men are like that'. 'Then why did you force me to marry?' 'Everyone has to get married. That's life.' Ever since I've been married, I feel odd, ill at ease, as one feels in a badly cut dress, which irks you without your knowing precisely where the trouble lies. But recently it has got much worse. There are days when I feel as though I were caught in a net; for two pins, I'd scream. I could break up everything, to find myself free and alone again.

Four years ago, my dearest, we were in Genoa. Yes, four years ago this week. Does this memory move you? I doubt it. I can assure you that for me it is worth the grief it cost me. And perhaps it is so dear to me because I paid so dearly for it.

I look forward to a friendly reply from you. But you have

accustomed me to renunciations.... And then, 'Women, full of memories, always dragging the past around like a nine-month belly, whereas man is eternal forgetfulness, the virile and child-like power of forgetfulness.'* No matter, never in my life have I waited as I wait for you now. May this letter bring you at least the assurance of all my tenderness.

Yours,

Solange

I I

Pierre Costals   to Madame Gaston Pégorier
Paris   *Paris*

10 October 1931

My dear Mme Gaston Pégorier,

You once said to me: 'The words you say to me are never the ones I expect.' Here are some more which are doubtless not the ones you expected.

Some years ago I had an impulse towards you; I took you. Afterwards I felt affection for you, I desired your well-being; there was a moment when I had it in my heart to love you very much. Then you wanted to transform this impulse, which was a natural thing, into a duty, that is into something unnatural and deadly; you sought to drag me – an irregular – on to ground which was not mine: you wanted to 'regularize' the position. And from that day onwards I also felt hatred for you: I say *also* because my affection remained. Until the day when I told you: 'Never.' From that day onward, I no longer felt hatred for you; I felt indifference, which I camouflaged as much as I could for some months more, out of a sentiment that you should have found quite unacceptable, but which you accepted nonetheless, because women accept anything, it's simply a matter of taking: this sentiment was charity. Until the day when I took myself by the scruff of the neck just as I was about to sink into a bottomless pit of altruism.

---

*Quotation from one of Costals' books (*Author's note*).

If I saw you again now, what would be my feeling for you?
It would still be, and would always be, simply charity: your
present suffering is a matter of indifference to me. On the
pretext that you have married an imbecile, you would like
me to become once more a prey to that charity which is the
cancer of man. Before you, and after you, I was and have
been happy. I was not happy 'during' you, because of that
charity and that duty. All around you there is health and
happiness, and you in the midst of it are misery and
disease: to me you were like a severed head on a golden
charger. You remember how I always thought that if I did not
marry you my future would be poisoned by regret for not
having done so. Well, in the past three years scarcely a
fortnight has gone by without my inventing God for a moment,
just long enough to throw myself on my knees beside my bed
and cry: 'O God, who gave me the strength not to marry her!
O God, who gave me the strength to resist the temptation of
charity!' And if, on receiving your letter, I said to myself
(what could be more human?): 'After three years she would
find me aged,' in a flash I answered myself: 'What matter,
since it isn't with her that I've aged.'

In the manuscript of a novel which has just been submitted to me by an unknown girl, I read this sentence: 'The
stupidity of women is like darkness over the earth.' (She might
equally have written: 'The love of women....') Ah! that
darkness is not the only darkness over the earth; there are
plenty of others. One of them is charity. Which makes an
artifice of what is worthless if not spontaneous. Which continually encroaches on love, which steals its prerogatives and
even its very features. Which turns smiles into grimaces. A
Persian poet has written: 'He who has been charitable to the
serpent cannot have seen that this was an injustice towards
the children of Adam.' In a more general sense I myself would
say: 'He who has shown charity cannot have known that this
was an injustice towards love.' My acts of charity fill me with
shame, which is why you have been one of my shames. I want
no more grimaces. There is nothing I desire more than to
rid myself of all those that I have been taught, for what is
called education is merely the teaching of grimaces. I am

doing my utmost to make daylight reign in me during the second part of my life, in place of that darkness which was there as it is over the earth, and to make my sunset a sort of dawn. Do not come and cast your shadow over it all again.

If this letter is harsh, unduly harsh, it is because one cannot go on indefinitely holding up a weight which is beyond one's strength. One goes on and on holding it, then the muscles give way, the weight falls, and if someone has put his foot in the wrong place, the weight crushes it. That, no doubt, is what women call 'betrayal'. You saw the weight fall on the foot of one of your congeners, the woman I showed you in my studio in Port-Royal. On the other hand, when one loves, the weight does not fall, because it is easy for one to bear it.

One day I definitely preferred myself to you, and from that day everything fell back into place. All the trouble sprang from the fact that there were times when I preferred you to myself. You tell me: 'I shall be for you whatever you want me to be.' I want you to be nothing to me. You wonder what remains of the affection I had for you. Nothing remains. If you knew the extent to which I do not love you, you would be appalled. You have left no trace in my substance; even your face has vanished. Although I owe you a few hours that were worthy of myself, your memory as a whole is painful to me. I remember all that was touching about you, and sometimes sublime, but none of it grips me any more – it's like a pair of pliers on which the screw has come loose. 'Esteem wears out, like love.' (Vauvenargues). The greater part of what concerns you has faded completely from my memory. If I happen to read on such and such a day in my engagement-book for 1927 that we went to the Théâtre Sarah Bernhardt together, not only does nothing – not an instant – of that whole evening float to the surface, but I could have sworn that we had never been to that theatre. And indeed it is well that it should be so. It has been said that memory is a muse. Oblivion must be a fairy.

And it's indifference, too, that you have felt for me in the past three years, in spite of this apparent recrudescence of passion provoked by M. Gaston Pégorier's absence in the Haute-Saône. And believe me, indifference, total, solid indifference, is a thoroughly healthy feeling between two people. Even when they have loved each other. Things become reabsorbed, and no more harm comes of it than from unanswered letters. This metamorphosis is not a function of man's woes, but of his virtues. I assure you, there's something intoxicating in feeling oneself in that state. It would be worth while loving if only to experience it some day. One feels as though one were flying through the air.

One of the reasons why I was able to put up with you so long was that you did not write me long letters. 'Misunderstood' or not, don't start down the slippery slope of letter-writing. I can do nothing for you: there is nothing one can do for those whom one does not love. Look elsewhere, the world is large, as I've told you many times. And if you need any consolation, tell yourself that at least you made me *live* for a whole year. You gave me feeling. So, until your dying day, you can console yourself with the thought that you will not have been superfluous on this earth: that much is established. Armed with this knowledge, go your way.

All the best,

C.

This letter remained unanswered. Costals never heard from Mme Pégorier again. All's well that ends well.

APPENDIX

Costals had just been re-reading some notes of his, a year old but unpublished, which he had found. And he mused:

'I go on thinking ill of women, and say so, and get carried away. Then a moment comes when I stop, blink, and ask myself "Where am I?" with the feeling that for some time now what I've been thinking and saying no longer squares with reality. Then I reproach myself, and take a vigorous mud-bath in humility and remorse. But when I come out of this bath, I'm surprised to find that I hadn't been mistaken at all, and that my alleged exaggerations corresponded exactly to the facts.

'For instance, a woman of sixty who has lived for forty years with her husband (of seventy), and who, while they go on cohabiting, eating face to face, starts separation proceedings, gets the bailiff to make an inventory of the house, has her husband's deed-box sealed up, and when he says: "This business will kill me", replies: "I know" – and all this out of jealousy, that is to say "love"....

'Or airmen's wives who tell you: "You think Georges has guts, but he's terrified in lifts, he wouldn't dare to reprimand the maid, and he does precisely what I tell him to. He's a child, etc."

'Or the young woman in Morocco whom I once heard say of her husband, slaving away up-country for ten hours a day: "René has to keep his nose to the grindstone. Now he knows what it costs to keep a wife."

'And similar instances *ad infinitum*. . . . One for every page of the calendar. No, it's when I think I've strayed too far from reality that I'm mistaken....'

Here is the text which the writer had just read:

The Lepers

SOME GRAVE MALADIES OF THE MODERN WEST
(Synopsis)

> Woman, what have I to do with thee? *Jesus to his mother.*

Unrealism. – Blinkers. Fear of reality, either from cowardice, or from idealistic inanity. When in fact it's reality that cleanses the soul. 'I throw into the waste-paper basket the documents about German rearmament which the military go on sending me.' (Briand to Stresemann, at Thoiry).

Dolorism. – The Apostle says: 'If ye be without chastisement, then are ye bastards and not sons.' The chastised rub their hands: down with the happy! The chastised affirm that one must suffer, as bad writers affirm that a novel must be badly written: it is a way of justifying themselves. Moral suffering is supposed to deepen one, when in fact it is not suffering that deepens,* but crisis: not at all the same thing. It provides people with a claim to consideration, to being fussed over, to forgiveness, one of the so-called essential ingredients of inner worth and of genius. A man cannot say he is happy without being considered a simpleton, or a vulgarian, or a humbug who wants others to envy him, or an insulter of the miseries of the human race. Whence the universal pose of suffering and 'anxiety', etc.: people realize that it's suffering that pays. Whereas the truth is that moral suffering is nearly always a sign either of physiological inferiority (it's only the weak who worry) or of intellectual inferiority (an intelligent person knows how to alleviate most of his own moral sufferings).

The desire to please. – Never saying what is, or what one thinks, but what one believes will please. The desire for approval is the common denominator of every individual in every *bourgeoisie*.

Gregariousness. – Fear and hatred of individual thought; and collective auto-suggestion. The world is riddled with clichés

---

*'For sorrow hath killed many, and *there is no profit* therein. – Ecclesiasticus.

as the vine is riddled with phylloxera. Everyone thinks in the same way at the same time, like puppets making the same gesture at the same time in response to the puppet-master.

Sentimentalism. – A substitute for reason and justice. The cheap morality and bogus uplift ('the threepenny opera') of religion, school and press.

Now, in each of these five sores of the body social, the same abundance of bacilli are to be found in the shape of *yoni*. In other words, all these sores are essentially feminine. Let us go over them again :

Unrealism. – 'I don't want to think about it' and 'It's to be hoped that' are two typically feminine expressions. Women are too infirm to bear reality : reality, for them, is an affliction. Whence the 'refuges' : love, religion, superstition, mythomania, convention,* idealism. Falsified both in face and body (because of their infirmity), they only feel at ease in a falsified universe. Men are more afraid of words than realities; women are afraid of both. Ostriches and women bury their heads in the sand and imagine they can no longer be seen. Men also bury their heads in the sand, but know they can be seen. In Hans Andersen's story, it was surely the women who were most enthusiastic in praise of the emperor's non-existent clothes; the men must have followed with some reluctance; and only the child was prepared to admit that the emperor was naked.

(Whence the success, in a society that gives women an exaggerated degree of influence, of an art – whether fiction, theatre or cinema – in which life is represented as it is not, and the loathing which that society feels for any art that represents life as it is.)†

---

*'Elegant women think a thing does not exist when it cannot be mentioned in society' – Nietzsche.

†Women authors. Their manuscripts always full of spelling and punctuation mistakes. They know how to spell and to punctuate, but they can no more *see* these errors in their manuscripts than they can see what stares them in the face in life. Like those mothers who, after a dozen years, have still not noticed that their son has a scar on his head or a birth-mark on his calf.

Footnote continued on next page.

Dolorism. – For long in a socially impoverished position, woman seized rapturously on the idea that suffering was an advancement and a benefit: the *yoni*-shaped bacillus and the cross-shaped bacillus have long been known to have certain affinities. No one reiterates more emphatically and more stubbornly that suffering is necessary; no one abuses more violently those who know how to avoid suffering, or is more tenacious in seeking out the chinks in their armour. 'I hate him because he does not suffer' (Mme Tolstoy on Tolstoy). The story of humanity, ever since Eve, is the story of the efforts made by woman to diminish man and make him suffer, so that he may become her equal.*

In the West, dominated by women, the cult of suffering. In the East, where man is master, the cult of wisdom.

The desire to please. – Woman wants to please, no matter what the price, no matter what the circumstances, no matter whom. (No need to elaborate.)

Gregariousness. – 'How different you are from all the others!' Every woman has heard that said to her by a man with his tongue hanging out. (Title for a novel: *Panting Tongues*.) When it's 'How like all the others you are!' that

---

For thirty years the chains that bar the platforms of Paris buses have let one through if one lifts them at one end. Yet a great many women, when they wish to board these buses, persist in pulling downwards instead of upwards, and eventually throw imploring looks at the passengers standing on the platform to get them to come to their aid, as a cat with a fish-bone stuck in its gums comes to you to have it pulled out after having torn its mouth to shreds trying to get it out itself. Yet *never* have we witnessed such a scene with a man in the part. I don't wish to infer too much from this. But it struck me as being worth remarking upon, however petty it may seem.

*You know nothing of feminine psychology, because you know nothing of suffering, because the satisfaction of the flesh (when *flesh that does not suffer is flesh still-born*) prevents you from despairing of everything ... A man may be this or that, but a woman will always remain a woman, *will always be able to inflict suffering which is more beautiful than love, ruin which is mightier than life*, on the strong, who are always the proudest and the stupidest.' (Letter from an unknown woman to Pierre Costals.)

she should have heard. The animal that secretes clichés most copiously is woman. Because, weak and lacking in self-confidence, she needs to feel the backing of majority opinion; because, lacking any ideas of her own, she needs to appropriate man's; because she is accustomed to saying what she thinks will please man. And yet, 'I'm not one of the herd' is a typical woman's remark. Could it then be that only the worst members of the herd cry out against it?

Sentimentalism. – When a man *really* loves a woman, the love he gives her is a different sort of love from that which she demands: she continually seeks to corrupt the love which the man gives her. It is women who have turned affection into a neurosis, and affectionate love – a divine emotion when it means tenderness, whether or not mixed with desire – into that laughable monstrosity which one might call 'Lurve'. Lurve is love-as-women-understand-it: absurdity, jealousy, histrionics, 'How do we stand?', the feminine anxiety with which women infect men, the need to be loved in return, the tendency to change to indifference, the tendency to change to hate – a whole inept scholasticism the object of which becomes so tenuous that one ends up by saying to oneself: 'But anyhow, what's it all about?' In short, one of the most ignoble products of the human race, a thousand times more vulgar and impure and maleficent than the sexual act in its simplicity, and the principal refuge of both man and woman against reason and conscience. Lurve, the European disease, the great Western hysteria.

The ancient Arabs used to crucify their slain enemy side by side with the carcass of a dog. If Lurve had a human form, it is thus that I would wish to crucify it.

*

A parenthesis.

Someone I know often feels, when in France, as lost as a man who has inadvertently strayed into a big drapery store thronged with chattering women: 'What am I doing here?' Some years ago I wrote in one of my essays: 'A feminine people, like the French....' Then I said to myself: 'Careful! perhaps that's an idle generalization; or perhaps one of my pet prejudices.' And I crossed it out.

But since then I've read this: 'There's something of woman in every Frenchman.' Who said that? Voltaire. And this: 'The role which Frenchmen play among men is that which women play in the human race as a whole.' Who said that? Goethe. And this: 'In every Frenchman, woman predominates. They are a decadent race.' Who said that? Tolstoy.

And I regretted not having had the courage of my convictions.

*

Let us resume.

This moral inferiority of woman, certain features of which we have noted and which is matched by a considerable number of physiological inferiorities (in a medical book I have in front of me, the bare enumeration of these inferiorities takes up ten lines), woman is herself aware of* – even without having to take into account the special container on liners into which she is invited to dispose of her 'towels and other bulky objects'. How can she fail to recognize that she belongs to a sorry race when she sees that she is always the asker, always the one who 'needs', always the one who flaps her wings and squawks for a beakful? (Her need to be loved, kissed, taken in someone's arms, is a veritable disease. How humiliating it is, this perpetual supplication, avowed or not, this perpetual mendicancy – camouflaged at times under the plumage of coquetry or disdain!) The sentiment of her inferiority secretly governs all her behaviour. Whence her tendency to engulf, to cling, to hoard, to seek assurance: it is as though she were in constant fear of being deprived; all she gives is the child, which she gives only after having received (and it is in that act of receiving, physiologists tell us, that

---

*'One of the facts that enabled me to establish my conception of individual psychology was the discovery of the more or less unconscious inferiority feeling that exists in all women and girls simply due to the fact that they are female. And this affects their psychic life to such a degree that they are always betraying traits of masculine protest, though often in a circuitous form, especially in the form of apparently feminine traits.' – Adler.

(Cows ride each other, though they get no pleasure from it, through a stupid imitation of the male.)

all her biological interest lies). Whence also the peculiar frenzy
with which women push themselves forward and grab and
cling, the tenacity with which they try to work their way into
your life or get you to do them a favour. (When, in a crowd,
you feel yourself being violently clutched or jostled, ten to
one it will be a woman or a child. Knowing their weakness,
the weak put all their strength into a gesture that called for
comparatively little.)

How explain, otherwise than by an inferiority complex, the
need, innate in almost every woman, to counterfeit herself –
to counterfeit her character (posing), her face (make-up), her
body (no need to go into details . . .), her natural smell (scent),
her handwriting? The strong do not lie, or rarely; they spare
themselves the trouble; they are honest, not to say cynical,
through disdain: 'We veracious ones,' the nobles of ancient
Greece used to say. And all races that are servile by nature,
or enslaved by circumstance, lie. How explain, otherwise than
by a sense of personal inadequacy, the need that obsesses
women to make themselves interesting, to affect sham moods –
always 'distinguished' ones? How explain, otherwise than by
a sentiment of physiological inferiority, the necessity they so
often feel to simulate sexual enjoyment.

And finally, it is not unusual for ambiguous women to get
the surgeon to change their sex. But even the bait of not
having to go to war never drives an ambiguous man to change
himself outright into a woman.

*

A civilization – ours – in which literature, whether popular
or academic, press, cinema, radio, popular song, are forever
harping on the slogan 'Woman must have her way', and have
ended up by making men believe it; in which, for centuries,
they have established, secured, envenomed this power of
woman, who would be harmless without them, and compelled
men and children to gape at her in wonder, through an immense
conspiracy of public opinion, morality, and clichés by the
million (thus the farmer and his daughter and the lad bang
away at the stallion with their sticks, to make him go to the
mare); all the social forces in coalition, a gigantic campaign of
ballyhoo which makes the publicity of big firms and the

propaganda of totalitarian states seem laughable by comparison; – and since the idolatry of woman means for a man the abandonment of his independence and his dignity, and the breakdown of all order, one feels the same sort of horror in the face of this ballyhoo as one feels on seeing an advertisement for some deadly alcohol. If, at least, women were proud and sensitive enough to tell their frightful knight-errants to go to blazes! If they would only greet with a hail of rotten tomatoes those cattle-drovers disguised as lecturers, or those film-directors dropping clichés like a tree shedding its leaves, whose milk-and-water patter dishonours them: 'Get away with you, you and your "victorious Eve". Defenders of your sort do us more harm than good. We need the respect that we deserve as human beings, but your gallantry makes us vomit.' Alas! not a sign of vomit. Even the most sensitive of them ask for more.

*

If woman reigns, in spite of her manifest unworthiness, in spite of her incompetence even in her own line – as witness her lack of insight, her weak judgement, her childish wiles – it is therefore only due to the stupidity of men.

This stupidity arises partly from desire. In desiring, a man flatters the object desired, in order to win its favours, and over-rates its charms in order to justify his lust, as well as the weakness it entails, in his own eyes and those of others.* But this stupidity is not necessarily implicit in desire. The peoples of antiquity, the peoples of the East, whose interest in woman no one would question, nevertheless put her in her proper place.

This stupidity derives especially from the after-effects of the ideology formerly applied to women: Christian love (fanatical belief in marriage), courtly love, romantic love, etc. (Develop).

Women play their game, and there is no cause to reproach them for it. The reproach should be aimed at men, for playing theirs badly. For letting themselves be imposed upon by these

---

*Whence the hue and cry raised by men themselves in the modern West against those who dispute the supremacy of women. For to demonstrate that that supremacy is unfounded is to brand them, indirectly, as nincompoops, since they created it. And then, just think of it, deflating the dreams of these gentlemen!

centuries of gynolatrous literature, not daring to be either clear-headed, truthful, or ruthless enough with women (everything that women and their toadies call 'caddish'), and all this either from a false sense of honour, because they are mesmerized, or from cowardice, because they are afraid public opinion will be against them if they act otherwise. Women are well aware of this, and so long as they are not brought forcibly face to face with what they are, as a dying man is brought face to face with death, they will shuffle and squirm and try to keep up the pretence.

One of the duties, therefore, of the modern European who wants to live rationally is the duty of *coarseness* in love. He must have the 'effrontery' to cut through those Gordian knots which women tie, those difficulties which are not difficulties at all. He must struggle against whatever there may be inside himself which reaches towards that swampy or mined terrain on to which she would entice him. He must oppose with the utmost firmness a *systematic frivolity* to her unhealthy complications and sublimations. He must cease to create for himself, where she is concerned, under the pretext of desire, idiotic obligations, I mean unjustifiable obligations. He must fight against the artificial reflexes of 'chivalry', by repeating to himself each time : 'If every human being has a right to respect, woman has a right to that respect, and no more. She has no right to *special* respect. There is no valid reason why a woman should be treated differently from a man.' He must oppose a harsh indifference, real or feigned, to all the vulgar tinsel of bogus uplift, bogus high-mindedness, bedroom idealism, Lurve-as-social-convention, all that that 'threepenny opera' which virtue turns into when it is conceived by the mind of woman, and laugh himself silly when women call him a lout because he pretends not to understand what they are talking about. In short, he must on the one hand *dishonour Lurve*, and on the other, to the extent that woman is not indispensable, *free himself* from her. And, after all that, he will see that women do not cease to come to him, that some of them, perhaps, come to him all the more readily. And he will take the leper in his arms, and enjoy her, and give her pleasure too – why not? poor kitten, – but without catching her leprosy.

At which, just as there is always some arch-unbeliever ready to throw black looks at those who eat meat on Good Friday, there will certainly be some male hog who will grunt: 'Alas for French chivalry!' And then you will remember that there was a Greek chivalry at one period of antiquity, a pre-Islamic Arab chivalry, a Persian chivalry at the time of Shah Nahmeh and the Beharistan, a German chivalry based on the cult of the hero, a Japanese chivalry with the samurai – all of them in the last degree authentic, by which we mean branded with the authentic chivalric absurdity, – and that in not one of them did women play *the smallest part* (any more than 'God' did, be it noted in passing).

And to all those who, 'rending their garments', yelp 'He has blasphemed; he has committed a crime against love!' we say further that it is not love that we are defaming, but its caricature, Lurve. Parental love and filial love, true friendship, even the love of 'God' and the love of humanity, such as they are to be found in certain lofty spirits; and even those sentiments which are deemed to be no more than pale reflections of love, to bear no relation to it whatsoever – the intellectual esteem of a disciple for his master, the graciousness of a superior to his subordinate, the comradeship of arms or adventure, the interest an educator takes in his pupil; and even sentiments which public opinion puts lower still, such as the friendship of a man for his dog or his horse, are sentiments altogether nobler and worthier of respect than Lurve.

*

> Progress comes about, not through women, but in spite of them.... Learning, reason, justice, all that is best in the patrimony of our species, is threatened by the advent of women. AMIEL, *Journal*.

That what we are saying here has been said many times before may be an argument against us, but what does it matter as long as it argues in favour of what we say? The civilization of which we have just laid bare one of the principal characteristics is not a Utopian one. It was, for thousands of years, that of the ancient world, which for centuries afterwards was praised to the skies, without anyone ever being aware that 'all the great things done by mankind in antiquity derived their strength from the fact that men found themselves side by side with other men, and no woman could lay claim to being, for man, the object of the closest and highest love, or even the sole object' (Nietzsche).* It is that of Asia, whose wisdom we praise, forgetting that the land 'whence cometh the light' is a land where woman has no place other than sexual. It rules the Moslem world, one of whose traditions tells us that the Prophet said: 'When he is in doubt, a Moslem consults his wife, so that he may do the opposite of what she advises' (quoted by Djami). Two thousand years of a different civilization, over only one part of the globe (Europe and the new World), against the millennia of that civilization. . . .†

Perhaps, to a future race, the era of woman's rule will

---

*And again:

'To be mistaken about the fundamental problem of man and woman, to deny the profound antagonism between the two and the necessity for an eternally hostile tension, to dream perhaps of equal rights, equal education, equal claims and obligations: those are the typical signs of shallow-mindedness. A man who has depth of mind as well as of desires, and also the depth of benevolence which is capable of severity and harshness . . . can only look on women as Orientals do . . . He must take his stand on the prodigious rationality of Asia, on the superiority of the instinct of Asia, as the Greeks did of old, those best heirs and pupils of Asia – those Greeks who . . . from Homer to the time of Pericles, joined the progress of culture and the growth of physical force to an even more oriental strictness towards women.' (Nietzsche, *Beyond Good and Evil.*)

These, almost word for word, are the views expressed by Napoleon on St Helena: 'We, the peoples of the West, have ruined everything by treating women too well. We have raised them, very wrongly, almost to be our equals. The peoples of the East have a sounder sense; they have declared them the virtual property of men, and indeed, nature has made them our slaves. It is only through our wrongheadedness that they have laid claim to being our rulers.'

†That the attempts made in the USSR to inject a bit of common sense into the 'couple' seem to be failing is not because they are 'unnatural', as our *bien-pensants* claim. For if Christianity has succeeded, anything unnatural can succeed.

appear as remote as the era of priestly rule seems to the men of today. Lurve will have disappeared as completely as the great saurians of the mesozoic period. The modern conception of the couple (sublimation, wrangling and frenzy) will arouse the same horrified amazement as marriage between brother and sister or the sacred prostitution of certain ancient civilizations arouse in us. It is possible that this period of health will last only for a time: civilizations are by nature ephemeral, like political régimes. The quantity of human stupidity probably remains constant; when it has been eradicated here, it springs up again there, like boils (what a staggering list one could draw up of the successive lunacies of humanity!), but it does happen that, between boils, there is a moment of respite. If a civilization in which woman no longer holds sway is no more than a respite in the furunculosis of our planet, one will nevertheless deserve credit for having been among those who brought it about.

'Well, you must admit it isn't too badly put,' he said cheerfully to the young woman over whose shoulder he had just re-read his thesis, which she was still holding in her pointed hands, her fore-arms resting on her hip-bones (half-Egyptian through her mother, she was built like those Egyptian figures one sees on monuments). 'Infamous race!' He kissed her head, the very scalp, underneath her hair, which had three different smells – on the crown of her head, on the temples, and where it met her forehead. 'Yes, you really belong to an infamous sex.' There was a silence. Then he added: 'Nevertheless I'm pleased with you for not yet having protested: "Pretty odd to write things you don't believe." '

'I haven't said it because I don't think it. But I admit I'm disconcerted. . . .'

'Everything I've written there I profoundly believe, and I've believed it since adolescence, since the age when one starts getting to know about people. But sometimes it seems to me that I could maintain with equal sincerity – that is to say with total sincerity – a completely opposite view of the question: a view that would demonstrate the grandeur of woman. Why? Because that maleficence and that absurdity and that grandeur all exist in women. Turn and turn about. Always turn and turn about. Sometimes, too, it seems to me that....

'Here, I'll tell you a story. There was once a boy in a boarding-school who was persecuted by one of the masters, who treated him with monstrous unfairness. One day, towards the end of the school year, the master sent for this boy, who appeared before him tense and bristling and said: "I suppose you're going to give me another wigging." The master replied: "No, I sent for you because I'm leaving the school for good, and we won't see each other again. And so I wanted to tell you that if I gave you a rough time it was because I liked you so much. Now give me your hand and go." They shook hands and parted. And, as he had said, they never saw each other again.'

'What's the point of that story?' asked the young woman, knitting her brows a little.

'Isn't it obvious?'

She had turned her face towards him, and she searched his eyes (like a real woman) not so much in order to understand as to see if she could find reassurance there.

But he, as always, was smiling at something else.

Fine works of fiction and non-fiction
available in Quality Paperback editions from Carroll & Graf